SQUADRON

FREDERICK E. SMITH

633 SQUADRON

633 SQUADRON: Operation Rhine Maiden

633 SQUADRON: Operation Crucible

CHANCELLOR
PRESS

633 Squadron
first published in Great Britain in 1956
by Hutchinson and Co. Ltd

633 Squadron: Operation Rhine Maiden
first published in Great Britain in 1975
by Cassell and Co. Ltd

633 Squadron: Operation Crucible
first published in Great Britain in 1977
by Cassell and Co. Ltd

This collected volume first published in Great Britain in 1994 by
Chancellor Press an imprint of
Reed Consumer Books Limited
Michelin House, 81 Fulham Road, London SW3 6RB
and Auckland, Melbourne, Singapore and Toronto

ISBN   1 85152 655 2

A CIP catalogue record for this book is available
from the British Library

Printed by William Clowes, Beccles, Suffolk

CONTENTS

CONTENTS

633
SQUADRON

To Des and Bob

The other two 'musketeers' of A Flight

With thanks to my good friends in Norway for their assistance

CHAPTER I

'I've always thought it one of the greatest stories of the war,' the young American said, his eyes shining. 'The way those boys went in, knowing what was coming to them. . . . Gee, what great guys they must have been!'

The innkeeper's eyes were growing reminiscent. 'They were,' he said. 'Great guys.'

'And every operation connected with the Black Fjord was carried out from here?'

'Yes; Sutton Craddock was made their base. They arrived in January '43, and began training for the job shortly afterwards.'

'So you'd meet the rest of the squadron – Gillibrand, Barrett, Bergman . . . all of them as well as Grenville himself?'

'Yes. I knew them all.'

The American shook his head in envy. 'Grenville has been my hero since I was a kid at school. I never thought that one day I'd be standing in the pub where he and his boys used to drink their beer.'

His eyes wandered round the lounge. Like the rest of the Black Swan it was of great age, with panelled walls and a timbered ceiling blackened by the smoke of centuries. Polished brass ornaments were everywhere, some shining golden in the soft lights from the shaded lamps, others winking back the firelight from the stone hearth. The counter against which the American and his friend were leaning was a massive structure, scarred and weathered, and at one end of it a large bowl of daffodils glowed with startling brightness against the pitch-black wood. Behind it a huge stand of oak shelves obstructed the view into the bar which lay beyond.

But the outstanding feature of the room was its photographs. These were hanging in double tiers round its panelled walls. There were pictures of aircraft: of a Boston, of a crashed Messerschmitt 110, of a graceful twin-edged plane with R.A.F. markings and cannon protruding from its sleek nose; there were photographs of airmen, some in flying-kit, others in uniform, nearly all young and nearly all smiling. Among them, seeming incongruous in their company, was the portrait of a tall, fair-headed naval lieutenant. In its way the room was a hall of fame: the innkeeper's tribute to courage, to the men he had known and loved.

The American drew in a deep breath and turned back eagerly. 'Tell us something about 'em, Pop. Tell us all you know about the Black Fjord job.'

'Haven't you read the war histories?' the innkeeper asked.

The American's voice was contemptuous. 'Of course, but you know what they

1

are. They're so cold-blooded they give you the creeps. Folks want to hear the real stuff – how those boys felt during their training, the girls they had, what they let out when they were drunk, how they felt on the last day. . . . The human stuff! One day some guy's going to put it all down, and what a story it's going to be.'

There was an odd light in the innkeeper's eyes now. 'You mean a biography that tells the stories behind the story.'

'That's just what I mean, Pop. And you must know a few of 'em yourself – a pub's a great place for hearing things. How about telling them to us?' The American motioned towards his companion, a young English pilot officer alongside him. 'Me and Danny here are pretty soft on 633 Squadron. We heard about your place a few weeks back and made up our minds to do a trip up here the first chance we got. We thought if we came across soon after opening time you might be able to spare us a few minutes. We're due back tomorrow, so don't let us down.'

The innkeeper, heavy of build and short-sighted, looked at each eager face in turn. Both men were young, no more than twenty-two or three. The American, who had introduced himself as Malcolm Daly, was slimly built with dark hair and humorous yet thoughtful eyes. He was wearing the uniform of the U.S.A.A.F. His friend in the R.A.F., Danny Johnson, was more stocky of build with sandy hair and a square, pleasant face. Both were still young enough to feel hero-worship, and the atmosphere of the room had brought its glow into their eyes. The innkeeper glanced at the clock, then nodded.

'All right,' he said. 'I was going to look after the bar until eight, when a friend who's staying with me is due back from Highgate. But I'll ask my girl to take over. She won't mind – we never do much business on a Monday, particularly in the lounge. Take your beers over to a table while I go and ask her.'

The two pilots went over to a table by the fire. Two minutes later the innkeeper returned. He had a thick folder and a photograph album under his arm. He put them down on the table in front of the two men.

'There you are,' he said to Daly. 'There's your biography. And here are some more photographs.'

Daly stared at him. 'Biography!'

The innkeeper smiled. 'Yes. I've already done what you said – written a biography of 633 Squadron's operation in the Black Fjord, or the Svartfjord as it's called in Norway.'

The American was dumbfounded for a moment. He picked up the folder and stared at it. The English boy was the first to speak.

'Are you going to go through it with us?' he asked eagerly.

The innkeeper settled his heavy body into a chair beside them. 'Yes; I've arranged it with Ivy. She's going to finish her tea in the bar and take care of both rooms. She'll manage all right – as I said, we get very few in on a Monday night.'

The eager mood of the two airmen had infected the innkeeper, and he was now as keen to talk as they were to listen. He opened the album and pointed to a photograph of two shell-torn aircraft. 'That's how two of the planes looked after getting back from Bergen. They flew four hundred miles like that. . . .'

At that moment a car engine sounded on the drive outside. It revved up once as if in protest, then died sullenly away. After an appreciable pause a man entered the lounge. The innkeeper half-turned, saw Ivy bustling through from the bar, and turned his attention back to the airmen.

The newcomer, wearing a trilby hat and an old belted mackintosh, hesitated in the doorway. The atmosphere of the room seemed to daze him with its impact, and the sight of the three men at the table to add further irresolution to his movements. He was turning back to the door when he shook his head almost angrily and approached Ivy at the counter. After a further glance at the engrossed innkeeper, he ordered a beer in a low, unfriendly voice.

Ivy, blonde, over-ripe, inquisitive in a good-natured way, eyed him with interest. In his middle thirties, she'd say, and not at all bad-lookin'. . . . A commercial traveller was her guess, having a drink to help him forget how badly things were going. . . . She watched him take his glass into the corner by the door, then shrugged and returned to the bar. The newcomer sat among the shadows, his head lowered, his eyes alternating between the photographs and the bespectacled innkeeper at the table.

The innkeeper closed the album and pushed it aside. The young American grinned. 'That was just to whet our appetites, Pop, huh? Now for the story. I can't wait – this place has got me. . . .'

The innkeeper was suddenly aware himself how the atmosphere had grown. The past was very much alive tonight – an invisible force, tugging at the sutured veins of his memory and starting the living blood flowing again.

As he drew the folder towards him, he suddenly thought of the newcomer and peered back across the room. His sort-sighted eyes detected the blurred, shadowy figure in the corner, and he wondered if he should invite him over. He finally decided against it: the war had not hit everyone alike. If he were interested he would surely come across without being asked. He would be able to hear what they were talking about clearly enough in the quiet room. . . .

As he turned back to the airmen, the light reflections from the framed photographs, distorted through the lenses of his spectacles, surrounded the room with dozens of luminous shapes. His mind, conditioned by the atmosphere of the room, gave him an instant simile. Like ghosts, he thought – their ghosts, gathering in silent company around them. But why had they come tonight, and what was the strange eagerness among them. . . ?

Both amused and irritated by his imagination, the innkeeper turned to the American. 'You're quite right about there being a great deal missed out of the war histories,' he said. 'Much of the truth could not be told at the time. In fact, it has taken me all these years to get permission to write this biography. Apart from the intelligence work and the organization behind the raid, it also tells the inside story of 633 Squadron – why they were nearly wiped out over Bergen, and the real reason for Grenville's attack on the building there. It might even explain why Gillibrand won himself a V.C. . . . Of course, no one can ever know the full workings of a man's mind in a battle crisis, but at least the facts help one to make some shrewd guesses. I think you'll find all those facts in here.'

3

There was respect as well as eagerness on the faces of his listeners now. 'You've got all that in?' Daly muttered.

'Yes; this is the complete story of the operation. It starts with 633 taking up their new base on the airfield opposite, and ends among the Focke-Wulfs and flak in the Black Fjord.'

There was a hush in the room as the innkeeper opened the folder. The ghosts nudged one another and drew nearer. . . .

And this, in somewhat greater detail, is the story they heard.

CHAPTER 2

633 Squadron took over its new airfield at Sutton Craddock on the 8th January, 1943. It was a bleak day with a spot of drizzle and a raw wind from the east. The deep low humming of the aircraft grew louder until the windows of the Black Swan were rattling with the noise. A crow, perched high on the crab-apple tree in the front garden, took fright and fled down the road like a startled enemy bandit.

The first Boston appeared out of the cloud. It was piloted by Grenville, and he brought it low, studying the layout of the airfield. He caught sight of the lone inn on the road alongside the field and wondered what it was. A Cockney voice suddenly came over the intercom.

'Looks as if the natives are friendly, skipper. See that girl down there, waving to us? Now ain't that nice . . . ?'

That was Hopkinson, his observer. Hoppy had the eyesight of a sparrow-hawk. Grenville's eyes, the only part of his face visible above his mask, crinkled in a brief smile as he waggled his wings in reply. Then Control came through again and once more his gaze became intent on the airfield. He completed a circuit, then came down to land. With flaps down and engines throttled back, the Boston swooped over the field and landed as gracefully as a ballerina. The rest of the squadron followed her down, scattering groups of sparrows like dry leaves in a wind.

The Black Swan across the way was an old country inn with thick whitewashed walls and a grey slate roof. Behind its front garden was the private porch that gave access to the living quarters. Alongside it a gravel drive led to its two public rooms, the bar and the lounge, both of which were at the side of the inn.

On hearing the approaching engines, Maisie, the barmaid, had run to the door of the bar. She was a big handsome girl with black hair, dark eyes, and bold features. She stood on the steps, waving a duster at each plane as it roared by. She was joined a few seconds later by the innkeeper, Joe Kearns. Kearns was a man in

4

his middle fifties, bespectacled, stout of build, with thinning white hair and a pleasant ruddy face. He stood peering up into the drizzle until the last plane had gone by.

It was a Bombay, full of administration and other ground-staff officers. Its black hulk passed right over them, the air whining through its struts and over its airfoils. Then it had landed, and the sky resolved itself into a formless ceiling again, devoid of shape or colour or noise.

Maisie's eyes were still sparkling with excitement as she drew reluctantly back into the bar.

'They looked fine, didn't they, coming in low like that? Did you see 'em waggling their wings – they saw me wavin' to them.' There was satisfaction in her strong, throaty voice.

A smile pulled at the corner of Joe Kearns' mouth. 'Yes; they saw you all right.'

There was an archness in Maisie's walk now as she stepped back to the bar. She flicked her duster reflectively over it.

'I wonder who they are. One of the guards we had last week said they were a crack squadron comin' here for special duties. The corporal with him gave him a nasty look, so there might be somethin' in it.'

'We'll probably get to know soon enough,' Kearns said, closing the door to keep out the drizzle.

Maisie's eyes turned dreamy. 'Gee; just suppose they've got some of those aces among them, like those you read about in the papers! Wouldn't that be wonderful?' She looked eagerly at Kearns. 'D'you think any of 'em will come over tonight?'

Kearns shook his head. 'I don't know, lass. They'll have their own messes, don't forget. But we're bound to get some over eventually.'

One of them, although not one of Maisie's aces, decided to go over that evening before dinner. He was Adams, the Station Intelligence Officer. Before leaving his billet he hastily checked his appearance in a mirror. The S.W.O. was a terror for smartness – there had been more than one case of senior officers being reported to the adjutant for untidy dress. . . .

The mirror showed a man in his middle forties with short legs, a plump round face, and spectacles. His service greatcoat added to his stoutness and the peaked cap made his face look owlish. Nothing could look less military and Adams turned away from the vision in distaste.

There had been no need to worry about his appearance, he thought, as he groped his way up to the camp entrance. The black-out was complete; he could have gone out in his shirt tails and no one would have known. Twice he wandered off the path into sticky mud, and once he stumbled heavily against a pile of stacked bricks. Nothing is more bleak or inhospitable than a newly-laid airfield, and he breathed a sigh of relief when he passed by the sentry at the entrance and started down the road.

Adams was something of a complex character. He hated war, yet would have given his right arm or a leg to have been young and fit enough for flying duties. Temperamentally he was unsuitable for Intelligence Work because of the romantic streak in his nature which constantly rebelled at having to keep silent over the deeds of courage he heard almost daily. He was a keen observer, highly imaginative, self-critical to a fault, and utterly contemptuous of his rôle in the war, being quite certain that the crews he interrogated shared his contempt. His wife was a woman fifteen years younger than himself – another indication of his inherent romanticism – and it was because of her he was making his present call at the Black Swan.

He stood now in front of the black-out curtain of the lounge, staring round at the panelled walls with their glinting brass ornaments. Maisie, reading a thriller behind the counter, looked up and quickly preened herself. He wasn't exactly the film star type, but still he was a squadron-leader and Maisie decided he deserved one of her Sunday-afternoon smiles.

'Good evenin', sir. What can I get you?'

Adams approached the counter. 'Good evening. Is the landlord about? I'd like a word with him, please.'

'The landlord, sir! That's Mr Kearns. Half a mo'. I'll give him a shout for you.'

With another bright smile, Maisie swung off to the side door, her skirt swirling invitingly about her legs.

'Joe,' she shouted. 'There's a gentleman from the aerodrome to see you. A squadron-leader.'

Kearns entered the bar, eyeing Adams curiously. 'Good evening, sir. What can I do for you?'

'I'm looking for a place for my wife,' Adams told him. 'I've just arrived today and one of the workmen said you had rooms here. What's the position?'

Kearns shook his white head regretfully. 'Sorry, sir; but I don't let rooms any more. I'm a widower and can't get the help to do the cookin' and that sort of thing. Help's hard to come by these days, you know.'

Adams looked disappointed. 'If it's only the cooking, I don't think my wife would mind doing her own.'

'It isn't only that, sir. There's the washing and the cleaning-up. . . . '

'Mrs Billan would help you out there,' Maisie interrupted. 'She said she'd give a hand if ever you were stuck.' The grateful look on Adams' face encouraged Maisie to continue. 'He'll never get a room in Highgate – it's full of evacuees. Go on – let him have one here. We'll manage.'

Kearns shifted uncomfortably. He was a kind-hearted man who always found difficulty in refusing a request. Maisie, exploiting his weakness ruthlessly, went on: 'It ain't right to keep a service man away from his wife, not when you've got empty rooms. It ain't patriotic.'

She winked at Adams who felt his face redden. Kearns scratched his head. 'You think your wife wouldn't mind doing her own cooking, sir?'

'I'm sure she wouldn't,' Adams said, who was not sure at all.

Kearns was still undecided. 'I hadn't intended to let them,' he muttered.

6

'Go on – let him look at them,' Maisie said. 'It's the least you can do for some-one who's fightin' for us.'

Adams felt himself flush again. Kearns gave way. 'All right, sir. Seeing how things are, I'll do it. You'd better come through and see what I've got.'

'That's better,' Maisie said cheerfully, opening the flap of the counter to let Adams through. 'It's up to us all to do what we can for the Services.'

Somewhat hastily Adams followed the landlord. He came back ten minutes later, looking pleased. He went round the counter, then approached Maisie, who leaned forward.

'Well; are you all fixed up?' she asked.

'Thanks to you, yes. What will you have to drink?'

'You don't have to buy me a drink for that.'

'I want to buy you a drink,' Adams said awkwardly. 'What will you have?'

Maisie surrendered gracefully. 'All right; if it'll make you feel better. I'll have a drop of gin – we managed to get a few bottles last week. Like a tot?'

'No; I'll have a pint of bitter, please.'

Maisie poured the drinks, then leaned voluptuously against the counter. 'Were you in one of the planes that passed over here this afternoon?'

Adams nodded. 'Yes. I was in the Bombay, the big one that came in last.'

'Did you see me wavin'?'

'Yes. We all saw you. I waved back, as a matter of fact.'

Maisie was pleased and was going to say so when the black-out curtain parted and two airmen appeared. One was a thinly built L.A.C., an old sweat with a long dismal face and a pointed nose. He was wearing a crumpled rag of a field service cap and a camouflaged ground-sheet as protection against the drizzle. His companion was a young A.C.2, very new-looking in his high-buttoned greatcoat. The strap of his gas-mask, running down from somewhere alongside his neck, appeared to be half-strangling him.

The A.C.2 was the first to notice the squadron-leader. He halted dead in his tracks like a rabbit seeing a stoat. The old sweat gave him a push.

'G'wan,' he hissed. 'This ain't Padgate. And it ain't out of bounds to airmen. Watcha afraid of . . . ?'

Then he saw Adams was looking at him and he made a vague up-and-down motion of his right hand. An enemy, wishing to discredit him, might have said it was a compromise salute.

'Evening, sir. Grim night, sir.'

'Good evening, McTyre,' Adams said, his blue eyes twinkling behind his spec-tacles.

With another surreptitious push McTyre sent the A.C.2 stumbling across the room to a table in the far corner. Muttering his contempt of fireballers who toady to authority, he pulled off his wet ground-sheet, revealing a uniform almost as greasy as his cap. His gas-mask, black wth oil, was slung over his left shoulder in officer fashion, and the top button of his tunic was open, revealing a black shoe-lace of tie struggling to hold together the frayed remains of a service shirt. Adams eyed him in fascination, thinking what unholy joy his appearance would bring to the S.W.O.

Still muttering, the old sweat dropped into a chair. Beside him the erk sat stiffly upright, his young, round face emerging hot and flushed from his buttoned-up collar. His eyes were glued on Adams.

Maisie had all the snobbishness of her kind for other ranks. 'Did they all come in today as well?'

'Some of them,' Adams said non-committally. Seeing she was making no move to serve them, he threw a half-crown on the counter.

'Take them a couple of beers, will you?' he said casually.

Maisie's eyes opened wide. 'My, is that the way you treat your blokes? Do you tuck 'em in bed as well?'

She filled two glasses and went over to the airmen. Adams drained his glass and picked up his gloves from the counter. 'See you later,' he said as she came back. 'And thank you again for your help.'

Maisie showed her disappointment. 'Are you goin' already? When's your wife coming?'

'Monday, I hope. I'm phoning her tonight and will drop in tomorrow to let you know.'

Seeing the young A.C.2 was rising, obviously trying to pluck up the courage to thank him, Adams moved hastily to the black-out curtain. 'Cheerio, and thank you again.'

'Cheerio,' Maisie sighed. She watched him go out, then turned to the two airmen. She gave a sarcastic laugh.

'No wonder you join the Air Force!'

McTyre scowled, picked up his beer, and slouched forward. 'Don't get any wrong ideas about us, kid. You know who we are?'

Maisie eyed him with both scorn and curiosity. 'Haven't a clue.'

'We're 633 Squadron. That's who we are.'

'Names and numbers mean nothing to me,' Maisie sniffed, inwardly impressed.

McTyre's face assumed the expression old sweats always assume before erks and civilians: a mixture of cynicism, bitterness and contempt.

'You ain't heard of 633? What's the matter with you? Ain't you English?'

'Don't get fresh with me,' Maisie snapped.

The young A.C.2 wandered to the bar. His eyes had not yet recovered from his being treated to a beer by a squadron-leader. McTyre jerked a grimy thumb at him.

'Just posted to us. Don't know the time yet.'

'I ain't surprised, with that clock of yours floating around in front of him,' Maisie threw back. 'What've you come to Sutton Craddock for, anyway?'

McTyre's face took on a secretive expression. He leaned forward. 'Special job, kid. Big stuff. Must be, or they wouldn't have sent us.'

'You ain't half got an opinion of yourself, haven't you? What's so wonderful about your squadron?'

McTyre's voice held all the bitterness of the unsung hero. 'If you read th' papers, you'd know. I keep telling you – there ain't a squadron in Blighty like ours.' He screwed up his long face for inspiration. It came – brilliantly. 'We're like . . . we're like the Guards in the Army, kid. The best! Ain't you heard of Grenville's raids on Rotterdam? Or on Emden and Brest? What's the matter with you. . . ?'

Maisie's eyes had suddenly rounded. 'Did you say Grenville? Roy Grenville?'

'That's right,' McTyre said, his expression triumphant now. 'Roy Grenville. He's our Squadron Commander. See what I mean now, kid?'

CHAPTER 3

Twelve hours later a small Norwegian fishing-boat drew alongside a jetty in a northern Scottish port. Except for a car, standing with dimmed lights, and two waiting men, the jetty was deserted. The boat's diesel engine went silent as she drifted slowly in, the wind soughing through her riggings. The two waiting men seized her mooring ropes, and a few seconds later the boat was firmly anchored to the quayside.

The two men on the jetty hurried back to their car, one settling behind the wheel, the other taking his seat in the back. The engine started up impatiently. A few seconds passed, then a man wearing a dark-blue fisherman's jersey leapt up from the boat and ran towards them. He was no sooner in the car than it pulled away, throwing him back into his seat. He felt his hand gripped tightly.

'Hello, my boy. How did it go this time?'

'Very well, sir.' The newcomer had a faint Norwegian accent.

'No trouble?'

'No, sir. Nothing.'

The darkness was giving way to the grey of the dawn, and both men could see the other's features. The Norwegian was a man in his late twenties, tall and broad, with an open, pleasant face and a shock of yellow hair. His questioner was an elderly man of soldierly appearance with iron-grey hair and a trim moustache. The epaulettes on his khaki greatcoat showed him to be a Brigadier.

He had a clipped controlled voice. 'Any more luck?' he asked quietly.

The Brigadier's hand gripped the young man's arm. 'Well done. We've had a bad week, wondering how things were going.' He paused, then went on: 'How are you feeling after the trip? Would you like a rest before the interrogation? We're all pretty keen to get started, of course, but I can arrange a rest if you need one.'

'No; I'm all right, sir. Where are we going now?'

'We've got a place in the country – it's only fifteen minutes from here. Anyway, you can have a long rest tomorrow. In fact, you should have a fairly easy time for the next two or three weeks. This is what we have laid on for you. . . .'

The Brigadier spoke for over ten minutes. 'You'll leave by train in two days' time,' he finished. 'When you get to Highgate, the Air Force will take you over. We've put an Air Commodore in the know, a chap called Davies, and he'll take you to the squadron's new base at Sutton Craddock. Once there, your job is to prevent curiosity. That could be a nuisance, so we've arranged for you to go as a naval lieutenant. The story will be circulated that you've been sent by the Admiralty as a liaison officer – to study Air Force procedure and also to tip off the squadron about enemy naval movements and so on. Most bomber squadrons get one sooner or later, and we think it will cover you up nicely. Of course you'll get more detailed instructions before you go, but is everything clear so far?'

'Quite clear. What squadron is it, sir?'

The Brigadier's voice expressed his satisfaction. 'We've done well for you there, although Bomber Comand didn't let them go without a fight. We've got 633 Squadron – Roy Grenville's boys. As you probably know they are one of Bomber Command's crack squadrons.' His tone grew serious again. 'They need to be, from what we hear.'

The Norwegian was looking puzzled. 'But Grenville's squadron uses Bostons, doesn't it? Surely they cannot carry heavy enough bombs for this job? And you say Sutton Craddock is down in North Yorkshire. Shouldn't they use a base in Scotland to cut down the range?'

Again the Brigadier lowered his voice. 'Jerry might start getting suspicious if a new light bomber squadron moved up into Scotland. He'll be wondering about 633, of course, but for the very reason you mention he won't guess its purpose.'

The doubt was still in the Norwegian's eyes. 'But I still do not understand, sir. How can they do this job in Bostons?'

'They won't have to,' the Brigadier told him. 'There's something very special coming along. Don't worry – they'll have the planes to get there.'

Back at Sutton Craddock that morning all the orderly disorder of a squadron on the move was at its height. An endless convoy of lorries were bringing in the stores. Thousands of gallons of high octane fuel were being poured into the petrol dump; hundreds of tons of equipment was being stacked into the workshops, the hangars, and the Nissen huts. The bomb-store at the far end of the airfield was being filled with 2,000-lb. A.P.'s, 1,000-lb. and 500-lb. M.C.'s, 250-lb. incendiaries, fragmentation bombs, S.C.I.'s, 4-lb. incendiaries, and dozens of different types of fuses and detonators. In the station armoury were being stored the spare Browning guns, the gun-sights, the belt-filling machines, the Mk. IX bomb-sights, the spare bomb-carriers, the bomb-pistols: all the hundred and one ancillaries that go with the weapons of a modern squadron.

In the workshops men toiled, heaved, and swore. Mechanics complained about their tool kits, lost in transit. Sweating N.C.O.s dashed from officers to men and from men back to officers again. As fast as stores were removed, fresh piles took their places as the lorries rolled in. New postings from training units wandered rain-soaked and glassy-eyed through the chaos, too dazed to palpitate at the yells and curses from red-faced N.C.O.s.

Everywhere it was the same. The Orderly Room looked as if a bomb had burst slap in the middle of the floor. Requisition forms, leave passes, ration slips: all the bumph so dear to Sergeant Whitton's heart was strewn in unbalanced heaps on desks, chairs and cupboards, and littered over the floor. Typewriters lay at odd dejected angles, clearly without hope of being used again. Men moved like nightmare figures, moving papers from A to B, wincing as another pile thudded on A again.

Panics came thick and fast. The Station Equipment Officer found a packing-case of men's underpants was incredibly filled with Bloomers Blue, Style 7, a grave mutation indeed. The Armament Officer found his harmonizing gear a shattered mess of twisted tubes and pulverized glass. The Maintenance Officer found that one of his bowsers had been routed to Scotland; and the Signals Officer found his dachshund pup, Hans, was missing. For safety Hans had been put in the care of three wireless mechanics who were bringing the Signals Van to the airfield. A pub had proved his downfall. While the three airmen were inside, having a hasty pint, Hans had spied a comely bitch pattering prettily down the pavement outside. With a yelp and a howl Hans had gone out of the window and hotfoot down the street after her. Result – Hans A.W.O.L., and sparks twittering round the Signal Officer's lips.

But at last order began to emerge. The example was set by the Station Disciplinary Officer, W/O Bertram (known from the C.O. down to the lowest erk as Bert the Bastard). After allotting his hundreds of airmen their billets, he set about putting an end to this nonsense. Superbly indifferent to the chaos raging around him he lowered his massive frame down on a packing-case and made out his first duty roster. The sight of those D.R.O.s was salutary. The guard-room rallied and made its first kill – an A.C.1 wearing a pair of civilian shoes. The Maintenance Officer contacted his bowser heading for the Western Isles, and said a few succinct words to its driver. Hans was discovered by an M.P. howling outside a house of low repute and brought back a sadder and wiser pup. The Intelligence and Navigation Officers found their charts and maps and began getting their offices in order. The Squadron Office, the Flight Offices, the Messes, the Cook House, the Crew Rooms: all started receiving their equipment at last. The familiar yellow gas detectors began appearing in their usual places, at the entrance to the E.T. rooms and the latrines. . . .

In short, 633 Squadron was rapidly becoming itself again.

CHAPTER 4

The station wagon drove into the gates of Sutton Craddock and halted. The M.P. on duty peered in, then stiffened to attention. A sergeant, already alerted, came out of the guard-house at the double, his boots clattering on the tarmac road. He skidded to a halt and saluted.

The driver, a pretty W.A.A.F. with a supercilious nose, leaned her forage cap and curls from the side window. 'Station Headquarters – the C.O.'s officer, please.'

The sergeant pointed along the road to a long, low brick building on the left. 'Second door, Miss, and take the first corridor to the right. . . .' Before he could finish the car shot away from him. He thought ponderously, then threw a discreet salute after it.

The Station Commander's office that morning was not its usual self. The rooms on either side of it had been emptied for the occasion and a security guard posted in the corridor and on the road outside the window, both men with instructions to look as inconspicuous as possible.

Barrett, the Station C.O., was standing restlessly at the window. Barrett was a heavily-built man of forty-two, with thinning hair, rather melancholy brown eyes, and a moustache large enough to earn him the nickname of Wally from his men. He was a South African by birth, his parents having settled in England during his early teens. He had joined the R.A.F. as a regular, and an apprentice-ship at Halton had been followed by a pre-war tour in both India and the Middle East. Although not imaginative, he was efficient, conscientious, and popular with his men. His ribbons included the A.F.C. and the D.F.C., the latter medal having been won over Kiel in the early days of the war when he had collected a chest wound that had grounded him for a long time. Because of it he was still under orders to fly as little as possible – an order that irked him, for he was a very keen pilot.

As he stood at the window the distant roar of engines as a Boston was run up for testing came to him. Queer business, this posting, he reflected. Too much secrecy for my liking. Anyway, maybe something would come out of the bag today. He certainly hoped so.

The station wagon pulled up outside with a squeal of brakes. Barrett gave it one look, then strode quickly to the door, motioning the sentry towards him.

'They're coming now,' he said gruffly. 'Don't let 'em see you're on guard. But keep a close watch once they're inside.'

He returned into his office and waited. A few seconds later he heard footsteps in the corridor, then a tap on the door.

Barrett knew the first of the two men who entered. It was Air Commodore Davies, an alert little man with a sharp intelligent face and quick darting eyes. In certain moods he resembled a truculent cockerel. Temper or not, he was a man Barrett held in high esteem. He came forward now with characteristic quick strides, his hand outstretched. He had a sharp, somewhat high-pitched voice.

'Hello, Barrett. How's everything going? Seeing daylight yet?'

'We're nearly out of the wood, sir. We're getting the kites air-tested today.'

'Good man. That's fine. Now I want you to meet Lieutenant Bergman. Lieutenant Bergman: this is Wing Commander Barrett, 633 Squadron's C.O.'

The Norwegian, tall and broad-shouldered in his naval uniform, stepped forward. Barrett took a look at his firm mouth and steady blue-grey eyes and decided he looked a good type. He held out his hand.

'Glad to meet you, Lieutenant.'

'I am very pleased to meet you, sir.'

Barrett noticed the foreign accent and wondered whether it had any connection with the conference to follow. He saw Davies looking at him.

'Where's Grenville and your Intelligence Officer?'

'They're both in the S.I.O.'s room, sir. I thought there might be something you wanted to tell me before they came in. I can get 'em here in half a minute.'

Davies shook his head. 'No; I don't think there's anything. Give them a call, will you?'

As Barrett spoke into his desk telephone, Bergman moved to the window, watching the airman who was sauntering up and down with the utmost unconcern before it. He caught Barrett's eye as the C.O. put the receiver down.

'One of your security men, sir?'

Barrett looked disappointed. 'Why, yes, he is, as a matter of fact.' He went resentfully to the window. 'I told the damn fool to look as inconspicuous as possible.'

Davies' bright eyes twinkled. 'I shouldn't worry too much, Barrett. Lieutenant Bergman has a nose for them. He needs to have, in his job.'

There was a tap on the door. 'Come in,' Barrett shouted. Bergman turned with him, watching with interest.

One of the men who entered was Adams, his eyes curious behind his spectacles at the sight of the naval officer. Bergman examined him, then turned his gaze on his companion. This one, he knew, would be Grenville.

Roy Grenville was twenty-six, slightly over medium height and compact of build. The force of his personality struck Bergman at once, that indefinable magnetism that makes a man a natural leader. Yet there was nothing about his appearance to conform with the popular conception of the ace pilot: he wore his uniform correctly and well. The same self-discipline showed in his expression and movements, indicating that here was a man who, after subjecting his mind and body to a hundred perils, had learned all their tricks, and now had both under rigid control. He looked an intelligent man who was applying all the power of his mind to the business of war with a ruthless disregard to its effects on himself.

Below his pilot's brevet was an impressive row of ribbons, including the D.S.O. and D.F.C.

Introductions were made and Bergman found himself shaking hands with Grenville. The pilot's eyes stared into his own, assessing him, coldly speculative on his rôle in the conference.

Davies, who knew Grenville, exchanged a few warm words with him, then took his place behind Barrett's desk. His quick, keen eyes flickered on each man in turn.

'The first thing I'm going to impress on you,' he began, 'is the need for absolute secrecy in everything you're going to hear. Not only Lieutenant Bergman's life, but the lives of hundreds of others could be lost by careless talk. In fact,' and his voice was grim, 'God knows just what isn't at stake in this show, so keep your mouths buttoned right up.'

He threw a glance at Bergman, smiling now. 'As you're going to find out in a moment, the Lieutenant here isn't quite all he seems. But as far as the rest of this squadron goes, he is a Norwegian Naval Officer who has come here to find out what makes the R.A.F. tick, and also to act as a liaison officer between you and naval affairs in northern waters. Most bomber squadrons get a naval officer sooner or later, and this is yours. Look after him and play up to him. That's something you *can* let out of the bag.'

He stared briefly out of the window, then turned to them again, his voice lower now. 'In actual fact Lieutenant Bergman is a liaison officer acting between the Norwegian Linge – that's their resistance movement – and our own Special Services. He used to spend most of his time over in Norway, tipping us off by wireless about shipping movements and that sort of thing. Now, however, he has handed those duties over to one of his assistants because he has made a discovery too important to be mentioned over the radio, even in code. During the last few months he has been nipping backwards and forwards, sometimes by sea, sometimes by air, to find out what more he can do about it and also, of course, to keep his resistance men organized. Now it seems things have gone far enough for us to be called in to help.

'Now I can't tell you what the job is going to be, because I don't know myself yet. Frankly, I was only told this little bit three days ago and then, I suspect' – and he threw a wry smile at Bergman – 'only because the powers-that-be decided it would look less suspicious if your squadron orders came through Group in the ordinary way instead of direct from Special Services. But this much I can tell you. . . .

'You're going to operate with these Norwegian patriots. You're going to drop supplies to them when they need them, and you're going to make any attacks Lieutenant Bergman thinks necessary. I hope he finds plenty necessary because then it'll help to justify your existence to Bomber Command, who loaned you to Special Services with the greatest reluctance. They don't know what is behind all this, either. But, according to Lieutenant Bergman and a certain gentleman I cannot name, you're going to be given the biggest job you've ever tackled within the next few months, and you have to start training for it shortly. No, don't ask me what it is – I haven't a clue. All I'm told is that it's immensely important and that you'll need to be trained to perfection to carry it out. Now I'm going to let Lieutenant Bergman take over for a minute or two. He might enlighten you a little more – we'll see. Lieutenant Bergman. . . . '

All three men watched the fair-headed Norwegian intently as he rose to address them, and all felt disappointment when he gave a rueful shake of his head.

'I am very sorry, gentlemen, but the Air Commodore has covered everything that I am allowed to tell you at the moment. Of course, when training starts, you will have to be told more, but until then I have the strictest instructions to say nothing about this discovery. I can only assure you that its importance cannot be exaggerated.'

He sat down apologetically. Davies shrugged his shoulders. 'Well; there it is – very hush-hush indeed. Your guesses are as good as mine.' He turned to Bergman. 'All right, you can't talk abou the big job. But what about the preliminary stuff leading up to it? What about that convoy you were talking about that has a bearing on it?'

'I'm waiting for news of it now. It should come through in the next day or two.'

Davies gave his attention now to Barrett and Grenville. 'From his contacts the Lieutenant has been tipped off that a fair-sized enemy convoy, anchored in a fjord to the north of Bergen, might be making a dash southwards in the next few days. There's no hope of getting it at anchor, but it'll be a different matter when it sails. It's obviously a job for us because, apart from the time factor, it will be at the wrong side of the minefields for the Navy. That's why I want you operational at the earliest opportunity; we must play safe. . . . Get your kites air-tested today and don't let your men wander far away. Lieutenant Bergman will give you all the details once I've gone so you'll be ready when the green light comes through. All right; any questions before I go?'

Grenville's face was expressionless, but Barrett was shuffling restlessly in his chair. Davies's keen eyes fixed on him.

'Any questions, Wing Commander?'

Barrett looked slightly uncomfortable. 'I don't quite follow how the machinery of this is going to work,' he said gruffly. 'I don't mean regarding the big job – we'll hear about that later – I mean on the preliminary stuff – such as the dropping of supplies or this shipping strike. Does the Lieutenant give his orders to me, or do they come through from Group?'

A delicate diplomatic point. Bergman, in appearance at least, was of junior rank to Barrett. Davies made it clear the point had not been overlooked.

'Orders will come through from Group, from me,' he said without undue emphasis. 'After I have given them, you can then approach the Lieutenant for the finer details. Sometimes – as in the case of this shipping strike – it may be necessary for him to attend the briefings. If so, I'll tell you. When that happens the crews must think he is there on Admiralty orders. Quite clear?'

Apparently it was. Barrett's moustache lost its temporary agitation as he sank back into his seat.

Adams spoke for the first time. 'I take it arrangements will be made for a full range of photographs and maps to be sent me, sir?'

'You'll be getting a cartload,' Davies told him. 'They should be on their way now. Anything else?'

His eyes moved on to Grenville, but the Squadron Commander's expression did not change. There was silence in the room, every man knowing the futility of asking the questions he had in mind. Davies nodded and picked up his gloves.

'Right; then I'm off. They haven't finished with me back there – God knows what else they have brewing for us. Keep on your toes in the meantime; the green light for this shipping strike might come on at any time.'

He paused at the door, his quick, bright eyes flickering from man to man. 'And mind you look after your new naval officer! From what I can gather he's worth more than a division of men just now.'

Barrett saw him out to his station wagon. As it pulled away down the tarmac road, an airman, coming out of the nearby Orderly Room, let out a wolf cry on seeing the pretty W.A.A.F. driver, only to freeze into horrified silence as Davies glanced out of the window. His consternation increased when he noticed Barrett not twenty yards away.

Barrett scowled and returned to his office. He put a call through to his Maintenance Officer, then turned to Grenville. 'Townsend says all the kites will be ready for air-testing by 15.00 except for M Mary. Some are ready now. You'd better go round and tip off your crews. No, wait. . . . Maybe we'd better first have a chat with Lieutenant Bergman about this strike, so we know what we're in for. Then you can take him round with you and introduce him to the boys. Adams, I'll want to see you again this afternoon. Say at 15.00 hours. . .'

Half-an-hour later Bergman accompanied Grenville to the Flight Offices. He felt a certain diffidence while walking along the tarmac with him: Grenville was taciturn and the Norwegian's own training had done nothing to make idle talk come easily. As a result they walked most of the way in silence.

It was a bitter afternoon, the wind probing bleakly among the Nissen huts and sweeping unmolested over the scarred, cement-stained ground. Over to the east a dark bank of clouds was massing, waiting impatiently for the brief winter day to end. As they came in sight of the airfield Bergman saw the squadron's Bostons at their dispersal points, each surrounded by its attentive mechanics.

A Naafi girl was coming out of A Flight office carrying a trayful of tea mugs as they approached. Grenville held back the door, motioning for Bergman to enter. The Norwegian went in curiously. The air was thick with cigarette smoke. Groups of Flight crews were clustered round the room, some playing cards, others swopping yarns. The flight commander, 'Teddy' Young, was sitting with his cap tipped over his eyes and feet up on his desk, miraculously dozing in spite of the blaring wireless and din around him. Young was an Australian who had worked his way over to England at the begining of the war with the express purpose of joining the R.A.F. He was a powerfully-built, ginger-headed man with a slow Australian drawl.

Someone shook him. He saw Grenville and rose at once. 'Hello, skipper,' he said, reaching out and turning off the wireless. 'What can I do for you?'

The Flight crews eyed one another curiously, clearly puzzled by the presence of a naval officer. Someone let out a raspberry, quickly suppressed as Grenville stared around. A respectful silence followed.

'I want you to get your kites air-tested as soon as possible,' Grenville said. 'And then keep your men within call. No twenty-four-hour passes.'

Young's expression was curious. 'What's coming up, skipper?'

'You'll hear that later,' Grenville said. 'All you have to do now is get your kites tested and keep your men within reach.'

Young shrugged but showed no resentment, a fact that told Bergman much about Grenville's popularity with his men.

'O.K., skipper. Fair enough. I'll keep 'em around.'

Grenville motioned casually to Bergman. 'By the way; this is Lieutenant Bergman. He's been sent to us by the Navy as a liaison officer. If you're nice to him he might get you some of those duty-free cigarettes.'

Laughs came, easing the slight tension. After brief introductions, Grenville took Bergman out, leaving Young phoning up the N.C.O. in charge of Maintenance.

They crossed over to B Flight office. B Flight was commanded by Sam Milner, an American who had joined the R.A.F. in 1939. Milner looked more like a professional man than a pilot, being neat and meticulous of appearance. Townsend, the Maintenance Officer and one of the station wits, said that even in flying kit Milner could make a pair of dangling earphones look like a doctor's stethoscope. Nevertheless, Milner was one of 633's top three pilots.

He nodded at Grenville's introduction and shook hands with Bergman. 'We wouldn't be doing any shipping strikes, would we, Lieutenant?' he drawled.

There was a groan from the crews in the office. A buzz of speculation broke out after the Norwegian and Grenville left them and went outside.

'That should cover the security angle,' Grenville said. 'Now we'd better see the adjutant about some quarters for you.'

Ignoring Bergman's protests that he could arrange this himself, Grenville led him towards the Administration block. The path they were taking took then near a Boston that was going up for air-testing. As they approached, its pilot opened up his two Cyclone engines, sending a cloud of gravel rattling against the metal roof of a Nissen hut.

Watching it, Bergman became aware of a disturbing sense of responsibility. All these highly trained men to whom he had been introduced were to risk their lives on the strength of his information in the weeks to come. Mistakes would mean losses, perhaps losses of friends. Until his own time came to go back into action, he knew he would be happier if allowed to share some of the missions with them.

He put a hand on Grenville's arm and tried to speak but the bellow of the engines drowned his voice. Grenville waited until the Boston rolled away, his face expressionless.

'Can you arrange for me to come with you on this shipping raid?' Bergman asked. 'There are men on the coast giving signals – it is something new and I would like to make certain it works satisfactorily.'

Grenville's voice was by nature curt. It was doubly so now. 'That's out of the question. Right out.'

'Why?' the Norwegian asked.

'You can't go on a shipping strike! To begin with we've no room for you and in any case it's far too dicey.'

'What do you mean by dicey? Dangerous?'

Understatement was Grenville's way. It was not easy now for him to give the facts. He pulled up the collar of his greatcoat, a gesture of irritation.

'Shipping strikes are always dicey. The flak is heavy and accurate, and you have to fly through it to get your target. That means losses, often heavy ones. It's quite obvious you couldn't be risked on a show like that.'

'But my life is no more important than yours, or your men's!'

'Davies didn't say that! His last words were that we should look after you. Taking you on a shipping strike would hardly be doing that.' Grenville looked down at his watch impatiently. 'Let's get over to the adjutant, please. I'd like to get my kite air-tested before lunch.'

Bergman checked him again. 'I don't think you understand. I'm not under Air Commodore Davies's orders. If I wish to go, I am quite free to do so. And I would like to go.'

Grenville, never patient of temper, was losing it now. 'And I'm saying you can't go. We've no spare kites for passengers; can't you get that into your head? And you can't go in anyone's place. Operational flying isn't a game for amateurs. A passenger could cause the death of the whole crew.' His voice became brutally frank. 'You do your job, Bergman, and let me do mine. Tell me what to sink, and I'll try to sink it. But don't go wanting a place in the grandstand, for God's sake.'

Bergman could also be stubborn. 'Why can't I go as a gunner? I have used machine-guns before. And perhaps before we go I could have an hour or two's instruction on how to use the turret.'

'Don't be a fool, man. You can't learn aerial gunnery in two hours.'

Bergman was determined not to use his power to demand a passage until the last resort. 'I know that, but it is not likely you will run into fighters on this raid, so that gunners will not be in action. And I might be needed to locate the convoy.' Feeling he had won a point, he went on quickly: 'Let me go, please. I would feel much happier sharing the raid with you. . . .'

Grenville did not miss the meaning or the sincerity of the Norwegian's last words. At that moment the Boston, which had been rolling down the runway, turned and began her take-off. A few seconds later she passed over them with a crackling roar. Grenville's eyes followed it, then dropped back on Bergman.

'I can see a point in your risking your neck to make sure the operation is a success,' he said curtly, refusing to concede, even to himself, that sentiment had in any way influenced his change of mind. 'If you think it will do that, then come along. I suppose we can manage somehow.'

Bergman showed his pleasure. 'Thank you. If you would introduce me to my pilot, perhaps I could go up with him on his tests this afternoon. . . . '

'If you go with anyone, you go with me,' Grenville said. Ignoring the Norwegian's thanks, he looked down again at his watch. 'I think we'd better do an air-test now, and fix up your quarters after lunch. Come on, then. I'll take you to the stores and you can draw your flying kit.'

Now that the affair was settled Grenville showed no resentment. Indeed his tone seemed more friendly, and Bergman ventured an unrelated question as they carried his flying kit and parachute towards the Squadron office.

'Do you know of any rooms to let in these parts? I have a sister I would like to get down here. We have not met for rather a long time.'

'You've got a sister over here?' Grenville asked in surprise.

'Yes. We were both in England when the Germans invaded Norway. I was at university at the time.'

'You'd better see Adams. He has just got his wife a room in an old pub opposite the airfield. As a matter of fact I believe she arrives today. He says there are other empty rooms. You should ask him to take you over.'

'I will,' Bergman nodded gratefully.

Grenville put a phone call through to his observer, the cheery, freckle-faced Hoppy, and then the two men changed into their flying clothes. Fifteen minutes later A Apple, the Boston with the distinctive red spinner caps, was thundering across the airfield and heading towards the distant clouds.

CHAPTER 5

Just after lunch Adams made his way down the road to the Black Swan. The east wind was stirring the bare twigs of the hedges, and he was grateful for the warmer air that met him as he entered the lounge. Kearns came round from the bar to greet him.

'Good afternoon,' Adams said. 'Has my wife arrived yet?'

'Aye, sir; she got in about an hour ago. Do you want me to give her a call?'

'No; don't bother. I'll go up and see her.'

'All right, sir. Come through this way.'

Adams tapped on the upstairs bedroom door, then entered. A slim, fashionably-dressed woman was sitting on the bed opposite him, smoking a cigarette. She was about thirty, with dark, well-groomed hair, and a narrow, elegant face. At her feet was an opened suitcase with half its contents strewn on the floor around her.

Adams closed the door and went over eagerly, bending down to kiss her. She let him touch her cheek, then turned away sharply. Adams' face dropped at once.

'Sorry I couldn't meet you in, darling,' he muttered. 'We had an urgent conference this morning – there wasn't a hope of getting away.'

Her voice was waspish. 'It took me over half an hour to get a taxi. I was frozen to the bone when I got here.'

'I'm sorry, darling. . . .'

She gave a sudden, violent shudder. 'I'm absolutely frozen. And this room's like an ice box.'

Adams looked around guiltily, noticing for the first time there was no fireplace. 'I'll get you a paraffin heater,' he said hastily.

'You'll have to get me something, or I'll never survive the winter.'

'There is a private lounge downstairs you can use, you know. It has a fire.'

'I've seen it. The landlord has shown me around.'

There was a brief silence. Adams wandered dismally over to the rear window and stared out. It overlooked the garden and the field behind the inn.

'I took a rear room because the one at the front overlooks the airfield,' he said. 'I thought this one would be quieter. I remember your saying at the last place how the planes kept you awake.'

She inhaled deeply on her cigarette, making no comment. Adams' eyes wandered round the room, taking in the old-fashioned marble-topped washstand, the ornate mahogany wardrobe and dressing-table, and the stiff-backed chairs. He looked back at his wife, Valerie. She had not moved, one slim leg was still crossed over the other, and her thin mouth was turned down at the corners. She was clearly in one of her moods.

Adams could not hide his disappointment. 'I thought you might like it here,' he muttered. 'I know things are a bit old-fashioned, but they could be worse and – '

She broke in with a sarcastic laugh. 'Old-fashioned? Have you seen the kitchen? It has a stone floor, bare walls, an old-type gas-stove that explodes in your face, and a sink that's fit for nothing but pig swill. And there are absolutely no facilities whatever for doing any washing.'

Adams nodded heavily. 'I know there are snags, but what could I do? Highgate is full of evacuees – it's hopeless even to look for a room there. Things are pretty difficult everywhere these days.'

He realized he had said the wrong thing as soon as the words came out. 'Don't tell me there's a war on,' she snapped. 'If you do, I'll scream.'

Adams recognized all the signs of a first-class quarrel. He looked hastily at his watch. 'I'll have to be getting back, I'm afraid. Barrett wants to see me again this afternoon.'

Valerie showed a spark of interest. 'Has it anything to do with your posting here?' When he nodded, she went on: 'What's behind this move? Has Barrett told you anything yet?'

Adams looked uncomfortable and did not speak. She stared at him. 'Well, what's the matter?'

'It's very hush-hush,' Adams muttered, shifting uncomfortably.

'What about that? You've told me things before. Why the secrecy now?'

Adams moved despairingly towards the door. 'Sorry, darling, but I can't talk about it. In any case I don't know very much. . . .'

'Things have gone pretty far when you can't trust your own wife, haven't they?'

For all his meekness Adams had a temper. It began to show now, in spite of himself. 'I'm not to blame for the Official Secrets Act, you know.'

Valerie's thin mouth curled. 'There's no need to shout. We don't want everyone in the place to know we're quarrelling.'

Adams took a deep breath, let it out slowly. 'The last thing I want to do is quarrel. It's simply that I'm not allowed to breathe a word of this to anyone – it's supposed to be too big.' He looked at his watch again. 'I'll have to go. I'll be over this evening, all being well.'

She rose. 'What do you intend doing tonight? Are you going to bring a few of the boys over?'

'Why, no; I hadn't planned to,' he muttered. 'I thought as it was our first evening we'd have it alone.'

She came nearer and stood beside him. Once more he found himself uncomfortably reminded that she was the taller of the two. She put a hand on his arm, her tone changing.

'I'd like a little company tonight, darling. It'll do me good. Bring one or two of the boys over, please.'

Adams remembered the projected shipping strike. 'There's a slight chance we may all be on duty tonight.' Then, seeing her expression, he went on hastily: 'Only a slight one. I think it'll be all right. Who would you like me to bring?'

'Oh, Jack Richardson. And what about Roy. . . ?'

'Roy has no time for Richardson, you know. In any case, I believe Richardson is Duty Officer tonight. I can ask Roy, but you know what it's like getting him to parties.'

Valerie pouted. 'I'm certain he'll come if you tell him I've just arrived and feel like company. Try him, anyway. Now who else can you ask?'

Her change of mood made a split in Adams' mind, one half of it thanking God and becoming co-operative, the other half turning hurt and resentful. The co-operative half won.

'We've had a Norwegian naval officer called Bergman attached to us. He told me over lunch he wants to find a room for his sister. Perhaps if he came over tonight, he could meet the landlord at the same time. He seems a nice chap and if he comes Roy may come too. I've got the idea Roy likes him.'

'Splendid, dear. That'll be lovely. You're really very sweet.' She lifted a hand and touched his cheek. 'I know I've been grumpy, but that long wait at the station was so upsetting. A little company tonight will put me right again.' With that she put up her face for him to kiss.

Adams went downstairs with his emotions in a tangle. He ran into Kearns in the hall.

'Everything all right, sir?'

'Yes; everything's fine,' Adams muttered, afraid the innkeeper's shrewd eyes were reading too much on his face.

'Don't you worry, sir,' Kearns said unexpectedly. 'We'll do our best to make her comfortable.'

Adams wondered afterwards why he did not deny the inference that he was worrying about anything, and realized it was because the ring of sympathy in the innkeeper's voice had come at a moment of need. His only thought at the time was that he liked the elderly man and would like to buy him a drink.

'I'm sure you will,' he said. At the door he turned back. 'We must have a drink and a chat together one of these nights.'

'Be glad to, sir,' Kearns said, looking pleased. 'Very glad to, indeed.'

Adams went out in the biting wind again. His only other clear reflection came at the camp entrance when the sentry presented arms. Irrelevantly but quite intensely, he realized he had never felt less worthy of a salute.

Probably because of the station order that prevented men going far afield, the public lounge was well-filled that night, and Valerie told Adams she preferred it to the quietness of the private sitting-room. Anyone without charity might have suspected that the number of unattached airmen sitting among the regular customers had some bearing on her choice. She was wearing a wine-coloured dress of light material with half-length sleeves, something totally inadequate for a winter evening, but the various admiring glances she received appeared to more than recompense her.

They had been in the lounge about fifteen minutes when Grenville and Bergman arrived. Valerie brightened up immediately on seeing Grenville.

'Hello, Roy. How nice to see you again.'

Grenville's face was expressionless as he took her hand. 'Hello, Val. You're looking well. This is Lieutenant Bergman, a naval officer attached to us. Lieutenant Bergman, Mrs Adams.'

Valerie's eyes had already appraised Bergman and her tone suggested approval. 'Delighted, Lieutenant. Please sit down, both of you. We're so glad you've come, aren't we, Frank? We were both bored to death. I'm afraid it's going to be very dull here.'

'Don't tell the lieutenant that,' Adams said, with a heavy laugh. 'He's hoping to get his sister here.'

'So I understand,' Valerie said. 'That'll be lovely. Where is your sister now?'

'In Scotland,' Bergman told her.

Valerie lifted pencilled eyebrows. 'Really! How nice for you. And you're going to get her a room here?'

'If I can, yes.'

Valerie wondered what Bergman, a Norwegian naval officer, was doing at the airfield. She was also curious to know how he came to have a sister in the country. If Grenville hadn't been there she would have asked outright, but Grenville was tight on security matters, something she had learned to her cost. She decided to tackle Adams later, and contented herself with an indirect question.

'Does she speak English as well as you, Lieutenant?'

Bergman smiled. 'Much better, I think.'

'It'll be lovely meeting her. When are you hoping to get her down?'

'Once I find a room, she can come at once,' Bergman told her. At that moment he noticed Kearns talking to Maisie behind the bar. 'Is that the innkeeper? Perhaps I could go over now and speak to him. . . .'

Valerie put a hand on his arm. 'We'll see everything is fixed up, don't worry. Have a drink with us first, and then one of us will take you over to him.' She turned her eyes on Adams.

Adams rose hastily. 'Yes, that's the idea. What will you all have?'

As Adams approached the bar, Maisie was in the last stages of an argument with Kearns. The innkeeper had brought a few bottles in to the lounge which he wanted displaying on the high shelves behind the counter. Knowing whoever put them up would have to stand on a chair and stretch upwards, he wanted to do the job himself, but Maisie would have none of it.

'I ain't got sciatica like you,' she told him. As he still protested she went on: 'Aw, let 'em look, if they want to. It ain't going to lose us the war, is it?'

Without further ado, she climbed on to a chair and motioned to him to pass the bottles up to her. As she reached upwards with the first one, displaying a generous length of leg, the black-out curtain was pulled aside and two Air Force warrant officers appeared. One saw Maisie and let out a howl.

'Hey, Jimmie. Take a look at this. We've found somethin' here, kid.'

The hum of conversation stopped as every eye turned on the speaker. The airmen knew him well; the civilians were soon to have that pleasure. The first thing they noticed was a broad craggy face, split open into an infectious grin, and topped by a mop of fair, unruly hair. It was Gillibrand of B Flight, one of Sam Milner's crack pilots. Everything about Gillibrand was big, his hands, feet, generosity, craziness and courage. He stood grinning at Maisie now, his unbuttoned overcoat swinging back and revealing the D.F.M. beneath his pilot's brevet.

His companion, Jimmie Willcox, provided a contrast in types. Willcox was a slim, dark-haired boy who could not have weighed more than nine stone, with a pale, sensitive face and wistful eyes and mouth. He looked no more than eighteen although he was actually twenty-two. At the moment he was blushing.

'What a sight to greet a feller on a winter night,' Gillibrand said.

Maisie turned, staring at him. 'What's the matter with you, you big gorilla? Ain't you ever seen legs before?'

'Not like yours, baby,' Gillibrand grinned, shouldering his way forward. 'They're really something.'

'What's the matter with all you Yanks? Don't they let you see women until you're twenty-one?'

'I'm not a Yank. I'm a cousin of yours, baby. I'm a Canadian.'

23

Maisie sniffed her disgust. 'Don't go calling yourself my cousin. I've got decent relations.'

Gillibrand motioned to the bottles. 'Go on, baby; don't stop. That was a great act.'

Maisie stepped down from the chair with dignity. 'I'll put the rest up when the wolves have gone,' she told Kearns.

The hum of conversation returned at a higher level, the bewildered locals throwing glances over their shoulders at Gillibrand, who was now talking to his observer. Adams paid for his drinks, put them on a tray, and returned to his table.

'What do you think of our mad Canadian?' he asked Bergman as he handed him his glass.

The Norwegian was laughing. 'He seems quite a character.'

'He's a character, all right,' Adams said, sitting down. 'He's completely crazy and a flying fool. If he sees a gun firing at him, he wants to fly down the barrel to get at the gunner's throat. Roy here could tell you some yarns about him.'

'Who is that with him?'

'That's his observer, Jimmie Willcox.'

Back at the counter Gillibrand was nudging Jimmie and pointing at Maisie, who was pretending to ignore him.

'It's always a good sign, kid, when they act toffee-nosed. Means you're doing all right. Watch me.' He approached Maisie. 'Hey, cousin! How 'bout having a drink with your relation from across the sea, huh?'

Maisie was very haughty. 'I'm particular who I drink with,' she said, nose in the air.

'What about my buddy here, then? He ain't done nothing to you.'

Maisie eyed the blushing Jimmie and softened. 'He's different. He's a gentleman.'

Gillibrand let out a howl of delight and pushed Jimmie forward. 'Kid, you're a success. Buy the girl a drink.'

'Stop pushin' him about,' Maisie snapped. 'Can't you see you're embarrassin' him.'

Gillibrand looked at Jimmie, then slapped him on the back. 'Just my way, son. No harm meant. Come on; let's go over and sit with the natives. Nothing like a few hayseeds to liven things up.'

He pulled his small companion across the room. As he saw Grenville, he flipped a respectful hand. 'Evenin', Skipper. Nice dive they've got here.'

Grenville nodded. The startled locals scattered as the Canadian went among them. Within a minute he had them all gaping as he plunged into a hair-raising story of the war.

Adams gave a laugh, the first relaxed sound he had made that evening. 'What a character! Look at their faces! They can't keep their eyes off him.'

Someone at the counter could not, either. Maisie caught Kearns looking at her and flushed: a rare thing for Maisie.

'Men who look at women like that shouldn't be allowed in decent pubs,' she said. 'It gives 'em a bad name.'

24

Kearns smiled. 'I don't think there's any harm in him, lass.'

Maisie sniffed. 'I wouldn't trust myself alone with him – not for five minutes, I wouldn't.'

There was a twinkle in Kearns' shrewd eyes. 'I'll bet you wouldn't, lass.'

Maisie glanced at him suspiciously, but his face was bland and innocent again.

Four hundred miles away, in the cold and darkness of the Northern winter, the convoy that was 633's target lay at anchor off Innvik. Innvik, a port six miles up the Svartfjord north of Bergen, was an ideal war-time anchorage. It was guarded from the air by the long precipitous mountains that flanked either side of the fjord, and protected from the sea by the rocky island of Utvik, a naval fortress lying four miles out from the coast. An additional protection was the winter darkness. From late November until February the sun did not rise high enough to clear the mountain tops, so leaving the water below in permanent gloom.

The convoy had been at Innvik for eight days. In that time it had discharged its cargo to a secret destination farther up the fjord, and replaced it by another. Except for one small hitch soon to be put right, all had gone well, and shortly the convoy would leave its haven and steal south down the long Norwegian coast, picking up other ships and an escort on the way. Its destination was Stettin in the Baltic, and in spite of the watchful British Navy and the probing planes of Coastal Command, the odds seemed greatly in favour of its reaching there safely. The long nights and the steep coastal mountains would offer it the protection they had given to so many ships before. And after delivering its valuable cargo of wood and metal ores in Stettin, it would return again to the Svartfjord with a cargo of even greater significance.

There seemed, then, every reason for enemy confidence and for the party which the Convoy Commander gave his officers before the serious business of briefing began. But he was not aware of what was taking place that very night only six miles away from his hotel.

Five hundred feet above the Svartfjord's dark and narrow mouth, a man was making his way through the snow towards a thick clump of dwarf birch that grew under a rock face. Reaching it he paused a moment to make certain he was not observed. Nothing moved in the snow around him, and satisfied he pushed his way into the trees.

'Olaf,' he called softly. 'Olaf; where are you?'

A deep voice at his elbow made him start with fear. 'I'm here, Jan Ericson, checking up you aren't a German.' A hearty laugh followed and Ericson felt his arm grasped. 'Come on, Jan. Take your skis off and come inside.'

Ericson was led through a thick camouflaged cover of conifer branches and foliage into a tent, in which both a paraffin lamp and a heater were burning. A camp-bed took up one side of the tent, a pile of provisions the other. Ericson knew that alongside this tent was another containing a battery-driven transmitter and receiver.

The paraffin lamp showed Ericson to be a slight man with quick, nervous eyes.

He was warmly dressed in a thick ski-suit, but his face appeared pale and cold. The wireless operator, Olaf Johansen, was a thick-set man in his early forties, with bushy eyebrows, a weather-beaten face, and a shock of untidy brown hair. He was wearing serge trousers and a leather windbreaker. As he entered the tent he threw a .38 revolver on the camp-bed.

'I heard our skis and thought the devils might have started night search parties in the hope of spotting a light.'

Ericson had a thin, breathless voice. 'Be careful. They had a Storch up the other day trying to locate you.'

Johansen grinned. 'I know. And I decreased my signal strength as he flew nearer and sent him off in the other direction. Don't worry about me – this rock face is a big protection, anyway. What about the convoy?'

'Alvin managed to see me for a few minutes today. A railwayman tipped him off – apparently the last consignment of ore has been held up because of a landslide blocking the line. But they expect to get it through on Wednesday and will sail on Thursday.'

The burly Johansen scratched his chin and grinned. 'Thursday, eh! That's good. That leaves us plenty of time. I'll let Bergman know tonight. Anything else? Any news from farther up the fjord?'

Ericson shook his head. 'No. Nothing yet.'

Johansen's rugged face was grim now. 'The moment you hear anything, let me know at once. You know how important it's supposed to be. Tell everyone to keep his ears open. Now; what about a hot drink? You look cold.'

Ericson shook his head. 'No; I must get back. The devils have put me on early shifts this week.'

'But you've plenty of time. Come on, man. Sit down and relax.'

'No, Olaf; I must go.'

Ericson was clearly nervous and Johansen made no further effort to detain him. He saw him out of the trees and watched his diminishing figure until it had vanished into the gloomy, snow-covered mountainside. Then he returned to his hide-out, and ten minutes later began tapping out his coded message to England.

On the surface nothing had changed. The mountains were as high, the darkness as unrevealing. Yet now the odds on the convoy reaching Stettin had appreciably dropped.

CHAPTER 6

As Bergman had said, his sister did not take long in coming to Sutton Craddock once a room had been found for her. She arrived on Tuesday morning. Bergman met her at the station and brought her to the Black Swan in a car Barrett had lent him.

They arrived just as Adams was stepping out of the front porch. With other members of the squadron that could be spared, Adams had been given a few hours' rest that morning in preparation for the long hours of duty that lay ahead. He was on his way back to camp when the car turned in on the drive. Although the glass was dropping fast, it was a clear morning with a pale blue sky and a wintry sun.

Bergman threw open the door and jumped out, waving a cheerful hand at Adams. 'Hello. Come and meet my sister. She would like to thank you for helping her get a room.'

At that moment a girl stepped out of the car, and Adams' romanticism made him draw in a sharp breath.

Hilde Bergman could not be taken for anything else but Scandinavian. She was bare-headed, and wore her mass of thick, blonde hair brushed up and over her ears. On many women it would have been too severe a style, on her it only served to reveal the perfect bone structure of her face, the foundation of lasting beauty. She had lovely, regular features, very composed for one so young, was tall and gracefully built, and was wearing a camel-hair coat with a light blue scarf at her throat. She came forward smiling, and as Adams took her hand he saw her eyes were a fine-grained texture of blue and grey. Looking into them was like gazing to the bottom of a sunlit Norwegian lake.

'I am very pleased to meet you, Squadron-Leader, and must thank you for helping Finn to get me this room.'

Adams had no sooner recovered his breath when he lost it again on hearing her voice. It had a mellow quality, it sang in his ears like a bronze bell, and her slight accent made it irresistible.

'I hope you like it here,' he managed.

'I know I shall. I am looking forward very much to meeting your wife, too. Finn has told me all about you both.'

Adams began remembering things again. There was Valerie – yes, he ought to introduce them. He glanced at his watch, then nodded.

'Val's in her room at the moment. Let me help you upstairs with your things, and I'll introduce you to her. She'll be able to show you around today.'

'You are certain you can spare the time?'

'Oh, yes. I'm a bit early; it's all right.'

Valerie received the girl quite cordially, and without quite knowing why, Adams was relieved. In his gratitude it did not occur to him that Bergman's presence might have had some influence on Valerie's behaviour. In anyone other than his wife Adams was a good judge of character, but loyalty was inclined to bias his judgement of her. He stayed until Hilde and Bergman had returned to the girl's room, then took his leave. In spite of the long and anxious hours awaiting him, he felt an odd lightness of heart as he made his way to the airfield.

Back in the inn Bergman helped his sister to unlock her suitcases. It was clear from both their expressions that they were delighted to be together again. They had always been deeply attached to one another, and their exile in England had strengthened that attachment. Now he was alone with her Bergman spoke in Norwegian.

'How do you like the inn?'

Her enthusiasm was spontaneous. 'Oh, very much, Finn. It's a charming old place.'

Bergman stared round at the heavy furniture and the old prints on the walls. 'I hope it's not going to be damp.'

'Oouf. . . . ' She made a gesture of impatience. 'You worry about me too much, Finn. It is nice and I am going to be very comfortable here.'

Bergman nodded and went to the window. He motioned her over. 'Have you seen this?'

She followed his eyes and saw the airfield across the road with its hangars, Nissen hut, and beyond them the Bostons at their dispersal points.

'Just the place for an agent, isn't it?' Bergman said humorously. 'Perhaps it's just as well you've taken it over.'

'Have any other rooms the same view?'

'Only one. The innkeeper's bedroom – directly above you. But Security have checked on him: he's all right. And both he and his barmaid have been warned to keep their mouths closed on anything they see.'

She watched his face closely as he was speaking. There was the faintest air of preoccupation about him – something she had noticed on first meeting him at the station. In one as trained in self-discipline as he, it usually meant only one thing.

'You're not going off again just as I have arrived here, are you?' she asked quietly.

He stared at her, then laughed. 'No; of couse I'm not. Why do you ask?'

She made a little fluttering movement of her right hand, a characteristic gesture. 'I do not know, but if you are not going it does not matter. . . .' She motioned towards the airfield. 'But I do not understand. Why have they attached you to the Air Force and why are you in naval uniform? Can you tell me, or is it something I should not know?'

He told her as much as Davies had told the others. 'That's as far as I dare go at the moment,' he finished. 'And even that much is very secret indeed.'

28

Her clear steady eyes, the eyes Adams was still thinking about, were shining very brightly now. 'But that is wonderful, Finn. It means you will be staying here – not going back. . . .'

He checked her quickly. 'It means I shall be here for a few weeks. That is why I asked you to come.'

'Only a few weeks. . . .'

He saw her disappointment and squeezed her arm. 'That's longer than we've been together since 1940. Let's count ourselves lucky and make the best of it, shall we?'

She made herself smile immediately. 'Of course we will. We will have a wonderful time. Tell me about everyone here. Have you made any friends yet?'

'Yes; I think so. There's Adams – I quite like him – and then there's Roy Grenville. I haven't told you, have I, that this is the famous 633 Squadron with Roy Grenville as Squadron Commander? You must have read about them in the newspapers.'

She nodded. 'Yes; I have. You say you and he have become friends?'

Bergman gave a rueful laugh. 'I like to think so, although it's not easy to be certain with anyone as curt of nature as Grenville. He's a strange chap in many ways.'

'What do you mean?'

'I don't know. . . . He gives me the impression of being a very intelligent man who has dedicated himself to this war. In peace-time I could imagine him as an explorer or an engineer – you know, the type that builds a bridge where no bridge has been built before. He has that sort of aggressiveness that every man needs to be a man. But, of course, aggressiveness can be used either way, to create or to destroy. The Nazis trained their youngsters to use it destructively. To defeat them we have to use ours the same way. I feel that is what Grenville has done – deliberately made himself into as efficient a fighting machine as a man can be.'

'You make him sound soulless,' she said.

Bergman shook his head. 'On the contrary, I keep getting the impression he bitterly resents what he has had to do, and so takes it out of the Germans all the more. But I may be hopelessly wrong about him; he may really like war for war's sake. He's a most difficult man to understand.'

'You seem to have tried hard enough,' She smiled.

'I've been seeing a good deal of him these last few days, that's probably why. He has taken me up with him a few times.'

She gave a start. 'You don't mean on raids?'

'Heavens, no. Just round and about. I asked him to.'

'Haven't you done enough flying?' she asked quietly.

Bergman shrugged. 'I'd never flown in Bostons before, and now I'm attached here I felt I ought to know something about them.'

There was a disturbed look in her eyes now. She watched him closely and noticed how his gaze kept wandering towards the distant planes.

They chatted for another ten minutes, then Bergman picked up his cap regretfully. 'I'm afraid I shall have to be getting back now.'

'Will you come over tonight?'

His eyes wandered to the window again. He hesitated, then shook his head. 'Things have worked out rather badly. I got some news through the other day that will keep us on duty tonight. It isn't quite definite yet – I shall get another message through later – but in any case we shall all be standing by. But I'll be over tomorrow at the first opportunity.'

'Why are you going with them on this raid?' she asked, keeping her voice steady.

Even Bergman's training could not prevent his giving a slight start. 'How did you know I was going?'

Hilde smiled faintly. 'It wasn't difficult to guess – not after you told me you'd been going up with Grenville. I should have known you wouldn't be content to sit back here while they went into danger.' Her tone changed, became puzzled. 'But why do they let you go? Your work is dangerous enough. Surely they do not need you once they have been given their target.'

Bergman shifted uncomfortably. 'There's nothing dangerous about this, particularly as I shall be flying with Grenville. Don't worry about it, please.'

Her recollection of some of Grenville's exploits did nothing to allay her anxiety, but she knew the futility of argument.

'Promise me you will be careful,' was all she said.

He reached out and pinched her cheek affectionately. 'I will. Have a good night's sleep and don't worry. I'll be over tomorrow and will bring Grenville with me. I'm hoping you'll like him. Bye-bye now. *Adjö da.*'

'*Adjö. Ta godt vare po deg selv.*''

She went to the window and looked out. A few seconds later he appeared on the road below, a tall figure in his naval great-coat. He looked back and waved. She watched him until the corner of the inn hid him from sight, then raised her eyes to the airfield. The wintry sun had already disappeared; a dark mass of clouds had rolled in from the east and turned the light bleak. The distant Bostons looked forbidding now, and the wind, edging through the window frame, sent a shiver through her.

Once more the Bostons went through their series of complicated tests. Mechanics fussed around them; D.I.s were filled in and signed. Crews left their warm, smoky offices and took their planes up for yet another flight trial. The last Boston, D Danny belonging to Jack Arthur of B Flight, came in just as the winter dusk, sprinkled with drizzle, was settling over the field. Archer taxied her over to his dispersal point, cut her engines, and climbed stiffly out, followed by his observer and air gunner. After a brief word with his maintenance N.C.O., he left the ground crew to make their final checks.

A petrol bowser came waddling alongside to top up D Danny's tanks. Armourers climbed into the nose and turret to arm the Browning guns with their long belts of ammunition. By 16.50 the last instrument check had been made, the last panel screw pressed down and turned. Every hornet of 633 Squadron was now ready.

The air crews ate early that evening. Directly after dinner they were ordered to the Briefing Room where they were given their instructions. Bergman, in his rôle of naval officer, tried to give his contribution as nautical a flavour as possible. When the briefing was over the crews were ordered to stand by in the crew rooms for further orders.

The wait that followed was of that restless, stomach-tightening order that frays nerves and jags tempers. Some men played cards, others talked volubly, yet others sat silent smoking cigarette after cigarette. Bergman was with Adams, Grenville and Barrett in the Operations Room. New to operational flying, the Norwegian was finding it difficult to control his nerves as he waited for the crucial message to come through.

At 20.00 hours a message came but it was not the one he wanted. The outcome was an order that all crews could stand down but must remain within instant call.

As always when an operation was delayed, the reaction on the crews was unfortunate. Keyed-up nerves had to slacken of their own accord and sometimes would not. The more experienced men went to their quarters where some managed to sleep. Others stayed in the crew rooms, playing cards, smoking, watching the clock. . . .

The hours dragged by to midnight, then in to the cold winter morning. Incessant tension had now had its effect, and the squadron lay in an uneasy, exhausted sleep. At 01.06 hours the Duty Sergeant was dreaming and turning restlessly over on his camp-bed. At that moment the bell of the teletype rang, bringing him awake with a start. He heard the clack-clack of the machine and the rustle of paper, and was on his feet and across the room in an instant.

633 Squadron swung into gear. The Duty Officer, making certain all outside communication was still cut, began making his phone calls. The Wing Commander, the Engineering Officer, the Station Armament Officer, the Navigation Officer . . . down the list he went, ticking each name in turn. Like a stone thrown into a pool, the initial alarm spread. Men awoke to the ringing of phones, cursed, and swung their feet to the ground. The chatter of voices grew. The Tannoy spluttered, barked, then blared forth triumphantly. 'All air crews report to the Operations Room immediately. Repeat: All air crews report to the Operations Room immediately. . . .' It was followed by the harsh hoot of a siren.

Crews felt that familiar dryness in their throats as they grabbed their flying kit. Lorries started up in the darkness, their engines barking in the bitter wind.

The strike was on.

The patter of rain could be heard on the blacked-out window of the private sitting-room. Occasionally a few drops found their way down the chimney, making the fire splutter. Valerie put aside her magazine and yawned.

'What a night! I think I'll have a cigarette and turn in.'

Hilde, reading a book in the armchair opposite, looked up with a smile. Valerie offered her a cigarette, then took one herself, putting it into a long holder before lighting it. She was an affected smoker and made something of a ritual over the operation. Inhaling deeply, she sank back into the armchair.

'They must be on a pretty important show or the weather would have cancelled it. You've no idea what time they are taking off, have you?'

Hilde shook her head.

'I suppose we'll just get off to sleep when they'll start up,' Valerie said. Her voice turned curious. 'Your brother won't be going with them, will he? As he is a Norwegian and in the Navy, I thought they might have been put on a shipping strike off the Norwegian coast.'

Hilde gave a slight start on hearing Valerie's surmise about Bergman. She was careful to avoid any reference to his movements in her reply.

'I don't know what the raid is on, Mrs Adams,' she said truthfully. 'My brother did not give me any details.'

Valerie waved her cigarette-holder impatiently. 'Don't be so formal, for heaven's sake. My name's Valerie.' She had not missed the girl's faint start and eyed her now with some malice. 'Oh; I know they don't like talking but women usually find things out sooner or later. You needn't worry about talking to me, you know. After all, I am the Station Intelligence Officer's wife.'

Valerie learned later that Hilde had the rare quality of frankness. She learned now that she was no idle gossip. The girl nodded her head but showed clearly she had no intention of discussing the subject any further. Valerie gave a brittle laugh and rose to her feet.

'Oh, well; if we don't feel like being sociable, I think I'll turn in. Good night.'

'Good night,' Hilde said quietly, and Valerie went out with a feeling of frustration.

The girl's eyes were troubled as she turned back to the fire, and the time slipped by unnoticed. A tap on the door made her start.

She turned to see Kearns standing in the doorway. He peered around the room, then entered. 'You alone tonight, Miss?'

'Mrs Adams has been with me, but she went to bed fifteen minutes ago.'

'Your brother couldn't get over?'

'No. Not tonight.'

Kearns motioned in the direction of the bar. 'We haven't had a single airman in tonight. Do you think there's something on, Miss?'

She shook her head slowly. 'They are not supposed to tell us, Mr Kearns.'

'Aye; and I've no business asking, for that matter,' the innkeeper said quickly. 'But I was in the last war myself and I can't help havin' an interest in the lads. They're as fine a crowd as I've seen anywhere. I like the look of that brother of yours too, Miss, if you don't mind my sayin' so.'

She gave him a sudden, bright smile. 'Thank you very much.'

Kearns, in his own way as impressed with her as Adams was, moved awkwardly back to the door. 'I'm goin' to make a cup of tea now – Maisie an' me always has a cup after closin' time. Will you have one, Miss?'

'Thank you – if it is no trouble.'

'No trouble at all, Miss. How do you like it? D'you drink it the same way as us, with milk and sugar?'

'Not with sugar, thank you. But otherwise the same.'

'All right, Miss. I'll bring it through in a few minutes. Just you wait here by the fire.'

He went back to the kitchen, to return five minutes later with a cup of tea and a plate of biscuits. He chatted a few minutes, then withdrew reluctantly to the door.

'If the planes ever keep you awake at nights, Miss, and you feel like a cup of tea or anything, don't be afraid of gettin' up and makin' one. You won't disturb any of us.'

'You've very kind,' she said softly.

'Not a bit, Miss. But I've got a son in the Army an' know how things can be. Good night, Miss.'

'Good night, Mr Kearns, and thank you.'

Hilde realized he had the same thought as Valerie, that her brother might be flying with the squadron. She drank her tea, then went up to her room. The blackout curtain was not in position, so she undressed in the dark. The sheets felt icy as she slipped between them. Outside the restless wind kept tapping a tree branch against her window. She tossed about for a long time, but at last fell into a fitful sleep.

She awoke with a start, unable at once to identify the noise that had awakened her. It came again, a queer honk-honk like the sound of wild geese, only louder. Jumping from her bed she ran to the window. It was still dark outside and she had to strain her eyes to see the dim silhouettes of the Nissen huts. She realized now that the sound was that of a siren.

The morning was bitterly cold and the draughts from the window stung her bare arms. She tore a blanket from the bed, wrapped it round her shoulders, and ran back to the window. A few lights were appearing on the airfield now and she could hear the sounds of intense activity: the slam of doors, men yelling orders, trucks starting up. . . .

Storm lanterns appeared out at the dispersal points and the Bostons came into view, their wet wings and bodies glistening like huge insects. Men were all around them, pulling covers away and opening hatches. One by one their engines fired and they began moving clumsily forward, trundling away into the darkness at the right of the field.

Two minutes more and the flarepath lights clicked on, blinding Hilde for a moment. They were followed by the distant crackling snarl of two revved engines. The noise grew louder as the first Boston came into sight, picking up speed as it came down the runway. It appeared sluggish at first, and three times its wheels lifted only to fall back on the glistening runway. It was moving at speed now, a black blur between the lights. Again its wheels broke free and this time with success. With a triumphant roar it cleared the distant fence and vanished into the darkness.

The others followed it. Hilde watched them all go, too fascinated to notice the cold. In the rectangle of lights they looked like darting fish with their shining, streamlined bodies. One by one they roared away until the last of them had vanished into the night. The flarepath went out like a candle being snuffed by a finger. All that was left was a deep drone of engines, and a minute later that too had gone, leaving nothing but silence and darkness behind.

CHAPTER 7

633 Squadron refuelled and bombed-up at Sumburgh in the Shetlands. Sumburgh had been alerted and carried out the operation in record time. The aircraft lined up for take-off the moment the last trolley train pulled away. The weather had deteriorated and icy rain was falling.

Grenville swung A Apple into position, nose in line with the flarepath, and waited for Control to release him. In the armoured nose compartment ahead was Hoppy, sitting with his navigational instruments and bombsight, and in the turret behind was Bergman with his Browning guns.

Bergman's excitement was growing. This was a new adventure for him and he was finding it hard to control his nerves. He peered out through his rain-splashed turret. The rest of the squadron were forming up behind them, their recognition lights glowing like watchful eyes.

A deep tremor ran through A Apple as her throttles were opened. The noise of her engines deafened Bergman and his stomach tightened as he felt the plane begin to move forward. This was it – the last take-off before the attack. Locked in his transparent cupola, watching the driving rain and the moving lights, he felt part of some fantastic nightmare.

In the pilot's compartment ahead, Grenville was holding A Apple in the centre of the runway. The Cyclones were gaining power now and the Boston was moving at speed, the lights on either side running into a blur. Sheets of water thrown up from the tarmac splattered against the perspex windscreen and hissed into spray against the driving propellers. The Boston was sluggish under her heavy load and Grenville felt her oleo legs grunting with the strain. He held her down, waiting for her controls to lighten.

The runway shortened like a ribbon snipped by giant shears. The Cyclones were screaming their hearts out now. Grenville's eyes were fixed ahead. There was a hill up in front there – he hoped the others would remember it. His lips moved as the Boston still held the runway. Come on, come on! Get up, you bitch. . . . The wheels smacked into a pool and sent a sheet of water over the windscreen, blinding him for a moment. He eased the stick back again, the Boston bounced, but more lightly this time. He held her down another five endless seconds, then tried again. She came up, dropped a couple of feet, then held steady. Another moment and the flarepath had fallen away and they were plunged in darkness.

Grenville grouped his squadron at 4,000 feet and let them out. No chance for low-level stuff – skimming the wave tops to avoid enemy detectors. Weather conditions were right against it, and would deteriorate the farther east they went. God knows what it would be like 200 miles farther out. . . .

Grenville had a word with Hoppy over the intercom to check his course. Hoppy's voice came back, as cheery and efficient as usual. Satisfied, Grenville then spoke to Bergman.

'Everything all right back there, Finn?'

Bergman tried to keep his voice steady. 'Everything fine, Roy, thank you.'

They flew on in silence. The squadron was in battle formation, two flights of six planes, each flight in ranks of three, line abreast. All the planes had their recognition lights on, the chances of fighter interception in this weather were virtually nil, the chance of collision a far greater one. Twenty long minutes passed and then a white wall swept at them from out of the darkness. Aircraft huddled closer together, their red-eyed crews peering anxiously through the white hell of driving sleet and snow.

Another fifteen minutes and Parsons of B Flight was in trouble. Ice cut out his starboard engine. By a miracle he avoided collision in the tightly packed formation and slithered down towards the invisible sea below. Above him the squadron vanished into the snow. There was no way he could contact them – R/T silence was strictly enforced on the way out to avoid giving warning to the enemy's monitoring system. He jettisoned his bombs but was still dragged down by ice and his load of petrol. It looked like curtains when, at less than 300 feet over the sea, his faulty engine picked up again. Reluctantly he turned back to Sumburgh.

Grenville was forced down lower. Down to 3,000, down to 2,000. . . . Still no sign of a break. A Apple was feeling the effects of the blizzard now. Her controls were growing sluggish and Grenville had to keep moving them to prevent their icing-up. Ice was flying off the airscrew tips and smashing like bullets against the metal-skinned fuselage. The cold was growing more intense, soaking like icy water through flying clothes, numbing hands and feet. . . .

Grenville's face was grim. Another quarter-of-an-hour of this might mean the loss of half his aircraft. Apart from the danger of engine failure, there was the growing threat of collision. A Apple was slithering about now like a man losing his reflexes. All the kites would be in a similar state, some probably worse. . . . Grenville dropped lower, damning the white filth that was blinding him. Davies was relying on them to get this convoy. So was Bergman. A hell of a thing it would be if their first job for the Norwegian was a failure. It might reflect on him. Certainly Bomber Command would have something caustic to say. . . .

Grenville cursed his helplessness as his reddened eyes stared out into the opaque, driving blizzard. Again A Apple skidded, forcing Grenville to make a violent and exaggerated movement of his controls to bring her straight again. It was no good, he realized bitterly. Another few minutes of this might mean disaster. He switched over to R/T and lifted his face mask. . . .

At that moment they broke out of the storm. From a suffocating white nightmare they were suddenly projected over a seemingly bottomless black void. With the ice breaking and shedding off their wings they swept on, once more a deadly threat to the unsuspecting convoy.

Each man expressed his relief according to his nature. Grenville had already accepted the good fortune and was now considering his battle plan afresh. Hoppy, completely confident in his pilot, began checking his instruments again. Bergman, who had forgotten his nervousness in his fear of losing the convoy, was now conscious of relief, and, paradoxically, nervousness again. Behind, in B Flight, Gillibrand's teeth clamped down on another wad of gum, his eyes glinting their pleasure at the fight to come. In front of him, Jimmie Willcox, alone in his hatch, was staring white-faced into the night, a nervous tremor racking his body.

Ten minutes more and according to Grenville's E.T.A. the Norwegian coast was approaching fast. Hitting snow again he led them up to 3,000. It proved only a squall and surprisingly they emerged into moonlight. Grenville quickly switched off his recognition lights, his pilots following his example. Then, taking advantage of the moon, he dropped down to ultra low-level, skimming low over the shimmering, icy waves. At this height the enemy could not pick them up with his detectors and Grenville was hoping for a surprise. Surprise was the essence of shipping strikes – the first attack to be made while the gunners were dozing or having a forbidden cigarette.

Another squall, sleet this time, then moonlight again. Bergman had a sense of unreality as he stared out at the dancing pathway of light along which they skimmed. This was a million miles from war: this was beautiful, ethereal, dream-like. Moonlight touched the graceful aircraft behind him, frosting their wings and edging their propellers' arcs with silver.

The pilots, however, had no time to admire the beauty of the scene. Grenville had the aircraft tightly bunched like a school of fish. It was dangerous work, calling for intense concentration and quick reflexes. To fly into the slipstream of the aircraft ahead, even for a second, meant almost certain death. The sea below was hungry, for all its frosted moonlight.

Grenville peered ahead. According to Hoppy the Norwegian coast must be close now. And it was a murderous place for aircraft at night. High mountains falling sheer into the sea, often too steep to hold snow, black and deadly. They had already taken a high toll of planes in this war. With face mask in position, ready to shout a warning, Bergman stared into the darkness with aching eyes.

Hoppy came through on the intercom. 'Three minutes past E.T.A., Skipper.' Three minutes, and still nothing! The moon was a curse now, dazzling the eyes and making the sky ahead appear darker by contrast. Would the mountain tops reflect it and give warning? Grenville did not know. He had the impression that A

Apple was travelling at twice her rated speed. The moonlit water below her was streaking by as if the plane were hurling itself to destruction.

Grenville cursed his imagination and stared again into the darkness. He thought he saw a faint light flash, far over past his starboard wingtip. He blinked quickly and looked again. Then Hoppy's excited voice came through.

'There's a light, Skipper. Over at two o'clock.'

Grenville led his pilots into a ninety-degree turn, a manoeuvre that only superbly trained pilots could have executed at that height. They headed south now; parallel to the still invisible coast. Grenville spoke to Bergman.

'Is that one of your men? Over there, at eleven o'clock?'

Owing to the position of his turret, Bergman had difficulty in seeing. Bergman swung farther over to starboard. Bergman saw the light now. It was flickering on and off, obviously signalling.

Bergman had an Aldis lamp in his turret and he sent a message back. The light went out, waited, then flickered again, falling astern as the Bostons droned on.

'Keep going,' Bergman told Grenville. 'The convoy passed here an hour ago. We'll get another message farther south.'

Less than four minutes later another light flashed at them. This one was high above them, clearly from a mountain top. It was bright and dangerously close. Bergman took its message and gave it to Grenville.

'Dead ahead, Roy. Minutes away.'

Grenville took a quick look around. The moon was on his port quarter. Ideally he should attack into it – it was always difficult for ship gunners to sight aircraft coming in against the moon. But that meant heading straight for the mountains. Too risky. He would attack on this course – if he remained lucky they would at least have the element of surprise with them.

They hit another snow squall. Grenville made a quick decision. He stayed low and switched on his landing lights so that they skipped over the heaving waves. His pilots followed his example, huddled together again for safety.

The snow thinned and fell away. They swept out into another moonlit gap and then they saw the convoy, dead ahead.

There were fifteen ships, perhaps more, lying like black-beetles on the frosty water. Not a light shone among them. Unaware as yet of their peril they steamed on in the protection of the darkness, the mountains, and the mine-fields.

Behind them 633 Squadron prepared to attack. The small shapes ahead began to grow out of the moonlit waves, to become larger, darker, and more solid. There was still no sign of alarm among them. Another three seconds and Grenville snapped on his R/T.

'Crossbow leader calling. Line Apple take a ship apiece in rear rank. Line Betty take the next rank. B Flight attack survivors. B Flight will follow in sixty seconds. Repeat. . . .'

Every aircraft was now under full boost. Every man was ready, his fatigue forgotten. They all knew what was expected of them; Grenville had put them through the drill often enough. Come in below deck level and form the nose or stern to avoid as much light flak as possible. Wait until she's towering above you, then back on your stick and over. . . . Let your eggs go, down her funnels if you can, and then get down on the water again and stay down. Jink low among the ships so if they fire at you they may hit one another. Then pick yourself another target and do it again. . . .

A searchlight suddenly blazed out from a small ship on the starboard flank. It was followed by another, then by three more. Lights began signalling frantically from the dark hulks. The first tracer came, red stuff, starting slowly as tracer always appears to do, but getting faster until it was snapping by like a vicious steel whip. Other gunners took alarm and also opened fire. A curtain of tracer came up now – red, yellow, all colours, glowing like beads on a dozen strings. Searchlights frantically swept the sky.

Both guns and searchlights were as yet angled too high. Now the rear ships were within range and Line Apple opened up with its combined twelve guns. The ships loomed nearer, nearer, enormous now against the luminous sky. . . . A jerk of the stick, a blurred impression of masts, winking guns, a bridge, a derrick, a jerk as if the Boston had been kicked in the belly, and then down again, still alive, screaming over the sea, ruffling the waves with the slipstream, dodging between the hulks of frantic ships. . . .

Grenville had picked himself the freighter dead ahead. He dropped the bombs himself, letting two go as the dark funnels yawned beneath him. As he went over an alert gunner raked him with a 7 mm., drilling a line of neat holes in his port wing. As he jinked away he heard an excited yell through his intercom from Bergman.

'*Se der*. You've got her! There she goes!'

The short time-delays had exploded and the red flash appeared to split the ship in two. The whole area was now a mad chaos of soaring tracer, exploding shells, and blazing ships. In the red light the Bostons looked like black-winged devils as they added to the havoc.

Grenville attacked a second ship with his remaining bombs. This attack was not successful; his bombs bounced and rolled off its heavily-timbered decks. He jinked away, passing near the small ship on the starboard flank of the convoy that had first sighted them. Flak and tracer was radiating from it like the quills of a porcupine. It turned its full fury on him, lashing the air with explosive and steel. Ugly red flashes burst all around, making A Apple shudder with the concussion.

Grenville swung violently out of range and the flak ship turned its attention on nearer aircraft. B Flight were coming in now and getting hell. Grenville, patrolling the perimeter of the action, saw that two other flack ships had closed in on the convoy. His earphones rang with a medley of shouts and curses. He made himself heard over the din.

'Crossbow leader here. No attacks to be made on enemy flak ships now joining convoy. Withdraw as soon as all bombs dropped and orbit three miles west. Repeat. No attacks to be made on enemy flak ships. . . .'

B Flight were having trouble. The tremendous barrage from the flak ships, helped by the now fully alerted gunners on the freighters, was driving them from their targets. A Boston was hit as it attacked a large freighter. From a streak of black lightning it turned into a cartwheel of fire as it received a direct hit in a fuel tank from a 37 mm. shell. It spun into the sea and vanished in a fountain of steam and spray.

Gillibrand's T Tommy was hit by the small flak ship as he made his run-in. A hole big enough to drop a football through suddenly appeared in his starboard wing. His big jaw clamped on his wad of gum, and he banked steeply over. To hell with orders – those bastards were asking for it. He came in low and at the stern of the floating gun platform. Everything on it opened up – quadruple automatic 20 mms., 37 mms., and its 7 mms. To Jimmie Willcox, staring down helplessly from his forward hatch, it was like flying into an exploding ammunition dump.

Gillibrand brought his stick back and howled over the erupting ship. He let his bombs go, then swung his controls hard over and skidded crazily to port, deceiving the gunners who were waiting for him to dip down astern. The port beam gunners were lining him up when both the bombs exploded. When the shattering glare had died down there was nothing on the sea but small pieces of wreckage and a pool of blazing oil. Gillibrand shifted his gum from one cheek to the other and grinned.

'Whaddya think of that, Jimmie boy? That fixed 'em, huh?'

The youngster's face was like a death mask. His teeth had bitten deeply into his lower lip and blood was trickling down his chin. He could feel the frantic pounding of his heart in his head, his hands and his feet. His stomach turned over, making him retch. He tried to reply, but only a whimper came from his lips. The intercom was kind to him, distorting the sound.

Gillibrand addressed his gunner as well as Jimmie. 'The R/T was u.s.! Don't forget it, you guys, or Grenville will take my hide off when we get back. Now what else is cookin' round these parts. . . ?'

From A Apple, circling the perimeter of the action, it was like looking down into hell. Gillibrand's T Tommy looked like a moth being pierced by a hundred white-hot needles as it attacked the flak ship, and its escape seemed a miracle. The flak ship exploded but the others were taking their toll. Another Boston of B Flight was hit when attacking a freighter. It went straight into the ship's beam, flaming petrol sweeping right over the deck above.

Grenville was swearing slowly and viciously. He gave a curt order to his crew. Hoppy's voice came back immediately. 'O.K., Skipper. I'm ready.'

In the dark turret, lit only by the glare of bursting shells and burning ships, Bergman's voice failed him. His whole body was aching from nervous strain; and his underclothes were soaked with perspiration and clinging coldly to his body. He thought of the warning Grenville had given him earlier, and managed a rueful grin in the darkness. This certainly did take some getting used to. . . .

Grenville's voice came again, as sharp as a whip. 'Are you ready, Finn? Do you understand what you have to do?'

Bergman managed it this time. 'Yes, Roy; I understand. I'm ready.'

'All right. Hang on then.'

A Apple echelonned away and plunged down into the centre of the convoy.

CHAPTER **8**

The Bostons returned to Sutton Craddock just after noon. Hilde was up in her room when she heard them. She ran downstairs and out on to the gravel drive. Maisie and Kearns were already there, having come out from the bar.

The hum grew louder, a deep throbbing note like that given by an organ with the lower stops out. There was nothing to see yet, low thick clouds effectively blanketed the sky. But as the hum grew louder irregularities in it could be heard as if some of the engines were missing. Over on the airfield a siren was wailing and ambulance and truck engines were starting up.

The noise was deafening now, a heavy roar that beat down on their temples. The first Boston came out of the clouds like a wraith. As it banked carefully over the road, they saw daylight through a jagged hole in its wing. It slid slowly out of sight behind the wooden fence, its engines coughing and the wind whining over its airfoils.

Another damaged plane followed it. Shrapnel scars showed on its fuselage and tail unit. One engine was missing alarmingly and sending out a thin stream of black smoke. It lowered itself as gingerly as a cat down a sloping roof, and vanished in turn behind the fence.

One by one the rest came in. Kearns stole a glance at Hilde. Her face was very pale and her eyes enormous as they followed the planes down. For all her natural composure she looked very young and vulnerable at that moment.

At last the sky was empty of sound again. Maisie, who had not spoken a word during this time, turned to Hilde. Her voice had a high-pitched, brittle ring. 'How many went out – d'you know? I didn't wake up until half of 'em had gone.'

'Twelve,' Hilde said.

Maisie's voice was suddenly hushed. 'Twelve! But only eight landed just now!'

Hilde nodded, then turned and went inside. Maisie stared at Kearns. 'That doesn't mean four have gone west, does it?'

Kearns shook his head heavily. 'I don't know, lass. We'll have to wait and see.'

The telephone in the hall rang fifteen minutes later. Kearns answered it, turning to Hilde who had appeared at the door of the sitting-room. His voice was relieved. 'It's for you, Miss. I think it's your brother.'

With a murmur of thanks she took the receiver from him. She spoke in Norwegian, her voice low and a little unsteady. Kearns moved off to the door that led into the public rooms. Maisie was standing there and he took her arm.

'Come on,' he muttered. 'Give the girl a bit of privacy.'

'There's something I want to ask her,' Maisie said. Ignoring his protests she drew closer to Hilde, hesitated, then reached out and touched her arm.

'Sorry to interrupt, Miss, but do me a favour, will you? Ask your brother if the big Canadian is all right. . . .'

Bergman came over to the inn just after three o'clock that afternoon. To his relief he found Hilde alone in the sitting-room. She came over to him at once, gripping his arm tightly for a moment.

He put a hand on her hair and ruffled it affectionately. '*Hallo, kjaere.* How is my favourite girl-friend today?'

She pressed his arm. 'Very pleased to see you. So pleased she'll forgive you for neglecting her for so long.'

He saw how pale she was and offered her a cigarette. She accepted his light, inhaled deeply, then turned to him. 'What was it like?' she asked quietly. 'Can you tell me or is it a secret?'

Bergman shook his head. 'No. As far as I'm concerned it isn't a secret any longer. The Censor will pass on the news to the papers just as if it had been a normal raid. To keep it hushed up would make things suspicious. It was an attack on a convoy off the Norwegian coast – what the Air Force call a shipping strike.'

Valerie's guess had been remarkably accurate, Hilde thought. She led Bergman over to one of the armchairs. 'Sit down and tell me all about it.'

Her eyes never left his face as he gave her brief details of the strike. He was sitting near the window and the bleak daylight showed up all his weariness. He finished his short account on a humorous note, telling her about Gillibrand.

'There was a tremendous row when they landed. Grenville was going to have him arrested but he swore his wireless had been faulty and he hadn't picked up Grenville's orders. His wireless mechanic bore him out. Just the same, I thought Grenville was going to arrest them both.'

'But why?'

Bergman laughed. 'Apparently this has happened before. Gillibrand talks his mechanic into putting in an unserviceable report. It's a risky game, with Grenville the Squadron Commander.'

For a moment the tension within Hilde eased. She laughed with him. 'I shall have to meet Gillibrand.'

'You'll find it difficult to miss him. He's a tremendous character.'

'And what was it like flying with Grenville?' she asked. 'So far you've made it sound as if all your plane did was fly about and let others do the fighting.'

Bergman's weary face became animated. 'Grenville was magnificent. I can't think of anyone else who would have got his squadron through in such weather.

41

And do you know what he did when he saw what the flak ships were doing to his planes?'

She shook her head, watching the enthusiasm glowing in his eyes.

'He ordered his planes to keep away, then kept flying near them himself to draw off their fire. And he kept it up until all his aircraft had dropped their bombs. I've never seen anything like it before.'

Hilde sat motionless a moment, then said quietly: 'Don't fly with him again, Finn. If you must go out with them, go with someone else. Please.'

Bergman read her thoughts and shook his head. 'He's not reckless, Hilde. He did that to save lives, not to risk them.'

'Your life was risked,' she reminded him.

Bergman shrugged impatiently. 'That wasn't his fault.'

She gave a quick, hopeless shake of her head. A burning coal fell on to the hearth. She picked it up with the tongs and threw it back into the fire.

'You lost four planes, didn't you?' she asked.

'Two. One lost contact with us and returned earlier, and another was pretty badly shot-up but got back to Sumburgh. We left it there to get repairs.'

'How many men is that?'

Bergman moved restlessly. 'Don't start getting morbid, please.'

'Please tell me,' she asked quietly.

He threw his cigarette into the fire, lit a fresh one. 'Six. And two gunners wounded and in hospital.'

She realized he was feeling the loss and changed the subject at once. 'Will you be coming over tonight? And are you bringing Grenville with you?'

'I would have liked to do so but he has a great deal of work to do. And then there is this party afterwards. . . .'

Her eyes widened. 'Party! What party?'

'They are having one in the Mess,' Bergman explained. 'It's a custom of Grenville's after a successful raid.'

She showed her bewilderment. 'But six of his men died today. Why does he want a party?'

Bergman shrugged. 'They can't afford to brood over those that have gone – they'd go crazy if they did. Grenville knows what he is doing.'

Hilde did not argue with him. 'Will you be going to this party too?' she asked, her voice low.

He nodded. 'I said I'd go over about eight. I must go, out of respect to Grenville if for nothing else. I'm sorry, particularly as I couldn't get over last night. But after this I should have a few free nights.'

She had risen and was staring down into the fire. Bergman rose, putting a hand on her shoulder. 'What's the matter?' he asked. 'You seem very quiet. What's worrying you?'

She turned to him, her eyes uncertain. 'I don't quite know. I think – ' Her hand fluttered in the gesture he knew so well. 'I think it is this friend of yours, Grenville. I believe I am a little afraid of him. . . .'

*

The naked bulb hanging from the ceiling gave off a harsh light that made Grenville's eyes ache. He was sitting at his desk reading a letter. He had almost finished it when he let out an exclamation and ripped it to pieces. Dropping his face into his hands he sat motionless for a moment, fingers pressed tightly into the thick dark hair over his temples. Then he picked up his pen and began writing again.

The letter took him over fifteen minutes to complete. He read it through again, shook his head, but this time folded it into an envelope which he put with five others that lay on his desk. Then he slumped back in his chair and lit a cigarette.

Thank God that was over. How he loathed the job, writing the same old platitudes, how they had died doing their duty, their courage in the face of enemy fire, and the rest of the bilge. What wife found any comfort in it when her children started asking where their father was? What mother gave a damn about courage as long as her son was alive and healthy? And that cant about them being remembered – that was a laugh. Who outside their own families was going to remember them after the war? Not a soul. No one liked being reminded of his debts, but there was one advantage in having them to the dead – you could forget 'em. . . .

Disjointed memories came to Grenville. The visiting journalist last year . . . puffed up little man . . . announcing pretentiously that at least the bereaved would have the pride of knowing their boys had died under a famous command . . . his look of amazement when Grenville had hit him . . . the fuss until Group had managed to hush it up. Pride! They'd damn him to hell for getting their boys killed, and who could blame them?

He swore viciously, jumping to his feet. It wasn't his fault, was it, if mothers had sons, and if men were damn fools enough to marry and have wives and children who could miss them. . . ?

Sweat trickled down his face, burning into the sores left by his face mask. He wiped a hand across his forehead, lowered it, and saw the sweat glistening on his fingers. He swore again, then glanced round the office in sudden alarm. Thank heaven he was alone.

The thought of others seeing him in this condition pulled him together. He was tired, that was all it was. He had ordered his crews to bed on their return: he should have gone himself. But he'd had to get in touch with Sumburgh about the wounded, Davies had wanted to talk with him, Adams had wanted to know how many damned rivets there'd been in the ships they'd sunk, these letters had had to be written – how the hell could a man sleep?

And now there was this party. He glanced down at his watch. Eight-thirty – it would be well on its way now. A party – on top of this! A couple of drinks and he'd want to puke his guts out. But it was his idea, wasn't it? The tough Grenville touch. . . .

He wondered where Bergman was. Probably still with his sister – he had said he might be a little late for the party. Quite a man, that Norwegian. He didn't like sitting back while others went into danger, although, if all Davies said was true, he'd earned himself a rest. He must have been scared to death when they went in

43

– that low-level stuff was hell for anyone green. But he'd taken it well, particularly at the end when they'd pin-pricked the flak ships. Not that he'd have hit anything with those guns of his except wave-tops, but he'd given it a bang. No one could do more than that.

Grenville wondered about his sister. She must know what his game was – it must be nerve-racking for her when he was over on the other side. He wondered what she was like. If she had half Bergman's courage, she'd be quite a girl. He looked at his watch again – there was still time to run over and meet her. Bergman would appreciate it, he knew that. They could have a quick drink, then he and Bergman could go to the Mess together. . . .

As always when he had made a decision Grenville acted promptly. He threw on his greatcoat, picked up the six letters, and gave them to the aircraftsman on duty in the Orderly Room. Then he made his way towards the camp entrance.

A bleak drizzle was blowing in from the east, and it was as black as the inside of a hat. He swore as his feet squelched in a patch of glutinous mud. As he passed the Mess he heard the muffled sounds of laughter and singing. The party was getting under way – in another two hours it would be a free-for-all as the boys worked off their tension. He walked quickly, trying to lose the ache in his back and legs. The guard at the gate recognized him and snapped to attention. He saluted back and turned right down the road outside. It was quiet here and he could hear the moisture dripping off the trees and soaking into the wet earth.

His eyes were accustomed to the darkness now and he saw the black silhouette of the inn looming up ahead of him. He had his hand on the door of the lounge when he paused. Why the devil had he chosen this of all nights to come over? He was in a filthy mood and couldn't be sociable if he tried! He took his hand off the latch, then swore again. Never turn back if you can help it, there's no easier habit to acquire. . . ! Get inside, say hello to her, then take Bergman over to the Mess! The party was the right idea after all – a few drinks would take away this tension and soften the edge on things. . . . Without giving himself time for further hesitation, Grenville pushed open the door and entered.

CHAPTER 9

Maisie was washing glasses behind the lounge bar when she heard the crash of metal. The half-dozen locals, yawning over their beers, jerked awake at the noise and followed her as she ducked under the counter and ran outside.

A small car was lurched up against the wall of the inn. Two figures were silhouetted against its lights, one huge, the other small. A rich Canadian voice sounded as Maisie approached the car.

'Aw; we'll leave it there, kid. The steering's gone for a burton. I'll get Chiefy to have a look at it tomorrow.'

'Hey, what's going on,' Maisie asked indignantly. 'You can't come busting up your car on our drive.'

Gillibrand swung round. A grin split his face from ear to ear. 'Waal, waal! If it ain't my little dream girl. Hiya, honey! How'r those big black eyes tonight? Shining bright for your cousin, huh?'

He slid his arm round her waist. Maisie backed hurriedly away. 'Don't you touch me. You're drunk.'

Gillibrand grinned again. 'Kid; you do yourself an injustice. I ain't gotta be drunk to make a pass at you. C'mon, Jimmie boy. Let's sink a couple here before joinin' the party, huh?'

The locals scattered as the burly Canadian entered the lounge, his arm around his small companion. They approached the bar behind which Maisie had taken refuge. She eyed Gillibrand cautiously.

'Now take it easy, see. We don't want no trouble here. This is a respectable place.'

Gillibrand draped himself over a stool, winking at his observer. 'What are you talkin' about, kid? Jimmie an' me have come to say hello and to have a little chat. Now what's wrong with that?'

'Just keep it that way, that's all,' Maisie sniffed. 'And don't try to be fresh again.'

Gillibrand's elbows shifted farther across the counter. 'Say, you look real pretty when you're mad.' He turned to Jimmie. 'Don't she, kid?'

The boy nodded, trying hard to smile. A lock of hair was hanging dismally over his eyes and his face had an unhealthy pallor. He looked as if he had had too much to drink and now wanted to be sick.

'Give us two beers, will you, honey?' Gillibrand said, 'and be matey and have a drink yourself.'

Maisie poured them two pints, then, after some hesitation, gave herself a small gin. Gillibrand winked at her. 'This is more like it, honey. This is nice.' He turned again to Jimmie. 'Bit different from this morning, ain't it, kid?'

The boy's lips moved in a caricature of a smile. 'A bit, yes.' He had a thin, shy voice.

Gillibrand grinned. 'You never thought we'd make it when we went for that flak ship, did you?'

Jimmie gave a cracked laugh. 'I didn't. I thought we'd bought it.'

The Canadian laughed and slapped him on the shoulder. 'Aw; you leave it to your Uncle Gillie – he'll always get you through. We showed 'em, and we'll show 'em again the next time they take a poke at us.'

Maisie was all curiosity now. 'What happened this morning? Can you tell me somethin' about it?'

Gillibrand winked. 'Waal, maybe a bit here and there – if you keep your mouth shut afterwards.'

45

'I won't say anythin',' Maisie promised. 'Honest, I won't. What did you raid?'

'Shipping off the Norwegian coast. An' we gave 'em hell. Jimmie'll tell you.'

Maisie threw a glance at the boy, who jerked his head nervously. 'Did you hit anything?' she asked.

Gillibrand let out a laugh. 'Did we hit anythin'. . . ! Hitler's one flak ship short tonight, baby. It took a crack at us and put a hole in my starboard wing, so I turned on the heat. The pieces are still comin' down.'

Maisie's black eyes were round and excited. 'Was that you who came in with a big hole in one wing?'

Gillibrand grinned. 'You were watchin', huh. Yeah, that was me. And that wasn't the only hole we got – Jimmie'll tell you. This is how it happened, kid. . . .'

When he had finished the story Maisie's mouth was a round O. 'Gee,' she managed. 'Just imagine that!'

Gillibrand waved a big hand. 'Aw, that's nothin'. I could tell you a hundred stories better than that. An' maybe I will some time. . . . Hey, what's the matter, kid? Where're you going?'

Jimmie had suddenly stumbled off towards the door. Gillibrand jumped from his stool and followed him. He returned alone two minutes later, shaking his head.

'Funny kid – wouldn't let me stay with him. Says he'll come back when he feels better.'

'You shouldn't let him drink so much,' Maisie said critically. 'He's only a kid, and doesn't look very strong.'

Gillibrand frowned. 'What can you do? He's gotta learn. This is a tough game – you gotta be tough to keep in it.'

'You won't toughen him up this way. I think this business this morning upset him. His eyes were like marbles when you were tellin' me about it.'

The Canadian's jaw suddenly tightened. 'Now wait a minute! That kid ain't afraid of anything, and don't you forget it. He's a good boy – see!'

'All right, all right,' Maisie said to pacify him. 'Then he's feeling queer because he missed a night's sleep and has had beer on top of it. Missing sleep does affect some people that way.'

Gillibrand's face cleared. 'That's different. That's sensible.' He stared at Maisie, then grinned again. 'You're all right, kid. How about you and me havin' a date one of these nights, huh?'

Maisie was surprised at her own caution. 'Ain't you got a wife or a girl friend?'

'I got a girl sure. . . . Everybody's got a girl. But she ain't here, that's the thing. She's down in London.'

Maisie tossed her head. 'I'm not the sort who plays second fiddle.'

'You won't be second fiddle, baby. Here you'll be my very best girl. An' I've got a car – we can have some nice long rides together. Won't that be somethin'?'

Maisie jerked a sarcastic thumb at the wall. 'You mean you had a car, don't you?'

'Don't worry; it'll patch up.' Gillibrand lifted his glass. 'Here's to them long summer nights we're goin' to spend together, baby.'

'Evenings,' Maisie said cautiously.

Gillibrand grinned. 'All right, honey. Here's to the evenings.'

Jimmie returned at that moment. His white face had a clammy appearance and his hand was trembling as he picked up his glass. Gillibrand reached over and took it from him.

'Leave that belly-wash alone, kid. Have somethin' to settle your stomach.' The Canadian turned to Maisie. 'What've you got for him, honey. Somethin' from under the counter, huh?'

Maisie half-filled a glass with brandy and slipped it to the boy. 'That'll make you feel better,' she said.

Jimmie thanked her and sipped at the neat spirit. The colour returned slowly to his cheeks. Maisie noticed the concern on the Canadian's face as he watched the youngster.

'That's better, kid?'

Jimmie nodded. 'Yes, thanks. I don't know what went wrong. . . . It must have been the car ride on top of the beer.'

'Yeah; that and the night's sleep you missed. Aw, it can happen to anybody. But you know, you ought to relax a bit. It ain't good to be tensed up all the time.'

Jimmie flushed. 'I'm not tensed up. There's nothing wrong with me.'

There was a shrill edge to his voice. Gillibrand waved a hand in good-natured protest. 'You don't have to tell me there's nothin' wrong with you. I know that, don't I? You've got me wrong. I'm advisin' you to enjoy yourself more. You want to get yourself a girl. . . . Now there's somethin'. Girls make you feel good, slacken off your nerves.' He looked at Maisie. 'Don't they, honey?'

'Do they? Don't ask me.'

''Course they do. An' heck, think how a guy would feel if he'd never had a girl and got the chopper. Why, he'd be up there, all bright an' shiny, pluckin' those strings and wishin' like hell all the time he hadn't missed out. It's waste, kid, that's what it is. Criminal waste.'

'Stop talking rubbish,' Maisie snapped, afraid that the boy would either break down again or take offence.

Jimmie appeared to have recovered, however, for he gave a wan smile. 'You'd better shut up or I'll take Maisie out,' he muttered. 'What'll you have – another beer?'

Gillibrand, delighted with the boy's show of spirit, was as fussy as a collie dog wagging its tail. 'Attaboy! That's better.' He grinned at Maisie. 'I'll have to watch him, hey, baby?'

''Course you'll have to watch him,' Maisie said, winking encouragingly at the boy. 'I like 'em quiet and well-behaved.'

The door latch clicked. Gillibrand turned around casually, then stiffened. Grenville was approaching the counter.

'Evenin', Skipper.'

Grenville nodded at him and Jimmie, then turned to Maisie. 'I'd like to see Lieutenant Bergman and his sister. May I go through?'

Conscious of the authoritative ring in his voice, Maisie hurried along the counter. 'Why, yes, sir. They're in the sitting-room, I think.' She lifted the flap of the counter. 'This way, sir. Through this door and across the hall. That door there, look, straight across. . . .'

Grenville nodded his thanks and crossed the hall. Maisie closed the door and returned to the others, her eyes eager with curiosity. 'Who was that? You called him skipper. He ain't Grenville, is he?'

Gillibrand bit off a wad of gum and grinned. 'That's the guy, honey. An' by the look of him he ain't exactly forgiven me for what happened this morning.'

Maisie shook her dark head in awe. 'That's Roy Grenville — and he ain't no older than my brother. Gee, can you believe it. . . ?'

Grenville knew at once she was Bergman's sister; there was a resemblance about her fine eyes and good forehead. She gave him a questioning smile from her armchair.

'You'll be Miss Bergman,' Grenville said, moving from the doorway. 'Lieutenant Bergman's sister.'

Her low-toned voice with its attractive accent gave him his assurance before she finished speaking. 'Yes; I am Hilde Bergman. Are you looking for my brother?'

He nodded. 'My name's Grenville. I thought your brother was over here.'

An odd, indefinable expression came into her eyes as he gave his name. There was a perceptible pause before she spoke again.

'Good evening, Squadron-Leader. Please take off your coat. Is there anything I can order for you?'

Grenville shook his head. 'No, thank you. Not now. And if you don't mind, I'll keep my coat on. I shan't be able to stay long.'

'Just as you wish, of course.' She motioned to the armchair opposite. 'I'm sorry my brother is not here, but he left for the camp a quarter of an hour ago. He said there was a party he had to attend.' Her eyes examined his face. 'I understood him to say you were giving it.'

In some indefinable way Grenville imagined her tone had changed slightly on hearing his name. He dropped into the chair, feeling his way cautiously.

'Yes; there is a bit of a party. That's why I can't stay. But I had a few minutes and thought I'd like to run over and meet you, and then perhaps take your brother back with me.' He changed the subject. 'Do you know this part of England at all?'

'No, I have never been in Yorkshire before.'

He motioned to the panelled walls. 'Do you like the inn? Are you comfortable?'

'Oh, yes. It is a lovely old place. I like it very much.'

For the first few minutes Grenville felt ill at ease, and his analytical mind, incessantly self-critical, gave him a reason. Before the war he would have enjoyed the company of such a girl. Now he felt gauche, out of place. It was the war, he told himself. Three years of it had coarsened him, both in his own eyes and the eyes of others. Now he was fit for nothing but Service life where rank so often took the place of culture and embarrassment for one's shortcomings could be kept at bay by the shouting of an order.

Gradually, however, the atmosphere of the room, with its old-world furniture, darkened wood, and gleaming brass, began to soak into him, relaxing his tight nerves. The warmth of the fire also had its effect, making his eyelids heavy. He studied the girl opposite him. She was beautiful! Her mass of hair was as bright as that of a child's. And her voice – if only he could lie back with closed eyes and listen to it! He was tired, and it was as soothing as a moonlit sky after a barrage of flak. With an effort he forced his eyes open, made himself talk.

'You haven't seen any ghosts in here yet?' he asked. 'Cavaliers, Roundheads, and that sort of thing?'

Hilde laughed. 'No, not yet. But I have not given up hope.'

'Do you usually travel about with your brother?'

She understood the significance of the question. 'When it is considered safe, yes.'

Grenville nodded. She knew – it was safe to talk. 'Then you'll have a pretty good idea why he has come here?'

'I know he is working with your squadron, but that is all.'

He wondered if she had heard about the shipping strike. Her question made it appear she had read his thoughts.

'How did my brother manage this morning? I know that he flew with you.'

There was no doubt about the sincerity of Grenville's reply. 'He did a fine job. It wasn't a pleasant trip and he took it well.'

She nodded. 'He told me nothing of his part in it, but he did mention your efforts to draw the fire from your men. He thought that very brave of you.'

Embarrassment immediately made Grenville's voice curt. 'I think he exaggerated a little. The danger wasn't as great as he imagined.'

She shook her head. 'My brother has seen too much danger to exaggerate it. He has had more than his share of it since the war started.'

What was that undertone in her voice? In one as composed as she it was difficult to place. . . . Then Grenville recognized it and instantly the rest was clear to him.

'It was your brother who wanted to come along,' he said, understanding now her apprehension. 'He insisted on it.'

He saw he had guessed correctly. He also saw that there was deep emotion in her, in spite of her natural gentleness.

She turned to face him. Her voice was still low in tone. 'You know why, don't you? That was because my brother cannot sit back and send others into danger. But he has to face dangers that none of you can share – terrible dangers. It is not fair that he should share yours too.'

Grenville shrugged. 'I quite agree with you. But whose fault is it?'

'It is the fault of those in command,' she said quietly. 'No one should be allowed to take him with them. No one should offer to take him.'

Excuses for himself never came easily to Grenville. 'You should tell this to your brother. There's nothing we can do.'

She turned her face away. 'How can I talk to him? When a man has a sense of duty like that, there is nothing a woman can do.'

Grenville's voice softened. 'It's true – brave men can be stubborn. But I shouldn't worry too much about it. He'll be all right.' He glanced down at his watch, then, surprised at his reluctance, rose to his feet. 'I'm afraid I shall have to be getting along.'

Hilde rose after him. There was a confused look in her eyes now. 'You are not quite as I imagined you. . . .' She paused, then went on hesitantly: 'Will you explain something to me?'

There was almost a wistful note in her voice. Grenville turned back. 'Yes, if I can. What is it?'

'I know that you lost six men today. Then why do you hold a party tonight? It is something I do not understand. . . .'

There was a devil in Grenville that liked playing up to another's unfavourable opinion of him. As a boy it had earned him many an unwarranted thrashing, and, perversely, thrived on the punishment. As a man it was more under control but in certain moods could be as wicked as ever. Her question, touching him where he was hypersensitive, put him in such a mood now.

'Why? Because I like parties. I like getting drunk – it's a hobby of mine. What has losing six men got to do with that?'

The disappointment in her eyes goaded the devil in him further. 'Don't worry about your brother,' he said. 'If he gets too drunk I'll see him to his bunk.'

Her lovely, steady eyes met his own, and for a moment he had the odd sensation he was sinking down into their blue-grey depths. Down, sinking deeper, very cool, very tranquil, very forgiving. . . .

He turned away with a sharp exclamation. Five minutes later he pushed open the door of the Mess. A cheer went up, startling him. The haze of tobacco smoke made him think of a shifting curtain between two worlds. He pushed his way through it and reached the bar. Someone pushed a filled glass into his hand and he drank deeply. The liquor sank into his stomach, warming his aching back and legs. This was the world he had chosen: this was the only world left – until it blew up in flame and broken spars around him! He lifted his glass and drank again.

Adams found himself in the innkeeper's kitchen that night. Since his wife's arrival he had developed a habit of joining Kearns over a cup of tea after the bar closed. Kearns was a restful person with his pipe and slow, contemplative voice, and Adams was growing attached to him. His kitchen, with its two rocking-chairs and its singing kettle, was becoming a brief sanctuary from the mad world across the road and (although Adams did not realize it yet) from the unsympathetic woman who was his wife. Instinct told Adams the innkeeper could be trusted and in the weeks to come he was to tell him more than was always discreet. It was a lucky thing for Adams his instinct did not betray him.

This was the first night he went below the surface. The reason was not difficult to find: he was half-drunk. Losses always hit Adams hard, and this was no exception. He would have liked to go to the party, but dared not trust himself to conceal his feelings. In any case, it would have made him feel impossibly old and futile. . . . With all his friends in the Mess and Valerie unsuitable company for such an occasion, there had been nothing for it but to drink alone, which he had done in a pub in Highgate. On his way back to camp a sudden impulse had made him enter the inn through a back door. Unknown to Valerie, he had now been with the innkeeper for over a quarter of an hour.

The warm quiet sympathy of the room was having its effect. Adams turned suddenly from the fire and faced the innkeeper.

'Did you notice the planes come back this afternoon?'

Kearns was packing his pipe. He paused. 'Aye, lad; we saw 'em all right. Some were lost, I hear.'

'Six men killed. I was sitting next to one of them at dinner last night. He was telling me what he was going to do when the war was over.' The sound of his own thick voice filled Adams with a vague disgust.

Kearns shook his head slowly. 'Aye; it's a terrible waste.'

'That's how it goes, week after week, month after month, until you're never quite sure who's alive and who's dead. Your memory starts playing tricks with you – you get the ghosts mixed up with the living.'

'Aye. War is a wicked thing, lad. A wicked thing.'

Adams found his emotions were in a tangle again. He leaned forward abruptly, the firelight gleaming on his spectacles. 'And yet, you know, I envy them. They do live before they die. They're not doing the same old job, growing old slowly, feeling old age coming on a bit more every winter. They get more out of life in a day than we get in a year.'

Kearns shook his head stubbornly. 'Don't say anything to make war sound better than it is, lad. War is a wicked thing. I know – I was in the last one.'

Adams' half-drunken voice became suddenly resentful. 'Oh; I know – I've been sitting on my backside too long listening to other people's exploits. I see the glamour because I'm an onlooker. . . . If I were in their flying boots I'd be scared to death. . . . All right, I agree with all that. But one thing I do know . . .'

'What's that, lad?' Kearns asked quietly.

'Just this. That those who come through will never find life the same again. Some won't know why, but I know. They'll never feel so strong, they'll never know blossom so white, they'll never find girls so lovely. And why? Because you never feel the real sweetness of life until you stand at the edge of death. . . . It's a paradox that makes me wonder if the whole business isn't one big, dirty joke.'

CHAPTER 10

Barrett stood by his office window, his blunt fingers drumming impatiently on the sill. He turned sharply at a tap on the door. 'Come in,' he shouted.

Grenville entered. Barrett waited until he had closed the door before speaking. 'I've just had Davies on the blower. He's got a special job for us as soon as the weather's suitable.'

'What is it this time? Another strike?'

'No, thank God. It's a single job, a recce.' Barrett paused, his gruff voice dropping. 'My guess is that it has to do with this big job everyone's so tight-lipped about. This is the gen I've got so far.'

He took Grenville over to his desk on which lay a large-scale map of Norway. He pointed a blunt, tobacco-stained finger at a point on the coast above the 61st Parallel.

'There's a fjord here called the Svartfjord. Apparently the convoy on which you dropped the hammer the other day sailed from it. It's very steep, is about twenty-five miles long, and at the back end there is a hydro-electric plant and a large camouflaged building. It's this building we have to photograph.'

Grenville looked up from the map, his face curious. 'You don't know what it is?'

Barrett grunted his disgust. 'No. They're as tight as a bull's arse in fly time about it. But it's obviously important – they've got an elaborate plan worked out to kid Jerry we don't know it's there and are flying over that way by accident. Davies has had it all worked out, and gave it to Bergman yesterday. In a few minutes we'll go and have a talk with him – he's with Adams at the moment. I called you in to talk about the crew. Davies said he'd like you to go yourself – the job's that important. But I said I'd like a word with you first.'

'Why?' Grenville asked.

Barrett looked slightly uncomfortable. 'It seems a rather dicey show to me. They don't want to send an escort for fear of making Jerry suspicious, and yet if it's that important he's bound to be on the alert. I don't fancy losing my Squadron Commander on some bloody mountain-top – not when I've got twenty-odd other pilots I can send.'

'They aren't likely to keep a constant patrol at 30,000 feet,' Grenville said.

'If you go, mind you stay up there,' Barrett grunted. 'If you can't see anything for shadows, never mind. Come back and let 'em organize something else. If you go lower they'll get you, as sure as hell.' He paused, frowning heavily. 'I asked Davies why they couldn't use a Spit for the job. He says they've tried twice, but drawn a blank each time. It seems this building is difficult to spot from the air unless you've someone with you who knows the landmarks. So we have to use old Popsy and take Bergman along as guide.'

Grenville started at the Norwegian's name. 'He's not going along, is he?'

Barrett nodded. 'That's the point of the idea. He leads you over the building and tells the photographer when to press his button.'

Grenville's face set. 'To hell with it! I took him with me on the strike; I don't want him again. Particularly on a job like this.'

Barrett stared at him. 'But I thought you said he did all right on the strike.'

'That was different. That was at night, in filthy weather. There wasn't a chance of fighter interception. But this will be in daylight. What happens if a patrol jumps us and I've no rear gunner?'

Barrett nodded his agreement. 'You're right, of course.' He stroked his moustaches thoughtfully. 'You couldn't manage without Hopkinson, could you? Let Bergman go in his place and take your regular gunner along?'

Grenville's voice was uncompromisingly curt. 'No; I couldn't. Let him keep out of this. We don't take staff-planning officers with us when we prang a target, do we? If we did we'd soon need Bombays instead of Bostons. Let Bergman do as the others do – give us the gen and then leave us alone. We'll get the photographs.'

Barrett scratched his head. 'I know how you feel, Roy. But I can't get round the orders. We haven't much of an argument, anyway. Two Spits have already failed on their own. We might do the same without Bergman.'

'Then you can count me out,' Grenville said abruptly. 'I don't want Bergman with me.'

Barrett nodded. 'All right, that suits me. As far as I'm concerned you're down with a heavy cold. Right – now who do you suggest? Milner?'

Grenville was silent, his face moody. Barrett stared at him, repeating his question. Grenville shook his head. 'Milner's down with the 'flu. I got word just before I came in.'

'Who else, then. Young? Gillibrand?'

Grenville gave a harsh laugh. 'Gillibrand! Are you trying to kill the bod? Gillibrand would probably go down and run his wheels over the bloody thing to see what it was made of.'

Barrett was growing impatient. 'What about one or two suggestions, then?'

Grenville made his reluctant decision. 'All right; I'll go,' he said abruptly. 'But keep him grounded in the future. We're not a transport squadron.'

In spite of his previous remarks, Barrett looked relieved. 'I suppose it is just as well,' he admitted. 'There'd probably be a hell of an inquest if anything happened and they found you hadn't gone with him. O.K.; then that's settled. You go on the first favourable met. report. Now come on over to Adams and Bergman and get the gen.'

Bergman and Adams were sitting over a pile of photographs and a map of Norway when Grenville and Barrett arrived. Adams had been fully briefed on the plan, and it was he who gave the details to Grenville.

He pointed to a cross on the map. 'You hit the coast here at a point eight miles north of Utvik as near 10.15 as possible. The time factor is very important, as you'll see in a minute. You must be over 30,000 feet as you come in. . . .' His myopic eyes lifted to Grenville's set face. 'That's one of the points I raised with the Air Commodore. Can you keep over 30,000 feet with a crew of three?'

Grenville shrugged. 'Davies can't have it both ways. If I must carry passengers, I obviously can't get so high.'

Bergman caught the black glance thrown his way and guessed its cause. He sat in uncomfortable silence. Barrett met Adams' eye and broke in hastily.

'I've told Townsend to take everything that's movable out of Popsy. We think she should make 30,000 feet, perhaps a bit more.'

Adams nodded and looked down at his map again. 'After crossing the coast you make straight for Hjelmestad, this small town here. The Germans have recently opened out an ordinance factory in Hjelmestad; we're hoping they'll assume this is the target for your reconnaissance. Allowing for your reduced airspeed we estimate it should take about five and a quarter minutes to reach it. You circle it once as if taking photographs, then start back south-west along this track,' and his finger pointed at a pencilled line on the map. 'That leads you right over and parallel to the Svartfjord whch, as you'll notice, runs in a south-westerly direction before turning west to the sea.

'Your track will take you along its first eight miles,' Adams went on. 'The building is here – right at the end of the fjord – but they want as many photographs as they can get so go on taking them until the fjord turns away. To avoid suspicion, you don't follow it but keep straight on and hit the coast here.'

'What are the Focke Wulfs doing during this time?' Grenville asked.

Adams felt the embarrassment he always felt when discussing the ways another man should risk his life. He coughed to hide it. 'That has all been considered in the time factor. We estimate you won't be over land more than fourteen minutes. Provided you aren't detected before you reach the coast, that gives you a fair escape margin. We know Jerry has got some of the very latest Fw 190 A-6's at Voss and Herdla, but even with them he can't reach 30,000 feet in that time. You should make it fairly comfortably.'

'You haven't got any performance figures on these new Focke-Wulfs yet?' Grenville asked.

'No; but however good they are they can hardly get up to 30,000 feet in much under twenty-five minutes.'

'It's cutting it pretty fine,' Barrett said anxiously.

'It is and it isn't,' Adams said. 'Fourteen minutes over the coast is a fairly generous estimate – it may take even less time.'

Grenville was studying the map and its details. 'Why is 10.15 so important? Couldn't we go in earlier?'

Adams shook his head. 'There's a very special reason for that. At this time of the year, the sun never reaches to the bottom of the Svartfjord. But there is a large glacier covering one of the mountains that overlooks the building. Because of its angle, between 10.15 and 10.45 it reflects the sun downwards just like a large mirror. It should give sufficient light for a photograph.'

Barrett's mouth had dropped open. 'Who the heck thought of that one?'

Adams motioned to the silent Norwegian. 'It's Lieutenant Bergman's idea. And one of his men over there has checked it for us. It works all right provided the weather is fine.'

Barrett's face was full of admiration. 'That's really smart. Lord, the brains that go into this business. . . ! O.K. Now let's all go over and see what Townsend is doing to old Popsy.'

Two days later a favourable weather report was received by wireless from one of Bergman's operators in Norway. That night P Popsy, a Boston with more powerful engines, took off on the first leg of her journey. She refuelled at Sumburgh, where her crew had breakfast, and took off again in daylight. It was a bright winter morning with a cloudless sky. A day when war seemed an impossible nightmare.

Grenville did not force the Boston up and they were half-way across the North Sea before she reached her maximum ceiling. At 29,800 feet she did not yaw too badly – a better height than he had dared hope for. And he might squeeze another 1,000 out of her before they reached the Norwegian coast – her fuel load would be lighter then. . . . To reach that height P Popsy had been stripped of everything not needed for the job in hand. All her armour had gone as well as her four front guns. Apart from the two Brownings in the rear turret, she was defenceless, relying on nothing but surprise and height to bring her safely through.

Alone in his turret, Bergman felt stunned by the immensity of the sky around him. He had never been at this height before and the experience was overwhelming. The congealed sea below looked like blue ice, without a wrinkle. The vast dome of sky was a cold pitiless blue and the sun brilliant, making his eyes ache in spite of his smoked glasses. The cold was intense, far worse than he had expected, and his hands and feet were in agony. Yet, in spite of the pain, he felt drowsy, lulled by the steady numbing roar of the engines and the gently swaying motion of the aircraft in the rarefied air. Behind him the exhaust gases of the engines were streaming out like the wake of a ship.

He remembered Grenville's warning and roused himself to keep watch below. If an enemy ship spotted them, it would wireless the coast for fighters, and if a patrol got up in time to meet them it would be curtains. But there was nothing below but the vast, empty sea.

In the pilot's seat Grenville was running over the plan of action. Provided they were not spotted on the way in, it seemed all right. You had to hand it to these people: they were thorough. That business of the glacier – that was clever. God – what a game it was. The tricks and the counter tricks. . . .

He shut his eyes tightly, then opened them again. His dashboard seemed blurred. His artificial horizon, altimeter, airspeed indicator, pressure gauge, temperature gauge, oil gauge – rows and rows of indicators and gauges and all quivering and indistinct. . . . It was this intense cold, affecting his nerve centres. His legs had a bone-chilled ache that was spreading up his back – he longed to stand up and stretch himself. He turned his oxygen full on for a moment and the instrument panel cleared.

He peered sideways, looking down the immense void to the flat, formless sea below. Weather perfect so far. . . . There was a band of mist down there at ten o'clock but it didn't seem to stretch far. It had better not. Any mist in the fjord or a cloud haze above it and they'd had it, glacier or no glacier. . . .

Hoppy's voice came through the intercom, as cheery as always. 'A couple of degrees off course, Skipper.'

Grenville swore. These damned navigators – they should try flying a kite dead on course. He checked with his compass, saw Hoppy was right, and swung the Boston gently to port. They droned on, a speck of dust in an immense blue void. . . .

At first it looked like a low-lying cloud, clinging to the edge of the sea. Five minutes later it became a snow-covered jagged coastline, looking like the outflung leg of a sea monster from their height. Grenville checked his course, swung slightly to port, then spoke to Bergman, with whom he had not exchanged a dozen words since leaving Sumburgh.

'That's your bay, isn't it, dead ahead? We go over it and straight on to Hjelmestad, right?'

Bergman checked the landmarks. 'That's right, Roy. Straight ahead on this course.'

'Keep your eyes open,' Grenville warned him. 'Particularly in the sun.'

Bergman stared about him until his eyes watered, but they seemed alone in the enormous void. The sunken mountains drew nearer, painfully slowly from that height, until at last they crossed the coast. Bergman experienced all the bitterness of the exile as he stared down. Below was his homeland, and yet for him to set foot on it was a desperate venture. His bitterness against the Nazis served his body like fuel, steeling it against the crippling cold.

The alert would have sounded now and German fighters would be leaping off from their snow-covered airfields. Yet the mountains of the Antarctic could not have looked more desolate than those that passed slowly under their wings as they approached Hjelmestad.

Bergman was tense in his turret, timing their flight from the coast to the town. It was just five minutes and eighteen seconds when Grenville spoke to him again.

'I'm starting to circle it now. O.K.?'

'O.K., Roy.'

The town was partly camouflaged under its covering of snow. From their height it looked little more than a hamlet squatting between two mountain ranges. They took a wide circle over it, their condensation trails and exhaust gases forming a gigantic ring. They had been flying so long now that the roar of the engines had faded into a neutral background. Bergman felt he had lost all contact with the earth and was floating bodiless in the vast, silent stratosphere.

Grenville's voice brought him back to reality. 'I'm turning off now for your fjord. Let Hoppy know when he can get cracking.'

Behind him Bergman saw the distant coastline tilt and wheel round as the Boston banked on to her new course. Mountain range after range slid below them, the fjords looking like pieces of bent silver wire threaded through them. Checking the landmarks was not easy for Bergman: they looked vastly different from this height than from the ground. But with the aid of a map he and Adams had studied earlier he saw they were now approaching the upper reaches of the Svartfjord.

He gave rapid instructions to both Grenville and Hoppy. Almost imperceptibly the Boston swung a few degrees to starboard. Bergman craned his neck sidewards. Two parallel mountain ranges, separated by a thread of silver, were sliding towards them. One mountain-peak was shining with a brilliance that made it stand out even from the surrounding snow. Bergman grabbed his mask.

'There it is! Straight ahead. If you watch you'll see the sun shining on the glacier. See it! If we're correct, it should be reflecting enough light downwards for us to take the photographs. The building is right below it.'

Grenville was silent. From his cockpit ahead of the main-plane, he could see something the Norwegian had missed – a thin film of strato-cirrus that was drifting slowly in over the fjord. It was no more than two miles wide and tenuous enough for the ground to be seen hazily through it. But it was more than enough to fog the camera plates. Hoppy confirmed this a moment later.

'That cloud's going to ball things up, Skipper. Can't we drop under it?'

Grenville cursed. Hardly a wisp of cloud all the way from the Shetlands, and yet there had to be one drifting right across their target. He eyed the strato-cirrus, making rapid calculations. It looked at about 24,000 feet – 6,000 feet below them. Not far, but it was those last few thousand feet that counted. Fighters would be swarming up now like tiger fish from the sea bed. They would reach 20,000 feet quickly but from then on their power curve would begin to fall away. If he dropped lower he was playing right into their hands.

He spoke sharply to Bergman. 'Now look! Forget the security stuff for the moment. We can go under that cloud, but it's going to be a gamble. We might make it, but so might the fighters. And if they get above us, it'll be curtains. Can this job wait for another day? Does it matter so much if a kite comes here under escort?'

'We want to avoid that if possible, Roy. It'll give too much away.'

'Then this thing is important enough for us all to risk our necks?'

'It's terribly important, Roy.'

'So you'd like me to go down and chance it.'

'I'd like you to, yes.'

Without another word Grenville pushed the nose of the Boston down. He did not dive steeply, they were still a mile or two from the end of the fjord and he did not want to make his descent conspicuous. The altimeter needle swung slowly round the dial – 29,000 feet ... 27,000 ... 25,000. ... Grenville's teeth were clenched and his hands sweating. The Focke Wulfs would think he had gone crazy. . . .

At 23,500 feet they reached the cloud, passing through it in a second. It was useless for concealment, yet would silhouette them perfectly to the climbing planes. There was no flak, a favourable sign. Jerry was not suspicious of their intentions and did not want to disclose the importance of the building below. Grenville straightened out and, following Hoppy's instructions, began tracking over the target. A few seconds later Hoppy began taking his photographs. Grenville, certain now that the building below was their ultimate target, stared down curiously.

The mountains flanking the narrow Svartfjord were clearly of great height. On its western side, right at the end of the fjord, was a bulbous-topped mountain capped by the glacier Bergman had pointed out. The glacier was easily distinguishable by its mirror-like brilliance. Directly below it, at the bottom end of the enormous *cul-de-sac*, Grenville could just make out a dark building through his binoculars. Although dwarfed by his altitude it was clearly one of considerable size. Surrounded on three sides by precipitous mountains, with its only ingress the deep and narrow Svartfjord, it looked completely impregnable.

Grenville could make nothing of its purpose. Slowly it fell behind them as they droned on. Grenville lifted his eyes, stared ahead. Some eight miles from the building the fjord turned sharply at thirty degrees to head straight for the sea. At this point it was joined by a tributary from the east, a deep gorge that split the flanking mountains and poured a stream of fresh water into the salt water of the Svartfjord. Trained in observation, Grenville studied the gorge almost unconsciously as it passed beneath them.

The Svartfjord angled away from them now as they continued on their undeviating course. Hoppy's voice came through. 'O.K., Skipper. Photographs taken. . . .'

Before he had finished speaking Grenville had put the Boston's nose up, fighting to regain the altitude they had lost. They were still within their time limit but God knows what 7,000 feet was worth to the Focke Wulfs. . . .

His eyes, sore with the strain, searched the sky incessantly. The strato-cirrus had been wider than he had thought and was still visible behind. As he turned his head, his heart gave an explosive thud. A brilliant spot flashed for a second on one side of the cloud, then darkened underneath it. . . .

They were here and had altitude on him. Only one thing to do – go down. As he slammed his stick forward, his brain was racing like the screaming engines in either wing. He snapped his orders to Bergman.

'Listen! They've made it – they'll be down on us in a minute or two. Switch on your reflector-sight and make sure your safety catches are off. Keep your head and don't fire until they're right on top of you. Try to remember all I told you about deflection. Don't panic, and keep telling me which side they're attacking from. I'll help you as we go along. O.K.?'

Bergman's mouth was suddenly dry. 'O.K., Roy.'

The Boston's nose dropped more steeply. Bergman's stomach lifted, making him feel short of breath. The noise was deafening, pressing into his ears like brutal fingers. He switched on his hooded reflector-sight and its orange ring glowed ominously before his eyes.

Grenville's voice again. 'Watch the sun!'

Bergman peered upwards through his smoked glasses. He thought he saw three black dots silhouetted against the blinding glare. The Boston was howling earthwards now, its wings and body trembling with the speed. To Bergman, looking back along the fuselage, it seemed the shuddering tail unit would break off at any moment.

Then he saw the Focke Wulfs clearly for the first time. One was close, already within a thousand yards, the other two more distant. He shouted to Grenville: 'Three of them – closing in on our tail. . . .'

Instantly Grenville pulled out of the headlong dive. A hand seemed to be clawing Bergman's entrails out and his spine felt crushed under the unnatural weight of his head. The Boston groaned in agony, rivets springing, paint cracking off its tortured wings, tailplanes whipped like the tail of a child's kite.

The Focke Wulf was still there, twenty-odd degrees to starboard. Bergman stared with fascination at its short quivering wings, its long transparent hood, and its huge radial engine. The olive-green upper surfaces of its wings, with their huge black crosses, showed vividly as it swung into position. In the brilliant sunlight it glowed like some great insect, beautiful and evil.

Grenville's voice came over the intercom. 'I'm turning to starboard to increase his curve of pursuit. He might black out. Watch him and when he shudders, fire.'

The Boston heeled over steeply. Bergman, crouched behind his sight, saw the Focke Wulf's wings tilt at a steeper angle as it tried to follow them. He understood Grenville's tactics now. At that speed a steep banking turn increased the *g*, particularly for the fighter which had to turn inside them to get the Boston in its fixed forward gunsight. Bergman felt the strain himself, the bone-crushing sensation in his spine again, the tearing at his eye sockets. The Focke Wulf's wing tilted more steeply. Bergman could see its pilot clearly now, crouched forward under his long transparent hood. The Focke Wulf was close – not more than three hundred yards away now. The Norwegian's spine cringed as he imagined his turret slowly sliding into the pilot's gunsight. At any moment now he would open up with his cannon. . . .

Then the 190 faltered. Bergman saw the sudden blind flutter of its wings, the helpless drop of its nose. The pilot had greyed out for a moment; this was his chance. He put his sight on the radial engine and fired one quick burst. His G.6 tracer curled by the Focke Wulf's starboard wing-tip. A quarter of ring relative speed. . . . He made the correction and fired a long four-second burst, twenty bullets a second hosing out from each of his Brownings. His tracer appeared to be striking but now the nose of the 190 was coming up, its pilot was recovering. . . . Bergman fired another frantic burst and this time a white stream of glycol began pouring from the fighter's exhausts. Its propeller stopped, it banked sharply away and began gliding earthwards.

Bergman let out an exultant yell as he fired another burst after it. 'I got him, Roy. He's broken off. I hit him – '

Grenville's voice cut his words off in his throat. 'Watch out, you fool. Watch out for the others.'

Bergman glanced back and his stomach shrank in fear. The two remaining 190's had closed in and were less than four hundred yards away. As he stared at them bright flashes ran along their wings. He twisted his guns back but was too late. Before his eyes the perspex turret splintered into white stars, he heard two shattering explosions and felt himself hurled backwards. There was a moment of intense pain, then nothing but red-streaked darkness.

Grenville felt the Boston shudder under the hammer blows of the cannon shells. A second later a shell tore through his hood. Air shrieked through the hole, buffeting his head backwards. Tracer flashed by like incandescent hail.

He threw the Boston into a spin to simulate loss of control. As always when near extinction, his brain became unnaturally lucid, gaining the ability to consider more than one problem at the same time. One half of it was thinking about Bergman. He didn't answer over the intercom; it looked as if he'd got the chopper. ... Condemning faces flashed before his eyes – Davies, Barrett, Hilde. Hilde. ... God! The other half of his mind was searching for a means of escape. Searching, discarding, selecting, all at fantastic speed. ...

There was one faint chance of survival. He leaned forward, his eyes searching the spinning, reeling mountains that were leaping upwards to crush them. For the moment the firing had ceased but he knew the 190's were following him down, ready to open up again if he pulled out. He watched his altimeter needle; 5,000 feet, 4,000, 3,500 – already below the level of some of those mountain-tops. If he didn't pull out now they were finished. ...

Groaning with the effort, the Boston came out of her spin. Instantly the Focke Wulfs hurled themselves at her again. Explosive shells probed for her fuel tanks, for her engines, for the flesh of her crew.

Ignoring the fire, Grenville searched for his objective. He found it not a mile ahead. Again he put the Boston's nose down. The scream of air through his shattered windscreen almost pierced his eardrums. A sunlit, snow-covered mountain peak flashed under his starboard wing, falling away dizzily in to a tremendous gorge. The Boston followed the drop down, plunging into it like a meteor.

Out of the sunlight now! Into the gorge, its towering walls fined smooth by the Boston's speed. Green water flashing below, foaming and cascading over the rocks. ...

Grenville's jaw clenched with satisfaction. He had made it – he was flying inland up the narrow gorge that ran into the Svartfjord. Now he had a chance, even though the 190's were still behind him, line astern, crazed with the lust to kill. The tremendous roar of the engines thundered across the narrow gorge, bringing down avalanche after avalanche of snow.

The stressed-skin fuselage of the Boston shivered under the impact of two more shells. Grenville dropped lower. Focke Wulf's guns set up at·two degrees . . . German thoroughness . . . forced pilots to fly low and so avoid tail gunners. Use it against them now. . . . That's it . . . he can't get you now without going lower still! Fox him . . . draw him down . . . he'll be watching you, not the gorge ahead. Here's a waterfall coming . . . hold it . . . hold her down . . . bit longer . . . longer. . . . Now!

Like a leaping salmon the Boston hurled herself up and over the waterfall. The 190 following behind had no chance. Before its pilot's reflexes could respond, the high shelf of rock was upon him. The plane vanished in an explosion of flame and spray. The pilot of the second Focke Wulf lost his nerve and pulled out into the sunlight above.

Grenville followed the gorge for its full length before emerging into a wide valley. There were no enemy aircraft in sight but he knew the hue and cry would be on. At zero height the Boston turned for the coast.

Hoppy's voice came hoarsely through the intercom. 'Lummy, Skipper; I thought we'd bought it that time. I could've washed me dirty feet in that water. How's Bergman? Is he hit bad?'

'We'll try to find out in a minute,' Grenville muttered.

Below the level of the tree tops, taking all possible cover, P Popsy headed for home.

CHAPTER II

The private sitting-room was empty when Maisie showed Grenville into it. The black-out curtain had not yet been drawn and the winter dusk was filling the room with shadows. A bright fire was burning on the hearth.

'She's in her room, sir,' Maisie said, touching her curls. 'If you'll wait here, I'll give her a call.'

Grenville nodded and went over to the window. The dusk was robbing both the earth and sky of colour. He could see nothing of the airfield for the high fence, the boundary between a peaceful Britain and a Britain at war. On this side human life was of the highest value, a thing above price. On the other side it was freely bartered away for destruction. And only a wooden fence separated the two. . . .

Grenville turned back and glanced round the room. The fire, sharpened by the cold, was making the brass ornaments wink cheerily. He stood motionless, listening to the silence of the old inn. It had the profound peaceful quality of old age.

Then he heard her footsteps outside, and felt his pulses quicken. She came in, recognized him, and drew slowly nearer. He gave himself no time for hesitation.

'I have some distressing news for you, Miss Bergman. Your brother has been wounded. . . . Not seriously,' he went on quickly as she lifted a hand sharply to her throat. 'But he will be in hospital for two or three weeks.'

She was a thoroughbred. She fought and conquered the tremor in her voice. 'What has happened?' She came forward again, making a fluttering movement with one hand. 'Please sit down.'

Grenville remained standing. 'It happened this morning. We were out on a photo reconnaissance. Three Focke Wulfs jumped us and your brother was hit. Not seriously, but he was wounded in the right shoulder and suffered concussion. He'll be all right in a week or two.'

'Where is he now?'

'I had to leave him in the Shetlands. They made arrangements to get him to hospital. I made certain he was all right before I left.'

'What did you do this time?' she asked quietly.

'I beg your pardon.'

Hilde looked him full in the face. There was a fine silt of resentment in her blue-grey eyes. 'I am sorry but I cannot help feeling bitter. My brother has had to fly many times since 1940 but his pilots, knowing the dangers he had to face on landing, have at least taken care of him in the air. With you he has had only two flights – on the first one you deliberately risked his life, on the second you come back with him wounded. I told you when we met that it was not fair he should share your dangers too, but it seems you took no notice.'

The tension of the fight had not yet worked out of Grenville. He was like a coiled spring, dangerous to handle. His hands tightened as he tried to control his temper.

'You don't think I tried to get him wounded, do you? This was his operation. My orders were that he should come on it, and this is the result.'

'What was the operation?'

'Ask your brother, not me,' Grenville said curtly. 'I was only the taxi-driver.'

Hilde moved over to the fireplace. With one arm on the mantelpiece she stared down. The firelight seemed eager to touch her, running its glow over her slim body, limning its contours in shadows. A welter of emotions suddenly surged up inside Grenville. None was defined, but all seemed to gear up with his tension, inciting him to some act that would explode it away and bring him relief.

Hardly aware of the movement, he drew closer to her. She looked up and saw how near he was standing. The firelight, growing in strength as the room darkened, shone full on his face, betraying much that the dusk had kept hidden. She saw the intense weariness in the shadows under his eyes, the resolution in the lines of his cheeks and jaw, the bitterness and strain round his mouth. She looked into his eyes, where the fire-glow was hot, and saw tiny miniatures of herself framed there.

She frowned slightly, shaking her head. 'I'm sorry. That was not fair of me. I should not say such things until I know more of what happened. . . .'

It was this retraction of hers that triggered off Grenville's impulse. That, and something which sprang without authority into her eyes on seeing the desire in his own.

He caught hold of her, jerking her towards him. Her mouth was parting in protest as he kissed her, and his lips imprisoned her words. He held her like this for a long moment, neither knowing nor caring whether she was struggling or not. His lips moved to her eyes, her forehead, her shining hair. She was lax now, her eyes closed and cheeks pale. She was crying something softly in Norwegian.

The light was suddenly switched on. For a moment Grenville did not know what had happened. Then he turned his bloodshot eyes on the door.

Valerie, in hat and coat, was standing there. Her voice was cold, spiteful. 'I'm sorry. I'd no idea what was happening, of course. . . .'

Hilde tore away, supporting herself against the mantelpiece. Grenville's face was murderous. Valerie thought he was about to strike her and drew back in sudden alarm. He hesitated, cursed, then made for the hall. Two seconds later the front door slammed shut. There was no quality of peace now in the silence that returned to the inn.

Bergman returned from hospital sixteen days later. It was a grey blustery day early in February when he entered Grenville's squadron office, his left hand outstretched. His right arm was held up in a sling under his naval mackintosh. A severely bruised cheek, still discoloured, gave a lop-sided effect to his smile.

'Hello, Roy. It's good to see you again.'

Grenville was on his feet, his own hand outstretched. For a moment, mixed with gladness, there had been a faint measure of uncertainty in his eyes. Now he was smiling, a rare smile that made him look almost boyish.

'Hello, Finn. I didn't expect you out quite so soon. Sit down and tell me all about it. Here, have a cigarette.'

Grenville's cordiality, unusual in one so taciturn, gave Bergman an assurance he had not felt before. Now he knew he had made a friend of Grenville, and his smile was an expression of his delight.

'It's good to be back. I've missed you all. Honestly, I really have.'

Grenville laughed. 'We haven't missed you quite so much. We've had a holiday from those crazy jobs of yours.'

Bergman was curious. 'Have you really had a rest? I know nothing has come through from my end, but I understood Bomber Command had borrowed you back in the meantime.'

Grenville gave a rueful nod. 'They did. We had to do a couple of Low Country jobs for them.'

'What were they like? Very tough?'

Grenville's face turned expressionless for a moment. 'So-so. They could have been worse.' He shrugged, then his voice lightened. 'Well; what are you bringing us? More trouble?'

'Later, perhaps. But at the moment I'm bringing you something good. I heard they were coming this morning and persuaded the doctors to let me out. I wanted to see them arrive. You'll have heard, I suppose?'

Grenville nodded. 'Yes; Davies told us last week.' He looked down at his watch. 'You've timed it well. They're due here any minute.' He lifted his eyes to the Norwegian's pleasant face. 'Will we be getting any more gen now?'

'Yes. The Air Commodore is going to come down, possibly tomorrow. He is going to tell you about the training he wants doing. It's pretty technical, of course – right outside my province.'

Grenville nodded, not labouring the point. He watched Bergman keenly. 'Have you seen your sister yet?'

'Yes; I called over on the way here.'

'Did she go to see you in hospital?'

Bergman looked surprised. 'Didn't you know? Haven't you been across?'

Grenville was toying with a ruler on his desk. 'I don't seem to have had much time. . . . But I saw she was kept informed about you.'

'Hilde told me. It was very decent of you, especially to arrange a trip for her. Anyway; I hope you'll be able to get over more now.' Bergman looked away, speaking with some diffidence. 'I'd like the two of you to get to know one another. She hasn't any real friends over here – that worries me in case something should go wrong on one of these trips of mine. I know you'd see she was all right.' He tuned back anxiously. 'You don't mind my saying that? I've no right to, of course. . . .'

'I shouldn't worry about her,' Grenville said abruptly. There was a short awkward silence. The sound of distant engines brought them both relief. Grenville jumped to his feet. 'This sounds like them now. Let's go out and take a look, shall we?'

They stood on the tarmac path, staring up at the grey, windswept sky. The sound of the engines was approaching fast, coming from the west. Grenville pointed over the hump-backed roofs of the Nissen huts.

'There they are!'

Two graceful shapes emerged from the low ceiling of cloud. They were long and slender with a high tailfin and shapely tapering wings. Their engines had a sweet, powerful note. They circled the airfield, banking steeply to follow its perimeter. One pilot feathered an engine and deliberately did a slow roll not a hundred feet above the wet grass.

'What a lovely job,' Grenville breathed.

The two planes drifted in to land, as light as thistledown. They braked, then taxied towards the Control Tower. Grenville nudged Bergman's arm.

'This looks like the job we've been waiting three years for. Let's go and have a closer look at her.'

They were not the only ones showing interest. Men were running towards the planes from all directions. The experts showed unqualified approval. The Maintenance Officer was running a hand dreamily along one of the 12-cylinder underslung Merlins like a man caressing a woman's smooth shoulder. The Armament Officer could have been staring upwards into paradise when he was given a glimpse of the huge bomb bay. Rumour after rumour spread among the air crews and mechanics. One rumour came to stay. This was the kite that eight days ago, on the 30th January, had bombed Berlin in daylight for the first time. . . . Air crews nudged one another, holding their breaths in prayer.

The A.T.A. pilot broke the wonderful news. Yes; this was the kite, and 633 were going to be re-equipped with her. They were lucky all right – she was a beauty. Her name? She was called the Mosquito. . . .

The phone call came from Grenville in the late afternoon. He had just taken up one of the Mosquitoes, and his eyes were still bright from her performance. He lifted the receiver, gave his name, then froze. Her voice was low, but even the interference on the line could not destroy its melody.

'I want to apologize for the things I said to you that afternoon. . . . I did not know, but now Finn has told me and I am very ashamed. Will you please forgive me?'

Grenville had to speak carefully: his voice was eager to betray him. 'I know how you felt. I'm the one to apologize. I was tensed up and very tired. . . .'

Her interruption was like a soft hand being placed over his mouth. 'There is nothing to forgive. Will you come over with Finn so that I know you have forgiven me?'

His mouth was dry. 'Yes. Yes, I will. As soon as possible.'

'Thank you. Then good-bye . . . for the moment.'

'Good-bye.'

Grenville lowered the receiver. He noticed with no surprise that his hand was trembling.

CHAPTER 12

Davies arrived the following morning, holding the same audience in Barrett's office as on the previous occasion. All his listeners noticed the change in him. He seemed less spry, to have lost something of his quicksilver. It seemed certain he had been told the purpose of the building in the Svartfjord, and was finding the knowledge a heavy burden. The implication made a deep impression on his audience. They listened in silence to his high-pitched voice.

'Well, gentlemen; you've got the first of your new aircraft.' His eyes travelled from Barrett to Grenville. 'As some of you have already found out, she's a beauty. In another week you'll be fully equipped. You won't be able to complain then that you haven't the tools to do the job because you'll have the finest light bomber in the skies today. First I want to say a few words about her.

'As you know, she recently did a daylight raid on Berlin. She was unarmed, relying successfully on her speed to bring her back safely. Wonderful job though she is, however, we've finally decided an unarmed kite, however fast, is a bit risky for the kind of jobs you might have to do. We next had a look at the fighter-bomber version, but the snag there is that the cannon breeches extend back into the bomb bay, so cutting down the bomb load considerably, and your bays, as you'll have noticed, have been converted to carry the maximum load of 4,000 lb. So we had a chat with the makers and they did a fine compromise job for us. To get the cannon in, they used two of the short-barrelled type and extended them in front of the nose. That gives room inside for the breeches. Of course, they couldn't give you four – with a full bomb load you'd be overweight – but they made up with two Brownings for good measure. Naturally, when you've got a full bomb load you won't get the same performance as the unarmed version, but you've got the satisfaction of knowing that once your bombs have gone, you've got a kite that can match any fighter Jerry can put up. Any questions so far?'

Everyone who had seen the new bomber had noticed one conspicuous thing about her. Grenville commented on it now.

'I noticed there is no hatch in the nose. How does the observer use his bomb-sight?'

'The answer to that one is that he doesn't,' Davies said. 'For the job you're going to do, a bombsight won't be any use. A damn good thing because the makers needed a solid nose for the cannon.' Seeing the puzzled frowns on three of his listeners' faces, he waved a hand. 'Don't worry about it – I'll explain everything later on. I've other things to talk about now.

'First, your conversion. I want it done quickly, because I want special squadron training to start in less than two weeks. It's going to mean a lot of work and a lot of reorganization – I know that. Your gunners, for example, are going to become redundant. They'll be posted. Your remaining pilots and observers are going to have a lot to learn – and they've got to learn it faster than anything has been learned in the Service before. Time is running short, and believe me, time is precious. This thing is bigger than I'd realized. Too damn big.'

There was a strained look in Davies' darting eyes as he continued. 'Once you are crewed up and have got your kits, we're sending you up on a daily trip to Scotland. A couple of routes are worked out for you which you'll always use to make things easier for the Observer Corps. Up there we have a deep valley with a special target site waiting for you. As near as possible it will resemble the target you're being trained to prang.'

His voice dropped, his eyes moving in turn from Grenville to Barrett and Adams. 'You've probably guessed by this time what that target is. I'm not allowed to tell you its purpose – I may never be allowed to – but I can say that you're out to destroy that building at the upper end of the Svartfjord. But' – and Davies paused expressively – 'No one else must know. Your crews are going to get curious when the training starts – when they do, tell them to belt up. No man outside you three must know the target. I can't stress enough the importance of secrecy. Any man breathing a word of this will be court martialled at once.'

He paused to let that sink in, then smiled wryly. 'Sorry to sound so tough, but that's the way it is. Now a few words about the training:

'This valley in Scotland is meant to represent the Svartfjord. Of course, it's nothing like so deep, but it's the nearest thing we've got like it in this country. At one end of it a target site is marked out. Not, as you would expect, at the bottom of the valley, but instead in a corrie in the mountainside, under an overhanging clump of trees. That's where you will practise dropping your bombs. The idea is to fly along the mountainside, bank steeply over, pull away, and as you go – release your bomb. Centrifugal force will then sling it at the target. You can see now how useless a bombsight would be. It's an entirely new technique and will take a hell of a lot of experiment and practice. But we think it can be done – in fact it must be done.' Davies's voice dropped even lower. 'Those of you who have seen the target and know how difficult pranging it in the ordinary way would be, might guess the idea behind this. If you do, keep it to yourselves. I'm not allowed to let the cat out of the bag until the final briefing.

'Right. In a few minutes we'll go into Adams' office and run over all the technical snags. In any case, I shall be going up to Scotland with you and will help out with the early experiments. But now I want to run quickly through the combined operation as Special Services and Lieutenant Bergman have planned it. Here is the general scheme.'

There was an expectant stir from the three hushed officers. Their eyes flickered for a moment on the fair-headed Bergman who was leaning in his chair, supporting his bandaged arm on his knee. His head was bent diffidently forward, his eyes staring down at the floor. They looked back at the small, serious-faced Air Commodore.

'If you haven't all seen the real thing, you've seen photographs of the target. It's at the bottom end of a hellishly deep fjord that is over twenty miles long. We know that Jerry doesn't believe we have a kite that can make a worthwhile attack on such a target, and until the Mossy came along he was right. However, he hasn't taken any chances – the target is too important. He knows that if an attack does come, the attacking force must fly inside the fjord for a considerable distance – probably from its mouth at the coast. No kite could prang the building from above and equally no kite could dive down on it – the mountains make both impossible. So Jerry has built flak posts all along the fjord sides. Lieutenant Bergman says he has everything lined up there – 88, 37, and 20 mm., the whole bag of tricks. If you've read your Tennyson, this is the Valley of Death. And if you flew down it as things are at the moment you'd end up in far worse shape than the Light Brigade. . . .

'Jerry, then, has been thorough. But our Special Services and Lieutenant Bergman haven't been sleeping either. The Norwegian patriots over there have been organized and are waiting. They know their job, all they want now are the tools to help them do it. And this is one of your next operations. . . .'

Again the stir of expectancy. The tension could be felt. Davies pointed a finger at the lowered head of Bergman. 'On a certain date in April, the Lieutenant will be dropped in Norway again. There he will contact the patriots and make certain everything is ready. He'll send a message through to us, and on receipt of it you will go out one night on a supply-dropping job. Among other things, the equipment you put down will consist of light machine-guns, ammunition and grenades. . . .' Davies gave a smile at the look on Grenville's face. 'I see some of you are beginning to fit the pieces together.

'Right. So far so good. The patriots have got tools and will make themselves ready. So will you. At a given date a week or two later, when everything has been checked and re-checked until it's as perfect as anything can be in this imperfect world, you'll go out before dawn – bombed up and ready. For weeks before this date you'll have been going out at the same time, so that no one around will take particular notice of you. But this will be the real thing. You'll be going out to smash that building in the Svartfjord.

'In the meantime Lieutenant Bergman and his men will be doing their stuff on the other side. They'll attack these gun outposts and overcome their crews in a surprise dawn attack. This will actually take place while you are airborne – the timing is most important. There's no chance of the patriots being able to hold these posts once reinforcements arrive, and the building is so important Jerry will move heaven and earth to get them back once he is alerted. Fortunately these outposts are in isolated places, mostly on high mountain slopes, so however fast Jerry moves he can't recapture them under an hour or two. And in that hour, gentlemen, you'll be batting down that fjord in those new Mossies of yours, heading straight for that building. You'll drop your special eggs in a special way – and then get out smartly. If all goes well, the building will be destroyed and the patriots will get away before the reinforcements arrive. That's the scheme and it has to succeed. No one must even consider failure – the alternatives are too grave.'

In the silence that followed Barrett's asthmatic breathing could be heard clearly. Satisfied that he had made the impression he desired, Davies ended on a lighter note.

'We'll prang it all right, don't worry about that. And afterwards we'll throw a party that'll go down in history.'

During the next two weeks 633 Squadron's conversion from Bostons to Mosquitoes went on apace. The air gunners were posted and their billets taken by a reserve of four pilots and four observers. Davies had these men sent as a precautionary measure. An emergency might arise, the squadron might be called on to fulfil some earlier mission, and if losses were sustained, they might find themselves short of trained men for the big occasion. A surplus of four crews, trained with the rest of the squadron, should cover all foreseeable emergencies. The wisdom of his move was to be apparent later.

By the 18th of February the crews were considered proficient enough to enter the second phase of their training. During this time Grenville, Adams and Barrett had all been up to Scotland to take a look at the valley from the ground, and during the last five days, with either Barrett or Davies as passenger, Grenville had made innumerable dummy attacks on the target.

At first it had appeared impossible even to fly close to the target, much less to throw a bomb on it, and it would have been impossible in any plane less manoeuvrable than the Mosquito. The target lay in a depression on the otherwise steep hillside and was overhung by a tree-covered ridge. The difficulty was not so much in making the run-in as in avoiding collision with the steep hill at the end of the valley. At first Grenville practised without bombs, trying to discover the correct approach and maximum safety air speed at which an attack could be made. After he had given near heart attacks to the watchers below, the outcome was an air speed of 280 m.p.h., a run-in over the last 200 yards with vertical wings, a tight 90 degree starboard turn to hurl the bomb outwards, then full throttle and a mad climb up and out of the valley.

The next problem was to find the precise moment to release a bomb. The pilot had to do this, and as things stood it was pure guesswork. On the third day Grenville had an idea. He lined up various points on his port engine nacelle with the target and dropped 11½ lb. practice bombs until he thought he had found a sighting spot. When he returned to Sutton Craddock that day, he had a mechanic paint a red mark on the nacelle. The next day, as he swung the Mosquito over and pulled her back, he waited until the red spot was in line with the target before giving Davies the signal. He learned afterwards from the two spotting quadrant huts that his smoke puff had landed in the middle of the target area.

That was good enough. Davies had already told him that in the Svartfjord a bomb within fifty yards of the target would be close enough. He ordered similar marks to be painted on the rest of the Mosquitoes. Later on, others would have to take their place when heavier bombs with a different trajectory were used, but the principle and application would remain the same.

With this experience and knowledge behind him, he was able to give his crews a detailed briefing on the morning of the 18th. After telling them what would be expected of them in the training weeks ahead, he went on:

'None of you will take any practice bombs today. We'll spend the afternoon going in and coming out of the valley. You'll find that quite difficult enough to start with – particularly the coming out! Make your first run-in at 250 m.p.h. – we'll work up speed later. Get fairly close to the target before banking away, but take it easy at first. We want bombs on the target, not bodies.

'Keep in touch with me all the time on your R/T, but don't talk unless you're the one going in. I don't want the channel blocked by a lot of chattering old women. And while on the subject of silence get this into your heads. This training and everything about it is hush-hush. I don't want a word spoken about it, either by mouth or letter. The first man caught talking won't know what has hit him. . . .'

The same instructions on security were issued to the ground staff and the training began. As Grenville had expected, it was hair-raising. The first planes to enter the valley went in confidently enough, only to come shooting out a few seconds later like nervous corks from bottles. His earphones were filled with mutters and curses as pilots strove desperately to avoid the hill at the end of the valley. In the two-hour practice that afternoon only Sam Milner and Gillibrand flew near enough the target to have successfully bombed it, and that at the cost of two trees from the ledge above. Gillibrand's T Tommy eventually limped home on one engine, a severed pine branch sticking aggressively out from the Coolant radiator in its starboard wing.

The next day went better. More pilots caught the knack of pulling their Mosquitoes round at the right time, and soon Grenville had them coming in at higher speeds. On the fourth day mechanics fitted light-series carriers and they went out with sixteen 11½ lb. practice bombs apiece. All went well that day, although few bombs went near the target. The following day brought tragedy. Dawson of A Flight, who, like Gillibrand, had been delaying his turn more and more for the sake of accuracy, did it once too often and went slap into the cliff. The blazing remains of his Mosquito went tumbling down to the moss-covered rocks below. Although the accident happened towards the end of the training session, Grenville made every pilot do one more run-in before returning home.

The Mess was quiet that night. Both Dawson and his observer had been popular and their deaths introduced a grimness into the training, something that had been lacking before among the light-hearted crews.

Inevitably there was an offender against the security regulations. Not three days after the training started a letter was brought to Grenville by the Station Censoring Officer. It was from an A.C.1 Atkins to his girl-friend, Ruby Sampson. After preliminary endearments, it read: *We've got some new kites now (what a job they are, ducks, you ought to see them) and now we've been put on some training stunt up in Scotland....*

Grenville did not bother to read on. The ruthless streak in him came to the surface at once. He ordered a full squadron parade and had the offender marched up and down the ranks. On his front and back he wore a placard bearing the words 'Take a good look at me. I am the B.F. who can't keep his mouth shut'. The unfortunate A.C.1 Atkins broke into tears before more than half his ordeal was over.

Drastic though the punishment, its effect was salutary. The letters that followed, from all ranks, were so austere in content they must have brought tears to many a neglected girl. But there was no stopping the rumours that circulated among the men inside the field. One of the most startling, voiced by no other than Gillibrand himself, was that they were training to bomb Hitler's Eagle's Nest in Bavaria.

'Stands out a mile,' Gillibrand said, winking at Jimmie. 'Can't be bombed from above, so we're gonna put 'em through the windows when he and Musso are having a girl party. Clear as the dew-drops on me Aunt Sally's nose.'

In this atmosphere of rumours and rising tension, the training went on.

CHAPTER 13

The battered saloon with the multi-coloured bonnet squealed to a halt outside the inn, its radiator-cap giving out a hapless wisp of steam. Gillibrand turned and thrust his wristlet watch under Maisie's nose.

'There y'are, honey. Twenty minutes early. What did I tell ya?'

Maisie shifted gingerly on the broken springs of her seat. 'I thought we were comin' back by car, not flyin'! Don't you ever drive like that again when I'm with you, d'you hear? I ain't been so scared in years.'

Gillibrand slapped her shoulder. 'Aw, you enjoyed it. I saw your eyes flashin' as we came round them corners. You were lovin' it, kid.'

Maisie eased herself off the seat. 'And I'm not goin' out with you again until you do something to this thing I'm sitting on. It ain't fit for a decent girl – the way it nips and pinches.'

Gillibrand grinned. 'I'll fix it. You won't know it when I get back from leave.'

Maisie took offence at once. 'Oh, sure. Now you're going off to see your girl-friend, you'll get it fixed. But it's been good enough for me all these weeks, hasn't it?'

'Now don't get all jealous, kid. You knew I was goin' down to see her on my leave. I ain't been holding out on you.'

Maisie sniffed, but inwardly had to admit the truth of what he said. She fell moodily silent. Gillibrand pushed a cigarette into her hand. 'Have a fag before you go, kid. An' cheer up. It'll soon pass – seven days ain't no time at all. Then we can start where we left off, huh?'

Maisie's eyes flashed. 'You've got a nerve. I'm supposed to sit around here for a week twiddlin' my fingers while you're necking a girl down in London. What do you think I am, a mug?'

Gillibrand pulled her towards him, nuzzling his nose against her cheek. 'You're a swell kid, that's what you are. Aw, hell; a guy can like two women, can't he? Some of those Eastern guys like hundreds. Give me a kiss, honey. That's better. . . .'

She returned his kiss fiercely. There was bitterness in her hot, dark eyes as she drew back and stared at him.

'I'm a fool,' she said thickly.

'Aw; stop talkin' like that.' He tried to pull her towards him again but this time she resisted.

'That's enough,' she muttered. 'Leave me alone now.' She motioned towards the airfield. 'How is it you're able to get leave? I thought you were pretty busy just now.'

Gillibrand grinned. 'So we are. But I'm takin' my kite in and out of cracks in the ground better than anyone else around here. That's the only reason they're givin' me leave. But seven days – hell, I'm due for a month!'

'What's Jimmie going to do while you're away?'

The grin left his face. He turned to her, frowning slightly. 'Matter of fact, that's one of the things I wanted to talk to you about. He might be a bit lonely at nights – he's too shy to make friends. How 'bout you looking after him – mothering him a bit, huh?'

She gave a harsh laugh. 'Me? A fine mother I'd make.'

'I dunno. I reckon you'd make a good 'un, kid. How 'bout trying it on Jimmie, anyway.'

Her cheeks reddened at his words. She took her resentment out of the boy. 'You talk as if he were a baby. What's the matter with him? He's only a couple of years younger than we are.'

Gillibrand shook his head. 'I ain't good at words, so it ain't easy to say. But that boy hasn't grown up somehow.'

'He's shy – I know that.'

'He's more than that, honey. He ain't faced life the way we have. He's kinda afraid of it. That's the way I see it, anyway.'

Maisie was staring at him. 'Go on,' she said.

He rubbed his big chin with his hand, then shrugged. 'That's all, I guess. There ain't any more.'

'You're lying,' she said. 'His nerve's gone, hasn't it?'

His face turned grim. 'I wouldn't let anyone else say that, kid.'

'I know you wouldn't. But that doesn't alter things. He's cracking up, and you know it.'

He scowled out through the windscreen into the dusk for a long moment, then nodded abruptly. 'Yeah; it's true. I've been tryin' to kid myself, but it ain't any use. He cracked up on our last op.'

'What happened?'

'Aw, we were sent out on a low-level prang over Holland. At that height you gotta watch the coast defences. If you don't pick your way through gaps in 'em carefully, they get you as sure as hell. We got in all right, but over Eindhoven there was a lot of flak and the kid folded up. He couldn't plot a course back, couldn't do nothin' at all. . . . So I had to bring the kite back on my own. I hadn't a hope of finding a gap, and we nearly got the hammer breakin' out. It was a close thing.'

Maisie's eyes were big, frightened. 'But didn't they ground him after that?'

Gillibrand's bushy eyebrows drew together. 'You don't think I reported him, d'ya? What d' you think I am, kid. A heel?'

'But what if he cracks again? You can't risk your life like that. . . .'

For a moment Gillibrand's grin returned. 'Now don't get scared, honey. I ain't going to get killed.' His expression changed, showing wonder. 'Gee; what that kid went through that night! I ain't seen anythin' like it before. He cried – honest he did! He sobbed for his ma! The poor little guy!'

Maisie's eyelashes were wet. 'But you can't keep him flying if he feels like that. It isn't fair to either of you. You're both going to get killed.'

Gillibrand frowned. 'You don't understand. He don't want to go L.M.F. Nobody wants that. He's more scared of that than anything.'

'But what are you going to do, then?'

He stared gloomily out into the early spring dusk. 'I don't know, honey. I've given it plenty of thought but ain't got nowhere. I can see why he's like this, but that ain't much help.'

'What do you mean?'

'Aw; it seems his mother died when he was a kid and he was put to live with an old aunt. She was the type with tight corsets – you know, wouldn't let him go to the movies, wouldn't let him play with the kids next door, kept him away from girls. . . . The poor little guy had never been further than the front room until this war came along. And then he ends up with people like me. It ain't fair!'

'Is that why you've kept pushing him around, encouraging him to drink and that sort of thing?'

Gillibrand nodded. 'Yeah; I see it this way – it's a tough war and you gotta be tough to last the pace. I thought that if I could pack enough confidence into the kid, he might be able to see it through. That's why I said he should get himself a girl, give her a kiss or two, make himself feel a man. . . . Aw, maybe I was wrong – I must have been wrong because he's cracked up anyway. But that was the general idea.'

Her eyes wandered over his craggy face. 'You're pretty fond of him, aren't you?'

He made a clumsy gesture with one huge hand. 'You know how it is. . . . You always get kinda attached to someone you bunk and fly with. Makes you feel responsible for 'em, somehow.'

It was growing dark inside the car now and her face was almost hidden in the shadows. 'You say you'd like me to look after him while you're on leave. What do you want me to do?'

He turned eagerly towards her. 'I don't like to think of the kid frettin' in his bunk in the evenings. If he came over here maybe you could talk to him and kid him up a bit – you know – make him feel somebody. And you must know a few girls round these parts. Couldn't you date him up with one? See what you can do, kid.'

'All right,' she said slowly. 'I'll see what I can do.'

He reached out, pulling her towards him. 'Gee, kid; you're really something. If it was anyone else but Joyce I'd take my leave here with you. I mean it, kid. You're a real honey.'

She returned his kisses with a fervour that startled him. Then, as suddenly, she pulled away and jumped from the car. Her voice sounded hoarse, indistinct.

'I'm late. I'll see you when you come back.'

Gillibrand leaned across the seat and waved to her. 'O.K., kid. Take care of yourself. Be seein' you, honey.'

She did not wait for the car to turn but ran quickly down the gravel drive to the inn. She was crying.

The first of the Anson's engines fired, scattering a flock of sparrows that had landed alongside its starboard wing-tip. Bergman, wearing a flying-suit, helmet, and parachute harness, turned to Grenville and held out his hand.

'Well, this is it, I suppose. Up to Scotland, wait for a good weather report, then off we go.' His accent sounded more pronounced than usual. 'Good-bye, Roy, and the best of luck.'

As always when under the stress of emotion, Grenville's tone was brusque. 'You need the luck, not us. Hang on to it and don't take any chances.'

Bergman smiled. 'I don't intend to get caught if I can help it.'

'Mind you don't,' Grenville said curtly.

The mechanics were having trouble with the port engine of the Anson. Twice it fired and then cut out. Both of the waiting men turned towards it. The moment was a painful one and they were glad of the diversion.

The engine fired again and this time its steady roar merged into that of its companion. Bergman turned his blue eyes back to Grenville.

'You won't forget about Hilde? You'll explain why I did not go over?'

Grenville nodded. 'I'll tell her. And don't worry about her. She'll be all right.'

Bergman smiled. 'I'm not worrying, Roy – not this time.' He gripped Grenville's hand again. 'Good-bye, Roy.'

'Cheerio,' Grenville said.

Their eyes held a moment, then Bergman turned for the plane. Grenville watched him enter it and did not move until the Anson had taken off and was climbing steadily over the distant trees. He returned to his office, sat in thought for a few minutes, then went to see Barrett.

'Will you want me this afternoon?' he asked.

'No, Roy, I don't think so. Take a couple of hours off if you like.'

'May I borrow your car?'

Although it was the first time Grenville had made the request for himself, he had no doubt of the answer. Barrett's generosity with his car was proverbial.

'You know where it is, Roy. Help yourself.'

Grenville returned to his office and 'phoned Hilde. 'Would you care to come out with me for a drive. I've got a couple of hours, and it's a fine day.'

Her low voice expressed her pleasure. 'I would like that very much, Roy. What time will you be coming over. . . ?'

Grenville picked her up at the inn fifteen minutes later. He felt a disturbing sensation of gladness as she approached the car. She was bare-headed and wearing a dove-grey coat thrown loosely round her shoulders. Her face was flushed with pleasure as she slid into the seat alongside him.

'This is a nice surprise, Roy.'

'I felt like getting away for a few hours,' He told her as he drove away. 'Is there anywhere particular you'd like to go?'

'No. Please go wherever you wish. I shall be quite happy.'

Grenville was aware of an odd lightness of heart. It was irrational because Bergman had gone and he thought a good deal of the Norwegian. Yet the feeling persisted, growing even stronger as the airfield fell back out of sight.

It was the day, he told himself. The may blossom was already out and lay sprinkled among the green hedgerows like powdered snow. The clouds had lost their winter gauntness, and the sun was shining with a richer gold. Spring was everywhere, in the white daisies, the nesting birds, in the wind stinging his cheek. But he could not deny that the catalyst that made him respond to its magic was by his side. She could have been the very repository of spring, with her peach-smooth cheeks, lustrous hair, and clear, shining eyes.

They chatted lightly for a little while, then fell into a long companionable silence in which words seemed unnecessary. They were driving over the moors with the sea a blue haze in the distance when she spoke to him again.

'You are looking happier today than I have seen you look for a long time, Roy. What has happened?'

Grenville's sense of guilt returned, particularly when he realized he had not yet given her the news. He kept his eyes on the twisting road ahead. 'Nothing,' he said. 'It must be the day – it's good to see the last of winter.'

She laughed. 'I thought you must have been given some nice dangerous raid to look forward to.'

The lightness of his mood, already threatened by the stinging memory of Bergman's departure, suddenly vanished. On an impulse he pulled up the car and turned towards her.

'Why do you say that?'

The happiness on her face faded at his expression. 'I'm sorry. Have I said something wrong?'

'You think I like war, don't you?'

He had already learned that she always spoke the truth, whatever the situation. She did now.

'Yes. I have thought so.'

'Why?'

His tone puzzled her, making her low voice uncertain. 'I'm not quite sure. Perhaps it is because you seem to spend so much time at the squadron, or perhaps it is because of what the others say.'

'What do they say?'

'That you are always thinking of war and working out new tactics. . . .'

'That's my job,' he said curtly.

Hilde hesitated again. 'Yes, I know. But none of the others work as hard as you. . . .' She put a hand on his arm. 'Please forget what I said. You were looking so happy a moment ago. Please smile again – it makes you look so young.'

His eyes pulled away from her, following the cloud shadows that were scurring over the undulating moors. He was resentful that she had the power to make him deny what he preferred others to believe, and his voice held that resentment.

'How can you think I enjoy this job – taking kids out to their deaths and then writing about it to their mothers afterwards?' He stared at her bitterly. 'What do you think I am?'

In spite of his words her eyes were shining. 'Please go on,' she breathed. He saw her expression and his tone changed abruptly.

'What does it matter? If you want to believe it, don't let me stop you.'

'You know I don't want to believe it,' she whispered. 'Please go on. There is so much about you I don't know. Tell me what you feel. . . . Tell me everything.'

His eyes were brooding on the distant sea. 'I hate war. But I also hate bullies – I always have. It's the one hate I've never been ashamed of. And just before the war I had a holiday over in Germany and saw what the Nazis were doing. When I got back I joined the Volunteer Reserve. A few months later the war broke out and that gave the Nazis a few more million people to beat up with their rubber truncheons. Somehow after that, everything else in life – marriage, a career – everything became unimportant until they were beaten and the whole filthy business was over.' His voice turned bitter again. 'I like to think there is a subtle difference between that and liking war.'

'Don't be angry with me,' she said quietly. 'I had no way of knowing this. You make everyone believe the reverse. Why do you do that, Roy?'

He could not have answered her if he had tried. Instead he told her about Bergman. As he had expected, she took the news without flinching although the loss showed deep in her eyes. She gave a slight, protesting shake of her head.

'I know he went this way thinking it would be easier for me, but I would have preferred him to say good-bye. I have a strange feeling about him; I have had it some time now. I feel he is going into great danger.'

'He'll be back in a few weeks,' Grenville told her.

She looked away, her eyes following the dipping flight of a sparrow. 'Well, he has gone, so there is nothing we can do,' she said quietly after a pause. 'I suppose it had to come, sooner or later.'

Courage was a quality Grenville could appreciate. He watched her in silence. She turned back to him abruptly, making herself smile again. 'We were talking about you, Roy. You said that to do your best in the war it is necessary to deny yourself everything else. Is that true? Would not some things make it a little easier to bear – perhaps even help you a little?'

'What things? A girl, a wife?' As soon as the words left his mouth Grenville realized how they had betrayed him.

Sadness tinged her faint smile. 'Perhaps even they might be of some help.'

He shook his head abruptly. 'No! I don't want any woman biting her nails over me every time I go out on a raid. I've enough to worry about as it it. A man's a fool to get mixed up with sentiment in war-time.'

'Can you prevent people being sentimental and biting their nails?' she asked softly.

Fear of his own emotions made Grenville unnecessarily harsh. 'You can if you prevent them getting any damn fool ideas. I've seen too many sobbing girl-friends and bereaved wives to want to give the world any more.'

She turned quickly away again, hiding her face. His next words, following the others like an echo, startled him. 'After the war it may be different, but no one can look that far ahead.'

She turned back to him immediately. Her voice had a soft, singing note. 'Some people can,' she said. 'Some people can wait a long time.'

Once again Grenville had the odd sensation he was sinking into the blue-grey depths of her eyes. It was very hushed in the car, with the sunlit moors the only witness to a promise she had dared make no clearer. It was, Grenville suddenly realized, a moment he would never forget.

CHAPTER 14

The hut was unbearably quiet. The naked electric bulb above, swinging on its flex in the draughts, shone down on Gillibrand's unmade bed, with its pile of folded blankets. Jimmie's eyes moved to the wall above it where the Canadian displayed his pin-ups. In his imagination they were staring back at him in contempt. They knew him: they were only displaying their charms to taunt him and bring him to ridicule. . . .

He turned away from their mocking gaze. The harsh light shone on his thin face. His skin was a muddy, unhealthy colour and his brown eyes were constantly moving, shifting at the slightest sound. There was something in his expression of a lost child who had strayed from his parents and suddenly found himself in an incomprehensively vast and perilous world. Once his lower lip began quivering and he dug his teeth punishingly into it. When he released it again there were two white dents that slowly turned an angry red.

It wasn't so bad as this when Gillie was here. Gillie didn't give you time to think. He was always pushing you about, making you do this and that, never leaving you alone. Sometimes it was irritating but it did help to take your mind off things. . . . What a wonderful thing to be like Gillie . . . afraid of nothing . . . doing anything you wanted to do without first thinking of the consequences.

Mind you, there had been times when he had hated Gillie. He had hated him when he attacked that flak ship. For weeks he had dreamed of that murderous flak, of steel cutting upwards through his body. . . . He jerked now at the memory and sweat formed inside his clenched hands. That hadn't been fair of Gillie. And it wasn't fair of him to take the chances he was taking up in Scotland. The way their kite had lurched when they hit that tree. . . . And a couple of days later . . . Dawson and Taylor . . . dying in flames for doing the same thing. . . .

Yet, on the other hand, you couldn't help feeling confidence in him. He gave it to you with that big laugh of his. He was so tough and sure of himself that he seemed indestructible.

But no one was indestructible! He'd kill them both sooner or later. And even if he wasn't so reckless, how long could you last in this game? At their last station, when they'd been operating on maximum and sustained effort for weeks on end, their losses in crews every two months had equalled their entire complement. So even if you were one of the lucky ones, like Gillie or Grenville, how long could you hope to last?

And now there was this new job coming up. From all the fuss and training it looked as if it might be one of those suicide raids.

Panic swept over the boy, bringing first a hot sweat, then a cold one. He couldn't go on; he couldn't stand the flak any longer. That raid on Eindhoven had finished him. If it hadn't been for Gillie all the squadron would have heard of it by now. But they all know he was on the way out – you could tell it by the way they avoided his eyes and the way they bought him drinks. They knew all right.

And soon the M.O. would know. And then he would be grounded and disgraced. The dreaded letters L.M.F. would appear for all time on his documents. Grounded for Lack of Moral Fibre – a denounced coward, an object of derision for any safe clerk or aircraftman. And it would not end there. Knowing himself, he knew that the final proof of his cowardice would torment him for the rest of his life.

His body, tortured by his thoughts, rocked backwards and forwards in his chair. Tears stung his eyes. It wasn't fair! It wasn't fair that other men were never expected to face enemy fire while he, who had already done twenty operations, could have L.M.F. put on his documents. It wasn't fair that some men grew up like Gillie and others like himself. His tear-stained, resentful eyes lifted to the pin-ups again. Gillie got everything out of life. Girls brightened up immediately on seeing Gillie but never showed a spark of interest in him. They knew; they could recognize a failure better than men. And they were less forgiving, particularly over cowardice.

He'd go crazy if he stayed in here much longer, and yet he couldn't face the Mess. He remembered what Gillie had said, that if he felt like company he should go over and have a chat with Maisie in the pub. . . . He'd like that – Maisie was very pretty – but how would she treat him? She'd always been friendly, but that might have been for Gillie's sake – she was crazy on him.

Jimmie was a good quarter-of-an-hour before making up his mind to go. After all, he finally argued, if she wasn't glad to see him he could always come straight back. . . .

There were no more than half a dozen customers in the lounge and he felt very conspicuous as he approached Maisie at the counter. But she gave him a bright smile.

'Hello, dear; I was wondering when you were coming to see me.' She motioned to one of the stools alongside the bar. 'Here, sit down and talk to me. What are you going to have – a beer?'

The boy nodded. 'Yes, please.' He hesitated, then went on with a rush, 'Will you have a drink with me?'

Maisie's dark eyebrows lifted in good-natured surprise. 'Say, you're getting the idea! 'Course I will, dear.'

She was pleased the boy had come over. Humming cheerfully she drew his beer, then bent forward and helped herself to a bottle underneath the counter.

She was wearing a black satin dress with a plunging neckline. As she bent forward Jimmie could see the deep cleft between her generous breasts. He found his eyes drawn down in guilty fascination.

'You'll be missing the big boy, I suppose.'

He realized with a shock that she was looking up at him and could see where his eyes were fixed. His face burned with colour.

'I'm sorry. . . . I mean yes. . . . Yes, I am. Very much.'

She threw a quick glance downwards and saw where his stare had rested. For a moment her dark eyes were amused.

'I'll bet you're missing him. What are you doing with yourself at nights?'

'Nothing, really,' the boy muttered. 'I haven't been out since Saturday.'

Maisie tut-tutted her disapproval. 'You could have come over to see me. I ain't far away.'

Jimmie's face was still flushed. His efforts to keep his eyes from her while he sipped at his beer were almost painful. Maisie did her best to put him at ease.

'You ought to go to the Trocadero in Highgate one of these nights,' she told him. 'That's where all the boys go. You can get a drink there, and there are plenty of girls.'

He looked surprised. 'Do the girls go alone?'

''Course they do. They go lookin' for men like you. A warrant officer and an observer at that – you couldn't go wrong.'

The look of longing faded from his eyes. 'It'd be no use my going there. I can't dance, and anyway I'm too shy with girls.'

Maisie gave a snort of disgust. 'You probably act the gentleman with 'em too much. You want to push 'em about a bit. Girls like a man to be a bit on the bossy side. . . .'

At that moment four locals entered the lounge. Maisie eyed them with dislike. 'Here they are – they'll probably start comin' in now you and me are havin' a nice chat. Don't go away, now! We've got plenty more to talk about.'

But after its deceptively quiet start, the evening proved a busy one and Maisie found little time to talk to the boy. Before closing time, however, she made him promise to come over on the following evening.

To her surprise he came early, and she was delighted to find his shyness with her a little less pronounced. She had the opportunity of a long talk with him before the lounge filled, and managed to get him talking a little about his life before the war. She discovered Gillibrand was right; he had lived an unnaturally protected childhood. He promised to come again and she imagined he was looking more confident when he said good-bye that night.

To Jimmie this was a novel and exciting experience, so much so that his sensitive nature began to exaggerate it. He began to question whether he was playing fair to Gillibrand in seeing so much of Maisie while the Canadian was away. The thought worried him and on the Thursday night he decided to ask Maisie's opinion. But at first his shyness proved too much and he drank more than usual to give himself false courage. By nine o'clock the floodgates of his mind were down and his eyes followed Maisie with both longing and devotion. Yet he was still worrying about his loyalty to Gillibrand and as soon as the opportunity came he put the question to her.

At first she was highly amused that the boy could see himself a serious rival to the big Canadian. Then she realized the question was confirmation that her campaign was succeeding. She had to be careful: his sensitive eyes were on her.... She used the amusement in her voice to advantage.

'Anything's fair in love and war,' she said. 'Why, that's one of the Big Boy's own sayings.' In spite of herself, bitterness crept into her voice. 'Heck; he ain't got any cause for jealousy; he's gone down to London to see his girl-friend. I'm only someone he passes his spare time with. Don't be so silly.'

Loyalty to Gillibrand and resentment at the Canadian's conduct made a confusion of the boy's mind. 'I hadn't thought of it like that,' he muttered. 'Then you think it's all right?'

''Course it is. You come here and see me whenever you like, whether he's here or not.'

The thought of himself competing against Gillibrand made the eagerness in Jimmie's eyes fade. Seeing his dejection, Maisie's voice rose. 'What's the matter with you? You take the same chances that he takes, don't you? You're doing just as important a job....'

As she spoke a nightmare vision returned to her. Gillie lost over enemy territory, struggling to find a course home as flak and fighters closed in, and this boy helpless with fear beside him. As her eyes cleared she saw tears quivering under Jimmie's lashes and realized that at any moment he was going to confess to his cracking nerves. Instinct told her it was the best thing he could do, but not here in the lounge. There was that cow Valerie Adams over in the corner. Her eyes had been on 'em all night. She wouldn't miss a thing....

Maisie laid a hand on the boy's sleeve. 'Listen, dear. I've got to wash these glasses now, but we'll have another chat later on when we can be nice and private. You stick around until closing-time and meet me outside near the front door. I'm finishing early tonight.'

Jimmie's face flushed, then went deathly white. Maisie's black eyes held his faltering gaze, her voice full and comforting.

'You needn't be afraid of me, dear. I'll take good care of you.'

The room was quiet after the boy's sobs. His tears had soaked through the front of her dress, wetting the smooth skin beneath. Now, with his agony spent, he was resting his head where his eyes had rested earlier. Her body had a warm smell, both stimulating and relaxing, and he shifted his face, trying to get even closer to her.

Maisie's voice was rich, confident. 'It feels better now, doesn't it?'

She had to strain her ears to catch his reply. 'Yes. Much better. . . .'

She had left the bedroom dark to make it easier for the boy to talk and to weep. Now she stroked his damp hair gently, like a mother soothing a child. Her fingers wandered down his face, touching his eyes and wiping away the last of his tears. His body jerked once, spasmodically, then quietened again as she drew his head closer to her breast.

'You must think me an awful coward,' he muttered.

'No; I don't. You're tired, that's all. You wanted someone to talk to, and now it's all right again. Isn't it?'

His face, a white blur in the darkness, lifted up to her own. 'I do feel better . . . much better. I'm awfully grateful. . . . Do you want me to go now?'

Instinct told her as sure as words the last thing needed of her. Her black eyes were unfathomable in the darkness. 'No. I want you to stay.'

He gave a gasp, almost one of protest. His body began trembling violently, yet she was conscious of a new strength rising into its weakness. She felt like a mother with a child at her breast, giving it strength from her strength. She bent over him, conscious of nothing but the ecstasy of sacrifice.

'There's nothing to be afraid of,' she said. 'Nothing at all.' And her full, firm mouth pressed against his lips, checking their trembling.

CHAPTER 15

The training of 633 Squadron went on right throughout April, but with two important changes. The first concerned their bomb load. Towards the end of March they had started dropping 1,000 lb. dummy bombs; now each Mosquito was loaded up daily with a single 4,000 lb. monster (the plane's maximum bomb load) and sent out to fling it into the target area. Twice a week lorries brought the specially-constructed dummies back from Scotland to be used again.

The second change concerned their time of take-off. Until now they had done the exercise in the middle of the day. Now they were ordered to be airborne at 04.30 hours every morning. To crews already heartily sick of the valley and all it stood for, this was a most unpopular change. To make matters worse (and more incomprehensible) such an early take-off meant they had to stoodge over the valley for over an hour before there was enough light to commence the exercise. On the surface the order was received with stoical resignation, but in the privacy of billets the comment from both air crews and ground personnel was lurid and descriptive.

There was one notable exception to this routine in the days that followed. It came on the 23rd April. When the Form D came through, rumours blazed around the airfield. This must be it! The Big Show was on! For hours the whole station sizzled like the fat in a frying-pan. Even the sight of the Supply Dropping Containers that the armourers were loading on to the Mosquitoes did not quell the excitement, although it considerably modified it. It all depended what was inside 'em. . . . Must be something important or there wouldn't be all those Redcaps hanging about.

The rumour was finally dispelled at the briefing of the crews that afternoon. It was not the Big Show. But it *was* an operation whose importance could not be exaggerated and one that had to be carried out with the utmost attention to detail.

The briefing was certainly detailed, for it lasted over two hours. Take-off was at 00.25 hours as it was to be a night operation. Prompt to the minute the occupants of the inn opposite heard the roar of the Mosquitoes' Merlins as one by one the planes climbed into the darkness. The long night hours dragged slowly by and dawn was breaking before the low, deep hum of the planes was heard again. Anxious eyes counted them as they dropped over the boundary fence to sink from sight. . . .

But all were back. The operation had been an outstanding success. No enemy opposition had been encountered and all s.d. containers had been dropped inside the target area. Crews dropped out of their Mosquitoes, almost disappointed by the anti-climax. If the Big Show was going to be as easy as this, what was all the fuss about, anyhow?

There was no suggestion of disappointment, however, in a country house not far from Sutton Craddock. When the news came through a certain Brigadier and Davies gave vent to their relief in ways characteristic of their temperaments. The Brigadier smiled, coughed, then wiped his neat moustache with fastidious care. Davies jumped up like a puppet on a string, spun jubilantly round, then sat down with some haste. The Brigadier, however, showed no contempt for such behaviour.

'Well done,' he said, instead. 'If anything had gone wrong in that operation, the whole thing might have fallen through. Congratulations.'

'If anything ever does go wrong it won't be 633's fault,' Davies said, his eyes shining with pride of his Service. 'Particularly with Grenville taking 'em out.'

The Brigadier nodded. 'So it seems. In fact, I think we should keep him on the ground now until the Big Show comes off – unless something exceptional crops up, of course. We can't afford to lose him at that stage.'

'I'll see to it,' Davies agreed.

'I also think it's time he was told the full story,' the Brigadier said. 'Will you bring him down next Wednesday morning after ten?'

'I'll fix that up. Next Wednesday at ten. . . .'

The Brigadier nodded again. Only his hand, doodling with a pencil on a pad before him, betrayed his hidden excitement. 'That operation last night got us over the last really big obstacle. All we need now is our fair share of luck. If we get that, it won't be long before the curtain goes up.'

The lounge of the Black Swan was full on the following Tuesday night. Maisie was serving at the counter and Gillibrand was draped over a stool alongside it. The Canadian's efforts at conversation were being thwarted by the demands of trade, and his usually good-natured face was sullen. Twice in the same minute he was interrupted. Once Maisie broke away to serve a pint of mild to a thirsty airman, a moment later she turned her head to answer the banter of an old countryman, one of her regular customers.

Gillibrand scowled. 'Say; what's the matter with you tonight? You know I ain't exactly been on top of the world lately. D'you have to talk to every other guy in the place?'

Maisie sniffed. 'It ain't my fault if your girl left you for someone else. Don't expect me to cry about it.'

Gillibrand stared at her moodily. 'You know, that was a funny business. It ain't happened to me before.'

'There's always a first time,' Maisie said with satisfaction. 'Maybe she found out what you were doin'. I don't blame her one bit.'

The Canadian's face darkened. 'I spent my leave lookin' for the guy she fell for. Gee; I'd have given a lot to have taken it out of his hide.'

'You'd better cut down on the drinking,' Maisie snapped, seeing the resentment flaring up in his muzzy eyes. Her voice turned curious. 'Where did you say Jimmie had gone tonight?'

'He said he was goin' into Highgate. Wouldn't come in here with me. I can't make out what's happened to that little guy. He ain't the same any more.'

Maisie's hand fingered an empty glass. 'What do you mean?'

'Aw; he seems to have more bounce an' cheek – he ain't so backward as he was.'

'Aren't you glad?'

'Sure I'm glad. Maybe the rest we're havin' is doin' the kid good. Only he doesn't have to quit goin' out with me, does he?'

'Maybe he feels it's better for him to go out on his own now and then,' Maisie suggested. 'He might learn to stand on his own better that way. You don't want to let it worry you.'

Gillibrand shook his head moodily. Then his face cleared. 'Anyway, kid, there ain't nothin' between the two of us now, is there? We've got a straight road ahead of us now, honey, ain't we?'

The glass with which Maisie had been toying suddenly slipped from her hand and broke into fragments at her feet. She looked down, then swept the pieces under the counter. When she lifted her black eyes to Gillibrand's flushed face again, there was still a residue of bitterness left in them.

'Did y' hear what I said, kid,' Gillibrand went on, with all the persistence of the half-drunk.

Her full lips twisted. 'I heard you. A straight road, you said.'

'That's it. That's the way it's goin' to be from now on. Just you and me, honey. . . .'

At that moment Joe Kearns came through from the bar. Unlike the lounge, the bar was having a quiet night; and the innkeeper kept relieving Maisie so that she could take orders from the tables, a privilege Kearns liked to extend to his customers whenever possible. Maisie caught his eye and turned back to Gillibrand.

'I'm going round for orders now. You'd better get back to camp and get your head down. You've had too much already.'

Gillibrand watched her morosely as she went round the counter into the lounge. She took orders from the more distant tables first and returned to them with a loaded tray. On her way she passed a table occupied by Valerie Adams. Valerie was having another of her intimate parties. Apart from Adams himself, there were two other officers present, one being the stocky, ginger-headed Equipment Officer, Jack Richardson. Adams did not care for Richardson, but Valerie expressed a liking for his somewhat carnal sense of humour. The knowledge he found her attractive might have been the real influence behind her taste. As things were Richardson had been drinking heavily, his hot eyes had been roving without opposition over Valerie, and he was in a self-assertive, pugnacious mood.

Seeing Maisie go by, he shouted at her to take an order. She waved a hand good-naturedly.

''Arf a mo', dear. One thing at a time. Won't be a minute!'

Valerie let out an exclamation of disgust. 'That girl! I've had nothing else but trouble with her ever since I've been here. She's impossibly common and cheeky.'

Adams shifted, then gave a conciliatory laugh. 'She's all right, Val. She's just a bit high-spirited, that's all.'

Valerie's small, hard eyes turned on him with instant hostility. 'Sorry. I'd forgotten you like that type.'

On her way back to them, Maisie was halted by two countrymen at an adjacent table. Richardson followed Valerie's eyes and scowled. He leaned sidewards and tapped Maisie's arm.

'What about that order? How long do people have to wait in this place?'

Maisie turned. She saw Valerie's disagreeable eyes fixed on her, guessed the cause of Richardson's impatience, and lost her temper. 'What's the matter with you?' she snapped. 'I told you I was comin' over. You ain't Hitler, are you?'

Richardson's hand closed tightly around Maisie's arm. 'Who the hell do you think you're talking to. . . ?'

A second later an arm like a descending pile-driver squashed him down in his chair. His bulging eyes stared upwards, to see Gillibrand's enraged face inches from his own.

'Touch that kid again, you earth-bound punk, and I'll ram your face through the table.' Gillibrand meant every word of it.

Richardson lay paralysed in his chair for a few seconds, then tried to rise. Maisie pulled frantically at the big Canadian who moved back reluctantly, his inflamed eyes still staring down.

'What d'you wanna do? Make somethin' of it?' he snarled.

Remembering Valerie's presence, Richardson half-rose from his chair, but pride succumbed to prudence at the look of unholy joy on the Canadian's face. He sat down again, trying to retrieve some dignity from the situation.

'I'm not brawling in here with you, Gillibrand. I'll have you arrested in a minute.'

Gillibrand thrust a jaw like the prow of an icebreaker into his face again. 'Go ahead and do it, punk. See what happens. I'll bust you all over the airfield, just as I'll bust anyone else who touches this kid,' and his eyes roved belligerently over the rest of the party.

The only one not intimidated was Valerie. She gave a sneering laugh. 'What are you trying to do? Make a good girl out of her?'

'She is a good girl,' Gillibrand scowled.

Valerie laughed. 'You needn't worry about anyone here touching her. If you're afraid of that, you want to go a little nearer home.'

Maisie's face suddenly went chalk-white. Valerie noticed her change of expression and nodded mockingly. 'Yes, dear; I know all about it. My room's right under yours, you know. It's surprising how much one can hear.'

Gillibrand's fuddled eyes were. moving from one to the other of the women. 'What're you gettin' at?' he growled. 'What's been happenin'?'

Valerie turned on him triumphantly. 'You should ask that little observer of yours. He'll be able to give you *all* the details.'

'What are y' talkin' about?' Gillibrand snarled. 'What's Jimmie got to do with it?'

Valerie pointed at Maisie. 'Ask her. It didn't take her long to find consolation when you were on leave. I suppose your friend was the first man that came along.'

Gillibrand's eyes blazed. He swung round on Maisie. 'You . . . and the kid? It's a lie. . . . Ain't it?'

Maisie's expression told him the truth. For a moment it seemed he would strike her. Then he turned away, his face murderous. He flung the black-out curtain aside and lurched out into the darkness.

Adams, his face white and ashamed, rose without a word and left the lounge. Maisie ran after the Canadian. She caught up with him on the drive and grabbed his arm.

'It wasn't the kid's fault – honest to God it wasn't. It was me. I thought it would help him – I thought it would help you both. . . .'

He heard nothing but her confession, and threw her away from him savagely. She struck the wall of the inn, almost collapsing from the shock. He stood before her, a denser shadow in the darkness, his breathing hoarse and uneven. 'Joyce . . . and you! And now the kid! What's happenin' to everybody? What's goin' on?'

Despair and terror made her plead with him. 'It wasn't Jimmie's fault. . . . Don't take it out of him. D'you hear? The kid wasn't to blame.'

Gillibrand turned and lurched away down the drive, his feet crunching piti-lessly on the gravel. Her hands reached out mutely after him, then dropped to her sides. The bricks of the wall were cold and rough. She put her cheek against them and sobbed.

Grenville opened the door of the Mess and paused there a moment. There was a good deal of noise going on – Parsons of B Flight had got news through that day that he was the father of a 9 lb. son and was throwing a party to wet the baby's ears. As Grenville turned to close the door there was a smash of glasses, a howl, then a roar of laughter.

The piano was the centre of the party's activities at the moment. As Grenville went forward, Parsons, a slim, fairheaded youngster of twenty-two with a wispy, insecure-looking moustache, was leaning unsteadily against it, giving a doleful rendering of Nellie Dean to the accompaniment of cheers, cat-calls, and boos. Catching sight of Grenville, he broke off and straightened himself with difficulty.

'Evenin', sir. Nice of you to come – ver' nice indeed. What'll you have to drink, sir?'

The noise around subsided as Grenville shook his hand. 'Nice work, Parsons. Congratulations. Let's hope the little chap doesn't turn out as big a toper as his pa, though. I'll have a whisky, thanks.'

The songs began again but with less abandon now. In an effort to ease the slight tension Grenville joined in, but soon fell silent. It was not the first time he had felt this curious sense of apartness – in spite of his efforts to suppress it, he had been feeling it more and more frequently over the last twelve months. It was this damned reputation the newspapers had given him: it affected the new young-sters, put them in awe of him. And, in turn, their attitude embarrassed him, made him curt, and so the thing got worse. . . .

Even among the old sweats there was that slight feeling. It wasn't too bad with them, of course, but it all added up and he didn't want it to add up. This was the life he had put everything into: he didn't want to become a creature apart in it.

But there was no escaping the fact that the party had become more self-conscious since his arrival. He had one more drink, then made his excuses. It seemed to him the young, uproarious voices took on an immediate tone of relief as he passed into the corridor outside, and the impression made him feel old.

He stood over the telephone a full fifteen seconds before picking it up. He was very conscious of the note of self-defence in his voice when he spoke to her.

'I thought I might come over for a few minutes if you weren't doing anything. But, of course, if you have any friends there. . . .'

Her low voice was full of understanding. 'I have no friends here, Roy. And the sitting-room is empty tonight – Valerie and her husband are in the lounge. Please come – as soon as you wish.'

The outline of the Mess merged into the darkness behind Grenville. His mind flashed back to his first meeting with her, acutely aware of the reversal in the order of things. He allowed the irony, but the significance he refused to consider. To escape his thoughts he walked quickly towards the Black Swan.

CHAPTER 16

Barrett frowned and gnawed at one end of his tobacco-stained moustache. He stared down again at the operation order on his desk. *Priority top secret stop . . . convoy anchored off Invik . . . believed to contain one Elbing class destroyer . . . unknown number of flak ships . . . one Mosquito to be provided immediately for photo reconnaissance. . . .*

Another similar job to the one Grenville and Bergman had carried out, he reflected. The convoy must have something to do with this building – probably bringing equipment to it. . . . Shouldn't be too difficult a job, but there was no mistaking the urgency and tone of the order. He had to send his best available men. . . . Well, neither Grenville nor Bergman were here this time. Bergman was already over on the other side and Grenville had gone with Davies to the conference. In any case, Roy was withdrawn from operations until further orders. . . . Who to send, then? Milner came to his mind at once and he was stretching his hand out to his telephone when he remembered. Milner's young English wife had been taken ill – the American had been given two days compassionate leave to see her. So he was out. . . .

Another name automatically stepped into his mind. Wonderful pilot if it wasn't for that confounded temperament of his. . . . And yet there didn't seem much that could go wrong on this job. The met. report enclosed with the order was excellent, and in a Mossy it should be a piece of cake. Straight out, photographs, and straight back . . . they shouldn't even see an enemy kite. On the other hand, if there was trouble, he was the man to fight himself out of it. . . .

The last thought decided Barrett. He put a call through to B flight office. 'Send me Warrant Officer Gillibrand right away,' he grunted. 'And tell his observer, Willcox, to come along with him.'

The mouth of the Svartfjord fell behind the high-flying Mosquito. Below it, the dark clusters of flak that disfigured the blue sky like some virulent pox drifted slowly away, sullen in defeat. The coastline, as jagged in outline as a shrapnel-torn wing, passed obliquely below the nose of the aircraft, giving way to the vast, congealed sea.

The operation had been a complete success and all the required photographs had been taken. The convoy had showed no hesitation in firing at the Mosquito –

it would have looked suspicious if it had not – but most of the flak had burst below them and no fighter had made their altitude. Gillibrand, looking huge and menacing in his flying-suit and oxygen-mask, turned his eyes on the small hunched figure of Jimmie alongside him and scowled. It had all been too damned easy. . . .

Freed from the necessity of concentrating, his mind began brooding again on what he had heard the previous night. It had been lucky for the kid that the booze had got him and that he'd passed out before the kid had got back to camp. . . . Maisie said it was her fault, and maybe most of it was, at that. . . . They were all the same – he was learnin' that fast enough. But hell, this kid had a mind of his own, hadn't he? He didn't have to do a lousy thing like that!

His thoughts goaded him and his hands tightened on the controls. He wasn't going to get away with it this easy! So the little punk thought he was a man, huh? All right, little tough guy. Let's take a look an' see just how tough you are. . . .

The Mosquito dipped its port wing with sudden purpose and veered down. The coastline, now far behind them, tilted until it was running parallel to their line of flight. The swinging compass steadied itself.

Gillibrand caught Jimmie's sidelong, startled glance. His lips drew back.

'You don't have to tell me we've gone off course, kid. You know what I'm going to do?'

The boy's eyes held a vague expression of alarm as he shook his head.

'I'm gonna pay you back, kid. I'm gonna see just how tough you've become all of a sudden. We're gonna have some fun, you an' me.'

Jimmie's voice was faint in the intercom. 'Our orders said we had to return straight back with the photographs. They're supposed to be important.'

Gillibrand laughed harshly. 'Gettin' yellow already, kid? The only one givin' orders up here is me. Just wait, kid. Wait until I've finished with you. You won't be so tough then. . . .'

The fury into which the Canadian had worked himself made no concession to caution or duty. He'd break this little punk if he had to fly the Mossy through the side of a battleship to do it. High in the infinite sky, the Mosquito droned southwards down the coast, a lone angry wasp looking for trouble.

There was a hush in the room as the Brigadier stopped speaking and the caw of a nesting rook in the elms outside could be heard clearly. For a few seconds even Grenville's self-control could not prevent his looking shocked.

'You'll understand now the importance of all we've been doing,' the Brigadier said quietly, offering both Davies and Grenville a cigarette. 'That building must be destroyed – we can't even contemplate failure. Knowing its importance puts a heavy responsibility on you, Grenville, I realize that, but I felt you should be told. I'd like to take the opportunity to say we have the fullest confidence in you. Are there any questions you would like to ask?'

Grenville nodded. 'When are you planning to send us in?'

'I'm not allowed to give you the exact date, but if everything goes well on the other side it will be in less than a month. It has to be because – '

The Brigadier broke off abruptly. Grenville followed his eyes and saw that a red bulb over the door was flickering urgently.

The Brigadier rose to his feet. 'That means a message has been sent through. Please excuse me while I see what it is.'

He came back two minutes later looking a different man. His face was quite grey and his mouth and cheeks pinched with shock. Both Grenville and Davies rose to their feet in alarm. The Brigadier motioned to the Air Commodore.

'Davies; will you come with me, please. I have some serious news for you.'

Davies flung an anxious look at Grenville and followed the Brigadier from the room. On their return Davies looked as white as the elderly soldier. He addressed Grenville at once, his voice urgent.

'When do your kites get back from Scotland?'

Grenville glanced at his watch. 'They should have been down eighty minutes ago.'

'Tell me – didn't you once train your men to do skip bombing – you know, precision stuff with time delays.'

Puzzled, Grenville nodded. 'Yes. We were given that Groningen prison job three months ago. Of course, we haven't done any in these new planes . . . '

'That's good enough,' Davies interrupted curtly. He nodded to the Brigadier and picked up the telephone. Ten seconds later he had Barrett on the line.

'Barrett! Davies here. I want your Mossies re-fuelled and armed in less than an hour. Yes, you can. Make 'em work like hell. The bombs are to be 500-lb. M.C.'s with eleven second delays. Got it? Right. Get your crews alerted. We'll be over as fast as we can and will give you the rest of the gen later. Now put me over to Adams, will you.'

After giving instructions to Adams on the maps and photographs needed for the briefing, Davies slammed down the receiver and turned to Grenville.

'That order grounding you is off. You'll have to lead 'em in. The job is to prang a certain wooden building in Bergen. Don't ask me why because no one is going to be told. There isn't any time to lay an escort on – as you heard, it's a rush job and there isn't a minute to lose. But if you go in at low level, surprise and speed should get you through. And if the worst comes to the worst, you've got armament on those Mossies of yours to fight back, thank God.'

At that moment a lieutenant entered the office, giving the Brigadier a dispatch-box. The Brigadier turned to Davies. 'These photographs will help your briefing. We'd better get along now. The car's waiting outside.'

'You're coming along too, are you, sir?'

'I must. Hurry, please.'

Less than half-an-hour later the station wagon screeched to a halt at the gates of Sutton Craddock. The sentry on duty had barely time to glance inside before it jerked away, to sit up against its brakes outside the Station Headquarters. The Brigadier, stern and pale, was already striding down the path when Davies gave Grenville his dismissal. His voice was half peremptory, half apologetic.

'We'll ring your office the moment we want you. In the meantime you'd better be getting yourself togged up.'

With that, Davies turned and ran after the Brigadier. Together they entered Barrett's office. Davies closed the door, quickly introduced the two men, then came to the point without preamble.

'Have you got everything moving?'

Barrett nodded. 'Apart from the briefing we should be ready for take-off in under an hour.'

Davies knew the magnitude of the task and nodded his appreciation. 'We'll have to make the briefing as short as possible. I'm afraid we have some unpleasant news and a filthy job for you. The Brigadier will give you the details.'

When the Brigadier had finished speaking, Barrett's ruddy face was as shocked and pale as anyone's.

'Good lord!' he muttered. 'Filthy isn't the word. Surely we don't have to carry things this far!'

Davies, highly-strung, needed no more to set him off. 'You don't think we'd give such an order unless it were absolutely necessary, do you? Don't be a fool, man.'

Barrett had a big man's slow but resentful temper. At another time he might have taken offence but he caught a glimpse of the Brigadier's face. There were lines of agony round the soldier's grey eyes and stern mouth. Barrett made his apology at once.

'Sorry,' he muttered awkwardly. 'It's just as bad for you, of course.'

The Brigadier looked his full age as he stared through the window. 'It is a very necessary order, I'm afraid. You know the Nazis as well as I; you can guess their reaction in a situation like this. They'll stop at nothing, and there's no doubt what is happening at this very moment – indeed, we know it's happening. That is why there isn't a second to lose.'

He turned towards Barrett, his voice sympathetic. 'I agree men shouldn't be asked to do such a thing. And they wouldn't be, if it weren't for devils like these Nazis. Your men are going out on an act of mercy, and that is the solemn truth.'

Barrett stood silent, then nodded slowly. 'At least the men won't know,' he muttered. Then he started. 'What about Grenville. You haven't told him, have you? Or doesn't he have to go?'

Davies answered the question. 'He'll have to lead them in, but we haven't told him, nor shall we. He's waiting in his office for orders now.'

'And what about Adams?'

Davies looked at the Brigadier, who nodded reluctantly. 'I think we'll have to tell him. But he'll have to keep it quiet or the morale of your crews will drop to zero.'

'That's what I'm afraid of,' Barrett muttered. He shifted, then set his jaw resolutely. 'I'd like to go on this show, sir. I think it's my duty to go.'

Davies was sympathetic, but shook his head. 'No. Particularly now that you know what the job is. Sorry, but I won't hear of it.' Noticing the Brigadier was growing impatient, he went on quickly: 'We'd better get over to Adams now. The Brigadier has some photographs we can use at the briefing.'

Barrett roused himself, moving his heavy body like a man in a nightmare. 'Yes; all right. He's standing by.'

Fifteen minutes later Davies, Adams and Barrett left to attend the briefing, which the Brigadier dared not attend for security reasons. As they went, his grey eyes fixed themselves almost beseechingly on Barrett.

'See that they make a good job of it, won't you? It would be terrible if it were only half-destroyed.'

Barrett's heavy face was grim. 'Don't worry, sir. We'll make it the devil's last party.'

CHAPTER 17

Gillibrand had flown south for over twenty minutes and was thirty miles due west of Bergen before he found himself a suitable target. The weather was less settled here, and heavy banks of cloud were throwing shadows on the sunlit sea below. He flew into a clear area and a tiny, dark object appeared to the right of his starboard spinner cap. He dropped lower and examined it through his binoculars. It was a minelayer, busy on the huge enemy mine-fields that protected the shipping lanes down the Norwegian coast. From this height the ship's wake, stretching out fanwise into the frozen sea, looked like the excrement of a caterpillar on some enormous leaf. The time was 14.07 hours.

Without hesitation Gillibrand put the Mosquito's nose down. The altimeter needle fell away as the airspeed indicator rose. 320 . . . 370 . . . 400 m.p.h. The sea was beginning to take shape now — slowly at first, then more quickly, its swell resembling the folds in a rucked-up sheet of cloth. At 8,000 feet Gillibrand had to pull up the nose slightly as the engines began to race. The whole plane was shuddering violently under the tremendous stress of the dive.

The ship was leaping upwards now. From a speck of driftwood it became a towering hulk with armoured superstructure, a squat funnel, and raised gun platforms: an impregnable metal castle rising from the blue-green sea. Gillibrand levelled out just above the waves, switching on his gunsight and his fire-and-safe button. From the corner of his eye he saw Jimmie, helpless in the hands of his pilot, staring with rigid gaze at the approaching terror.

The ship was massive in Gillibrand's gunsight now, hurling itself at him. A sudden rapid staccato of flashes ran up and down its full length, and steel lashed the waves below the plane into a seething mist of spray. With teeth bared, Gillibrand pressed his gun button. The two Hispano cannon, aided by the twin Brownings, kicked back viciously as they pumped a total of twenty shells a second into the camouflaged hull of the mine-layer.

Incoherent pictures flashed before the terrified boy's eyes like the snatches from some crazy film. Cannon shells exploding in the water . . . rising higher . . . raking the ship's superstructure and gun platforms. . . . A man in a navy-blue jersey clutching his stomach in agony and toppling from one of the platforms to the deck below. . . . Two other men, crouching behind a pom-pom, being hurled backwards, a shambles of quivering flesh and spouting blood. . . . A lifeboat dropping away from its davits . . . a four-barrelled pom-pom hurling shells right at their windscreen. . . .

Then the smoking, erupting nightmare vanished and only the shadowy blue-green sea lay ahead. But the shells followed them, stabbing vengefully through the fuselage and hammering into the armour protecting their backs. Jimmie's body was racked with a violent nervous tremor. His terrified eyes pleaded mutely with Gillibrand, but the Canadian only laughed. The sea before them swirled crazily, the centrifugal force crushed the boy back into his seat, and the terror was back again, dead ahead. . . .

The minelayer was sending out frantic calls to the coast defence for fighters. As the Mosquito came back the ship's gunners opened up with everything they had. Through his gunsight Gillibrand saw a wall of tracer hurling itself at him. A shell ricocheted off his hood, another smashed through the instrument panel and passed between himself and the cringing boy. Grinning his hate, he opened fire again. Once more the Mosquito shuddered under the violent recoil. Bullets and shells sliced among the superstructure and deck timbers, cutting down men as a scythe cuts down grass. The base of the transmitting wireless aerial came into Gillibrand's sights. His shells were searching it out when suddenly the Mosquito was flung upwards by a tremendous explosion under its fuselage.

The minelayer spun down out of sight in a whirling chaos of smoke, masts, and spitting guns. The Mosquito, completely out of control, snaked upwards like a damaged rocket. Fighting desperately, Gillibrand managed to straighten it out at 5,000 feet. The minelayer was still snarling viciously at them, and he drew out of range to take stock of the damage.

Half his instruments were smashed. Those still intact began settling down nervously after the shock. His port engine was belching smoke alarmingly. As he watched it, a jet of flame appeared under its shattered cowling. Quickly he feathered the propeller and switched on the fire extinguisher. Dirty grey foam appeared, flying back in spume from the wing. With a grunt of relief he saw the flames die down and vanish. Then he turned towards Jimmie.

For a moment he thought the boy had fainted. He was lying limply against his straps. Gillibrand reached out and shook him roughly. The boy's face-mask slipped down and Gillibrand saw blood on his lips. Instantly the Canadian knew terror.

'Jimmie! What's happened, kid? Jimmie. . . !'

He shook the boy again. Jimmie stirred, tried to straighten up, and his face contorted in agony. His frightened eyes turned on Gillibrand – eyes as transparent as those of a child. He tried to speak, but the blood only flowed faster from his lips.

'Kid! For Christ's sake. What is it, boy?'

Jimmie's eyes moved mutely to the first-aid kit. Suddenly Gillibrand understood. Holding the stick with his knees, he undid the canvas pack and pulled out one of the tiny morphia hypodermic tubes. He pulled back the boy's sleeve and jabbed the needle into the flesh, squeezing until the tube was empty.

The boy's head slumped back in relief. Blood trickled from his chin to the collar of his flying-suit. Gillibrand leaned over him.

'Jimmie! Say somethin' to me, kid. For God's sake say somethin' . . .'

The boy did not move or speak. With fear choking his throat, Gillibrand swung the crippled plane round and headed back for Sutton Craddock. He flew like a madman, his blue eyes glaring rigidly ahead. The time was 14.12 hours.

The twelve closely-grouped Mosquitoes swept over the coastal town of Whitby like a tornado. A car halted, its four passengers staring upwards from its windows and waving excitedly. A man on a bicycle turned his head in fright, ran into the kerb, and tumbled in a heap on the pavement. The planes skimmed a cliff, leapt over a golden strip of beach, then were over the sea, glancing over the wave tops like a shoal of flying fish.

Impressions registered themselves on the retina of Grenville's mind in spite of his preoccupation over the task ahead. The ruins of the Abbey, pointing to the sky with gentle, admonishing fingers. . . . A fishing boat rolling gently in the swell, probably crabbing. . . . A flock of seagulls clustered around some object, their turning wings white against the blue sea. They flashed by and then there was nothing but the sea – the sea that was like a barren plain, stretching to infinity.

To Grenville the operation was a complete mystery. He had been told no more than his crews had been told at the briefing – that a certain building in Bergen had to be destroyed and the ways of finding it. Nothing more except Barrett's few mumbled words before take-off. There had been an oddly apologetic look on his face.

'Sorry Davies won't let me come along, Roy. But do a good job, will you? Blow it right out of the ground. We don't want anything left standing. . . .'

Barrett had been apologetic. Why? Grenville felt his irritation rising. Surely, after all the Brigadier had told him that morning, he could know what was behind this job! What was all the secrecy about?

The Mosquitoes were in battle formation, two tight lines of six aircraft apiece. They were flying at economical cruising speed without boost, so low that their slipstreams were ruffling the wave tops and leaving a wake behind them. Every pilot's eyes were fixed on the water ahead: a slip in concentration at that height meant certain death. The observers were kept busy switching on fuel cocks, keeping a watchful eye on gauges, and ceaselessly scanning the sea and sky around them.

Ninety minutes passed and they ran into an area scattered with medium-level cloud. The waves were higher and it had grown cold – a reminder that even towards the end of April Norway was still in the grip of winter. As they passed under the clouds a sharp shower of rain brought their visibility down to a few yards. The planes drew closer, wingtip to wingtip, nose to tail, a phalanx of screaming engines and hurtling wings. Observers sat tensed, straining to pierce the grey curtain that pelted horizontally by them. The rain hid the distant mine-layer that was limping back to port with seventeen casualties on board, and by the time they broke from it she had vanished hull down over the horizon.

A break in the clouds and a blue sky again. Their shadows returned to the sea, like pursuing sharks that had re-discovered their prey. Hoppy looked at his watch. It was 14.17 hours.

'Eight minutes to E.T.A., skipper.'

A distant snow-cap, shining in the sunlight, suspended over the horizon like a cloud. . . . Observers nudged their pilots, pointing. There it is! Enemy coast ahead. . . .

A chain of grey islands grew out of the sea and flashed by. The Oygarden group – leading straight to Bergen. Hoppy pin-pointed the mountain ahead and gave Grenville a correction. The squadron turned four degrees to port. They leap-frogged the islands and hugged the channels between them. Four minutes . . . five . . . six. . . . Going down a wide channel now . . . houses among the rocks on either side . . . a glimpse of camouflaged oil tanks . . . a smoking chimney. . . . Mountains mushrooming upwards . . . forests springing up green from the sea. . . . Into a wide bay now . . . a forty-five degree turn to starboard . . . and ahead the skyline was laced with the masts of ships. Beyond the ships was a mass of buildings, sweeping nearer at breakneck speed.

Bergen, dead ahead. Grenville was crouched forward in his seat, his gunsight and camera-gun switched on, bombs fused. No time now to wonder on the purpose of the raid. Another half minute and they would be screaming over the interlaced streets of the city, searching for one building out of the thousands that flashed by. . . .

A startled voice suddenly broke the R/T silence. 'Bandits, Skipper! In the sun! Break port . . .'

Grenville allowed himself one quick look around. Twenty plus Focke Wulfs were diving out of the sun, their red spinner caps like mouths agape with anti-cipation. An ambush: God! He switched his eyes upwards. A filigree pattern of contrails was pointed ominously down at them. More up there . . . dozens of them . . . alerted and belting down. . . .

Only superb training saved the squadron from that initial attack. Not 300 feet over the city Grenville led them into a tight turn. His orders came snapping over the R/T.

'Swordfish leader calling . . . defensive circle . . . work back to cloud base. . . .'

The break to port had fouled the 190's surprise attack. Before they could press home a second, the Mosquitoes had formed a huge defensive circle, each plane covering the tail of the one ahead.

Grenville over the radio again. 'Swordfish leader . . . jettison bombs.'

There was no hope of getting through to the target. The sky was full of enemy fighters, converging from all directions. A hail of bombs fell away from the Mosquitoes into the bay below, further scattering the small boats that were racing for shelter. A few seconds later the delay-fused bombs began exploding like depth charges, throwing up columns of spray.

Out over the islands the battle began in earnest. The Focke Wulfs, short-winged, vicious, pressed home their attacks savagely, but Grenville's defensive tactics frustrated them time and time again. The sky was like a great aquarium tank with dozens of red-nosed fish swarming round a huge, spinning jellyfish – darting, biting, tearing, but unable to get a decisive hold. The sky was laced with snapping tracer and the black threads from smoking exhausts.

A Mosquito was hit. Its starboard engine stopped, sending out a white cloud of glycol. Another burst of cannon hit the same wing and the white cloud turned to black. Tendrils of flame appeared, curling round the wing like a claw. A violent explosion, and the Mosquito spun helplessly away. Another explosion, tearing away the other wing, and the smoking fuselage plunged down like a dart into the sea. No one baled out. The remaining Mosquitoes closed the gap, the circle growing smaller.

A Focke Wulf, too eager to make a kill, caught the full vengeful blast of two cannon and two machine-guns right in its main tanks beneath the cockpit floor. It exploded like a bomb, leaving only an oily black cloud and a mass of fluttering debris. A hoarse voice bellowed out exultantly over the R/T: 'I got him! See that! I got the bastard. . . .'

Two other Focke Wulfs, their pilots intent on the same Mosquito and drawn together by its climbing turn, collided and spun down in a tangled mass of flame and wreckage. The top-level reinforcements had arrived now, cluttering up the sky with enemy aircraft. Their very numbers were against them, causing them to get in each other's way. But Mosquito after Mosquito was hit; man after man wounded. . . .

'Tighten up. Keep formation. Nearly there now. . . .' Grenville's voice kept coming over the R/T, encouraging his men. Seeing the squadron's objective the 190's pressed home their attacks with increased ferocity, attacking in pairs now. Staccato flashes ran along their clipped wings from the firing of their cannon.

The dark clouds, heavy with rain, lay over to the west, shadowing the sea. They were no more than three miles away now, a sanctuary from the hell of flame and steel. But three miles could be eternity with forty plus Focke Wulfs barring the way. They came snarling in again and the Mosquitoes shuddered under the impact.

CHAPTER 18

Gillibrand rubbed his bloodshot eyes and stared through his windscreen again. It was the English coast and never before had he been so glad to see it. Green-couched, with patches of woods, it slid gently over the horizon to drive back the pitiless sea.

With his face-mask slippery with sweat, the Canadian leaned over Jimmie and touched his shoulder.

'Here's the coast now. . . . Stick it a bit longer, kid; we're nearly home. They'll fix you up – you'll be fine in a couple of weeks.'

Morphia had kept the boy dozing most of the way back. He awoke now, his face drawn with pain. As he tried to follow Gillibrand's pointing finger, the Mosquito hit a bump, jerking his body against its straps. The abrupt movement forced fresh blood from his lips, sending it oozing out over the congealed crust round his mouth.

Gillibrand's big hands closed convulsively around his control stick. He stared round the shattered cockpit with hating eyes, damning the aircraft, whipping it on with every tensed muscle in his huge body. If there was another airfield nearer than Sutton Craddock he could put the kid down on it, but there was nothing around here. . . . His eyes strayed to the boy's slumped body and a wave of panic swept over him. The kid mustn't die. . . . D'you hear, God – he mustn't die. . . . Sweat poured from him, draining his strength away until he felt weak and sick. That afternoon, for the first time in his life, Gillibrand knew fear.

Sutton Craddock came into sight at last, sliding upwards behind its belt of trees. They had got his message – the ambulance and the fire-tenders were standing by. Ignoring Control he came in cross-wind, working his way down on his one red-hot engine. In spite of his care, the Mosquito made two high bounces before settling down, and from the corner of his eye he saw Jimmie jerk in agony. Cursing, he braked, switched off his engine and turned to the boy.

After the roar of the Merlins, the silence had a muffled heavy quality through which the distant wail of the ambulance sounded thin and unreal. Gillibrand unbuckled Jimmie's straps and caught his slumping body in his arms.

'We've made it, kid. We're home. You'll be O.K. now.'

The blood on the boy's face was like a smear of red ink across a sheet of parchment. He did not move or speak.

Gillibrand's voice rose hysterically. 'Kid, say somethin' to me. D'you hear? Say something, kid.'

Jimmie's eyes opened wearily. He stared upwards at Gillibrand, looking puzzled. Then his crusted lips moved, trying to smile. Gillibrand lowered his head to listen.

The sounds were as faint as the flutter of a moth's wing. 'It's all right, Gillie. Don't worry. . . .'

'Don't worry. . . . Listen, kid. I'm sorry. I don't know why I did it. There ain't a skirt in the world worth your little finger. . . . You can have 'em all, kid – honest to God. Only don't die. . . .'

Jimmie's head sagged back. Gillibrand glared down, willing him to live. 'Don't die, kid. For God's sake don't die!'

The boy's lips moved again. 'It's funny, Gillie. . . . I'm not a bit afraid. Tell her, will you? Tell her I'm not afraid. . . .'

The wonder of it was still in his eyes when he died.

Adams saw him lurching down the tarmac, throwing off helpers as a wounded bear shakes off dogs. His helmet was pulled back exposing his yellow hair which was matted with sweat. There was a streak of oil down his face and a red stain down the front of his flying suit. But it was his eyes that drew Adams' gaze. They were glaring straight ahead with the look of a man who had been given a glimpse into hell and knew for the rest of his life he would be haunted by the memory.

Adams approached him. 'What happened, Gillibrand?'

The glaring blue eyes never shifted their stare as the Canadian lurched on. Adams took a deep breath and caught hold of his arm.

'Gillibrand! What happened?'

The Canadian swung round, his face murderous. In spite of himself Adams drew back, expecting a blow. Two long seconds passed, then Gillibrand jerked his arm savagely away and lurched down the tarmac.

It was only contempt for himself that drove Adams on. He caught hold of the Canadian's arm again and forced a ring of authority into his voice.

'I want a report on what happened straight away. Not later – now, in my office. Come on!'

Discipline succeeded where sympathy had failed. Gillibrand turned to face him, his wild eyes puzzled now.

Adams gave him no time to recover. 'Come on. This is important.'

Feeling as if he had a savage animal on a leash, Adams led Gillibrand into his office and closed the door. He motioned the pilot into a chair alongside his desk, put a phone call through to the Naafi for tea, then took a seat himself. He threw a cigarette across the desk, then pulled out a large official questionnaire. He kept his voice authoritative and impersonal.

'The first thing is – did you get the photographs.'

The Canadian looked dazed now. He nodded like an automaton. 'Yeah. We got 'em.'

Adams filled in the standard details on the form, then looked up. 'See anything unusual on the way out?'

'Nothin' but sea and sky.'

'Apart from the convoy, was there any other activity in the fjord?'

'Didn't see any.'

'Any opposition from it?'

'The usual flak from the ships. Nothin' else.'

As Adams made notes on the form, the Canadian's dazed eyes wandered round the office. 'Where's the skipper?' he muttered.

The question was understandable. In his rôle of Squadron Commander Grenville was usually present at interrogations. Adams explained briefly.

'While you were out, we were given an emergency job – a raid on a building in Bergen. They're due back any time now – they didn't leave long after you.' Adams paused, looking at his watch. 'All right. You took the photographs and got out. You were due back round about 15.45. It's now 16.40. What happened in that extra time?'

Gillibrand did not appear to hear the question. His square, oil-streaked face reminded Adams of a bemused schoolboy confronted with a simple yet baffling problem.

'Did you say Bergen?' the Canadian muttered.

Adams nodded. 'They went out at low-level. Why? What's worrying you?'

Whatever had sparked the question in the Canadian's brain clearly eluded him now. His eyes turned dull and he shook his head mechanically. 'Don't know. Nothin', I suppose.'

It was not the first time Adams had interrogated men in the last stages of physical and nervous exhaustion, and he knew the symptoms well. He was relieved when the Naafi girl brought in tea and sandwiches. He shoved them in front of Gillibrand.

Gillibrand sipped at the hot sweet tea but pushed the sandwiches aside. The smell of his flying-suit came to Adams' nostrils, a mixture of oil, grease, cordite and a hundred other indefinable things. Even at that moment something in Adams stirred in envy. He motioned to the sandwiches.

'Don't you want anything to eat?'

Gillibrand shook his head. 'No; I ain't hungry.'

Adams inhaled deeply on his cigarette. The question had to be asked – he deferred it as long as possible. 'What happened after you left the fjord,' he asked. And very gently: 'What happened to your observer?'

Fatigue had dulled Gillibrand's mind like an anaesthetic, but this sudden reminder brought both memory and agony back. The cup in his hand jerked sideways, spilling tea down his flying suit. His blue eyes blazed their protest.

'You ran into trouble somewhere,' Adams went on, trying to conceal his apprehension. 'What happened?'

Gillibrand's madness returned. He leapt to his feet with a curse. 'What the hell is it to you? What's it matter now. . . ?'

'I must know,' Adams said gently. 'A man has been killed – I must know what happened.'

Ignoring him, Gillibrand turned and lurched for the door. Words were falling from his lips like blood from a re-opened wound. 'Yeah . . . I'd forgottten. The kid's dead. . . . The little feller. . . . Oh, my Christ . . .'

He flung open the door and stumbled out. At that moment a siren screamed. He stopped dead, his bloodshot eyes staring around, trying to understand. The fire-tenders started up again and the ambulance began to wail. Under and through the noise came a deep irregular hum that grew louder as he listened. He turned his eyes upwards and saw the arrival home of the Mosquitoes. . . .

They were flying in an open protective box, guarding the two planes in their centre. Now, under instructions from Control, they began to orbit the airfield while the two badly-hit planes were given priority down.

Adams joined Gillibrand outside the office, his eyes huge behind his thick spectacles. On the airfield ahead the ambulance, accompanied by the Medical Officer in his jeep, was speeding to the distant end of the runway. One of the fire-tenders was moving in the same direction, the firemen on its running-boards looking like men from another planet in their grotesque asbestos suits.

The first crippled Mosquito appeared over the boundary fence. Its approach was going to lead it right over the two watching men. Staring upwards they could see the blackened scars on its engine cowlings, the wingtip that was half torn away, the tail unit riddled and tattered. It looked like a toy plane that had been dragged through a thorn bush.

They felt the chill of its shadow as it passed over them, the wind whining over its airfoils. Its starboard engine faltered for a second, the torn wing dipped, and Adams felt his breath lock in his throat. Somehow it skidded level again, both engines coughing like a man trying to clear his flooded lungs. It levelled off at least 100 feet above the airfield as if its pilot had decided to make a fresh approach. At that moment the starboard engine cut right out and the damaged wing dropped as though pulled down by wire. . . .

There was an agonized pause that seemed to last minutes. Then a rending crash that tore through nerves like a bulldozer through soil. The Mosquito struck wing first, cartwheeled over, and fell tail forward, furrowing the ground for at least fifty yards. There was a dull coughing explosion, a vivid streak of light, then an outflung cloud of oily smoke shot through with avid tongues of fire.

A fire truck raced up and thrust its radiator almost into the flames, hurling carbonic foam through its high-pressure nozzles. Swinging their axes like madmen, the firemen leapt into the flames, ignoring the danger from white-hot wing tanks and unspent cannon shells. But nothing moved in the furnace that was the cockpit. The stench of burning rubber drifted across the airfield, making Adams retch.

The second Mosquito made its approach. It was flying on only one engine, its dead propeller as stiffly upright as a tombstone. The broken spars and ragged cloth hanging under its fuselage made Adams think of the dragging entrails of a crippled bird. With half its control surfaces shot away, it was having the utmost difficulty in avoiding stalling as its flying speed dropped for the landing. Its wheels hit the runway with a thud that made Adams wince, there was a sharp crack as a tyre burst, and the plane leapt 20 feet into the air. It crashed down heavily,

633 Squadron

heavily, one wingtip digging into the ground and tearing off as if made of card-board. The rest of the plane ground-looped to the accompaniment of snapping spars and tearing fabric. There was an ominous hissing as petrol came into contact with the white-hot engine, but this time a fire truck had a chance and used it well. The crew rammed their nozzles right on to the smoking engines, covering them in foam. The danger of fire passed. The observer staggered from the shattered fuselage, then went straight back for his comrade. But the pilot was beyond aid. The firemen brought him out, as limp and broken as a child's doll.

Gillibrand started forward and after a second's hesitation Adams followed him, trying to keep up with the half-crazed Canadian. Gillibrand ran out on the field, then halted, his eyes staring up wildly at the smoke-blackened sky. A thin streak of saliva was trickling from his mouth. A Mosquito, with two mechanics holding its wingtips protectingly, came taxi-ing in their direction, its battle-scarred fuselage jolting over the uneven ground. Gillibrand, massive in his flying suit, turned and ran towards it.

Two men tumbled out of the plane. One was Teddy Young, the A Flight commander. His powerful shoulders were sagging with exhaustion. His observer was one of the reserve crews, a youngster named Reynolds whose blue eyes were still stupefied with the fear of death. As Gillibrand and Adams approached, the boy caught hold of the trailing edge of the wing to steady himself. He leaned down, vomiting from reaction.

Young peered at them through swollen eyes. He moistened his dry lips and tried to grin. His voice was little more than a croak.

'Hiya. I guess there's no place like home, after all.'

Gillibrand's voice was even thicker. 'What happened?'

The Australian's lips twisted. 'We only ran into half the Hun Air Force over Bergen, that's all.'

'You mean they were waitin' for you?'

'Yeah. Some bastard must have alerted 'em. Don't ask me how any of us got back. What about a smoke, cobber. You got one?'

But Gillibrand was stumbling away, wild-eyed and haggard. Later Adams wondered why he had not understood the Canadian's torment over the news. But his mind at the time was full of the sight and sound of crashing aircraft, of dead and wounded friends. The Mosquitoes were still coming down and the ambulance making trip after trip to the casualty station. The airfield was a chaos of shot-up aircraft, shouting men, and wailing sirens. Some panic-stricken member of the Control staff kept firing off red Very lights, making Adams' tight nerves jump each time they soared overhead. The fire crews were still busy among the wreckage of the crashed Mosquitoes, and the sullen smoke, stinking of melted rubber, was drifting like a pall across the field.

Adams turned his short-sighted gaze back to Young. The tension was working out of the Australian now, and he was gazing after Gillibrand resentfully.

'What's the matter with him? Can't he give a guy a smoke?'

Adams thrust a packet forward. 'Here. Help yourself.'

100

Young muttered his thanks and went over to his observer. 'Have a fag, Danny. Make you feel better.'

Reynolds shook his head. He tried to speak but failed. The whites of his eyes showed as he retched again, and Young caught hold of his arm.

'Give me a hand with him, will you?' he said to Adams.

Adams nodded and took Reynolds' other arm. The youngster tried to fight them off but the Australian quietened him. 'Nothing to be ashamed of, kid. I've puked often enough myself. You'll be O.K. after a drink.'

As Adams slung the observer's arm round his shoulder, he caught sight of two more men in flying clothes walking away from a battle-torn Mosquito. One was Grenville, the very immobility of his twisted face testifying to the pent-up emotions within him. His companion was Hoppy. Hoppy's right shoulder and arm were soaked in blood, and smears of it made a red and grey patchwork of his flying suit. His thin, pointed face was drawn with pain, but a grin was locked around the cigarette in his mouth. With his uninjured arm he waved aside the solicitous attention of a crowd of mechanics. His shrill Cockney laugh came echoing back to Adams.

'Those 190's put up a black today, Skipper. Used a shrimping net with an 'ole in the bottom . . . I'll bet they caught 'ell when they got back.'

A shudder ran through Adams. The thing inside him was groaning at the waste and glorying at the courage. Fighting to keep his emotions under control, he helped the still-retching Reynolds off the field.

A thin thread of desperation ran through Davies' high-pitched authoritative voice.

'Grenville, this thing is so urgent that if there was enough daylight left, I'd order the lot of you back tonight. As it is, you take them back at 04.15 hours so that you can attack at dawn. That's an order.'

There was no compromise in Grenville's reply. 'I'm not taking them back in a few hours' time. Those boys need rest – what's left of them. You'll have to send someone else.'

Davies was fully aware of Grenville's fatigue and for one of his temperament showed commendable patience. 'I keep telling you – there isn't anyone else to send. These Mosquitoes are still a new job – we've very few squadrons equipped with them and you're the only one with the experience to do this job. Don't argue any more. Get some sleep now and you'll feel better in the morning.'

Grenville leaned forward, an aggressive movement. 'Jerry must have been alerted about something or he wouldn't have been there waiting for us. Whatever it was, now we've had a crack, he'll be doubly careful and keep a patrol up, certainly for twenty-four hours. If I take back what's left of my boys, in the state they and their kites are in, not one of them will get back. I'm not doing it, and that's final.'

Davies' eyes were bright with shame and anger. 'You realize this is insubordination? That I can have you arrested for disobeying an order?'

Grenville's resentment went out of control. 'You can do just what the hell you like; it won't make any difference. I'm not taking those boys out again until they're fully rested and their kits are repaired. As they are, they'd never even get to Bergen in the dark, much less be able to fight half Jerry's Air Force. What's the matter with you? Do you want to murder them?'

Their eyes locked across the table. The silence reminded Adams of a time he had lain dazed alongside an unexploded bomb while the dust settled around him. He watched the tableau in fascination. The office was his own, the Intelligence Room. Alongside him was Grenville, still in his flying clothes, oil-smudged and battle-weary. Opposite him at the other side of the long table were Barrett, the Brigadier and Davies. All wore different expressions. Barrett had sweat on his forehead, and his heavy breathing betrayed his anguish. The Brigadier looked old and straight and very soldierly. Davies was quivering with anger now and two red spots glowed high upon his cheeks.

Each of them, according to his background, was feeling a slightly different reaction to Grenville's insubordination, yet each had a deep sympathy for it, knowing its cause. But, like Adams, they knew something that Grenville did not know, a thing so compelling it could not allow personal feelings to stand in the way.

Because of this Adams felt no resentment at Davies's threat, wince at it though he did. He knew the urgency, the desperate race against time.

The Brigadier, laying a restraining hand on Davies's arm, turned his grey eyes on Grenville's defiant face. His voice was almost fatherly in its tone.

'I know how inhuman it must sound to you, Grenville, but believe me we wouldn't ask you unless it was desperately important. Having to wait until dawn is a tragedy in itself' – the grief in his tone was unmistakable – 'It may well mean it is too late. But we have to hope for the best, and that leaves us no option but to send you back.'

'Why is it so important?' Grenville gritted. 'Why is a building in Bergen more important than these boys' lives? What's in it?'

In the silence that returned to the room, Adams could hear the distant clang of metal on metal as mechanics worked feverishly on the engine of some damaged Mosquito. He saw from their expressions that both the Brigadier and Davies were tempted to answer, but neither spoke.

Receiving no reply, Grenville lurched to his feet, staring bitterly at Davies. 'You can tell the guard they'll find me in my room.'

He stood to attention a moment, then left the office. There was a short silence in which none of the remaining men met each other's eyes. Then Davies turned his ashamed face towards the Brigadier.

'He'll be court-martialled, of course. We'll put the squadron in charge of another commander. But I must warn you there may be only half-a-dozen planes serviceable by the morning.'

The Brigadier was staring down at the table. He lifted his head at Davies's words, his eyes oddly bright.

'You can't arrest him, Davies. He is doing it for his men.'

In spite of his anger, Davies looked relieved. He threw a glance at Barrett, who nodded and said gruffly:

'I'm afraid my sympathies are with Roy, sir. It will be pretty near suicide for the boys as things are.' As he paused Barrett was dully aware of the irony. Here was a real chance for him to fly on operations again, and he didn't want to go – not on this job.

'I'll take 'em out,' he said, nevertheless. 'I'll scratch up all the kites I can and give it a bang.'

Hope stirred on the Brigadier's face, but Davies shook his head regretfully.

'No, Barrett. It isn't everyone's kind of job. Grenville is one of the few men I know who might have pulled it off. That's the trouble. . . .'

'You've nothing to lose,' Barrett argued, crushing down his relief. 'Let me have a crack at it.'

Desperate though the situation was, Davies knew this was no remedy. 'Sorry,' he said, trying not to wound too deeply. 'You and I are a bit past this sort of thing. It wouldn't work out.'

Barrett sat silent a moment, then reached for his cap. 'Then let me go and talk to Roy. We've been together a long time. He might listen to me.'

Davies hesitated, but the Brigadier gave an eager nod. 'Yes. Let him go, please.'

Barrett paused at the door. 'You know, Grenville's a queer devil. Can I handle him my own way?'

'You mean tell him?' Davies asked, startled.

Barrett nodded. Davies turned inquiringly towards the Brigadier. The silence lasted perhaps five seconds – seconds which beat on the temples of the breathless Adams like leaden hammers. Then the Brigadier nodded slowly.

'All right. Do what you think best.'

Barrett nodded. The door closed and he was gone.

CHAPTER 19

'Now relax a minute and listen to me.'

There was nothing subtle about Barrett, which in the circumstances was probably as well. He pushed Grenville back into his chair and lowered his own heavy body down on the bed, ignoring the spring that twanged its protest. This wasn't going to be a pleasant job, but if it wasn't done Grenville might easily get himself arrested. To prevent that happening, Barrett was prepared to go a long way. . . .

'Roy,' he said bluntly. 'You've got to take 'em back in the morning.'

'You're wasting your time, Don. I meant what I said back there.'

Barrett nodded absent-mindedly. He took a match from his pocket and began picking at a tooth with it. After the operation he paid detailed attention to his moustache before eyeing Grenville again.

'Roy,' he said. 'Do you remember Charley, that big collie I had last year?'

Grenville stared at him as if he had gone crazy.

'Well, do you?'

'Of course I do.'

Barrett nodded reflectively. 'That was a fine dog – I liked him. I've got a soft spot for dogs – most of the time I prefer 'em to people. I did Charley. You remember what happened to him?'

'He was run over by a truck, wasn't he?'

'That's right. I thought at first he'd get over it, but he was in pain, Roy – something was bust in his back. I tried for a couple of weeks to fix him but he got worse and worse. I used to lie awake at nights listening to him whimpering, poor devil. I stuck it as long as I could, and then one morning I shot him. And I'll tell you this, Roy – I couldn't have felt it more if he'd been one of my best friends.'

Grenville's face was sullen, impatient. 'What are you telling me this for?'

Barrett sat up a little straighter on the bed. 'I'm trying to say that sometimes you have to be cruel to be kind. That sometimes you have to kill something you like to put it out of its misery.'

'We all know that, don't we? What's the point?'

Barrett shook his head. 'No, we don't. We know it applies to animals, but we don't think of it applying to people. It doesn't apply in peace-time, of course, except when there are doctors around. I've heard it said they sometimes do it – on the quiet, naturally. . . .'

Grenville's voice was tight. 'What in hell are you trying to say?'

Barrett took a deep breath. 'You know what the Gestapo are like, don't you, Roy? You know what they do to anyone who has information they want. Well, supposing a friend of yours was caught by them, and in pain, and you couldn't rescue him – what would you do, Roy? What would you do if you had a plane and some bombs to drop?'

Under the smudges of oil Grenville's face was chalk-white now. 'For God's sake come out with it straight, Don. What has happened?'

Barrett rose from the bed and put a big rough hand on Grenville's shoulder. 'I'm sorry, Roy, because I know you and he became good friends. But that building in Bergen is occupied by the Gestapo and they've got Bergman and another poor devil inside it. They took Bergman in early this morning. . . .'

It was nearly seven o'clock and quite dark outside when Adams heard footsteps approaching his office. He was alone, sitting in the same chair he had occupied when Davies and the Brigadier had left him half-an-hour earlier. An ashtray, half full of cigarette butts, was at his side, and he had a freshly-lit cigarette in his hand. He was staring into the haze of smoke before him, utterly lost in his thoughts when he heard the footsteps. Instantly a thrill of nervousness ran through him, and he felt his heart pounding in his throat and temples. A second later the curtain across the door was flung aside.

It was Grenville, alone. He was still in his flying clothes, still grimy and reeking from the smoke of battle. He stood a moment at the door, and Adams could not find the courage to meet his eyes.

The silence, full of mute tortured emotions, frightened Adams. He wanted to speak but could think of nothing to say. Panic swept over him: he wanted to jump up and run. He cleared his throat, agonizingly conscious of the inanity of his words.

'Hello, Roy. What can I do for you?'

The sound of his voice, cracked though it was, gave him back some of his moral courage. He lifted his eyes to Grenville's face and shuddered at what he saw. A man on the rack could have looked this way at his torturers. . . .

'Barrett has told you,' he muttered, knowing the answer as he asked the question.

Grenville came forward like an automaton, reached the edge of the table, and stood looking down. His voice was like the snarl of an animal.

'Damn you, yes. The one honest man among the lot of you.'

Adams made no attempt to excuse himself. 'What are you going to do?' he muttered. 'Are you going to take them out again?'

Grenville's swollen eyes blazed with fury. 'By God; I'm not. I wouldn't take them now if they were a hundred per cent fit and had two serviceable kites apiece. There's a limit to filth, Adams, even in this war.'

Adams wondered afterwards how he found the courage to argue. 'This is an act of mercy, Roy. That's how we all see it.'

Grenville's reply was vicious and unprintable. Adams hesitated, then asked the question that was puzzling him.

'If you're not going, Roy, then what have you come for?'

Grenville's hands were resting on the table in front of the Intelligence Officer. Adams watched them in fascination as they bunched up into tight fists, the knuckles standing out above the oil-blackened skin like white rocks. Grenville's reply came down on him like a whip.

'I never said *I* wasn't going, Adams. I've come to look over the photographs and maps again. I'm taking off at 04.15 hours.'

Adams looked up aghast. 'Not alone?'

Grenville sneered. 'How can I take someone along now that I know what the job is? Tell me that, Adams.'

Adams knew what he meant. He sat silent.

'Come on, Adams. You all want the job doing. Get those maps and photographs out. I want to run over it all again. I want to do a good job – a nice, efficient execution.'

The nightmare began. Adams opened a drawer and took out the relevant material. Grenville pulled one of the photographs from him and pointed at it.

105

'That's the building, isn't it?'

Adams nodded. 'Yes; it's a sort of annex to the main Gestapo Headquarters. As you can see, this building is on a piece of waste land quite near the railway station. You can pin-point it on your way in from the docks by using the Nautical School in the Nordnes Parken as a marker. Straight on you come to the National Theatre, which is almost alongside the main Gestapo Headquarters at the top end of the Ole Bulls Plasse, a wide avenue with flower-beds and trees down the centre. At the other end of the Plasse is a tiny park, and then a small octagonal lake.' He unfolded a large-scale map. 'Here it is, the Lille Lungegardsvann. Right behind it is the waste land with the building, and beyond that is a lake or fjord called the Store Lungegardsvann. You'll have to be careful over there. Jerry has plenty of flak both alongside the station and over near this bridge, the Strombro. . . . Here are photographs of the Nautical School and the theatre. . . .'

Grenville studied the photographs a moment, then threw them aside. 'I'm not planning to come in from the docks. They'll be guarding their approaches. I want a route in from the north.' He pointed at the map. 'What's this valley here, behind the city?'

Adams studied his notes. 'That's the Isdalen Pass between two of the surrounding mountains. There's a lake in it called the Svartediket with a reservoir – it provides Bergen with its fresh water. The pass comes out into the Store Lungegardsvann.'

'It looks quite deep. How high are the mountains on either side?'

'Ulrikken on the east side is over 2,000 feet. The other one is about the same.'

'Where does this Isdalen Pass lead from?'

'It comes from the Arna district, up here.'

Grenville nodded, his eyes moving up the map, following the fjords out to the sea north of Bergen. 'This is my way in,' he said at last, tracing a route with his finger. 'If I keep on the deck I'll have the islands or mountains covering me on both flanks most of the way. Wait a minute; where's Herdla? That's one of Jerry's airfields, isn't it?'

'You're all right. Herdla's farther south, down here. . . .'

Grenville's questions came for over twenty minutes. His final ones were about the building itself.

'You say it's wooden?'

'Yes. Until the Gestapo took it over it was used as a warehouse. It's three stories high and about fifty feet long – it shouldn't be difficult to destroy if you get through all right.'

Grenville's lips twisted. 'No; it shouldn't be a bit difficult to blow up a place like that.'

Adams cracked then. 'Take someone with you, Roy. For God's sake don't do it alone.'

'Why not? I've a better chance of getting through that way.'

'It isn't that. I know how things are between you and Hilde – I'm not blind. You're never going to forgive yourself if you do it alone. The Brigadier told us this sort of thing has had to be done before, but never by one man. . . . If you take a couple of planes with you, or even an observer, it won't seem so personal.'

Grenville's eyes burned their contempt. 'Share out the guilt a bit – is that it, Adams? No; let's rather keep all the filth in one place.'

He looked down at his watch, and his tone suddenly changed. 'Barrett said they took him inside early this morning. Is that what you heard?'

Adams nodded. 'Yes; they were seen arriving with him just after dawn. They took in a second man called Ericson later in the day – the message about him came through when you were on the raid.'

'So he's been in there all day. And I can't do anything for him before dawn. Ten more hours, Frank. . . . That's a long time. . . .'

His words and the agony in them came as a shock to Adams. He had to look away, his teeth sinking deeply into his lips. When he turned back, Grenville was standing at the door.

'Thanks for the gen, Frank,' he said curtly. 'If all goes well I'll drop in tomorrow and let you know how things have gone. Cheerio.'

'Cheerio, Roy,' Adams whispered. The door closed, and in the silence that followed Adams could hear the tick-tick of his watch as it whipped on the stumbling seconds.

Hilde came out of the sitting-room the instant Adams entered the hall. Although she smiled at him, he did not miss the deep disappointment in her eyes on recognizing him instead of Grenville. Her face was pale and there was a tremor of unsteadiness in her voice.

'We've all been wondering when someone would be coming over. What happened today, Frank? Are you able to tell me?'

Adams had hoped to avoid seeing her, and now her words sent a shock through him, stiffening his features. It was a few seconds before he realized she was talking about the squadron's homecoming that afternoon – a tragedy he had almost forgotten in the events that had followed it.

'They had a special job to do,' he muttered. 'Something went wrong and they ran into trouble. But Grenville's all right – he's quite safe. . . . I'd forgotten – you'd see it all from here.'

Her eyes had closed thankfully on hearing of Grenville's safety. As they opened again Adams saw in them the memory of that blood-drenched afternoon. 'Yes,' she said unsteadily. 'We saw both the planes crash.'

In spite of himself, his gaze was drawn to her face. She was lovely . . . lovely and young, too young to be mixed up in anything as hellish as this. Suddenly he felt trapped, felt her blue-grey eyes were getting right into his mind, reading the secret there. . . . The palms of his hands grew sticky. She mustn't find out – it could turn her mind. He had to get away. . . .

'Where's Valerie?' he blurted. 'In the lounge?'

'Yes; I believe so.'

Adams had been given two hours off duty in preparation for the sleepless night ahead. His thoughts had tormented him, making him feel like a conspirator in a murder, and he had fled the airfield in an effort to escape them. Desperately needing solace, he had made instinctively for the inn; and had he been asked why he would have given the answer that his wife was there. Now he knew he had not come to see Valerie, particularly if she was in the lounge. . . .

'Where's the landlord?' he asked.

Hilde pointed at the kitchen door, which was closed. 'The bar has been very quiet tonight as there have been no airmen over. I believe he is making tea.'

Adams thanked her and started down the hall. She made a fluttering motion of her hand, stopping him. 'Please. Is the Canadian, Gillibrand, safe? Maisie has been worrying about him.'

A vision of Gillibrand's frantic face came to Adams. He hesitated, then nodded. 'Yes; he's back all right. But he lost his observer today, so naturally he's rather upset.'

A spasm of pain crossed the girl's face. 'Do you mean the young boy he called Jimmie?'

Adams nodded. 'Gillie was pretty broken up about it when I saw him, so you might tip Maisie off. He might be a bit difficult to handle at first.'

'I understand and I will tell her,' the girl said. She hesitated, then went on quietly: 'And Roy is all right? Nothing like that has happened to him?'

Adams felt trapped again. 'No; he's quite safe.'

'I thought he might have come over for a little while. Do you know why he has not?' As soon as she had spoken, the girl flushed, then went pale.

'He's had a bad day,' Adams muttered. 'And he's on duty tonight. Most of us are. I've only come over for an hour myself.'

He knew his voice was giving him away. He wanted to turn and run. She gave a helpless shake of her head.

'It is so difficult with Roy. He does not seem to realize how much one worries about him. And one is so helpless, sitting about here. Oh, *denne fryktelige ventingen.* . . .'

It was her breakdown into Norwegian that went through Adams' guard. In some odd way it lent intense expression to her loneliness. Under the shaded bulb of the hall, she looked very young and clean and vulnerable, and Adams could bear it no longer. He stumbled away, feeling blindly for the kitchen door.

'I'm sorry. I must see . . . the landlord. Excuse me.'

He lurched into the kitchen, closing the door to hide her from his sight. He remembered Grenville's words. Filthy? – even the knowledge made one feel that. Unclean and tainted. . . .

He tried to see round the kitchen. From a shapeless blur the familiar face of Kearns slowly took shape, eyeing him with concern.

'What's the matter, Frank? What's happened, lad?'

Adams tried to speak, but the sound that came from his throat alarmed him. He gritted his teeth and closed his eyes tightly.

'Frank, lad; what is it? Here, sit down.'

Adams sat down, gripping the arms of the chair for support. He sat motionless for a full thirty seconds, breathing heavily. Then he looked up at the solicitous face of Kearns.

'You're right, Joe. War is vile. Dear God, it is. Unspeakably vile.'

CHAPTER **20**

The last of the locals said good-night to Maisie and closed the bar door. After the low hum of conversation the room seemed very silent. Maisie stared around it and suddenly shivered. She didn't want to be alone – not after what Miss Bergman had told her. . . .

She latched the door, and mechanically began collecting up the empty glasses. How could the kid be dead? Why, he'd been in here drinking beer only a couple of nights ago, looking better than she'd seen him look before. And two weeks before that she'd kissed him up there in her room, and felt his tears soaking through her dress. . . . He couldn't be dead, cold and grey in the soil. People couldn't go as quickly as that. It didn't make sense.

The shock was wearing off now, and dullness giving way to both grief and panic. How was Gillie taking it? Mr Adams had promised to try to get him to come over, but he might be holding it against her more than ever now. Surely not – surely he could see now how unimportant it had been. Beside men's lives it was nothing. . . . But some men didn't see it that way – not men like Gillie.

She put the empty glasses into the sink, turned on the cold water, and let it run over her hot wrists. She was worried about Gillie. He'd thought an awful lot about that boy – he might go right off the deep end if she didn't get a chance to talk to him first. Why couldn't he see she'd done it for him as well as for the kid? Why hadn't he come over already? She was frightened. . . .

Anxiety and hopelessness hung over her like a blanket, dulling her eyes and ears. She did not hear the stumbling footsteps on the drive outside: it was the sound of the latch being tried that awakened her. She looked up in unbelief, her heart pounding madly. Switching off the lights, she ran forward and unlatched the door.

Gillibrand staggered inside, swaying drunkenly in the darkness. Maisie closed the door, switched on one of the lights, and led him to a chair. Tearing a scarf away from his throat, he dropped into it, breathing heavily.

She knelt down beside him. His cap had fallen back, letting his tangled yellow hair fall over his forehead. Under the scarf his collar was undone, and there was a shadow of beard on his cheeks. He looked very drunk.

She threw her arms around him, pressing her wet face against his shoulder. 'Thanks ever so much for comin'. . . . I didn't think you would. I'm sorry, darling. Miss Bergman told me. . . . The poor little kid. . . .'

His huge body suddenly writhed, pulling away from her. She misunderstood and became frantic. 'Don't, Gillie! It wasn't the way you thought. I did it for you as well as him – honest I did. I was scared for you both. Don't hate me for it, Gillie. Please don't hate me.'

He lifted his face, and the agony in it made her catch her breath. She saw now that only his body was drunk, not his mind. He made a sound that could have come from a trapped animal.

'Yeah, the kid's dead. Passed out just after we landed. Can't get used to it, somehow. Seems all wrong. . . .'

She clutched hold of him again, talking as a woman talks to a distressed child, using words of comfort without meaning. Again he pulled away.

'They sent th' kid and me out on a recce job. We got the photos O.K., but I was sore with him and went lookin' for trouble. Found a minelayer off Bergen and attacked it. An' the kid got hit. . . .'

She did not understand and went on trying to comfort him. He shook his head, ignoring her.

'I got him back, but he passed out a couple of minutes after we landed. He got a few words out – said I had to tell you something.'

'Me?' she breathed, suddenly hushed.

'Yeah. He said I had to tell you he wasn't afraid any more. . . . That's why I came over.'

Maisie's black eyes were huge with wonder. 'He said that?'

'Yeah. I guess he was sayin' thanks. He was, too.'

Tears rolled unchecked down her face at the miracle of it.

'Yeah. . . . And then I found out that the rest of the boys had gone out to prang some place in Bergen. Bergen, mind you. I saw 'em come back an' that finished me.'

The spasm that ran through his body made Maisie apprehensive in spite of what she had just heard 'Why?' she asked.

Gillibrand's blue eyes filled with agony again. 'Why? Don't you see – it was the minelayer I attacked that alerted those fighters and put 'em up. If I hadn't gone lookin' for trouble, the boys would have got through O.K.'

Her voice sharpened with alarm. 'You mustn't tell them, do you hear? You mustn't tell them or they'll court martial you.'

He stared dully down at the table. 'I ain't goin' to tell them, kid. I've thought about it and decided it wouldn't help them or me. No; that ain't the way out. . . .'

'It wasn't your fault,' she said, relieved. 'It was just bad luck.'

He gave a slow, drunken shake of his head. 'You ain't got it yet. I went for that layer because I wanted to punish th' kid. I wanted to hear him squeal; I wanted to frighten and break him up again. Now do you get it?'

Suddenly she drew back as if struck with a whip. 'You're drunk,' she breathed.

'That's why you're saying this.' Her voice rose hysterically. 'It is the drink, isn't it?'

He lifted his bleary face upwards. 'No, honey. I ain't that drunk, although I've been tryin' hard enough. I killed that boy – killed him as sure as if I'd stuck a knife in him.'

She shrank back as if from a leper. Her hushed voice was incredulous. 'You mean you killed that decent little kid because of that. . . .'

He saw her expression and lurched to his feet. 'I know how you feel. And you're right, too. You helped him to live, an' I helped him to die, and nothin' can change that now. Nothin' at all because he's dead. I'm gettin' along now, kid. S' long. . . .'

And he stumbled out into the darkness.

Five hours later a party of four men, huddled together for comfort, watched a lone Mosquito heading down the flarepath. With screaming engines, it hurled its bomb-packed fuselage over the airfield fence with an abandonment that made all four men wince. None of them met the others' eyes as they turned away, nor did they speak. Their ears were filled with the sound of those engines, now fading into the silence of the night sky.

CHAPTER 21

The dawn broke grey and cold, and the wavetops below the Mosquito snapped like the fangs of hungry animals. Grenville peered anxiously at the lightening horizon. He was ten minutes late to his E.T.A. – either he was off course or the meteorological forecast had underestimated the strength of the head winds. He hoped fervently it was the latter, although any delay, whatever the cause, would be serious enough if the Focke Wulfs came up at dawn.

He was flying at just under 1,000 feet, and as the light improved he dropped down to one hundred. He dared not go lower in his present condition. Strain and lack of sleep had slowed his reflexes: during the last hour he had kept turning his oxygen on every few minutes to keep himself awake.

It was another five minutes before he sighted land. At first it was a fog bank that appeared, clinging to the sea like a dusty cobweb. As he lifted the Mosquito over it, conical peaks rose from its flat surface like tiny islands. Instantly his eyes lifted to search the sky above. It appeared empty and he gazed down again. The fog patch passed below him, as did the islands it was shrouding, but he knew now that he was not far from the coast. The tiny peaks were part of the Oygarden group, the long fence of islands that lay outside Bergen and the Nordhordland district.

Another line of islands appeared, an unbroken chain this time with banks of fog swirling in their hollows. Grenville leap-frogged over them, banked steeply, and dropped down another fifty feet. He was flying south-south-east now, with the islands guarding his right flank.

Now that his target was drawing near his fatigue left him. Since leaving Sutton Craddock he had lived a nightmare, either fighting off sleep or fighting off thoughts that clawed his mind like torturer's hooks. Now, with no observer to assist him, he was too busy to think, and was thankful for it. Increasing his boost, he dropped right down on the water, the black and grey islets of rock flashing by in a blur of speed. He caught sight of a fisherman's wooden house, half-a-dozen goats feeding on a patch of bright grass, a clump of shrub, a cluster of windswept trees. . . .

A larger island appeared . . . a small jetty . . . two fishing-boats at anchor . . . a hamlet . . . a woman waving an apron from the front door of a house. . . .

Two minutes more and land soared up on either side of him. Petrol tanks swept by . . . a group of large, camouflaged buildings . . . three tall, smoking chimneys. Not 200 yards from his port wing-tip a freighter was making her way up channel, her bow wash white against the shadowy sea. Grenville caught a glimpse of a brace of multiple pom-poms on her boat deck before his speed swept him by. No shots were fired and thirty seconds later a shoulder of land hid the ship from sight.

The channel broadened as a tributary flowed into it from the east, then narrowed again. The land on either side rose higher, became mountainous with denser vegetation of scrub and pines. Houses became more frequent, typical Norwegian country houses with wooden frames and high-sloping roofs. Grenville was in a fjord now and the water below him was calmer. His slipstream shivered a wake behind him as he streaked not 30 feet above it.

He drew back his stick and a town flashed below him. That would be Garnes. Garnes, and not a shot fired at him yet! He made a little altitude and scanned the sky above. Still no sign of fighters! He went down again, his eyes probing the green, birch-covered mountainside on his right.

He found the valley and banked steeply into it. Trees flashed under him, mountains towered on either side. The Isdalen Pass! Rocks . . . bright grass . . . trees . . . then a long sheet of water. Svartediket! The green-wooded mountain on his left was Ulrikken. A cold, sadistic voice inside his mind suddenly began to mock him. 'Are you wondering what it feels like to be an executioner? Well, you'll soon know. You're nearly there now. Nearly there . . .' He tried to blank his mind to it. The woods and water of the pass flashed by. . . . 'Nearly there,' the voice mocked again. 'Nearly there.'

Quite abruptly he was there. The pass fell away and Bergen, beautiful in its cradle of seven mountains, lay below him. Opposite was Lovstakken, a long massive ridge that ran to the U-boat pens south of the city. Below was a broad lake –

what had Adams called it? The Store Lungegardsvann. It was dotted with small boats of all types. On its far side was a bridge – that would be the Strombro. Watch that – there were flak posts on it! On this side of the lake were railway lines and the station. Flak there too, although none of it had started up yet. . . .

He had banked steeply to starboard on leaving the pass and was over the centre of the city before he got all his landmarks. Behind him he caught sight of the small octagonal lake Adams had mentioned. It was near the railway station, and behind it was a piece of waste ground. . . .

Gritting his teeth, he threw the Mosquito into a sharp 180-degree turn to port. Bergen, clean-looking in the early morning light, swam in a dizzy arc under his vertical wingtip. When he straightened out he was flying inland again along the Lovstakken range, with Bergen on his port side. From the corner of his eye he caught sight of other landmarks: the Nautical School in the Nordnes Parken, the green roof of the National Theatre, the wide, tree-lined avenue of the Ole Bulls Plasse. . . . But he needed no markers now. His target was in sight, standing alone like a diseased thing on the waste land between the two lakes.

The first flak appeared, coming up from the docks, a red, yellow and green chain that seemed about to hit him between the eyes before curving away. As if it were a signal, flak opened up from all directions – not for nothing was Bergen considered to be one of the best defended ports in occupied Europe! Within seconds his Mosquito was bracketed by a cloud of bursting shells, making him take violent evasive action.

As he approached the Strombro Bridge, a fan-shaped cluster of white bursts opened out dead ahead. How could he make a run-in across the lake with all this stuff lined up. . . ? With these flak posts on the bridge and the others on the railway opposite, they'd be able to catch him in a cross-fire. He wouldn't have a chance. . . .

He made a split-second decision. Switching on his gunsight, he dived straight at the bridge, opening fire with both cannon and machine-guns. Tracer came upwards in blinding sheets – he felt he was flying right into the barrels of the murderous guns. Just as he believed himself finished, panic-stricken grey shapes rose from the gun-pits and fled before the fury of his attack. His shells burst among them, mowing them down. Three men, seeing the flame-spitting thunderbolt howling down on them, leaped straight from the bridge into the water below.

Drenched in sweat, Grenville pulled the Mosquito out of her dive and sent her rocketing up the slopes of Ulrikken. The ferocity of the fire from the bridge had now greatly diminished: he had to press home his attack before the crews were rallied.

The Mosquito rolled over on the top of her dive and came plunging down again, the tight skin on her wings and fuselage drumming with speed. Behind Grenville the green slopes of Ulrikken streamed dizzily away. He was travelling at well over 400 m.p.h. when he pulled out over the lake, lowering the Mosquito down until her belly nearly touched the water. He opened his bomb doors, clicked down his selector switches, and fixed the building at the far end of the lake dead in the centre of his gunsight. Then he had nothing to do but wait. In the few endless seconds that his Mosquito took to flash over the shivering water, the voice in his mind began torturing him again.

'It won't be long now. Just a few more seconds – if you get through, of course. . . . I wonder if he'll guess it's you that is killing him. . . .'

The accuracy of the guns alongside the railway was terrifying. Three posts got Grenville's range at once. The water below him seethed as shells tore it into spray, blurring his windshield and hissing into steam on his red-hot engines. White puffs enveloped him, interspersed by black ones as the murderous 37mms. joined in. A shell went clean through his bomb hatch without exploding, ricocheting off a 500-lb. bomb. Another one burst near the starboard engine, making the Mosquito wince as shrapnel tore through its wing. A blinding flash came from the instrument panel, followed by an explosion that almost shattered Grenville's eardrums. There was the smell of cordite and burning rubber . . . sparks spluttering from a damaged contact box. Outside, tracer soared through the smoke like coloured streamers, graceful to watch and death to touch.

Grenville was hunched down in his seat to gain what protection he could from his armour plating. His legs were affected by an intense nervous convulsion and his toes clenched up inside his flying boots. He had to get through . . . he had to get through. . . . He gritted the words over and over as the flak thunder increased around him. 'Of course you must', the devil voice jeered back. 'An executioner shouldn't be late for his appointment. . . .'

The building was huge in Grenville's gunsight when a party of black-uniformed figures began pouring out from it. Instantly loathing drove all other emotions from Grenville's mind. Here were the bullies he had always hated: here were Bergman's torturers, running for their lives! He kicked the rudder bar, brought them into his sights, and fired a long vicious burst, his thumb tight down on the button. The Mosquito shuddered under the tremendous kicking recoil. Grenville sawed on the rudder bar, hosing the stream of shells and bullets among the screaming men. The effect was murderous. The earth itself was churned into furrows and men were thrown into shapeless heaps of bloody flesh and charred rags.

The building swung back into Grenville's sights again. His 20mm. shells smashed through its wooden walls, doing enormous damage. Two hundred yards . . . one-fifty yards . . . the lake fell away, he was over the waste land now. One hundred yards . . . fifty. . . . Now! He pressed the bomb release and jerked back on the stick. The Mosquito screamed upwards, missing the roof of the building by less than ten feet.

The four bombs, tail-fused and falling horizontally, hit the ground and bounded forward like flat stones on water. They smashed through the wall of the wooden building as if it had been cardboard and disappeared within.

The wide avenue of the Ole Bulls Plasse streamed under Grenville like a green ribbon. Ignoring the vengeful flak that was still following him, he banked steeply to look back. He was counting to himself . . . seven . . . eight . . . nine . . . ten. . . .

At eleven there were four simultaneous explosions that disintegrated the building, hurled it upwards in a mushroom of red-cored smoke and splintered wood.

Although the flak by the bridge would be reorganized now, Grenville was prepared to make a second attack for Bergman's sake if anything was left standing. But there was nothing on the waste ground but four blackened craters and a blazing pile of debris. No one could have survived that holocaust.

Reaction hit him as he stared down. His stomach retched, jerking his body against his harness. His eyes felt as if nails were being driven though them into his brain. The physical pain he welcomed; it was an ally against the worse pain within.

It was the instinct of self-preservation plus his innate flying habits that saved him at that moment. Before making his attack he had noticed patches of fog hanging round the southern slopes of Lovstakken and among the fjords and islands beyond. Now, without conscious thought, he flew over Lovstakken, dived down among these patches, and worked his way round their fringes towards the coast.

He was only just in time. The hundreds of flak bursts that pock-marked the sky had barely lost their separate identity before the first flight of Focke Wulfs came howling in. With snarling engines they darted over the city like dogs sniffing for a scent. Then, at a given signal, they hurled themselves over Lovstakken and into the chase. The vengeful roar of their engines followed the Mosquito out to sea and faded with it.

CHAPTER 22

It came again, and in some odd way Grenville knew it was a nightmare. Yet the knowledge only heightened his feeling of trapped terror. He was coming in to land after his raid on Bergen. His undercarriage would not lock down, the hydraulic mechanism had been damaged by shrapnel. Nor would it fully retract, which meant the crooked wheels were a menace to a belly landing.

He thought for a moment of doing some steep dives in an effort to force the undercart down, but his tired mind rejected the idea at once. The shattered Mosquito might disintegrate and in any case he was weary . . . weary. . . . He had to get down before the black cloud floating at the corners of his eyes closed over and blinded him. There wasn't much time left.

He heard his tired voice speaking to Control. 'I'm coming in for a belly landing. Please stand by. Switching off. . . .'

The field swam dizzily before his eyes as he banked up-wind. The Mosquito answered sluggishly: shrapnel had sprung a hinge in the starboard aileron, making lateral control difficult. To make certain he would not be trapped in a flaming coffin, he reached out to jettison the escape hatch but it would not budge. He tugged again but it was tightly jammed and he was tired. . . .

A vision flashed in front of him as he dropped lower. Priestman piling up yesterday morning – the blackened scars in the grass lay dead ahead. From the corner of his eye he saw the crash wagon and ambulance following his shadow along the runway.

God, the field seemed to be coming up fast! His reactions were slow, deceiving him. He switched off both engines and pulled the stick back. Easy, easy, don't let her stall. Hold it. . . . Hold it. . . . Now!

The Mosquito bounced a full fifteen feet, nearly snapping Grenville's neck with shock. The wooden fuselage buckled and splintered like a bamboo cane, the wings crumpled like papier mâché. Another tremendous jerk and this time Grenville was flung forward, his harness snapping with the strain. He managed to half-cover his face with his hands before it was smashed into the gunsight. There was a sickening pain in his lower jaw . . . the taste of blood . . . the feel of a broken tooth on his tongue. . . .

Then only pain and silence. No, not silence. The hiss of petrol vapourizing on the white-hot engines. Get me out! For God's sake, get me out!

Frantic hands suddenly pulled at him, bringing a shock of pain through his head. Blackness for a moment, then a vague confused picture of the shattered Mosquito twenty yards away with firemen playing pumps and extinguishers on her. His last impression before unconsciousness was that of a thin black column of smoke rising from the disembowelled port engine. . . .

He knew what the nightmare was going to do to him, and tried desperately to awake. But the thing held him tightly, forcing him to watch. The column of smoke belched and burst into a red-cored explosion. Now he was over Bergen, looking down on the thing he had done, seeing the four smoking craters and the heap of flaming wreckage. The fire seemed to reach up and burn every corner of his cringing mind.

He awoke then, and soaked in cold sweat lay trying to identify his surroundings. But his mind was still too dazed: the figures in the grey mist that swirled around him were out of focus and unreal. He tried to call to them, but his lips were still and would not move. A few minutes later darkness and the nightmare swooped down on him again.

Just after 16.00 hours that same Thursday Davies entered the Intelligence Room. There was a peaked look about his sharp face, and the usual briskness was absent from his movements. He motioned to Adams to remain seated, and tossing his cap on the table, sat down opposite him.

'I've just come from seeing Grenville,' he said, catching the anxious question in Adams' eyes. 'They've put him in Stanhope Hospital in Highgate. He'll be all right in a few days. He got a nasty crack on the head and face when his harness snapped, and a wrenched shoulder into the bargain. The head injury is the worst – there was slight concussion and he's been a bit delirious – but they say none of it is serious. Anyway, I told them to keep him there a few days. The rest won't do him any harm.'

Adams nodded his relief. 'He was lucky. I never thought he'd come out of it alive.'

'His type are hard to kill,' Davies said with some pride.

'Particularly when they don't much care about living.' Adams had not meant to say it – the words slipped out – and his plump face turned crimson when Davies's eyes fixed themselves resentfully on him.

'I didn't know the rest of the story when I ordered him out. And it might have been better if you hadn't told it to us last night. I felt enough of a murderer as things were.'

'I should have kept it to myself, I know,' Adams muttered.

The aggressiveness left Davies's voice at once. 'I don't blame you. Some things are better shared. I don't suppose I'd have been able to keep it quiet myself.' His tone changed, became awed. 'My God; the guts of the man. He'll get a bar to his D.S.O. if I've got any say in it.'

Adams winced at the suggestion. 'It might be better to leave that for a while, sir. I'm pretty certain he wouldn't want it – not for this.'

Davies nodded reluctantly. 'I suppose you're right. But it seems damnable there isn't some reward one can give him.'

'Have you seen the camera films yet?' Adams asked.

Davies showed some of his old spirit. 'They were the first thing I went to see when I got back. God, man, aren't they terrific? The way he slaughtered those devils as they came running out. . . .'

Adams nodded. He had seen the films as soon as they were developed. Grenville's hate had come out through them, holding him in horrified fascination.

'It's a pity he had no way of photographing the destruction of the target,' he said.

Davies lowered his voice. 'The Brigadier got confirmation two hours ago. That's what I came to tell you.'

Adams knew his face had paled. He tried to keep his voice steady. 'Was it completely successful?'

Davies held his eyes grimly. 'Yes. Completely.'

'Does everything go on as before, then? Or don't you know yet?'

Davies hesitated a moment before replying. 'The Brigadier seems optimistic again. None of the patriots has been arrested yet, so it doesn't look as if anybody talked, God bless 'em. Yes; if nothing else happens we shall go on as planned. We must; we've no option.'

'Isn't all this damage to our planes going to delay us?'

Davies picked up his cap and rose to his feet. 'It's been a blow, but we've got to get over it somehow. Barrett must keep everyone working until they're airworthy again. I don't know the exact date we're supposed to go, but for some reason or other it has to be before the end of May.' His voice was grave. 'After that the Brigadier reckons our chances of success are greatly reduced, perhaps gone altogether. So we've no choice but to be ready.'

Grenville awoke from his doze and stared round the room. The walls were cream-washed, sterile and blank. A small cabinet stood alongside his bed, its glass surface littered with bottles. A polished electric stove stood near the half-open door. The air held the faint smell of antiseptics.

He lifted a hand to his head. They had removed some of the bandages, but his jaw and mouth were still bound up, making it impossible to have a smoke. He shifted restlessly. Three days of this was more than enough. He'd have another go at that confounded doctor when he came tonight. . . .

Something tapped on the window, and his eyes moved sharply towards it. At first nothing was visible but a rectangular patch of sunlit blue sky. Then, as he watched, the bough of a flowering almond moved across the glass, tapping gently as it passed by. It had no leaves, just a thin branch and a cluster of pink blossoms that waved like a magic wand in front of the blue sky.

Grenville watched it in fascination. The ward sister's voice outside the door made him start. 'Yes; you can go in; he is awake. But only ten minutes, please. And don't expect him to talk to you – his face is still bandaged up.'

'Thank you.'

Grenville's breath stopped at the sound of the second voice. His head jerked sidewards, then he lay motionless, only his eyes moving as she approached his bedside. She was wearing a grey, slim-fitting coat with a blue scarf at her throat, and was carrying a large leather bag. A sunbeam made her uncovered hair shine with golden light. A faint perfume came from her, driving back the smell of the antiseptics.

His panic-stricken mind searched desperately for comfort. Her appearance, her smile . . . she could not know yet. Thank God for that. . . .

'I had to come to see you,' she said, as the door closed, leaving them alone. 'Frank told me where you were.'

Damn Adams. He wanted to close his eyes to save himself looking at her, but could not. She took three packets of twenty cigarettes from the bag she was carrying and laid them on the cabinet alongside him.

'It is very little,' she said apologetically, 'but they were all I could buy.'

To get them she would have had to queue up at half the tobacconists in Highgate. Don't make it worse, please! Don't do things for me. . . ! Grenville wanted to beg her to leave, but could force nothing from his bandaged mouth. His eyes, the only part of his face visible, stared up at her mutely. She misunderstood their expression and looked anxious.

'Frank said you were not seriously injured – I had not expected to see you so bandaged. Are you in much pain?'

He shook his head. Her grave, blue-grey eyes did not lighten. 'For a while I almost hoped you were more seriously hurt, because then you would not have had to fly for a long, long time. . . .' She smiled at him sadly. 'Why could you not have broken an arm or a leg, Roy? It would have made me very happy.'

As if ashamed of her seriousness, she flushed and took a large bunch of daffodils from the bag at her feet. She went over to a water bowl on the window-ledge and began arranging them.

'They brighten a room,' she said defensively. 'I picked them this morning from Mr Kearns' garden. You should see his fruit trees – the sun has brought out all the blossom.'

He caught sight of the pink almond blossom again, nodding above her shining head, and emotion struck him like a blow. He lay half-dazed as she told him more about the innkeeper's garden.

She finished arranging the flowers and turned back to his bedside, smiling. 'You know, Roy, it is rather nice for me to do all the talking and to know that you cannot argue with me. It makes the words come easier, somehow.'

The ward sister tapped on the door at that moment. Hilde's face saddened at the reminder. She hesitated, then laid a hand on his forehead. Grenville lay motionless, hardly breathing, not daring to think.

'I'm coming to see you again as soon as I can,' she said. 'They say I may come on Tuesday.'

Grenville moved his head sidewards, like a dazed boxer trying to avoid a blow. Three more days – she would know by then! Her voice came from far away, yet with the purity of a bronze bell.

'Somehow it is easier to ask you now. Roy, when you are better, please do not be long in coming to see me. It is so very lonely without you. Good-bye. *Gud velsigne deg.*'

She kissed his forehead, then ran quickly from the room. Grenville closed his eyes. Something like acid was running into them, blinding him.

CHAPTER 23

Two mornings later the Dispersal Hut alongside the Southern perimeter of the airfield was unusually quiet – only one Mosquito standing ready for take-off with filled tanks and loaded guns. She was the outcome of an order from Group for 633 to provide a plane for meteorological duties.

With the rest of the squadron still feverishly licking its wounds, Barrett had had no option but to cancel the dawn training flights. Six of his aircraft were undergoing major repairs in the hangars (where ground crews had been working day and night since the battle over Bergen), and the rest were dispersed around the field with cowled engines, waiting for daylight to bring another swarm of mechanics to attend to their repairs. Nevertheless, Barrett was hoping to resume training in four days' time. Townsend, the Maintenance Officer, thought his mind had gone.

Shortly before dawn a five-hundredweight truck from the Transport Section pulled up outside the hut with a grunt of brakes. Two men, Gillibrand and his new observer, leapt from the tailboard, sparks showing from their cigarettes as they landed on the tarmac. Both were wearing flying suits and harness. They pulled down their parachutes, then Gillibrand thumped a huge hand against the tin side of the truck. 'O.K., Mac. Take it away.'

The yawning driver threw in his gears and the five-hundredweight lumbered away. Gillibrand made for the hut without a word. The observer shivered and followed him. A cold, gusty wind was blowing, rocking the Mosquito's wings. It was growing lighter and objects began appearing out of the darkness: the sand-bagged shelter near the hut, the nearby gun-post, the shadowy outline of the Control Tower.

A chink of yellow light shone under the door of the hut. Gillibrand pushed his way inside. It was warmer in there: someone had lit the stove which was giving off clouds of sulphurous smoke. Above it hung a naked electric bulb, which was shining down on a group of mechanics who were warming their hands round mugs of tea. They looked around at the newcomers and muttered their greetings, their sleep-encrusted eyes a little wary of Gillibrand. Once Gillie had been one of the boys, but since he had lost his observer he wanted watching. . . .

The Canadian tossed his parachute on a chair, then turned to the mechanics. 'Well; what about some char?'

The diminutive corporal in charge of the fitters jumped up, took two mugs down from a shelf, and filled them with black tea. He slopped in condensed milk from a half-opened tin and handed the mugs to the two men.

'Chilly out 'ere this mornin', sir,' he offered Gillibrand.

Gillibrand nodded without speaking, lifted the mug to his lips and drained it. The naked light, with its uncompromising shadows, made him look a grim and formidable figure. His heavy brows shadowed his eyes, sinking them into his skull. Lines showed round his nose and mouth, and a bristle of beard on his massive jaw added to the grim-visaged effect. His young sergeant observer, just posted to the squadron, looked subdued and unhappy alongside him.

Gillibrand handed the mug back to the corporal, then jerked a thumb towards the door. 'You'd better be gettin' her started up, hadn't you?'

The corporal looked surprised and glanced down at his watch. 'She's been warmed up, sir. I thought you wasn't due off for another quarter of an hour.'

'Never mind. Get her runnin' now. I want an early start.'

The corporal nodded and gave an order to two of his men. They put their mugs down and went out sullenly. The corporal handed the D.I. to Gillibrand.

'She's O.K., sir. We've given her a good check.'

Gillibrand barely glanced at the form before shoving it back. He dropped on a bench, his eyes brooding on the smoking stove. The observer, looking embarrassed, began fishing inside his flying suit for cigarettes. The corporal offered him one in sympathy before going out to his men. As he left the hut the first of the Mosquito's Merlins coughed and fired.

The sergeant hesitated, then followed him outside. It was almost daylight now. The eastern horizon was a blaze of red fire, shot with the black smoke of clouds. At the distant end of the field a row of poplars stood out against it in dark relief. The second engine fired, throwing mud and pebbles against the side of the hut. The cold blast made the sergeant shiver again.

Gillibrand came out of the hut, carrying both parachutes. He tossed one at the sergeant and jerked his thumb at the Mosquito. The sergeant stamped on his cigarette and followed him. He was half-way to the plane when the Canadian halted, lifting his head like a Great Dane sniffing danger.

The next moment the sergeant saw them himself – Messerschmitt 110's, two lines of them, one line coming straight down the airfield perimeter towards the dispersal hut. . . . As his eyes froze on them, the nose of the leading plane lit up with stabbing flashes.

A huge hand grabbed his arm, he was almost lifted off his feet, and a moment later found himself slumped inside the sandbagged shelter with Gillibrand alongside him. Another second and the startled mechanics tumbled over the parapet and dropped beside them.

The noise of the engines and cannon fire came in brutal waves, hammering the men down among the sandbags. Tracer whiplashed over them and smashed into the nearby gun-post. A thin scream sounded over the din. Gillibrand's face was murderous as he glared over the parapet.

The strategy of the 110's was already clear. Their first target was not the planes or the airfield, but the gun-posts on its perimeter. They were making their attack in two lines astern, one line strafing the south boundary posts, the other line attacking the north ones. The unfortunate gun crews, with a year's immunity from attack behind them, were caught completely napping. Only one Hispano opened up, and its gunner died not five seconds later with a bullet in his throat.

With the skill of rehearsal behind the manoeuvre, the two lines of 110's completed their attack on the two boundaries, swung in a tight arc, and made for the remaining east and west posts. Here, with a few seconds of warning to prepare them, the gunners put up more resistance, and one 110 sheered off, trailing black smoke. But lack of battle practice was all too evident, and the tough 110's were allowed to press their attacks right into the muzzles of the guns. Post after post was blasted and destroyed.

Gillibrand saw the outcome. With all flak cover gone, the airfield would be wide open. And the Messerschmitts were carrying more than long-range tanks under their slim bellies. . . . It would be good-bye Mr Chips – planes, crews, erks, the lot. . . .

He leapt over the sandbagged parapet, bent double, and ran for the Mosquito. Running under its wings he snatched away the chocks, then heaved himself up into the fuselage and into his seat. No time to turn up-wind, no time to use the runway. . . . With over 3,000 revs, full boost, and flaps right down, he released the brakes and gave the Mosquito her head. She bucked and reared like a maddened horse, but somehow he kept her nose straight. Through his windshield he saw the 110's were making another attack on two gun-posts that were holding out stubbornly. His tight lips moved. Just a few seconds more, boys. . . . That's all I want. A chance to pay back. Give it to me, boys. . . . That's all I want. A chance to pay back. Give it to me, boys. . . .

The Mosquito's tail was up now and her controls lightening. But a Messerschmitt saw him, banked steeply, and came in like a winged devil. There was nothing Gillibrand could do but hold on and pray. The 110's height saved him: its pilot had no air space to jockey into position. He could only take a split-second, full-radius deflection in the hope his cone of fire would take care of any error.

It nearly did. The Mosquito's tailplanes were riddled like a sieve, only a miracle saving the control wires. Baffled, the 110's pilot gave the alarm over his R/T and went into a climbing turn for another attack. The rest of the bandits, their job on the flak posts completed, turned to blast the lone Mosquito from their path.

But Gillibrand was airborne now, back in his element. With one wing-tip clipping the grass he turned into the astonished 110's, scattering them right and left to avoid collision. In the confusion he settled on the tail of one of them and opened fire with both cannon and machine-guns. At point-blank range his fire did terrible damage, shattering the tail planes and ripping open the fuselage like a tin-can. The 110 rolled over and plunged into a clump of trees. Blazing petrol swept over them, setting them aflame like giant torches.

Putting his weight on his stick, Gillibrand reversed his turn, his Mosquito skidding round like a car on ice. The pale-blue underbelly of a 110 appeared from nowhere in his sights. He was close enough to see the blue oxide flames from its exhausts and the patch scar from some earlier encounter under one wing. Everything seemed to slow down for a second, the 110's propellers waving like arms as it struggled to escape. The luminous graticule of Gillibrand's sight moved deliberately to a spot between its wings. He steadied his controls – then pressed his gun button exultantly.

The clear picture blurred and disintegrated before his eyes. Only a violent jerk on his stick saved him from collision. As he plunged through the cloud of oily smoke interspersed with flaming wreckage, the acrid smell of it came to his nostrils. He glanced sidewards, saw the attack had led him some distance from the airfield and that one or two of the 110's were steadying themselves to make a bombing run. With a growl he rolled the Mosquito over and went plunging back.

Down below all was confusion. Men were crouched behind shelters, lying under beds, gaping from windows. Others were bawling orders no one could hear for the tremendous racket of engines and cannon fire. Over in the inn all its inhabitants, in various stages of undress, had invaded Hilde's bedroom; and, blind to their own danger, were standing alongside her, craning their necks to follow Gillibrand's fantastic manoeuvres.

There was even more confusion among the Messerschmitts. The R/T channel was swamped by cursing voices. The Squadron Commander was growing frantic with anxiety. The attack had been timed to seconds: already his planes should have dropped their bombs and been heading back for home. Spitfires would have been alerted minutes ago. . . . But no one could make a bombing run for this madman: he broke up every attack before it could be made. The Commander shouted his call sign above the din and gave his orders. . . .

Messerschmitts closed in on either side of Gillibrand, trying to box him in. The Canadian's answer was simply to turn into the plane outside his starboard wing. Its terrified pilot broke away, almost crashing into a telegraph pole. His nerves were further shattered by the burst of shells Gillibrand sent after him which missed his port engine by inches.

The battle raged on for another thirty seconds with 110 after 110 trying to make a run-in on its target, and Gillibrand foiling each attempt with complete disregard for his life. Some bombs did fall, but they were released without aim and did little damage. The very madness of Gillibrand's manoeuvres made them successful, bewildering the enemy pilots. Yet the odds were so great there could have been only one outcome had a different noise not made itself heard through the colossal din. A small, shark-like body leapt over the distant poplars and fastened itself with incredible venom to the tail of one of the Messerschmitts. Another followed it, and yet another. Spitfires! Hundreds of watching eyes below glowed their relief.

The German Squadron Commander gave orders to break off the action. But he was a brave man, and goaded with the knowledge that only one plane had stood between him and success. He at least could make some atonement. Snatching his opportunity in the confusion, he dived over the poplars and headed straight for the distant hangars.

Gillibrand, watching for nothing else, turned on a wing-tip and dived after him. The slim body of the 110 grew in his gunsight – 500 yards . . . 400 . . . 350. . . . He pressed his gun button and heard only the clank of breechblocks and the whine of compressed air. He pressed again. No use! His ammunition was finished.

The 110 had levelled out and was making her run-in. Gillibrand was not fifty feet above her. He could see the pilot clearly, looking like a huge insect in his goggles as he stared backwards. In the nose his observer would be lying over his bombsight, waiting with his thumb on the button. . . .

Everything slowed down once more for Gillibrand, and in the early morning light everything became very clear. The plane, with its huge black crosses and turning propellers, the hangars beyond it, and the Nissen huts of the airmen. . . . And beyond them the familiar road leading to the inn with its flowers, its white apple trees, with Maisie. . . . Spring below . . . bitter-sweet at that moment beyond all understanding.

One last look, and then Gillibrand pushed his stick forward. He hit the 110 between the tailplane and cockpit, cutting its fuselage almost in two. Locked together, both planes spun into the ground not seventy yards from the Control Tower. There was a sheet of flame, followed by an explosion that showered bricks and mud as far as the men's billets by the road. No court martial was needed for Gillibrand now.

CHAPTER 24

Davies could not wait a minute longer to ask his question. 'Before you go on, sir – doesn't this attack mean they've found out everything?'

The Brigadier's grey eyes rose from his table. 'No. Not by any means.'

'But surely it must. There hasn't been an attack of that strength on one of our British airfields for over a year. And this was no hit-or-miss affair. It had been carefully rehearsed beforehand.'

It was at moments like these that the different temperaments of the two men, so often complementary, fell out of step. Davies was wishing the Brigadier wouldn't be so damned tight-lipped and stoical, and the Brigadier was regretting Davies's dramatic instinct that could never resist discussing all the possibilities of a rich situation aloud – a habit doubly irritating on occasions such as this when he might possibly be right.

'I agree the attack was planned and that it was no coincidence 633 received it,' the Brigadier conceded. 'But that doesn't mean the enemy knows very much. Look at it this way – they saw you try to raid Bergen and would recognize your squadron markings. If they didn't know then what your target was, they would know the next morning when Grenville went in alone. After that they would guess you had some connection with Bergman. But if Bergman and Ericson didn't talk – and we've no reason to believe they did – how would they learn any details? Their suspicions are aroused, that is all, and the stakes are so high that they've played safe by trying to wipe you out.'

Davies shifted uneasily in his chair. 'I'm not sure they don't know more. I can't see them risking a whole squadron of 110's just on a vague suspicion.'

The Brigadier was silent for a moment. 'There is a possibility they may know more, of course,' he said quietly. 'But what are we to do – you know the importance of the target as well as I. So far none of the patriots has been arrested, and they've got a leader to take Bergman's place. So what alternative have we got but to carry on as before?'

Davies snapped his fingers, impatient with himself. 'I'd forgotten about the patriots. Of course, that's proof enough Jerry doesn't know very much.' His tone became brisk as he tried to destroy any impression of pessimism he might have created. 'As long as they are there to silence those flak posts, we'll prang the thing all right. Sorry – I see your point now.'

'What is the latest news from the squadron?' The Brigadier asked.

'Barrett's hoping to have the kites serviceable by the weekend. Crew replacements are his biggest headache because altogether he lost more in killed and wounded than he had in reserve. Obviously we can't give any new men the training the others have had, but we'll do our best with them. I've organized it with Barrett that where a replacement comes into a plane he has a trained man alongside him. And as fast as the kites become serviceable the new men will be taken up to Scotland and put through the drill. By Monday at the latest we hope to start the full squadron flights again.'

'Have replacements arrived yet for the planes you have lost?'

'A.T.A. tell me they'll be along at any time. That top priority order did the trick, of course.'

The Brigadier leaned forward. 'And what about Grenville? How is he getting along?'

'He'll be there all right,' Davies told him. 'He's back with the squadron now.'

The Brigadier showed his surprise. 'Already? But I thought you'd given orders for him to remain a week in hospital.'

'I did,' Davies muttered, shifting uneasily again. 'But it seemed Miss Bergman went to the hospital to visit him.' He saw a shocked look appear in the Brigadier's eyes. 'She didn't know about her brother at the time – as you know, the wire only arrived yesterday – but apparently she told Grenville she was going to pay him another visit shortly. He couldn't stand it, I suppose, and returned to camp. In the circumstances I thought it better for the Station M.O. to attend to him. He's got the bandages off now, in any case.'

The Brigadier nodded slowly. 'How is he taking it?'

Davies shrugged. 'It's difficult to tell – you know Grenville. But Adams thinks it has hit him hard.'

'Hard enough to affect his morale?'

The sharpness of Davies's reply betrayed his resentment of a war in which courage had to be evaluated as coldly as this. 'I shouldn't worry about his morale. He'll attack the bloody thing because it is his duty to attack it. After what he has done already, I don't think anyone should have any doubts about that.'

The strain was telling on all of them, the Brigadier thought. It was as well there was not much longer to wait. . . .

'No one could admire Grenville and his boys more than I,' he said quietly. 'His raid on Bergen, that magnificent sacrifice of Gillibrand's yesterday: everything is quite beyond any praise of mine. But you know the importance of this raid – at the risk of appearing soulless we can't afford to overlook anything, particularly the morale of the man who is going to lead it.'

Davies was quite disarmed by this reply. 'I don't think you've anything to worry about on that score. He'll probably try all the harder to prang it for all the misery it has caused. I know I would.'

Satisfied, the Brigadier drew Davies towards a large contour model of the Svartfjord and district that lay on the end of his table.

'This model has been built up from photographs received from your men and from patriots on the other side. Here is exactly what I want your lads to do. . . .'

Less than an hour later the Brigadier shoved aside a pile of papers and looked up at Davies. 'Well, that's everything. The contour model and the photographs will be sent to Adams under armed escort this afternoon. Let Barrett and Grenville see them, and tell them and Adams all I have just told you. But not a word to another soul until the briefing. Tell Adams to keep this model out of sight and to have a security guard round his office day and night. I think to make quite certain no one gets a look at it, the four of you should take turns in sleeping there.'

Davies nodded. 'What about these special bombs? When do we get them?'

'We can't give them to you yet, because the moment they go into your bomb-store your armourers will become curious and start talking. They'll arrive the night before the raid and go straight onto your aircraft. It won't matter then who talks, because, in addition to your own security safeguards, we shall send a crowd of our men down for the night.'

'And you want us to commence our full squadron training flights again as soon as all the kites are serviceable, and to keep them up every dawn until the day of the raid?'

'That's right. Then no one outside the airfield can guess which morning is zero hour.'

Davies felt his heart thumping excitedly in his wrists and ankles. He took a deep breath. 'And when is zero hour? That's the one thing you haven't told me?'

'They'll go in on the 14th,' the Brigadier said quietly. 'At 06.45 hours to be precise. That will give the patriots just enough daylight to do their job first. If all goes well, the gun-posts will be in their hands by 06.45. The rest of it will be up to your boys. For all our sakes, let's hope they do a good job.'

Davies stared around for a calendar. He eventually found one on the wall directly opposite him. The high-pitched sound of his own voice startled him. 'The 14th! But that's only nine days off!'

'We can't afford to leave it a day longer.' The Brigadier paused, not for effect but to compose his own anxious voice. 'Well, can you give your new men enough training in that time? Are you going to be ready?'

Anticipation of the battle ahead drove away Davies's doubts. He was quivering now like an aggressive bantam cock. 'Don't worry, sir. One way or another, we'll make it!'

'Hey; you up there! McTyre!'

McTyre, the old sweat, wedged on the wing alongside the stripped-down engine of a Mosquito, poked his long, sharp nose cautiously over the leading edge. He saw the bow-legged, unwelcome figure of Corporal Martin, one of the S.W.O.'s underlings, leaning on his bicycle below, and instantly his mind, allergic to M.P.'s, began searching for a reason. Unable to find one, he replied truculently.

'Whatcha want?'

'You! You've got to report to the S.W.O.'s office at 14.00 hours sharp. That's in fifteen minutes.'

'What for? Can't yer see I'm busy?'

The corporal grinned sardonically. 'Not 'alf as busy as you'll be after Bert's seen you. You're in trouble, mate.'

'What've I done this time?'

'Bert made an inspection of the billets this mornin'. He found your bed not made up, fag-ends all over the floor, and half a bottle of beer in your locker.'

McTyre gaped down incredulously. 'Yer mean he's been snoopin' round the billets at a time like this. . . .'

'Gotta keep discipline,' the corporal pointed out.

'Discipline!' McTyre nearly choked. He waved a scandalized arm round the perimeter of the airfield where other Mosquitoes were being repaired. 'Look at 'em all! shot to 'ell! How many of 'em would ever fly again if it wasn't for us? Here we are, workin' day and night, workin' ourselves to skin and bone, and he goes worryin' about a fag-end and an empty beer bottle. . . .'

'Half empty,' the corporal insisted.

'Here we are, riskin' our lives out 'ere, never knowing when them 110's are coming again, and he goes muckin' about in our billets. . . . It's terrible. Ain't it terrible?' McTyre demanded of the young, chubby face that suddenly popped up at the other side of the fuselage.

The young erk swallowed, nodded, saw the corporal frown, and popped down out of sight again. McTyre shook his head in bitter disgust.

'It's terrible! Makes yer wonder what yer're fightin' for. Snoopin' about while men are riskin' their lives, crawlin' around looking for fag-ends. . . . What's the matter with you all? Can't yer find anythin' better to do?'

The corporal saw the dignity of his own office was now coming under fire and took swift retaliatory action.

'That's enough of that. It ain't my fault you've got dirty habits. You mind what you're sayin', see.'

'Dirty habits,' McTyre growled, wiping his oily hands down the legs of his overalls. 'You wouldn't 'ave the guts to say that if you didn't have two tapes on your arm.'

But the corporal was not staying any longer to argue. He threw his bow legs over his bicycle and started away. '14.00 hours,' he shouted back. 'And don't be late.'

McTyre slid down the wing and rolled off. He was joined a few seconds later by the young A.C.2. 'Well; what d'you think of that?' McTyre demanded. 'See what I mean now about Bert?'

The erk nodded. McTyre pulled a blackened fag-end from the top pocket of his overalls, looked round furtively, then lit it. 'A bastard through and through,' he grunted. 'I ain't ever told you about him and the duck, 'ave I?'

'Duck?' The A.C.2 asked curiously. 'What duck?'

McTyre gave a bitter laugh and motioned the erk nearer. 'Listen to this, kid, and you'll see what you're up against. Fair frightens yer, it does, to think a man can be so low. . . . It happened at our last station – before your time. About a quarter of a mile down the road there was a small wood; and as me and my mate was courtin' a couple of local girls, we used to nip into it on the summer nights for a cuddle or two. Behind the wood was a field that didn't seem to belong to nobody, and right in the middle of the field was a pond.

'Well, the four of us were in there one evenin' in August when Jim suddenly nudges my arm. I look round and of all the people in the world I see Bert walkin' across the field towards the pond. He was alone and whistlin' to someone or other. We couldn't catch on, an' were beginning to think maybe his conscience had driven him that way when a little duck came waddlin' out of a clump of grass straight towards him. An' Bert leans down and gives it some food from his pocket.'

McTyre shook his head at the memory. 'You could've knocked me down with a feather if I hadn't been lyin' down already. We don't say nothin'; we just watch him. He puts some more food on the grass, pats the duck for a while, then after about ten minutes goes back the way he came. . . .

'Jim, who was a bit of a Bible-puncher, said it proved what he'd always believed – that every man had some good in him somewhere. He said Bert must be lonely in the camp, an' this was an outlet for his feelings. Jim said it made him feel better towards Bert now, more sympathetic, like. Me; I didn't know what to think.

'Anyway, this duck business went on for months. It must've been a nightly routine because every time we took the girls in the wood we saw Bert about the same time, round about eight o'clock. He'd feed the blooming thing, pat it, even play with it the way you'd play with a dog. Jim was real sorry for him by this time, and I was startin' to get that way myself. The girls thought he was a nice man and must have a very kind heart to come all this way at night to feed a lonely little duck. Can y' imagine it. . . ?

'Well, the months went by and it got a bit too cold for us in the woods at night, so we didn't see so much of Bert. But every now and then I'd have a squint, and sure enough, rain or snow, he kept goin' to that pond every night. I began to think Jim must be right – any man who went to all that trouble for a little duck must have a heart tucked away somewhere. Not that it was a little 'un now, mind you. It was gettin' as fat as a pig with all the food he'd been stuffin' into it.

'Christmas came, an' it was as cold as the clappers with everything frozen up. Do you know what duty Bert gave me on Christmas Eve, kid?'

The youngster shook his head.

'Goin' round the camp pulling W.C. chains to keep 'em working! Yeah, that was Bert!' McTyre took a deep breath, and blew smoke out through his long nose at the memory. 'And even that didn't convince me. Every time I pulled a chain I'd think about the duck and forgive 'im.'

'Christmas morning I was off duty at eight. At a minute past eight I was gettin' my pass from the Guard Room. As I went out of the gate I saw Bert goin' down the road ahead of me. My bus stop was down that way, so I followed him. When he reached the wood he turned off into the field, and curious now because he was off schedule, I hid behind some bushes and watched him. He looked around, didn't see anybody, then walked across the snow towards the pond. He let out a whistle, and sure enough that duck came waddlin' up just like a dog glad to see 'em. So 'elp me; you could see the trust on the bloomin' thing's face. I stood there watching, thinking maybe Bert had come over early to give it a Christmas present or something. But I was wrong, kid. By the centre I was wrong! Do you know what he did?'

The erk shook his young, puzzled face.

For one moment McTyre paused, as if reluctant to destroy such cherubic innocence. Then he gave a cynical grin and hitched up his overalls. 'All right; then I'll tell yer, kid. I'll tell yer how I know Bert's a bastard through an' through.'

And tell McTyre did before slouching away to see the villain of the piece in person. The shocked expression on the young erk's face left him in no doubt that he had proved his point.

CHAPTER 25

Adams closed the door of Grenville's billet with some attention to detail, painfully aware of his procrastination. He turned slowly, inwardly wincing at the unfriendly stare that met him.

'What do you want?'

Adams was not completely certain what he wanted – that was part of the trouble – and having had too much to drink did not help matters. His eyes, distressed and slightly puzzled, began wandering round the billet as if soliciting aid. None came from the tallboy in the opposite corner, none from the few photographs of planes and crews on the walls, and the flying suit hanging from a peg near the bed seemed positively contemptuous. The photograph on the top of Grenville's locker gave him great hopes until his short-sighted eyes discovered it to be of an elderly, white-haired woman. Adams felt a sense of injustice at the odds. It was going to be very, very difficult. . . .

'What's the matter with you? What do you want?'

Adams glanced hastily back at the bed on which Grenville, fully-clothed but for his tunic, had risen on one elbow to stare at him. A heavy shadow from the reading-lamp on the locker lay over the pilot's forehead and eyes, giving his severely bruised face an almost satanic expression. Adams discovered the words he had so carefully memorized on the way over from the inn had all fled in dismay, leaving him sorely tempted to follow them. He cleared his dry throat and blurted out the first thing that came to him.

'I've come to you about Hilde, Roy.'

The sudden silence hurt his ears. Then Grenville rose higher on his pillow. 'What do you mean?'

Adams braced himself. This was it, now or never. He took three jerky steps forward. 'Roy; I like that girl. She's the nicest kid I've known in years.' His own words brought a shock to Adams, confirming the suspicion that so far he had avoided meeting face to face. But there was no time to consider himself and Valerie now. That would have to wait until later. Ignoring the regret that lay like a heavy bruise in his mind, he went on: 'I can't bear seeing her being hurt like this. There's a limit to anything. . . .'

'Go on,' Grenville said, watching him with that devil's face from the shadows.

'As you know, the poor kid got the news about her brother last week. She took it well – too well, somehow. She doesn't talk about it, doesn't cry, doesn't say anything – but you can feel how bad it is underneath. And we can't do anything: not a damned thing. That's why I'm here tonight – to ask you to come over to see her.'

Grenville was sitting upright on his bed now. Adams saw his expression and went on with a rush.

'You're making it ten times worse for her, Roy. She must know you've heard about Finn – it's over a week now – and yet you haven't been to see her. To her it must seem as if the whole world has let her down. That's the look she gets in her eyes sometimes and I can't stand it. . . .' Tears suddenly blinded Adams. He blinked them back, cursing the treachery of the drink that was making him maudlin. 'She's never said a word about you, but I know what she's thinking. For God's sake go over and help her, Roy, before it's too late. You're the one person that can. You don't have to tell her what happened. . . .'

'Get out of here, you drunken sot,' Grenville said, with sudden viciousness.

Adams waved a plump hand in a half-protest, then let it fall to his side. 'Call me what you like, Roy, but do me this one favour.'

Grenville was on his feet now and moving threateningly forward. 'I said get out, damn you.'

Adams drew back one step, then stood his ground, dazed at his courage. As if in reward memory returned to him, bringing back some of his prepared arguments. He snatched gratefully at one. 'What about Bergman? You and he were good friends. How would he feel if he knew you'd never gone to see her?'

Grenville halted. The sound of his breathing came to Adams, harsh and uneven.

'You know what he'd want,' Adams went on with renewed hope. 'He'd want you to comfort his sister. Any man would.'

The purple and yellow bruises stood out evilly against the pale background of Grenville's face. His swollen lips sneered at Adams.

'You fool. What comfort can *I* bring her? I killed Bergman, remember?'

Adams caught the despair as well as the derision in Grenville's voice, and relief brought weakness to his legs. The worst was over: now he had a chance. He motioned to a chair and sank into it without opposition from Grenville.

'Roy; you've got to look at it differently.' As he spoke Adams realized how sober he had become. 'You were ordered to destroy that building. That alone excuses you from blame. . . .'

Contempt blazed in Grenville's eyes. 'Don't tell me that, Adams.'

'But it's true.'

'True be damned. If it were true there wouldn't be a guilty man in this war. Every Nazi who tortures his prisoners could be excused: every S.A. devil who throws children into gas-chambers could plead innocence. A man has a greater moral duty to himself than to the State, and you know it. I didn't kill Bergman because of an order, damn you.'

Adams wetted his dry lips. 'All right. But you did kill him to save him from torture. You can't deny that.'

Grenville's laugh was not pleasant to hear. 'And is that what you want me to tell Hilde – that he was being tortured? Or has the telegram already given her those little details?'

Adams was silent. Grenville jeered at him. 'You want me to go over and console her! I'm to tell her that everything's all right, that her brother didn't die in action as she thinks, but was put in a torture chamber where half a dozen sadists went to work on him. That we didn't like this at all in case he talked, and so I, being the squadron's best murderer, was sent out to finish him off. Well; is that what you want?'

The arguments Adams had prepared earlier had covered no more ground than this, and he felt defeat close at hand. And the intense hunger of Grenville's eyes made him miserably aware that it was not only the girl he was failing. . . .

'Get out, you fat fool,' Grenville suddenly gritted. 'Get out and leave me alone.'

In his desperation, Adams' words stumbled over themselves like a small child's running feet. 'I didn't want you to tell her anything of your part in his death. . . . But if you can't see her without doing it, then even that's better than not seeing her at all. Her brother's dead, but you're alive, Roy. You're the one thing she has left. . . . It'll be a shock for her to hear it, I know, but later on she'll be more proud of him than ever. And she'll understand why you did it and think even more of you too.'

'What a fool you are,' Grenville sneered.

'But can't you see – it's better for her to know the truth than to think the whole world has let her down. Her brother's loss she can understand now – she knows he is dead – but she will never understand why she has lost you. Why haven't you bothered to go over – you, the one person in the world who can comfort her? She'll wonder that for the rest of her life. It's enough to break the kid's faith in everything. Can't you see that?'

Grenville's face was very pale. 'Why should I matter so much to her?'

'Why? How can anybody answer that? Why do people care for one another – God knows why. But she's got you deep in her system and unless she knows why you're acting this way, it's going to ruin the kid. Think of her feelings' – Adams was shouting now – 'Damn it, if you'd ever been in love you wouldn't need telling all this. She doesn't know the job is coming off tomorrow night, but she must know it's coming off soon. She knows you might not come back from it, and yet the precious minutes are ticking by without her seeing you. . . . It's enough to turn her mind. Blast you; you've got to see her. If you don't, I'll tell her the whole story myself. I will; I mean it.'

Grenville's reply was not the vicious one Adams had expected. Low, with all anger gone, it caught him completely by surprise.

'There's something you don't know, Frank. When I first took Finn up with me, she thought I was exposing him to unnecessary danger and told me so. Now you're trying to tell me she'll forgive me for deliberately killing him. You're wrong. She'll get the shock of finding out the truth, she'll loathe me, and she'll discover what happened to Finn in the bargain. How is any of that going to help her?'

'Better loathe you and get you out of her system than go on fretting about you for the rest of her life,' Adams said, the sweat trickling down his face. 'But she won't loathe you. She'll understand. Go and find out, for God's sake.'

At his words Grenville's expression had suddenly changed. He stared at Adams for a long moment with an indefinable look in his eyes. Then, without speaking he eased his stiff shoulder into his tunic and picked up his cap.

'Are you going over?' Adams breathed.

Grenville turned back at the door, his lips twisting. 'Yes; I'll go and put things right. I don't like being a disease in anyone's system.' A second later the door slammed behind him.

Adams sank weakly back into the chair, not certain from Grenville's expression whether to feel relief or anxiety.

CHAPTER 26

Grenville waited in the hall while the innkeeper went upstairs to call her.

'Miss Bergman! There's Squadron-Leader Grenville to see you. . . .'

She came running breathlessly down the stairs, pausing on the bottom step. Her face was pale, and Grenville saw the glisten of crushed tears under her lashes. With an impatient movement of her hand, she brushed them away. She gave a smile, and the courage of it pierced him like a knife.

'Hello, Roy. How good it is to see you again.'

'Hello, Hilde. Sorry I've been so long in coming over.'

As he stepped forward, the shaded hall-light fell on his face, revealing its heavy bruises. She let out a low exclamation of concern.

'Your face – does it hurt you very much?'

He shook his head, glancing towards the sitting-room door. 'No; I'm all right now.'

Her face clouded as she followed his eyes. 'Valerie is in there – listening to a radio play. It will be difficult to talk. . . . Shall we go upstairs to my room? It will be quiet there.'

He did not want that, but could think of no suitable protest. In silence he followed her up the stairs and into her room. As he had feared, its atmosphere caught him at once. She had not lived long in the room, but it had already taken her personality for its own. It lay all around him, in the restful murmur of a clock, the graceful fold of a curtain, the white shoulder of a pillow. He felt trapped and afraid.

'I came to talk about Finn,' he muttered.'I should have come before, but somehow . . .'

'You had not fully recovered from your wounds,' she said quickly. Relief came into her eyes, and he realized she had already found an excuse for his behaviour.

'It wasn't that,' he protested, but she cut off his words with a fluttering gesture of her hand.

'There's no need to apologize. I quite understand. You were not fully recovered, and the news came as a shock to you. I had forgotten what good friends you and he were.'

There was a ring of self-condemnation in her voice. Grenville realized she would always find an excuse for him if an excuse could be found. This was what Adams had meant by saying he was deep in her system. That look in her eyes on coming down the stairs had been another symptom of it.

He knew the feeling himself. It was like having another life inside one, crying for the birth his raid had made impossible. Adams had been right: it must not be left to torture her throughout the years. One way or another it had to be killed. The truth would do that, but would also hurt her too deeply. There was another and better way. . . .

Her voice was like the sweet chiming of a clock heard through the grip of a nightmare.

'What is it, Roy? What are you thinking?'

She was standing no more than a yard from him, her eyes fixed with concern on his face. He noticed for the first time that she was wearing a simple black frock that unintentionally set off the whiteness of her skin and the bright gold of her hair. The faint perfume that always clung around her drifted towards him, evoking a thought-image as clear as the one given by his eyes. The one image superimposed on the other made her more real than reality.

'Why are you looking at me like that?' she asked again, uncertainly.

His mind answered her. Why? Because this is the last time I shall see you like this. In a few seconds the thing that makes your eyes warm when you look at me will be dead, and you will never be the same again, not to me. . . .

Another moment and he knew he could never find the strength to do it. He dragged his eyes from her and looked down at his watch.

'I haven't got long,' he muttered. 'I only dropped in for a few minutes.'

'You are going – so soon. . . ?'

He nodded, not meeting her eyes. 'I'm afraid I must. The boys are throwing a party in Highgate, and I've promised to take a friend of mine along. I'm late as it is – she's already been waiting over half-an-hour.' His voice was deliberate with meaning. 'It's as well we're old friends or there'd be trouble.'

She looked dazed, unable to understand. He went on quickly.

'She moved up here a couple of weeks ago. Got herself a room in Highgate.'

He saw the delayed action of the shock strike her now. Her words were as involuntary as a cry of pain.

'A girl! But I had no idea. . . . You have never spoken of her before.'

Grenville forced a sheepish grin, believing the bruised skin round his lips would split with the effort. 'I should have mentioned it, I suppose. Sorry if you got any wrong ideas.'

'But the things you said that day in the car. . . . You said you did not want anyone worrying about you. You made it sound – '

'I made it sound simpler than it was,' he broke in roughly.

Her voice had a dead sound. 'So when you said that after the war things might be different, you were talking of – ' She suddenly turned away, moving as if blinded. Her hand moved in the fluttering gesture he knew so well, then fell helplessly to her side. It was a few seconds before she turned back to face him. Her face appeared frozen with shock, but tears were falling down her cheeks like the beads from a broken necklace. She made no sound with them, and the silence was like a tightening cord round Grenville's temples. He had to speak to break it.

'After all, I've never pretended to be over-keen. You can't say that I have.'

Her eyes closed to hide her shame. 'That is true. But I misunderstood the reason. . . . I see now. . . . The fault has been mine, not yours.'

Grenville had been praying for anger, not forgiveness. He turned quickly to pick up his cap, hiding his face. He heard her voice again, still bewildered.

'But it is so hard to believe. . . . You have never been unkind before. Why have you chosen this time to tell me? Why not before, or . . . or even a little later? I would so much like to know that.'

Grenville knew now that there was no gentle way of killing anything. He lifted the knife and struck. 'Surely that's obvious enough. I didn't tell you before because it was quite pleasant and I was enjoying it. I'm telling you now because she has come here, and it has to end at once. That's why. Sorry.'

He dared not hold out his hand, dared not touch her. At the door he paused and turned back, with the excuse he was making certain of his murder. But his eyes failed him: he saw nothing but the white blur of her face and the misted brightness of her hair. Then he was outside, with the black fields and pitiless stars a part of the agony that racked him.

CHAPTER **27**

The briefing-room was packed to capacity. At one side of the table on the platform, a group of men were conferring quietly. Among them were Davies, Barrett and Grenville. The silence was aggravated by the shuffle of feet, the whispers of conversation, and the scratching of matches. In the centre of the table stood the contour model of the Svartfjord, covered with a cloth. Nervous eyes pulled away from it, examined the empty black-board alongside it, then wandered round the walls, which were covered with diagrams of German aircraft set in gunsights with the correct aiming deflections. Battle slogans were everywhere, giving such admonitions as: 'It's the One you don't see who gets You', 'Always watch the Hun in the Sun', 'Remember your Cockpit Drill' as well as the ubiquitous 'Careless Talk costs Lives'. From the ceiling dangled scale models of Focke-Wulfs, Dorniers, and Messerschmidtts as well as Allied aircraft, all of them turning uneasily in the rising smoke from over thirty cigarettes. Eyes wandered back to the covered model on the table. The tension could be felt, catching at the throat.

The group on the platform reached agreement, and Davies moved forward to face his young audience. The low mutters among the air crews ceased abruptly. There was a red spot on each of Davies's high cheekbones and a bright glint in his eyes. His sharp, high-pitched voice added to the tension.

'Well, chaps; here it is – the big show you've been waiting for. You've had a lousy time training for it – all this getting up before dawn and stoodging around in the dark over Scotland must have made you fed up to the back teeth. And your having to throw your bombs into a corrie in the side of a valley must have made it seem an even bigger muck-up. Well; now I'm going to try to fit all the pieces together. Here we go. . . .'

Davies stepped back alongside the covered model of the Svartfjord. 'In a few minutes I'm going to let you all come up here to take a closer look at this thing. But for the moment you'll have to be content with a long-range view while I explain what it's all about.'

He pulled the cloth away. The young faces before him craned forward, both curious and apprehensive. Someone coughed loudly, relieving his tension. Davies picked up a pointer.

'This is the scale model of a certain fjord in Norway. It's very deep and narrow, over 20 miles long, and ends as a *cul-de-sac* at its eastern end. It is this end, the far one, that we're chiefly concerned with. A high waterfall drops down here and gives power to a hydro-electric plant at the bottom of the fjord. Built around this plant is another building the Germans have put up, a massive affair with walls nearly as thick as U-boat pens. This is our target. Keep it in mind while I explain the rest of the scenery.'

His pointer moved to a mountain on the side of the fjord, directly alongside the hydro-electric plant. 'This mountain is called the Trollfjell. It rises steeply to over 2,500 feet, retreats in to a corrie a couple of hundred feet deep. Then bulges out again into a massive, overhanging summit. On this summit is a glacier called the Trollisen. The whole thing resembles a man's chest, neck, and head. Like this. . . .'

Davies made a quick sketch on the blackboard. 'Here you are! The chest is the side of the fjord, the neck the corrie, and the head the overhanging summit. Add the glacier on the top and that gives you a crop of white hair. That's how the mountain and glacier got their names – Troll is a kind of Norwegian gremlin.' Davies paused, giving a puckish smile that made him look more than ever like a gremlin himself. 'This job gives you a chance to get your own back on one of the little beggars.'

He moved forward to the front of the platform again. 'Later on you'll be given all your wireless, navigational and bombing gen in detail, and after that Squadron-Leader Grenville will give you his personal orders. But I'm going to explain the job to you first so you know all the whys and wherefores, and know what is expected of you. So listen carefully.

'Tomorrow morning you are going to take off before dawn just as you have been doing throughout your training. You're even going to fly north on the same track for ten minutes. After that you start playing a different game. Instead of going to Scotland, you're going to Norway, and instead of carrying dummies, you'll each have a special bomb apiece in your bomb bays. These bombs arrived five minutes ago and will be loaded straight on to your kites.

'Right – you're on your way and scheduled to reach the mouth of the fjord at 06.45 hours, from now on known as Z hour. Meanwhile at Z hour minus thirty, a very brave band of Norwegian patriots will be clearing the way for you.' Davies went on to explain the task of the underground forces. 'If all goes well they will have the guns out of action by the time you arrive. You fly straight in and make for the other end of the fjord. Once there the fun starts.

'I don't think I need stress by this time that you don't drop your bombs on the target. As I've told you, it has massive walls and a very thick roof. You're flying low, and it would be impossible to achieve sufficient penetration to do any damage even if your bombs were designed for that sort of job, which they are not. Instead, we have quite a different scheme. . . .'

Davies went back to the blackboard and made another sketch. 'As you've heard, this summit overhangs the fjord. Naturally, before the Germans built their project, they sent geologists up to check on it. Their reports were that it was safe enough and there were no risks of accidents. That was enough for the Germans –

they needed this site badly because of the hydro-electric plant. So the project was built – a top priority job. Now I'm not allowed to tell you much, but I can say this. As you know, German scientists are working just as hard as our own to discover new weapons, and, like ourselves, hope to find something that will end the war quickly. Well, in this building, using some of the energy and by-products of the hydro-electric plant alongside, the Germans are on to something big. Something so big, in fact, that it might have a far-reaching effect on the outcome of the war if it isn't destroyed.'

Davies's sharp eyes travelled slowly round the arc of breathless crews, letting the point sink home. His voice became brisk once more. 'All right. Back to the old gremlin's head again. The German geologists passed it as safe, but we heard an interesting story through Intelligence channels. A Norwegian geologist, who examined it before the hydro-electric plant was built, says there is a fissure at the back of it. Normally this fissure is completely covered by snow and ice, but every summer the ice retreats a little, and apparently the summer he made his examination was an exceptionally warm one. He was able to study the fissure in detail and found that the perennial dripping of water had hollowed it out inside to a considerable depth. However, after very careful study, it was decided there was no danger of the overhang falling through natural causes, and the Norwegians went on to build their hydro-electric plant.'

Davies eyed the puzzled faces before him with grim amusement. 'I know! You're all wonderng what the devil all this geology has to do with your prang tomorrow. The answer to that is everything! Because you're going to use this knowledge to chop off old Trollfjell's head and drop it right on top of the target.'

There was a sudden buzz of amazement among the pilots and observers. Davies gave them a few moments to recover before holding up his hand.

'Here is a non-scientific explanation. You know the way you've been dropping – a better word is hurling – your bombs into a corrie in the side of a valley. Well, tomorrow morning you're going to hurl these special bombs in to the corrie under old Trollfjell's head. These bombs have been specially designed to give maximum blast effect, or, to put it another way, to start severe shock waves.

'Now shock waves are greatly magnified in effect when they enter solids like earth or rock – they become tremendously destructive. Normally the blast from a surface bomb goes upwards into the air where it is wasted. But in this case the shock waves from your bombs will go upwards into this overhang, and shiver up to the fissure like a seismic disturbance.

'Our scientists haven't been able to calculate exactly how many bombs it will take, but they are confident that a succession of explosions will fracture that fissure more and more until the front part of the overhang comes crashing down. To put it inaccurately but graphically, the shock punch from your bombs will throw old Trollfjell's head backwards, his neck will snap like a carrot, and another redskin will bite the dust. . . .'

The excitement among the crews was intense now. Davies held up his hand again for silence. 'You'll guess now that everything has been most carefully worked out. The date, for example, is most important. At this time in May the snow and ice on the summit is ideal for an avalanche. It is beginning to thaw, but still has lost nothing of its mass and weight. If part of the overhang goes, the ice and snow goes with it, and that'll be curtains for anything in the fjord below.'

He laid down his chalk and dusted his hands. 'Just to tuck in all the loose ends, I'll add that this scheme has the full approval of the Norwegian Government. The loss of the power plant will be a serious one to them, but the alternative is too grim to consider. Right – now you'd all better come up and take a closer look at your gremlin.'

Pilots and observers clustered round the contour model, taking notes and drawing sketches. When all were satisfied Davies waved them back into their seats. 'All right – now for the technical details. Don't miss anything. We can't afford a single boob.'

Detailed instructions were given by the Senior Signals Officer, the Navigational Officer and the Armament Officer, the crews again making careful notes. Barrett made a short address. Then they were all taken into the Operations Room, where photographs of the fjord were projected on to a screen. Maps were scrutinized and E.T.A.'s chalked up on a blackboard. Before the crews returned to the Briefing Room Adams presented each observer with his wallet, making him check that it contained the full complement of maps and charts.

It was well over an hour before Grenville himself came to the front of the platform. Immediately there was a subtle change in the atmosphere. Previously an onlooker might have gained the impression that the crews had given their attention more to the duties and office of the speakers than to the speakers themselves. Now the man facing them was their battle leader: the pilot who was always the first to fly into danger, the pilot more accomplished than themselves, the pilot on whose judgement their lives depended. Their attention now was born of both a personal and a professional respect.

Grenville's cultured, if forceful, voice was at odd variance with his battered appearance. If the usual touch of devil-may-care humour he used before an operation was less marked this evening, none of his listeners thought his tone unfitting to the occasion.

'We shall be using our full strength of fifteen Mosquitoes and will fly in battle formation, sections of three, line abreast. It shouldn't be difficult to keep visual contact because the Met. forecast is good, and, in case you don't know, the sky in those latitudes is always luminous at this time of the year.

'The essence of this raid is strategy and surprise. For that reason it is not considered expedient to have a fighter escort on the way out. Coming back is a different matter and, as you have already been told, we have a rendezvous with long-range Spitfires over the sea.

'All signals on the way out are to be visual only – there must be strict R/T silence. Keep close contact until I fire one green Very light. That means you fall back in line astern. I shall make that signal just before we enter the fjord and we shall enter it at forty second intervals. The reason is that your bombs will have eleven seconds delays – if you make your attacks too soon after the other bloke you might find the mountain falling on top of you. So remember – forty seconds intervals!

'Watch out near the mouth of the Svartfjord. There's an enemy naval base on the island of Utvik, and I don't want any fool going close to have a look what those funny-looking trees are. They aren't trees – they're 88 mms., so keep away!

'We're not expecting too much flak, but if there are any posts still in enemy hands, the Green sections from each flight will engage them. Watch out for the target itself – it might pack a few guns on its roof and of course the patriots won't be able to silence them.

'When you drop your bomb, remember all you have practised. Get as far inside the corrie and as much underneath the overhang as you can – we want to give it the maximum shock possible. Once you've dropped your bomb, beat it straight out of the east end of the fjord or you'll clutter up air space, and that's one of the things we shall be short of.

'When you come out of the fjord, keep a sharp look out for enemy fighters. We're hoping to have finished before they arrive, but you never know. If they are there, form a defensive circle directly south of the fjord. If they aren't, head straight for the kelk factory on the island south of Utvik. You shouldn't be able to miss it – the Intelligence Boys say it has a smoking chimney and stands out white against the black rocks. We shall reform over it.

'The Code word I shall send back to base when old Trollfjell's head falls will be 'sneeze'. When you hear that you can start getting ready for a party.

'Every navigator will keep an individual log so that he can bring his plane home alone if necessary, and everyone will synchronize his watch before take-off. The squadron call sign will be Vesuvius and the station call-sign Dudley. Any questions?'

There were three. Grenville answered them, then threw a glance at Davies. The slow shake of the Air Commodore's head said everything. Nothing more could be done now but send them out and pray. All that had gone before, the courage of Bergman and his men in discovering the building, their sufferings, the frantic efforts to discover a way of destroying it, the scheming, planning, designing, the race against time: all had led to this. A single squadron; a handful of boys. More depended on their skill and courage than one dared consider.

Grenville turned back to his men, his voice curt. 'There is just one more thing. Some brave men have already died in making this raid possible. For their sakes, and for more than their sakes, it has to succeed. We've been specially chosen to do it, and that means, if it is humanly possible, we shall do it.' His uncompromising eyes travelled slowly round the arc of hushed men. 'We pull it off whatever happens. Is that quite clear?'

Nods, a pause, then Grenville's voice again on a more cheerful note. 'Right, chaps; that's all. Off you go to bed. You'll be called at 03.30 hours sharp. Good luck.'

CHAPTER 28

It was cold in the Operations Room the following morning, and no amount of attention could coax any heat from the radiators. Nevertheless, none of the four waiting men could pull himself away to make enquiries about the heating plant. They were scattered all over the room. Adams was sitting huddled in a chair near to one of the dead radiators, Davies was at the foot of the huge operational map that almost covered one wall, the Brigadier was seated at the end of the long table, and Marsden, the Chief Signals Officer, with headphones at his ears and a message-pad before him, was hunched over a small table at the opposite side of the room.

Adams shivered and shrugged himself deeper into his greatcoat. It seemed to be growing colder, and the bluish-white light from the fluorescent tubes did nothing to improve matters. Adams tried to close his weary eyes but they opened immediately as if on springs. The stark, shimmering light, merciless to his fatigue, gave the room and its occupants a touch of unreality. The Brigadier looked like a pale waxen statue as he stared unblinkingly at Marsden. He was wearing no greatcoat, but the intensity of his concentration appeared to make him unaware of physical discomfort. In complete contrast Davies, sitting under the huge map on which had been pencilled the track lines of the squadron, was fidgeting about like a schoolboy in church. He too was watching Marsden, whose earphones and transmitter key were connected to Signals. Marsden had been listening in for over ninety minutes, but as yet no message had come through.

Another ten minutes passed by. In the silence the tapping of Davies' fingers on the arm of his chair was like a monotonous jungle drum. Adams would have shouted at him to stop if one shouted such things at Air Commodores. As it was he hunched down farther in his seat and tried again to close his eyes.

A sudden metallic crackle sounded in the earphones, amplified by the silent room. All four men jerked upright as if pulled by the same string. The crackle grew louder, then died away. Marsden stared round apologetically. 'Static,' he muttered, lowering his head again.

Davies swore. Another minute, then he jumped to his feet. 'It's confounded cold,' he said, looking around for agreement. No one answered, leaving Adams with an immediate sense of guilt. The Signals Officer wasn't expected to reply, the Brigadier was above coercion – didn't that leave him with the baby? But it was too late to answer now. Davies frowned peevishly, began pacing up and down in front of the map, and Adams suppressed a groan. This was going to be worse than the chair tapping.

At the end of his tenth oscillation, Davies halted and turned his sharp, resentful eyes on Adams. 'I wonder how Barrett is getting on.'

The testiness in his voice told Adams this was his last chance. 'Yes; I wonder,' he muttered.

Davies did not appear to notice the inadequacy of his reply. 'I shouldn't have been fool enough to let him go,' he said resentfully. 'But he'd worked himself a pretty cast-iron case.'

In spite of the reserve crews and the replacements that had been rushed to the squadron after the disaster at Bergen, 633 had found itself one trained pilot short. As Davies had previously said he wanted every serviceable plane in the air, this had been Barrett's chance. He had offered to fly without a command; and when Davies had reminded him about his weakened chest, he had pointed out that the raid was to be carried out at low-level throughout, which should mean no undue strain on him. Davies had had his doubts, but in the circumstances had felt forced to agree. Now he was regretting his decision.

'The idiot will probably go and kill himself. He'll probably ram his kite into the side of the mountain.'

Adams was inclined to agree, but knew better than to say so. He nodded uncomfortably, shuffling in his chair to avoid Davies's stare.

Davies looked at his watch, then up at the wall map. 'If everything's going all right, they should be coming up to the coast in less than fifteen minutes. Hear that, Marsden?'

The Signals Officer turned his head briefly and nodded. The Brigadier showed signs of life. He looked down at his own watch, then took a handkerchief from his pocket and dabbed at his moustache with meticulous care. Adams tried to visualize the scene out there – the dawn sky and sea, the roar of lifting engines, the approaching enemy coast; but his imagination, usually so reliable, refused to help him this morning. The blue-white glare of the fluorescent lamps, the waiting figures, the tense, anxious *safety* of the room: he could not escape from any of it. He felt betrayed and his sense of inferiority deepened.

The telephone alongside Marsden gave a sudden buzz, an urgent sound that made Adams jump. A second later the Brigadier was at the table, taking the receiver from Marsden. As he leaned forward to take the message, a premonition of disaster shot through Adams like the stab from a decayed tooth.

'Hello,' the Brigadier called. 'Hedgerow speaking. . . .' Adams guessed this was a password. 'Hello, Graham; what is it? What's that. . . .' The Brigadier's clipped voice was suddenly tense, shocked. In the hush the metallic rasp of the voice on the phone could be heard clearly. The words were not distinct but their urgency was unmistakable.

Davies drew near, his bright eyes and jerky movements reminding Adams, even at that moment, of a nervous cockerel. The Brigadier let out a sudden gasp of dismay, an event of such significance that Davies turned pale. Adams jumped to his feet, waiting anxiously alongside the Air Commodore.

The Brigadier dropped the receiver and turned towards Davies. His face was grey and drawn, with a look about his eyes that shocked the others.

141

'Get in touch with Grenville at once! Tell him to turn back. Quickly! There's no time to lose.'

Davies started. 'Why? What's happened?'

It was clearly an effort for the Brigadier to speak. 'We've just had a message from one of our Norwegian agents over there. He was wounded, but managed to escape and reach his transmitter. . . .'

Davies's voice was suddenly shrill. 'Don't tell me they haven't managed to capture the flak posts!'

The Brigadier shook his head heavily. 'Worse than that, I'm afraid. They haven't even had the chance to try. The Gestapo rounded up every man during the night.'

Davies stared at the Brigadier in horror. 'Rounded them up! But how? How could they know. . . ?' His voice trailed off as he remembered.

'Torture will get anything from a man if he suffers it long enough,' the Brigadier said wearily. 'We've always known that. It wasn't Bergman who talked – it was Ericson, the poor devil they captured later that day. The Gestapo must have passed on the news before Grenville destroyed the place. . . .' His voice sharpened. 'Hurry, man, and warn him. Can't you see, the whole thing is a trap. After failing in their attack on your airfield, they've deliberately delayed capturing the patriots until the last minute. If it wasn't for this message the squadron would fly into a death trap.'

'My God, you're right,' Davies muttered. He nodded to Marsden, who immediately sent out the Station call sign to the squadron. While they were waiting for a reply, Davies turned back to the Brigadier.

'There'll be everything waiting for them – fighters, the lot. For all we know they might be among them now. We can't receive their R/T at this range.'

The Brigadier had himself under control again. 'I don't think that's likely, not yet. Remember – they don't know we have been warned. I think they will let the squadron fly right into the fjord before showing their hand. Once they're inside Jerry can close the net and they haven't a chance.'

Davies shuddered at the mental picture of the Mosquitoes trapped among a hundred guns. The buzz of morse in Marsden's earphones came as a welcome relief. It was Grenville, acknowledging their call.

'Thank God,' Davies muttered, snatching a pencil from Adams' pocket. 'Here, send this.' He wrote on the pad. *Dudley calling. Patriots captured. Guns still in enemy hands. Return to base immediately.*

Marsden tapped out the message.

'Send it again,' Davies ordered, taking no chances.

Marsden obeyed, the transmitter key jerking up and down under his practised fingers.

There was a pause of perhaps fifteen seconds, then Marsden's earphones buzzed again. Three pairs of eyes followed his pencil as it traced out words on the pad.

Vesuvius leader calling. Request permission to attack alone.

Adams felt sick. Davies turned towards the Brigadier, his eyes unnaturally bright. 'Grenville's offering to go in alone. What shall I tell him?'

For a moment a wild flicker of hope had sprung into the Brigadier's eyes. It died as he shook his head. 'No; it would be suicide. And even if he got through it's most unlikely one bomb would bring it down. Tell him to come back.'

One bomb useless, Davies wrote on the pad. *Return to base, Dudley.*

Silence followed this transmission. All four men looked at one another uneasily. 'What's happened now?' Davies muttered. 'Don't say the Focke Wulfs have got them.' He was just about to order Marsden to transmit again when the earphones were buzzing afresh. Words grew on the pad.

Vesuvius leader here. Have called for volunteers. Squadron will go in with me. Believe we have chance. Request permission. . . .

Nothing, not even the magnitude of the disaster, could keep the glowing pride from Davies's voice now. 'They've all volunteered to go in with him, sir – every man jack of 'em. What do you want now?'

Adams' imagination came back when he wanted it least. Mosquitoes entering that black fjord . . . running the gauntlet of a hundred guns that could weave an unbreakable web of steel from wall to wall . . . the vision brought the sweat out of him, cold though the morning was. He wanted to shout his protests to the Brigadier: instead he stared at him mutely, pleading with his eyes.

The Brigadier, overcome by emotion at the news, had swung abruptly away. The few words he spoke, when he could speak at all, were the outward expression of the conflict raging inside him.

'There'll never be another chance! After this they'll make it impossible to get near the place. And it's so desperately important. . . .'

So are those lives, Adams wanted to shout. You can't send them in there now. It's murder. Plain bloody murder. . . .

It was full thirty seconds before the Brigadier faced them again. 'If they have volunteered, then I must say yes.' He paused, then went on quietly: 'I'm very sorry – please believe that.'

He walked over to the long table and stood stiffly before it, his back towards them. Davies's voice had a dry, proud sob in it as he looked down at Marsden.

Permission granted. God bless you all. Dudley.

God help you, you mean, Adams thought bitterly.

143

CHAPTER 29

The Mosquitoes were riding as tight as a troup of horsemen, stirrup to stirrup, nose to tail. Every man was aware of an odd kinship between himself and his machine that morning. The powerful engines seemed to merge their vitality into his own, the speeding wings to be an extension of his young, powerful arms. It was a madly intoxicating feeling.

Even Grenville felt it, and his mind, coldly analytical, dissected the reasons. One was the morning. White columns of cumulus towering into a blue sky ... sea-washed islands with patches of dazzling green ... grey-blue sea streaming under their wings. Spring always had the magic quality that made a man feel godlike.

There were other factors bound up in it too. One of them he had often felt before, in the spring before a raid. To walk out to one's plane with the smell of spring in one's nostrils and the knowledge that impossibly soon one would be flying into a sky stinking of death – to do that was to know the real bitter-sweetness of life.

Then there was the spirit of sacrifice. It gave men a feeling of unity and purpose that was near ecstasy. It might well be the greatest ecstasy a man could experience. The trouble was that to sustain it one had to fight shoulder to shoulder with one's comrades, or it had a way of betraying one and letting in the fear of death. And in the air one had always to fight alone.

'Five minutes more to the coast, sir. And Utvik at two o'clock.'

Grenville's mind returned from the abstract. That was Phillips, his new observer, playing safe. He glanced at him briefly. Phillips had a sallow complexion, a pencil-thin moustache, and dark, intense eyes. He looked the keen, earnest type. He wasn't new to operational flying, of course, or he would not have been sent to them at this time, but he'd had little training for this job. Grenville had managed to take him three times up to Scotland, and that was all. He must be feeling more than nervous, particularly after the news from base. ... At the same time Grenville was glad Hoppy was tucked away safely in hospital.

He took a long, careful look at the dazzling white clouds ahead, but could see nothing. They'd be up there, all right, waiting for the trap to close before coming down. His job was to keep them there as long as he could.

Telling Phillips to keep his eyes open, Grenville swung nearer the rocky island of Utvik. He passed close enough to catch a glimpse of a harbour, the camouflaged shapes of oil tanks, and a couple of destroyers, but no flak opposed them as they swept by. His lips pressed tightly together. No doubt now that the trap was laid.

He swung five degrees to port and the high mountains flanking the Svartfjord lay dead ahead. He fired a Verey light and his crews began falling back in line astern as if preparing to enter the fjord. He had given them their new orders during the last ten minutes – enemy R/T would have picked them up, of course, but he was hoping there had been no time to put out a general alarm. If the Focke Wulfs received advance warning of their intentions, they wouldn't have a chance.

As he watched the rapidly approaching mountains, a vision of the waiting gun crews came to him. They had everything in that fjord: batteries of 20 mm. in both double and quadruple mountings, at least three dozen 37 mms., an unknown number of 88 mms. near the target, and all with predictors. . . . The gun muzzles would be swinging about like the heads of waiting cobras as the Mosquitoes drew nearer the trap.

Phillips stabbed a finger upwards. Fearful that the Focke Wulfs had been told this new plan and were making a swift counter attack, Grenville glanced upwards, only to see a black speck dodging back into the towering cumulus north of the Svartfjord. He nodded his relief. Better they were hiding on that side than the south, although there might be more than one squadron up there. . . .

The entrance of the Svartfjord was taking detailed shape now, the grim, soaring rocks, the dense clumps of birch, the seagulls cluttered around some object in the water. . . . Beyond the entrance he could see the twisting, shadowy fjord beckoning them in.

Out of the sun now, into the shadow of the mountains, the entrance only 200 yards away. . . . A seagull smacked right into his windscreen, sliding off in a mass of blood and feathers. A second more, the arms of the fjord were almost around him – then Grenville suddenly flung his Mosquito into a tight, ninety-degree turn. The right flank of the fjord reeled under his vertical port wing, not fifty yards away. Another ninety degree turn a few seconds later, to port this time, and the line of Mosquitoes were now speeding inland parallel to the fjord, with its own flanking mountains protecting them.

Grenville knew the alarm would be up now. The fox had dodged the trap: now the hound would come baying down. But as yet he could not see the 190's; the mountains on either side hid them from view.

Birch, patches of scrub, rocks, flashed beneath them. They were in a wide valley. A stream ran under them for half a mile, its clear water reflecting back their racing shadows. A bridge shot by, a white-painted house, a clump of fruit trees laden with blossom. . . . Then the land began rising again, black rocks showing through the grass, patches of snow appearing. . . .

Grenville's eyes were intent upon the steep mountain range on his left, the one flanking the Svartfjord. The responsibility made his whole body clammy with sweat. One mistake on his part now and the mission was a hopeless failure. It would fail anyway, he reminded himself, without the X factor, luck. . . .

He ordered the planes behind him to throttle back and increase further the distance between themselves. He forced his memory alert as his eyes probed the unfolding mountain range. A minute gone, a minute and a half. . . . Nearly half the range covered and still no break in it. Had he missed it? He fought back panic, gritting his teeth. The ground below was shelving steeply upwards now, there were thick patches of snow on the mountain-tops above him. Two minutes . . . two minutes and a quarter . . . the Focke Wulfs were now overdue. Where was it?

Then he caught sight of the blacker rift among the early morning shadows. His voice snapped out over the R/T.

'Attention, all Vesuvius aircraft. Follow me at twenty seconds intervals. Repeat time alteration – *twenty* seconds! Notify me the moment you enter the main fjord. Green Sections one and two go over and attack flak posts. Going in now. . . .'

He banked steeply, saw the massive rocks leaping towards him, and for one ghastly moment though he had made a mistake. Then, with a deafening roar, the walls of the gorge closed around the shuddering plane.

It was a little easier this time than the last because now the gorge was falling away from him. He shot over the waterfall into which the Focke Wulf had crashed and plunged on, followed by the rushing water. The noise of his engines, reverberating from the steep walls of rock, made the Mosquito tremble. Trees and bushes, growing precariously from crevices, reached out and seemed to touch his wingtips.

Relaxing for a few seconds, Grenville reviewed his plan while his body flew the plane instinctively. The six members of his Green Sections, who had jettisoned their bombs to make their planes more manoeuvreable, should emerge over the fjord at approximately the same time as he entered it. Their job was to harass the guns, to make things a little easier for the squadron following behind. They would provide only a slight diversion: Grenville had no illusions regarding the nightmare ahead. By entering the fjord *via* the gorge they had avoided Innvik and twelve miles of the fjord, which meant they had by-passed perhaps half of the waiting guns. Theoretically that doubled their chances. But a devil voice in his mind reminded him that double zero was still nought. . . .

The thoughts blazed in his mind with the clarity and suddenness of a photo-flash. Then they changed, fixing themselves on Phillips again. Poor devil; what an introduction to a new squadron! Wonder what he was thinking. . . .

The gorge widened, then quite suddenly fell away, its stream plunging a sheer 700 feet to the bottom of the Svartfjord.

The sensation was like walking over a cliff edge. Instinctively Phillips gasped and drew back. Grenville banked steeply, gave his engines full boost, and waited for the inferno to begin. . . .

In the split-second before the gun crews recovered from their surprise, he had an unmolested view of the Svartfjord from the inside. Here, barely eight miles from its eastern end, it was a grim and savage place. From the black water below that looked like oil, the mountains shelved steeply upwards, their lower slopes covered in birch and scrub, their upper slopes rising as sheer as the walls of some enormous prison. Impressions registered themselves indelibly on Grenville's mind in that final moment before hell broke loose. The grey clefts among the black rocks caused by melting snow . . . the rock-falls that had left inverted funnels of scree . . . the wisps of snow in crevices . . . the golden ledge of sunlight far above . . . a waterfall up there, bursting into a rainbow. . . .

Then it came. A huge eye suddenly winked from the shadowy mountainside and a glowing chain of shells came swirling towards them. Two more guns opened out on the opposite side of the fjord, then one from above. A line of red-cored white puffs burst dead ahead, making both men flinch back. A vicious explosion made the Mosquito rear like a frightened horse.

Now every gun within range had opened out, vieing with one another for the kill; 20 mm parabolas made dazzling white bridges under which the Mosquito tried to dive. Tracer squirted out from clumps of trees and from rocky eyries, lacing the fjord with a deadly net of steel. Shells came reaching out, slowly at first, then with diabolical speed, clawing for their eyes. A succession of black explosions rocked the Mosquito, and shrapnel gashed her port wing; 37 mm now, trying to bracket her. . . .

Grenville had never seen flak like this before. Thank God his Green sections were up there, ready to attack. If only there was an escort to help them. . . . He spoke into his microphone.

'Vesuvius leader calling Green sections. Attack now. Go.'

The distraction they caused could not help him. They could not pin-point the guns until they opened fire on him, and before they could make their attack he would be either past or shot down. But it should afford some relief to those behind. His earphones crackled a moment later.

'M Mother calling, Skipper. Am in fjord now.'

That was Milner, twenty seconds behind him. One half of Grenville's mind was on his mission, checking, calculating, deducing: the other half was engrossed with the business of keeping alive. A massive rock face, black-bearded with trees, thrust itself at him from out of the smoke. He hugged it closely, trying to find cover from the flak, and nearly impaled himself on a double-pronged fork of tracer that stabbed upwards from a clump of trees. He saw the shuddering flashes open up and instinctively slammed his stick forward, kicking the rudder bar at the same time. The Mosquito skidded away, a whiplash of steel snapping two feet above its fuselage. The twin barrels swung down viciously, but Grenville had banked into the cliff again and his speed carried him to safety behind a rock shoulder.

Sweat poured into his eyes, almost blinding him. That was one flak post that had to be destroyed. . . . He gave orders to his Green sections, inwardly cursing the shakiness of his voice.

He found himself counting and realized that some cell of his mind had been doing so ever since hearing Milner enter the fjord. Twenty seconds then . . . now thirty-one, thirty-two, thirty-three. . . . In distance covered about two and a half miles. At least five more to the target.

The lichen-stained rocky walls of the fjord streamed by, their shadows lit up by the rapid flashes of automatic guns. Another mountain spur deflected the fjord from its course. Grenville took this one wide, kicking his rudder bar left and right as he went by. The fire this time came from two posts on the rock face above them. Dazzled by the tracer, Grenville and Phillips crouched down. Coloured lights flashed by the perspex windshield, deadly white puffs cast a hail of shrapnel in all directions. There was a sharp metallic crack, a jerk, and the smell of burnt rubber and cordite. A hollow voice echoed round Grenville's mind as if his skull were a cavern. This is it! Here it comes. . . !

But miraculously they were past and still alive. The fjord widened as the spur fell behind them and the fury of the flak lessened for a moment.

'F Freddy calling, Skipper. Have just entered fjord.'

That was his number 3, Ayliffe. He listened again to the monotonous voice still counting in his mind. Only forty-five seconds since he had entered hell! He glanced back. The fjord appeared blocked with an impenetrable curtain of smoke trails and bursting shells. Six lines of tracer were converging on an invisible point, probably Milner. Nearer, looking frail and tiny against the massive rocks, a Mosquito was diving on a flak post with all four guns ablaze. Far above he saw a black speck soaring over the jagged rim of the fjord – either another of his Mosquitoes or a Focke Wulf, he did not know which. His lips drew back painfully as he remembered the Focke Wulfs. They would not venture into this hell of flame and shrapnel, but they would be waiting up there to pick off any survivors. They were a problem to which he had found no answer. But they could wait: they were a full minute away.

As his Number 4 announced his successful entry into the fjord, the mountains closed in. A row of flashes appeared above an approaching treeline. God; how many guns were there in this place. . . ? Grenville thew a sidelong glance at Phillips. The observer's sallow face was shiny with sweat and a white spot of saliva hung at one corner of his mouth. He was sitting with his knees bunched up and his body strained forward as if he were in an electric chair. He caught Grenville's eyes and tried to smile. The poor devil . . . sitting there helpless . . . waiting for it. What a filthy job!

The fjord straightened out again, and at last Grenville could see Trollfjell. It was at eleven o'clock, a mountain that from this angle looked oddly like a man, with a woolly chest of trees, a gaunt grey neck and high above a massive bulging head with a cap of ice. Alongside it, at the extreme end of the fjord, was the high waterfall that fed power into the hydro-electric plant below, and built round this plant was the huge concrete building that was their target. On the banks of the fjord, half-hidden by birch and firs, were dozens of small huts which Grenville guessed to be living quarters.

But there was no time for curiosity. At this last line of defence the flak posts were more numerous than ever, and their gunners no longer exultant but desperate. The tiger had broken through its trap and its prize lay dead ahead. The entire area around the building lit up with the flash of guns, and their stunning thunder brought minor avalanches down from the surrounding heights. Luminous balls of tracer criss-crossed the sky around the weaving plane, the coloured glow from their shells reflecting back from the dark water below. The Mosquito shuddered and rocked like a cockleshell caught in a typhoon.

Grenville heard his Number 5 calling, but now his whole attention was focused on the mountain that was leaping forward at nearly five miles a minute. It loomed nearer, crushingly near – so near that he could see the flak shells hitting it and sending rock splinters flying like shrapnel.

Phillips had opened his bomb doors and he could feel them quivering in the air-flow. The red light on his bomb distributor panel was glowing, and Phillips had fused the bomb. Air-speed was right, everything was ready. . . .

The Mosquito flashed into the rock-strewn corrie. Below it were the wooded slopes that led down to the water, above it was the massive overhang with its millions of tons of rock and ice. Oblivious now of the raging flak, Grenville pin-pointed his aiming mark – a huge boulder where the neck curved outwards. He watched the red paint-mark on his port nacelle, speaking slowly into his inter-com.

'Coming up now . . . easy . . . easy.' The Mosquito was on her side now, her wings vertical with the cliff. The red mark was almost in line with the boulder. 'Ready . . . ready. . . .' With all his strength Grenville pulled the Mosquito away. 'Now!' he shouted, and Phillips pressed the bomb release.

CHAPTER 30

The Mosquito shot away as if ricocheting from the rocks. The huge bomb, re-leased in the steep turn, catapulted away to crash among the debris of loose rocks at the foot of the overhang.

Grenville felt himself rammed into his seat by the g. Invisible fingers clawed at his eyes and cheeks, and for a few seconds everything turned grey before him. Then he found himself shooting across the fjord like a rocket with the vengeful flak following him. The imperturbable voice in his mind was counting again. Three . . . four . . . five. . . . He pulled back on the stick, going into a steep climb-ing turn that lifted him towards the blue sky above.

Six . . . seven . . . eight. . . . The flak was following him up. A blinding flash burst dead ahead, and long gashes appeared near the port wing root. Not a second later another shell burst in the nose, shrapnel ripping through pneumatic pipes and electric cables. The cockpit filled with the stink of cordite and fumes from the escaping hydraulic fluid. Air screamed through the shattered nose, adding a banshee wail to the sound of the engines.

Nine . . . ten. . . . The Mosquito suddenly burst out into the clean morning sunlight. Flak still followed it like lava being tossed up from the bowels of a volcano. Grenville should have taken cover over the rim of the ridge, but instead he turned back. Eleven . . . his mind chanted.

Half a second later the bomb went off. Every detail below became etched in brilliant light. The volcanic appearance of the fjord was increased by the cloud of stones and rubble thrown upwards by the tremendous explosion. The Mosquito reared and almost turned over in the blast. Still dazed from the flak, Grenville fought the controls, his eyes on Trollfjell.

But the massive overhang had not moved, although small falls of rock and ice were still sprinkling from it. Milner came over the radio. 'Am going in now, Skipper.'

Twenty seconds was a perilous margin between attacks. Grenville had known it, but because of the waiting Focke-Wulfs it had been imperative to get the planes into the fjord as quickly as possible. He had gambled on the mountain spurs protecting the attacking plane from the explosion ahead and it seemed he had been right. Of course, there was danger from rock falls, but that was nothing compared with the flak.

From above Milner's tiny Mosquito looked like a dragonfly being pierced by a dozen brightly-coloured pins. Somehow it got through and vanished for a breathless moment into the deep shadows under Trollfjell. Then it came shooting out and began corkscrewing upwards.

'O.K., Skipper. Bomb gone.'

Grenville was just congratulating Milner when a row of eight black bursts cut the climbing Mosquito in two. Her right wing tore off at the root, fluttering away like a leaf. The asymmetrical fuselage spun down, trailing black smoke and a shred of flame from its port engine. The flame lengthened, brightened, there was a sudden brilliant flash, then nothing but a glowing ball of fire that dropped like a plummet into the dark mass of trees below.

As if in revenge, the bomb Milner had planted burst two seconds later. This time a heavy sheet of snow cascaded from the summit and fell among the shrubs on its lower slopes. But the massive head of Trollfjell still towered over the smoke and falling debris.

A medley of shouts over the R/T brought Grenville's stunned mind back to the present.

'Focke Wulfs at eight o'clock. . . !'

'Look out, Green two! Break port!'

Grenville realized the Focke Wulfs were among his Green sections and remembered his own danger. His tight turn came just in time – red tracer snapping by his port wing-tip. A green and black Focke Wulf dived by: he was about to attack it in turn when he remembered his own orders. Every plane that survived the attack on the mountain had to go back to help the others through. As another 190 came snarling at him, he dived away into the shadows of the fjord. The Focke Wulf did not follow him.

Flying as he now was in the opposite direction to Trollfjell, the flak did not pay him much attention for the moment. He turned to Phillips and saw with a shock that the observer was slumped forward in his harness. As Grenville pulled him back his head lolled sidewards, showing the front of his flying suit to be sticky with blood. Grenville had no way of knowing how seriously he was hurt, and could do nothing for him at the moment. He checked his controls. It seemed nothing vital had been hit, although his trimmer controls appeared to have gone.

He stared down. Far below Ayliffe was commencing his run-in on Trollfjell. The flak caught him the moment he stopped weaving. A thin stream of burning glycol from his starboard exhaust showed white against the shadows. It turned black a second later . . . a thin tongue of fire licked back . . . lengthened . . . a bright explosion among the rocks. Gone.

Not three seconds later, far up the fjord, flak got his Number 4. The curving plume of flame and smoke, the pathetic shower of sparks against a rock face, they could mean nothing else.

Whatever the cost, they had to get more bombs on Trollfjell! Grenville called up his Green sections, only to hear Young's Australian drawl come back wearily:

'We're doing our best, Skipper. But there's only Archer and me left. . . .'

And not ten seconds later Archer went, caught by a 190 as he came up blinded after attacking a 20 mm post on a rock shelf.

Two spitting barrels came into Grenville's gunsight. He pressed his attack so close he was able to see the discarded shell cases leaping out from the recoiling breeches, and the crouching loaders with their clips of ammunition. He opened fire and his shells cut down men, splintered trees, ricocheted off rocks. Only his two cannon were firing, the shell that had burst in the nose must have cut the pneumatic leads to his Brownings. He pulled away, looking for another post. Through the animal fury that was shaking his body, a cool untouched part of his brain was analysing the reports that were coming over the radio, and giving orders both to himself and his crews. Number 5 had planted his bomb success-fully, had turned back up the fjord, then gone silent – probably shot down. Number 6 had also got through to Trollfjell, but appeared to have crashed into it after planting its bomb. Seven, eight, and nine were still on their way.

Trollfjell was still there – Grenville could see its ugly head in the distance as he raged over a mountain shoulder. Bitterness was swilling about inside him like acid. What fool had thought of this idea? Throwing men against a mountain in the hope of bringing it down. . . .

The Focke Wulfs above were buzzing about like flies over a jam-pot. Occasion-ally one of them would screw up enough courage to venture down over the rim of the inferno, only to draw back hastily a few seconds later. But they were ready, waiting like hawks for any survivors.

'I've had it, Skipper. Sorry. . . .' That was young Parsons – Parsons who was so proud of his baby. He was hit as he cleared the last mountain spur. His smoking Mosquito tried to pancake into the fjord, crashed in a cloud of steam, and turned over. Only one yellow Mae West showed among the bubbling black water.

The loss of his crews was driving Grenville frantic. He called down Young, the last survivor of his Green sections, and ordered him to escort Number 9 while he flew ahead of Number 8. Perhaps by flying in pairs, with fifty yards between each plane and less than twenty seconds between each pair, they might thin out the intensity of the fire.

Number 8 was Barrett. As Grenville dived over him to take up position, he saw the Wing Commander's squirrel-brown moustache clearly as Barrett leaned back and waved at him. His gruff voice came cheerfully over the radio.

'Quite a party, Roy. Everything but the dancing girls.'

Grenville tried to remember the sites of the flak posts as he led Barrett by them. The fire from them was thinned a little, but only relatively. Not a mile behind them Young followed, leading his Number 9.

The smell of leaking hydraulic fluid was severe now. Grenville pulled up his oxygen-mask, somehow managed to do the same for Phillips, and turned the taps on to emergency. His heart was hammering both from the tension and the sheer physical effort of throwing the Mosquito about in the narrow fjord.

The last mountain spur approached, and with it the flak post that had got Parsons. Its multiple pom-pom gave Grenville a burst, then, as if knowing who was carrying the bomb, turned its full fury on Barrett. A flash on his port engine, and a piece of cowling was torn away. Another flash, and a leg of his under-carriage dropped like a broken claw. Then they were past.

Grenville's mouth was dry. 'You all right, Don?'

'Still around, Roy. Now where's that gremlin?'

The massed flak posts round the building opened up like the roll of drums before an execution. Two shells went right through Grenville's tailplane without exploding. Barrett's voice came longingly over the radio.

'Hell, Roy; wouldn't it be just the job to drop the bloody thing right on top of 'em?'

Grenville led him almost under the massive overhang before turning away. He was unable to see Barrett drop his bomb, but heard his excited voice a few seconds later.

'Right on the button, Roy, or as near as damn it, anyway. Now let's get out of here.'

Doubting Barrett's skill, Grenville could only hope he had been as accurate as he believed. He fought for height through the thundering flak, Barrett followed him. As they climbed higher the flak lessened as the gun-posts, knowing now they carried only one bomb apiece, concentrated on the planes yet to come in.

Just under the lip of the fjord Grenville levelled out and waited for Barrett's B Bobby, with its dangling undercarriage, to come alongside him.

'Any second now, Roy. Watch for it,' Barrett called.

Grenville held little hope of bringing down Trollfjell now, and was busy watching the sky for fighters. Barrett was staring intently down. The familiar blinding flash came, the upflung shower of rocks, the blast, and then Barrett's hysterical voice.

'Roy! It's going! The bloody thing's going. Look!'

Startled, Grenville looked down. The massive head of Trollfjell appeared to be wobbling drunkenly. Then, as if split by some enormous mason's chisel, the front section of it slipped away and toppled into the void below.

The noise could be heard over the roar of the engines, an earth-shaking thunder as thousands of tons of rock, followed by the dislodged mass of the glacier, plunged 3,000 feet into the fjord. An irresistible force, terrifying to watch. . . .

It hit the lower slopes and bounded forward like a tidal wave. It swept over trees, huts, flak posts, hydro-electric plant and concrete building, grinding them and crushing them as a steamroller flattens an ant heap. It set off enormous echoes that reverberated across the fjord for minutes.

'God,' Barrett said, awestruck.

All the firing had stopped. Even the Focke Wulfs had broken off their vigilance to stare down aghast. But one flak post commander, more phlegmatic or perhaps more revengeful than the rest that had survived, saw the Mosquitoes approaching and snapped out orders that pulled his shocked crew together.

Grenville had just finished transmitting the code word that would send Davies delirious with pride when he saw the red flashes open up dead ahead of them. He yelled a warning to Barrett and swung sharply away. But Barrett's reflexes had lost their edge through lack of combat flying and he turned too late. Tracer stitched a line of holes the full length of his fuselage. . . .

Even then it seemed no harm had been done. His Mosquito flew over the post and swept on along the range.

Grenville's voice was sharp with anxiety. 'Don; are you all right?'

No answer. Grenville flew closer until he was right alongside.

'Don! How bad is it?'

He could see through B Bobby's transparent hood now. The observer was lolling sidewards against his harness and Barrett was huddled over the stick.

'Don! For God's sake. . . . Get the hatch away. Try to bale out!'

A ghost voice answered, a million miles away. 'No . . . good, Roy. No . . . good.'

The whisper died away and the Mosquito's nose dropped wearily. Steeper . . . steeper . . . one wing dipping as she went. Down . . . down . . . out of sight. A red glow staining the shadows of the fjord. . . .

Grenville went back to look for the gun-post. His face was that of a devil. With the target destroyed and his crews virtually wiped out, he was at last able to give full vent to his bitterness. He set the flak post with exquisite care in his gunsight as he came back along the ridge. It was not enough to blast it with shells, however: pure hate is never satisfied with long-range killing. He was going to hurl the Mosquito's white-hot engines on the crew, to impale them on the struts of its fuselage, to smash them to pulp with the impact of his own flesh. They were to be killed for many things, not least for letting him live when so many others had died.

The crew were inside his luminous sight now, warmly dressed, crouching behind the quadruple 20 mm with a mountain hut behind them. The four automatic guns were already firing, doing mortal damage to his Mosquito, but he noticed the shells no more than a berserk fighter notices the blows of his opponent. A white-faced loader carrying ammunition clips halted, staring upwards in terrified fascination. Grenville's pressure on the gun-button was as savage as if it had been on the windpipe of an enemy. The loader was flung away, unrecognizable now as anything human. Grenville swung his rudder bar, mowing men down with meticulous care. Crouched behind his gunsight he urged his plane on to destruction. A gunner lost his nerve and began running. That won't help you.... Nothing can help you now. Faster.... Faster, you bitch....

It was a small thing that prevented the final tragedy. A shell, bursting under the starboard wing, that made the Mosquito lurch sidewards.... Grenville corrected the movement immediately, but its suddenness had thrown the unconscious Phillips towards him and the observer's head nudged his arm....

The contact pierced the mist of hate round Grenville's mind. It was as if the unconscious man were pleading for his life. One could sacrifice a conscious man, a nod from him and the thing was done. But not this....

With a curse he jerked back on the stick. The shell-torn, smoking Mosquito pulled away not ten feet above the stricken gun-post. Grenville's duty now was to get Phillips home – he knew it, and his bitterness was complete. Duty lay on him like the curse of Cain.

With one engine feathered and his starboard aileron dragging loose, he struggled painfully to clear the snow-topped mountains. But the Focke Wulfs were waiting. Crippled, with the last of his ammunition gone, he was helpless against them. A burst of 7 mm. sent a stab of agony through his legs, smashing them from the rudder bar. He manged to side-slip away, but he was tired ... tired.... A Focke Wulf came weaving in for the kill, its pilot's eyes cold behind his gunsight. He fired at point-blank range.

One burst was enough. The Mosquito's weakened tailplane broke away and its surviving engine choked and died. It struck the mountain-top, skidded forward under its speed, then suddenly vanished in an enormous flurry of snow. A few seconds later all that showed to the circling aircraft was a pathetic tangle of spars and the flaming mass of a broken-off engine. The battle of the Svartfjord was over.

CHAPTER 31

The innkeeper slowly closed the folder. 'Every man who took part in that action was decorated, and Grenville got the V.C.' His eyes lifted upwards. 'And there you are. That's the whole story.'

The two young airmen were spellbound, too awed for the moment to speak. The innkeeper took a glance round the lounge while he waited for the questions he knew must come. The fire was burning red now, deepening the glow from the shaded lamps. No one else was present but the car driver, who was still sitting in the corner among the shadows. The room was hushed, and the atmosphere even more intense than it had been earlier. An odd shudder ran through the innkeeper as again the reflections from the photographs swam in his vision. . . .

The English boy found his voice first, stealing the question from his friend's lips. 'What about the girls? What happened to them?'

The innkeeper nodded. 'Maisie stayed on here for another eighteen months, then got herself married to another Canadian airman. This one came through all right, and she went back with him in 1945. She has two children now, a boy and a girl. I think she's happy.'

The American found his voice now. 'That's good to know,' he said huskily. 'And what about Hilde?'

'She didn't stay here long after the raid. Like everyone else she thought Grenville had been killed. She went into the Services and stayed in uniform for the rest of the war.'

Daly was opening his mouth to ask another question when his friend again interrupted him. 'Just what did happen to Grenville? How was it he escaped? I've never been sure of that.'

'Rocks tore off both wings, so keeping the burning engines away from the fuselage. The deep snow did the rest by cushioning the effects of the crash.'

'Grenville must have been convinced he wasn't meant to die after that.'

'He must indeed. Of course, like Phillips he was badly wounded and in prison hospital for a long time.'

'They thought over here he was dead, didn't they?'

'Yes. They believed it for over two months.'

The American could not be withheld any longer. 'Hilde – that's the kid I want to hear more about! What happened? Surely she met Grenville when he got back?'

The innkeeper shook his head heavily. 'She has never seen him since that last night before the raid.'

Daly looked shocked. Then he exploded. 'But why? Why the hell didn't some-one tell her the truth? Why didn't this guy Adams have the guts to tell her?'

'He did tell her,' the innkeeper said quietly. 'But it was two days before he found out what Grenville had said. He knew Grenville had no girl-friend, he knew the whole thing was a pack of lies and told her so. He told her everything. . . .'

Daly's voice was hushed. 'How did she take it?'

'It was a shock to her, but she took it as he'd always believed she would. But then it was too late.'

'But it wasn't too late! Grenville came back. Couldn't something have been done then?'

'It wasn't her fault; it was Grenville's. You're forgetting his state of mind. It was he who had always believed there was an impassable barrier between himself and Hilde, and two years brooding in a prison camp did nothing to change his mind.'

'But if someone had told him she understood!'

'Someone did tell him, but he would not believe it. He was too bitter.'

'But in time he would have come round if they'd kept at him. . . .'

'There was no way of keeping at him. Once he had given his story to In-telligence he was discharged, and then everyone lost touch with him. Letters came back undelivered; nobody knew if he was alive or dead. And to my knowledge nobody knows to this day.'

The silence had a finality about it that brought a sudden chill to the room.

'It's a long time ago,' the innkeeper said wearily. 'And yet at times it seems only yesterday. Nothing has ever seemed as real since.'

'What about Adams and his wife? How did they get on?' The American's tone betrayed little interest; like the innkeeper he was only talking now to drive off the silence.

'Yes; I can even tell you that. They were divorced in 1948.'

One question had been in Daly's mind ever since the innkeeper had laid down the manuscript, but it had had to take second place until more urgent ones were answered. Now he leaned forward curiously.

'There's one thing I can't make out, Pop. You say that Kearns was a man in his fifties. O.K.; I guess you're in your fifties too. But you weren't ten years ago. And there's something else, too. How did you find out all the details – all that hap-pened in the Intelligence Room, the Operations Room, and in the house in the country? And how did you find out all the technical stuff? You tell it as if you'd been one of the boys.'

The innkeeper took off his thick glasses and wiped them. 'I realized some time ago that you hadn't been told my name, and was rather hoping you wouldn't ask.' His weak eyes looked at them almost apologetically. 'It's quite simple, really. You see, I'm Adams. . . .'

There is always a shock in discovering that in real life characters have a way of living on beyond the final curtain. Both airmen felt it now.

'You're Adams,' The American muttered.

'Yes. I bought the pub just after the war. The old man and I had become good friends and he gave me first option when he sold.' The years had weathered away Adams' bitterness; there was barely a trace of it in his voice as he went on: 'It was one of the things Valerie and I quarrelled about. She didn't like the idea of being a country publican's wife, and perhaps one can't blame her – it can be quiet here in the winter.'

'Why did you buy it?' the English pilot asked curiously.

Adams hesitated. 'I don't really know.' Then he smiled. 'Perhaps because I'm a big of a sentimentalist. Perhaps that was it.'

'Was it you who told Grenville?'

'Yes; it was me. I wrote him in prison camp, telling him everything, and I had another go at him when he was ordered to give us the full story of the raid. But he wouldn't discuss her at all. I wrote him quite a few times afterwards, too, but all my letters were returned address unknown.'

The American moved unhappily in his chair. 'It's a waste,' he muttered. 'Two people kept apart like that – I don't like it.'

Adams gave a faint smile. It was not difficult to recognize another sentimentalist.

'Where is Hilde now?' Daly asked. 'Back in Norway?'

'Yes. She lives with a cousin in Bergen.' Adams tapped the manuscript in front of him, smiling ruefully. 'It wasn't easy to get her permission to include her in this book. Of course, I haven't used any of the girls' true Christian names – theirs are the only fictional names in the book – but she was still very hesitant. I think only one thing changed her mind.'

'What was that?'

'I pointed out that if it were published, Grenville might read it and realize how wrong he had been. I'm pretty certain that was the only reason she gave in.'

Daly winced. 'The poor kid,' he muttered. Then he looked at Adams eagerly. 'But you're right. It could bring him back – even after all these years. When is it to be published?'

Adams' reply startled him 'It's already published. It came out on the sixth of this month.'

'And you've heard nothing from him yet?'

Adams shook his head.

'Maybe he wouldn't know where to find you,' Daly suggested.

'Oh, he knows I am here. I had already bought the pub when I last saw him in 1945.'

Daly was young. He refused to give up hope. 'There's still plenty of time. Supposing he did come back – could you get hold of Hilde easily?'

'Oh, yes. We keep in touch. In fact, she comes over here every spring to stay with me.'

'Here?' Daly said horsely. 'Every spring? Why?'

Adams smiled quietly. 'Why? Why do people keep their memories alive? Why do they keep souvenirs and photographs? Tell me that and I'll tell you why she comes over here every spring.'

The young American did not need telling. He was staring at the huge bowl of daffodils on the counter with an awed, almost frightened look in his eyes.

Adams nodded. 'Yes. This year as well. She has been here over a week now. Of course' – this was a trifle wistfully – 'we have become good friends over the years. I like to think that has a little to do with her coming.' He glanced at his watch. 'She went into town this afternoon. The bus is late; she should have been back over ten minutes ago.'

None of them had noticed how emotion had been clawing at the face of the man in the corner. Nor did they notice how he started now at Adams' words. He only drew their attention five minutes later when light, hurrying footsteps on the gravel outside brought him sharply to his feet. Adams caught the abrupt movement, heard his harsh, expectant breathing, and peered at him curiously. Slowly the white, intent face swam into focus. Adams gave one incredulous gasp, and then the lounge door opened. . . .

Half an hour later they had all gone from the lounge, and Adams stood alone behind the bar. Something inside him was still trembling, still glorying, still weeping a little. In the glistening blur before his eyes, the lights from the photographs had diffused and become his ghosts again. They were as gay now as they had bene in the old days – laughing, joking, congratulating one another. Then, one by one, they waved to him and slipped out. They were the dead who wanted the living to live, and for years their leader's loneliness had been their sorrow. They had joined him this night with a long-held wish, and at last they had seen that wish granted.

They could all rest well now.

OPERATION RHINE MAIDEN

To

my old and dear friend

JOHNNIE GEMMELL,

who will be greatly missed

The author wishes to acknowledge his debt to the authors of the following works of reference:

Bekker, *The Luftwaffe War Diaries* (Macdonald); Adolf Galland, *The First and the Last* (Methuen); Alfred Price, *Instruments of Darkness* (Wm Kimber); Richards and Saunders, *Royal Air Force 1939-1945* (H.M.S.O.); C. Martin Sharp and Martin F. Bowyer, *Mosquito* (Faber); Sir C. Webster and N. Frankland, *The Strategic Air Offensive against Germany 1939-1945* (H.M.S.O.).

And, last but not least, to his good friend Group Captain T. G. Mahaddie, D.S.O., D.F.C., A.F.C.

CHAPTER I

The small group of mechanics, all smoking cigarettes, were standing in the summer sunshine outside a dispersal hut. An FBVI Mosquito with modifications was at rest twenty yards away. Beneath its nose a young Aircraftman IInd Class, whose chubby face was shining in the heat, was trying to replace a gun bay panel. As he struggled to locate the spring-loaded screws, a Leading Aircraftman detached himself from the group. An old sweat with a long, dismal face and a sharp nose, he was wearing a filthy pair of overalls held together at the waist by a single button. Ducking his head he gazed at the sweating youngster.

'Takin' your time, aren't you?'

'I'm going as quick as I can,' the ACII muttered.

'You'd better get a jildi on, mate. If Chiefy has to ground this kite, he'll have the lot of us workin' on it all night. And then you'll be real popular.'

The youngster was having difficulty in lining up the screws with their sockets. 'Couldn't you hold the panel for me?' he asked tentatively.

The old sweat, by name McTyre, looked shocked. 'You want to get me into trouble, Ellis? I'm a fitter, not a bloody armourer.'

'But I only want it holding while I fasten the screws,' the young ACII wailed.

McTyre was clearly shaken by the youngster's readiness to bend the sacred lines of demarcation. 'Out of the question, mate. By the centre . . .' Shaking his head, the old sweat retreated to the group of mechanics. 'You hear that? He'll be askin' Chiefy to give 'im a hand next.'

A telephone was heard ringing. A corporal ran into the dispersal hut, to return fifteen seconds later. 'Hey, Ellis. Is that gun serviceable yet?'

The cherubim-faced youngster had got the panel on at last. 'Yes, I think so, corp.'

The corporal went back to the telephone. McTyre met him in the hut doorway as he was coming out. 'Is it right Lacy's not flyin' with Harvey today?'

'Yeh. Lacy's got appendicitis.'

'Who's flyin' in his place?'

'One of the sprogs. Blackburn.'

McTyre gave a whistle. 'Christ! That'll make Harvey happy.'

By this time Ellis was carrying his equipment away from the nose of the Mosquito. When the way was clear McTyre stepped loftily forward and climbed into the cockpit. A few seconds later the starboard engine fired, following by the port. A flight of starlings, grubbing in the short grass near by, took off with a clatter of wings.

The Merlins began to thunder as McTyre warmed them up. A shower of dust and stones made the group of mechanics take shelter on the lee side of the hut. Three minutes later McTyre waved an underling into the cockpit and swung his legs to the ground. As he scribbled his initials on the Form 700 that the corporal pushed at him, the roar of the engines died into a rhythmical murmur. It allowed the mechanics to hear the roar of other Merlins around the airfield where the same routine was being carried out.

A 25-cwt. transport began circling the perimeter track, dropping off crews at their dispersal points. A second vehicle, a station wagon befitting a Flight Commander, drew up a few yards from McTyre whose muted wolf whistle at the pretty Waaf driver brought only a toss of curls.

The tall, powerfully-built pilot who jumped out was Frank Harvey, A Flight Commander and Acting Squadron Commander for the operation. With the warm evening obviating the need for flying clothes, he was wearing service uniform. A Yorkshireman with withdrawn eyes and a face that was all planes and angles, Harvey was not famous for his sociability at the best of times. This evening his mood was forbidding as he dragged his parachute from the station wagon.

Two other men followed him out. One, a stocky youngster carrying a canvas bag as well as his parachute, was Blackburn, Harvey's new navigator and the innocent cause of the Yorkshireman's mood. The other man was 'Sandy' Powell, an affable Australian who, like Harvey, was a survivor from the original squadron. Wounded over Bergen, he had been hospitalized during the climactic raid, an accident that had probably saved his life. Harvey's dourness was an obstacle to friendship, but Powell was the closest to a friend on the squadron that the Yorkshireman had, and, although Harvey would have died rather than admit it, he valued the Australian accordingly.

As Harvey started for the dispersal hut, Powell caught his arm. 'Wait a minute. You still haven't given me the name of those gee-gees.'

Harvey did his best to be affable. 'You can have 'em when we get back.'

'You kidding? What if you get the chop?'

Harvey gave an impatient scowl. 'It's Sun King for the two-thirty and Jason II for the three o'clock. The other one's Blue something – maybe Blue Stocking. I'll have to check on it.'

'Great. If they come up we're in Scarborough tomorrow night for dinner. O.K.?'

Harvey nodded, humped his parachute over one shoulder, and started again for the dispersal hut. As the stocky Blackburn followed somewhat ruefully after him, Powell clapped him on the shoulder. 'You'll be all right, cobber. His bark's worse than his bite.'

Blackburn gave him a grateful look, and Powell ran back to the station wagon, which shot away. At the dispersal hut Harvey barely glanced at the Form 700 before signing it and shoving it back at the corporal. Ignoring Blackburn he strode over to the Mosquito, ordered the mechanic out, and took his place in the pilot's seat. Feeling the eyes of the ground crew on him, Blackburn took a deep breath, threw his bag and parachute through the open cockpit door, and pulled himself in after them. Almost instantly the two Merlins began to roar as Harvey tested them. A green Very light soared up from the Control Tower and D-Danny began to roll forward.

McTyre was grinning unsympathetically. 'I'd hate to be in his shoes. Harvey looks mad enough to pitch him into the drink.'

Ellis, still new and young enough to feel wonder at it all, ventured a question. 'Where are they going, Mac?'

McTyre gave him a look of pity. 'You've helped to bomb up the bloody thing and don't know where they're going?'

'Nobody's told me,' the young armourer complained.

Across the airfield Mosquito after Mosquito was moving from its hard-standing and taxi-ing in procession for take-off. As another Very light soared from the Control Tower, Harvey's D-Danny came swooping along the runway and climbed into the sunlit evening sky with a crackling roar. McTyre jerked an oily thumb eastward. 'They're goin' to prang a Jerry convoy. Somewhere off the Danish coast.' As another of the graceful planes took off and banked around the airfield, the old sweat followed its flight with a rare pride.

'Look at 'em, mate. Miracle kites, that's what they are. Made of wood and yet able to outfly anything Jerry can put up. And carry a 4,000-lb. cookie if they want to.'

The youngster's ingenuous blue eyes, bright with envy, watched the orbiting planes break and follow Harvey eastward. Flying in a loose gaggle, they swept so low over the fields that their shadows pursued them like sharks. Reaching the coast just south of Flamborough Head, they leapt over a sunlit beach still sprinkled with holidaymakers. Men leapt to their feet and excited girls waved towels. The gaggle swept over a line of inshore fishing boats, then the sea that led to the enemy coast reached out blue and dangerous before them. Within seconds they were only a cluster of specks to the watching holidaymakers. The time was 19.15 hours. The month was July 1943.

It was later the same evening that Frank Adams, the Station Intelligence Officer, took a walk round the airfield perimeter. Since the teleprinters had started clacking that afternoon he had been working at full stretch, and in an hour or less, when the squadron returned, de-briefing might keep him busy until midnight. This was the lull period when the ground staff could take a breather, and Adams had discovered that a walk helped to ease his tension.

The murmur of voices drifting towards him told him that inside the dispersal huts mechanics were smoking cigarettes and brewing cups of tea. The distant row of poplars were black against the fading sky and an arrowhead of homing birds was winging its way towards Bishop's Wood. Adams glanced at his watch. The evenings would begin closing in soon. In less than three months those icy, north-east winds would be back, probing through the Nissen huts and sweeping un-molested across the cement-stained ground. Adams had never been able to decide which season he preferred since putting on uniform. In spite of its discomforts, winter did at least match the black mood of war.

The turf-lined mound on Adams' left was the bomb dump. As he passed a gun-post he could feel the crew watching him and had to restrain his impulse to call out a greeting. That most other ranks found familiarity from officers an embarrassment was another unwelcome fact Adams had learned.

He walked until a hillock hid him from the gun-post, then pushed through a tangle of sweet-smelling grass to the perimeter fence. The fence here was only three feet high and down the road, set back behind its garden, he could see the Black Swan. With all the personnel of the airfield on duty tonight, its bars would be almost empty.

In the hedgerow across the quiet road a blackbird had begun its evening song. With the sentimentalist in him unable to equate such moments with war, Adams found his thoughts turning paradoxically to the time ten weeks previously when the aircrews of 633 Squadron, weighing their lives against the threat to their country, had chosen to fly straight into the murderous steel trap of the Swart-fjord.

It had been an evening of equal beauty when the armourers had loaded the earthquake bombs into the waiting Mosquitoes. And Adams could distinctly remember hearing a blackbird singing during the cold dawn vigil when he, Davies and the Brigadier had waited for survivors. Blackbirds seemed an integral part of Sutton Craddock, but when only one crippled Mosquito had landed and the full extent of the disaster was known, Adams had wondered bitterly what the hell they had to sing about.

It was a memory that was still painful to Adams, yet certain scenes of it were etched for ever on his mind. The numbed expression of Marsden, the Signals Officer, as he tried to understand that he would never see ninety per cent of his friends again. The mercurial Davies, struggling to balance the loss against his euphoria at the success of the mission. The elderly Brigadier's shame at the relief he could not hide. But of all the fragmented memories, the most painful was Hilde Bergman's reaction on hearing Grenville had not returned. There had been the small fluttering motion of her hand that Adams had come to know so well and now epitomized her grief. The few unsteady steps she had taken across the room, her single sob, and then, incredibly, her melodic voice addressing him.

'Thank you for coming over to tell me, Frank. I know how painful all this must be for you.'

That she could think of him at such a moment and express sympathy had been the breaking point for Adams. Wanting above all else to comfort her, he had instead stumbled back to his billet where, cursing his cowardice, he had drunk almost a full bottle of whisky. It had not helped. The next twenty-four hours had contained all the elements of a black nightmare for Adams.

His eyes focused again over the perimeter fence. Two months had not been long enough to hide the fire-blackened scars in the cornfield where Gillibrand had made his supreme sacrifice, although when the field was ploughed in the autumn the scars would disappear. While the sentimentalist in Adams protested at the thought, the realist in him knew the world seldom sorrowed long over its martyrs.

He stirred impatiently at his habit of extracting melancholy from memory. The news he had been able to give Hilde three days ago ought to have erased some of the sadness of the past. He had heard from the Red Cross that Grenville, although seriously wounded, was making good progress in a German prison hospital. Adams had run all the way to the Black Swan to tell Hilde. Her reaction had made Adams think of his childhood and the tale of the Sleeping Beauty who had come back to shining life at the kiss from her Prince. 'I have felt it, Frank. But it is something I have never dared to believe.'

Adams told her that apart from Harvey and his observer who had escaped capture and been brought back to England by the Norwegian Linge, the Red Cross reported only two other men alive in German hands. Her decision when the full import of Grenville's survival had sunk in had dismayed Adams but not surprised him. 'I've wasted enough time feeling sorry for myself, Frank. Now I must go and make myself useful like the rest of you.' She had phoned a military nursing unit in Whitby and had left Sutton Craddock only that morning.

Perhaps, then, there was an excuse for his mood tonight, Adams thought. When his wife, Valerie, had decided to leave the Black Swan and live with her parents until the war ended, Adams had been free to spend his off-duty time as he wished and much of it had been spent seeing Hilde. They had become close friends and after a day or night assessing how many enemy aircraft had been shot down, how many German factories had been destroyed, or how some young friend had been killed, Adams' need to see the girl had often been as urgent as a wounded man needing a sedative. He sometimes felt the madness of war would go on for ever and the realization tonight that he would have to face it without her was crushing.

About to sit on the top rail of the fence, Adams decided it was too rickety. As he leaned his elbows on it instead, he remembered almost with surprise that it was Sunday. In the village churches that dotted the Yorkshire countryside the faithful would be in their pews reaffirming their allegiance to the Prince of Peace. Listening to the blackbird's song again Adams discovered that a coarse background of sound was adulterating it. Back where the shadows were thickening between the billets and hangars, orders were being shouted and engines were starting up. With a sigh Adams pushed himself away from the fence. Signals must have been alerted that the squadron was nearing its base and Sue Spencer, his assistant, must be wondering what had happened to him.

An unmilitary figure with his spectacles and stocky build, Adams started back along the perimeter track. In the dusk ahead the activity was quickening. As the dim lights of the Control Tower came on, darkness seemed to close in and envelop the airfield.

As Adams passed one of the sandbagged gunposts he heard the hum of an approaching aircraft. A moment later he saw its navigation lights in the darkening sky and he quickened his stride. Half a minute later the Mosquito passed over him with a roar of engines and began orbiting the field.

Hurrying now, Adams passed a row of Nissen huts and the transport park. To the east he could hear more aircraft approaching. As he crossed the tarmac apron in front of No. 1 hangar, he passed close to a frail monoplane. It was a Miles Messenger, flown in two hours ago by Air Commodore Davies. Davies, a small, alert man with a choleric temperament, had been the link man with the Special Operations Executive in the Swartfjord affair. An officer with a high pride in his service, Davies had a particular affection for 633 Squadron and consequently, in the way of love, was prone to criticize it when it fell below his expectations. A goodlooking young Wing Commander had flown in with him but as Davies had offered no introductions, Adams could only speculate on the reason for the visit. For the last ninety minutes they had been closeted in the Control Tower with Henderson. Henderson, nick-named 'Pop' by the crews, was a huge, middle-aged Scot who had taken over the squadron after Barrett's death. A taciturn man, he exercised his authority with the minimum of fuss and so was a popular C.O.

As Adams was passing the door of the Control Tower the landing lights flashed on, a dazzling corridor of brilliance that made Adams' eyes blink behind his spectacles. Navigation lights flashing, the first Mosquito began its landing approach. Engines purring and airfoils whining, it positioned itself between the two rows of lights and sank down. There was the squeal of tyres and brakes and the graceful shape disappeared into the luminous haze at the far end of the field.

The second Mosquito appeared to have suffered damage and Adams paused to watch it. One engine was coughing like a man with asthma and there was an unsteadiness in its approach as it entered the lane of lights. But its wheels were locked down and it was sinking into a safe landing when, to Adams' horror, a dark shape hurled itself out of the darkness like a hawk on a pigeon. The hammer of cannon fire was followed by a muffled explosion and a great gush of flame. The stricken Mosquito lurched helplessly and crashed fifty yards to the left of the landing lights. As the fireball slithered along the ground it left behind it huge patches of burning petrol and wreckage.

The German night intruder, who had carried out his mission so successfully, escaped into the darkness before the stunned crews above or the ground staff below knew what was happening. One gunner did let go a burst of Hispano cannon fire but the wildly-aimed shells were a greater threat to the orbiting Mosquitoes than the Ju.88. In the few seconds of chaos that followed, men ran in panic for the air-raid shelters and other men yelled orders that no one obeyed. From the platform of the Control Tower someone was firing pointless Very lights into the red-stained sky.

Then training asserted itself. As if a giant's black sleeve had swept across the field, the landing lights went out, giving Adams a moment of vertigo. Around him men were assuming their duties and fire engines and an ambulance were already gathering speed in their dash to the distant funeral pyre.

The Control Tower door burst open and Davies, Henderson and the young Wing Commander appeared. Seeing Adams, Davies ran over to him. 'How many of the bastards are there? Any idea?'

'Only one, I think,' Adams said, hating the unsteadiness of his voice.

Henderson joined them. The swinging headlights of a fast-moving ambulance momentarily lit up his face. Normally ruddy, it was pale and shocked. 'Let's hope you're right.' As he turned to flag down a crash wagon, Davies caught his arm.

'There's no point to it, Jock. You'd be wasting your time.'

For a moment it seemed Henderson might resist. Then his huge body relaxed. 'I suppose you're right.' His Scots voice held a dash of resentment.

Overhead the orbiting Mosquitoes had switched off their navigation lights. Adams' imagination lifted him up there. Weary from hours of action, in imminent danger of collision with their comrades, the crews had no way of knowing if other intruders were waiting to pounce on them when they came in to land. Turning to Henderson, whose shocked eyes were still fixed on the burning aircraft, Adams found his question difficult to ask.

'Do you know who it was, sir?'

Henderson nodded. 'Yes. It was Sandy Powell and Irving.'

'Sandy Powell! Oh, Christ,' Adams breathed.

Davies, birdlike in his quick glance at both men, gave neither time for reflection. He pushed Henderson and the young Wing Commander, who had not spoken, towards the Control Tower. 'If we don't get the rest of 'em down, there might be another disaster. Come on.'

The three men disappeared through the door. Over on the airfield crash wagons were now pouring foam on the wreckage. With a last look Adams followed them inside.

CHAPTER 2

The atmosphere in the Intelligence Room that evening had a hardness that a sharp knife might have had difficulty in cutting. Adams was seated at a large table. A detailed map of the Danish province of Jutland was spread out before him. His assistant, Sue Spencer, was seated at a table against the opposite wall. She was a tall, willowy girl whose sensitive face and gentle voice belied her efficiency. At the opposite end of the long hut, standing on either side of the door, were two groups of aircrew, and it was from them that the tension was radiating. Afraid of an eruption at any moment, Adams was finding concentration on his task a problem.

His method of interrogation was to give the crews some small privacy when they spoke to him, his belief being that privacy made them more likely to discuss their own mistakes and the mistakes of their comrades. Stan Baldwin, lapsed Catholic from Barbados, called his hut the 'Confessional' and the name had taken on.

Hopkinson was the navigator Adams was interrogating. Hoppy, as he was affectionately known among the older aircrew members, had once been Grenville's navigator but an injury received in an earlier mission had kept him out of the Swartfjord raid. A small astute Cockney with a pinched face and the eyes of a sparrowhawk, he was wearing flying overalls which carried an evocative smell of combat – oil, cordite, and a dozen other indefinable odours – to Adams' nostrils. Condemned to ground duties by his eyesight and his age, Adams had discovered that the odours always stirred envy in him, and this envy puzzled him because in general Adams found war abhorrent.

He stole another quick glance at the two groups of aircrew. Their sullen muttering and antagonistic glances at one another made him think of the two electrodes of a giant condenser into which an overcharge of current had been poured. Apprehensive, he glanced up at Hopkinson again. Usually one of the most cheerful men on the station, the Cockney was looking disgusted and resentful.

'So you don't think any ships were hit?' Adams asked.

Hopkinson's laugh was caustic. 'It would have needed a miracle, wouldn't it?'

'Why?'

'I've just told you. Because there was a bloody great smokescreen right over the convoy.'

'But that means they must have had wind of your coming.'

'Of course they'd wind of it. Is anyone surprised?'

With Hopkinson usually a helpful as well as a polite collaborator, and with everyone shocked by the intruder attack, Adams had thought it prudent to allow a loose rein. Now he decided things were getting out of hand.

'All right. You're not happy and you've shown it. Now pull yourself together and tell me specifically what went wrong. And while we're being civil to one another, put that cigarette out.'

The jolt to Hopkinson was the more severe because it came from Adams, usually the mildest of men. His nicotine-stained fingers holding the smoking cigarette ground it into an ashtray on the desk. 'I thought you'd already heard about the flak ship,' the Cockney muttered suddenly.

'If you'd been keeping your eyes open instead of grumbling to those old sweats of yours, you'd have realized you're the first navigator I've interrogated. What flak ship?'

'The one you warned us about at our briefing.'

Adams gave a start. 'The one south of the convoy?'

'Yes. You pointed out that if it sighted us it would tip off the convoy. That's what happened.'

Adams winced. The German convoy, protected from the Royal Navy by off-shore minefields, was believed to be carrying precious iron ore from Narvik to the Baltic ports. Adams was not looking forward to the rocket Group would dispatch when it learned the convoy was now safe in the Skagerrak.

'But you were routed well north of it. So how did it see you?'

'You're forgetting Harvey was given a sprog navigator. The fool took us in sight of it. I spotted the bloody thing on the horizon and broke R/T silence to warn Harvey, but he decided to keep going and hope for the best. We didn't run into any fighters, thank Christ – maybe they thought we were making for the coast – but the convoy hadn't taken any chances. The smoke was like a London pea-souper when we reached it.'

'How can you be sure it wasn't your R/T that alerted them?' Adams asked.

Hopkinson tried unsuccessfully to hide his contempt at the question. 'A Jerry flak ship doesn't miss two gaggles of Mossies only six or seven miles away. With the Banff Wing scaring the shit out of them, that's what they're looking for all the time.'

Although Adams knew he was right, he felt a need to put in a word for the un-fortunate Blackburn. 'By the time you got there the convoy and the flak ship can't have been more than thirty miles apart. It's not difficult to drift a few miles off course over the sea – as a navigator you know that well enough.'

Hopkinson's lack of charity was as uncharacteristic as was Adams' severity. 'I know this – if it isn't one bloody thing, it's another. Christ knows when we last hit the button. The lads have had a bellyful. Once we were a squadron. Now we're just a shower.'

Hiding his thoughts beneath a frown, Adams tapped his questionnaire with a pencil. 'Let's make that the last of the moans, shall we? What type were the des-troyers?'

'Elbings, I think,' the Cockney muttered.

'Any flak ships in the escort?'

'I saw one. There might have been others.'

'Was there much flak?'

'Enough for me.'

'Radar controlled?'

'It had to be in all that smoke.'

'Any damage?'

'I didn't see any. I saw them hit Powell though. Just under his starboard engine.'

'Did he start straight back?'

'No, he dropped his bombs first. Then Harvey told him to piss off. Not that it did him much good,' Hopkinson added as an afterthought.

Adams wrote it down. At the nearby table Sue Spencer had finished inter-rogating a freckle-faced navigator and a tall young pilot was now walking down the Nissen hut towards her. As he neared the girl, Adams, who could not resist a sideward glance, saw that her eyes held a faint trace of moisture.

It was a scene Adams had witnessed at least a dozen times as the girl gave silent thanksgiving for the pilot's return. Worship seemed the only appropriate word to express Sue Spencer's feelings for Tony St Claire, and yet Adams felt even a hardened cynic would excuse its extravagance, for the slim young officer with the Byronic head and long, sensitive hands was the handsomest man Adams had ever seen. Nor was his artistic appearance deceptive. After studying the piano at the Royal College of Music, St Claire had just been making a name for himself on the concert platform when the war had claimed him for service. In the six weeks since the young pilot's posting to Sutton Craddock, Adams had more than once pondered on the unfairness of a world that could pour such lavish gifts on one man and leave others so impoverished.

Only a trained observer would have noticed how Sue Spencer brushed her hand against St Claire's as she handed him a leaflet. Occasionally Adams had felt a certain professional unease at allowing the girl to interrogate him: at the same time he knew she was not one to put personal relationships before her duty. Watching their faces in that brief moment and knowing they were already together in that magic world where he always walked alone, Adams felt a tug of pain as he turned back to Hopkinson.

'Did you see Millburn and Gabby get hit?'

'No. But that wasn't anything serious, was it?'

'Gabby got a scratch and a bang in the ribs and the M.O. sent him back to the County Hospital for an X-ray. We're expecting him back tonight. Have your photographs gone in?'

A sudden shout interrupted Hopkinson's reply. The voice had a north-country accent that was exaggerated by anger. 'You! St Claire. Over here! At the double!'

The sullen hum of conversation stopped dead as all eyes turned on the doorway. Looking enraged enough to commit murder, Harvey was moving stiff-legged into the hut. Hiding his apprehension well, St Claire turned away from the startled Sue Spencer and approached him. 'Yes, sir?'

Adams could hear the Yorkshireman's heavy breathing. 'You bastard,' Harvey gritted.

St Claire's good-looking face turned pale. 'I beg your pardon, sir.'

Harvey was trembling with fury as he moved to within three feet of the young pilot officer. 'Don't beg pardon me, you bastard. I ought to bloody kill you.'

There was a low gasp as Sue Spencer rose to her feet. Afraid she would intervene Adams caught her arm. Down the hut, although he was as shaken as the girl, St Claire was giving no ground. 'You keep on abusing me, sir, but I still don't know what I have done.'

A large vein was visible on the Yorkshireman's forehead as he fought for control. 'You wouldn't know, would you, you stupid sod. What orders did I give you after Powell was hit?'

'You said I had to fly back with him.'

'That's right. And what do you think that was for – to play a duet with him?' The loss of his friend was almost choking Harvey. 'Your job was to provide him with cover. And what happened? You let a bloody intruder give him the chop.'

A few cries of assent rose from the smaller group and loud shouts of protest from the larger. As the dismayed Adams watched he saw a big pilot officer with a shock of black hair detach himself from the latter group. Tommy Millburn, an American of Irish descent, had joined the RAF before the United States had entered the war and in spite of repeated overtures from the 8th Air Force and the promise of pay that was astronomical by British standards, Millburn had resolutely refused to exchange uniforms. Rich with humour and the darling of the Waafs, the American was showing the quixotic side of his nature as he faced Harvey.

'You've got it all wrong, sir. That Ju.88 wasn't behind Powell – he came in at ninety degrees. I was right behind St Claire and saw the Hun cross the flarepath. There was nothing anybody could have done.'

Frustrated by a witness who could clear St Claire, Harvey was only too glad to turn his resentment on to the American. 'So you were right behind the dreamy bastard! What were you doing? Listening to him playing Beethoven?'

A fighter to his fingertips, Millburn was only too willing to trade punches with the Flight Commander. 'No one could have stopped that 88. Why don't you ask the guys on the ground? They must have seen it too.'

There was a shout of agreement from the larger group. Knowing his case was lost but his pain still demanding a victim, Harvey moved closer to the American. 'Neither of you thought of helping him down? Or giving him cover on either flank?'

Millburn's contempt was pure provocation. 'How could we know an intruder was waiting for him? Control thought he was fit to land on his own and so did Powell. Anyway, what difference would it have made? If we'd been in line with Powell that Hun would have got one of us as well. Maybe both.'

It was the wrong thing to say. Harvey rammed his incensed face into Millburn's. 'I'll tell you what difference it would have made. I'd trade half a dozen of your lot for Powell, Millburn. Any day of the week.'

Millburn's cheeks paled. As men shouted their protest it seemed for a moment that the American might put himself straight in front of a court martial. Instead, regaining control with an effort, he muttered something and turned away. Instantly Harvey grabbed his arm and swung him round.

'Don't you turn away from me, Millburn! Not until you've been given permission.'

His tug was the spark to the powderkeg. With a curse Millburn shoved him away. Eyes blazing with relief, Harvey was moving in to a fight that would have destroyed his career when an urgent bellow halted him.

'Harvey! Millburn! Attention!'

Training made both men stiffen. The horrified Adams, who by this time was running down the hut, saw Henderson inside the doorway. The bluff Scot was looking incredulous as he came forward. 'What the hell's going on in here? What do you two think you're doing?'

When neither man spoke, Henderson turned his anger on Adams. 'You – Adams! This is your office. Can't you keep order in it?'

Seeing that Davies and the young Wing Commander had followed Henderson into the hut, Adams was able to appreciate even more the big Scotsman's indignation. 'I'm sorry, sir. That intruder raid seems to have upset everyone's nerves. I think you'll find it's only a misunderstanding.'

Henderson was taking in the two groups of airmen and the expressions of Harvey and Millburn. Acutely conscious that the splenetic Davies was dying to get in on the act, he knew he had to act fast and firmly. The Intelligence Officer's explanation, weak though it sounded to Adams, gave the Scot the excuse he needed.

'It'd bloody better be,' he said grimly, turning to Harvey and Millburn. 'You two get to my office. I'll be along in a minute. If you exchange another word on the way, you're straight in front of a court martial. Understand?'

The two men nodded. Glancing at one another, they went out. Feeling Davies's critical eyes on him, Henderson turned to the hushed crews. 'As none of you appear to have hit anything, I'm cancelling this de-briefing session. Go to the Ops. Room and wait for me. It's time you and me had a long talk. That means no one leaves the airfield tonight. All right — move!'

As the men filed silently out Henderson turned his attention on Adams. 'I want you to stay but not your assistant.'

The shaken girl collected her papers and left. The door had barely closed before Davies, whose efforts to remain silent had almost choked him, came forward like a truculent cockerel.

'That was a bloody disgraceful scene, Adams. A Flight Commander brawling with a pilot officer. . . . Christ, this is a military establishment, not a taproom. What the hell was it about?'

Adams could see no harm in telling the truth. 'It's the old problem, sir. When Harvey's navigator was taken ill, we had to give him a fresher, a man called Blackburn. It seems the youngster's mistake gave the convoy the tip-off.'

'That doesn't call for a punch-up, does it? Where do St Claire and that American fit in?'

Adams could only hope he wasn't making matters worse. 'St Claire and Millburn were following Powell down. It wasn't their fault — I saw myself that the 88 attacked across the flarepath — but Harvey thought they hadn't given Powell cover. I suppose it was one thing piling on another — Harvey and Powell were friends.'

Davies swore and swung round on Henderson. 'This isn't a squadron — it's a pack of squabbling mongrels. You've got to sort it out, Henderson. And bloody quick at that.'

Somehow the Scot hid his displeasure. 'Yes, sir. I'll do my best.'

'You do that,' Davies snapped. 'Once this was the best squadron in the Group. I want it the best again. So I'd like some fingers pulled out. All right?'

Henderson's burly face turned red. 'I said yes, sir!'

Giving him a sharp look, Davies motioned the young pilot forward and turned back to Adams. 'You two had better be introduced. Adams, meet Wing Commander Moore. You'll be seeing a good deal of him in the future because he's your new Squadron Commander.'

CHAPTER 3

Adams' start and the glance he gave Henderson brought a terse nod from Davies. 'I know. Harvey's not going to like it, but that's something he'll have to live with. In any case, after this ding-dong tonight he must know he's blown any chance he had.'

Adams held out his hand. The man facing him was fresh-complexioned, with wavy fair hair and a good forehead. A very English face was Adams' first thought – the kind one associates with cricket matches and regattas at Henley. He had a small scar on his right cheek, and the crinkles round his eyes when he smiled suggested he was somewhat older than the squadron average – perhaps twenty-six or -seven. He was slim in build and his uniform was beautifully tailored, but any suggestions that the wrappings were more impressive than the contents were dispelled by the DSO and DFC ribbons beneath his pilot's brevet. His reaction to the fracas and Davies' sarcasm had been little more than a quirk of the mouth. With storms eddying all around him, Adams found this composure a most attractive feature.

He said the first thing that came to him and wanted to kick himself for it half a second later. 'You've picked quite a night to arrive.'

Moore's voice was much what he expected. English, cultured, and laconic. 'These things happen.'

Davies jumped in quickly at that. 'They bloody shouldn't.' He turned to Henderson. 'Mind if I come to the bollocking?'

The big Scot made no attempt to hide his lack of enthusiasm. 'If you want to.'

'I do. I've a few things I want to say myself. And we can introduce Moore to them. All right?'

Henderson sighed audibly. 'All right, sir.'

'What about Harvey and that American? You going to talk to them first?'

'Yes, I suppose I'd better.'

'You wouldn't like me to handle that while you go along to the Ops. Room?'

This time Adams was certain he saw Moore's lips quirk as the big Scot reacted. 'No, sir. It's a Station disciplinary matter and I'd rather take care of it myself. But of course you're welcome as an observer.'

Davies glowered. 'No. I'll make a couple of phone calls instead. I suppose I am allowed to use the Adjutant's office?' he asked sarcastically.

'Of course, sir.' Henderson's face was pink but expressionless as he turned to Moore. 'If you don't mind waiting here, I'll collect you on my way back. If there's anything you want to know in the meantime, Adams will take care of you.'

175

Looking like two dogs — one very large and one very small — who had squabbled over a bone, the two men left the hut. Unsure what Moore's half-smile signified, Adams proceeded with caution. 'Feel like a seat while you're waiting?'

The two men sank into a couple of chairs that flanked the long hut. As the younger man pulled out a cigarette case, Adams shook his head.

'No, thanks. I'm a pipe-smoker myself.'

Moore extracted a cigarette and snapped the case closed. 'Don't they say pipes are more soothing for the nerves?'

Adams could not help following the cigarette case back into the Wing Commander's inner pocket. Unless it was a fake — and spurious possessions did not seem to go hand in hand with this self-confident young man — the metal was gold. Before Adams could think of a reply, the need was taken from him as Moore flicked on an equally expensive lighter.

'Talking about nerves, this seems a pretty edgy squadron. What's your version of it?'

Knowing that both Davies and Henderson must have briefed him, Adams proceeded carefully. 'I feel that any squadron that's suffered the losses we've suffered would have the same problems.'

Somewhat to his surprise, the young officer nodded. 'You're probably right. I'm told you have ten left of your original crews. Tell me again how that number's made up, will you?'

'Ten until tonight,' Adams said with some bitterness. 'Young and his navigator were the only ones who flew back from the Swartfjord. He's now B Flight Commander. Harvey and his navigator, Lacy, escaped capture after being shot down and were smuggled back to the U.K. by the Norwegians. The other six come from crews wounded over Bergen before the Swartfjord raid who have now come back to us from hospital.'

'So you needed massive replacements?'

'Right. And with the newspapers having plastered 633 Squadron's sacrifice in the Swartfjord on every front page, it's hardly surprising they didn't arrive here full of confidence.'

The young officer looked sceptical. 'You're not suggesting they saw this as a suicide unit?'

'No. But they saw it as an élite one. And with the Press constantly reminding them of it, it's not surprising they arrived here feeling inadequate.'

'Did the old sweats behave like a *corps d'élite*?'

'They're a bit clannish,' Adams admitted. 'With their common bond of survival, I suppose it's natural in one way. And with three times their number of recruits pouring in, self-protection must have had some part in it.'

'So the recruits felt they were being patronized, got chips on their shoulders, and things have got steadily worse?'

Either he knew something about men, Adams thought, or else Davies's briefing had been very perceptive. Rightly or wrongly, the recruits had felt themselves patronized. And the old sweats, mistaking their resentment for envy, had started

176

making comparisons. As comparisons, in the nature of things, could hardly be anything else but unfavourable, they had closed their ranks even further. Polarization of the two groups had led to bad feeling and inefficiency, inefficiency to a series of abortive missions, recriminations to even more drastic polarization. Before Adams could comment further on the vicious circle, Moore put another question to him.

'What action did your last Squadron Commander take to put things right?'

Sweet nothing would have been Adams' reply if he hadn't disliked speaking ill of the dead. Alan Prentice, sent to the squadron a week after Grenville had been reported missing, had been a stiff, unimaginative officer, and although he had led the squadron courageously enough, he had been at sea in handling the psychological tensions that were tearing it apart. So his death in action three weeks previously had been no setback to the squadron's difficult convalescence, unless one argued that it had led to Harvey's temporary accession to the leadership. What that had done to squadron morale, in particular his behaviour tonight, Adams was still trying to sort out in his mind.

'I believe he thought that time would put things right,' was the best Adams could say for the unfortunate Prentice.

Moore did not pursue the subject. 'How do the ground crews line up?'

'They tend to make matters worse. In Grenville's day they were members of an élite force and could look down their nose at other squadrons. Now the other erks are taking their revenge and ours don't like it. We try to keep them in line but they show their contempt of the new men in a hundred ways.'

Moore was examining Adams' round, bespectacled face. 'What would you like to see done?'

The directness of the question surprised Adams. 'Me? I suppose I'd like to see them pull off a few successful operations. Their tails would come up and they might get a new respect for one another.' Conscious of the obviousness of his solution, Adams suddenly felt embarrassed. 'I know it's oversimple but I can't think of anything else.'

The younger man gave no sign of noticing his discomfort. 'Fair enough, but what comes first – the chicken or the egg? I suppose all the old sweats fly together?' When Adams nodded, Moore went on quietly: 'Have you ever thought there might be a solution there?'

Adams gave a jump. 'You don't mean split up the crews?'

'Not so much the crews as the flights. That way they might gain a new respect for one another.'

Harvey loomed large in Adams' mind. An ambitious man, the Yorkshireman must have had high hopes that his role of Squadron Commander would be substantiated, yet in a few minutes he would learn he had been used only until Group had found a man more to their taste. After such a day of disaster, it was hard to visualize what his reaction would be to his replacement's suggestion.

'I'm afraid you'd have a revolution on your hands. You know how crews stick together. And most of the old sweats are in Harvey's flight. He'd go berserk if he lost them.'

Moore's shrug suggested nothing could worry him less. 'Tell me about your kites. They're a modification of the FBVI fighter-bomber, aren't they?'

'Yes, but by leaving in only the two outer cannon and giving us the short-barrelled version, the manufacturers have given us a longer bomb bay and room for a bombsight in the cockpit. It's a bit of a squeeze but it does make us a very flexible unit.'

Moore nodded. 'How long have you been with the squadron?'

Adams had to think. 'Over sixteen months.'

'Then you must know the men as well or better than anyone. Will you advise me on reshuffling the flights?'

Adams procrastinated. 'Have you discussed this with the Old Man?'

'Not yet. But I'm sure he won't object. I've been told I've got a relatively free hand to sort things out.'

'I'm a coward,' Adams told him. 'I'll give you my advice but only on condition you don't tell even the station cat.'

Moore gave his likeable smile. 'It's a deal. When? After the C.O. has introduced me to the men?'

'If you like,' Adams slanted a glance at his crowded desk. 'In any case I'll be here for at least an hour – I haven't filled in my reports yet.'

'Fine. Then I'll be back.'

Adams hesitated, then decided to say it. 'Don't be too hard on Harvey and the old sweats. They've taken a hell of a beating and I think half their trouble is they're miserable that the squadron has slipped so much.'

He saw a twinkle in the younger man's eyes. 'Do you know something, Adams?'

'What?'

'You're just as sold on the old crowd as those erks you were talking about.'

Behind his spectacles Adams looked resentful. 'They were a fine crowd. So what's wrong with admiring them?'

'Nothing. Except I'm wondering what the difference is between you and the others.'

'I don't blame the new men. That's the difference.'

'Don't blame them for what? For not matching up?'

Discovering his muscles were tight, Adams made himself relax. 'All right, you've made your point. I'll watch it and be as objective as I can.'

'Good man.'

Heavy footsteps sounded outside, and a moment later the burly figure of Henderson appeared in the doorway. His expression suggested he had got something off his mind and was feeling the better for it.

'You ready, Moore?'

'Coming, sir.' With a friendly nod at Adams, the immaculate young officer walked unhurriedly towards the door. Watching him with a certain grudging respect, Adams, prone to irrelevant thoughts at such moments, found himself wishing he knew the name of his tailor.

*

The bright moonlight made the woods an eerie place of old light and jet-black shadows. The hoot of the distant train, reverberating among the mountains, added to the atmosphere. Hidden in a bush among the trees that flanked the cutting, Hausmann pulled aside a branch. The moonlight enabled him to see the single-line railway track that ran past him. Fifty yards down the track a heavy steel gate, linked to a high mesh fence, straddled it. Both were glinting dully in the moonlight. Defences could not be seen because of the darkness, but from the lights that had appeared when the guard was changed an hour ago, Hausmann knew there was a large blockhouse only thirty yards from the gate.

His eyes followed the high mesh fence that disappeared into the woods on either side of the track. Probably electrified and surrounding the entire valley, was his guess. He gave the railway track his attention again. Once it passed the steel gates, the tall firs closed tightly on either side, giving the appearance that the track was running into a dark tunnel. Probably it was, Hausmann thought. If the valley held the secret he and his comrades believed, German thoroughness would almost certainly ensure the track was camouflaged from the air.

The mournful hoot of the train sounded again. This time, as he listened, Hausmann could pick out the rhythmical pounding of its steam engine. With sounds carrying far in the mountain air, he knew it was still some distance away, but now it seemed certain this heavily-guarded valley was its destination.

He let the branch swing back into place, but not before the moonlight showed a weatherbeaten face and a burly, middle-aged figure wearing a pair of workman's overalls. As he sank back, a sharp root that had been jabbing into his body for the last ninety minutes no matter what position he assumed, took on new venom and dug into his right groin. With a silent curse he drew himself forward and took the pressure on his thigh. The sudden movement brought a loud clatter as a jay in the trees above took fright and flew away. Holding his breath, Hausmann drew the branch aside again, but to his relief no signs of alarm showed at the gate.

He wondered what Meyer and Rall were doing. They had been gone forty minutes: surely they had determined the extent of the fence by this time. On the other hand, the woods here were dense and vast: it was easy enough to get lost in them in the daylight, never mind at night.

A pain in his left leg was growing by the minute. Günter Hausmann suffered from arthritis which, although seldom severe enough to incapacitate him, could cause considerable pain when he was subjected to damp, and heavy dew was an integral part of summer night in these parts. He could feel its wetness as leaves brushed his face and knew that in the morning he would have difficulty in getting to work. The bloody war, he thought, that made a man of his age crawl about damp woods when he ought to be in bed with some plump woman. It was typical of his character that Hausmann could concern himself with rheumatism when one security slip could end in torture and death.

There was a singing in the telephone wires that ran alongside the track. As the wind dropped, the wail of the train was heard again. By this time Hausmann knew it had passed through the small town at the head of the approach valley: the rumble of its freight cars and pounding of its engine had taken on a sterner note as it began its climb through the mountains. Under the waiting man the ground began to tremble.

Half a minute later a dazzling light shone through the bush as an arc light above the gates was switched on. Drawing the branch cautiously aside, Hausmann saw that the massive barrier, the high fence, the grim blockhouse, and a platoon of soldiers were standing out like a stage set against the black woods. To a yell of orders, the soldiers ran forward and manned the gates.

A shaded blue headlight appeared among the trees to Hausmann's right. Edging forward, he watched the freight train approach the gates. Although it was travelling slowly, the red glow of its firebox and the dull glint of its metal surfaces gave an impression of crushing weight and power. As it came opposite him there was a hiss of vacuum brakes. With a clanking of couplings and screech of metal wheels, the chain of wagons halted in front of the grass. As a searchlight flashed on and began playing down the track, Hausmann ducked back out of sight.

At the gates the driver and fireman were called down from the engine to show their papers. Soldiers from the blockhouse began moving down the train, shining their torches into and under the freight cars. The search for possible intruders was exhaustive: even soldiers who were manning the flak wagon at the rear of the train were called down for interrogation.

Fifteen minutes passed before the train was cleared and the steel gates opened. When the tail light of the flak wagon disappeared into the woods, Hausmann began counting in an effort to see how far the train ran into the woods before reaching its destination. As he counted, the steel gates swung back across the track and the arc light went out. He had reached only nine seconds when far into the valley there was a bright flash and a dull explosion. Dogs began barking immediately and there was a fusillade of automatic fire. Showing alarm, Hausmann backed a few yards into the woods. Then, forgetting his aching leg, he began to run.

'There it is!' Rall's whisper had a youthful sound as he raised an arm. His taller companion, little more than a shadow behind him, pushed forward to his side. Thirty yards ahead was a corridor of felled trees and down its centre the heavy-gauge wire of a mesh fence glinted in the moonlight. Meyer's whisper suggested an older man. Both men spoke in German, their native tongue.

'So it does go right down the valley. Probably all the way round. Let's go back and tell Hausmann.'

Below them they could hear the freight train penetrating deeper into the valley. Rall caught Meyer's arm. 'We've got to find out what's going on down there. Let me take a closer look. If it's not electrified, we can come back with wire cutters.'

Meyer hesitated, then nodded. 'Be careful. There might be guards on the other side.'

Rall's white teeth flashed in the shadows. 'I've a date tomorrow night. You think I'm going to miss it?'

The youth crept forward while Meyer kept watch. A night breeze, bringing the sound of the train nearer, seemed to emphasize the size and loneliness of the woods. The youth managed to keep in shadow until he reached the bright corridor of moonlight that lay between him and the fence. As he paused, Meyer straightened anxiously. 'That's enough. You can see all you want from there.'

Rall either did not hear him or ignored his advice. Bending low, he began running towards the fence. He was half-way towards it when there was an eruption of flame and a shattering explosion that threw his body like a rag doll against a felled tree.

For a moment Meyer was too horrified to move. Then he ran to the edge of the moonlit corridor. One glance at the dead youth was enough: he drew back gagging. As his ears recovered from the explosion he heard the barking of dogs, followed by automatic fire. Fighting to control his stomach, he ran back into the trees and made for the valley entrance.

He took a path that led him away from the fence, but the sound of dogs and shouting men was growing louder. He thanked God they came from the other side of the fence but he knew there must be access points along it, and if his presence were suspected and the dogs released ahead of him, he was as good as dead. Stumbling and falling, running until he felt his heart would burst, he kept going until the sounds grew faint behind him. By the time he reached his prearranged rendezvous with Hausmann he was retching again, this time from exhaustion.

'Mines,' he gasped. 'All along the fence. The youngster ran right on top of one.'

As he dropped to the ground Hausmann's fingers dug into his shoulder. 'Could he talk?'

'Talk? Christ – what with?'

Hausmann relaxed. 'Then they can't be sure. It could have been anybody – a forester or a poacher.'

Chest heaving painfully, Meyer managed to sit up. Lean in build, he had gaunt, sardonic features. 'Did you get a look at the wagons?'

'Yes. They were covered with tarpaulins but their serial numbers tallied.'

Hausmann motioned him to be quiet. The dogs had ceased barking and the train could no longer be heard. Yet the deep silence was broken by the distant sound of machinery and the throb of powerful engines. Coming from the vast stretch of forest, the sound was both mysterious and intimidating. Hausmann listened a moment, then put an urgent arm beneath Meyer's shoulder. 'Come on. We must get a message through to London.'

The weary Meyer stumbled alongside him. As they disappeared a night breeze swept down the valley, agitating the tall firs and drowning the alien sound. When the breeze dropped, the woods were silent again.

CHAPTER 4

'Parade! Attention!'

There was a loud rumble of chairs and benches as the crews rose. Henderson, his ruddy face still showing resentment, waited at the foot of the platform for Davies to precede him before starting towards the end door of the Operations Room. Towering a good eight inches over the diminutive Davies and weighing at least a hundred pounds more, the Scot had the thought they must look a bloody ridiculous pair, particularly as they had unconsciously fallen into step. In his sensitive mood he wondered if Moore, who had stayed behind to chat with Young, wasn't being smart in avoiding the walk up the aisle with them. A suspicious glance at the crews showed their faces were expressionless but nevertheless Henderson broke step before they reached the door.

It was held open by Marsden, the Station Signals Officer. Giving him a nod, Henderson followed Davies outside, not failing to hear the muted cat-calls and murmurs of discontent the second he was out of sight. Nor did Davies either. The red spots on his cheekbones made him look more like a truculent cockerel than ever as he turned to the C.O.

'You've got your fair share of comedians among that lot. If you take my advice you'll keep swinging the big stick from now on. Otherwise they could get on top of you.'

Although he needed to clench his jaw to do it, the big Scot kept silent. Outside on the airfield the rescue crews were still sifting through the wreckage to find the remains of Powell and his navigator. 'The bastards!' Davies snapped to no one in particular. 'A bloody dirty way to fight.'

As things stood Henderson could see no percentage in reminding him that both sides practised it. Still bristling from the indiscipline he had witnessed, Davies marched stiff-legged across the tarmac to the Headquarters Block and down the corridor to the C.O.'s office. There, as if setting an example to all who abused protocol, he waited for Henderson to open the door and invite him inside. Muttering to himself, he tossed his cap on the Scot's crowded desk.

'I'll say this – you laid it on. Let's hope it makes 'em pull finger in the future.'

Henderson decided it was time to speak up for his team. 'There's nothing basically wrong with these lads, sir. They've had a run of bad luck and it's had an effect on them but they'll pull through.'

Davies scowled. 'They'd better, Jock, because I had to fight every sod from the C.-in-C. down to get this squadron. Nobody seemed able to grasp that one day a vital target might come along that only an élite squadron could clobber. Then

182

that Swartfjord job arrived – and Christ, wasn't that important – and the boys did me proud.' With memory ousting all else, Davies' birdlike eyes turned as bright as new pennies. 'Nobody else could have done that job, Jock – not the Army, the Navy, or Main Force itself. This squadron did it – *my* squadron. So doesn't that give me the right to jump on 'em when they start falling from grace?'

Recognizing love and pride when he saw them, Henderson was mollified. 'These boys won't let you down, sir. Just give them a bit more time and you'll find out.'

Davies' remark was addressed to himself more than Henderson. 'That's the trouble. Time's running out.'

The Scot's ears pricked up. 'Does that mean another big job's coming along?'

Regretting his lapse, Davies gave another scowl to cover it. 'If we don't pull finger we won't have 'em for any job, big or small. There are dozens of gloating bastards up top who can't wait to shove 'em back in Main Force again.'

Henderson's eyes were on his face. 'Is that why you've brought in Moore?'

'Yes. If anyone can make a team of them, he will. But he might be a bit drastic at first – in fact I've told him to be. Back him up, will you, Jock? He knows what he's doing and I must have a first-class unit again.' Before Henderson could comment, Davies went on: 'You know who he is, don't you?'

'No. Who?'

'You must have heard of Moore's Footwear. Shops in every town in the U.K., Army contracts, the lot. He's the only son.'

The Scot grimaced. 'At least he shouldn't have problems meeting his Mess bills.'

'Loaded,' Davies told him. 'Somehow his old man's kept the business private. Rumour has it he's on his last legs, so any day the lad could inherit the lot.'

'Let's hope it doesn't take his mind off the job,' Henderson said, conscious of his malice.

'Not a chance of that. He was one of Pathfinder Force's top men and you know what that means. I'd nearly to use dynamite to get him here.'

At that moment the phone rang and the Scot picked up the receiver. 'Oh, hello, Bill. What's your problem?'

Davies, whose sharp eyes missed nothing, saw Henderson's brow furrow as he listened. 'Marsh? Yes, of course I remember. But you know what my orders were.'

The indecipherable metallic voice made hurried explanations. After hesitating, Henderson appeared to relent. 'All right. Let him go. But no one else. Got it?'

Before the caller could reply he slammed the receiver down. 'Trouble?' Davies asked casually.

'No,' the Scot said shortly. 'An administration matter. It's settled now.'

Davies changed the subject. 'I'd like a favour, Jock. Can I borrow your office for the night?'

Looking surprised, Henderson glanced down at his watch. 'You mean you want to work?'

'No. I want to sleep in here. Will you arrange to have a bed brought in?' Catching Henderson's look, Davies decided some explanation was called for. 'I'm expecting an important phone call but it won't come until the early morning. So there's no point in your staying up.'

'I don't mind,' the curious Scot offered.

'No. In any case it's something I have to handle alone. Fix it up, will you?'

Henderson had two thoughts as he dropped into his chair and picked up the receiver. One was that he was now certain the Old Man had something big up his sleeve. The other was that the request for a charpoy would start the rumour that he was knocking off a Waaf in his office. Not wanting to hear the Duty Officer's surprise, he let the receiver fall the moment he made his demand known. 'Anything else, sir?'

'No. I've got all my kit with me.' Davies was picking up his cap from the desk. 'Now what about a drink?'

Henderson, who could be tactful in spite of his bluff exterior, hesitated. 'You mean in the Mess?'

'Where else?'

'You don't feel after all that's happened tonight, it might be a good idea to stay out and let the lads blow off a bit of steam?'

Davies stared at him. 'Because you've given 'em a bollocking? Good God, no. Face 'em and let 'em know you meant every word of it.'

About to argue and then realizing the futility, the burly Scot gave a semi-humorous shrug and followed Davies outside.

Unlike Young, Frank Harvey did not stay in the Operations Room to talk to Moore. As soon as Davies and Henderson had disappeared outside, he pushed back his chair and followed them. Conscious that men were nudging one another as they watched him, he looked neither left nor right. Out in the corridor he saw that Davies had not yet reached the exit door and he paused. The last thing in the world the Yorkshireman wanted at that moment was an exchange of words with either.

As dangerous as a goaded animal, he gave a start and swung round as a hand tapped his arm. For one who possessed his full measure of Irish temper, Millburn was looking contrite. 'I'm sorry, sir. I'd forgotten back in the Intelligence Room that you and Powell were friends.'

'What the hell had that to do with it?'

Seeing how things were, Millburn took it cautiously. 'I guess it makes me understand better how you feel. Only I had to put in a word for St Claire. The kid really wasn't to blame.'

'So you said.'

Although the American felt he was hammering at a brick wall he decided he might as well say it all. 'It's tough about the job too. I guess all the guys feel the same way.'

The crews were now leaving the Operations Room and their glances at the two men were curious as they jostled past. The embittered Harvey jerked a thumb. 'They look it, don't they? Don't give me a load of crap, Millburn.'

The embarrassed American was wishing he'd never surrendered to his impulse. 'You are coming over to the Mess, aren't you? Taff Wilson got a case of whisky today.'

Harvey swung away. 'No. I'm turning in.'

Glad the painful scene was over, Millburn watched the Yorkshireman's power-ful figure clump down the corridor and disappear. They came all shapes and sizes, the American thought, but that awkward sonofabitch led the field. Then thoughts of Harvey vanished as a hand clapped across his shoulders and pushed him for-ward. 'You brooding about the bollocking, Yank? Forget it. There's whisky in the Mess.'

The dog began barking when Harvey was still fifty yards from his billet. As he pushed open the door it rushed forward and leapt against his legs. Closing the door he switched on the light. The dog, a large black mongrel with Labrador leanings, tried to leap up and lick his face. Pushing it away, Harvey stripped off his tunic. The dog, sensing his distress, ceased its fussing and watched him anxiously as he dropped on the iron-framed bed.

Christ, he thought, what a day. A ballsed-up operation, Powell's death, and now this. After they'd raised his hopes by letting him lead the squadron for nearly three weeks. Harvey's big hands closed into fists but before he could release the dam gates of his bitterness he saw again the funeral pyre that had incinerated Powell and Irving. His exclamation of protest as he jumped to his feet and went to his locker brought a bark from the anxious dog. Discovering he had locked the doors earlier, Harvey put a foot against one door and heaved on the other. With a rendering of wood the lock burst open. Pulling out a bottle of whisky and a tin mug, he returned to the bed where he tore off his tie. A mat of chest hair showed as he unbuttoned his shirt and ran a hand round his sweating neck. Staring down at his wet palm, he cursed and swilled whisky into the mug.

The neat spirit warmed his stomach and for a moment the blood-red image in his mind faded. Before it could return he grabbed and held on to his resentment. The hatred it engendered was like an analgesic and Harvey surrendered himself to it.

The effing, sodding country – nothing ever changed. When Prentice had got the chop they'd used him as a stop-gap. Now, with the heat off, things were back to normal. You could sweat your guts dry with fear, you could fly until the oxygen burned your lungs out, but the moment they looked at your documents and saw your background, up went their bloody toffee noses. They called in the boys with the old school ties like this bugger Moore and you were out on your arse.

Harvey raised the mug again. You could always tell 'em. Their looks, their accent, their manner – most of all their manner. Harvey, who was nobody's fool, knew that education and polish gave a man the confidence he could never have, but it was knowledge that only put a sharp point on his bitterness. The bastards denied you that polish and then punished you for the rest of your life because you lacked it.

The whisky was warming the Yorkshireman's hostility as well as his stomach. You had to hand it to 'em, though. They hadn't survived down the centuries for nothing. Carrots were their secret. Dangle one before a donkey and he'd follow you to hell and back. They were doing it now. Every newsreel and broadcast told you the war was destroying for ever the old class system, and if we all fought hard enough and won it, we'd all march shoulder to shoulder into a bright egalitarian future. Harvey gave a belch of disgust. When the war was over, the toffee-nosed bastards would climb back into their Daimlers and managerial chairs, and buggers like himself would be back in the factories and coal mines.

Another vision of Powell's funeral pyre came to Harvey as he slumped back on the bed. As he stiffened, the anxious dog barked and tried to jump up alongside him. Harvey wiped an arm across his sweating face. Better the bitter prewar memories than that.

His eyes settled on a faded photograph on a chest of drawers. The middle-aged woman was plump and dowdy, the balding man showing unease in his Sunday-best suit. Kicked from arsehole to breakfast time all their lives and as poor as church mice, the poor sods. To give him and his kid brother, Jack, a Christmas stocking they'd had to put a sixpence a week away in a Christmas Club from January to December. If he or Jack had torn a shirt or a pair of shorts in play, it had been a major disaster. Yet in his entire life Harvey could never remember hearing either of them complain. His mother had sometimes cried but that had been for other reasons than self-pity. That was as far as Harvey could think about his mother: as always his mind shied away from the painful memories.

His father, Arthur Harvey, was a veteran of Ypres and the Somme. Although he had known nothing but menial work and poverty since leaving school he had tried to rejoin the Army on the outbreak of war. Disappointed by his rejection, he had joined the Home Guard. In Harvey's harsh terms – and oblivious of the fact he himself was an RAF volunteer reservist – his father was being loyal to the very bastards who had shit on him. Today, in his middle fifties, Arthur Harvey was a vanman receiving less than fifty shillings a week. With his younger son, Jack, crippled in North Africa and now back home receiving only a private's disability allowance, he would have been unable to keep the home together without the allowance Frank Harvey sent him.

Harvey had long ago decided there wasn't a single institution of society he could believe in. Parliament, the Law, and the Police were in his judgment a Machiavellian syndicate to help predators rob the poor and then protect the loot they seized. The Church's primary function, in spite of the casting of pious eyes upwards, was the preservation of its power and the power of its sponsors. What was that prayer in the Anglican High Church Service? 'Thank God for the gift of great leaders.' Ramsay MacDonald, Stanley Baldwin, Neville Chamberlain – Thank you very much, dear God! Something Harvey had once read had made him grin with pleasure – that the greatest charlatans in any society were those who wore the gowns, be they white, pulpit-black, or lined with ermine. The fact that the wide net could embrace doctors and university dons had not diminished the Yorkshireman's approval.

By the time Harvey had drained the second mug of whisky, his thoughts were as blurred as the outlines of the sparsely-furnished billet. Attempting to get cigarettes from his tunic pocket, he fell back on the bed and his hard laugh echoed round the room. 'Hey, Sam. I'm drunk! I'm bloody pie-eyed drunk!'

The delighted dog reacted instantly with a fusillade of barks. Abandoning his attempt, Harvey tried to swing his legs up instead. It took him two attempts before he was able to lie back full length on the blankets. More confident of him now, the dog jumped up and when it was not pushed away, crept up to lay its head on the man's chest, a position it often assumed when the Yorkshireman was sleeping. The dog lay quiet for a minute, then reached up and licked the man's face. There was no response. Harvey was fast asleep.

CHAPTER 5

The Black Swan was quiet that night. Maisie, the barmaid, a big, handsome girl with dark hair and bold features, was leaning moodily against the counter of the lounge. A massive structure, the bar was scarred and weathered by centuries of used. The lounge beyond it, like the rest of the old inn, was also of great age, and had panelled walls and a timbered ceiling. Wooden tables, the cross-sections of some huge and ancient tree, stood round the walls. Like all the timber in the room they had the rich black patina that came from centuries of wood and tobacco smoke. Copper and brass ornaments flanked the wide stone hearth while others winked back light from the massive beam that made the lintel over the bar.

The girl was wearing a thin but tight-fitting sweater that accentuated her large breasts. The only other occupants of the lounge were four locals who were playing dominoes at a table near the fireplace. At the opposite side of the room blackout curtains were drawn across a huge mullioned window.

The public bar was hidden from the girl by a stand of oak shelves but she could hear the voices of the half-dozen farm labourers who were playing darts there. Usually jocular, they sounded muted tonight. As the girl listened a door opened and closed and a voice called out a greeting. Reacting immediately she hurried to the end of the counter where she had a view into the bar. Her face clouding, she drifted back to her original position and moodily lit a cigarette.

The innkeeper came round from the bar a minute later. Stoutly-built, with a countryman's ruddy face and thinning white hair, Joe Kearns was a man in his middle fifties. Like the girl he had a North Yorkshire accent.

'Young Jack Wilkinson has just come in. Seems he's had a word with the Special Policeman on the gate. No one's been allowed out of camp tonight.'

The girl nodded sarcastically at the near-empty lounge. 'Jack's always first with the news. Didn't he find out what happened?'

'The S.P. wouldn't say. But Jerry attacked 'em, I'm sure of it. I heard gunfire just before the crash.'

The girl shifted restlessly. 'So we still don't know who it was?'

Kearns shook his head. 'What makes it worse they'd all got back. I counted 'em going out and coming home.'

The girl's generous mouth was sullen. 'You'd think someone would phone us and let us know.'

'You know better than that, lass. They put a blackout on the station when there's an emergency on.'

The sound of an opening door made both of them turn but it was only one of the domino players going to the toilet. Kearns pulled out a huge pocket watch, then nodded at the remaining three men.

'Make that their lot tonight. We mightn't get a delivery tomorrow and I don't want the lads to go short when they're allowed over.'

Maisie nodded and Kearns returned to the public bar. As the man returned from the toilet, one of his companions showed him an empty glass. The man, wearing a sports coat and corduroy trousers, nodded and approached the counter.

'What about another round, luv?'

Maisie gave him a stare. 'What's the matter, Jack Foster? Can't you count? You've already had your two pints.'

'Come on, luv. You can't be short tonight. Give us another round and have a drink yourself.'

'I'm surprised at you, Jack Foster. If everyone tried to get more than his ration, where would the country be?'

'You don't ration that RAF crowd when they come over,' the man complained.

Maisie bristled instantly. 'I should bloody think not. Those lads earn their beer.' Stalking from behind the counter she approached the men's table. 'Come on, you lot. I'm closing up now.'

Grumbling, but without malice, the men packed up their dominoes and said their goodnights to her. Listening at the door to their cheerful voices growing fainter, the girl caught the scent of geraniums and on impulse walked down the garden to the wicker gate. Over the wooden fence opposite she could see the Control Tower and the roofs of the hangars. With the airfield unusually quiet, the distant sound of a crane and the clink of metal were audible. Guessing the nature of the sounds the girl stood listening while a light breeze rustled the leaves of the crab apple tree behind her. It carried on it a smell of burnt rubber that drowned the scent of the flowers.

*

The small man wearing a service shirt and slacks was standing in front of a mirror on the billet wall. His right shirt sleeve was rolled back and he was peering at the back of his forearm. As he held it up to the mirror he showed his dissatisfaction and rubbed it with something he was holding in his left hand. This time he appeared more pleased with the result. As he was about to rub again the billet door suddenly crashed open and Millburn entered. Dishevelled and clearly drunk, the American stumbled over the step. His cap clinging precariously to his shock of black hair, he peered at the small man then gave a wide grin.

'So you're back, kid. Hiya. How'd it go?'

The other airman, startled by the unexpected visit, had whipped his left hand behind his back. His voice had an undertone of guilt as well as a Welsh accent. 'Not too bad, boyo. It can't have been, because they let me out.'

Millburn waved a hand vaguely at the billet door. 'You've missed a great party, kid. A whole case of whisky. We've drunk the lot.'

The Welshman showed his disgust. 'Greedy sods. You could have kept a bottle for me.'

A wiry man with sharp features that looked comically young or shrewdly old at will, Johnnie Gabriel was one of 633 Squadron's characters. Nicknamed Gabby or The Gremlin either because of his appearance or his madcap pranks, his youthful image was in fact an illusion because at 28 he was the oldest aircrew member on the Station. In the late thirties he had flown as a fighter pilot for the Government in the Spanish Civil War and had shot down three planes before being shot down himself and captured. When threatened with death by firing squad, he had offered to fly for Franco and incredibly his offer had been accepted. The first time Gabby had flown solo he had flown straight out of Spain into France.

At the outbreak of World War II, Gabby had volunteered to fly for the RAF, not unreasonably expecting to receive pilot training. Instead, in its infinite wisdom, the RAF had kept him waiting in civvie street for eighteen months and then, to his high indignation, trained him as a navigator instead. His present rank of pilot officer was the same rank that his pilot, Millburn, held.

Incongruous in appearance as the American and the small Welshman were, they were an inseparable couple and notorious on the station for their mad pranks and tireless pursuit of women. Unlike most of the other recruits, who had come straight from the pool, they had served for six months on a Mitchell Squadron which in April 1943 had been posted to the Middle East. At that time Millburn had been in hospital recovering from a foot wound and Gabby's protestations had been so vehement that he had been allowed to remain in the U.K. until his pilot was fit again. The outcome had been a posting to the famous 633 Squadron which at the time had flattered and delighted the two men. Now, faced with the dissension that threatened the very existence of the unit, they were less happy with their posting.

Sensing with a drunk's perception there was something wrong with the Welshman, Millburn showed concern and lurched towards him. 'What'd they say about your back, kid? It isn't broken or anything, is it?'

'Of course it isn't bloody broken. But I've got a hell of a bruise.'

Millburn gave him a lecherous grin. 'You didn't waste your time in there, did you, kid? You've got a couple of nurses lined up for us?'

'Not nurses,' Gabby told him. 'But there was a bint in the Waiting Room I chatted up. Her mother was having a finger stitched and this girl was waiting for her.'

'Nice looking?'

'Great. Long blonde hair and all the trimmings. Looked like Veronica Lake.'

'I go for Veronica Lake. She got a girl friend?'

Gabby nodded. 'I said we'd see 'em on Saturday if we're not flying.'

'What's the girl friend like?' Millburn asked suspiciously.

'How do I know? Gwen said she's all right. But you don't have to come if you don't want to.'

Grunting something, the American sank down heavily on his bed. 'I'm in trouble, kid. I had a scrap with Harvey and Pop Henderson heard it. Called us both in and gave us hell.'

Gabby was edging towards his locker. 'What was it about?'

'Harvey was going for St Claire. Said it was his fault Powell got the chop. He's as touchy as hell tonight. Maybe this new skipper's got something to do with it.'

Gabby halted. 'New skipper?'

'Don't you know anything, kid?' Then Millburn remembered. 'The Old Man had us in the Ops. Room while you were away. Tore us off a strip for not pulling together and then introduced us to this new guy, Moore.'

'Moore?'

'Yeah.' Millburn grinned maliciously. 'He looks like one of your upper crust. Got a row of gongs, though.'

'Harvey must be shaken up.'

'You're not kidding. He didn't come into the Mess tonight.' It was then Millburn noticed Gabby's rolled-up sleeve and the hand he was still holding behind his back. 'What the hell are you doing?'

Gabby's start and look of guilt was all the big American needed. Moving fast for a man in his condition he grabbed the indignant Gabby by the arm and stared down at it. A thin weal, raw and inflamed, ran across the outer forearm. Glancing round, the puzzled Millburn saw a discarded bandage lying over the back of a chair. 'What's the idea?'

As the small Welshman tried to pull away, the American spun him round and forced his other hand open. He stared down at the toothbrush that Gabby had been trying to hide, then let out an enormous guffaw. 'You little bastard! Now I've seen everything.'

Caught in the act, Gabby reacted defiantly. 'Listen who's talking! If I were in your outfit they'd give me the Purple Heart for this.'

Millburn's hysterical laugh was echoing round the billet. 'You were rubbing it, weren't you? Making it worse so you could show it off to the broads.' Howling with laughter he released Gabby and collapsed on the bed.

'Jesus Christ, the Conquering Hero. . . . Pity it's not across your arse, kid. Then you could give 'em a real eyeful.' Millburn wiped tears from his eyes. 'I can't wait to tell this to the boys.'

Gabby looked aghast. 'You wouldn't do that?'

'Kid, I couldn't stop myself. It's a lulu.'

'You do and our date's off,' Gabby threatened.

Alcoholic cunning came to Millburn's aid when he saw Gabby was serious. 'I'll make a deal with you, kid.'

'What kind of deal?'

'I have Veronica Lake on Saturday and you get the blind date. Right?'

Gabby, who in spite of his stature liked tall girls, did not give in without a fight. 'You could lose out. The other one might be terrific.'

'Yeah, that's likely. You've caught me that way before, you little bum. Make up your mind. It's Veronica Lake or I'll take your arm and that toothbrush and lay 'em both on the Mess table.'

Gabby's voice was bitter. 'Now I know why you don't join the Yank Air Force. They're too bloody smart to have you.'

'Right. Is it a deal?'

'It's a deal,' the small Welshman choked.

CHAPTER 6

The blackout in Wilberforce Street, Highgate, was complete that night. The only light Julie Marsh could see as she sat at the windows of the upstairs room was the moonlight glistening on the roofs of the prim, semi-detached houses. Wilberforce Street lay in the suburbs of the small Yorkshire market town, and its inhabitants were mostly elderly and law-abiding citizens.

In the semi-darkness of the sitting room the girl's hands were picking fretfully at the arms of her chair. As she heard the sound of an engine her pale face appeared at the window. Seeing it was only a car moving down the street with hooded headlights she turned restlessly and entered a bedroom where she tip-toed to a cot and listened. Satisfied the child was asleep she adjusted the coverings and withdrew.

Holding her watch to the moonlit window she saw it was almost midnight. Time for the news if she wanted to hear it again. She did not and yet she switched on the battered old radio that stood on a small table near the fireplace. Music sounded for a couple of minutes and then the announcer's voice she had come both to need and fear. 'This is the late night news read by Alvar Lidell. The battle

in the Orel sector is still raging and latest reports indicate the Russians are in-
flicting heavy losses on the enemy and are advancing on all fronts. In the Pacific
the Americans claim to have shot down 45 Japanese bombers over the Central
Solomons. In Italy the Canadians have captured Caltagirone. . . .'

Years of war had taught Julie March to sift through the propaganda and only
hear what was relevant to her. The relevance came at the end of the bulletin. 'This
evening, light aircraft of Bomber Command struck at enemy shipping off the
Danish coast. Enemy merchant ships were damaged and one believed sunk. Only
one of our aircraft is missing.'

That was what it had come to now, the girl thought. Suffering was measured in
numbers. One missing aircraft was nothing – if it were a Mosquito it meant only
two bereaved families. Fifty missing aircraft were different. Fifty plus was bad –
unless the results came up to expectations in which case the losses in military
terms were still insignificant.

The girl could taste blood where she had bitten her lip. She had been listening
to the news bulletins since nine o'clock and with Peter still not home had convinced herself the light aircraft referred to belonged to his squadron, for she knew
they had used 633 on shipping strikes in Danish waters before.

Feeling panic clawing at her she tried to obey Peter's appeal to stay calm.
Ninety-nine times out of a hundred, he had told her, there was an innocent reason
why he was late. It might be a hold-up at de-briefing or an unexpected order to
see the Flight Commander. It might very easily be a breakdown of his old motor-
bike. There were dozens of innocuous things that could make him late.

If only he were able to contact her, the girl thought. Needing a target for her
pent-up emotion, she found one. Why hadn't those two old bitches downstairs
got a telephone? For the rent they charged they ought to have one in every room.
Although Julie knew that half the time Peter would not be allowed to phone her,
reason had no place in her resentment. You saw selfish bitches like them every
day. Women whose husbands had no more dangerous jobs than running the local
bank or cinema and yet who grumbled because the sound of our own planes kept
them awake. The war had split society right down the middle. On the one hand
profiteers were making a killing from it and their wives were gloating over their
newly-found wealth. On the other hand were mugs like Peter and herself, living in
two threadbare rooms and wondering if each day would be the end of their
world.

Julie Marsh discovered she was trembling and went to the sideboard for the
pills the doctor had prescribed her. Needing water, she started downstairs to the
kitchen she shared with the elderly sisters. They had long retired to bed and six
months of conditioning made the girl tip-toe down the staircase. Then she
realized what she was doing and a sudden rush of defiance made her leave the
kitchen door open as she ran the tap. The jet of water, drumming into an enamel
basin, drowned noises from the street and it was only when she heard the sound
of a motorcycle being leaned against the passage wall outside that she knew her
vigil was over for one more night. Forgetting the blackout, she fumbled with the

lock and tore the door open. As a uniformed figure appeared in the rectangle of darkness, she flung herself forward. 'Oh, thank God, Peter. Thank God!'

He could feel the trembling of her thin body. 'I'm sorry, love. I knew you'd be worried.'

'Worried! . . .' She was holding him with the urgency of one trying to press through the barrier of flesh to make the only unity death could not sever. He made an effort to enter the kitchen but her arms were binding him like vines. His rush of impatience shocked him. 'Careful, love, for Christ's sake! There's light streaming out all over the garden.' As her arms slackened he disengaged them and closed the door. 'That's better. Another minute and you'd have had the police round.'

Marsh was a 24-year-old pilot officer. Orphaned in his late teens, he had been studying to become an accountant when he met Julie at a Christmas dance in 1938. Discovering she was an orphan herself and that they shared the same serious-minded tastes, Marsh had fallen in love with the girl almost at first sight and they had married while he had been waiting his call-up into the RAF. At the time Julie had been living with an ageing aunt and it had been agreed she should remain there until Marsh's pay would allow them to rent their own home.

Their child, Mark, had been born one month after Marsh's posting to 633 Squadron and had been a disastrous turning-point in their marriage. Until then Julie had seemed to bear his aircrew activities if not with equanimity at least with the nervous fortitude other pilots' wives displayed. But with the birth of Mark had been born a fear that no pleas of Marsh's, no visit to the doctor, no frantic calls on the Church for help, could diminish. With only her old aunt for a relative, what would happen to her child if Marsh were killed?

It proved a fear as progressive as a chronic disease. On his doctor's advice Marsh had asked for living-out permission. Although in general aircrews were not allowed to have their wives within forty miles of their airfields, Barrett, the old C.O., had let himself be influenced by medical reports, and Marsh had found two rooms for the girl in Highgate.

It was a move the young pilot officer had regretted almost as soon as it was made. Now Julie had facts as well as imagination to torture her, and her discovery that Marsh was a member of an élite squadron, with all that status implied, did nothing to help her. As the unit had trained for its climactic mission in the Swartfjord her neurotic apprehensions had grown, and it had come as a relief when Marsh had been seriously wounded in the arm during the ambush over Bergen. Longing for him to be grounded, she had secretly prayed for amputation and so had added guilt to her neurosis. Instead Marsh had made a complete recovery and now that he was back on active service every day was a crucifixion for Julie.

Marsh had lost count of the times the girl had begged him to ask for ground duties and his procrastination was not helped by the fact he had flown over forty missions. In Main Force he would have automatically qualified for a rest: in an élite squadron it was almost a prerequisite that one stayed on for a second tour because a high degree of efficiency could only be obtained with experienced crews. Nor had the situation been helped by 633's terrible mauling in the Swartfjord. With such a small nucleus of survivors to build on, Davies had practically insisted that all men volunteer for a second tour, and now, as things stood between the older crews and the new, the survivors would bitterly resent one of their members shaming them by withdrawing from combat.

Yet the strain on the young pilot officer was great. Unlike most of his comrades who, in spite of their experience, seldom thought of personal death because they were young enough to believe themselves immortal, Marsh was made to think of death every time he returned home. And death contained no subconscious illusions of glory. Knowing what it would do to the girl, Marsh feared it not for its pain or its mystery but for its stark breach of faith. He was needed, and so death would keep him chained to the earth in an attempt to expiate it. That Marsh could hold such thoughts was perhaps the best evidence of his deteriorating health and the love he had for this sick and frightened girl.

In appearance he was thinly-built with a sallow face and thin locks of black hair that tended to straggle over his bony forehead. Strain and battle fatigue showed in his withdrawn eyes, nervous movements, and sudden bouts of irritation.

Hurt and confused by his tone, Julie had drawn back into the kitchen. 'Have you had anything to eat?'

He tried to make amends. 'Yes, love. But I wouldn't mind a cup of coffee.'

Glad to have a task, the girl turned to a cupboard that hung over an enamel-topped table. As she fumbled inside, a tin tumbled down with a loud clatter. 'Watch it, for Christ's sake,' Marsh muttered, picking up the tin. He was returning it to the cupboard when he heard a door creak. Looking dismayed, the young couple turned to see a woman of late middle age advancing down the hall towards them. With curlers in her frizzled hair and her mottled legs thrust into a pair of fluffy slippers, the apparition was wrapped in a grey woollen dressing gown that in her displeasure she was wearing like a suit of mail. Her initial attack was directed at the white-faced girl.

'Really, Mrs Marsh, I do feel you ought to be more considerate. Do you know what the time is?'

The girl's voice had a cracked sound. 'Yes, Miss Taylor. I know what the time is.'

'Then how do you justify this kind of behaviour? First you come clattering down the stairs and wake me and my sister up and now you make all this noise in the kitchen. You're not thinking of cooking a meal at this time of night, are you?'

'No, Miss Taylor. I'm making my husband a cup of coffee.'

'Then do you have to make so much noise?' The elderly woman, who was in fact the younger of the two sisters, transferred her resentment to the dismayed young man. 'It's very late, Mr Marsh. Nearly half-past twelve.'

The trembling Julie pushed past Marsh before he could answer. 'Unfortunately the enemy aren't very considerate about the time, Miss Taylor. Sometimes they sail their ships and fly their aircraft right through the night.'

The unexpected counter-attack made the woman stiffen. 'There's no need for sarcasm, Mrs Marsh. We're just as aware as you are what the Germans do.'

Marsh moved fast before the situation got out of hand. 'My wife's a little overwrought tonight, Miss Taylor. She knew I'd been out on a raid and was worried because I'm late home.'

He received a sniff of disapproval. 'Mrs Marsh gets overwrought a little too easily, Mr Marsh. I think you should explain to her that my sister and I can hardly be blamed for the war or that you are in the Air Force.'

Marsh felt the girl contract and squeezed her arm warningly. 'No one's blaming you, Miss Taylor.'

'Most people of our age wouldn't dream of taking in a young couple with a baby. Loss of one's privacy is quite a sacrifice at our age, you know.'

'We know that, Miss Taylor. And we do appreciate it.'

'I'm glad of that, Mr Marsh. Because with Highgate crowded with evacuees accommodation isn't easy to find these days.'

The girl's eyes were tightly closed. You're doing this for me, aren't you, Peter? You fly out day after day and put your life on the line and then have to come back and crawl on your belly to people like this. Just for the privilege of being with me for a few hours. Julie Marsh suddenly felt sick as she listened to the woman's mollified voice. 'If you really need a cup of coffee, please be as quick as you can about it. My sister and I find it very difficult to sleep when someone is pottering about in the kitchen.'

The girl waited until the door closed before opening her eyes. 'Dear God Almighty,' she breathed. 'Is this what the war is all about? Protecting the possessions of millions of people like that?'

He sighed. 'Never mind the coffee. Let's go to bed.'

For the first time she saw how weary he looked. 'No. First you're going to have a drink and something to eat.'

Upstairs the room was chilly: the old house with its stone walls exuded dankness even in the summer. With the one-bag-a-week ration of coal firmly in the hands of the Taylor sisters, and with the Allocation Board arguing that Marsh was taken care of by the RAF and his wife ought not to be billeted so near the airfield, heating was another problem the young pilot officer could only try to push to the back of his mind until the autumn.

He was drawing back the cot blankets but, afraid he would waken the child, Julie pulled him away. 'I didn't get him to sleep until nine o'clock. I think a tooth is bothering him.'

Marsh moved reluctantly away and stripped off his uniform, the gaslight giving his thin arms and torso a pallid appearance. By the time he had climbed into his pyjamas Julie was already in bed. As he turned off the gaslight and opened the blackout curtains to let the moonlight in, she turned back the bedclothes for him. He sank down beside her with a sigh. 'Heavens, that's good.'

She reached out and felt his hand. 'You feel cold.'

I am cold, he thought, his mind on Powell and Irving and the way they had died. Her question was the one he had been expecting since his arrival home. 'It was you who lost that aircraft, wasn't it?'

'No,' he lied.

'Yes it was. I can always tell. Who was it?'

He lay staring at the ceiling. With his eyes now accustomed to the moonlight he could just make out the damp stain in the corner caused by the rain the previous day. 'Have you told Miss Taylor about the ceiling? It's got to be fixed before the autumn.'

'Yes. But they said it's difficult to get workmen with a war on.'

He gave a groan. 'Not that again.'

There was no way of side-tracking her. 'Who was it, Peter? You've got to tell me. Otherwise I'll be wondering all night.'

Someone has to help her, Marsh thought in panic, but who? The medicos she had seen had fobbed her off with pills that only made her feel worse afterwards and the churchmen had made her feel guilty for not having faith that her husband, who statistically should already be dead, would live to be a hundred and fifty. The only name that offered hope was Squadron Leader Adams. Unlike any other Administration officer that Marsh had known, Adams seemed genuinely concerned with the problems of his men, and the one time Marsh had confided in him had brought Adams straight round to No. 30. Not being present at the interview, Marsh had never known what Adams had said, but for at least a week afterwards Julie had seemed brighter. Marsh made a mental note to see Adams the next day.

'I have told you,' he said. 'We all got back. All fifteen of us.'

Her hand, gripping his own tightly, brought a lump to his throat. It was all so bloody pitiful – she did not believe him and yet desperately wanted to. Perhaps if he made love to her it would release the tension in them both. Her voice, small with shame, checked him as he was turning towards her. 'I was an awful coward tonight, Peter. I was certain it was you.'

Suddenly, as real as if it were in the bedroom, he caught the smell of burnt flesh that had hung around the ashes of the Mosquito. He sank back. 'We were dropping leaflets from 30,000 feet over France. You can't have anything safer than that. They haven't a fighter that can touch us.'

At least it was as good a lie as any to sleep on, he thought. As he kissed her he tasted the salt of her fear. 'Are you going to sleep now?'

'Yes,' she whispered. It was another lie: how did one resolve one's desperate need for rest when every second with him was so precious?

He kissed her again. 'Good girl. Dream about that leave I'm getting. It's only six weeks away.'

For a moment she did not speak. Then she held out her arms to him. 'I love you, Peter,' she whispered.

At that he made love to her. Afterwards, with hands entwined, they lay quietly side by side in the old-fashioned bed with its brass fittings. Their bodies had just been one but their minds were already a thousand miles apart in their thoughts and fears. Both were too young to know their loneliness was shared by all mankind.

CHAPTER 7

A moonbeam was slanting across Henderson's office when the scrambler telephone rang. In precise time it was 02.46 hours. A comical figure in striped pyjamas, Davies leapt from his camp bed and promptly stubbed his toe against a chair. Cursing loudly he limped towards the desk and snatched up the receiver. His irascibility died at the voice that greeted him and it was nearly three minutes before he spoke again. His tone had changed to sobriety and a barely-concealed excitement. 'That's bad luck, sir. But at least we know our suspicions were right. Yes; I'll organize that right away. With luck I should have the photographs by noon or thereabouts. How shall I get them to you?'

As Davies listened to the reply, his sore toe was rubbing itself ruefully against his bare ankle. 'I agree, sir – it'll be more convenient. Right, providing all goes well I'll drive round with the plates tomorrow afternoon. Yes; I'll organize that too – I'm pretty certain there's room. No, we'll keep that hush-hush but it's going to be difficult not to tell Henderson and Adams about the valley: can I play that as it comes? I can – good. What's that? The squadron? Oh, Christ, no. You've nothing to worry about there. When we want 'em they'll be ready. All right, sir – I'll see you tomorrow.'

Lowering the receiver, Davies stood motionless for a moment. Out of uniform, his small pyjama-clad body looked oddly vulnerable. Nothing to worry about – Christ. You know your trouble, Davies? You're a sentimentalist as far as this squadron is concerned and unless you're lucky or Moore is a miracle worker, they're going to drop you right into it. And then those bastards up top will have your guts for garters. Suppressing a sigh. Davies picked up the second telephone.

'Hello, switchboard. This is Air Commodore Davies. I want you to get me the Photo-Reconnaissance Unit base at Benson. What's that? Of course I know the time, you silly little man! Pull your finger out and put me through.'

The Waaf sergeant at the sunlit window gave a start. A pretty girl with freckles, she was finding it difficult to hide her excitement. 'I think some of them are coming now, sir.'

Moore, who was inspecting a plan of the station with Adams at his elbow, did not look up. 'Are they, sergeant? How many?'

'Eight, sir.'

'Is the Flight Commander, Harvey, among them?'

'Yes, sir.'

Moore slanted an amused glance at Adams. 'It sounds like your old sweats. Good. There's nothing like killing all the birds with one stone.'

Adams wondered at the young man's imperturbability. After helping him with the crew reorganization the previous evening, he had agreed to give Moore a conducted tour of the airfield. Believing the new lists would not go up in the Flight offices until Harvey had a chance to see them, Adams had suggested the tour was made directly after breakfast. Now, trapped with Moore in the Squadron Office, with over half of A Flight marching in for a showdown, Adams was feeling like a criminal caught in the act.

The flushed Waaf moved to her ante-room door. 'What shall I do, sir? Let them in one at a time?'

Appearing not to hear her, Moore was pointing at the station blueprint. 'What's that?'

'Our SCI stores,' Adams told him. 'We keep them away from the bomb dump. Just in case.'

'I take it they're inspected regularly?' As Adams nodded, Moore's voice ran on with no change of inflection. 'No, sergeant. Let 'em all in together if that's what they want.'

Adams could now hear the tramp of outraged feet in the corridor. Giving him an agitated glance, the girl ran into her office. A moment later Adams heard a door flung open. The gruff voice that followed made him wince. 'I want to see the Squadron Commander.'

The girl sounded breathless. 'I'll see if he's free, sir.'

For a reply there was a cross between a growl and a snarl. The flustered Waaf appeared in the ante-room doorway. 'Flight Commander Harvey would like to see you, sir.'

Adams, aware of his cowardice, broke in quickly. 'Would you like to handle this alone?'

'No. It shouldn't take more than a couple of minutes.' Expecting Moore to keep Harvey waiting in a gambit to draw his steam, Adams was surprised when the young Squadron Commander gave the Waaf a nod. 'Ask him to come in, will you, sergeant?'

The glowering figure of Harvey, wearing a uniform that had known much wear and tear in Mosquito cockpits, entered the office. Already on his feet, Moore held out an amiable hand. 'Hello, Harvey. I'm sorry we didn't get the chance of a chat last night. But it's good of you to come along like this and introduce yourself.'

The coolness of it took Adams' breath away. As Harvey stopped dead in his tracks, Adams had an incongruous vision of a fighting bull, breathing fire and brimstone, being confronted by a smiling matador holding a bouquet of flowers.

The handshake the Yorkshireman was compelled to make was little more than a hostile crunching of palms. Before any more courtesies could frustrate him, he launched his attack.

*

'I've come about these new flight lists pinned up in the office. Are you responsible?'

'Yes, of course.'

'You gone out of your mind? You've not only split up the flights, you've even split up some of the crews. What the hell's the idea?'

Moore indicated a chair. 'Like to sit down while you discuss it?'

The Yorkshireman's face was as blank as a fell in a thunderstorm. 'No, I wouldn't. You've only been here five minutes. How the hell can you learn anything about my crews in that time?'

Moore dropped into his chair and sat back. 'It was a bit of a problem, I admit. But I managed to get expert advice.'

Harvey's glare almost knocked Adams' spectacles off. 'From him?'

'There are plenty of people on the station who know your crews, Harvey. So it wasn't difficult to put two and two together.'

'And get what? Five, six, a bloody dozen? You come barging in, tear apart lads who've been flying together for months, even years, and stick sprogs in their places. Do you realize how the lads in my flight feel? If you don't pull those flight lists down, every man-jack of 'em will ask for a posting.'

Moore nodded at the ante-room door behind which sullen voices could be heard. 'Are those your men?'

'Yes.'

'Which ones? The crew who flew under Grenville?'

'That's right. When this was a real squadron.'

'Do they want to see me?'

'To a bloody man.'

'Then call them in. It'll save time that way.'

Glaring at Moore suspiciously, Harvey stalked to the door and gave a growl. Led by Hopkinson, men began filing into the office. Some looked openly rebellious, all looked upset. Among the latter was Peter Marsh. Moore, who had risen to his feet again, gave each man a smile. 'This is an informal get-together, chaps, so take what chairs there are and smoke if you want to.'

Although a few puzzled glances were exchanged, no one took advantage of his offer. Giving no sign he noticed, Moore seated himself again. Standing fascinated by a filing cabinet, Adams saw Hopkinson throw a glance at Harvey and then step forward. He guessed the Cockney, as Grenville's old navigator, had been chosen to speak for the rest of the flight.

'We're here about these new crew lists, sir. We can't make any sense out of 'em. As things stand we've got one good flight. Split us up and all we've got is a shower.'

'Go on,' Moore encouraged as a mutter of assent ran round the office.

'Splittin' up the flights is bad enough. But you've broken up some of the crews as well.' Hopkinson nodded at a rangy, satirical-faced New Zealander. 'I've been flyin' with Andy Larkin ever since I came out of hospital. Now you've given him one of the sprog navigators. Where does that leave me?'

Moore's laugh surprised even Adams. 'You've all my sympathy, Hopkinson. A new boy arrives one evening and the next day wholesale changes are made. It does seem a bit of a bastard, I agree.'

Although Harvey's scowl deepened at this show of forebearance, it clearly threw Hopkinson. 'We're sore because we're the old crowd who flew with Grenville. It's bad enough to change flights: it's the bloody end to be crewed up with a fresher.'

Moore nodded sympathetically. 'I agree. Losing your crew mate is worse than losing your girlfriend. That's why it's only done when necessary. I'm sorry you're one of the victims, Hopkinson.'

A puzzled murmur ran round the office. Hopkinson voiced the men's bewilderment. 'Can I get somethin' straight, sir? Was it you who made those changes or wasn't it?'

'Oh, I made them. With help, of course.'

'Then I don't bloody get it,' Hopkinson said bluntly.

With a laugh, Moore walked round to the front of the desk and leaned against it. Watching his performance with admiration, Adams found himself thinking of a young college tutor lecturing his students. 'It's really quite simple. Wellington used to do it in all his battles. And it was very effective.'

'Did what, sir?' The open-mouthed question came from Bernard Ross, a Scottish navigator.

'When Wellington had a lot of rookies – and he was always given half-trained troops – he used to slip in one seasoned soldier among every three or four of 'em. That way he never had a completely inexperienced battle line and of course the recruits soon learned all the tricks from the veterans. I suppose in botany they'd call it self-propagation.'

Another of the 'old' hands – in this case a 21-year-old called Frank Day whose pink cheeks suggested only a passing acquaintance with a razor, was frowning. 'What has that to do with us, sir?'

'That's easy. You are one of the seasoned veterans. When a fresher has you around, either as a member of his crew or in the kite alongside him, he feels much more confidence.'

Adams could have sworn he saw the youngster grow a couple of inches. 'I see. Thank you, sir.'

Moore's gaze travelled round the eight men, most of whom were now listening intently. 'The truth is, this squadron can't afford the luxury of super crews all flying in the same flight any longer. Look at the situation as it stands. A Flight have four experienced crews. B Flight has only two, Young and Millburn, and although Millburn is experienced he tends to associate himself with the more recent arrivals. If I transfer two of your crews to B Flight and at the same time split the two remaining experienced crews into two units, I have in effect four experienced crews in each flight, a far better balance. Doesn't it make sense?'

Seeing from the men's expressions and the couple of hesitant nods that Moore's argument was gaining ground, Harvey launched a counter-attack.

'That's all theory. In practice look what happened to me yesterday with a sprog navigator. It'll be bloody chaos. No one will know his arse from his elbow.'

His pugnacity earned no more than a grin from Moore. 'Then we'll have to teach everyone the difference, won't we? I've asked Air Commodore Davies to take us off ops. for a few days.' As the men gave an interested stir, Moore went on: 'We'll spend them getting to know one another better. I want you all in the Ops. Room at 11.00 hours to brief you on a practice exercise. In the meantime get your kites air-tested. Any more questions?'

'Yes.' As expected, the growl came from Harvey. 'Does the C.O. know about this?'

'Of course. I had to get authorization from him before I could ask Davies to take us off ops.'

'I didn't mean that. Does he approve of your buggering about with the crews?'

'He had a few reservations, just as we all have, but he felt it was worth a trial.'

It answered the question Adams had asked himself. 'So he's not as sold on it as you are?'

'I'm not sure I know what you mean by sold. He's given his permission for it to go ahead. That means he will back its enforcement. Is that what you are asking?'

For the first time Adams felt the iron fist in the velvet glove. Harvey's grim expression suggested he felt it as well. 'It's not going to work. It's better you know it now than later.'

Ignoring him, Moore glanced round the half-circle of thoughtful faces. 'As the survivors of the old squadron, you must be more aware than anybody there's a need for change. I don't believe what's happened recently is your fault or even the fault of the new men. I believe it's one of those things that happen to any squadron that suffers the casualties you've suffered. 617 were in an even worse mess after the dam raids – at one time it looked as if they might be disbanded. But they've pulled through and become a crack squadron again and so will you. But because you're the seasoned crews I need your co-operation and it's my guess you'll give it. All right, that's all. You can get your kites tested now.'

Looking more rueful now than militant, the men began filing from the office. Seeing Harvey was still standing his ground, Hopkinson hesitated, then said something and followed the others out. Moore, who had walked back behind his desk, feigned surprise on seeing Harvey still there.

'Is there something I haven't covered?'

Although deserted by his army, Harvey was still defiant. 'This isn't the way to improve squadron morale. You're only going to make more problems.'

'Have you any better suggestions for improving it?'

'Yes. Give those bloody freshers a dressing down. Tell them to stop thinkin' they know everything.'

Moore grinned at him. 'But I'm giving you the chance to do that. Right inside your flight office.'

Harvey's temper broke. 'I'm warning you. I'm not taking this and neither will my lads when they see through your flannel.'

Moore's voice checked him in the doorway. 'Harvey, let me give you some advice. If you have thoughts of influencing your men against me, I would think again. Otherwise you'll find yourself in very serious trouble. Do I make myself clear?'

For a moment the Yorkshireman's huge frame seemed to expand in the doorway. Then, with a curse, he lurched out. As Adams released his breath he received a comical glance from Moore.

'I don't think he approves of me, do you?'

'Whether he approves or not, you talked the others round.'

'Not all. Don't forget there are still the new men.'

'Do you think they'll also make a protest?'

'From what I saw in your office last night, I wouldn't be surprised.'

Before Adams could reply Moore's phone rang. 'Moore here. Oh, hello, sir. Yes; he's with me now.'

He replaced the receiver thirty seconds later. 'We'll have to postpone the crew briefing. That was Davies; he wants us both in his office later in the morning.'

'What time?' Adams asked.

'He can't say exactly. It seems there's a PR Mossie dropping in some time before lunch with photographs. Davies wants us when the photographs are developed.'

Suspicions that had collected almost unnoticed in Adams' mind since the previous evening suddenly surfaced. Davies' prolonged stay at the airfield, his anxiety to get the squadron shipshape, Moore's almost indecent haste in reshuffling the crews, and now this PR Mossie. . . . 'Do you think Davies has something lined up for us?'

Moore's shrug gave nothing away. 'If he has, perhaps he'll tell us about it when the photographs arrive. What about this inspection tour of ours? Have we still time to make it?'

Convinced now that he was right, Adams could only hope Davies knew how deep the squadron's troubles went. 'We can try. It's up to you.'

At that moment the Waaf sergeant put her freckled face round the door. 'Pilot Officer Millburn's on the phone, sir. He's asking if he and some others can have an interview.'

Moore's laugh was aimed at Adams. 'There goes our tour. Let's try to make it this afternoon.' He turned to the girl. 'All right, sergeant. But tell them to hurry it up.'

Adams moved towards the door. 'I'll go and catch up with my work in the meantime. Shall I drop in when the Mossie lands?'

'If you would. Then we can go to the C.O.'s office together.'

CHAPTER 8

Adams heard the Mosquito just after 11.30 hours and walked out on the tarmac in front of No. 1 hangar. The dazzling morning sky made his eyes blink behind his spectacles and he was a few seconds spotting the aircraft. Painted sky blue, it was banking gracefully over the gunposts along the southern perimeter. As Adams watched, it banked more steeply and began flattening out for a landing.

His eyes lowered to two jeeps that were waiting on the airfield. The moment the Mosquito's wheels touched the runway, the jeeps began moving forward. As the aircraft lost its forward momentum its propellers became golden bangles in the sunlight. The jeeps had now made contact and were running alongside the taxi-ing plane. A man was standing up in the leading jeep and waving an arm. Obeying his signals, the sky-blue aircraft turned off the runway and came to a half alongside a dispersal hut. The pilot and observer climbed into the first jeep which drove off immediately for the Headquarters Block. The second jeep parked between the aircraft's stationary propellers and Adams saw a mechanic and a Waaf jump out and remove the camera pack. Half a minute later the jeep span round and headed at speed towards the photographic section.

In his turn Adams made for the Squadron Commander's office. The freckle-faced Waaf was checking her curls in a mirror on the wall as he entered. 'Tell Wing Commander Moore that the PR Mossie has landed, will you?'

'He's gone to see the Armament Officer, sir. He shouldn't be more than a few minutes.'

'How did his interview with Millburn and company go?'

The girl's giggle told Adams she had fallen for the debonair Moore. 'He told them it was important they flew with the older members because, as they'd been at OTU more recently, they were better acquainted with the latest equipment.'

Adams stared at her. 'Did it work?'

'It seemed to cool them down. It's the way he does it, sir. I think he could charm the birds from the trees if he wanted to.'

Walking with Moore five minutes later to the C.O.'s office, Adams asked the question that had been worrying him for the last two hours. 'That business about Wellington. Did he really space his seasoned veterans out like that?'

Moore's amused laugh echoed down the corridor. 'I haven't the faintest idea. But it sounds the kind of thing he might have done, don't you think?'

Unteroffizier Klaus's earphones crackled. 'Wildcat Two! Steer 122 degrees for practice interception. Altitude 1,600 metres. Grid reference Anne-Marie 15.'

'Got that, Fritz?' Klaus asked in his throat microphone.

Behind him little Fritz Neumann already had his map open and was tracing his finger along the intersecting A and M references. 'Ludwigshafen,' he announced.

The Bavarian countryside with its mountains, forests, and ripening rye fields tilted and revolved as Klaus set the Me.110 on its new course. A pleasant-faced young man, Klaus was wearing shorts, for the July day was hot and the cupola of the 110 had a hothouse effect. His shirt was a South African bush jacket on which his girl friend, Heidi, had sewn his insignia of rank and his pilot's wings. Klaus, young in years but old in experience, had flown in North Africa the previous year and the bush jacket was a gift from a South African he had shot down near Benghazi. The plane had been a Mitchell and all its crew had survived. Klaus had entertained them at his airfield that evening and before the drinking had ended he and the South African pilot had exchanged shirts like rugby players after a hard-fought match. As the Mitchell had been his first kill Klaus had looked on the bush jacket as a lucky charm and even during the winter had worn it under his flying suit.

With his kills now totalling six, the young German felt he had reason to believe in the efficacy of the souvenir. Four more kills and he would be an ace and receive the Iron Cross. The difference that decoration made! Even a small man like Kuhnel, who couldn't scale 130 lb., had seemed to grow six inches once it dangled around his neck. And the effect on girls was magnetic. Klaus had promised himself he would notch up his tenth kill before his leave in August when he and Heidi were to be married. To go home and greet Heidi an ace and a hero seemed to young Klaus the ultimate in human happiness.

Fighter control came in somewhat snappishly: 'Wildcat Two. You're drifting off course. Turn on to 122 degrees.'

The order roused Klaus from his dreams of glory and he turned and gazed into every quarter of the blue sky. Satisfied it was clear of hostile aircraft, he threw a glance back at Neumann. 'Anything showing yet?'

The radar operator was peering at his three opaque screens. 'No. We must still be out of range.'

Klaus felt the Messerschmitt yaw slightly and swore as he corrected her. The cause was the contraption of aerials and reflectors sticking out of the 110's nose. Part of her Lichtenstein air-borne radar, it reduced her speed by at least eight knots and made her more clumsy to handle. At the same time, Klaus reflected, the cat's eyes that the radar set provided more than made up for its defects. Since his transfer to a night fighter squadron he had made four kills in as many weeks and all had been four-engined bombers. Many of his comrades had been equally successful: the *Tommis* were taking a terrific beating. Klaus's one fear was that their losses under the Kummhuber defences would stop them coming and so frustrate his ambitions.

Like the target plane it was stalking for practice, the 110 was under the control of 'Kassel', one of the many Kummhuber radar stations that by July 1943 formed a complete defence chain from Denmark to the Swiss frontier. Picking up an approaching bomber on its 'Freya' beam, a station would hand over its image to one of its 'giant Würzburg' beams when the plane came within their range. With a second 'giant Würzburg' locked on to radar-equipped Me.110s or Ju.88s whose nightly task was to patrol the beacons, the fighter controllers could vector their hunting aircraft near enough to an unsuspecting bomber for their air-borne radar to take over. Kassel was one of the latest beacons, built in depth behind the main radar chain, to take care of any Allied bombers who broke through into the heart of the Reich.

Fritz Neumann could hear Klaus humming the latest popular song through the intercom. Neumann was a Bavarian from the small town of Bad Heilbrunn at the foot of the Austrian Alps. At school he had wanted to be a journalist but the war had scotched that ambition. As a member of the Jungvolk he had been in Hamburg during the early 1941 RAF raids, and although they had been small-scale compared to what was to come later, the sights the impressionable Neumann had seen had determined him to join the Luftwaffe. He had hoped to become a pilot but there had been a glut of pilot cadets at that time and he had been trained as a navigator instead. During this time the bombing offensive on Germany had greatly increased in severity and a desire for revenge on the *Tommi* flyers had been strong in the young Bavarian. From navigational school he had been sent for a two months' course on radar equipment before his posting to the Pool. There he had been crewed up with Klaus whose North African tour had ended in a spectacular crash that had killed Klaus's navigator and brought the young pilot back to Germany in a flying ambulance. Somewhat prone to hero-worship, Fritz had at first been flattered at becoming Klaus's navigator. Now his hero-worship, if not altogether gone, was growing thin.

For now that Fritz Neumann had become an experienced airman and taken part in the destruction of four Allied aircraft, his desire for revenge had totally vanished. These days he saw the enemy as men like himself – ordered by their political leaders to do a filthy job and doing it at the risk of their lives. He had never dared tell Klaus that more than once he had retched when he saw the Messerschmitt's cannon shells rake open the belly of a helpless bomber and flames engulf its wounded occupants. At such times he envied Klaus who, like so many other fighter pilots, seemed to see enemy aircraft as clay pigeons to be shot down for sport rather than vehicles containing men of flesh and blood like himself. Sometimes Neumann wondered if the very imagination that had made him sob for revenge in the flaming streets of Hamburg was now responsible for his feeling of identity with the *Tommi* fliers whose charred bodies were strewn over France and Germany.

The huge, blue mirror of Lake Constance lay to the right of the 110. It fell behind as 'Kassel', whose instructions were coming through more frequently, made Klaus turn thirty degrees north. 'Any luck yet?' he asked Neumann.

Neumann was scanning the screens of his 'Emil-Emil', the night-fighters' code name for their Lichtenstein radar, with some exasperation. The fighter controller's instructions to Klaus told him they should be well within A.I. range of their target. 'Nothing yet,' he called back. 'I think these mountains must be interfering with the blips.'

Klaus switched off his R/T so his words wouldn't reach Kassel. 'If the stupid fools had set the exercise at 3,500 metres instead of on the deck, there wouldn't be any problems. Forget the Emil and look out of the bloody window.'

Neumann was about to obey when he saw a flicker of light appear on one of his screens. He made quick adjustments to his controls. 'Got it,' he shouted. 'Range 5,000 metres.'

Klaus had spotted the target plane visually at almost the same moment. It was an old Dornier 11 flying over a wooded hill. He switched on the R/T to inform Kassel that contact had been made and pushed forward the yellow throttle knobs. The note of the engines rose a full octave. Behind him, to satisfy Kassel and the demands of the exercise, Neumann was giving instructions from his radar set but Klaus was paying little attention. Swinging in a wide arc on the slower Dornier, he approached it on a parallel head-on course. At a closing speed of over five hundred miles an hour the Dornier grew from a black speck to twenty tons of power-packed metal in seconds. Klaus waited his moment and just before the two aircraft shot past one another he banked steeply into a half-circle and pulled up under the Dornier's tail.

He could not resist putting his thumb on his cannon firing button as he crept in closer. Two hundred metres, one-fifty, one hundred. . . . He was now in the perfect position for the kill, so close he could see the penumbra of the sunlight round the turning propellers, the blue oxide flame of the exhausts, the patched scars from old battles on the bomber's wings and fuselage. The graticule of his sights moved to the junction of body and wings. In his mind's eye he pressed the firing button and the aircraft reeled away like a stricken fish. It took a yell from Neumann to pull him together. 'Look out! You're getting too close.'

With a smile Klaus swung the stick over and the Messerschmitt dived away. Only four more bombers needed and over a month to go before his leave. He would double, perhaps treble, that number of kills before then.

CHAPTER 9

The two rooms on either side of the C.O.'s office had been vacated of staff when Moore and Adams came down the corridor. An S.P. posted on guard stiffened to attention. Certain now that his suspicions were well-founded, Adams followed Moore into his office. Davies, who with Henderson alongside him was bending over a map on the desk, glanced up irascibly.

'You've both taken your time, haven't you?'

Moore's voice was imperturbable. 'You said when the photographs were developed, sir. Are they here?'

Davies scowled. 'No. But they bloody well ought to be by this time.'

Taking the hint Henderson picked up a telephone and put a call through to the photographic section. While he was talking Adams noticed two young airmen standing in the corner by the door. Although they had removed their helmets, both were wearing flying suits which suggested they had been flying at altitude. Now back on the ground they were looking uncomfortably warm. One was tall, dark-haired, and sported a huge moustache. His colleague had sandy hair and a nose that looked as if it had been bent in a rugby scrum.

As Henderson replaced the receiver, Davies motioned Adams and Moore towards the map. They saw it was a largescale map of Bavaria with a red ring drawn round an area west of Salzburg. Davies jabbed a finger at the ring. 'I want you to take a look at that. It's where these two PR wallahs have just been.'

Neither man could see anything but the contours of mountains and the dots of Alpine villages as Henderson passed on the news of the photographs to Davies. 'They hope to have the plates over within ten minutes, sir.'

As Davies gave an ambiguous grunt, Moore turned to the two PR airmen. 'What was the trip like?'

The taller man answered him. Very self-possessed, he sounded in accent and manner as if he had just returned from a successful conference in the City. 'Frightfully good, sir. Top-class weather all the way. Lucky, really, because we only got wind of the job early this morning.'

'That's all the notice I could give 'em,' Davies snapped to no one in particular. Then, to the pilot and navigator: 'Tell us again what you saw.'

At the pilot's glance, the sandy-haired navigator stepped forward. Adams caught a lilt of Welsh in his voice as he stood over the map. 'There wasn't very much, sir. Just a railway track running from this village up into the valley' – the navigator's finger traced a line between two mountain contours – 'but then it vanished into the woods.'

'No suspicious buildings of any kind?'

'There was something that might have been a blockhouse, sir. But apart from that, only a few farms and forest huts.'

'What about firebreaks?'

'Yes, sir, there were some of them. But don't all woods have them?'

Davies shifted his gaze to the pilot. 'Did you say there was no flak at all?'

'Not over the valley.' The pilot's quip was clearly intended for his Celtic colleague. 'It was as quiet as a Swansea Sunday.'

Davies' scowl suggested he did not approve of this young man's self-possession. 'Some people have it easy, don't they? All right, you'd better go and have something to eat until we've seen these photographs. Remember your briefing. Not a word about this to a soul – not even your mothers. Off you go.'

The two men nodded. As they disappeared outside, a Mosquito climbed over the building with a crackling roar.

'Air-testing?' Davies asked.

Moore nodded. Through the window Adams could see a second Mosquito taxi-ing towards the runway. Davies sounded curious.

'How did they take your shuffle-up?'

'Not too badly.'

'Think they'll settle down in a couple of days?'

'I'm hoping so, sir.'

'So am I,' Davies growled. Motioning to the men nearer again, he lowered his voice. 'What I'm about to tell you is something you don't even tell yourself once you've left this room. Understand?'

Both men nodded.

'All right. Here it is. As you must have heard, there have been rumours buzzing about for years that the Jerries are miles ahead of us in rocketry and recently a Waaf Intelligence Officer, Babington-Smith, has identified what looks like a flying bomb of some kind on a ramp at Peenemünde in the Baltic. They're keeping tight-lipped about it but I gather PR kites have located factories and laboratories there as well, so we can assume it's due for a Main Force raid at any time. That's one side of it. We're on to something a bit different. It seems Jerry's clearing house for reports on secret weapons, code-named ZWB, has been infiltrated by one of our agents and he's confirmed that Jerry is developing an entire range of rockets: rocket fighters, long-range bombardment rockets, radar-controlled flak rockets, and Christ knows what else. Until now, apart from Peenemünde which is believed to be specializing only in this flying bomb, no one has known where these developments are taking place. However, we've known for some time that a certain factory near Hoffenscheim in north Germany is turning out servomechanisms and our agents have been trying to trace their destination. With the rerouting Jerry does with his wagons, you can imagine the problem and until a week ago they'd had no dice. Then, by sheer chance, someone discovered a high-security zone in Southern Bavaria. Agents were put on surveillance there and the outcome is disturbing.'

Letting the point sink home Davies lit a cigarette and as an afterthought offered the packet round. As the three men declined, another Mosquito could be heard taking off on its air-test. Glancing upwards, Davies waited until the roar of engines faded.

'I don't have to tell you that our aircraft losses are climbing again. Jerry's a resilient sod and he's pulling out all the stops to defend the Fatherland. At the moment it's not his flak but his fighters that are the main threat. The Yanks are taking a hell of a beating on their daylight raids and the radar-controlled night fighters are clobbering us hard. If losses continue to rise, Jerry could win back control of his air space and that wouldn't only put paid to our policy of strategic bombing but would also have a drastic effect on our invasion plans. And if invasion is delayed another year or so, who knows the effect it might have on Russia and the fate of Europe. So the stakes are bloody high.'

Satisfied from his listeners' faces that he had their full attention, Davies laid a finger on the map again. 'Which brings us back to this Bavarian valley. Although Jerry is working on a dozen rocket projects, we've reason to believe he is giving top priority to two. One is a bombardment rocket that can be radar controlled for about forty miles. Imagine what that would do to an invasion fleet. The other, code-named Rhine Maiden, is a radar-controlled anti-aircraft rocket with a proximity fuse. If we don't like their fighters, imagine what these bastards would do to us. Our armament and speed would be useless and among tightly-packed formations such as the Yanks use, their effect would be catastrophic.'

In the tight hush that followed Davies' revelations, Adams felt that someone was expected to ask a question. 'You're saying that these servomechanisms have been traced to this valley, sir?'

'Correct. I got the news last night. A train entered the valley and its wagon numbers corresponded with those seen leaving Hoffenscheim.'

'Do the agents know the exact location of the plant?' Moore asked.

'No. You know what those Bavarian valleys are like – all high mountains and bloody huge forests. You've only to lop off the lower branches of the firs and you can hide a railway track and anything else in 'em. And the population's sparse. That's why we've only just discovered it's a security area. The peasants have probably been told it's a training centre or some guff like that.' Irascible again, Davies swung round on Henderson. 'Where the hell are those photographs?'

The Scot was turning back to the telephone when running footsteps were heard in the corridor, followed by a half-hearted challenge by the S.P. Pushing past Adams, Davies yanked the door open, to reveal a breathless Waaf carrying a tin box. Davies' bark made the girl jump as if the S.P. had pinched her bottom.

'You've taken your time, haven't you?'

'We've been as quick as possible, sir.'

'How have they come out?'

'Quite well, sir. We've enlarged two of the best as you asked.'

Davies snatched the box from her. 'All right. Off you go.'

As Adams closed the door, Davies put the box on the office floor and opened it. As he lifted out the first photograph, a wet print sandwiched between two plates of glass, he gave a satisfied grunt. 'That PR pilot was right. We have been bloody lucky with the weather.' He examined the rest of the prints, then, motioning Henderson to clear the desk, laid two prints on it. 'The one on the left is of the main valley and the town at its entrance, Ruhpolding. The other is a blow-up of the town itself.'

The other three men gathered round him curiously. The first photograph, taken from a great height, made the Bavarian landscape resemble a heavily-wrinkled tablecloth. A short, wide valley occupied the centre of the print and Adams knew that the dark shadows on the flanking mountainsides were dense forests. Half-way along its length the valley bifurcated, the eastern leg of the Y being longer and narrower than the western. Davies laid the point of a pencil on the parent valley entrance.

'Ruhpolding's here. Now take a look at the blow-up. This is the railway station. I've already been told that the line used to end here. Now see where it goes,' and his pencil ran up the photograph and off the glass.

He replaced the print with two others. The first was a long-range shot of the eastern branch of the valley. The sides were densely wooded and although minute squares of fields dotted its length, most of the floor was dense in timber. The second print was a blow-up of the junction of the two valleys and heavy enlargement showed a cotton-thin black line swinging into the eastern leg. Tracing it Davies gave an exclamation of triumph. 'You see. It ends in a forest. Doesn't that prove that it has to mean something?'

Henderson was looking doubtful. 'It could be just for removing timber. Or it could go right through the valley to somewhere else.'

'Then why the hell would they throw a high-security net round it?'

The unconvinced Scot gazed down at the photographs. 'What security measures have they taken?'

Adams was studying the thin lines of firebreaks that were criss-crossing the timber. Two ran along the mountains that flanked the valley and two others lay across it, forming a huge rectangle. He pointed them out. 'These firebreaks look a bit too symmetrical. Could there be fences along them?'

Adams had never expected to get a beam of approval from Davies but he received one now. 'That's good work, Adams. Our tip-off says the fence is mined and that the trains have to pass through a check-point before they enter the valley. So you see Jerry's security is tighter than a bull's arse in fly time.'

'What's our first move?' Henderson asked.

'First we have to be certain we're right about the nature of the target and where it's sited. That's a job for our agents and with all this tight security they've got a problem. Our problem – assuming our guesses are correct – is that we don't know how long the plant has been there and what stage its research has reached. So time could be running out for us.'

Adams, still euphoric from Davies' praise, interrupted him. 'Excuse me, sir, but if the target is so important and time is at a premium, wouldn't the simplest thing be to send in a force of heavies?'

The glance he received was withering. 'Send in thousands of trained men and millions of pounds' worth of machinery without knowing what we're bombing? Into a narrow valley as far away as Berlin? You losing your grip, Adams?'

'Sorry, sir. I didn't give it proper thought,' Adams said hastily.

'You can say that again. Christ, they're queuing up in front of Harris with their priorities. We've not even certain it's not an elaborate spoof – Jerry's clever enough – and then think what clots we'd look! But in any case heavies could never bomb this place at night, even if they used Pathfinders and knew what they were bombing. Don't you know those forests stretch for miles?'

Moore's intervention brought Adams relief. 'Have you considered B.17s? They would solve your daylight problem.'

Davies' scowl was an admission he had dabbled with the idea of calling on the Americans for help. 'No one would choose an out-of-the-way valley like this out of pure cussedness. We feel it's a hundred to one the plant is sited so a high-level raid can't touch it. And if it has to be done at low level, Mossies are the only kites with the necessary range and capability.'

Nodding, Moore spanned the map with his hand. 'I make it around six hundred miles. More with dog-legs.'

Davies expressed his uneasiness in irritability. 'I know that.'

'What time of day would the attack have to be made?'

'The experts think about noon. In the early morning and evening the mountains throw too many shadows.'

'That's what I thought. So it would mean a round trip of 1,200 miles in day-light over enemy territory with a low-level attack thrown in. As things are at the moment, I'd say it was just about impossible.'

Although Adams was shocked by the risks involved in the operation, it was clear Davies had not expected his young Squadron Commander to hold the same doubts.

'Nothing's impossible, for Christ's sake. We're working on it, and if the job has to be done, we'll find a way. But as far as the primary target goes we can't do any-thing until our agents confirm their suspicions and then pinpoint the target for us. Unfortunately that might take some time although they're making it a top priority job.'

'How can they get near the plant if security is so tight?' Adams had the temerity to ask.

'Leave their problems to them,' Davies snapped. 'You're going to have enough of your own because I'm making the entire operation this squadron's pigeon. Your first job, now we know where the servomechanisms are going, is to flatten the Hoffenscheim factory. This might give our agents a bit of breathing space to do their stuff. Also, as Hoffenscheim is in a valley, it'll give your lads a taste of what the real job might be like. After that, if the agents are still in the dark, we'll clobber another factory that's making gyros. It's on the outskirts of Miesbach, near the Swiss frontier. Even if we're wrong about the whole thing, it won't do any harm to knock out two of Jerry's highly-specialized factories. You'll get more details later. All right?'

The three men nodded. Adams, the only man other than Davies who had been present at a similar briefing four months ago, was feeling the same dry throat and sense of presentiment. Moving from face to face, Davies' eyes stopped on Moore.

'I hope it's clear now why I want this shakedown doing fast. If Jerry's research is completed before we've the chance to hit him and his blueprints go out to fac-tories all over Germany, we can forget about stopping production. In three months he'll have his long-range rockets targeted on our Channel ports and his Rhine Maidens will be knocking us and the Yanks out of the sky like pheasants, so work your boys until they drop. Plenty of low-level stuff. Use the Loch Ness range if you like – I'll get clearance for you. Your deadline for Hoffenscheim is 06.00 hours on Thursday. O.K.?'

'Yes, sir.'

Satisfied the urgency of the situation had sunk in, Davies stood back from the desk. 'Then that's it for the moment. I'm away for a day or two but will be back before Thursday. In the meantime, not a word to the fleas on the station cat. Off you go.'

As Adams followed Moore into the corridor, Davies appeared in the doorway. 'Hang on, Adams. You're pretty friendly with the innkeeper of the Black Swan, aren't you?'

Adams showed his surprise. 'Yes, sir.'

'What's the accommodation situation over there? Do you know?'

'He hasn't anyone at the moment. He doesn't like letting rooms because it's impossible to get help to do the cooking.'

'But wasn't your wife over there for a time? And Miss Bergman?'

Adams saw this was going to be difficult. 'I could ask him, sir. As a favour.'

'I'd like you to. For two weeks. Starting on Thursday.'

'You mean for yourself, sir?'

'What the hell would I want a room for? No; it's for a girl.'

'A girl? I see, sir.'

'Don't look so bloody salacious, Adams! I'm not planning myself a bit of crumpet across the road. It's the daughter of some friends of ours. Swiss people who came over to this country in 1939. The girl teaches German and until now hasn't been north of the Thames, so while the schoolkids are on holiday I promised to see if I could fix her up. The moors might suit her because she likes walking and she'll also get a chance of meeting some young people from the station. Anyway, it's the best I can do, so speak to the innkeeper for me, will you?'

'Yes, sir. I'll do it right away.'

'Good man. Tell him I'll take care of the bill. Her name's Reinhardt, by the way. Anna Reinhardt.'

Both excited and apprehensive at Davies' disclosures, Adams would have given much to discuss them with Moore as the two men walked down the corridor, but with Orderly Room staff passing by he contented himself with the remark: 'Am I right in thinking you'd a hint of this when you arrived?'

Moore glanced round them before answering. 'A hint but that's all. I hadn't any details.'

Satisfied, Adams changed the subject. 'As you've cancelled the briefing of the crews until this afternoon, what about coming over to the Black Swan with me? We've just time for a quick one before lunch.'

Half-expecting a refusal, he was gratified by Moore's reply. 'Why not? It'll be my last chance to relax this week. Let's take a look at this famous pub of yours.'

CHAPTER 10

As Adams led Moore into the pub lounge, Maisie was chatting to two young farm labourers at the counter. The only other occupants were two middle-aged couples drinking beer at a table near the fireplace. The girl's eyes brightened at the sight of Adams and she gave a shout. 'Joe! Frank's here.'

Conscious that all six people in the lounge had suspended conversation to watch them, Adams led Moore forward. As Kearns came hurrying in from the public bar, his greeting expressed his relief.

'Hello, Frank. It seems a long time since Saturday.'

Privately Adams agreed with him. 'Hello, Joe. One way and another we've been kept busy. Let me introduce our new Squadron Commander – Wing Commander Moore.'

As Kearns shook hands with the pilot, Maisie was taking in his appearance. Under thirty, good-looking, a row of medals a mile long, and a scar on his cheek that made Maisie think of a romantic film she had once seen in which students gave one another sabre cuts to attract women. Forgetting the two young labourers, she took a quick glance at herself in a mirror behind the bar. Although as concerned as ever about the crash the previous evening – and beneath her sweater Maisie had a heart as big as her mammaries – the sex in her could always be relied on to lighten her mood if a presentable man came into her orbit. As Adams turned to her, she smoothed down her sweater.

'This is Maisie. If you're extra nice to her, she sometimes reaches beneath the counter and finds a bottle of whisky.'

Maisie leaned her hemispheroids provocatively over the counter and offered her hand in the way she had seen it done on films.

'I'm pleased to meet you, sir, I'm sure.'

Moore gave her a smile. 'I'm pleased to meet you, Maisie.'

Too posh for her, Maisie was thinking without the slightest resentment. You'd only to look at his uniform and listen to his voice to know that. But who cared? The fun was in the trying, wasn't it? There was an archness in her movements as she stood back.

'What would you gentlemen like to drink?'

Kearns gave a chuckle. 'After what Frank said, I don't think we've much choice, lass.'

Winking at the two officers, Maisie leaned voluptuously down, to reappear fifteen seconds later with two half-filled glasses of whisky. Her tone changed as she saw hope light up the faces of the watching locals. 'It's no use you lot lookin' at me like that! It's the last of the bottle and there's no more due for another week.'

At any other time Kearns would have asked Adams about the accident the previous evening but with Moore an unknown factor and with civilians present, he decided to wait until he and Adams were alone. Maisie, however, had no such inhibitions.

'What was the trouble last night? We heard 'em come back and then there was some firing and a terrific crash. We could see flames from upstairs.'

Unsure of Moore himself, Adams decided to make the locals his excuse and slanted a warning glance in their direction. 'I'm afraid it's all a bit hush-hush at the moment.'

His expression made Maisie forget her role of the femme fatale. 'Someone was killed, wasn't he? Is it anyone we knew?'

Kearns took her by the arm. 'We'll find that out soon enough, lass. Run in and take my place in the bar, will you?'

The girl hesitated, then, with a troubled look at Adams, obeyed. Kearns addressed his apologetic murmur to Moore. 'Sorry about that, sir. But the lass is as fond of the lads as I am and it's a strain not knowing what happened.'

Adams was glad he had another subject to broach. 'Joe, have you ever met Air Commodore Davies?'

Kearns had to think. 'I seem to remember he came over here once. Is he a small man?' As Adams nodded, Kearns glanced at Moore and judged his man to a nicety. 'With all respect, as spry and sharp as a fox terrier?'

Both men laughed. 'You've got him,' Adams said. 'He wants to know if you'll let him have a room for a couple of weeks. From Thursday.' As the innkeeper's mouth opened in protest, Adams went on quickly: 'I told him the difficulty you have in getting help but the snag is he knows my wife and Hilde were here recently. So I had to say I'd ask you.'

Although recognizing Adams' problem, Kearns was looking doubtful. 'It's very difficult, Frank. Mrs Billan might help again but I'd have to ask her first. The trouble is, a man makes more work than a woman.'

Adams saw a ray of hope. 'It isn't for him. It's for the daughter of some family friends of his.' He went on to explain. 'The girl's Swiss. Aren't they supposed to be very domesticated?'

The piety of his hope made the innkeeper's eyes twinkle. 'Let me have a word with Maisie. She's in touch with all the help around here.'

He returned a minute later. 'All right, Frank. Maisie thinks Mrs Billan will help but if she won't the two of us will manage. You did say it was only for a fortnight?'

Adams was moved to relief. 'That's all. Thanks, Joe. I appreciate it.' He glanced at Moore. 'Time for another?'

Moore emptied his glass and set it down on the counter. 'No; I must get back now. I've still a few jobs to do before the fireworks start this afternoon.' He turned to the white-headed innkeeper. 'Nice to have met you. I'm hoping you'll see plenty more of me in the weeks ahead.'

'I hope so too, sir. Good luck in your new job.'

Maisie, who had been keeping an ear open for their departure, popped her head round the corner. 'If you two come in this evenin', I might find half a bottle of brandy in the cupboard.'

Moore was smiling. 'Keep it until the weekend, will you? By then we'll appreciate it.' He glanced back at Kearns. 'Don't worry if you don't see many of the boys in here for a few days. As a new man I have to show them my way of doing things and it'll probably keep us busy until the weekend. Then I'm hoping things will get back to normal.'

Kearns hid his curiosity well. 'I see, sir. Thanks for letting us know.'

As the innkeeper stood watching the two men go out, Maisie left the bar and joined him. 'What did Frank say he was?'

'He's the new Squadron Commander. Roy Grenville's old job.' Kearns' expression was reflective as he packed flakes of tobacco into a blackened pipe. 'I hope he'll handle the squadron as well. Things haven't been the same since Grenville went.'

Maisie's big eyes were dreamy. 'I don't know how he'll handle the boys but one thing's for certain, he could handle me. Did you ever see such a dreamboat?'

The Waaf with freckles put her head round the door. 'Pilot officer Hopkinson's here, sir.'

Moore lowered a file of papers and sat back in his chair. 'Tell him to come in, sergeant.'

The Cockney, still looking resentful, marched in and saluted. 'You wanted to see me, sir.'

Moore indicated a chair. 'Yes. Sit down and make yourself comfortable. Smoke?'

The Cockney remained standing. 'No, thanks, sir.'

Grinning wryly, Moore leaned back. 'You're sore with me, aren't you, Hopkinson? You're angry because I've split up your partnership with Larkin and puzzled why I haven't crewed you with anyone else. Right?'

'If you say so, sir.'

'I think it's a fair guess. Now I'm going to explain my reasons and you'll understand why I couldn't give them in front of the others. I'd like you to fly with me.'

This time Hopkinson reacted. 'With you?'

'Don't look so surprised. From all I'm told you're the best navigator on the station. And as Squadron Commander I can't afford to lose my way, can I?'

Hopkinson's expression said clearly that it was going to take more than flattery to win him over. 'Someone's been stringin' you along. There's a half a dozen navigators here as good as me.'

'Grenville didn't think so. And the way I see it, if you were good enough for him, you ought to be good enough for me.'

The implied compliment to his old skipper, the surest way of modifying the Cockney's resentment, brought a frown to his bony face. 'Can I ask a question, sir?'

'Why not?'

'Why didn't you bring your old navigator with you?'

'I couldn't. He finished his second tour of ops. a month ago. As he was a married man they wouldn't let him volunteer for a third.'

'Where was that, sir?'

'Warboys.'

Hopkinson gave a start. 'Warboys? Were you in Pathfinders?'

Moore looked almost apologetic as he nodded. 'Johnnie got me in the middle of his first tour and was stuck with me until they stood him down. It came as a wrench to us but there was nothing either of us could do.'

The rapid calculations Hopkinson was making brought a new respect to his voice although it retained its characteristic Cockney bluntness.

'If you know what it feels like, I don't see why you've done it to me and Larkin.'

Moore's eyes lifted to his face. 'That's easy to answer. My job is to make this squadron a first-class unit again and that means I can't let individuals' preferences stand in my way. This afternoon we're starting a shakedown programme that's going to continue non-stop until Wednesday evening. For that and everything that comes later I need your co-operation because, whatever you say, you're the best navigator on the station. At the same time I don't like making a man fly with me.' Moore's lips quirked humorously. 'I don't suppose you'd care to volunteer, would you?'

Hopkinson shuffled uneasily. In the silence a trapped fly could be heard buzzing in the sunlit window. Making an effort to look resigned, the Cockney gave a shrug. 'I suppose there's no harm in givin' it a try.'

Moore relaxed and the charismatic smile that made the Waaf sergeant dream of cots and cottages reached across the desk to the frowning navigator. 'Thanks, Hopkinson. I don't think you'll regret it. Now let's get over to the Ops. Room and start the briefing.'

In a certain large country house not far from Sutton Craddock the security staff were on their toes that afternoon. At the main gate sentries were scrutinizing with extra care the credentials of all visitors whether local tradesmen, artisans, or service personnel. The armed guards with Alsatian dogs who patrolled the inside of the high walls were keeping a watch that would have made it difficult for a squirrel to enter the estate undetected. Davies, who was driving a staff car borrowed from Sutton Craddock, was stopped half-way down the drive as well as at the main gate before he reached the house.

The courtyard on which he parked contained four other cars, one a large American staff car. As he jumped out, a briefcase in his hand, a young Army lieutenant approached him, saluted, and led him down a flight of stone steps to a large lawn surrounded by flower beds. Two uniformed men were sitting at a table in the centre of the lawn, and as Davies approached, the elder of them came forward and held out his hand. He was a Brigadier of distinguished appearance with iron-grey hair and a small, trimmed moustache. An officer in SOE, his role was to work with Davies, the RAF's nominated representative, when close inter-service co-operation was needed. An outstanding example of this co-operation had been the Swartfjord operation. With the Brigadier very British and stiff upper-lipped and Davies volatile, hypersensitive and quick-tempered, it had all the surface appearances of a shot-gun marriage. Instead, by some mystical symbiosis, the two men worked well together and had complete confidence in the other's judgments.

'You're looking well, Davies.' The soldier had a quiet, clipped voice that matched his appearance. 'Come over and meet General Staines.'

The man that rose from the table weighed at least fifteen stone and every ounce of it looked like bone and muscle. In his early fifties, he had spiky iron-grey hair and the face of a boxer. His gravelly voice had a Texan accent. 'Glad to meet you, Davies.'

Davies saluted, then took the big hand that was offered him. 'It's good of you to come, General.'

The American shrugged. 'Your people said it was important, so I guess I didn't have much choice.'

The Brigadier, who had caught the eye of a waiter hovering nearby, turned to the Air Commodore. 'What will you have to drink, Davies?'

Davies saw there were two half-filled glasses standing on the table. 'Nothing for me, thank you, sir.' Seeing the American staring at him, he felt an explanation was necessary. 'Drinking during the day always gives me a headache.'

The Texan pushed a cigar case towards him. 'Then have a smoke.'

Feeling he was on trial, Davies opened the case and pulled out something that resembled a toy airship. Discovering with relief his lips could just encircle it, he struck a match and inhaled cautiously. Seeing the Texan's eyes on him, Davies was determined to die rather than cough. When to his surprise he did neither, his normal perky confidence returned.

'Thank you, General. They're milder than I expected.'

Staines pulled one out for himself, bit off the end, and lit it. 'They're my midday smokes. I go for the heavier stuff after dinner.' Releasing an expansive blue cloud, he settled back in his chair. 'O.K., let's get down to business. The Brigadier has filled me in with the Intelligence details. I understand you've brought some photographs.'

Opening his briefcase, Davies passed the prints to the two men. Staines studied them, then pushed them back with a grunt. 'All they tell us is that we can't see anything. But I'll grant you that rail track looks suspicious.'

'We're nearly one hundred per cent certain the establishment is there,' the Brigadier said quietly.

'O.K., suppose it is. Are you telling me you're expecting your boys to go all that way in daylight? And then bomb at low level? Jesus, it's not that far from Salzburg.'

'We are using a Mosquito squadron,' Davies pointed out.

'I don't care what the hell you're using. The Kraut controllers will vector fighters all the way across Europe. When they come down they'll be slaughtered.'

Davies nodded. 'That's why we need your help. If you lay on a Fortress raid in the Munich area it's certain to draw all their available fighters.'

'Not if this rocket establishment is as important as you both think. What happens if they give a couple of Focke Wulf squadrons the job of looking after you?'

'We think we can avoid that happening.'

'How?'

Davies spent a couple of minutes explaining. When he finished Staines looked thoughtful. 'It might work. Only how many of our ships are you thinking of?'

Davies cast a glance at the Brigadier, then took a deep breath. 'To work it has to be a major effort. We'd like a minimum of one hundred and fifty. Preferably two hundred.'

The Texan gave a loud laugh of disbelief. 'Two hundred B.17s! You've got to be kidding, Davies! What's happened to the RAF? You gone out of business or something?'

Davies stated the obvious. 'Our heavies are designed for night bombing: they haven't the armament to fly all that way by day.'

Staines's tough face was a study. 'You know the range of our Thunderbolt escort? Even with wing tanks we can only reach Cologne. After that we'd get hammered all the way.'

The Brigadier's quiet voice drew the American's attention. 'We appreciate your losses would be heavy, General. But they have to be weighed against the threat of these rockets which our experts think is very grave indeed.'

'O.K., that's as maybe. But we can't release that to the Press, can we? So how do I justify a hundred or two hundred American ships carrying out a support role for one British squadron? If we lost half a dozen the Press would crucify us, and we'd lose a hell of a lot more than that.'

'The Press won't know about us,' Davies said. 'Not if you pick yourself a legitimate target in the Munich area.'

Staines was frowning. 'Why can't we hit this valley ourselves? Then I'll have a real case to put to Eaker.'

'We wish you could,' the Brigadier told him. 'But our agents have gone into it very thoroughly and assure us the configuration of the valley makes it impossible for heavy bombers to make the raid. It has to be done by highly manoeuvrable light bombers.'

The Texan ran a hand over his spiky hair before putting his question to Davies. 'What outfit are you using?'

'633 Squadron. One of our highly specialized units.'

The Texan gave a start. 'The outfit that did the Swartfjord job?'

Davies could not keep the pride from his voice. 'That's the one, sir.'

For a moment the tough American looked impressed. 'That was one hell of a job. No question about it.' His shrewd blue eyes moved from the Brigadier to Davies and back to the soldier before he spoke again. 'So you think this job's important?'

The Brigadier nodded. 'We think the Allied air strategy and perhaps the invasion itself could be affected if these rockets are allowed to go into production. But

218

I must warn you that it might not be possible to give you more than twenty-four hours' notice once the target is located.'

The Texan raised his bushy eyebrows. 'Why not?'

'We haven't been told yet. But it seems all the notice our agents are prepared to guarantee us.'

Staines ran a hand over his spiky hair again. 'A hundred and fifty plus B.17s . . . twenty-four hours to put 'em on the line. . . . Jesus, you two really give me a case to put to Eaker. If I pull this off I'll expect a recommendation for that Victoria Cross of yours.'

Davies found the temptation irresistible. 'I'd stress the threat of those A.A. rockets among your formations, General. They'd make daylight bombing almost impossible.'

A less assured character than Davies would have blushed at the look he received. 'What the hell do you think I'm going to sell him – the benefit of playing footsy with the British? What's the code name of this A.A. rocket again?'

'Rhine Maiden, sir.'

The American emptied his glass, then heaved his big body from the chair. 'O.K. Leave it with me and I'll see what I can do.'

CHAPTER II

For that day and the two that followed the men of 633 Squadron felt as if a tornado had hit them. Moore's message, fully endorsed by the Station Commander, was as succinct as any message could be. After its heroic efforts in the Spring the squadron had suffered a reaction but its period of convalescence was now over. A massive shake-up and stocktaking would commence, and from now on a hundred per cent effort would be expected from every man.

The message went like a battle order from officers and NCOs down to the lowest erks in the pecking order. Engine fitters like McTyre found themselves doing an exhaustive inventory of their spares and then indignantly checking every individual part to establish its reliability. Crews were sent round the labyrinths of the bomb dump to check for exudation among the older bombs and to list the available stock of pyrotechnics, detonators and fuses. Bomb armourers were made to check the serviceability of pistols, bomb racks, hoists, bomb-sights, and all the other multitudinous offensive equipment that made up a Mosquito squadron. Gun armourers were dispatched to the range to check the harmonization of all serviceable aircraft and to test spare Brownings and 20mm. cannon, and on their weary return made to strip and oil every propellant unit from Very pistols to signal mortars.

All over the airfield tradesmen were similarly employed. Transport Pool drivers were made to check their vehicles as thoroughly as if preparing to take them into action. Ground gunners were tested on latest German aircraft silhouettes and sent to the range for practice. Photographers had to list their stocks and check every camera; radio operators had to strip and re-tune their sets. Nor was the shake-down limited to the tradesmen. The Clothing Store was made to carry out a stocktaking that would have done credit to Marks and Spencers. The Catering Officer had to match his stocklists with his stores, and great was the consternation thereof. Even Burt the Bastard, the Station Disciplinary Officer, and the Guard Room were not exempted from the shakedown. Before long a rumour ran round the airfield that even the resident blackbirds were lining up for inspection.

To add to the ground crews' resentment, maintenance of the aircraft had to be carried on at the same time. With the Mosquitoes flying as if they were on maximum effort, this meant men working in the evenings and in most cases far into the night.

Yet if resentment was felt on the ground it was nothing to what was felt among the aircrews, old sweats and new men alike, on the first day of the shake-up. Taking the squadron over the moors in the late afternoon, Moore made no attempt to lead them into the complicated drills that those who knew his record expected. Instead, to get the men used to his orders and to familiarize them with his methods, he gave them simple formation practice. Although it was a mere prelude to what was to follow, to men who had flown in action – and that included every man who flew that day – the drilling was an insult, and in spite of the feeling that ran between the reshuffled crews, men took time off their personal feuds to roundly condemn his behaviour.

If on their arrival back at Sutton Craddock they believed their day was over they were bitterly disappointed. During the exercise, cursing armourers had been out on the airfield filling up 11½lb. practice bombs with smoke-producing stannic chloride. It was a job armourers hated for the chemical was evil-smelling and an irritant to eyes and skin. As the Mosquitoes landed, light-series carriers were hoisted into their bomb bays and these in turn were loaded up with the practice bombs. At the same time bowsers discharged high-octane fuel into the aircrafts' tanks. The choked-up aircrews had barely time for a cup of tea before they were ordered back to Moore who was waiting for them on the airfield. After a quick briefing, he led them into the air again.

This time his destination was Scotland. Ordering the Mosquitoes into line astern, he led them like a file of soldiers between mountains and into steep-sided valleys. After half an hour of this he set a course to Loch Ness where the quadrant huts of a bombing range had been warned to expect them.

Here at both medium and high level Moore sent in each aircraft to test its navigator's and pilot's skill. Most crews obtained reasonable results but some of the newly-assorted ones had problems. Among them, to the Yorkshireman's chagrin and fury, were Harvey and his new navigator, Blackburn. Clashing over methods of finding wind direction, they saw their bombs falling thousands of feet away from the yellow target. The curses and condemnations that filled the R/T channel brought no more than a smile from Moore, who knew the problems minor enough to be solved in a day once the rival factions lost their bloody-mindedness towards one another.

With each aircraft carrying sixteen bombs apiece, the exercise was a long one and before Mosquito No. 16 had dropped its last bomb the Highland mountains were black and the western sky aflame. Although it was dusk when the crews landed, their day was still not over. Lindsay, the Station Armament Officer, had been ordered to give the crews a refresher lecture on the latest bombs and pyro-technics, and after a quick meal the men were sent to join him in the Ops. Room. Faced with derisory howls and comments, Lindsay could not make himself heard until Moore entered the room and laconically announced that written tests would be given to all crews that weekend and any man who failed them would suffer a curtailment of his freedom until his knowledge improved. Although the hostile silence that followed appeared to have no effect on the imperturbable Moore, it reminded Lindsay of an ocean groundswell before a storm.

The second day brought no relief, in fact the pressure was intensified. Three more flights to Scotland were laid on, and on each Moore stiffened the exercises. On the first flight he led the squadron out on another high-level bombing exercise over the Loch Ness target. This was carried out in two stages, the first at 20,000 feet and the second at 25,000 feet. On the second trip he led the Mosquitoes in line astern through the Highland mountains until their coolant radiators were almost brushing the tree tops and then into a low-level attack on the loch target. On the last flight rockets were used against a special target set up alongside a lake. The day was rounded off by another lecture, this time given by Moore him-self, on the latest Pathfinder techniques using ground and sky target indicators.

A gusty wind and a falling barometer on Wednesday morning gave warning that the weather was changing. It was also the morning Harvey's temper ex-ploded. Directly after breakfast he came storming unannounced into Moore's office.

'We're not going up to Scotland again, are we?'

Moore, dragging his flying suit out from a locker, turned unhurriedly. 'I'm afraid we are. Is something wrong?'

'Too true something's wrong. I've had a bellyful of being drilled as if I were a rookie at Padgate. Haven't you been told that some of us have flown among mountains a bloody sight more dangerous than those Scottish gnat bites?'

'I know your record, Harvey.'

'Then how about showing us some respect? Take the new men if you like but stop treating the rest of us as if we were at OTU. What does it do to you – appeal to your ego or something?'

With some sympathy for the Yorkshireman's anger, Moore was wondering why this man of all his crews could get under his skin so easily. He made an extra effort to be patient.

'I know it's irksome for you and the others, but stick it out a bit longer, will

221

you? I can't practice with half a team and I have a good reason for what I'm doing.'

'Is that what you think we are – a football team?' Cursing his disgust, Harvey went to the door and turned. 'You can play a reserve today. I'm dropping myself.'

Moore met his eyes and held them. 'Wrong. You're playing and that's a direct order. Do I make myself clear?'

In the hush that followed the bellow of a Merlin under test could be heard. The seconds seemed endless before Harvey cursed thickly and withdrew. The slam of the ante-room door made the building shake on its foundations.

The weather allowed Moore only two practice flights that day but both exercises were unusual enough to intrigue even the incensed Harvey. The Mosquitoes were led at low level through the Scottish mountains until fifteen miles from the Loch Ness target where they were ordered up to 2,500 feet. From that height they were brought down in a shallow dive, to release their practice bombs at 1,000 feet and continue the dive until they were no more than a hundred feet above the Loch. Twisting through the valleys they stayed at low level until called on to repeat the exercise.

Both exercises ended with gunnery practice on a sea target off the Lossiemouth coast. Rain was falling steadily as they returned to Sutton Craddock and the relieved crews heard that flying was cancelled for the rest of the day.

With all sixteen Mosquitoes to service there was still no respite for the ground crews, however. Squatting on his Mosquito's wing, with rain dripping off his long nose and down his cape, McTyre gave vent to feelings shared by most of his colleagues.

'Talk about a sodding new broom sweepin' clean! What's the stupid bastard trying to do – kill us off before our time?'

The corporal fitter, enjoying the privilege of rank by sheltering under the wing, grinned at him. 'Maybe he's a Jerry in disguise, Mac.'

'Stranger things than that have happened, mate,' McTyre said darkly. 'Look at us lot out here. If we don't get pneumonia in this bloody rain it'll only be because we'll get rheumatic fever first.'

Under the nose the cherubim-faced Ellis was struggling to free the ill-fitting 20mm. gun panel. 'Did you know Air Commodore Davies is back, Mac? I saw him get out of a car when I went to armoury.'

McTyre's long nose twitched like a greyhound scenting a fox. 'Again? Then something big's comin' off. There's always trouble when that little sod's around.'

'Who needs trouble when we've got Moore,' the corporal grinned.

Feelings were as high in A Flight crew room where the weary pilots and navigators were slumped in chairs. Grumbles and derogatory comments on Moore were heard coming from even mild-tempered men like St Claire and Marsh. As Hopkinson entered he saw to his surprise that Larkin and his new navigator, Richards, were drinking tea together. The satirical New Zealander raised a malicious hand on sighting Hopkinson. 'Greeting, most favoured one. How does it feel to fly with Nero?'

Hoppy looked uncertain whether to scowl or grin. 'You know something? If I had to fly round those bloody mountains once more I'd get hairy knees.'

'You'd get more than that, my Cockney sparrow. You'd grow a sporran. Wouldn't he, sprog,' Larkin demanded fiercely of his new navigator.

Richards, a plump young man with auburn hair, seemed surprisingly uninjured by the epithet. 'I think I've grown one myself, skipper.'

'You hear that?' Larkin asked of all and sundry. 'Those highlands have given my sprog navigator a sporran. And our Cockney sparrow's got hairy knees.'

'I'd say he deserved them, man.' The comment came from Stan Baldwin. Negro ex-accountant from Barbados, Baldwin was a comparative rarity even to a service that drew members from all quarters of the Commonwealth. An ebony-faced, heavily-built man with a rich sense of humour, his favourite story was that every time he and his pilot, Paddy Machin, went on a night operation Machin would turn anxious and keep asking if he was still there.

'Why do you say that, my sun-burned friend?' Larkin asked him.

Baldwin showed superb teeth in a wide grin. 'Man, anyone who shows that Pathfinder how to play silly buggers with us in those mountains deserves to get hairy. I hope he gets hairy all over.'

Hoppy grinned weakly as cheers and catcalls came from old sweats and new men alike. Even Harvey, who had appeared in the doorway, was seen to be grinning. Larkin turned towards him with a groan. 'What is it now, skipper? More lessons?'

The Yorkshireman shook his head. 'He must be sick of you lot. You're stood down for the rest of the day.'

There was a howl of relief. 'You mean we can go out?' someone asked.

'Why not? You're off duty until the morning.'

In the general euphoria that followed Larkin was seen cuffing the plump Richards' face and Clifford, another old sweat, was heard offering his new navigator a lift into town. Similar scenes were in evidence in B Flight crew room. If the crews missed the implications, they were not lost on the officer who entered Adams' 'Confessional' half an hour later. Hanging up his raincoat, he approached the Intelligence Officer's desk. 'Well, what's your verdict?'

Adams, who had been working as hard as anyone during the last three days, was unsure of Moore's question. 'It's looking good. The average error on the range today was under seventy yards.'

At Moore's impatient gesture, Adams understood. 'You mean the crews? Oh, yes, it's working. They're still a bit cliquey, of course, but most of their hostility to one another appears to have gone. Those training exercises of yours must be therapeutic.'

Moore was looking amused. 'You know there's more to it than that. I saw your face in the Mess last night when they were all trying to avoid me.'

Adams shuffled uneasily in his chair. 'What's your point? That their hostility has transferred itself to you?'

'What else?'

223

'It's only a temporary thing,' Adams muttered. 'It'll go as soon as they get to know you better.' Then he caught Moore's quizzical expression and gave a start. 'You wanted it this way, didn't you?'

Moore shrugged and reached out for the bombing report. 'They say you can't beat a common dislike for drawing men together.'

Adams was about to reply when the telephone rang. 'Yes, sir. He's here now. I'll tell him.' Replacing the receiver he glanced up at Moore.

'That was the C.O. He and Davies want a word with us right away. They intend laying on the Hoffenscheim job as soon as the weather clears.'

CHAPTER 12

The dog, sitting upright in the passenger seat of the car, gave an impatient bark. Harvey glanced at it and grinned.

'Shut up, you stupid bugger.'

A torn rubber on the left-hand wiper, giving a blurred image of the rainswept road ahead, was the cause of the dog's complaint. At the sound of Harvey's voice it wagged its tail and attempted to paw the windscreen. Instead it slipped and stumbled into the well beneath the seat. Looking crestfallen, it scrambled back and wagged its tail at Harvey, who grinned again.

'Serve you right for being such a moaner, mate.'

The car was a bull-nosed Morris the Yorkshireman had picked up for thirty pounds when he was promoted to Flight Commander. Its main function before Powell's death had been to transport both men to local race meetings, a pastime they shared, and to take them to Highgate where Harvey was friendly with a middle-aged bricklayer and his family. The family consisted of Jack Lewis, his wife Mary, two sons and a daughter. Both sons were in the Army; the girl, Sarah, who had recently left school, was still at home. Once and sometimes twice a week the shirt-sleeved Harvey could be found in the kitchen helping the family to wash up the evening dishes. To those at the station who saw him as a hard, uncompromising officer, the sight would have provoked either disbelief or hilarity, as Harvey was uncomfortably aware. Powell, however, who had visited the family somewhat less frequently than Harvey, had kept the Yorkshireman's visits a secret to the day of his death.

For Harvey, whose father lived too far away to be visited except on a long weekend pass, the visits had become as necessary as the companionship of Sam, his dog. Elevated by war to command men better educated than himself, secretly embarrassed by the military conferences and Mess functions and their upper-class overtones, the Yorkshireman found relief and even security in his visits to the bricklayer's house.

Today, Wednesday, had been his first opportunity to inform the family of Powell's death. Sarah's reaction had confirmed Harvey's long-held belief that the girl had a crush on the Australian. Shock had turned into hysteria, forcing Mary Lewis to take the girl to her room. With Jack Lewis on fire-watching duty that night, Harvey had stayed long enough to ensure the girl had quietened down and then, on Lewis's suggestion, had slipped out to have a pint with him at the local before the bricklayer reported to the Town Hall for duty. Left alone in the pub, which held painful memories of Powell, Harvey had found himself growing increasingly restive and moody. Finally, on an impulse that was entirely self-punishing, he had bundled Sam into his car and started back to the station.

With rain falling steadily from an overcast sky, the evening was drawing in early as the old Morris laboured up the long hill that led from Highgate. From its crest, on fine days, the southern reaches of the Yorkshire Moors were just visible. Today the wide counterpane of small fields and dales that lay between them and Sutton Craddock looked as if a spider's web had been drawn across it. It was a sight many members of the squadron would have found depressing but Harvey found an affinity with it. It was not the first time Harvey had been glad the war had not taken him from his native soil.

He was a third of the way to the airfield when he saw a stationary taxi at the road side. A man with a brace was struggling with the rear wheel and a woman wearing a mackintosh and head scarf was standing beside him. On seeing the Morris the man dropped the brace and signalled the car to stop. Braking, Harvey leaned across Sam and wound down the window.

'Puncture?'

The taxi driver, his jacket black with rain, nodded his disgust. 'I can't get the bloody wheel nuts loose.' Then he noticed Harvey's RAF mackintosh. 'Are you going to the station, sir?'

'Yes.'

'Then would you give my fare a lift? She's got a room booked at the Black Swan. Give my office a ring too, will you? Here's the number.'

Harvey glanced at the smudged card the man pushed at him and slipped it into his coat pocket. 'All right. Tell her to jump in.'

Through the rain-streaked windscreen he watched the man drag a suitcase from the taxi and follow the woman to the Morris. As he leaned across Sam again to throw open the door the dog gave a bark of protest. 'Put the suitcase on the back seat,' he told the driver. As the man obeyed, the Yorkshireman picked up the indignant Sam and deposited him alongside the suitcase. He then acknowledged the waiting woman.

'Jump in.'

'You are very kind.' Her voice had an attractive foreign accent that Harvey could not place. She gave money to the taxi driver and then climbed in beside him. Nodding at the man, Harvey revved the engine and pulled away. With a sigh of relief the woman lifted her hands and removed her scarf.

'It is good to get out of the rain. Is it true you are going near to the Black Swan?'

'Yes.' Glancing at her Harvey saw she was young with swept-back dark hair and an oval, intelligent face.

'I hope it isn't far out of your way.'

'No. It's right next to the airfield.'

'How far away is that?'

'Six, perhaps seven miles. No more.'

'You are stationed at the airfield, of course?'

Harvey was unaware of the grimness of his nod. 'Aye, I'm stationed there.'

In the awkward silence that followed he could feel the girl assessing him. One who always found small talk with women difficult, Harvey was relieved when she broke the silence.

'What is the Black Swan like?'

'It's not the Savoy. But it's homely and old-worldly, if you like that kind of thing.'

'I do.'

'Then you shouldn't find it too bad.' Before another silence could fall Harvey made an effort. 'Do you know someone at the airfield?'

'Yes.'

'Might I ask who?'

'Air Commodore Davies.'

Harvey could not conceal his start. 'You know Davies?'

'Yes. His family and mine are friends.'

'But I thought his home was in Kent.'

'It is. But I am on holiday and he kindly arranged for me to stay here for a couple of weeks.'

Harvey was nothing if not blunt. 'He must be out of his mind. What the hell is there here for a girl on holiday?'

'He knows I love walking and felt I would like the moors. They're not far from here, are they?'

'Not too far. But you'll need to pick your weather.' Harvey's nod was at the slanting rain. 'They don't make you very welcome on days like this.'

Her answer made him stare at her. 'Like all things with character, I suppose they have their moods.'

'They have their moods all right.' His laugh was harsh. 'Some of 'em black and surly.'

'Yet you like them, don't you?'

'What makes you think that?'

'The way you talk about them. Some men pay compliments that way.'

Wondering how anyone could discover the truth about him so quickly, Harvey began throwing up his defences. 'I was born in this part of the world, so it's different for me. In a couple of days you'll probably hate the place.'

'What makes you so sure of that?'

'For one thing you're foreign, aren't you?'

'Yes.'

'What nationality?'

'Swiss.'

'Swiss what?'

'I don't know what you mean.'

'Swiss Italian, Swiss French or Swiss German?'

'My family are of German stock.'

'German,' Harvey repeated, as the girl looked full at him.

'Yes. Pure German. Does it offend you?'

Harvey was getting over his surprise. 'What do you mean – offend me?'

'That I am a German. Most people in this country today do not like Germans, Swiss or otherwise.'

Harvey's laugh was harsh again. 'We'd have to be sick or something if we liked them, wouldn't we? Seeing we spend most of our working time trying to kill 'em.'

The girl was gazing at him as if she had not seen him properly before. 'I suppose that is true. If one felt nothing about one's enemies, war would be an even greater obscenity than it is.'

Her words made Harvey start. The nearside wheels of the Morris hit a pool and sent water cascading over the verge. With a muttered curse he pulled the car back to the crown of the road. 'So you think war's an obscenity?'

'Don't you?'

It was a question that brought out the perversity in Harvey that was always close to the surface. 'Not particularly. In peacetime the rottenness of the world is often hidden. In wartime it comes out into the open. I'm not sure I don't prefer it that way. At least you know who your enemies are. Or think you do.'

'Think you know,' she repeated. 'Don't you believe the Nazis are your enemies?'

'Maybe they are. But they aren't my only ones.' Suddenly realizing how he was giving himself away, Harvey turned his attention to the road.

Her eyes were moving over his morose face. 'You must have had a very unhappy life to think like that.'

The astonished Harvey was wondering how you could want to hurt someone whom you had only known a few minutes. 'Why must people like you always rush to Freud? Has Davies had an unhappy life? Because in case you don't know he's about the keenest Hun killer I've met.'

Her gaze moved to the stone hedge where a crow, disturbed by the approaching car, was flapping away into the rain. 'Arthur has never hidden from us that he doesn't like the Germany of today. But I know he distinguishes between the ordinary Germans and those who support the Nazis.'

To hear Davies being called Arthur was enough to bring any Flight Commander down to earth, thought Harvey as the Morris crested another hill and the Control Tower of Sutton Craddock became visible through the murk. 'Sorry. I don't know why I'm talking this way. I'm not even sure I know what I'm talking about. Blame it on the weather, will you?'

'You don't need to apologize. People should always say what they think – or how can one get to know them?'

Harvey found he was smiling for the first time that week. 'Then you ought to get on well with the folks around here. They also believe in saying what they think.'

He liked her laugh. It was contained and yet spontaneous. 'And you said I wouldn't like it here. Now I know you are wrong.'

Less than two minutes later Harvey braked outside the private gate of the inn. As he opened the rear car door he found the girl talking to Sam. 'What is your dog called?' she asked him.

'Sam.'

She gave a laugh of pleasure. 'I think he likes me. Look, he's licking my hand.'

He dragged out the suitcase. 'You're honoured. By and large he doesn't think much of people.'

She appeared to be about to say something, then climbed from the car instead. As a loud gust of shouting and laughter came from the inn she glanced inquiringly at him. 'What is it? A party?'

From the corner of his eye the Yorkshireman was watching two sergeants who were passing the car on their way to the pub. Catching sight of him and the girl, one man nudged the other and whispered a comment. The sight made Harvey brusque.

'It'll be noisy tonight. The lads have been under pressure this week and they're letting off steam. Things will get back to normal tomorrow.'

Closing the door on the barking Sam, he followed the girl down the path. Although the loose mackintosh hid her figure, he saw she was tall and walked well. Opening the front door of the inn he led her into an oak-panelled hall that was in semi-darkness. On the right was a well-worn staircase, on the left an antique table and a wall telephone. Ahead were three doors. One, glass-panelled, only partly concealed the light and gaiety of the bars it served. Putting down the suitcase Harvey struck a bell that stood on the table. He had to strike it twice more before the door opened and a perspiring Kearns appeared. For a moment the din was deafening and among the milling airmen Harvey caught sight of Millburn and Gabby jammed tight against the bar. Then Kearns closed the door and hurried forward.

'Sorry, Mr Harvey, but it's murder in there tonight. What can I do for you?'

The girl took a step forward. 'Are you Mr Kearns?'

'That's right, Miss.'

'I believe Air Commodore Davies has made a reservation for me. My name is Reinhardt.'

'Oh, yes, Miss. The room's all ready for you. Sorry we're in such a state tonight.'

The girl gave him a smile. 'Why are you sorry? Everyone seems very happy.'

'I think they are, Miss. But I hope the noise doesn't disturb you too much.'

'Don't let it worry you. I'm sure it won't.'

Clearly impressed by her manner and good looks, Kearns helped her remove her mackintosh. Beneath it she was wearing a green costume that set off her tall, supple body and dark hair. Picking up the suitcase Kearns hurried up the stairs. 'I'll show you your room now and as soon as the rush dies down I'll see you get dinner.'

The girl glanced at Harvey. 'If you are in a hurry I will phone the taxi people for you.'

'There's no need,' he told her. 'I've plenty of time.'

In his hurry to get back to the bar, Kearns was already halfway up the staircase. 'Your room's Number Two, Miss.'

'Thank you,' she called. 'I'll be up in a moment.' Turning back to Harvey she held out her hand. 'Now we know each other's names. Mine is Anna Reinhardt. And you are Mr Harvey.'

There was a grace about her that made Harvey feel clumsy. 'Frank Harvey. Would you like me to tell Davies that you've arrived?'

'It is not necessary. He said he would phone me after nine-thirty.'

Still uncertain of her relationship with Davies, Harvey could only hope his question was not too obvious. 'Will you be seeing much of him while you're here?'

The semi-darkness of the hall hid from him the smile that for a moment touched her lips. 'It is not likely. Arthur is a friend of my family but he is far too important a man to have much time to spend with me. Although I am hoping he will take me out to dinner one evening.'

Harvey took a deep breath. 'Then would you care to have a drink with me when you've unpacked your things?'

She cast a rueful glance at the glass-panelled door. 'It looks very crowded in there. And I have been travelling since this morning.'

Nothing more was needed to change Harvey's mood. 'Sorry. I shouldn't have asked. I hope you enjoy your stay and don't find our aircraft too noisy.'

He was at the telephone and fumbling for the taxi-driver's card when her hand touched his sleeve. 'You are a very sensitive man, aren't you? I did not refuse to have a drink with you. I only meant I would prefer it when I am less tired.'

Harvey was suddenly aware she had the greyest eyes he had ever seen. Gazing into them, he was lost. 'You said you liked walking. Would you care to go on the moors when the weather clears? We could drive to Pickering or Whitby and – '

Her smile came before he could finish. 'Yes. Very much. When?'

'Can I phone you? We never know from day to day when we're flying.'

'Of course. Thank you for asking me. Now I had better go and look at my room. Auf Wiedersehen.'

Harvey watched her until she had vanished upstairs before making the phone call. As he walked down the road towards the station entrance the rain ceased and he could smell the nettles. He took a deep breath and held it. The weather was changing. It would be a fine day tomorrow.

229

CHAPTER 13

Davies, newly-shaved and impatient, was standing near the open door of Henderson's office. Hearing footsteps hurrying down the corridor he turned to the three men by the window. 'Remember, as far as these two go, this is just another job. The same applies when we go into the crew briefing afterwards. Watch what you say. All right?'

Henderson, Adams and Moore nodded. Ten seconds later there was a tap on the door and Harvey and Young appeared. Although neither had expected the early morning call, the Australian was the only one showing its effects. He had celebrated the end of the training stint with Millburn and Gabby the previous evening, and the pouches under his eyes showed it. Davies' sharp eyes were on him as he answered the salutes of the two flight commanders.

'You didn't expect this early call, did you, Young?'

'No, sir.'

'I can bloody see you didn't. What were you on last night – meths?'

Young made a brave attempt to grin. 'No, sir. Just the usual swill.'

'You must get a different brew to what I get, lad. Unless you had a bath in it. Can you see?'

'Yes, sir.'

The grunt Davies gave suggested scepticism as he walked over to the desk. A large map of Western Europe was pinned on the wall alongside it. Picking up a ruler, Davies motioned the two men nearer.

'We've got a job for you today. Before we go in and brief the crews we thought we'd run over the finer details with you. The target's here' – and Davies held the ruler to the map – 'An engineering factory at a place called Hoffenscheim on the old German-Belgium frontier. It's not on the scale of the factories in the Ruhr but it's important because it specializes in precision engineering. You've been chosen for the job because it's situated in a narrowish wooded valley, but as this valley runs east to west you shouldn't have any approach problems providing your navigation is good. All right so far?'

Both flight commanders nodded. Davies moved the ruler across the map. 'The distance from the enemy coast is around one hundred miles, so we've decided to make it a low-level job all the way.' Seeing both men start, Davies nodded. 'I know it means surrendering your altitude superiority but this way you'll get beneath his radar defences. The reasoning goes that to precision bomb the target you'll have to come down to low level anyway, and if Jerry's radar could track you all the way to the target, he could have a reception committee waiting for you. Whereas by keeping on the deck we hope surprise and speed will keep you out of trouble.'

Neither flight commander looked wholly convinced. Davies' eyes were on Harvey. 'You got a question, Harvey?'

'Yes, sir. If we're going all the way on the deck we're going to need diversions. Have we got any?'

'If you'd give me a bloody chance, I'll come to 'em,' Davies snapped. His pointer lifted to the coast of Jutland. 'Up here – above latitude 55 – the Banff Wing will be out on a sweep. Further south II Fighter Group will be carrying out an offensive patrol over the Netherlands. 12 Group are going to do the same over Belgium and Northern France. Best of all we've picked a day when the Yanks are hoping to clobber Frankfurt.'

'Hoping?' Harvey interrupted.

Davies gave him a scowl. 'The Met. boys say there's still plenty of thin cloud about, particularly below latitude 50. However it's expected to clear around midday, perhaps before. The plan is that you cross the enemy coast fifteen minutes after the last of the B.17s. That way, if Jerry's defences are on their toes, and they usually are, most of his fighters will be chasing the B.17s.'

'Poor bloody Yanks,' Young ventured.

Davies allowed the general laugh to die down before continuing. 'Lindsay will go into the details of your armament but as I understand it you'll be carrying four 500-pounders apiece. Two will be General Purpose and the other two Semi Armour Piercing. You're taking SAPs in case there is any heavy machinery about. Also the heavier shrapnel will do more damage. I think Lindsay's tail-fusing with 5.5 second delays, but you must check on this to make certain your kites are far enough apart on the run-in: we don't want you blowing one another up. You'll drop all four stores in one salvo. So unless you make a balls of it you'll only do one bombing run. As for ammo, you'll be carrying full tanks for your Brownings and Hispano, although we're not expecting you'll need them. Don't forget before take-off to check your crews have set their bomb sights for low level or they'll clobber Berlin instead of Hoffenscheim. All right, Moore – you want to finish it off?'

His back to the window, Adams saw Harvey's face cloud in dislike as the immaculate figure of Moore stepped forward. Taking the ruler from Davies, he turned amiably towards his two flight commanders.

'With luck I'm hoping we'll get away by noon. After take-off I want your men to climb to 1,500 feet and form behind me in echelon right according to your numbers. I shall lead you at that height to Manston where we shall dive right to the deck and make a dirty dash straight for the target. Your navigators will get all details of this track at their briefing. But – and this is the answer if either of you thought I was playing silly buggers over Scotland yesterday – we won't be keeping on the deck all the way. You both know how difficult it is to sight a target, much less avoid over-shooting it, when you're flying at low level. As soon as we reach Viviers – that's about twenty miles from the valley – we're going to make a steep climb to 2,500 feet. Then we'll begin a shallow dive on the target. It has to be shallow because you both know one can't bomb from a steeply-diving Mosquito. This way we'll have time to identify the target before we clobber it. Any questions so far?'

Young nodded. 'What's the idea of flying in echelon right all the way to Manston, skipper?'

'This is because we now know that Jerry's long-range radar can pick us up almost as soon as we start orbiting our airfields. If we fly south in echelon right, our images superimpose themselves on his screen and give him the impression we're heavies. So once we dive beneath his screen at Manston he'll assume we've only been air-testing and have landed again.'

Surprise and grudging respect appeared on the faces of both flight commanders. Before Moore could continue, Harvey's gruff voice checked him.

'I'm not happy about the climb to 2,500 feet before we reach the target. According to that map Hoffenscheim is on the south-east fringe of the Ruhr and that means a hell of a lot of fighter stations close by. This climb could give them the chance to reach us.'

Moore gave him an amiable nod. 'That's one of the reasons we wanted to consult you both before the briefing. I agree it does give them an extra minute or two. But look at it the other way. By making it easier for us to identify the target and so avoid over-shooting it, we might spend far less time over it than if we have to stooge around in a search. If you think about it, I'm sure you'll agree it's the best choice.'

When Harvey did not reply, Moore went on: 'We're not expecting much opposition. Intelligence believes they've only two small flak posts, and a couple of 500-pounders apiece ought to see them off. In fact with any luck at all we'll clobber them before their radar sets are warmed up. I'll take care of them myself, but if I make a mess of it, then Millburn will take over. Then you come in at pre-set intervals, concentrating on the factory. Orbit afterwards at 2,000 feet until you get my all-clear, then get down to the deck again and make for home. Your navigators will get a track that takes us north-east to Breda and then over to Norwich. This is to make certain Jerry isn't waiting for us on our homeward leg. Now – any questions?'

'What about flak ships on the way out?' It was Young.

Moore glanced at Adams, who pushed himself away from the window. 'You pass between a couple code-named Hermann and Otto. Our reports say Hermann's a new ship with much heavier armament. So you're routed nearer Otto to give Hermann the benefit of the doubt.'

Davies interrupted impatiently. '12 Group have promised to take care of them, haven't they?'

Adams was thinking of the muted cat-calls and hollow laughs that the crews would make if Davies made the same comment at the briefing. Bomber crews had little if any respect for their fighter colleagues' ground support. 'Yes, sir. But we still think it's wise to keep well away from Hermann.'

Harvey, whose silent hostility towards Moore had been a feature of the interview, returned with his earlier complaint. 'On a normal low-level operation with all these diversions I'd agree we shouldn't have too much trouble. But if we make this climb on the way out, then I feel we ought to have a fighter escort.'

It was the kind of remark a flight commander was allowed to make when alone in his Squadron Commander's office but not, because of its implied criticism, in front of others. Davies, with red spots beginning to glow in his cheeks, intervened sharply.

'You've got a fair share of complaints today, haven't you, Harvey? You're not getting a fighter escort because we don't think you're going to need one. All right?'

Seeing Henderson wanted a word with the two flight commanders, Moore stepped aside. Aware Davies' eyes were on him, the big Scot trod warily. 'See your kites are air-tested as soon as possible in case the mist clears quickly. We don't want you to miss the Yanks because they could give you a clear run to the target.' Torn between his wish for success and the need to keep secret the target's larger importance, Henderson mixed his metaphors with some effect. 'As you know, we've a lot to live up to and now we've had this spell of training there'll be plenty of people watching to see how we perform. So turn the wick up a bit and bring your boys back with their tails wagging. All right – let's get to the briefing.'

After receiving their detailed briefing and carrying out their air test, the sixteen operational crews of 633 Squadron had no option but to wait for the weather to clear. Few welcomed the delay, particularly those blessed or cursed with vivid imaginations. The morning sky with its bright film of cloud would have been ideal for their mission. But as the sun shredded away layer after layer of moisture, Larkin's gloomy prophecy was shared by most of the crews. 'By the time the Yanks have made up their minds we're going to look like goldfish swimming about at the bottom of a lighted tank.'

The way men spent the stomach-tightening wait gave some indication of their characters. St Claire had gone into the Mess after completing his air test. Adams, hearing the sound of a Chopin nocturne being played on the piano as he passed the door, glanced inside. The young artist was seated at the piano in the far corner with Sue Spencer beside him. The girl's expression made Adams feel like a Peeping Tom. Moved, he drew back out of sight and listened until the haunting melody died away.

Harvey had gone back to his billet. Lying on the bunk with his eyes closed, he was running over the briefing session again. Aware his dislike of Moore was an incentive to criticism, he had nevertheless been sincere in his complaint that the attack held built-in risks. One of Harvey's virtues, which Moore had had no time to discover, was his responsibility to the men in his flight. Even those who disliked him admitted he looked after his men like a hen her chicks. It was the reason that pilots like Marsh, who had no death-or-glory ambitions, valued him as a

flight commander. To the Yorkshireman the only justification for the risk Moore
was taking was a target of special strategic importance.

The thought made his eyes open. Could it be that? It was true that Davies had
offered an explanation but somehow it had sounded thin to Harvey. He had
taken more notice of Davies' presence at the briefing. It was feasible an Air Commodore found a raid on a precision engineering plant a special occasion but
Harvey had his doubts.

He closed his eyes again. Special target or not, the war would go on and one
side of him was not sorry. The thought of stepping out of his flight commander's
uniform to become a builder's clerk again had long been one of Harvey's secret
dreads. What a bloody world, he reflected, when men dreaded peace because of
the humiliation it brought them. He lit a cigarette, thought about Anna Reinhardt, and found his mental abrasions became less painful.

At the same moment Moore, seated at his desk in the Squadron Office, was
staring at a telegram that had arrived ten minutes ago. 'Your father passed away
at 2 a.m. His last thoughts were of you and the future. Funeral next Wednesday
at Cotsmere. Please try to attend. Your loving mother.'

Moore's hands were trembling as they held the telegram. The sight surprised
him. For over three years he had seen friend after friend killed, some in ways that
beggared description. During that same time in the seventy-nine missions he had
flown he must have been responsible for the deaths of hundreds of enemy soldiers
and civilians. They were not statistics Moore liked to dwell on but they were the
ones the young pilot felt he had a moral obligation to face. Death was anything
but a stranger to him and yet although he had known for months that his father
was seriously ill, the telegram still had the power to shock him.

He rose and walked over to the window where he could see a young ACII chat-
ting up one of the Waafs. It was the severance of the umbilical cord, he thought.
While the father lived, the child that lived on in the son saw him as a final refuge.
When death took him away, the son knew that he stood alone at last.

And not in a personal sense only. Now John Moore was dead, the empire he
had built became the son's responsibility. Exigency arrangements would keep it
ticking over until the war ended but if Ian Moore survived, the livelihood of thousands of workers would depend on him having the same business sagacity as his
father. The prospect which for a long time had been a cloud on Moore's horizon
was suddenly a forbidding mountain. With Harvey having the same apprehensions about the end of the war but for entirely opposite reasons, the situation was
not without its irony.

Another loner, Marsh, was sitting out on the airfield in the weak sunlight that
was now filtering through the clouds. The young pilot officer had a book on his
knees but his thoughts were back in Highgate. On his arrival home the previous
evening he had found Julie almost hysterical. The baby had been unwell and cried
most of the day, and the younger Miss Taylor had complained at the noise. It had
taken Marsh half the night to calm Julie, and the couple had barely fallen into an

exhausted sleep before an S.P. had hammered on the front door and told Marsh to report immediately to the airfield. The outcome had been another indignant complaint from Miss Taylor and near panic from Julie at what the recall might presage. With no time to reassure the girl before he left and fearful how she might react during the long day, Marsh felt as if the weight of the world was resting on his young shoulders. The fact he might help or even cure the distraught girl by requesting to be taken off flying duties did nothing to help his state of mind.

The rest of the crews were trying to take their minds off the raid in more physical ways. Some were playing cards and darts in the crew rooms. Others were playing football with members of the ground staff. As Gabby slid a neat pass to Millburn, whose boot missed the ball completely but almost took a corporal's head off, the Welshman gave a yell of derision.

'You clumsy pillock. My kid sister could have put that one in.'

The American, whose tousled black hair was wet with sweat, glared at the sharp-tongued Gabby. 'Why don't you Limeys play real football? Then I could scatter little punks like you all over the field.'

When 12.00 hours arrived with no news, the crews were called in for an early lunch. They had just sat down when the bell of the teletype brought the Duty Officer to his feet. He read the orders on the rapidly-moving paper and began making his terse phone calls. A minute later Tannoy loudspeakers spluttered, then blared the alert. Cursing men snatched up what food they could carry and ran to the crew rooms for their flying gear and parachutes.

The indecipherable Tannoy voices could be heard from the upstairs front bedroom of the Black Swan. Switching off the radio, Anna Reinhardt ran to the window. Over the russet leaves of a crab apple tree it was possible to see into the airfield where the scene was one of great activity. NCOs were yelling orders, men were climbing into trucks, and one by one, with their characteristic coughs, Merlins were firing at the dispersal points. As the girl watched she saw the first Mosquito begin trundling southwards down the field. Another plane followed it a few seconds later. By this time the concentrated sound of thirty-two Merlins was making the windows of the inn rattle.

The leading Mosquito had reached the far end of the runway and was waiting for flight permission. As a green Very light soared from the Control Tower its engines began booming and it started forward. Weighed down by its bombload it dropped its wheels twice to the runway before it broke free with a triumphant roar. As it dipped a wing and passed over the pub, the girl saw its wheels locking back into their nacelles. The second plane rose eight seconds later, followed by fourteen more at regular intervals. The sky was now free of cloud, and as the sun shone on the streamlined bodies the girl thought of deadly barracudas streaking towards a distant victim. She stood listening at the window until the deep drone of the engines died away.

CHAPTER 14

'Flak ship at two o'clock, skipper,' Hopkinson said.

Moore, who had already seen the ship, gave a nod. The sixteen Mosquitoes were flying line-astern across the Channel. Since dog-legging at Manston, they had gone down so low their slipstreams were ruffling the blue-green swell. Every pilot's eyes were fixed on the waves ahead: one slip in concentration at this height meant certain death. The navigators were keeping a watch on the gauges and constantly scanning the sky above.

The flak ship Otto was less than three miles away and Moore knew that warning of their approach was already being radioed back. In fifteen minutes fighters would be scrambling from Dutch and Belgian airfields. With luck, the zero height which the Mosquitoes were flying would make them difficult to find and pursue. Difficult that was, Moore thought, until they climbed into the open sky near Viviers.

The second flak ship, Hermann, was now visible on the port quarter. Otto however was nearer and the menacing steel hulk of the floating gun platform was beginning to tower out of the sea. Every armoured post along its deck contained radar-controlled guns and Moore knew these would already be lined up on the approaching Mosquitoes.

Climbing up a couple of hundred feet Moore waggled his wings. With radio silence enforced it was a prearranged signal for the squadron to open out. As the pilots obeyed, a rapid staccato of flashes, visible even in the bright sunlight, ran along the side of the ship.

Spread out and skimming over the waves like a shoal of flying fish, the Mosquitoes were making as difficult a target as possible, but the flak crews showed their experience by concentrating on each Mosquito in turn as it flashed past their port beam. For a few seconds the sea below A-Apple, Moore's aircraft, seethed with spray and a sharp explosion made the Mosquito rock. Then the fury of the attack turned on Young who was flying at Number 2.

With the pressure taken off him Moore was able to see that some fire was coming from Hermann, but with the Mosquitoes flying no higher than the masts of Otto, the gunners were clearly afraid of hitting their companion ship. Marsh, who was flying Number 12, had a shell burst beneath his port engine, and as he almost lost control a vision of Julie's condemning face flashed before his eyes.

At the speed the Mosquitoes were travelling, the action was over in seconds. Hopkinson, staring back through the perspex blister, was trying to count the aircraft as they swung back in line astern. 'I think they all got through, skipper.'

Although both men were in their shirtsleeves they were sweating. The Mosquito was a warm aircraft and at zero altitude in summer the heat could be stifling.

The flat Belgian coast with its wide sandy beaches was now rushing towards them. Although their point of entry had been carefully plotted Moore caught a glimpse of beach defences and a massive gun emplacement as they skimmed over Hitler's Western Wall. Abandoned holiday villas, nestling among sand dunes, flashed past.

Like all his crews, Moore's concentration was intense. Images flashed and faded on the retina of his eyes in rapid succession. A cobbled road, streaming below like a grey river. A horse and cart. A small enemy convoy of camouflaged trucks. A church steeple. A railway track swinging in beneath them. Half a dozen civilians waiting at a small station. Excited arms gesticulating.

The railway track swinging away northwards. A blur of fields, some green, some golden. A pond with cattle drinking. A canal with bridges. A yell from Hoppy – power cables ahead. Up and down to the canal again. A column of grey-clad soldiers marching alongside it. At this height they were real – one could feel their jack-booted threat.

The canal bending away south. Trees thickening and hills rising ahead. Must be the Ardennes. Down a shallow valley – sunlight glistening on a river. Who said Belgium was all cobble stones and factories? Wonder what the fishing's like?

Six more minutes and Hopkinson tapped Moore's arm. 'Viviers, skipper!' Over at ten o'clock Moore saw a smoke haze. If any fighters had tried to follow them, they would know it in a moment.

As Moore put A-Apple into a steep climb, the pilots and navigators behind him shared an ambivalence of emotion. Relief from the killing concentration of hedge-hopping was mixed with apprehension that they were now entering the enemy monitoring screens.

From 2,500 feet it was possible to see the great plain of Liège, the northern limit of the Ardennes forests. The amorphous sprawl of buildings covered by a thin film of smoke was Viviers. Below and to the right of the Mosquitoes the densely wooded hills of the Ardennes spread to the horizon. Catching Moore's glance, Hoppy expressed a confidence he did not feel. 'I think we're on track, skipper.'

Both pilots and navigators were now turning their heads ceaselessly in their watch for fighters. As Harvey had rightly said, there were many airfields near the great industrial complex of the Ruhr and all must have had warning that a squadron of low-flying bombers had penetrated the coastal defences. The question was whether the German Observer Corps had been able to follow their route. Liverish black spots appeared and disappeared into the great blue bowl of sky as men rubbed their watering eyes and stared again. The white-hot sun drew their gaze like a magnet. Life-giving to the burgeoning earth below, it was a constant source of death to bomber crews.

Even at that height the smoke haze that hung permanently over the Ruhr was visible to the north-east. Below, farms and hamlets had returned to the landscape. A town set among low hills appeared and Hopkinson led Moore towards it. As it swept past they caught a glimpse of a ruin on a hilltop and picturesque, half-timbered houses flanking a river. 'Monschau,' Hopkinson called with relief.

The line of Mosquitoes swept on towards a chain of low hills. As they fell behind, Hoppy gave a yell of triumph and pointed. 'Hoffenscheim! One o'clock!' More hills rose ahead. A wide valley shaped like a boomerang ran east and west between them. On its floor was an untidy sprawl of factories and industrial buildings. Climbing up the hillsides were housing estates. A railway track ran into the valley, spread out in a network to feed the factory complex, and wound on into the hills.

Moore knew that if the town were Hoffenscheim the engineering plant must lie round the bend in the valley. He also realized that the Mosquitoes' speed was going to make it impossible to identify the target and attack it simultaneously. Keeping radio silence in case Hoppy was mistaken, he opened A-Apple's throttles and swept along the rail track into the valley.

The small industrial town, used to the Ruhr being attacked at night, was caught completely by surprise. Workmen, finishing their lunch in factory yards, watched the aircraft streak past in blank amazement. Men on shift work, lying in the sun in their back gardens, decided the planes must be their own and closed their eyes again.

Factories and smoking chimneys flowed past Moore's wingtips. He caught a glimpse of a small marshalling yard with stationary freight wagons. Then A-Apple's wings tilted as Moore followed the southward bend of the valley. As a hill shoulder fell away the engineering plant came into sight.

It stood perhaps three-quarters of a mile from the steeply-rising hills to the south. Although Adams had said it was small in Ruhr terms, it looked formidable enough with its smelting furnaces, pressing mills, machine shops, and dozens of smoking chimneys. Hoppy, feverishly checking his photographs, gave a yell of affirmation. 'We're O.K. skipper. This is it.'

Moore had already identified one flak post, a concrete tower built up above the trees on the hill shoulder. As A-Apple swept down the valley he spotted the second, a squat blockhouse set alongside the rail track at the western end of the complex. He switched on his R/T. 'Zero One to Pygmalion. We'll attack on a reciprocal course. Follow me at twelve-second intervals. Good luck.'

A-Apple went into a steep climb and began to turn. Led by Young the string of Mosquitoes followed and began to orbit over the western approaches of the valley. Beside Moore, Hopkinson had abandoned his photographs for the bombsight. His metallic voice sounded in Moore's earphones. 'O.K. skipper. Ready when you are.'

Below, a siren was hooting hysterically. Frantic gun crews had now reached their charges and were turning on radar sets and tugging off gun covers. Inside the factory workmen switched off lathes and ran towards the deep shelters.

Banking steeply, Moore put A-Apple into a shallow dive. Fast though his circuit had been, the gunners in the nearby post were already firing and a glowing chain of shells was swirling upwards. Lining the Mosquito's nose on the flak post, Moore flicked a switch. 'Bomb doors open.'

Beneath him he could feel the doors trembling in the slipstream. Peering into the bombsight, Hoppy was chanting his instructions as he guided the first gun post into the sights. 'Main switch on. One and two selected and fused. Left, left. . . . Steady, steady. . . .'

The engineering complex was rising from the valley floor like a grotesque castle as the diving Mosquito swept towards it. By this time the flak tower on the hill had also commenced firing and a line of black bursts swung A-Apple off course and cut a gouge in her port wing. Automatic 37mms. and almost dead on target. . . . Moore could feel the sweat running down his face as he listened to Hopkinson's instructions. 'Right, skipper. Right. . . . Hold it there.'

Unable to take evasive action until its bombs fell away, the Mosquito was bracketed in black explosions for seemingly endless seconds until the flak post entered Hopkinson's sights. Then he yelled 'Bombs gone' and A-Apple reared like a frightened horse as two 500-lb bombs, one GP and one SAP, fell simultaneously and plunged towards the blockhouse.

Sweeping on towards their second target, neither man could see how accurate their aim had been but the crews above saw spurts of dust and gravel rise less than twenty yards from the blockhouse as the bombs struck. Although the gunners must have known their fate, they continued firing at A-Apple as it swept over the factory towards the second flak post. With the Mosquito's speed giving him only a few seconds in which to act, Hoppy's instructions came thick and fast.

'Left, left, skipper. Right. . . . A bit more. Hold it there. Steady. . . .'

Aware now of their peril, the flak-tower gunners were throwing everything they had at A-Apple. Swirling shells appeared to start lazily from the hill, only to snap at vicious speed past the perspex blister. Forcing himself to concentrate Hopkinson squinted down the bombsight and pressed the release. Two more bombs plunged down and disappeared into the trees but the hail of shells followed A-Apple as it leap-frogged the hill shoulder and dived for cover. That same moment two black mushrooms of smoke and debris erupted from the far side of the plant. As A-Apple flashed over the shocked town and clawed for height, two more explosions, this time heard through the roar of the Merlins, came from the hillside. When the four black clouds subsided, both flak posts had ceased firing. Bathed in sweat, Moore lifted his face mask. 'Zero One to Pygmalion. In you go.'

Young gave his navigator a nod, peeled off, and dived into the valley. As the huge complex of buildings rushed towards him he saw that only two guns were still firing, a couple of light machine guns high up on the roof whose thin threads of tracer looked innocuous after the flak posts. Moore might be an eager-beaver, the Australian was thinking, but by taking all the risks himself he'd reduced the job to a piece of cake. Dropping all his 500-lb bombs in a salvo, Young went into a steep climb, then banked steeply in an effort to gaze over his wingtips. 'See where they fell, Woody?' he was asking his navigator when four flashes ripped two storage sheds apart and tossed them into the air. Three seconds later the Mosquito rocked like a ship at sea from the heavy explosions.

Bomb doors lowered, the third Mosquito had already begun its attack. Its four bombs fell in a line across a large foundry. As smoke and flame belched upwards, a chimney was seen toppling over. Half-way down, it disintegrated into tons of bricks which half-buried a transport yard.

One after another the Mosquitoes made their strike. By the time the last of Young's flight was peeling off to attack, a great pall of black smoke lay over the valley. As the Mosquito made its approach a parabola of coloured shells reached out towards it from the hillside to the south. Hopkinson sounded startled. 'You see that, skipper?'

All the crews realized immediately what had happened. Because of the dense trees on the southern ridge, the PR photographs had failed to pick out this third flak post. With its crews lulled into carelessness by months of inactivity, the post had either been unattended while the men enjoyed the sunshine or some mechanical failure had kept the guns out of action. From the hail of shells now being pumped out, the inference was the crews were doing their best to make amends.

Orbiting above the valley, Moore watched the attacking Mosquito vanish into the smoke of the stricken plant, then emerge unscathed. Relaxing, he changed his mind about ordering an attack on the flak post. Unlike the earlier ones, it was not only farther from the plant but had a much more difficult target as the Mosquitoes swept from right to left across its field of fire. In brutal military terms the risk of an aircraft being shot down was greater if sent to attack the post than to attack the plant. Moreover, with the engineering complex now almost entirely covered by smoke, it was impossible to see how much of it remained undamaged. Conscious of the need to destroy as much capacity as possible, Moore decided to concentrate on the primary target.

Not so Harvey. With all his flight yet to make their attack, the Yorkshireman decided the flak post had to be taken out. For a moment he debated whether to seek Moore's permission, then he clicked off his R/T switch. With he and Moore back-to-front in everything they thought and did, it was more than likely the bastard would refuse it. 'The flak post's our target,' he told Blackburn. 'Set your distributor to "stick" and make sure all four bombs are fused when I open the doors. Never mind your bombsight – drop 'em when I tell you.'

Blackburn sounded a trifle breathless. 'O.K., skipper.'

Knowing the rest of his flight would stay in orbit until he had completed his attack, Harvey peeled away and made for the pall of smoke. As D-Danny's airspeed increased and the smoke began swirling around its wingtips, a glowing chain of shells reached out from the port quarter. It was followed by a double fork of tracer a couple of seconds later. Holding the Mosquito on course until it almost disappeared into the smoke, Harvey suddenly banked steeply and hurled it straight at the flak post. 'Bomb doors open!' he yelled.

Orbiting above Moore caught sight of the manoeuvre. 'Zero One to Red Leader. You are not to attack flak post. Repeat. Do not attack flak post!'

Harvey could not hear nor would he have obeyed if he had. Dead ahead of him the flak post was spitting shells like a snake spitting venom. Some streaked past the Mosquito like white-hot meteorites. Others burst around it and threw out nets of lethal shrapnel. Feeling his mouth turning dry, Harvey cursed, lined up the post in his gunsights and pressed the firing button. The massive crash and recoil of the Hispano cannons and Brownings seemed to momentarily check the Mosquito before it threw itself forward again. Although Harvey found relief in striking back, the impact of the Mosquito's fire, equal to that of a three-ton truck hitting a brick wall at 50 mph, had no effect on the heavily-armoured post. Two seconds later the Yorkshireman had to release the firing button as he levelled the aircraft from its dive.

The lower slopes of the hillside were now streaking past. From the corner of his eyes Harvey saw the dry pebbled bed of a water-course. With its guns elevated, the flak tower was pouring up everything it had and to the crews above the Mosquito looked like an insect being pierced by brightly-coloured pins. A shell ricocheted from an engine nacelle and another took a couple of square feet from the starboard wingtip. Big hands gripping the control column as if it were the throat of his enemy, Harvey was counting: 'three . . . four . . . five . . . Now!'

Like a stone skimming on water the Mosquito bounced four times as its bombs fell at half-second intervals and vanished into the trees. As Harvey heaved back on the column to clear the rising hill, a shell smashed into the armour plating at his back and filled the cockpit with fumes. Then the fury of the fire fell away as the Mosquito found shelter on the opposite side of the hill. The four explosions sounded like heavy doors being slammed as Harvey climbed up towards Moore and the other orbiting Mosquitoes. Spouts of black smoke together with rocks and entire trees erupted from the ground. Westward along the valley, obeying instructions, the first Mosquito of Harvey's flight had already commenced its bombing run. As it reached the drifting smoke and no tracer attacked it, Harvey's big jaw clamped in satisfaction. With any luck at all, his lads should now have a clear passage. The Yorkshireman looked almost benign as he turned to the pale-faced Blackburn. 'You feeling O.K.?'

The stocky young navigator managed a smile. 'I think so, skipper.'

Harvey gave him a grim wink. 'You did all right, lad. Keep it up.'

Sinking back into his seat Blackburn looked unable to decide which incident had shaken him the most: the flak post's fury or the Yorkshireman's praise.

One after the other, as safe now as if on a practice run, the aircraft of Harvey's flight flew along the valley and dropped their bombs. From 2,500 feet Hopkinson was taking photographs. The last Mosquito was just commencing its bombing run when a startled voice sounded in Moore's headphones. 'Bandits, Pygmalion Leader! In the sun!'

Turning his head, Moore caught a glimpse of a blurred black shape dropping at incredible speed towards the circling Mosquitoes. Before the white-hot sun forced his eyes away he saw two more. His orders stilled the startled voices that were filling the R/T channel. 'Red One-Six – jettison bombs and join defensive circle. At the double!'

The crew of Red One-Six were two of the despised 'freshers'. Startled by the alarm, the navigator forgot to click down his main switch and wasted precious seconds trying to release his bombs before discovering his error. By the time the bombs fell the Mosquito was less than half a mile from the great pall of smoke.

The enemy fighters were Focke Wulf 190s, the advance guard of a squadron based near Maastricht. For the last seventy minutes they had answered urgent call after call as scores of British fighters harried miscellaneous targets in Northern Europe. Frustrated by the diversity of the fighter sweeps, they had at last come face to face with *Tommi* and although their numbers were only four, they had no intention of holding back until their comrades arrived. Seeing the lone V-Victor still down in the valley, the Focke Wulf leader went plunging after it like a kestrel. Ignoring the odds, the remaining three 190s attacked the circle of Mosquitoes with guns blazing.

Freed from their bomb load, the Mosquitoes could hold their own against any German fighter and the defensive tactics they were employing enabled them to cover the tail of their comrades ahead. As one Focke Wulf, eager to inflict some retribution for the damage below, picked out a Mosquito and dived on it, Millburn, only 150 yards behind, lined up his reflector sight and fired. The blast of cannon and Brownings hit the main fuel tank, and the 190 disintegrated into a ball of black smoke and scraps of wreckage. Millburn's yell made earphones rattle. 'See that, you guys? I got one.'

But although the defensive circle could hold against such small odds, Moore knew it would be a different story if the remainder of the 190 *Gruppe* caught up with them now. Gazing down he saw the Focke Wulf leader had now fastened on the tail of V-Victor whose crew had not yet had time to close their bomb doors. Harvey, also an anxious observer, saw the fighter's tracer lance out like the tongue of a chameleon and strike the Mosquito's starboard engine. As a white thread of glycol began to stream down, Harvey cursed, broke circle, and went plunging down.

To save V-Victor he had to open fire at over 500 yards. Seeing tracer snapping past his port wing, the Focke Wulf pilot lost interest in V-Victor and tried to break to starboard but another burst of fire made him kick his rudder bar back again. Seeing the dense smoke cloud he dived into it for sanctuary. V-Victor, freed from the savage attack, was thankfully climbing for the relative safety of the circle. Harvey, with the tenacity of his kind, flew right through the smoke after his prey and followed the 190 down the valley. Unable to shake him off the Focke Wulf went down to tree-top level and headed for the chimneys of Hoffenscheim. For a moment it seemed Harvey might follow him. Instead he banked reluctantly and climbed after V-Victor into the circle. Watching them, Moore waited a few more seconds, then raised his mask. 'Zero One to Pygmalion. That's it, the party's over. Follow me home.'

Pushing his control column forward he dived north-east towards Breda. Like a severed noose unfolding, the circle of Mosquitoes broke and streamed after him. They were only just in time: the rest of the Focke Wulf squadron was less than a minute away. Streaking into the valley like angry hornets they banked over the burning plant, latched again on the call sign of their colleagues, and headed after them. As the vengeful roar of their engines faded, the summer day was left to the wail of fire engines and the muffled thumps of fires and explosions.

CHAPTER 15

Over by a dispersal hut a group of mechanics had turned and were gazing expectantly at the southern sky. Motioning Adams and Henderson to break off their conversation, Davies listened. For a moment the only sounds were the distant scream of an electric drill and the background singing of birds. Then, as Davies gave Henderson a nod, a hooter sounded and the engines of crash wagons and ambulances started up. Climbing into a jeep that was standing beside them, the three officers waited for the Mosquitoes to appear.

At the inn Anna had been passing the time reading. Now, hearing the commotion on the airfield, she ran to the open window. The first Mosquito appeared over the poplars at the southern end of the field. As it banked with a shattering roar over the inn the girl saw that its port wingtip was heavily gouged and black scars disfigured its sleek fuselage. Her eyes followed it as it circled the field and settled down to land. Dust rose as its tyres squealed on the far end of the runway. Other aircraft were now orbiting the field. The first Mosquito taxied from the runway to its dispersal point. The three senior officers, who had identified its number, were already bounding towards it in their jeep. As they came alongside its two engines spluttered and died. Hopkinson appeared and dropped to the ground, followed by Moore. As the debonair squadron commander allowed a mechanic to help him remove his parachute harness, Davies jumped from the jeep and hurried towards him.

'Well – how did it go?'

Moore was suffering the temporary loss of hearing caused by two power-packed Merlins at close range. 'Sorry, sir. I can't hear you.'

Davies put his mouth to Moore's ear. 'How did it go?' he bawled.

Moore grinned. 'I think we gave it a good clobbering.'

'How good?'

'There wasn't any wind to clear the smoke, which was pretty dense, but I'd say three-quarters of the buildings were hit.'

Davies' eyebrows shot up a full half-inch. 'Three-quarters! You're certain?'

'Pretty certain,' Moore, whose ears were now recovering, glanced at a corporal and Waaf who were removing the photograph pack. 'We did our best to get photographs. They might tell us more.'

'There'll be a PR Mossie going over once the commotion's died,' Davies told him. His excitement communicated itself to Henderson and Adams who were now at his elbow. 'If three-quarters has been damaged, we'll be dead unlucky if it doesn't slow things down for a week or two.' Then, realizing how close he had been to breaking security, the small Air Commodore frowned at Moore. 'If the smoke was that dense, how can you be so sure?'

'It wasn't a small target and all the boys had to do was drop their bombs on it. There was practically no opposition.'

Davies jerked a thumb at the powder-blackened scars on the Mosquito's fuselage. 'What's this? Scotch mist?'

'That was from the flak posts,' Moore explained. 'Once they were knocked out it was a piece of cake.'

As Davies' twinkling eyes met Henderson's, the big Scot got in his question at last. 'Any casualties, Moore?'

'No, sir. We got away lightly. MacDougall and Briggs had their starboard engine hit by a 190 but they got back to Manston. Neither was hurt.'

With his mind eased on that vital issue Henderson looked as delighted as Davies. 'Then it's been a big success?'

'I think so,' Moore admitted. His eyes were on a Mosquito with a missing starboard wingtip that was coming gingerly in to land. His attention was jerked back by Davies who, drawing nearer, pitched his question low enough not to reach the mechanics working on A-Apple.

'What's your verdict on the lads? Are they going to make the grade or not?'

To the delight of both Henderson and Adams, Moore pretended to be surprised by the question. 'I'm not sure I know what you mean, sir. I'd take these crews anywhere. They're a first-class unit.'

It was a rebuke that made Davies scowl with pleasure and Henderson look as if he had been presented with a crate of Highland Dew. As the Scot drew Adams' attention to the deep gouge in the port wing, Moore excused himself and walked over to Hopkinson who was chatting to the Waaf photographer.

'Go over and tell Harvey I want to see him in my office, will you?'

Hopkinson's grin was wry. 'Before or after de-briefing?'

'Before. In other words, now.'

As Moore turned, he almost knocked over the small figure of Davies who had followed him. The Air Commodore's voice was sharp with suspicion. 'What do you want Harvey for?'

The good-looking Moore gave him a blank glance. 'Nothing in particular, sir.'

'Come off it, Moore. I saw your face when you watched him coming in. And he's had a clobbering. What happened?'

'It's nothing important, sir. Only a small misunderstanding that can be put right in a few words.'

Seeing he was getting nowhere, Davies gave a grunt of displeasure. 'It had better be. Because this squadron and what it has to do is more important than one bloody-minded flight commander. If you have any more trouble with him, you're to let me know. Is that clear?'

'Quite clear, sir.'

Giving Moore a suspicious glance, Davies turned away. He was half-way towards Henderson and Adams when his eyes fell on the shell holes in the fuselage. Halting, he jabbed an irascible finger at them. 'There's one other thing. There'll be no more of this nonsense. I can't spare you and you know it; so in the future when a dicey job comes along, you delegate it. Understand?'

When no answer came, he span round. Instead of being at his elbow Moore was exchanging words with Adams who had walked round to examine the other side of the shell-torn Mosquito. Unable this time to hear what confidences were being exchanged, Davies gave a snort and strode off towards the jeep.

Expecting trouble and in no mood to avoid it, Harvey gave the freckle-faced Waaf no chance to announce him. Giving the adjoining door a thump with his fist, he marched into Moore's office. Straight from his aircraft he was wearing no tunic, and his rolled-up shirt-sleeves revealed powerful, sinewy arms. 'I hear you want to see me.'

Moore, seated behind his desk, showed no sign of the anger he was feeling. He glanced at the flushed Waaf who, after trying to stop Harvey, was now standing undecided at the door. 'Close the door behind you, sergeant, and don't let anyone in.'

'Yes, sir.' As the girl obeyed and the door closed, Moore turned back to the truculent Yorkshireman. 'I'm assuming you know why I've sent for you.'

'I've no idea. Tell me.'

Moore's stare moved up slowly to the man's aggressive face. 'You know what my answer is to that, Harvey?'

'No.'

'I don't believe you.'

The Yorkshireman gave a start, then his voice turned hoarse with fury. 'You calling me a liar?'

'If you deny knowing why I sent for you, yes. My orders were to leave that flak tower on the southern hillside alone. You deliberately disobeyed them. I want to know why.'

'I never heard your orders. That's why.'

'If you're saying your radio was u.s., don't. I had it checked five minutes after you landed.'

Harvey gave another start. 'You what?'

'I had your radio checked. So let's begin again. Why did you disobey my orders?'

'I've just told you. I never heard your orders. I'd switched my R/T off.'

It was Moore's turn to stare. 'You did what?'

'I switched it off. There was so much chattering over it I couldn't hear myself think.'

'You, a flight commander, switched off your R/T in the middle of an operation. Don't you know that's an offence in itself?'

'What the hell was there to hear? We'd all been briefed. In fact I had two bloody briefings.'

Once again Moore, whose self-control was his pride, was wondering why this belligerent man could upset him so easily. He picked up a pencil from the desk and studied it for a moment before answering. 'One reason you leave your R/T on is that you can hear my orders. And my orders were to leave that third flak tower alone.'

Harvey's laugh was derisory. 'Then it was a good job I didn't hear you, wasn't it? Because it was a bloody daft order.'

Holding himself under tight rein, Moore gazed at him almost thoughtfully. 'Tell me why it was a daft order.'

'Tell you why? Christ, not five minutes earlier you'd played the Lone Ranger and tackled two gun posts on your own. Why did you feel *that* was necessary? Because they were throwing flowers up at us?'

'Those two posts were right alongside the plant. And they covered either approach. The post you attacked was further away and had only a beam shot at us. You took a greater risk in attacking it than by leaving it alone.'

'How the hell do you know? I might have lost a couple of my crews if we'd played it your way.'

Moore took a deep breath. 'Harvey, when you fly with me, you obey my orders. Whether you like them or not, you obey them. You've been in the Services long enough to know those are the rules of the game. So will you stop pulling different ways and let us both get on with the job?'

He received another laugh of dislike. 'Your orders – right or wrong? You know what I believe, Moore? You staged that affair today to show us all how tough you are. And you're fighting mad because someone else took the limelight from you. Why don't you admit it?'

Moore's chair fell over as he jumped to his feet. With battle tension still tight in both men, the atmosphere caught at the throat of the breathless Waaf listening at the door. Moore's loss of control showed in his tone as well as his words.

'It's clear enough why you hate my guts, Harvey. You were hoping to get this job and you didn't. Someday, if you can ever take that chip off your shoulder, you'll understand why you were passed over. Until then you'll obey my orders or Christ help you.'

Harvey looked as if he had been struck in the face. With a tremendous effort that drained the blood from his cheeks, he went to the door and turned.

'You think you know my reasons for hating your guts? You bloody tailor's dummy, you wouldn't understand my reasons in a thousand years.'

The slam of the door behind him almost brought the roof down. Unaware of the deep wounds his words had reopened in the Yorkshireman, Moore was standing pale-faced and motionless. It took a sharp crack to make him start and glance down. The pencil had fractured in his hand.

A tap on the billet door made Moore turn. In his shirt-sleeves, he was putting on his tie in front of a mirror. 'Come in.'

To his surprise Henderson appeared in the doorway, followed by Adams. The big Scot was looking a trifle embarrassed. 'Sorry about this, Moore, but it can't wait.'

Although the chair Moore offered him was the best one available, it creaked protestingly as Henderson lowered his weight on it. Confronted with a choice between the only other chair and the bed, Adams somewhat hesitantly chose the bed. Hiding his curiosity, Moore turned back to the C.O. 'Can I offer you a drink, sir?'

The Scot shook his head. 'No, thanks. I'll probably have a tankful this evening.' His question, although clearly a digression from his main purpose, held its full content of curiosity. 'Is it true you're standing the party tonight?'

Moore resumed knotting his tie. 'I've suggested it to the Catering Officer. You've no objections, have you?'

Henderson looked surprised. 'Why should I have objections? I'm just wondering why you should pay for us drunken bastards to celebrate a success you made possible.'

Moore sounded almost curt as he reached for his tunic. 'Sorry, but I don't see it that way. The boys put up a good show so why shouldn't they get a chance to relax. I can afford it.'

Adams' myopic eyes had moved to two photographs standing on a locker by the bedside. In the foreground of one was a middle-aged woman of distinguished appearance cutting roses from a large bush. The warmness of her smile suggested she was on close terms with the photographer, possibly Moore himself. The background showed the lawns, forecourt, and terraces of a large country house. The second portrait was that of a white-haired elderly man seated at a desk. Behind him was a wall of tooled leather books. Although both photographs were set in modest frames, their contents unmistakably spelt out wealth and privilege.

Adams was suddenly aware Henderson was grinning at him. 'Never let it be said a Scotsman turned down a free dram. All right, Moore, it's your party. But put a limit on the booze or some of 'em won't be fit to fly for a week. Have you seen Davies since the de-briefing?'

'Davies? No.'

Henderson, who was lighting a cigarette, released a rueful cloud of smoke. 'He's seen me. He's got a bee in his bonnet that you had trouble with Harvey. He told me to have a word with Adams after the de-briefing and then report back to him.'

'Report back about what?'

Henderson was viewing Moore's innocence with some scepticism. 'Come off it, Moore. You're forgetting every pilot and navigator in the squadron saw him disobey your order. They're all clamming up but even a hairy-kneed Scot can put two and two together. Do you want me to spell it out or will you tell me in your own words?'

Realizing he already knew the facts, Moore shrugged. 'It was one of those occasions when either of us could have been right. I thought we stood a bigger chance of losing a kite by attacking the flak post than by leaving it alone. Harvey thought otherwise.'

'So he disobeyed your direct order and attacked it?'

'Not my direct order. He never heard it.'

'You're not saying he used that corny yarn that his radio was u.s.?'

'No. It wasn't turned on.'

Henderson's chair gave a startled creak. 'Wasn't turned on? Jam Bang over the target! That's a disciplinary act in itself. Didn't you tell him so?'

'I tore him off a strip in my office fifteen minutes after we landed.'

'How did he react?'

Moore gave a wry grimace. 'We had a bit of a ding-dong, I'm afraid. Not that it matters if it helps clear the air.'

Henderson swore and turned to Adams. 'I'll have the bastard posted. It's the only way.'

Adams, who realized he was not expected to offer advice, contented himself by making non-committal sounds and pretended to repack his pipe. Moore, who had gone over to the window, spoke without glancing back. 'I'd rather you didn't.'

Henderson swung back. 'What was that?'

'I said I'd rather you didn't post him.'

'Why, for Christ's sake?'

'I think he's a good flight commander.'

Henderson stared at him. 'He nearly clobbers a fellow officer and then disobeys your orders in front of the entire squadron! He's the best!'

'You're forgetting the reason he nearly clobbered Millburn, aren't you?'

'No. I know Powell was his friend.'

'That's what I thought at the time but now I see there was more to it. He's got a strong protective streak towards his men. That was why he went for the flak post today.'

'It was still against your orders.'

'Yes, but who knows I was right? If he hadn't silenced those guns they might have shot down a couple of kites.'

Henderson swore again. 'You're not supposed to be a prophet. You gave an order and he disobeyed it – that's the point at issue. Anyway, how can you be so sure he was that altruistic? Perhaps he just wanted to show the others he's as good as you are.'

Adams saw Moore shake his head. 'No. He did it again later when the 190s arrived. He took a big chance helping MacDougall and Briggs – if the other 190s had followed him down, we probably couldn't have saved him.'

The Scot was beginning to show impatience. 'You sound as if you like him.'

Moore's laugh was rueful. 'Hardly. On a personal level we're like two dogs with their hackles up.'

'Then that's it,' Henderson grunted. 'I'll get the bastard transferred. The squadron's starting to pull together at last – I'm not risking the entire barrel going sour for one rotten apple.'

'Harvey won't turn the barrel sour,' Moore said. 'Not after what happened today.'

Watching Henderson, Adams was certain the Scot understood even though his question seemed to deny it. 'What's that supposed to mean?'

'Harvey isn't in charge of old sweats now. Today his flight contained four fresher crews. Yet he still risked his life twice to keep them out of trouble. What's more, everyone saw it. How can that turn the barrel sour?'

Adams felt that integrity demanded some statement from him at this juncture. 'It is true, sir, that at the de-briefing all the men were showing respect for the way he helped MacDougall and Briggs.'

Henderson muttered something rude and moved towards the door. It was a good fifteen seconds before he turned, and to their surprise both men saw he was grinning maliciously. 'What d'ye ken? Harvey the peacemaker! There's a thought to raise Davies' blood pressure.'

His chuckle died away as his eyes fixed on Moore. 'All right, you can keep him for the moment but don't think this'll be the end of your trouble with him. That's as sure as that Millburn and Gabby will get pissed on your free booze tonight.'

The two men listened to his anticipatory footsteps retreating down the corridor. Adams returned Moore's smile. 'He can't wait to tell Davies. I think he's browned off at being told how to handle his men. Is Davies going to the party tonight?'

'No. He's seeing this Swiss girl over at the pub. For some reason I've been invited to join them.'

Adams, who had not been told of Moore's bereavement, looked offended at the news. 'That doesn't mean you're going to miss the party, does it?'

Moore crushed a cigarette in the ashtray. 'I wasn't coming in any case.'

'But that's ridiculous. It's your party. Can't you come after you've met this girl? As Davies is letting us stand down tomorrow, it's sure to go on all night?'

Moore's sudden abruptness startled Adams. 'For Christ's sake, I'm not going. Let's leave it there, shall we?'

The sensitive Adams nodded and moved towards the door. As he opened it, Moore checked him. 'Sorry, Frank. I'll explain later.'

Adams was always quick to forgive. 'That's all right. It's none of my business anyway.'

Moore was frowning heavily. 'I've noticed you're a pretty shrewd judge of people and what makes them tick. Tell me why Harvey and I don't get along. Why does he get into my hair more than anyone I've ever known?'

Impressed by the tolerance the young Squadron Commander had displayed so far, Adams was curious himself. 'I've no idea. Unless it's just the two of you are on entirely different wavelengths. It does happen sometimes.'

CHAPTER 16

With the ground staff as well as the air crews benefiting from Moore's gesture, the Black Swan was quiet that evening. The Squadron Commander found Davies and Anna Reinhardt in the private lounge, the only occupants in an old-world room of blackened beams and glinting brass. They were seated at a table beneath the window and an evening sunbeam set them in deep shadow. As Moore accepted Davies' invitation to draw up a chair he had the impression the couple had been deep in conversation before his arrival.

The girl's appearance came as a surprise to him. Although he had not given the matter much thought, he had expected to meet an older woman if only because of her friendship with the middle-aged Davies. Instead the girl who held out a slim hand to him was no more than twenty-four or twenty-five. She was wearing a black dress and the dark hair that Harvey had admired was now swept up into a French roll. With her only jewellery an emerald brooch, she looked as regal as a queen.

'Like a drink?' Davies asked. Before Moore could reply he reached for a bell push, then dropped back on the window seat. 'Is the party under way yet?'

Moore smiled. 'There were audible hints it was as I came by the mess.'

'The Squadron are having a bit of a celebration tonight,' Davies told the girl. 'It could get out of hand later – let's hope the noise doesn't drift across here and keep you awake.'

'Shouldn't you both be there?' she asked.

'No. We've other things to do.' Davies turned back to Moore. 'Sorry if I misled you but this wasn't meant to be a social occasion. I've a special reason for wanting you to meet Miss Reinhardt.'

Curious, Moore waited, but at that moment Maisie entered the lounge. Catching sight of the young squadron leader, her face brightened and there was an archness in her steps as she approached the window. 'Hello, sir. What can I do for you?'

Moore smiled up at the girl. 'What can I have?'

The girl's roguish expression gave him a different answer to her words. 'I think I can find you a whisky, sir.'

'Then that's what I'll have. Thank you.'

Maisie turned her big lashes on Davies. 'What about you and the lady, sir? Can I bring you another round?'

As Davies nodded the girl picked up the empty glasses, gave Moore a sidelong look, and made for the door, her skirts swirling invitingly around her legs. Davies was about to make a comment when he remembered the girl alongside him and gave a grunt instead. 'Well, they say it's a friendly pub.'

Moore, managing to keep his face straight, met the girl's grey eyes and saw they were laughing. 'Yes, it is, sir. Very friendly.'

Seeing the glance the couple exchanged, Davies frowned. 'What's all this nonsense about Harvey? You don't seriously think he's a good flight commander, do you?'

'Yes, sir. I do.'

Neither man had noticed the girl's slight start. 'You're turning soft, Moore,' Davies said contemptuously. 'He's the sort that enjoys causing trouble.' Before Moore could reply he turned to the girl. 'We're talking about a character we've got who puts the back up of everyone he meets. I want Moore to get rid of him.'

The girl hid her curiosity with a laugh. 'You make him sound quite interesting.'

'Interesting be damned,' Davies grunted. 'He's probably a Bolshie if the truth were known. But we've more important things to talk about than Harvey. As I told you earlier, Moore, Anna's come up here for a holiday and I'm hoping she'll enjoy herself. But there's no reason why we shouldn't kill two birds with one stone and that's why I asked you over tonight. You remember that second specialist factory I want clobbering? Well, Anna knows the place and has agreed to brief us before she goes back.'

Seeing Moore's curiosity, Davies felt some explanation was necessary. 'Her father's a well-known architect and before the war he used to get commissions from all over Europe. He had two in England in the early thirties. That's why Anna's English is so good – she went to an English school for over three years. Then he got a commission from Munich. Anna went to university there and on her vacations used to take parties of English and American tourists round Bavarian places of interest. Miesbach was one of those places. Am I coming through?'

Uncertain how much the girl knew and yet feeling it highly unlikely that Davies would have told her the wider importance of the Miesbach factory, Moore contented himself with a 'Yes, sir.'

At that moment Maisie entered with the drinks. As she fussed about the table with all her attention focused on Moore, Anna was silently assessing the young Squadron Commander. A girl to whom a man's physical appearance meant little, she found his scar a relief in a face that might otherwise have been too good-looking. His ease of behaviour coupled with the vaguest hint of shyness, made her remember a comment her father had once made about the English upper class. 'They have the rare ability to express self-confidence and vulnerability at the same time. And that makes them very formidable, Liebchen, particularly with women.' The impertinence of such an early assessment amused the girl. Apart from what Davies had told her about the young pilot, there had been time to learn only one more thing about him – he had a sense of humour.

Davies waited until Maisie had swung her skirts round the hall door before returning to his theme. 'Before Anna came up here I got her to search through her souvenirs and she found photographs and brochures of the town. Add them to her own knowledge of the place and we're in business.'

251

The mellow shaft of sunlight, filled with shining dust motes, was now slanting directly on the girl. Tinted by it, her smooth neck, composed features and piled-up dark hair were rising like a flower from the black calyx of her dress. Davies' voice drove away Moore's fanciful thoughts.

'I can't give you our reason at the moment but we're not carrying out this raid for a few more days. However, when the green light comes, I'll call in Henderson and Adams, and Anna will give us a briefing. Until then not a word to anyone.'

Moore contented himself with a nod. Davies, who had lapsed into his usual terseness when discussing service matters, made an attempt to be convivial as he turned back to the girl.

'How were your parents before you left?'

'Quite well. My father keeps getting twinges of arthritis but for that' – the girl was smiling – 'he blames the English weather. They both sent their regards to you.'

'I must get to see them on my next leave,' Davies glanced at his watch, then drained his glass. 'I'll have to be going.' As Moore rose with him, the Air Commodore made an impatient gesture. 'No, you don't need to come. Stay and buy Anna a drink.'

Embarrassed, Moore turned to her. 'I wish I could, Miss Reinhardt, but I have some rather important letters to write tonight. May we make it some other time?'

The girl, who had been told by Davies of his bereavement, nodded sympathetically. 'Of course. Give me a ring when you are free.'

Meaning well but more suited by nature to a military two-step than a quadrille, Davies made his suggestion sound like an order. 'Why leave it so vague? Anna's on holiday and you're not flying tomorrow. So why not ask her out to dinner?'

Moore managed to keep his face expressionless. 'I'd enjoy that very much, Miss Reinhardt. May I?'

There were mischievous lights in her eyes as she turned to Davies. 'I'm sorry, Arthur. If Wing Commander Moore would care to take me out some other evening, I'd be very happy to go. But it so happens I have a date tomorrow.'

Davies looked both curious and irritable. 'A date? Already? Who with?'

'An officer called Frank Harvey. He's taking me for a drive on the moors in the afternoon and to dinner at night.'

Davies jumped as if a large dog had suddenly leapt from the shadows and bitten him. 'Who?'

'Frank Harvey. The pilot you were talking about earlier.'

For once it seemed Davies was caught speechless. 'How in hell did you meet Harvey?'

'He was kind enough to pick me up when my taxi broke down yesterday. And today he phoned to make a date.'

'Harvey,' Davies breathed with the air of a man haunted by a name. 'You don't know what you're doing, girl. An afternoon and evening with him and you'll be a Bolshie with a fur cap on your head.'

When the girl only smiled Davies marched stiff-legged to the door. His growl was addressed to Moore. 'Well, are you coming or not?'

Without waiting to hear his question answered he stalked out into the hall. Which was as well or he might have noticed the smiles that Moore and the girl were exchanging.

Gabby gave a leer of contempt. 'Easy, boyo. Dead easy!'

Hopkinson grinned scornfully. 'You think so?'

'I know it, boyo. A piece of cake.'

The Officers' Mess that night was a shock to the senses with its noise and drunken hilarity. With the squadron's run of bad luck ended, its members were celebrating in time-honoured fashion. A dozen of the older officers, Adams among them, were clustered round the piano where the Armament Officer, no mean pianist, was playing every request thrown at him. In a far corner a party of younger officers were playing a revised version of the Eton Wall Game with a turnip someone had stolen from the kitchen. Every half-minute or so a ruck of struggling men would surge into the party of songsters but miraculously their cohesion would return when the wave had receded. In the opposite corner half a dozen men were surrounding a chair on which a young pilot was standing. They had stretched out a rope from wall to wall and were loudly encouraging the pilot who was preparing to walk it. A final group of hardened drinkers, which included Millburn, Gabby and Hopkinson, were propping up the bar. Waiters, volunteers for the night, weaved glassy-eyed through the turbulence and dropped almost as many glasses as they delivered.

Someone yelled for 'Old-fashioned Anson' and the versatile Lindsay picked up the tune. The song was popular and within seconds even the wall-game players were bawling it at the top of their lungs. Adams, whose innate romanticism was always compounded by alcohol, felt the tug of memory as the singing swelled up and filled every corner of the room. This was like the old times when Gillibrand had led the bawdy choruses. The indefinable camaraderie of the fighting man that transcends fear, self-interest, or the love of women. An intoxication that made a man feel a giant and ready to make any sacrifice for his friends or his country. Because it was a manifestation of war, Adams knew it was a dangerous drug and that he should not glory in it but tonight his heart betrayed his mind. The ranks were closing at last: the squadron was becoming a unit again. At the other side of the singing group Henderson's face showed that the Scot had the same thoughts. At that moment Adams had only one regret: that Moore was not present to witness his handiwork.

The song ended and horseplay was rejoined with additional vigour. Gabby jabbed a finger again at the rope and its would-be walker. 'A piece of cake,' he repeated. 'Not worth walking across the room to watch.'

'Think you can do better?' Hopkinson taunted. 'You're too pissed to walk a chalk line on the floor.'

Nothing more was needed to stir the Welshman's aggression. 'Who's pissed, you Cockney twit? I've walked things a bloody sight more dangerous than that. Haven't I, mush?' He asked Millburn who was turning from the bar towards them.

The American, his black hair dishevelled, grinned and thrust a glass of whisky into the Welshman's hand. 'Sure you have, kid. You're a regular little Houdini.'

'But I bloody have,' Gabby repeated with the insistence of the half-drunk. 'What about that church tower near Cromer? You said I couldn't do it with that Force Seven wind blowing. Well – did I walk round it or didn't I?'

Millburn's eyes twinkled at the half-circle of grinning faces. 'You did, kid. You nearly broke your goddamned neck but you did.'

'And how high was it?' the Welshman demanded.

'Oh, a hundred feet, I guess. Maybe more.'

Gabby thrust his sharp nose at the sceptical Hopkinson. 'You hear that? A hundred feet!' He jabbed a finger again at the tightrope. 'And how high's that? Three bloody feet.'

'You still couldn't walk it,' Hopkinson insisted.

Across the Mess the young officer, a broomstick extended in his hands, pushed a stockinged foot gingerly out on the rope. He took two quick steps, swayed unsteadily to a chorus of cheers, took two more, then tumbled in a heap to the floor. At the howl of derision that arose, Gabby turned triumphantly towards Hopkinson. 'That's why he flies like a kite without a tail. No sense of balance.'

'I've a pound to say you can't do any better,' Hoppy said.

The challenge was clearly an affront to the drunken Welshman's pride. 'Three feet above the deck? I could do it with my eyes closed, you Cockney pillock.'

'All right. Do it on something higher.'

'Such as?'

As Hopkinson grinned there was a gasp from the onlookers. 'There's always the water tower.'

It took a minute for the challenge to sink in. Then Gabby beamed. 'You're on. Once round the parapet. For three quid.'

For a moment Hopkinson was taken aback. 'You're bullshitting.'

Gabby fumbled in his tunic pocket and pulled out a couple of crumpled notes. He turned to the grinning Millburn. 'Lend me a quid.'

The American gave him a note and held three more up to the gathering crowd. 'Three quid on little Houdini. Who's on?'

A buzz of excitement rose as men began laying bets. As Gabby, grinning vacuously, downed his whisky and pushed away from the bar, a man caught his arm. St Claire, one of the few officers still reasonably sober, had overheard the challenge.

'Don't be a fool, Gabby. You'll kill yourself.'

The Welshman pushed him away. 'Make yourself some money, boyo. Put three quid on me.'

St Claire followed him. 'You'll kill yourself. The stones round the tank are bevelled. You'll slide straight off if you try to walk round them.'

Gabby paused and focused on him. 'You're sure of that?'

'Positive,' St Claire lied. 'I've flown over the tower enough, haven't I?'

Gabby frowned. 'Any one else noticed it?'

Simpson, St Claire's navigator, caught his pilot's eye and quickly added his own corroboration. 'It's true. The stones are definitely bevelled.'

Hopkinson looked relieved the bet was off but the grinning Millburn, who was even drunker than Gabby, put his mouth to the Welshman's ear. A moment later the triumphant Gabby swung round. 'Don't put your money back yet, boyo. What about the cannon butts?'

Hopkinson looked puzzled. 'The cannon butts?'

'The wall at the back. I'll walk from one end to the other. O.K.?'

'But there's a bloody great pile of sand to fall on,' Hoppy objected.

'Not at the back there isn't. It's a straight drop of thirty feet. Maybe more.' Seeing Hopkinson's hesitation, Gabby misjudged its cause. 'A minute ago you said I couldn't walk along a chalk line. You're getting scared now, aren't you, mush?'

Taunted himself, Hopkinson forgot his misgivings. 'You can't walk any sort of line, you Welsh pisspot. You're swaying on your feet now.'

Gabby gave a yelp of indignation. 'You taking me on or backing out?'

'I'm taking you on. But don't blame me when we pick up the pieces.'

As the crowd of onlookers surged excitedly towards the Mess entrance, Gabby cast a glance at the older officers still singing around the piano. 'Take it easy or they'll bugger it up. Go out a few at a time.'

Outside the crowd regrouped and with Gabby, Millburn and Hopkinson in the van started across the airfield towards the distant cannon butts. The night was dark, with patchy cloud and starlight, and a gusting wind was chilling the crews manning the gun posts. They gazed with astonishment at the drunken, jostling crowd that passed below them. News that Gabby was up to one of his madcap pranks had spread to both the sergeants' and the airmen's messes, and by the time the butts were reached the crowd numbered a hundred men.

Built to take the impact of 20-mm shells, the butts consisted of a high bank of sand backed by a 35-ft brick wall. Behind the wall the drop was sheer to the metallized surface of the perimeter road. A loud cheer rose as Gabby removed his tunic and climbed over the fence into the butts. Half-way up the steep bank of sand he turned. 'Come up here and gimme a hand!'

Millburn and three other men followed him, sinking almost up to their knees in the sand. At the top of the bank there was still six feet of bare wall and it took three of them to hoist the Welshman up. The crowd cheered again as he jack-knifed over the wall and then squirmed round to sit on it straddle-legged. The cheer turned into a gasp of excitement as a gust of wind made him grab the wall with both hands. Below, Sue Spencer had joined St Claire and her face was pale as she gripped the tall young pilot's arm. 'Shouldn't one of us tell the C.O. or the Adjutant? Otherwise he's going to kill himself.'

St Claire hesitated, then shook his head. 'We can't do that. But some of the men have gone to fetch blankets. They might help to break his fall if he slips.'

Two men carrying service blankets were already running towards the butts. Yelling for others to follow them, they ran round the back of the wall and threw the blankets open. From this vantage point the black wall rose like the face of a

255

cliff. On top of it the small figure of Gabby was silhouetted against the stars. Gripping the edges of a blanket, six men tried somewhat ludicrously to position themselves beneath him. Grinning onlookers followed and offered their advice:

'He'll need a bloody bombsight to land on that, mate.'

'Why not chuck him up a parachute?'

'That'll never stop him. He'll keep going all the way to Aussie land.'

Five seconds later a great cheer sent birds clattering from trees into the night sky. Gabby, who had got his breath back at last, was attempting to rise to his feet. As a gust of wind made him grab again at the top of the wall St Claire glanced back at the dark shapes of the Administration Buildings and the Control Tower. He had little hope that the size and noise of the crowd would draw the attention of some senior officer. Most of them were in the Mess, but in any case the butts were a good four hundred yards from the airfield's main buildings and the wind was carrying sound away from them. As Sue's hand tightened spasmodically on his arm, the young artist bitterly regretted he had not broken the unwritten law that governed such madcap pranks as he watched Gabby, arms out-stretched, begin his long walk along the wall.

High up on the bank of sand Millburn was sobering fast and growing restive as he watched Gabby take his first few uncertain steps. As the Welshman paused and swayed, he turned to the three men alongside him. 'I'm going up too. Gimme a hand.'

The men stared at one another, then obeyed. Dropping face down over the top of the wall, Millburn saw the sheer drop to the perimeter track and muttered a subdued 'Christ!' Recovering, he wriggled round, put one cautious leg behind him, and not daring to look down, pushed himself to his feet.

A fresh buzz of excitement rose from the crowd. Here and there the muted screams of the Waafs could be heard. Sue Spencer sounded horrified. 'What's Tommy doing? Has everyone gone mad?'

It was unlikely there was one aircrew member among the crowd who did not understand Millburn's behaviour. A man shared his comrade's danger in the same way he shared his beer and his cigarettes even when that danger was a self-imposed act of foolhardiness. With the philosophy containing a romanticism that most women found absurd, St Claire made no attempt to answer the girl's question.

Fascinated by the spectacle, even the drunks in the crowd went silent and Gabby's indignant voice could be heard over the wind. 'What's the game, Yank? You think you're sharing the stakes?'

Arms outstretched for balance, a sheer black drop on his right side, and the wind a personal enemy, Millburn was now as sober as he had ever been. 'Look where you're going, you little bastard,' he gritted. 'And keep your bloody mouth shut.'

A man who thrived on excitement as a schoolboy thrives on icecream, Gabby began to move swiftly along the wall. Sue Spencer turned incredulously towards St Claire. 'He's not singing, is he?'

St Claire was listening. 'It sounds like it.'

'Singing,' the girl breathed. 'I don't believe it.'

The American, whose purpose was to grab hold of the drunken gremlin if he should slip, felt his heart miss a beat as Gabby swayed uncertainly. As Millburn struggled desperately to reach him, Gabby's off-key chant floated back.

> 'A man came home one evening,
> After working hard all day,
> He found the fire had gone out,
> And his wife had run away. . . .'

'Belt up, you Welsh moron,' Millburn hissed, now only four feet away but still too distant to lend aid. 'Belt up and watch what you're doing or I'll clobber you for sure.'

The excitement was increasing the Welshman's drunkenness rather than sobering him. Grinning back at Millburn he actually balanced on one leg for a couple of seconds before starting forward and recommencing his song.

> 'Twas then he took to drinking,
> What else was he to do,
> He mixed with bad companions,
> And became a burglar too. . . .'

In spite of the chilly wind Millburn could feel the sweat trickling down his face. Cursing himself for his part in the madcap act, he shuffled after the chanting gremlin. 'Don't go so bloody fast,' he gritted.

Gabby had actually reached the transverse wall that acted as a buttress when his luck ran out. As he turned to grin his triumph, a sudden gust of wind caught him off balance. Seeing him swaying backwards, Millburn acted instinctively. Throwing himself forward he managed to grab the Welshman's shirt but only at the cost of his own balance. Keeping a bulldog grip on the shirt, he lunged out in desperation and flung himself over the other side of the wall. His weight dragged the Welshman after him and in a flailing of arms and legs the two men plunged down into the sand, to screams of alarm and a drunken cheer.

They rolled half-way down the bank before disentangling themselves. Spluttering and wiping his face, Gabby began to laugh. Reacting, Millburn gave a howl of rage. 'You horrible little gremlin! I'm going to kill you.'

Sand was thick in his dark hair and plastered all over his sweating face. As he tried to reach the Welshman his legs sank into the sand and he fell back. Taking another look at him Gabby realized he meant business and scrambled indignantly down the bank. 'What's the matter with you? You're the one who suggested the bloody wall.'

Neither reason nor any other scruple could have halted Millburn at that moment. As his raging figure came plunging down the bank Gabby gave a yelp of dismay, scrambled over the fence and dived into the hysterical crowd. Breathing sand and fire, Millburn vaulted out of the butts and charged after him.

CHAPTER 17

Harvey paused on the crest of the hill. 'Feel like a rest? Or do you want to go on?'

It was not tiredness but the view that made the girl sink down. To the north and west the moors were covered in heather and cloud shadows. Far to her right the sea was visible between the folds of two hills. The sunlit air was still and filled with the singing of skylarks.

'Sit on this. The ground might be damp.' Harvey was indicating a gas cape he had laid down. Obeying him, she leaned forward and wrapped her arms around her knees, a characteristic posture. Thirty yards down the hillside, Sam, who was nuzzling through the heather, noticed they had halted and gave an impatient bark. When neither stirred he grumbled and started back.

'I think Sam likes the moors as much as you do,' she said.

She could feel his eyes on her. She was wearing a green cotton blouse and fawn skirt. He lit a cigarette before answering. 'What about you? Are you enjoying yourself?'

She turned. Bareheaded, he was sitting on his tunic a few feet behind her. 'Of course I am. Why do you need to ask such a question?'

Instead of answering he lay back and stared up at the July sky. The dazzling banks of cumulus that drifted past only accentuated its height and clarity. The dog appeared and gave her bare arm a generous lick. As she rubbed its ears, it sank down beside her.

'There was a party at the airfield last night, wasn't there?' she asked as she bent over the dog

'Yes. How did you know?'

'Air Commodore Davies told me. Did you go?'

'No.'

She was suddenly aware why she had mentioned the party. 'Why not?'

For a moment his voice was gruff and hostile. 'Because I didn't want to.' Then, less brusquely: 'I had some friends to see in Highgate.'

'I met your new Squadron Commander last night. Arthur Davies brought him over.'

'Why?'

She did not want to lie to him but Davies' instructions left her no choice. 'I suppose Arthur just wanted me to meet him.'

258

The sudden harshness of his laugh made the dog lift his head uneasily. 'Oh, I see. He wants you to have some nice, upper-class company while you're here. Did Moore ask you to go out with him?'

'Yes, but only because Arthur virtually ordered him to. He was as embarrassed as I was.'

'Oh, come off it. When are you seeing him?'

'I don't know.'

'But you've just said he asked you.'

His change of behaviour both puzzled and annoyed her. 'If you must know, he asked me to go out with him today.'

'Why didn't you say yes? I wouldn't have held you to a promise. All you had to do was ring me.'

'Why on earth would I do a thing like that?'

His laugh jarred her. 'I'd have thought Moore was every girl's dream of paradise. A bachelor, clean-cut, well-educated, and stinking with money. Didn't Davies tell you he paid for the party last night?'

'Is that why you didn't go?' she asked.

His hard face stared at her aggressively. 'I could have worse reasons, couldn't I?'

'I don't know. Moore seemed a nice enough person to me.'

'He would, wouldn't he? Good-looking and the heir to a fortune.'

'I suppose you do realize you are insulting me?'

With a growl Harvey sank back on his jacket. 'Don't blame me. Blame the way the world operates.'

'Why do you dislike Ian Moore so much? Is it a personal thing or is it only dislike of what he represents?'

'*Only?*' The word was a denunciation.

'Does that mean it isn't personal?'

'For Christ's sake! If you're going to talk about Moore all the afternoon, you might as well have gone out with him in the first place.'

'It's not Moore I want to talk about. I'm curious to know why you're so bitter towards people like him.'

He exhaled smoke resentfully. 'Well, you can stay curious as far as I'm concerned.'

Her wish to make peace surprised her. 'I'm sorry. I know I've no right to ask you such questions.' Bending over the dog again she ran her fingers through its wiry coat. 'I think I must blame the war. It leaves one with such little time to learn about people.'

It was a change of tone that for a moment made her sound alone and vulnerable, and it was enough for the loner in Harvey to respond. 'That's all right,' he muttered. 'I just don't want to talk about it, that's all.' A man who found apologizing an effort of will, he frowned and glanced away before making his gruff compromise. 'Forget it if I was rude a minute ago, will you? I get carried away sometimes.'

She gave him a forgiving smile, then turned back to the sunlit hills. Cloud shadows were moving across them like armies and with her arms wrapped around her knees she watched them in fascination. It was the dog, shifting its position in the heather, that broke the spell. Glancing at Harvey and believing him asleep, she lay back on the cape. As she half-closed her eyes the sunlight splintered on her lashes into iridescent shafts and whirls. With the hum of insects a distant organ note, her eyes turned heavy and closed.

When she awoke the organ note was louder and more insistent. Drugged with sun and sleep she sat upright, trying to trace the sound. Harvey's voice made her start. 'It's all right. It's one of ours.'

He was lying on one elbow. From the cigarette in his hand, he appeared to have been awake some time. At his nod she glanced westward. A four-engined aircraft was moving south over the ridge of hills.

'A Lancaster,' he told her. 'Doing an air-test.'

She noticed now how far the sun had moved. 'I must have been asleep some time.'

'Over an hour.'

'Haven't you slept?'

He was watching the steady progress of the Lancaster. 'I think I dozed off for a while. Can't be sure. I saw three others ten minutes ago. There'll be a Main Force raid on tonight.' With one of the abrupt changes of mood that characterized him, he turned towards her half-mockingly. 'More Terror-Flyers over the Fatherland. How do you feel about us?'

She knew he had been wanting to ask the question since their first meeting. 'You mean how do I feel because I'm of German descent?'

'Yes.'

She hesitated. 'I'm not happy about the bombing, if that is what you mean.'

'No one expects you to be happy. But do you resent it?'

'No. I know the Nazis have to be defeated.'

'Then you see a difference between the Nazis and the Germans?'

'Of course. Nazism has been imposed on the Germans.'

'They didn't have to accept it if they didn't want to.'

'Hadn't history something to do with that?'

'Never mind history. The Germans accepted Nazism because it promised them wealth and power. So shouldn't they take some of the blame?'

She was aware he was provoking her. At the same time she wondered if she was being fair to him in the answer she gave. 'It isn't only Germans who can be seduced by promises. But in any case how can you speak for an entire people? Even in the democracies there are some who do not like the way they are governed. Then think how many more there are in Germany who hate Nazism.'

His harsh laugh was full of respect. 'At least you're right about democracies. We've got a bloody nerve to be throwing stones around.'

His resurgence of bitterness made her wish she had not made the point. 'You must not make the mistake of thinking things are as bad here as in Germany. I spent some time there before the war. This is paradise compared to life under the Nazis.'

'Paradise?' he sneered. 'Here? You should have seen this country in the thirties.'

'I did see it. I learned my English here.' Seeing his sceptical glance she went on: 'We moved about a great deal when I was young because my father is an architect. We spent over a year in Plymouth and nearly three years in Canterbury.'

His nod was full of disgust. 'In the south. I thought so. If you'd been up in these parts you'd have different ideas about paradise.'

'Nothing is as bad as Nazism,' she said quietly. 'Take the word of someone who has seen it first hand.'

A small bird, landing on a bush close to them, checked his reply. To her surprise he motioned her to keep still. Balancing like an acrobat on a swaying twig, the bird lifted a wing and preened itself. Then its bright, alert eyes caught sight of the sleeping dog and with a chirrup it launched itself upwards and flew inland.

Harvey jumped to his feet and stood watching it. Tieless, with his shirtsleeves rolled up and his tall, bony body braced against the summer sky, she thought he looked more like a farmer than a soldier. A moment passed and then he gave an embarrassed laugh. 'Sorry about that. But it was a dipper. You don't see many of them in this part of the world.'

He straightened again and gazed across the moors in the direction the bird had flown. She saw his shirt tighten as he took in a deep appreciative breath. 'God,' he said. 'What a perfect day.'

There was a catch in her laugh as she rose. The reflections of the moors were still in his blue, puzzled eyes as she faced him. 'I'm glad that happened.'

'What?' he muttered.

'The way your mood changed when you saw that bird. You are a fraud. You don't hate this country as you pretend to do. You love it. Passionately.'

He turned away; then, with a curse, he ripped up a clump of heather and thrust it almost into her face. 'All right. I love this! And this!' And a sweep of his arm embraced the moors and the distant sea. 'Why shouldn't I? No one's spoiled them. But the rest!' He almost choked on the words as he swung away. 'They've laid their dirty fingermarks on everything else, haven't they?'

Startled by his outcry the dog had jumped up and was barking. Glad of the interruption he cuffed its ears and quietened it. As she stood watching him, it was suddenly clear to her why she had an affinity with this lonely, embittered man.

'You don't need to fight me,' she said quietly. 'Who could understand you better? Don't I have much the same problem as you?'

CHAPTER 18

The front gate of No. 30 Wilberforce Street, Highgate, had a notice that read: No Tradesmen and No Vendors. Wincing at its antagonism Adams pushed the gate open, crossed the path, and pressed the door bell.

He had to press it three times before the slide of a bolt and the rattle of a chain brought him encouragement. The woman who faced him was the archetypal elderly spinster with primly-permed hair, a voluminous blouse, tweed skirt and brogues.

'Yes. What do you want?'

'Good afternoon. I have an appointment with Mrs Marsh.'

'Are you Squadron Leader Adams?'

'That's right, Miss Taylor. I met your sister when I visited Mrs Marsh a few weeks ago.'

The woman's eyes moved from the rings on his sleeve to the crest on his cap. Adams, who suffered a permanent complex about his non-military appearance, decided she was finding it difficult to believe he was not a tradesman. Behind her was a hall and staircase decorated in sombre shades of brown. A large mahogany hallstand stood against the side wall. With a last stare at Adams the woman withdrew to the foot of the staircase.

'Mrs Marsh. There's that officer to see you. Squadron Leader Adams.'

Adams heard a girl's voice on the landing above. The woman gave him a nod and stood aside. 'You'll find her upstairs. The second door on the left.'

Feeling her eyes on his back, Adams started up the stairs. Half-way up he encountered two sepia photographs set in identical oval frames. One featured a bulky man in a frock coat, all bristling moustaches and Imperial arrogance, and Adams had barely recovered from the confrontation when he ran into the haughty stare of a *mem-sahib* wearing pearls and a Victorian hair-do.

Reaching the landing with some relief he found Julie Marsh, baby in arms, waiting at her sitting room door to greet him. Adams held out his hand.

'Hello, Mrs Marsh. It's good to see you again.'

As the girl struggled to free a hand, Adams saw he had made the wrong move and closed quickly on the baby instead. 'How's young Marsh getting along?'

Nervousness made the girl sound breathless. 'He's not very good today, I'm afraid. That was why I couldn't get downstairs to let you in. I've just had to change him.'

Adams, who had already noticed the smell of vomit that surrounded the child, wished he did not sound so hearty. 'Never mind. We all have our bad days, don't we? How old is he now?'

'Nearly nine months.' The girl backed into the sitting room. 'Won't you come in?'

Adams followed her into the combined sitting room and kitchen where the girl indicated an armchair. 'If you care to sit down I'll make a cup of tea.'

Adams sank into the armchair. Its padding was compressed and he could feel the pressure of a spring. Julie, after gazing round the room somewhat helplessly, excused herself and took the baby into the bedroom. Barely five seconds passed before there was a loud wail. Hearing the girl trying to soothe the infant, Adams hesitated, then made his gesture.

'Why don't you give Mark to me?' he called out. 'Then you'll have your hands free to make the tea.'

She appeared in the doorway with the wailing bundle. 'Are you sure you don't mind?'

'Not a bit,' Adams lied.

Somewhat hesitantly she deposited the bundle on Adams' lap. Leaning forward Adams drew back the blanket with one finger. The small, red face that appeared told Adams beyond any doubt that his intrusion was resented. Seeing him at the same time, the infant let out a howl of outrage, stiffened, and kicked its feet furiously against the arm of the chair.

Busy filling a kettle at the sink, Julie glanced back anxiously. 'If you could rock him a little he might settle down.'

Hoping fervently the infant would not exact revenge by peeing on him, Adams obeyed. The effect was counter-productive: the yells turned hysterical but with no other recourse open to him Adams went on rocking. Setting the filled kettle on a gas ring the girl hurried towards him.

'I'll give him some orange juice. That usually quietens him.'

The subterfuge worked and the replenished infant was replaced in his cot. Adams was at last able to pay her attention. Her dress, cheap but neat, suggested she had made some effort to be presentable but her hair looked straggly and needed combing. Months of stress had given her skin an unhealthy pallor and her face had a pinched appearance that made her look older than her years.

She handed him a cup of tea, then sank on the settee as if the effort of coping with him and the baby was too much. 'I'm sorry I haven't any cakes. I meant to go out this morning to the shops but it was difficult with Mark off-colour.'

Adams was wondering how to begin. 'I never eat between meals. I have to think about my figure.' As the girl made an effort to smile, he took the plunge. 'You do know why I've come, don't you?'

Her nod was jerky. 'Yes. Peter told me he was going to ask you.'

'Is there anything you would like to say to me first? It will all be in confidence, of course.'

The girl hesitated, then shook her head. 'What is there to say? I want Peter to give up flying and he says he can't. I think he'd like to but he's too ashamed to ask. I can't see why.'

Adams took the first gentle step forward. 'It is difficult for him, you know.'

'Why?' Her voice was suddenly hostile. 'He's done forty-four trips. That's a tour and a half. On other squadrons men are rested after thirty operations.'

'I'm afraid that's your answer. This isn't an ordinary squadron. Like the Pathfinders, crews can only achieve maximum proficiency by staying on beyond their normal tour.'

'But that's unfair! Most men don't live to finish a tour. Twelve raids is the average. Peter's done nearly four times that number.'

Adams realized the size of the task facing him. 'I'm afraid that's why he is so valuable. We've recently had to bring in a large number of new men, so the experienced crews like Peter are worth their weight in gold.'

The suddenness with which her emotion died and her eyes filled with tears told Adams the state of her nerves. 'What's the use? You all say the same things.'

Adams tried a different approach. 'Aren't you rather looking on the dark side of things? Have you ever thought how lucky Peter is to be flying the Mosquito? It's probably the safest plane in the RAF. It can get up higher than any German fighter and it can also go faster. This gives him a far better chance of survival than if he were flying heavy bombers.'

Adams was conscious of his blunder even before the girl's bitter reply. 'Peter has said this to me too. But it didn't help in May, did it? One plane back – from an entire squadron! If Peter hadn't been in hospital at the time, he'd already be dead.'

'That was an exceptional operation. In the normal run-of-the-mill raids, Mosquito losses are well below the Main Force average.'

Hypersensitive to a degree when discussing other men's lives, Adams imagined the girl's resentful eyes rested a moment on his wingless left shoulder. 'You've just said this is a special squadron. That means it carries out special operations.'

In desperation at the hash he was making of things, Adams played the liar. 'The May raid was exceptional because of its importance and because the Germans had caught wind of it. It doesn't mean the squadron is going to be given anything as dangerous in the future.'

The girl was staring blindly at the worn carpet between them. With Adams having disappointed her, she had withdrawn into her private world and was no longer listening to him. Disgusted by his lies and his failure, Adams took another sip of tea and found it was growing cold. The feeling he was letting the young pilot down brought a plea from him when a minute or two of silence might have been wiser.

'I know how hard it is but have you ever tried to see it from Peter's point of view? He's part of an élite group – the few who survived from the old squadron – and a part of him can't help being proud of it. Also men grow very close in wartime and try not to let one another down. I know how desperately he wants to ease your mind but it is a huge step for a pilot to ask to be grounded. In fact it's just possible it might be the worst thing we can ask of him.'

Her expression made Adams realize he now sounded more like an enemy than an ally. Resentment drew on the last dregs of her nervous energy. 'Men with their stupid pride and fear of being thought a coward. . . . What do I care what people think of him? Who'll remember any of this in ten years' time? I want a father for my baby, not a dead hero.'

The difference between man and woman, Adams thought, frozen in his chair. The woman who since the dawn of time has resolved her morality within the walls of her cave and the children's mouths she has to feed. The man, out-going and finding both survival and success needing collective effort, adopting a morality that takes into account the interests of his fellow-hunters. One morality rational and therefore often selfish. The other equally rational and yet often sentimental. On occasions such as this totally incompatible.

With her efforts to show a brave face spent, the girl was now sobbing uncontrollably. More upset than he could remember, Adams forgot his role as a senior RAF officer. 'I know how you feel. It's my job to talk to these boys before they go out on a raid and I can't think how many times I've asked myself how men can find glory in killing one another.'

He broke off, too horrified by his confession to know if the girl had heard him or not. A glance at her made him doubt it: her sobs appeared to be tearing her thin body apart. Adams stole an uneasy glance over his shoulder. The door was ajar and the girl's distress must surely be heard downstairs. Then Adams reviled himself. It was a poor man who weighed up his personal interests when a fellow human being was suffering like this. Dropping on the settee, Adams put an arm around the girl's shoulders and defied any dragons who might see him.

'You mustn't torture yourself this way. The worst doesn't usually happen, you know. I don't believe it will happen to Peter.'

She tried to speak but her sobs choked her. Adams drew her closer. 'What exactly were you hoping I could do, Julie?'

'I'm not sure. . . . Couldn't you talk to his Flight Commander . . . or perhaps to the C.O. himself?'

'I could, but you must see they will do nothing until Peter himself asks to be grounded.'

'Then talk to Peter for me. Please.'

'I already have, Julie. I advised him to go straight to the C.O.'

'Then try again. Please. I can't go on like this much longer.'

Adams could feel the wetness of her tears on his cheek. 'I will. And if I can think of anything else, I'll let you know. But I don't want to disappoint you, so please don't bank on it.'

Her lack of response told him that that was unlikely. Not allowing her to go downstairs with him, he remembered little more of his exit than the haunted, tear-ravaged girl saying goodbye to him at her sitting room door. In fact Adams' mind only began to function again on his drive back to Sutton Craddock. In the entire history of war were there ever more pathetic victims than these young fliers and their wives? The monstrous daily charade of women waving goodbye to their husbands as if they were going to the office instead of into mortal danger contained all the elements of pure sadism. For the rest of that day and a considerable part of the night Adams remembered the girl's bitter remark that all the present heroism would soon be forgotten. He had the feeling she was right and it upset him. Adams, the idealist, would have liked these young couples to be remembered forever.

CHAPTER 19

With a cheerful toot of its siren, the pleasure boat nudged the pier and swung in alongside it. Behind it the Chiemsee was bright and blue in the July sunlight. As a gang-plank rattled down, the brass band on the pier, all shiny faces and glinting instruments, took a deep breath and burst into a popular tune. With café tables crowded, children playing, and soldiers on leave sauntering up and down with their girl friends, the scene was relaxed and colourful. The war was still a long way from Bavaria and people were making the most of the Sunday afternoon.

Outside a café back on the main road that ran to Prien a burly man nudged his companion's foot under the table as the first passengers disembarked. 'As you'd expect, the arrogant bastards are the first off.'

The two men, wearing local defence force uniforms, were Hausmann and Meyer. Both worked in the timber yards during the week but like the rest of their fellow workers wore the defence force para-military uniforms in the evenings and on weekends. Although most of the men were over military age or medically un-fit, the uniform staved off embarrassing questions as to why they were not in the Services. For Hausmann and Meyer their uniforms were a shield against a more serious embarrassment.

The burly Hausmann was watching a party of four high-ranking German officers who were walking up the pier. Local girls were clinging to their arms. Although the officers were sharing jokes with the girls, there was an arrogance about them that made civilians move aside. His back to the pier, Meyer took a sip of beer.

'Is it the Herrenchiemsee boat?'

'Yes.'

The gaunt-faced Meyer had a satirical sense of humour. 'That fits. They'll have been strutting up and down the corridors imagining themselves Louis XIV.'

The party had reached the pier entrance. As they moved towards two large cars parked there, Hausmann nudged Meyer again. 'He's the tall one with a girl on each arm.'

Meyer turned casually. The officer Hausmann indicated was a slim and erect man in his late thirties. Arrogant-featured, he had a schläger scar on his right cheekbone. His manner and the deference shown him by the rest of his party made it clear he was their superior in more than rank. Waiting for one of his fellow officers to open the rear door of the larger car, he stepped inside. The two giggling girls followed him a couple of seconds later. Hausmann glanced back at Meyer.

'Colonel von Löwerherz. Wealthy with an aristocratic background. Studied at Heidelberg and was brilliant. Used to be a designer at Mercedes Benz. Now he's Co-ordinator of Research and Development, so he has access to all parts of the project. His weakness is women and rumour has it he's a sadistic bastard. He's in Prien most weekends and doesn't waste any time. We've learned that on at least three occasions he's taken a woman back to Ruhpolding.' Hausmann allowed himself a brief grin. 'He must find the weekends too far apart. It's against all the rules of course, but apparently his technical know-how, aristocratic background and rank allow him to get away with it.'

Meyer's gaunt face betrayed his frustration. 'Three little tarts get taken right inside and we can't even manage a look through the bloody fence. Can't we question them in some way?'

Hausmann shrugged. 'How can we do that without making them suspicious? Anyway, what would be the point? They wouldn't be interested in what was going on, and Löwerherz would hardly take them on a conducted tour.'

Back at the pier entrance the two cars were now moving away. As they swept past the café both men looked engrossed in their beer. Hausmann waited until they vanished round a bend before leaning forward again. 'London have been in touch while you were in Munich. And this is the idea they've come up with.'

He spoke in a low tone for nearly three minutes. When he finished Meyer was showing both shock and disgust. 'You haven't agreed to this, have you?'

Hausmann's own distaste for the scheme did nothing to improve his temper. 'What the hell can I do about it? I'm here to obey orders, not give them.'

'But it's inhuman. No one has the right to ask another human being to do a thing like that.'

'Apparently no one has asked. It's Lorenz's own idea.'

'Knowing Lorenz, it probably is. But London shouldn't agree to it.'

'What alternative have they got? We haven't come up with any ideas ourselves.'

'Maybe we haven't. But this one's suicidal. For Christ's sake, Hausmann, have a word with. . . .'

Hausmann's expression made Meyer break off in mid-sentence. A young Gestapo officer had come round the corner of the café and Meyer's raised voice had caught his attention. Both men froze as he approached their table. He paused behind Meyer's chair as if to question him, then appeared to change his mind and walked on. He was twenty yards down the pavement before Hausmann drew breath again. 'Have you gone out of your bloody mind?'

'Sorry,' Meyer muttered. 'Only it's a filthy thing to ask anyone to do.'

Nerves and twinges of arthritis made Hausmann uncharacteristically short-

267

tempered. 'It's a filthy world – or haven't you heard? And it could be a damn sight filthier unless we can break this security and locate that plant.' He glanced at his watch. 'I'm on duty in an hour, so the rest is up to you. Get into Prien and follow Löwerherz around. Find out his haunts and everyone he sees. Keep on him all night if necessary because we've only got this weekend and next to get the information London needs. O.K.?'

Meyer nodded and emptied his glass. Down the pier the band had broken into a rousing march. As Hausmann rose, another twinge of arthritis made him grab hold of the table. 'It's those damned damp forests,' he growled at Meyer's inquiry. 'If we don't get this business settled soon I'll be in worse shape than my old mother.'

Davies straightened up from the photographs and brochures that covered the bed. 'All right, that's your target. Any more questions?'

When no one spoke he nodded at Anna, who began collecting up the briefing material, and moved into the centre of the room. Henderson, Adams and Moore, the other men present, hesitated a moment and then followed him. Seeing Henderson give Moore an apologetic glance, Davies turned irritable.

'Someone say something, for Christ's sake.'

Henderson's comment was addressed to Moore. 'You wanted to get away tomorrow, didn't you?'

'What's that?' Davies asked.

The Scot turned to him somewhat disapprovingly. 'He was going on leave tomorrow to attend his father's funeral.'

Davies allowed himself a single moment of compassion. 'Sorry, Moore. It's damned bad luck. But that's how things go.' Dropping the disappointment as another casualty of war he went on: 'You're all being bloody coy about this raid, aren't you?'

Challenged, Henderson took the plunge. 'I suppose that's because it seems a hell of a long trip, sir.'

'It is a hell of a long trip,' Davies snapped. 'But what else can we do? Until the green light comes, we have to slow down production somehow.' He turned to Moore. 'What do you think? You're the one that has to go.'

All eyes turned on Moore who took a few seconds to answer. 'With a bit of luck we ought to get there all right. But as we have to go down to five thousand feet or under to obtain accuracy, I think we must expect losses.'

'You mean their radar will track you to the target?'

'Yes. I know you've plenty of other activity planned tomorrow night but they can't miss picking us up if we penetrate as deeply as this. And that means night fighters will be waiting when we go down.'

To avoid his expression betraying him, Davies turned to the window. 'So it's primarily a problem of their tracking system?'

Moore looked surprised at the question. 'That and their night fighters. When isn't it the problem?'

Instead of answering Davies gave himself a few seconds more at the window before turning back. 'Maybe when it comes to the night it won't be as bad as you think. I'll have another word with the three of you before we brief the crews tomorrow afternoon. In the meantime, if you've no more questions, let's thank Miss Reinhardt for her help and leave the pub as unobtrusively as possible. There's no point in making people curious.'

Thanking the girl, Henderson and Adams left first. As Davies led Moore to the door, the young pilot turned back. 'I understand Harvey is on duty tonight. So I'm wondering if I might be sneaky and ask for that dinner date you promised me?'

Anna returned his smile. 'I'd like that very much, Wing Commander.'

'Good. What time will suit you? Seven o'clock?'

'Yes. I'll be ready. Thank you.'

Davies followed Moore out on the landing, then reappeared in the doorway. 'You're starting to get some sense at last,' he grunted.

She laughed at him. 'I'm relieved to hear you say that, Arthur.'

Davies gave her a wink and closed the door behind him. Left alone the girl drifted across to the window. From it she could see Henderson and Adams walking down the road to the airfield. The field itself was sunlit but a bank of dark clouds were massing over the southern perimeter and a Mosquito flying on air-test could be seen silhouetted against them. The girl was about to turn on the radio when her telephone rang. 'Hello, Miss.' The voice was Maisie's. 'Someone from the airfield wants a word with you.'

The someone was Harvey. 'Anna? Hello. I thought I'd phone while I had the chance – you never know in this game when they're going to cut communications.'

'Hello, Frank. I'm glad you did.'

'It doesn't look as if I'll get a chance to come over today but what's the situation tomorrow?'

'I'm not doing anything if that's what you mean.'

'Then am I going to see you?'

Aware he knew nothing yet about the forthcoming raid she chose her words carefully. 'If you'd like to. What about the morning?'

'The morning?' Harvey sounded disappointed. 'If we're not flying, couldn't we make it the afternoon or the evening?'

'Yes, of course. But it would be good to see you in the morning if you can manage it.'

When other men might have made egotistical assumptions, it was typical of Harvey that he only sounded puzzled. 'All right. Around 10.30?'

She was trying to resolve this inhibited, diffident man with the belligerent trouble-maker portrayed by Davies and failing on every count. They talked for nearly five minutes before Harvey was interrupted. 'Sorry, Anna, but there's a bit of a flap on. I'll have to go.'

She was surprised to hear her voice pull him back. 'Don't forget about the morning. Come as early as you can.'

She lowered the receiver and as if the airfield were a magnet found herself drawn to the window again. The bank of clouds, moving rapidly, had now covered the sun and in its shadow the entire aspect of the airfield had changed. Hangars and Nissen huts, whose outlines had been softened by the sunlight, now looked gaunt and impermanent. Stains of oil on the runways, refracting prismatic lights, were now ugly bruises on grey flesh. As the Mosquito under air-test flittered like a shadow across the threatening sky, a chill ran through the girl.

CHAPTER **20**

Across the packed room the three-piece band was playing 'Only Forever'. Waiters, some with trays held above their heads, were struggling through the circle of tables. On the small maple dance floor, locked together in the fashion of the time, couples were doing their best not to collide with one another. Although a number of civilians were present, servicemen and their girl friends were in the majority. A blue haze of tobacco smoke hung over the tables and the air was filled with the frenetic chatter and laughter of wartime.

Moore's eyes were on the girl seated opposite him. An American sergeant and his girl, ignoring the fox-trot tempo, were jitterbugging on the crowded floor, and she was watching their performance with amusement. She was wearing a green evening dress that set off to perfection her dark hair and creamy skin, and Moore, who had already decided she was the most unusual girl he had ever met, was wondering whether it was her appearance or her personality that intrigued him the most. He gave her a rueful grin as she turned back.

'I'm afraid it's hardly the Dorchester but it's the best we've got in these parts.'

Her grey eyes reproved him. 'Don't apologize for it. I'm enjoying myself.'

'You are? That's marvellous. I suppose the food wasn't too bad. Would you care to dance?'

'If you promise not to jitterbug. I don't think there is room on the floor for two of us.'

'Jitterbugging isn't my style. I'm the close-in, smoochy type.'

A dimple came into her cheek. 'I'm not sure I know what that means.'

Smiling, he led her towards the floor. 'Come and find out.'

He was not surprised to discover she danced well. As the floor grew more crowded, dancing turned into little more than a shuffle, but with her tall and supple body pressed against him Moore had no complaints and it was nearly fifteen minutes before he led her back to their table. Seeing the champagne bottle was empty he checked a passing waiter. 'Bring another bottle, will you?'

He ignored the girl's protest as he sat back. 'You mustn't argue. This is a special occasion.'

'It is?'

Moore's eyes were admiring her. 'It is for me. It isn't every day I get the chance to take out an Air Commodore's beautiful girl friend.'

She took his banter the way it was intended. 'Poor Arthur. He never seems able to relax, does he?'

'He doesn't need to. He enjoys his work. God knows what he'll do when the war's over.'

'I think you are right. He will be very bored.'

Moore's mood changed. Lighting a cigarette, he frowned down at it. 'He won't be the only one. A good many of us are going to find peacetime difficult to take.'

'But why? Surely you can't like all this destruction and killing?'

His smile was wry. 'Between the two of us it disgusts me.'

'Then why will you find peacetime so difficult?'

He shifted in his chair before answering. 'I suppose with me it's because I dread responsibility.'

'Does your father's death mean you are now head of the company?'

He wondered how much Davies had told her. 'Yes, I'm afraid it does.'

'And you don't like that?'

Never one to share his forebodings easily, Moore wondered at the special qualities of this girl who could make him admit them now. 'Frankly, I dread it. Thousands of men and their families dependent on me for their livelihood. . . . I'm a coward – it'll turn me old before my time.' Then he saw she was laughing. 'What's the joke?'

'You are a Squadron Commander. Every time you lead your men out on a raid you are responsible for their lives. Yet you are afraid of being responsible for their livelihood. Can't you see how funny that is?'

He laughed with her. 'It's a different kind of responsibility. I'm not the strategist, only a tactician. But as the Chairman of the company I'll be responsible for policy every inch of the way. And that thought frightens the life out of me.'

'I still think it is very funny,' she told him.

Over on the dance floor there was a loud cheer as the American and his partner completed their marathon dance. Moore's question came as the girl turned to look. 'Anna! Why did Davies arrange for you to come here?'

For a moment her gaze remained on the group of cheering servicemen as if she had not heard him. Then, without haste, she turned back. 'Arthur told you why. I came for a holiday and also to tell you all I know about Miesbach.'

'But Davies could have had you interrogated at home and had the photographs sent to us. There was no need for you to waste your leave here.'

'I am not wasting it. I wanted to see this part of England.'

'A northern market town? An airfield?'

'No. The scenery. It is very beautiful up here.'

'There's beautiful scenery in the south.'

271

'I know that. But I wanted to see another part of the country. Is that so strange?'

It wasn't at all strange, Moore thought, wondering why he was asking his questions. 'Where did you go yesterday?'

'To the moors. Somewhere near Whitby, I believe.'

'What did you think of them?'

'They are everything I expected. Very beautiful.'

The question came before Moore could check it. 'How did you get on with Harvey?'

She picked up her glass of champagne. 'Quite well, I think.'

'You didn't find him a difficult character?'

He discovered that instead of avoiding a challenge her inclination was to meet it half-way. 'Are you another who doesn't like him?'

He avoided a direct answer. 'One can't deny he has a pretty large chip on his shoulder.'

'Perhaps there is a reason for that chip.'

'Perhaps. But he's not the only man in the war who's had a hard life. Half of my squadron are working class but they don't go round acting like martyrs.'

'Perhaps his life was harder than most.' At his glance she shook her head. 'No, he did not speak about it. But I am sure something has happened to make him the way he is.'

'Aren't you a bit suspicious of people who blame society for their behaviour? Isn't it often an excuse to hide their own short-comings?'

Although it was a remark made deliberately to disturb her composure he found the tables were turned as her grey eyes met his own. 'But Harvey does not use it as an excuse. He will not talk about it.'

'But the inference is there, isn't it?'

'It is easy for you to talk this way – society has been kind to you. For that reason it is easier for you to fight to preserve that society.'

Although quietly delivered, it was a rebuke that made him smile wryly. 'You're very frank.'

'Would you want me to be anything else?'

'No. I like you as you are. But if Harvey is so bitter with society, why does he fight for it? We're not Nazi Germany. He wouldn't be shot if he were a conscientious objector.'

'Haven't you ever thought this could be one of the conflicts he suffers from? He believes he hates England for her indifference and yet deep inside he might love her passionately. I think he does. Not the society but the fields, the hedgerows, the villages – the visions men have when they think of England.'

Moore was trying to associate visions of rural England with the brooding Harvey and failing on every count. 'Isn't that rather romantic?'

She smiled at her analogy. 'Isn't love itself romantic? Harvey makes me think of a man in love with a cruel mistress. He curses her and wants to escape but must always be there when she needs him.'

'He seems to interest you very much,' Moore said curiously.

'He does. I have not met many men like him.'

'You will if you stay in this country long enough. We've got more than our fair share of them.'

Her quiet reply made him start. 'Then you are lucky.'

'Lucky?' Moore had to glance at the girl's earnest face to be certain she was not teasing him. 'Warts and all, I'll take Harvey as a flight commander because a good part of his bloody-mindness rubs off on the enemy. But in peacetime his type are a menace. Harvey would call a strike if someone took just a minute off his tea break.'

'He probably would,' she said quietly. 'But is it a bad thing to defend one's rights?'

'Oh, come off it!' Moore's sudden outburst of impatience was uncharacteristic. 'When I was a boy I remember seeing someone like Harvey take a swing at my father simply because he was trying to rationalize a production line. Don't tell me that's defending one's rights. It's just bloody-minded obstructionism.'

It was a moment before she answered him. 'Have you ever thought that men like that are the price one has to pay for democracy?'

He stared at her. 'Now I know you're pulling my leg.'

'No, I'm serious. Men who can't be cowed by authority can't be conquered by authoritarianism. If there had been half a million of them in Germany ten years ago – perhaps only a few thousand – there would be no Nazism today.'

'There might be Communism though, mightn't there?'

She saw he was recovering his good humour and allowed herself a smile. 'I find that rather funny. I doubt if Harvey knows what a Communist is.'

'If he doesn't, he's trying hard,' was Moore's wry comment.

'I think you're wrong to lump Harvey with the kind of man who struck your father. I believe he has a much deeper reason for his bitterness towards society.'

Too intelligent to miss her inference, Moore gave a sudden start. 'What are you getting at? That I might dislike Harvey because when I was a boy I saw someone like him strike my father?'

She held his stare without flinching. 'It is possible, isn't it?'

His laugh was a mixture of disbelief and respect. 'I suppose anything's possible. Are you sure you're not a teacher of psychology?'

For the first time she showed embarrassment. 'I have no right to make such suggestions. But it was you who began talking about Harvey.'

'I don't mind your suggestions. As a matter of fact I'm grateful for them. As I said earlier – Harvey's a good flight commander and acts like a father to his men. When you come across a man like that you resent not liking him.'

'You are very generous to someone you don't like and who doesn't like you. I don't think you would find Harvey so generous.'

His reply teased her. 'You're forgetting your own credo. Everything is that much easier when society has made you the top dog. Remember?'

The dimple reappeared in her cheek. 'You can't deny it's true, can you?'

'I'm not denying anything. But you have got Harvey insured all ways.' Moore's smile turned quizzical. 'Harvey – the pillar of democracy! The archetypal Saxon defending his rights against the Norman oppressor! I must tell this to Davies. He'll never be the same man again!'

She laughed with him. 'I'd rather you didn't. It might come between our two families.'

It was approaching midnight when they made the journey back to Sutton Craddock. Although its roof and walls were silvered by the waning moon, the inn had a stillness that made her turn to him. 'I'm sorry I can't invite you inside for a cup of coffee but Mr Kearns and Maisie are usually in bed well before this time.'

He nodded and slipped an arm around her shoulders. For a minute or more she responded to his kisses with a warmth that surprised him. Then abruptly she drew back. Her expression in the shadowy car gave him the thought – until he dismissed it as absurd – that the evening had induced her to discard her armour of self-discipline and that she was suddenly alarmed by its absence.

'What is it, Anna?'

For a moment she did not respond. Then she began fumbling for the door handle. 'I must go now.'

He checked her. 'It isn't Harvey, is it? Or someone else?'

Her exclamation of distress was in German. 'I cannot talk about it. Please do not ask me.'

His hand fell away from her arm. 'Very well. Am I going to see you again?'

'Yes, of course. You can always phone me. Thank you for the evening. I have enjoyed it very much.'

He made no further effort to detain her. With the car door open, she suddenly turned back. 'You and Harvey – you will both come back tomorrow night, won't you?'

It took him a moment to understand what she meant. 'Don't be silly. Of course we shall come back.'

Outside she paused by the wicker gate. Although she was a lovely monochrome picture in the moonlight, there was a loneliness in her expression Moore had not seen before. As he was telling himself it was a trick of the light she turned and hurried up the gravel path.

He waited until she had disappeared into the inn before reversing the car and driving to the airfield. It was just on midnight when he entered his billet. Although it was a habit of his to listen to the late news, he made no attempt to switch on his radio. Instead he undressed, slipped into bed, and lay gazing up at the dark ceiling.

CHAPTER 21

The staff car pulled up with a squeal of brakes outside the Administration Block. A young Leading Aircraftman chatting up a pretty Waaf near the entrance stiffened as Davies, with the agility of a man half his age, leapt from the car and came bounding forward. Trousers flapping round his legs, he snapped a salute at the frozen couple and disappeared into the building. As he hurried down the corridor he glanced at his watch and his footsteps quickened. Five seconds later he reached the C.O.'s office, rapped on the door and threw it open.

The room was full of the officers who conducted crew briefings. Among them were Henderson, Moore, Adams, and the two flight commanders, Harvey and Young. Ignoring the salutes, Davies slung a briefcase on the desk and turned. 'You all heard the BBC news this morning?'

When some of the men shook their heads Davies marched over to a radio perched on a filing cabinet and switched it on. A boisterous chorus of singing indicated the end of Workers' Playtime. Turning the volume down for a moment, Davies glanced at Henderson. 'Everything going all right, Jock?'

'Yes, sir. Everything's fine.'

'What time are you holding the briefing?'

'Directly after the men have had their evening meal.'

'I take it the Target Indicators have arrived.'

'Yes. They came an hour ago.'

Davies' eyes shifted to Moore. 'Your men do understand this technique of bombing on flares?'

'Yes, sir. We did an exercise last week.'

'Who are you using as backers-up?'

'Harvey and Young, sir.'

Davies slanted a look of dislike at the heavy-jowled Harvey. 'You're sure they've got it buttoned-up? If the flares go down in the wrong place you could end up dropping bombs in Lake Constance.'

'They both know what to do, sir. They're experienced pilots.'

Before the scowling Davies could reply, the chorus of singing turned into a loud cheer, then faded away. Reaching out hurriedly, Davies turned up the volume. Six pips sounded and then the measured, resonant voice of the news reader. As Davies motioned for silence, the intrigued officers crowded nearer to listen.

'Last night over seven hundred of our heavy bombers raided the important

275

enemy port of Hamburg. Great damage was done and crews reported that the entire centre of the city was set ablaze. Because of new defensive tactics employed, our losses were slight. In all only twelve aircraft failed to return.'

A stir of excitement ran through the listening men. As their questioning voices arose, Davies turned off the radio and swung round.

'Sensational, isn't it? 1.5 per cent casualties. Until last night our average losses over Hamburg have been six per cent. So last night we saved around thirty-five heavies.'

Henderson asked the question all wanted to ask. 'How, sir?'

The grinning Davies was revelling in the moment. 'Anyone got a new packet of cigarettes?'

As the officers stared at one another Lindsay shrugged and held out a packet of Player's Navy Cut. Opening it Davies pulled out a strip of tin foil. 'You won't be seeing this stuff in cigarette packets much longer.' Releasing the foil he allowed it to flutter to the ground. 'That's how it's done. Too bloody simple, isn't it?'

He grinned again at the blank stares he received. 'Tin foil's the secret. If bundles of it are thrown out every minute by an approaching heavy, they reflect back the impulses from Jerry's radar beams and throw his direction-finding to hell. We've known about it a long time but no one dared use it until we were sure it would benefit us more than Jerry. Now the time has come and Butch Harris chose Hamburg as his first target.' Davies turned his exultant eyes on Moore. 'That's why I set up this raid on Miesbach — I knew it wasn't going to be as dangerous as it sounded. Once the Hamburg raid was over and the cat out of the bag, you could get the benefit of it.'

Excitement was growing among the listening officers. Adams put the question they all wanted to ask. 'Does it affect all types of radar, sir?'

'Everything except long-range detectors,' Davies told him. 'That means his searchlights and gun predictors as well as his night fighters' Airborne Interception Equipment. From what I heard early this morning his searchlights were all over the place and his flak fire a shambles. It's been given the code-name "Window" and sounds like the greatest thing since Father Christmas. Of course Jerry will find a counter to it in a month or two but until he does we're going to make hay while the sun shines. You can't carry the stuff yourselves because there isn't room for the bundles in a Mossie cockpit but you can still benefit from it as you will see in a minute.'

Quelling their curiosity with difficulty, his listeners watched him unlatch his briefcase and pull out a file. Opening it, he gave his attention first to Moore and his two flight commanders.

'Let's take the attack first. As you know, because accuracy is so important on this operation we're using the Pathfinder technique. Wing Commander Moore will corner the factory with green target indicators and the rest of the squadron will bomb within those flares. But because flares burn out or get buried beneath falling rubble, it's important you two backers-up keep a beady eye on things. If Moore's flares don't suffer any damage, back up with your own at the intervals given you. If they go out earlier than they should, make certain they are replaced before any more bombs are dropped. When you do the main briefing this afternoon, be sure all the men understand this because we don't want any bombs wasted. O.K.?'

As the three men nodded Davies flipped over a page in the file. 'All right – now to the ways and means of getting there. Here is a list of our activity tonight. Up north we've got 4 Group and the Canadians doing a spot of mine-laying in the Baltic. 8 Group will be doing their nightly milk-run to Berlin and they're also laying a spoof raid on Karlsruhe. But the operation that's going to help you most is a Main Force raid on Augsburg. Your run is timed so that you'll approach Jerry's radar beacons at the time the bomber stream is running through them. Main Force will be twenty-five miles north of you, so you don't need to worry too much about collisions, but their presence alone ought to draw every fighter for two hundred miles. Better than that, however, they'll be dropping "window" from the moment they're within range of the beacons. Which we believe will make your trip a picnic.'

While talking, Davies had been watching Harvey examine the large map of Europe on the wall. His sharp question made the Yorkshireman turn. 'What's the trouble, Harvey? You found something to gripe about?'

The gruff voice that answered him was Harvey's characteristic response to attack. 'I'm thinking we can't keep twenty-five miles from the heavies all the way. What happens when we peel off for Miesbach?'

'For Christ's sake – you're getting cover ninety per cent of the way! Do you want your hand holding over the target as well?' Aware he had shown his dislike of Harvey too openly, Davies turned back irritably to the others. 'What do they say – you can't please everybody? Because this is the first time the night fighters in the south have encountered "window" we believe they'll spend the night chasing their arses. But however it turns out, it ought to be a damn sight easier operation than you expected. Any more questions or gripes?'

When nobody spoke Davies handed the file to Henderson and picked up his briefcase. 'All right, Jock. Take over, will you? I have to run off now to see somebody but I'll be back in time for the crew briefing.'

Klaus gazed around the night sky disconsolately. A month ago, even a fortnight ago, it would have seemed impossible that he might go with Heidi to the altar without his Iron Cross. Now the odds seemed all in its favour. Why, of all places, had he to be stationed in Bavaria? The Reich stretched from the Russian steppes to the French seaboard, from the Arctic Circle to the foot of Italy, and nearly everywhere there was air activity. In Russia it was well known that even third-rate pilots were registering two and three kills a week, and in Belgium and Northern Germany it was action all the time.

Hamburg seemed to be the latest battle centre. It was true rumours were running wild that the *Tommis* had introduced a new radar interference device but it took more than rumours to convince Klaus that if he were in the air with six or seven hundred *Tommi* bombers he wouldn't make his presence felt.

What infuriated Klaus and his younger colleagues were the reports that selected squadrons of night fighters had recently been given freedom from the chains of the radar beacons. Using them as mere assembly points, the fighters were being allowed to follow the bomber streams to their targets. Not only did the tactics, christened Wild Boar, give the fighters longer contact with the bombers, but over their objectives the backdrop of fires and search-lights made them an easier target. The new system meant refuelling at remote airfields but the risks entailed were a small price to pay for the extra kills being recorded. However all the fortunate squadrons were based in the north where enemy activity was high. In the south, as sleepy as the country it protected, the old Kummhuber 'tied-system' still held sway.

Behind Klaus, little Fritz Neumann was also in low spirits, although for a very different reason. Earlier that day he had received news that his mother had suffered a severe embolism and been rushed to hospital. Fritz had put in immediately for compassionate leave but felt his chances of getting it before Klaus became due for leave himself were nil.

With little to do until a bomber entered Kassel's radar beam Fritz gazed out through the cupola. It was a good night for bombers, he noted, with a low, waning moon, plenty of breaks in the clouds for star navigation, and reasonable cover from searchlights and fighters. The Messerschmitt was circling the station at 20,000 feet and the clouds had an eerie appearance in the faint moonlight. A black hole in them directly below made Fritz think of a drop into a bottomless dungeon. As he peered into it, a narrow smear of light appeared, to go out like a snuffed match thirty seconds later. A night fighter taking off, was Fritz's guess, and he felt a sense of comradeship in the thought.

The feeling died as he gazed upwards at the spangled dome of stars. Millions of them, all icy and impersonal, and reaching up to infinity and beyond. This was the time Fritz always felt lonely. Waiting for the bombers to come and aware that one night you could be the one slithering down that terrifying hole to oblivion. Tonight, with his mother close to death, Fritz marvelled at the madness of men who could deliberately create suffering when so much suffering existed already.

Feeling it was a thought with an undertone of disloyalty he tried to push it away, then shrugged. Why bother? Thousands of other men must think the same. Yet when the moment came only a handful failed to press the trigger or drive home the knife and they were shot as traitors or reviled as cranks. Man was a victim of both his destructive instincts and his moral cowardice.

As if to prove his point, Fritz bent attentively over his A.I. set as a sharp voice crackled in his earphones. 'Bearcat Two! A hostile force is approaching. Steer Zero Six Five. Altitude 6,400 metres. . . .'

Before the Controller at Kassel had completed his instructions the eager Klaus was banking on a wingtip. Settling on its new compass course like a wolf taking scent, the black 110 raced across the starlit sky. When a correction came fifteen seconds later it veered five degrees and streaked on, its exhaust stacks aflame.

Back at Kassel the Fighter Controller discovered his calf was itching. Intent on vectoring Bearcat II towards its first victim, he rubbed the afflicted spot with his foot. The blue co-ordinates on the Seeburg Table representing Klaus's 110 had travelled another five miles nearer the eight red traces that were British bombers when the Controller forgot his itching calf and gave a grunt of shock.

'What the hell's happening? The bastards look as if they're spawning in mid-air.'

His assistant, who had been fine-tuning the radio, swung round to see the eight traces had burst into a thousand and turned the entire screen luminous. 'What is it? Interference?'

'It must be. But what's causing it?'

While the two men stared at the flashing screen, other beacons in the defence chain were experiencing the same phenomenon. Shouts and curses rang out, some reaching out across the air to the puzzled fighter pilots.

'This can't be happening, Max. It's crazy.'

'Christ, there are thousands of the bastards!'

Hearing the tumult, Klaus turned to Fritz. 'What do you make of it?'

'It must be the interference the *Tommis* used over Hamburg.'

'But how the hell does it work?'

Before Fritz could answer the Fighter Controller at Kassel recovered his poise. 'Bearcat Two! I can't vector you because of interference. Try to make contact on your Emil-Emil.'

In other words we're on our own, Klaus thought with mixed feelings. 'You hear that, Fritz? Get that scanner of yours working.'

Ahead, its upper layer silvered by moonlight and its belly dark and sullen, a long bank of cloud stretched from horizon to horizon. The muscles of Klaus's face tightened as he estimated its height. 6,800 metres and maybe more. Even the elements were on the *Tommis'* side tonight.

Fritz's first contact came when the ghostly peaks of the clouds were swirling beneath them. 'I've got something, Hans. Six hostiles. No, eight.... 6,000 metres.'

Klaus felt his mouth water. 'What bearing?'

The radar operator ignored his sharp question. '4,000 metres ... 2,000 metres ... they've gone past!'

'Gone past? What the hell are you talking about?'

'They've gone past. At a hell of a speed.'

'But we're behind them. So how could they go past?'

Fritz's voice quickened. 'Another contact. 8,000, 6,000, 4,000, 1,000.... This is crazy! They've gone past too.'

'But they'd have to be flying on a reciprocal course to do that. Are you sure there's nothing wrong with your set?'

Before Fritz could answer his screens lit up again. This time there were too many traces to count. 'It's hopeless, Hans. According to my set there are thousands of hostiles flying in different directions.'

Biting his lip, Klaus stared down at the sullen vastness of the cloud. The *Tommis* were inside it somewhere and although it was a hundred-to-one chance of making contact with them without A.I. help, he wasn't going to fart about any longer while Fritz reported ghost images. He pushed his stick forward and cloud vapour was swirling past his wingtips when Control came on again.

'Attention, Bearcat Two. There are more hostiles south of Beacon Kassel. Passing through map reference Hans-Wolfgang on a bearing of approximately 150. Speed and number indefinite because of interference but are believed to be a much smaller force. The main force is your priority but if contact is impossible, seek out the new hostiles.'

Klaus kicked the rudder, drew back on the column, and the 110 came howling out of the cloud. As he rammed the throttles right up to the gate he heard Fritz's uneasy voice.

'Didn't he say the main force had priority?'

Klaus switched off the R/T before replying. 'Forget what he said. If we can't depend on your Emil, we have to see the bastards. And there's much clearer weather to the south.'

CHAPTER 22

With the moon hidden behind the bank of cloud, the Überlingen stretched to the south and east like a vast sheet of unpolished steel. Miesbach, a solid shadow around its western reaches, lay huddled under the cover of darkness. For nearly three minutes the night sky above the town had been filled with the roar of engines as Mosquito after Mosquito arrived and began orbiting at pre-set heights. Flying in the lowest orbit of the stack, Moore had been giving time for any stragglers to arrive. The stack was now complete, from Moore at 4,000 feet to Marsh at 14,000.

Uncertain as to whether it was the target or only the assembly point, Miesbach was playing it safe. Air Raid wardens were frantically ensuring not a light was visible. Defence crews, tensely watching the darkened moon, were standing ready beside their unlit searchlights and warmed-up flak guns. Townsfolk, huddled in basements and shelters, were talking in whispers and swallowing to lubricate their dry throats. Tension was like a static charge in the warm night air.

At 7,000 feet Millburn and Gabby, who had arrived a minute ahead of their ETA, were high enough to see the red glow that was Augsburg, the Main Force target. As the Welshman looked away he saw a tiny flame appear in the sky east of the glow. At that distance it looked no more than a burning match being dropped from a giant's fingers. Gabby's comment was cynical. 'That's one poor bastard Davies' Father Christmas hasn't saved. Do you think it's working?'

Millburn, a dark shape in the eerie blue light of the cockpit, shrugged. 'It's been quiet enough so far.'

'So what? Since when could Jerry intercept us at 35,000 feet? Harvey was right, boyo. This is where it counts.'

Millburn pushed a stick of chewing gum into his mouth. 'Some guys expect everything. If we get a clear passage here and back, I'm not complaining.'

'You know what I think,' Gabby said maliciously. 'All that tinfoil will do to Jerry is make life easier for him. They say he's getting low on bumph. I'll lay odds he's already got his Strength-through-Joy Boys running around collecting it.'

Millburn grinned. 'It's a bit on the flimsy side, isn't it? And kinda narrow.'

'Then he'll probably melt it down for tin cans. Jerry's an ingenious bastard, boyo.'

'If you're so worried about bandits, stop nattering and keep your eyes open.'

Gabby, who was in a touchy Celtic mood that night, took instant umbrage. 'You make a lot of noise for a taxi driver, Yank. Without me you couldn't go from Leeds to Liverpool without getting lost.'

'Sour grapes'll get you nowhere, kid. It's like with women – some guys have it and others don't. So why bellyache so much?'

Gabby scowled darkly. 'What would happen if an 88 got me tonight? How would you get home? Go on – tell me!'

The grinning American turned to him. 'All right, kid, I will. I'd go down on the deck and backtrack that tinfoil. Didn't you know that's what it's for? So we can get rid of little ponces of navigators who're always bellyaching.'

At the base of the stack Moore was ready to lay his target indicators. As Hopkinson, crouched over the flare chute, gave him a nod, he levelled A-Apple and swept over the centre of the town.

'O.K., Hoppy. Let's have some light.'

The barometrically-fused, hooded flare slid down the chute and fell to its preset height of 2,500 feet where its parachute broke free. At the same time its magnesium candle burst into brilliant luminescence and hung suspended in space.

The effect was startling. A petrified vision, the town seemed to leap upwards and freeze in the icy light. Set in relief by their jet-black shadows, factories, streets, even flak batteries with their toy crews, could be seen. To St Claire, the artist, who was circling at 6,500 feet, the effect was that of a black cloak being torn from a naked body.

Hopkinson had no time for such fantasies even had his Cockney mind indulged in them. Dropping a second flare from the chute he edged forward and peered down. Five seconds late he gave a yell. 'There it is, skipper. Over to the right. At two o'clock.'

Moore dipped a wingtip to take a look. Along the northern bank of the lake was a complex of factories, railway sidings and docks. As A-Apple swept towards the complex Hoppy's confident voice came again.

'We're O.K. Our target's over on the far side. Three parallel sheds and a rail siding. Just like the photographs.'

Waiting to hear no more, Moore put A-Apple's nose down. It was the moment the petrified Miesbach came to life. Not knowing whether the flares expressed uncertainty on the part of the *Tommis*, so that they might still sweep past, the defence crews had held their fire. Now, as Moore dived into the light, their last doubt vanished and every flak battery in and around the town began firing. To Hopkinson, concentrating on the target ahead, coloured chains of tracer seemed to be coming up from every point of the compass. A series of explosions rocked the Mosquito and shell fragments beat a tattoo on her wings. Five seconds later three searchlights coned her. If the cursing Hopkinson, a veteran of forty-three operations, had not already pulled down his smoked goggles, their combined 21,000,000 candle power would have blinded him.

'Skipper, for Christ's sake call some of the others down. We can't take all this stick ourselves or we'll never make it.'

The heavy defences of the town had come as a surprise to Moore. Before he could react to Hopkinson's entreaty, four more Mosquitoes dived down beneath the hooded flares. Harvey had sized up the situation and brought down three other crews with him.

A-Apple was jinking violently to escape the searchlights. Two slid off like fingers trying to hold a slippery fish. The third clung on tenaciously, forcing Moore to dive and then bank on a wingtip. The manoeuvre lost the searchlight but forced A-Apple to swing east in a wide arc to make a fresh approach on the factory. With the two flares now close to the ground, Moore ordered his high-level Mosquitoes to drop four more. As they ignited Hopkinson guided him back to their target.

On the perimeter of the flares, the factory was a study of elongated shadows. To gain greater accuracy Moore dived down to 1,200 feet, a target for every light gun in the district. Like nets thrown up to ensnare a bird, tracer soared up from flak posts and factory roofs. As he drove the Mosquito on Moore could feel his toes clenched up inside his flying boots. 'O.K., Hoppy. Drop it!'

A-Apple reeled from a sharp explosion as the first target indicator fell away. It burst in a huge splash of green fire on the factory's railway siding. The second fell fifty feet from the corner of a large shed. As Moore banked and banked again, Hopkinson dropped two more T.I.s to complete the square. His relieved yell made Moore's earphones rattle.

'I feel like a ping-pong ball in a shooting gallery, skipper. Let's get the hell out of here.'

'All right, Hoppy. We'll drop our GPs later.'

Followed by the flak, A-Apple clawed for the cover of darkness. Still orbiting at 7,000 feet Millburn gave a grin of appreciation. 'You've got to hand it to that guy – he's got some hard bark on him.'

The flares were dying out and as the town sank back into darkness the only lights came from searchlights and gun flashes. Yet the very darkness that brought an illusion of safety to the townsfolk only emphasized the square of green fire burning within the factory complex. Orbiting at 8,000 feet Moore directed his crews towards it. As each Mosquito, flying at 4,500 feet, swept over the squares it dropped a stick of bombs.

Heavy explosions and fires betrayed the damage that was being done. Seeing one of the target indicators die out as a factory wall toppled over it, Moore called in Teddy Young. The experienced Australian dropped his T.I. within twenty yards of the original marker and completed the square for good measure. In less than thirty seconds the raid was in progress again.

When Peter Marsh, flying No. 16, was called down great clouds of crimson smoke and flames almost hid the factory from view. But the flak was still heavy and a couple of seconds after Marsh's navigator had released his bombs a chain of 37mms. bracketed the Mosquito. An explosion at the rear of the starboard engine sent something spinning off into space and a massive crump beneath the fuselage almost turned the plane over. As Marsh fought for control he could smell cordite and burning rubber. Heart in his mouth, he tested the controls and then turned gingerly away. As he began climbing he heard Moore's sharp voice. 'Marsh! What's the damage?'

'I think it's my undercart, skipper, and I've lost the exhaust shroud on my starboard engine.'

'Can you make it home?'

Marsh hoped the R/T static would mask his unsteady voice. 'I hope so, skipper.'

'All right, get on your way.' Moore was about to wish the hapless crew good luck when a distant cry of shock checked him. It was followed by a voice hideously distorted by terror and despair. 'We're hit, skipper . . . Finished. Look out for the bandits.'

The cry came from one of the Mosquitoes already making its way home. As Moore and Hopkinson stared round they saw a flame appear in the night sky. Rapidly expanding into a long tongue of fire it slithered down and vanished into the hills west of the town.

The fires at Miesbach were staining the Überlingen red and forming a crimson cloud in the night sky. Klaus had spotted the fires five minutes ago and although the 110 was flying under full boost he was trying to urge it along even faster with his body.

'See any *Tommis* yet, Fritz?'

'Not from here. Perhaps they've finished and gone home.'

Klaus winced. 'We'd have had a contact of some kind, wouldn't we?'

'Not if they're Mosquitoes. They could be three thousand metres above us by this time.'

The knowledge Fritz could be right did nothing to improve Klaus's temper. 'Sometimes I think you don't want to find the bastards. How do you know they're not doing a dog-leg home?'

About to ask how they were going to overtake Mosquitoes if they were, Fritz decided it was wiser to keep quiet. To the south, shaken by the raid that had taken place so near to their frontier, Swiss gunners were firing shells that exploded like red poppies in the sky. As he turned back to his radar set Fritz gave a start. 'Hans, I've got a reading! A clear one.'

Adrenalin began pumping immediately through Klaus's bloodstream. 'Hang on to it, for Christ's sake. What's its range?'

'Maximum. But it's closing fast. I think it's a Mosquito.'

Exultant one moment, Klaus cursed the next as the stars vanished and dark cotton wool pressed against the cupola. He breathed a sigh of relief ten seconds later as the 110 swept out into an enormous chasm of starlight. At a word from Fritz he broke to port, then circled in a wide arc to starboard until he had completed 180 degrees. He could still see no shape in the vast black bowl of the sky. But if Fritz was reading his Emil correctly he should now be behind the hostile bomber.

His nerves were tight as he waited for Fritz's readings. If the hostile was a Mosquito and it had enough fuel, it could both outpace and outclimb him. But if its fuel reserves were low it might just be flying within his own maximum speed.

Fritz had begun his counting again. '7,000 metres. . . .' A pause and then: '6,500 . . . 6,200 . . . 6,000.' Klaus's jaw clamped with relief. Luck was with him at last.

He spotted the Mosquito ninety seconds later. Its dark shape, climbing all the time, was three hundred feet ahead of him at eleven o'clock. Klaus touched the rudder and drew the stick back an inch. Gently, he told himself. Don't get over-keen or you might lose it.

Like a cat creeping on its prey, he closed the range to a hundred and fifty yards. The Mosquito's crew, Elliot and Jameson, a solicitor's clerk from London and an apprentice printer from Salford, flew on unsuspectingly. Their 'boozer', the red bulb on the dashboard activated by the AI set of an approaching radar-controlled fighter, gave two weak blinks and then went dead, the victim of a short in the receiver. With both men gazing intently out into the night sky, neither noticed its abortive alarm.

With only seconds of life left to them the two young men were allowing their thoughts to wander. Elliot, who had played for the Harlequins before the war, was wondering if he would be picked by the Group for their trial in two weeks' time. Jameson, the apprentice printer, was wondering what he could buy his girl friend f. r her birthday next week.

Beneath them Klaus had crept forward until the 110 was almost directly below the Mosquito. Then, with a cry of a man driving home a spear, he hauled back on the stick and pressed down hard on his firing button. With a crash that seemed to split the sky open, three heavy Orlikon cannon raked the Mosquito from nose to tail.

The effect was almost indescribable. The first shells blasted off the Mosquito's nose and released a howling banshee into the cockpit that turned loose objects like charts into lethal projectiles. The ones that followed sliced open the fuselage like some giant buzz saw. A shell pierced the buttocks of Jameson and burst somewhere in the region of his lungs. The right leg of Elliot was blown off, and he sat staring blankly at the pumping stump. Hydraulic and oil pipe lines burst like arteries and began discharging their vital fluid. The stricken aircraft lurched like a pole-axed animal, then miraculously righted itself as the dying Elliot croaked out his warning. Then Klaus fired a second burst and the port tanks caught fire.

Satisfied, Klaus allowed the 110 to fall away. When he righted it the Mosquito was little more than a blazing torch falling into the hills. Klaus's exultant shout, the cry of the German fighter who had made a kill, made Fritz's earphones rattle. 'Pauka! Pauka!'

Hidden behind his radar set, Fritz was silently retching. When that *Tommi* bomber hit the ground, they would need sacks to pick up the pieces of meat. Yet it too had probably killed men tonight, and if he, Fritz, had not helped to destroy it, it might have killed women and children tomorrow. There was no stopping the lunatic game now – as each side provided the other with more justification for revenge the slaughter grew more vicious and indiscriminate. As Fritz gagged again, Klaus expressed his jubilation aloud.

'Eight, Fritz. Only two more to go and I've still a fortnight left.'

Ten kills – anything between thirty and seventy men slaughtered. In a mad world, Fritz thought, what better basis on which to build a marriage and have children? As if to mock him, traces flickered on his screens again.

'I've got two more readings, Hans.'

Still quivering from excitement, Klaus gave a laugh of disbelief. '*Two* more!'

'Yes. They're heading this way.'

'Then put me behind the bastards! As fast as you can!'

Fighting his stomach, Fritz concentrated on his A.I. set again. Five seconds later the 110's port wingtip dropped and the deadly black shape cut across the summer night like a reaper's scythe.

CHAPTER 23

Harvey peered through the windshield at the dark shape and twin exhausts three hundred yards ahead of him. 'Marsh! It's me, Harvey. What shape are you in?'

Marsh exchanged a glance of disbelief with his navigator. 'Hello, Skipper. How did you find us?'

'You've an exhaust shroud missing, remember? What other damage is there?'

'The engines seem O.K. but I think there must be elevator and aileron damage – she's very sluggish.'

'That's probably because your undercart's half down. Listen – I'm going to try to give you cover home. We can see you as long as the weather stays clear – if it closes in we'll have to work something out. Don't use your R/T unless it's necessary – we don't want to make it easy for the bastards. Just keep an eye on your boozer. O.K.?'

Marsh's voice could not hide his relief. 'Thanks, skipper.'

Sinking back into his seat Harvey turned to Blackburn. 'Don't go to sleep for the next two hours,' he grunted. 'We might have visitors.'

Blackburn, tense in his seat, swallowed before answering. 'No, skipper.'

The two Mosquitoes droned on through the starlit sky. With Marsh's crippled plane doing no more than 230 knots, Harvey was finding his own sluggish on the controls. Two bloody beetles floundering across the surface of a pond, he thought. With God knows how many hungry birds on the hunt for food.

Unlike the rest of the squadron who, after dropping their bombs, had started for home, Harvey had remained behind to see how his flight fared and so had witnessed Marsh being hit by flak. A professional, the Yorkshireman bore no resentment that Moore had allowed the young pilot to find his way home alone. Moore's job was to stay and assess the damage to the factory, and even if his crews had been present and volunteered to a man to give Marsh cover, no responsible Squadron Commander would have sanctioned the gesture. Apart from the difficulty of keeping contact at night, Marsh's crippled Mosquito would have to limp back at the altitude in which the enemy night fighters were at their deadliest, and without A.I. equipment two Mosquitoes would be as vulnerable as one. Like any other raiding party in enemy territory, bomber crews accepted the hazard that if they were hit they were on their own and Marsh was no exception.

Harvey had no quarrel with the reasoning behind the unwritten law but tonight could not obey it. A man protective by nature, his impulse was reinforced by his knowledge of Marsh's personal problems. The reason he gave himself was that Marsh's exhaust shroud was missing. The exposed flame would make it easier to keep contact and so the effort was worth making. The fact that the same flame might attract fighters as blood attracts sharks, Harvey chose to ignore.

As he watched the flickering exhausts ahead of him he tried to work out the pros and cons. His hope was that in spite of their jammed radar equipment the majority of the night fighters would go on trying to track the heavies both to and from their target. If they did, there was a chance Marsh and he might sneak through unobserved. On the other hand there was always the chance that some pilots, like the one who had shot down Elliot, might have decided that the pickings were easier to the south where the weather was clearer and the radar interference less marked. The real facts were anyone's guess.

Harvey's main ambition at that moment was to reach the cloud front they had passed over on their way to Miesbach. Met. had told them it would widen during the night and spread north – and in fact it had already doused the crescent moon half an hour ago. Not only would it give reasonable cover against fighters but the bomber stream would be returning through it and Harvey remembered they would be dropping 'window' until out of range of the enemy beacons. If he and Marsh could latch on to the stream, the odds on their getting home would rise dramatically.

In R-Robert the numbness Marsh had been feeling since the flak had crippled him was wearing off. Everything indicated that this was the trip Julie feared, the one when his luck ran out. Over and beyond his personal fear of death, Marsh had his greater fear. If he was killed and Julie's mind snapped – and he was certain it would – what would happen to her and the baby? Sweat began to run down the young pilot's body. Dear Christ, I mustn't be killed. Not until they're both safe. Please take me back to them.

Fear that his anguish was showing made him glance guiltily across the cockpit. Seeing Douglas, his navigator, staring anxiously out into the darkness, he sank back in relief. Knowing there were still four hundred miles to the coast, Douglas was probably as scared as he was. Then Marsh shook his head. Douglas wasn't married. He had no hostages to fate.

His envy turned immediately to guilt. He loved Julie and it wasn't her fault the war had torn her nerves into shreds. Marsh had discovered that many men, by blaming the war for their family's problems, were able to carry those problems lightly. It was something Marsh could not do. If you loved someone, you cared. Here or at the far end of the world.

The baby's sobs fell into a whimper and died away. Holding her breath, Julie tip-toed to the cot and laid the child down. Replacing the coverlet she sank wearily on the edge of her bed.

It was 3 a.m. and she had hardly slept. Lying in bed she had been tortured by fears for Peter. Then Mark had woken up and, perhaps sensing her overwrought condition, had fretted for over an hour. As a result the girl was now physically as well as nervously exhausted.

A thin figure in her nightdress she moved to the window and drew aside the blackout curtain. Although the gardens of Wilberforce Street, with their small lawns and patriotic vegetable patches, were in shadow, the waning moon gave a faint sheen to the roofs of garden sheds and the houses that stood opposite.

Her eyes lifted to the hard, glittering stars that the moon could not extinguish. Those same stars would be gazing down on Peter and indifferent to whether he lived or died. A shiver ran through the girl and her heart rate increased. Both she and Peter had been wicked to bring a child into such a pitiless world.

For the hundredth time that night she wondered where Peter was. As it was a night raid he was probably over Germany. Two lonely men in a tiny wooden box, plunging through a sky filled with searching enemies while below them an entire nation willed their death. The realities were terrifying enough before her feverish imagination added its own hazards. Engine failure, navigation error, maintenance neglect, a structural defect, any of these and a dozen more could be added to the massive defensive strength the Germans could muster over their own territory. If Peter should escape this time, what chance did he have of escaping next week or next month? The people who lectured her for her lack of faith either lied about the odds against him or were blindly ignorant of them. Even if Peter were a different kind of man, the outlook would be no better.

It was an ironical fact that while Julie Marsh lived in constant fear of Peter's death in action, she could at no time accept him as a fighting soldier. Men like the big, brooding Harvey or the handsome, devil-may-care Millburn one could see any night at the cinema, charging a machine gun nest single-handed or clubbing half a dozen Japs to death with a rifle butt. But to Julie, Peter was still the gentle accountant's clerk who had been almost too shy to ask her for a date. The fact that every night over Germany the skies were filled with men like Peter giving battle to the enemy was lost on the girl. To her, Peter was miscast, a stripling among men, and it was one of the reasons she felt no guilt in begging him to give up operational flying.

But she knew now that he never would. False pride, perhaps the hope he might grow one day into someone like Harvey or Millburn, kept him going. The knowledge that he had a baby and that she, Julie, needed him made no difference. A sudden massive spasm of resentment made her body contract. Damn him! Damn him! If she had to go on suffering this torment with no hope of his survival at the end of it, then it was better he died tonight!

The thought was like a massive explosion in her mind, leaving the room hushed and her face pale and shocked. God in Heaven, what have I done? If he doesn't return now I shall know I have killed him. . . . Closing her eyes she concentrated until she felt her brain would burst. Dear God, please listen. I didn't mean that about Peter. I don't know where the thought came from but it wasn't from me. I love Peter. So please forgive me and bring him safely home!

When she opened her eyes her nightdress was icy with perspiration. Her prayers had brought some relief but she knew a new fear had been created alongside the old. If Peter were killed now she would never be sure whether or not she was the cause. Why had the thought come to her? Was she going mad?

She glanced at her watch. It would be dawn in two hours. Allow him another three hours for de-briefing and the journey from Sutton Craddock and he should be home by 8 o'clock. No, give him another hour. If he were not home by 9 o'clock she would have reason to fear the worst.·

A movement in the garden caught her eye. A black cat was creeping soundlessly along the wall beneath the window. As she watched in fascination it suddenly leapt down and bounded forward in one movement. A second later the girl imagined she heard the faintest of cries rise from the garden.

Hand at her throat, she backed away. The whimper she gave as she threw herself on the bed was a sound of pure terror.

'Peter! Look!'

The sharp cry came from Douglas. Red pulsations from the bulb on the dashboard were suddenly staining the cockpit interior and the navigator's alarmed face. Torn brutally from his thoughts of Julie, Marsh was paralysed for a moment. Then he snatched at his mask.

'Skipper! Do you have a contact on your boozer?'

Harvey sounded both startled and puzzled. 'No. Have you?'

'Yes. A strong one. Maybe your set's not so sensitive or it's u.s.'

Harvey's grim answer came five seconds later. 'We've got it now. All right, start a banking search. But take it slowly in case I lose you and for Christ's sake don't go off course.'

Ahead the flickering exhaust tilted as R-Robert banked to port. Without taking his eyes off the plane as he followed it, Harvey addressed the pale-faced Blackburn. 'We'll probably be the first he'll try to take, so keep your eyes skinned. Underneath and behind – the bastard might come in either way.'

As the Mosquitoes zig-zagged across the sky both pilots lowered one wing and then the other to give their navigators a view below. In the black sky behind them Fritz noticed the manoeuvres on his screen. 'They've started to take evasive action, Klaus.'

Neither German was surprised. For some time now German night-fighter crews had known the *Tommis* were carrying an A.I. detection device although as yet they did not know how it worked. The important thing, Klaus was thinking, was to make certain it did not help them to escape. As Fritz estimated the range at 1,000 metres, Klaus made his first visual contact, a slim black shape arching across the starlit sky ahead and above him.

'There's one of them! See him? He's swinging over to 2 o'clock.'

'Shall I switch off the Emil?'

'No. Let's get in closer first in case I lose him. I'll tell you when.'

Fritz sounded puzzled. 'What are they?'

'Mosquitoes. I'm sure of it.'

'But why are they only doing 370 kph?'

'I suppose they got damaged in the raid and they're trying to sneak home.'

Fritz could understand Klaus's excitement. Among fellow pilots if not by High Command, the high-performance Mosquitoes were considered a greater prize than Lancasters. At the same time Fritz shared the respect most of his kind had for the versatile wooden aircraft. 'One might be giving the other cover. So take it easy when you go in.'

Klaus grinned. 'At night? If he is, he's a bloody fool. Doesn't he knew he's likely to be picked off first?'

The two Mosquitoes were now dipping their wings constantly in their efforts to locate their hunter. Like blind man's buff, Harvey was thinking, his big hands gripping the control column. Two blind men on one side and on the other a man with eyes that could see in the dark. . . . 'Marsh, listen. If he attacks me first – and if the bastard is any good he will – then you piss off. No heroics. You've got the crippled kite, so you get the hell out of here the moment he opens fire. That's an order.'

Marsh caught a glimpse of Douglas's expression in the red, pulsating light and read his thoughts. Maybe he was a moody bastard and maybe he could be bloodyminded too. But when it counted Harvey was there.

'Marsh! Do you hear me?'

'Yes, skipper. I heard. Thanks.'

None of the four men was certain who would be attacked first. If the hunter made the deduction the leading plane was the only one crippled, he might give it priority under the argument that a bird in hand was worth two in the bush. All four men hoped that if the worst happened it would be swift. An aircraft could take minutes to reach the earth from 20,000 feet and minutes could be an eternity in a tortured, screaming body.

With tension as tight as a bowstring the cat-and-mouse chase continued. Ahead it looked as if a mountain had risen into the sky and was hiding the stars from horizon to horizon. Sweating freely, Harvey tried to estimate how long it would take them to reach the cloud front. Five seconds later he growled at his own stupidity. The enemy pilot would be making his own calculations and be certain to attack in good time. As if to prove him right the pulsating red light suddenly went out, the sign the hunter was close enough to switch off his A.I. for fear of damage. Although he had been expecting it for the last minute, Harvey was momentarily frozen in the darkness. Then his urgent but steady voice reached out across the black sky to Marsh.

'Steady, lad. He can't be far away now.'

The attack came as Harvey had known it would, very suddenly. The blackness beneath his Mosquito was ripped apart by a series of vivid flashes, and although the Yorkshireman's response was almost instantaneous there was a deafening explosion at the rear of the cockpit which hurled both men against their straps. A second shell smashed brutally between their legs and exploded somewhere beneath the instrument panel. In a second the cockpit was full of choking fumes. As the half-stunned Harvey fought for breath, the Mosquito went out of control and spun earthwards. As it passed him, Klaus gave a yell of triumph and followed it down. The other *Tommi* might have the chance to reach the cloud before he could climb back but that couldn't be helped. He mustn't let this, his ninth kill, escape.

For Marsh the way to life was open again and no one could have condemned him had he taken it. He had Harvey's express order to escape and moreover there was a strong possibility his crippled plane might break up in combat. And beyond those clouds were Julie and the baby. For a moment the temptation was like the tearing of flesh. Then the young man whom Julie could never see as a soldier pushed the control column forward.

A second burst of fire from Klaus had brought flames from Harvey's port engine. With the stunned Yorkshireman still unable to take evasive action, Klaus closed in for the kill. The thought of the crippled Mosquito following him down never entered his mind because he believed the darkness made pursuit impossible.

What the excitement of the chase made him forget was that the burning engine of Harvey's plane silhouetted the 110 to any aircraft diving after it. In addition his last burst of fire had given Marsh a reference point. It was little more than a flitting shadow but enough for Marsh to sight on.

His first burst, which brought startled shouts from both Klaus and Fritz, ripped past the fuselage like a flight of luminous arrows. His second burst passed beneath the violently banking 110. Neither attack appeared to do any harm except to Klaus's temper. Yelling at Fritz to get his scanners working, Klaus came raging round to take revenge on the crippled *Tommi* who had shown such impertinence.

It was then that his starboard engine coughed and died. The first burst of fire that had seemed innocuous had in fact severed the armoured fuel lines. There was no fire because the shells had been armour-piercing instead of incendiary, but the effect was a useless power unit. In vain Klaus put the 110 into a dive in an attempt to re-start. Unlike the Mosquito, which remained capable of a high performance even on one engine, the 110 had no such power reserve and it was soon clear to the frustrated Klaus he had no chance of a re-engagement. All his skill would now be needed to find a landing field. Nor was there any question of his claiming the first Mosquito as a kill. Fritz had already reported that its engine fire had gone out as its pilot switched on his extinguisher.

As Klaus was about to ask the Controller to give him a fix he gave a grunt of disbelief. His other engine was playing up now. Oil or coolant trouble – whatever it was the thermometer needle was steadily climbing. Cursing his luck he asked the Controller to vector him towards the nearest airfield.

Keeping a wary eye on the gauge he lowered the 110 down. As the needle entered the red zone the danger of fire forced him to throttle back. Below, the defence systems were now alerted and two searchlights were laying their luminous beams in the direction of the nearest airfield. By this time Klaus knew he was not going to make it: the overheated engine could be seen glowing in the darkness. At 5,000 feet, in a series of enormous bangs that both men felt would tear the wing off, it seized up. In the silence that followed the men could hear the forbidding scream of the airfoils. Hidden by his radar set, Fritz crossed himself.

All Klaus could do now was steer towards one of the searchlights and hope its crew would choose him a reasonable landing site. As he drew nearer he saw the horizontal beam was lying across a field of rye. Conscious that one mistake would be his last, he dived more steeply to avoid overshooting, then levelled off and lowered the 110 into the surrealistic flare path. The searchlight crew ducked down as the plane, airfoils screaming, passed no more than thirty feet over their heads.

The rye was tall and hid the undulations of the field. Klaus's landing was good and for the first hundred yards, although juddering violently on its oleo legs, the 110 remained intact. Then one wheel dropped into a hole, the port wingtip struck the ground, and with a massive rending of stressed metal and spars, the plane ground-looped, half rose on its nose, and crashed down again.

Although half-stunned, both men were able to climb out and run a safe distance from the ominously-smoking plane. A trickle of blood was running down Fritz's face and Klaus was nursing a badly-bruised arm. In the distance the shouts of the searchlight crews could be heard as they ran towards the field. Seeing Klaus's expression and thankful for the pilot's skill, Fritz felt a word of comfort not out of place.

'We're lucky. It could have been a hell of a sight worse. And we're certain to get a new plane fitted out well before you go on leave.'

Klaus did not answer. His young face, petulant with disappointment and anger, was gazing vengefully up at the night sky.

CHAPTER 24

The siren that awoke Anna sounded just before dawn. The sky was clear as she threw open her bedroom window although red pennants on the eastern horizon foretold a deterioration in the weather later. The two windsocks showed the breeze was fresh and southerly. Across the airfield ground crews who had been snatching a few hours sleep were emerging from billets and dispersal huts. Engines were starting up and a couple of ambulances were already moving alongside a runway. Ten seconds later a crash wagon followed them.

As Anna threw on a wrap against the morning chill, the first Mosquito flew in. Wheels and flaps down, it swooped so low over the inn the girl could see the blackened scars of flak on the underside of its fuselage. There was a cloud of spray and a squeal of rubber as its wheels touched the runway. Half a mile down the field, all grace gone now it was earthbound, it turned and taxied towards its dispersal point.

One by one at irregular intervals the Mosquitoes came back. The sun was above the horizon and turning the dew on the crab apple into crystal gems when the thirteenth Mosquito, like a weary traveller in sight of home, swept towards the inn. Although its wings bore flak damage, they wagged a couple of times before it settled down on the landing strip. Leaning from the window Anna saw a buxom figure in a dressing gown waving from the wicker gate below. Early though it was, Maisie was not one to let the squadron's return go unwelcomed.

As the Mosquito came to rest at its dispersal point a tense silence settled over the field. Groups of men formed, their eyes on the empty sky. When five more minutes passed their tension turned into resignation and they began to disperse. Below Maisie drew back disconsolately from the gate and vanished into the inn. Discovering she was chilled to the bone, Anna closed the window.

Three aircraft missing. She was wishing now that she had found out beforehand the identification numbers of Harvey and Moore. She reached for the telephone, then drew back her hand. The crews would be at de-briefing; for her to interfere with personal questions would be an unpardonable act in Davies' eyes.

On going down to breakfast she had hopes that Maisie might know whom the missing planes belonged to, but the subdued girl had seen only the last three Mosquitoes fly in. Returning restlessly to her room, Anna was listening to the news when her telephone rang. She ran across to it. 'Hello.'

'There's a call from the airfield for you, Miss.'

Her heart was beating hard as she waited. 'Hello. Anna?' It was Moore. 'I'm sorry to phone you so early but I wondered if I could come across to see you.'

Her pleasure at hearing his voice was countered by a sudden numbness. 'Yes, of course. When will you come?'

'Right away, if I may.'

'I see. Come straight up to my room. I will have coffee sent up.'

Her face gave nothing away when she went downstairs to make her request. The curious Maisie brought up a coffee tray and had barely left the bedroom when Moore entered. Her first impression was how much older he looked. His hair was dishevelled and his eyes bloodshot from strain. He had shed his flying suit but the uniform beneath was not the immaculate one she had become accustomed to. It was old and oil-stained and smelt of combat in its every crease. For once Moore looked the combatant pilot that he was.

His smile was wry as he paused in the centre of the room. 'Sorry about this. I know it's a poor time to visit a girl.'

It was the kind of deliberate banality she had learned to expect from the British when emotion was involved. She indicated the tray on her bedside table.

'Will you have coffee?'

'Yes, thanks.'

'Black or white?'

'Black, please.'

From the corner of her eye she saw him pull out a packet of cigarettes and then hesitate.

'Please smoke if you wish to,' she said.

As she began pouring she heard a match strike and the sound of his inhaling. 'You know why I've come, don't you?'

She handed him his cup of coffee before answering. 'I think so. Harvey hasn't come back, has he?'

He seemed puzzled by her self-control. Inhaling again, he walked across to the window. 'No. I'm afraid he hasn't.'

'Does that mean he is dead?'

He took a sip of coffee, then laid the cup and saucer on the window ledge. 'I'm afraid it's too early to say what happened.'

'Then no one saw him shot down?'

'No. When he was last seen over the target area he appeared to be all right.

293

After that we don't know what happened because each of us made our own way home. But one of my boys heard him talking on R/T to Marsh, a member of his flight.'

'What does that mean?'

'Marsh had been crippled by flak fire. We think the fool tried to escort him home.'

Every muscle in her body stiffened. 'The fool?'

The tension of the night had not yet worked out of Moore. His bloodshot eyes accepted her challenge and threw it back. 'Yes. No one can give cover at night. If it were possible I'd have seen Marsh got it. It only means the cover is the first to be shot down.'

She believed him and yet found she was shivering with resentment. 'You don't see it as a brave gesture?'

'Bravery's not enough. It was stupid. No one can match German night fighters without A.I. equipment. All he did was throw good money after bad. And there's no profit in that.'

It was a remark Harvey himself could have made but her desire to hurt him made no concession to fairness although afterwards her comment appalled her. 'Perhaps men like Harvey aren't so interested in profit. Perhaps they had a different education and upbringing. Have you thought of that?'

At first he appeared to find difficulty in believing what she had said. Then his cheeks turned pale. Grinding out his cigarette in an ashtray, he started for the door, only to pause as he reached her. Close enough to see dislike as well as fatigue on his good-looking face, she was about to apologize when with a curse he jerked her towards him and kissed her full on the mouth. Unsure of him, she tried to break away but the grip of his arms was too fierce and she had to wait for the paroxysm of emotion to die away. As his grip slackened, the telephone rang. Answering it, she held out the receiver.

'It's the airfield. For you.'

Discovering she was trembling she crossed over to the mantelpiece and leaned against it. Behind her his voice was expressing relief. 'Thanks for letting me know, Frank. Yes, I'll be right over.'

He was gazing at her as she turned. 'That was Adams. They've just received news that Harvey's safe. He landed on an emergency airfield.'

A small ornament stood on the mantelpiece and she fingered it for a moment before speaking. 'What about the other crew?'

'They ran out of petrol just after crossing the coast and had to crash land. Marsh is badly shaken up but he's alive. His navigator's dead.'

He went to the door. 'They're flying Harvey back some time this morning. After we've had a word with him, I'll see he comes over.'

As if they were challenging one another, their eyes met and held. Then he turned and the door closed behind him.

It was nearly noon when a small single-engined aircraft circled the airfield and landed. Expecting Harvey's arrival, Anna was sitting in a deckchair in the garden behind the inn. Putting down her book she went upstairs to her room. From it she could see the aircraft taxi-ing to the nearest hangar. In spite of its distance away, she felt certain she recognized the big-boned figure of Harvey as two men jumped out.

Knowing Moore would not keep him long she stayed at the window waiting for him. To her surprise he had still made no attempt to contact her when Maisie rang the lunch bell. Concerned at his behaviour she returned to her room after lunch and put a call through to the airfield.

The moment he spoke she knew she had given him offence. 'Hello. What is it?'

'Frank, why haven't you come over to see me? I've been worried about you.'

'Sorry. But I've been busy since I got back.'

'Didn't Ian Moore ask you to come over?'

His reaction at her mention of Moore told her everything. 'What the hell has it to do with Moore?'

'I want to see you, Frank. Please come over as soon as you can.'

In the pause that followed his pride seemed at war with his wishes. 'All right,' he said sullenly. 'I'll see what I can do.'

She was back on the lawn when he appeared half an hour later. As he crossed the grass she saw there was a heavy contusion on his left cheek. She rose quickly. 'You've been hurt. I didn't know.'

He gave a shrug of indifference. 'It's only a bruise. What do you want?'

'Want?'

'Yes. Why do you want to see me?'

'What a strange question. I thought we were friends.'

'So did I,' he said bitterly.

She walked right up to him. 'Someone saw me having dinner with Moore, didn't they? Is that why you didn't come across yesterday morning?'

He avoided her eyes. 'What do you think?'

'Frank, there's something you must understand. I'm free to go out with anyone I like. So I wasn't going behind your back when I had dinner with Moore.'

He cursed and swung away. 'Go out with the bugger every night if you want to. I know he's got a damn sight more to give you than I have.'

She did not know whether to be angry with him or sympathetic. 'Frank, you're acting like a jealous child. It doesn't make any difference to me how wealthy a man is. I went out with Moore because I'd promised to go out with him.' She drew another deckchair alongside her own. 'Now please sit down. You must be worn out.'

When he still did not respond she found herself searching for conversation that would prevent his leaving. 'Where's Sam today?'

'In the billet. Asleep.'

'I hear he sometimes flies with you. Is that true?'

'Sometimes.'

She caught hold of his hand. 'Sit down, Frank, please. I'm worried about you.'

Muttering something she could not catch he ignored the chair but sank down on the grass. It was, she realized, a compromise amnesty. 'I intended telling you I'd had dinner with Moore,' she said. 'But so far I haven't had the chance.'

His eyes, sunken and half-closed with fatigue, were following the clouds crossing the sky. Her thoughts had a bitter flavour as she watched him. He was a man to whom responsibility was a sacred trust, who would put his life between an enemy and a friend. Yet he was also a man hounded by a sense of inferiority that could diminish those qualities to those who did not understand him. The greatest evil of privilege was not the uneven distribution of wealth, she thought. It was the crippling of personality.

'Tell me what happened,' she said after a minute had passed.

He turned his head. 'Nothing much. One of my kids got his exhaust shroud knocked off by flak and was showing up like a roman candle. As I had to come back the same way home I thought I'd keep him company.'

Her eyes were on his swollen face. 'How did you get that injury?'

His laugh was self-derisive. 'A hell of an escort I turned out to be. A night fighter clobbered me and young Marsh had to turn back and give me a hand.'

'That was just what Moore said would happen. By trying to help him you made yourself the first target.'

His look of dislike returned. 'Moore might have been a bloody Pathfinder but he doesn't know everything.'

'What do you mean?'

'He doesn't know much about his men. Young Marsh is carrying a hell of a load. The doctor reckons his wife will go mental with worry if he doesn't pack up operational flying. And to make things worse they have a kid of nine months. Adams keeps on having a go at me but what the hell can I do.'

'Can't you recommend that he's grounded?'

Harvey's voice had never been more gruff. 'No, I bloody can't. It's something a man has to do himself. Otherwise you might do him more harm than good.'

She could understand that. When the malicious whispers began and the self-doubts followed, the cure might be as destructive as the illness. 'His navigator was killed this morning, wasn't he?'

'Yes. We stayed with him until he put his kite down in a field. It didn't look too bad a prang – there wasn't enough fuel left for a fire – but he was the only one who got out. Later on we got a police report that his navigator's neck had been broken. That won't make him feel any better either – they were close friends.'

She winced. 'Was Marsh hurt?'

'No. Only bruised and shocked. They took him to the nearest hospital. I'd like to have seen him but they put him under sedation. So I . . . .' Harvey broke off, then his breath sucked in. 'Jesus Christ!'

As he leapt to his feet she rose with him, oddly frightened. 'What is it?'

'His wife – Julie,' he muttered. 'I wonder if anyone's thought to get in touch with her.'

'Can't you phone her from here?'

'The people she stays with aren't on the phone.' Harvey was showing more alarm than he had shown throughout his entire ordeal over Germany. 'I'll have to go. I'll take Adams with me.'

'Let me come too,' she pleaded.

Ignoring her he began running down the gravel path to the gate. She hesitated a moment, then ran after him.

Over at Group Headquarters, Davies was deep in conversation on a scrambler telephone. His appearance suggested relief and excitement. 'So they've got the ground prepared at last, have they?'

The Brigadier's clipped words were the gentlest of reminders that scrambler or no scrambler their dialogue should be as uncommunicative as possible. 'Yes. The next stage begins tomorrow.'

'Tomorrow?'

'Yes. The participants will be notified later today.'

Although surprised, Davies decided he had better play it as cautiously as the Brigadier. 'How long is the next stage expected to take?'

'We're hoping no more than a week to ten days. The final stage is more difficult to assess. However, let's take first things first. The briefing will take place tomorrow night at the usual place. In the meantime there is one more thing I want you to do.' The Brigadier spoke for a couple of minutes before ending: 'In view of his importance in the affair, I feel he ought to attend. If it is done in the way I suggest, it should look like a perfectly natural occurrence. Do you agree?'

Davies was thinking it might cause some speculation among those close at hand and then realized that that very speculation would be a cover itself. 'I'll see to it, sir. Have you spoken to the Americans yet?'

'Yes, they're being kept fully informed. Of course, like you they'd prefer definite dates but I'm afraid there are too many imponderables for that. Is there anything else you'd like to know before I ring off?'

Excited that events were on the move at last, Davies was mentally rubbing his hands. 'No, I can't think of anything.'

'Very well. Then we'll meet tomorrow night.'

CHAPTER 25

Abandoning the bell Harvey hammered on the door with his fist. Embarrassed, Adams made an attempt to restrain him. 'Give them time, for heavens sake. They're two elderly spinsters.'

Ignoring him Harvey was about to assault the door again when a chain rattled and the younger Miss Taylor appeared.

'What on earth are you doing? Trying to break the door down?'

Harvey took an aggressive step forward. 'We want to see Mrs Marsh. It's urgent.'

'Do you, indeed? You don't have to smash the door down. I've a good mind to complain to your Commanding Officer.' Giving the black-faced Harvey a glare, Miss Taylor went to the foot of the stairs. 'Mrs Marsh! There's Squadron Leader Adams and a man and a woman to see you. In a great hurry from the way they're behaving.'

There was no reply. The woman called again, then strode back to the doorway. 'She must be out. She does sometimes go shopping on Tuesday mornings.'

Harvey's eyes were on the hat and coat the woman was still wearing. 'When did you last see her?'

'Yesterday evening.'

'You haven't seen her this morning?'

'No. But that's not unusual. She often sleeps late and my sister and I have spent the morning with our cousin. In fact we've only been back a couple of minutes before you arrived. Why are you asking all these questions?'

Adams broke in in an attempt to lower the temperature. 'I'm sorry, Miss Taylor but we're very worried about Mrs Marsh. Are you saying she's been alone all the morning?'

'Of course she's been alone. Why shouldn't she be? She's a woman, not a child.'

At Harvey's growl, Adams felt like a man trying to hold back a bear with a piece of string. 'May we go upstairs for a moment? Just to make certain she is all right.'

A glance at the scowling Harvey decided the woman. 'No, you can't. I don't know this man and I'm not having strangers wandering all over my house. In any case, why shouldn't she be all right? I'll get her to phone you when she comes home.'

Before she could close the door Anna stepped forward. 'I don't think you understand, Miss Taylor. Her husband has been hurt and she doesn't know yet. We've come to break the news and to reassure her he'll soon be out of hospital.'

Before the hesitating woman could change her mind, Harvey's patience exploded. With a snarl he shoved aside both the door and the squealing woman and went up the stairs three at a time. Not daring to think what they were doing, the dazed Adams followed him with Anna close on his heels.

Harvey had already disappeared into the bedroom when they entered the empty sitting room. Anna was about to follow the Yorkshireman when he appeared in the doorway. His appearance shocked her: the bruise looked huge and livid on his pale face. With a curse he lurched towards her, half-dragged her out on the landing, and pushed her roughly against the wall.

'Don't go into that bedroom! You hear me? I'm going to get an ambulance.'

As he ran downstairs the startled Miss Taylor tried to question him but he ignored her and disappeared into the street. Anna, who ran straight back into the apartment, saw Adams was approaching the bedroom door. As he reached it he stiffened, then began gagging. 'Oh, my God!'

She waited to hear no more. Pushing Adams aside as he tried to stop her, she ran into the room.

The air was heavy and close that evening with yellow clouds prematurely darkening the sky. As Anna sank wearily on her bed, Harvey crossed over to the window and threw it open. A crow, taking a rest on the crab apple, gave a caw of indignation at the disturbance and flapped away towards the airfield.

Loosening his tie, Harvey lit a cigarette. His laugh made the girl wince. 'So that's that. Another sample of man's inhumanity to man.'

For a moment reaction made it an effort to answer him. With Adams they had remained at the hospital until it was certain no more news on the girl would be forthcoming that day. The theory of the doctors was that the half-crazed girl had given her baby the last of her sleeping tablets before slashing her own wrists. A fit of vomiting, coming after Julie had lost consciousness, had undoubtedly saved the baby's life but the girl was in a more critical condition. Although given massive blood transfusions, she was still unconscious and it would be another twenty-four hours before an assessment of her chances could be made.

'At least we got there in time to give her a chance,' Anna said. 'And we know the baby is safe.'

He gave a shudder of hatred. 'It's no thanks to those two old bitches, is it? They knew the job Marsh was doing but although they were sharp enough to grab his rent they couldn't help him by keeping an eye on the girl. That's what it's all about, isn't it? Sod you Jack.' Harvey was breathing like a man trying to rid his lungs of a pestilence. 'And they tell us man's born in the image of God. If he is, Christ help us.'

Since their discovery of the stricken girl his mood had grown blacker as the day wore on. Even on the harsh terms of the tragedy Anna was finding it difficult to accept a bitterness of this magnitude. 'You mustn't take it so personally. You did all you could to prevent it happening.'

From his glance she might have been an enemy. 'Did I? Then why the hell didn't I remember to get news to her earlier?'

'You can't remember everything. You'd just spent the night risking your life for her husband. It was the others, the ones who were safe on the ground, who should have remembered.'

Her resentful words reminded Harvey of Adams. A sensitive man at the best of times, the Intelligence Officer had looked as if his moment of forgetfulness would haunt him for the rest of his life. 'They were thinking about us. You can't expect them to think of wives and girl friends as well.'

'Then neither can you. You're the least guilty of anyone. When you get over the shock you'll realize that.'

299

His brooding voice suggested he had not been listening. 'It's going to be hell for Marsh when he hears about it.'

'When will they tell him?'

'Adams is going to ask Henderson to wait until he gets back. It shouldn't be more than a day or two. The poor sod can't help her and he'll go out of his mind trapped in a hospital two hundred miles away.'

'Will Henderson agree?'

'Christ knows. People do queer things, don't they? He might prefer to pass the buck to someone down there. Not that he needs to.'

'I suppose by that you mean you intend breaking the news yourself,' she said quietly.

His aggression leapt back. 'Why not? He's one of my men, isn't he?'

Not for the first time she wondered how a man could feel such bitterness towards his fellow men and yet be so protective towards them. 'You can't carry every load. No one's got that strong a back.'

'I've done a great job so far, haven't I?' he sneered. 'If you hadn't had the presence of mind to put tourniquets on the girl while I was downstairs yelling for help, she'd had been dead before she reached the hospital.'

Again she was angry with him. 'The only reason I thought of tourniquets was because I've had a nurse's training. Stop blaming yourself. You're making a sin of it.'

The tortured thing inside him was only too ready to take offence. 'What the hell do you expect – one of Jesus's little sunbeams?' Cursing, he snatched up his cap. 'I'm getting back to camp. Give Moore a ring. Nothing affects that bastard – he'll cheer up in no time.'

Controlling her nerves with an effort, she rose and went to the door. 'Sit down while I fetch us both a drink.'

'Don't bother. I can get all the drink I want in the Mess.'

'Frank, we've both had a shock today – that's why we're acting like this. Please sit down until I get back.'

He muttered something, hesitated, then flung his cap into a corner of the room. 'For Christ's sake – you don't let up, do you? All right. But ask Maisie to look under the bloody counter.'

As the girl disappeared Harvey lit another cigarette and turned moodily away. Every protective element in his make-up resented the part the girl had been called to play in the harrowing affair. At the same time her willingness to help and her resourcefulness had deeply impressed him. Although unaware of it in his present mood, the Yorkshireman had lost his heart without trace to this capable and courageous girl.

She returned three minutes later with a couple of glasses half-filled with whisky. 'Maisie's an angel,' she smiled.

'Aye, she is,' he muttered, taking a glass from her. 'And so she's another one the bloody world has kicked in the guts.'

She dropped on the bed and watched him. The cords of his neck stood out as he half-emptied the glass. As he slumped into a chair she had hopes the neat spirit was acting as a tranquillizer. Instead, as his eyes rose to challenge her, she realized it was inflaming rather than mellowing his mood.

'Do you know what drove that kid to suicide today?' When she did not speak his arm swung out like a man swinging a sword. 'It wasn't just her fear of young Marsh being killed. It was that filthy world out there. If those two old bitches had shown her some charity she could have lived with it. Even if buggers like me had gone to see her occasionally instead of getting pissed in the Mess it would have helped. But no – she was left to sweat it out alone. It's not the fear or the pain or the hunger that kills – it's the feeling nobody cares. Once you believe the world's as callous as that, who the hell wants to go on living in it?'

She swallowed to ease the dryness of her throat. 'Do you feel that yourself sometimes? That nobody cares?'

'Me?' His derisive laugh jarred the heavy evening air. 'What the hell have I to do with it? I learned how to be a loner when I was knee high. But some never can. When they find out what an uncharitable world it is, they can't face it.' He took another gulp of whisky and a cough almost drowned his words. 'People like my old woman.'

She realized that the events of the day had somehow inflamed the festering sore within him and his pain needed relief. At the same time his old, distrusting self was bitterly resenting his weakness. Afraid of slamming the door that had unexpectedly swung open, she moved with great care. 'Tell me about your mother, Frank. And your father. I'd like to know them better.'

He stared at her, then jumped up and went back to the window. The first breath of the storm stirred the blackout curtains. As they sank back against the wall he exhaled smoke.

'It's bloody morbid, going back into the past like this. Why don't we go downstairs and have a drink with the boys?'

His offer was a measure of his desperation, for she knew how much he disliked sharing her company with his colleagues. 'Please, Frank. As a favour.'

His bruised face had a baleful appearance as he turned to her. 'Why do you want to hear about my parents? You feel like going slumming?'

Unable to find a suitable reply she did not answer him. With his hostility finding no opposition his desperation seemed to grow. 'You know what my parents were?'

She shook her head.

'They were a pair of bloody criminals.' At her start his voice jeered at her. 'That's right. Criminals! Stupid and uneducated but worst of all, poor. And that's the worst crime you can commit in this bloody world. Or didn't you know that?'

As she relaxed, he lifted his glass again. 'Want to hear any more? Or is that enough?'

'No, I want to hear more,' she said quietly.

'Then you're crazy. What's interesting about a couple of old fools?'

'I'd like to decide that myself if you'll give me the chance.'

Defeated but offering a last gesture of defiance he slumped back in the chair and lit another cigarette. 'What the hell do you want to know?'

'Tell me the things you remember most. When you were a child.'

His swollen face twisted. 'The thing I remember most was moving from house to house to find one we could afford. I believe the old man had a job before the Depression but he lost it with three million others. Then there was the old woman selling her bits of furniture. Their idea was to open up a pastry shop. Looking back it was a crazy idea – if they hadn't money to buy decent food, who else had? – but the daft old fools never did have any business sense. Although looking at it another way, what alternative did they have? Every factory had a queue of men a hundred yards long outside its gates and the old man had been trudging round 'em for years.'

She was afraid to move or speak as his sullen voice led her down the dark corridors of memory.

'The old woman was the hardest worker I've ever known but she had one obsession – an onyx table her father had left her. It was a handsome thing but looked bloody ridiculous in the rat-holes we lived in. She wouldn't part with it, however, although it might have brought in enough money to buy a shop. You only needed a few quid in those days because everyone else was getting rid of 'em, but although she wasn't well she preferred to take in washing and go out charing rather than sell it.' Defending his mother now, he lifted his bruised face. 'When you're really poor, you need something to value. Maybe it has something to do with self-respect or security, or maybe it's a life-line. I know the old woman felt selfish in keeping it but as it was the only thing of value she had, my father never thought of asking her to part with it.'

He ground out his cigarette and lit another. When he started again his voice had subtly changed as if his bitterness had momentarily slid away and he was living his childhood days again.

'By selling nearly everything they had, they finally got their shop. It had to succeed, so they put everything into it. My father was up every morning at 5 o'clock to light the ovens; my mother never finished until 9 in the evenings. For six years it was hand-to-mouth living. No one took a tram if he could walk – every penny counted. Holidays were something you read about. The incredible thing was' – his laugh was meant to be derisive but in fact was full of pride – 'they made it. They managed to pay a woman to work in the bakehouse and even bought a second-hand van for twenty quid. They began thinking about employing someone to look after the shop so we could have a holiday. And then, bingo, it blew up around their ears.'

The light was fading fast and a rumble of thunder sounded. 'What happened, Frank?'

His laugh was a sound she knew she would always remember. 'The system took over, love. A quarter of a mile down the road one of the City Fathers had a grocery and bottle store. I suppose he'd been watching us for years to see if the struggle was paying off. When he saw it was he got himself a few ovens and a

302

couple of bakers and put the boot in. It's as easy as hell if you've got the capital. You just undercut the other poor sod until he folds up. It's called good healthy competition. Only they don't tell you how the bastards get their money. This one had made his by fiddling municipal contracts.'

His expression told her she was near the source of his bitterness. The curtains at the window stirred again. 'Did they go bankrupt?'

'Of course they did. No one would buy the shop now this alderman bastard was bleeding it to death. They had to stop trading and sell the stock and fittings to pay the bills. When they got the debts down to sixty pounds, my mother tried to sell her table, but now that everyone knew the mess we were in, no one offered more than a few quid. While she was trying to find an honest buyer the Receiver was called in and it went anyway.'

'You are saying they lost their personal possessions because they went bankrupt?'

His gibing voice mocked her. 'Why not? I told you my people were stupid old buggers. They'd never heard of limited liability and even if they had, they'd never have crawled behind it. To them a debt was something you paid in full no matter what it cost you. So when the Receiver's hearing was over, all they had was a bit of kitchenware and the beds we slept in. And none of that was much use when the landlord kicked us out into the street.'

She was finding it difficult to believe what she was hearing. 'You were made homeless too?'

'Why not?' he sneered. 'We'd no money. Who wants people without it? Worst of all we'd gone bankrupt. So even the couple of friends they approached for help said they were sorry but they had relatives staying with them that week.'

'But why was going bankrupt such a crime? It wasn't their fault.'

A vein was swollen on his forehead. 'You don't know how the system works, do you? It's not enough to have a power structure that means the wealthy always win. You have to make sure the peasants don't see through it. So you condition them to feel ashamed of the debts you've driven them into. Where we lived it was a hell of a disgrace to go bankrupt. My poor old mum went around with her head down as if she'd been caught stealing the Crown Jewels.'

'Where did you go to live?' she asked in the silence that followed.

He swung away but not before she saw the sweat on his forehead. 'They put us in a couple of hostels,' he muttered. 'My father and I in one, my mother in another.'

'How old were you at this time?'

'I don't remember. Fourteen. Maybe fifteen.'

'But you were still at school.'

'Yes. I'd got a scholarship to a secondary school and although it was a hell of a sacrifice for them they wouldn't let me give it up and find a job.'

With his background she had often wondered how he had obtained his education. A flash of lightning lit up the window and rain began pattering on the leaves of the crab apple. Although she flinched from the pain it would give him, instinct told her the last door of his memory must be opened.

303

'Your mother must have suffered at being separated from both of you like that.'

He started as if a knife had been driven into him. 'Of course she suffered. It was the first time she and the old man had been apart.'

She braced herself. 'It killed her, didn't it, Frank?'

The bruise seemed to rise from his pale, sweating face as if it had a life of its own. As a loud peal of thunder sounded, she thought for one bizarre moment he would leap from his chair and strike her. Instead his eyes closed and he sank back. As the peal of thunder died she could hear his heavy breathing. She crossed over to him and stood beside his chair.

'What happened? Did she commit suicide?'

He nodded, his eyes still closed. His jaw muscles were bunched like a man fighting a life-and-death struggle. As the rain began drumming down she went to the window and spent a few seconds closing it. When she glanced back he was fumbling in his tunic pocket for cigarettes. 'I'm sorry, Frank, but you've held that inside you too long.'

'Aye,' he muttered. 'You could be right.'

She pushed the cigarettes back into his pocket. 'You've had a hellish twenty-four hours. Come and rest for a while.'

For a moment he resisted her. Then he allowed her to lead him to the bed where she helped him remove his tunic and shoes. 'Lie back and close your eyes.'

Exhausted by emotion he tried to argue and sank back instead. His forehead felt feverish as she ran a hand across it. Her touch seemed to dissolve his tension and he felt himself sinking into a voluptuous brown sea. Although he did not want to leave her his weariness was too great to resist. As he sank slowly down he heard the strident ring of the telephone. Although it drew him back to the surface he was not fully awake when she answered it.

'Yes. Who? Oh, yes, thank you. Please tell him to wait a moment. I'll come downstairs to speak to him.'

With a backward glance at Harvey, the girl slipped from the room. When she returned four minutes later he was sitting up in bed. 'Was that the phone?'

Half-asleep he missed the unsteadiness of her voice. 'Yes. It was for me.' To hide her expression she crossed over to the dressing table where she spent a few seconds fumbling in a drawer. When she turned back to him her face was composed again. 'I thought you were supposed to be asleep,' she chided.

He sank back but as she approached the bed she saw he was staring at the ceiling. Aware of his suspicions, she knew only a lie would comfort him. 'I took it downstairs so as not to disturb you. It was Arthur Davies. He wants to come over tomorrow morning to see me. That's all it was.'

She saw his features relax and his eyes close again. She sank down on the bed alongside him and as sleep quietened his breathing she reached out and touched his arm. A gesture too gentle to disturb, it suggested an impulsive desire to remain in contact with him. A flash of lightning showed her face was pale and strained. For long minutes she sat motionless, lost in some desolate world of her own. Then, with a sigh, she rose and began undressing.

Her white body, with a flat stomach and long, slender legs, returned to the bedside. Her shapely breasts lifted as she raised both hands to release her hair. In a black cascade it tumbled down her smooth back.

She drew back the coverlet with care and slid into bed. To avoid disturbing the sleeping Harvey she kept as far away as possible but a lock of hair slid like silk across his cheek. Drugged as he was by exhaustion, some magic of communication made him stir and reach out a hand. As it made contact with her naked shoulder he gave a start and awoke. 'Anna!'

She turned and leaned over him. 'I'm here. What is it?'

'You're cold,' he muttered. 'Why are you cold?'

She put a hand on his lips and whispered to him. Obeying her he undressed and rejoined her in bed. Now he could feel the entire nakedness of her, the firmness of her breasts, the smooth length of her thighs. His desire was a throbbing ache and yet Harvey, who had never known such love for a woman before, was held back by uncertainty.

'There's something wrong, isn't there? What is it?'

She pressed closer to him and her lips touched his bruised cheek. 'Why do you ask such foolish questions?'

His head lifted from the pillow. 'You're not doing this because of what I told you? Because if you are. . . .'

Her denial was spontaneous and fierce. 'No! No, no, no! Stop talking like this.'

She saw he was still not convinced. As his head dropped back she ran a hand across his forehead. 'What are you afraid of?'

His tough, battered face tried to grin up at her. 'This is one time I have to be sure. I happen to be in love with you.'

Tears filled her eyes. 'You can be sure,' she whispered.

'Then tell me why you're trembling like this.'

Her sudden cry startled them both. 'Stop asking these questions! Just put your arms round me and don't talk any more.' Then, seeing her outburst had fed rather than allayed his doubts, she forced a laugh. 'You don't know much about women, do you, Frank?'

'What does that mean'

'Don't you know that women often act this way when they're happy?'

'Happy about what?'

She bent down and kissed him. 'I was crying because you trusted me with the story of your mother. Can't you understand that?'

As he searched her face she kissed him again. This time his wish to believe her was too strong. Gently she slid beneath him, her hands running through his hair and down his naked back. He was the one who was trembling now and the implications in a man so strong reached into the depths of her womanhood. As his blue eyes, oddly vulnerable in their masculine setting, gazed down she reached beneath him and drew him forward.

The fervour of her love-making surprised them both, tossing them about like two branches in a cataract. The climax was a shuddering drop into a whirlpool of storm-tossed water and glittering droplets of sunlight. Yet thirty seconds later, when his eyes opened to gaze into her own, she wondered if the very intensity of her love-making had betrayed her.

Footsteps sounded on the road outside as Maisie sent the last of the airmen home. A young man's voice could be heard telling a ribald joke. The laughter that followed faded as the group of men crossed the road and made for their barracks. Harvey, dressing in the dark, slipped into his tunic and approached the bed.

'I'm not sure what's on tomorrow but I'll ring you the first chance I get.'

She was glad he had not turned on the light. 'Yes. Please do.'

He bent down to kiss her. 'God, it's hard to go,' he muttered.

She caught hold of his hand and gripped it tightly. 'You will take care of yourself, won't you?'

He misunderstood her as he was meant to do. 'It's not likely there's an operation tomorrow or Adams would have contacted me.'

'I'm glad. But in future don't take any more risks like you took last night, will you?'

Again Harvey was puzzled by her behaviour. 'You don't have to worry about me. Don't you know I'm bullet-proof?'

Smiling at his clumsy attempt to reassure her she kissed his hand, then pushed him gently away. 'Of course you are. I'm just being sentimental, that is all. Now you had better go.' At the door he heard her voice again, an unsteady whisper, 'Auf Wiedersehen, Liebchen.'

It was one of the few times he had heard her speak German and its emotional undertones disturbed him. 'Are you sure there's nothing wrong?'

'Yes. Don't worry about me. God bless you, Frank.'

He hesitated, then, impatient with himself, closed the door and hurried downstairs. Left alone she sat motionless until his footsteps sounded on the gravel path below. Then a sudden urgency stirred her and she ran to the window. The sky was still heavily overcast and she could see only the silhouettes of the hangars and Control Tower. As the wicker gate clicked, the shadowy figure of Harvey could be seen walking down the road towards the airfield entrance. Half-way there he turned and although she knew he could not see her at the darkened window, she waved. A moment later his shadow merged with the shadows at the camp entrance and the sound of his footsteps died away.

She walked to her small table and sat there. Inside the inn she heard footsteps on the creaking staircase and a door close. Outside, raindrops were dripping mournfully from the eaves and pattering on the leaves of the crab apple. The silence seemed to close in and isolate her in time and space.

Stirring herself with an effort, she drew the curtains, switched on the light, and carried a notepad over to the table. The task she had set herself appeared immensely difficult. Four times she tore sheets from the pad and threw them away, and when the letter was completed at last and she read it through she gave a cry of despair and buried her face in her hands.

CHAPTER 26

Harvey turned briskly down the path that led to Adams' 'Confessional'. Pattering alongside him, Sam paused to cock his leg against a gas detector post. Coming in the other direction, with mugs, knives, and forks in their hands, were McTyre and Ellis. Last in and last out of breakfast as usual, McTyre, with his dishevelled hair, unshaven chin, and unpolished buttons, was a sight to make any self-respecting S.P.'s mouth water. Seeing the big Flight Commander turn down the path, McTyre was about to make a smart detour by the Photographic Section when he heard Harvey whistling. The unprecedented sound either stunned the old sweat or brought out the touch of bravado to which he was prone from time to time. Giving the faltering Ellis a shove he shambled on down the path, transferring his mug and cutlery from right hand to left as he went. Three yards from the briskly-stepping Harvey he brought up his arm in what for McTyre was a respectable salute.

The glance the Yorkshireman gave the two airmen was almost benign. 'Morning, McTyre. Morning, Ellis. You going to find out what's rattling in my starboard engine today, McTyre?'

McTyre halted. 'I'll find it, sir. No need to worry.'

Harvey grinned. 'You'd better find it bloody fast because if something drops off I'll have your giblets for dogmeat. All right?'

'Just relax, sir. Leave it to me.'

Nodding at both of them, Harvey turned down the path that led between two small flower beds to Adams' sanctum. McTyre nudged the speechless Ellis' arm as the couple moved on. 'You ever seen 'im as friendly as that before, mush?'

'Never,' the youngster said truthfully.

His long nose as curious as a pointer's, McTyre watched Harvey and the dog enter the Intelligence Room. 'I wonder what the 'ell it is? Maybe he's heard they're postin' him to Burma or the Russian Front.'

Inside the 'Confessional' Harvey was approaching Adams' huge desk. 'The Old Man gave me a buzz ten minutes ago and said I had to see you. You know what it's about?'

Adams, still shocked and full of guilt at Julie's attempted suicide, was taking in the Yorkshireman's cheerful appearance with some surprise. 'Yes. He wants me to brief you.' Before Harvey could comment, Adams' tone changed. 'Have you heard anything from the hospital this morning?'

'I phoned half an hour ago,' Harvey told him. 'They said there was a slight improvement.'

Adams, who had spoken to the hospital three times during the night, looked worried. 'After all the blood transfusions she's had she ought to be sitting up in bed by this time. The doctors have a theory she doesn't want to recover.'

Twenty-four hours ago Harvey would have shared his concern. Today he found pessimism difficult. 'She'll feel differently when Marsh gets back and visits her.' He nodded at the photographs that littered Adams' desk. 'What's all this bumph for?'

Adams made an effort to concentrate on the task in hand. 'Didn't the Old Man tell you that you're to lead a training exercise up to Scotland this afternoon?'

'A training session? This afternoon?' For a moment Harvey's disappointment and dislike of Moore broke through. 'Doesn't the Wonder Boy give us our lessons any more?'

'He went off on leave this morning. He hasn't had a chance to go home since his father died.'

Harvey gave a shrug of sarcasm. 'Who would tell me? I'm only the bloody Senior Flight Commander.' He picked up a photograph. 'What's the exercise?'

'A simulated low-level attack in a wooded valley. The Observer Corps have got everything marked out for you. You're to use 11½lb. practice bombs. Accuracy's very important.'

Harvey was studying the photographs which were all of the same valley. 'It's bloody narrow, isn't it?'

'Fairly narrow,' Adams admitted, continuing quickly. 'It's not our choice. Group sent the photographs last night.'

Harvey's bruised face frowned at him. 'You know what the job is?'

Adams hesitated. 'I've got an idea, yes. But it's very hush-hush at the moment.'

'On whose instructions? Moore's?'

'No. Davies'.'

Harvey's resentment cooled. 'So it's something big?'

To Adams' relief the sound of an aircraft taking off brought a change in Harvey's questioning. The noise, little more than a purr compared with the throaty roar of a Mosquito's Merlins, made the Yorkshireman glance at him.

'Davies,' Adams ventured. 'He said he was off somewhere or other this morning.'

Harvey strode to the window and peered out. His expression as he returned to the desk puzzled Adams — of late Davies' comings and goings had become so frequent that the squadron had grown used to them.

'Is he expected back this morning?'

'This morning?' Adams looked surprised. 'Nobody said anything. But I shouldn't think so.'

'Are you sure?'

The Yorkshireman's insistence puzzled Adams. 'Nothing's sure with Davies. But there's no reason for him to come back today that I know of — not unless he wants to see how the exercise has gone.' Feeling a change in Harvey's mood and unable to account for it, Adams indicated a chair. 'If you'd like to take the weight off your legs, I'll run through the details.'

He talked to Harvey for ten minutes. His feeling the Flight Commander's mind was on other things persisted – twice he had to repeat details that normally Harvey would have taken in his stride. But by the time the briefing was over the Yorkshireman appeared to have recovered something of his earlier mood. 'Did you say the Old Man wants the crews briefed this morning?'

Adams nodded. 'Will 11.00 hours suit you?'

'I'd rather make it 12.00 hours. I've a couple of things to do this morning. Will that be O.K.?'

'I don't see why not. Providing the air-tests are done beforehand.'

Harvey pushed back his chair. 'They'll be done. See you here at 12.00 hours then.'

Calling Sam, he was half-way down the hut before Adams remembered. 'You do know that Henderson has agreed to keep quiet about Julie until Marsh gets back?'

Harvey turned. 'Yes, thank Christ. The M.O. told me at breakfast.'

He glanced at his watch as he left the hut. There was plenty of time to organize the exercise and nip over the road to explain the situation to Anna. Giving Sam a playful cuff round the ears, Harvey went to his flight office. He was on the phone talking to his Flight Sergeant when a young S.P. knocked on the door and entered. Finishing his conversation, Harvey replaced the receiver.

'Yes?'

The S.P. saluted, then held out a letter. 'This was dropped in the Guardroom this morning, sir.'

Harvey gazed down at the envelope. Addressed to him, it was written in a handwriting he did not recognize. 'Do you know who brought it?'

The S.P. looked embarrassed. 'No, sir. It was there when we came on duty.'

'You mean it had been forgotten?'

'I'm afraid so, sir.'

Harvey scowled. 'All right. I'll see to it.'

The S.P. thankfully withdrew. Dropping into his chair Harvey tore open the envelope. As his eyes ran down the brief letter he gave a grunt of shock. A moment later his chair clattered over as he leapt to his feet and ran from the office. Startled by his behaviour, Sam gave a bark and scampered after him. Ignoring the sentry's salute as well as the startled glances of airmen and Waafs, Harvey ran out of the station and down the road to the Black Swan. Breathing heavily he reached the front porch only to find the oak door bolted. He had to hammer three times on the iron knocker before Joe Kearns appeared. Still in his shirtsleeves, the innkeeper looked startled by the Yorkshireman's urgency.

'What's the trouble, Mr Harvey?'

'I've come about Miss Reinhardt. Has she left yet?'

'Yes. Didn't you know? She went just after seven-thirty this morning.'

The panting Harvey cursed. 'Do you know the time of her train?'

As Kearns hesitated, Maisie appeared in the panelled hall. Drawn to the door by curiosity, an apron round her shapely hips, she could guess why Kearns was reluctant to answer Harvey's question and pushed herself forward. Although a kind-hearted girl, Maisie considered herself a realist.

'She didn't go by train. That new Squadron Commander of yours called for her.'

Harvey's violent start confirmed Kearns's suspicions. 'You mean he took her to the station?'

Maisie shrugged. 'No. I think she was going all the way with him, wherever that was.'

The Yorkshireman's swollen face turned thunderblack at the suggestion. 'Why the hell should you think that?'

It was a reaction that would have made a lesser girl draw back. In Maisie it produced a hostility she was to regret almost at once. 'Because it looked that way, that's why. They'd both got their luggage in the car. And anyway, there isn't a train going to London at that time in the morning.'

Without another word Harvey swung away. Meeting Kearns's glance, Maisie looked immediately defensive. 'He wanted to know, didn't he? An' anyway, what's wrong with a girl taking a lift? It isn't exactly the end of the world, is it?'

Kearns did not answer. His eyes were on the tall, big-boned figure of Harvey. With the anxious dog gazing up at him, he was walking heavy-footed down the road as if from the death of a dream.

The Mosquito was darting through the mountains like a swift chasing gnats. Banking left, then skidding right round an outcrop of rock, it entered a valley and flattened down to zero height over a narrow but fast-flowing river. On either side dense forests of firs shivered to the roar and fury of the aircraft's passing. Inside it Harvey was hunched over the control column like a man who was demonstrating his hatred of life. At his side young Blackburn was as tense as a man in a dentist's chair as he glanced again at the pilot's huge and forbidding figure.

Ahead, a mountain spur diverted the river a full forty degrees. Holding on course until it seemed the Mosquito would crash into the shelving rock face, Harvey swung the column over and heaved it back. Hanging on its wingtips, curving in its flight like a bent bow, the plane flew parallel to the rock face for a few seconds, did a reverse bank, then swooped down to the treetops again. Fighting to keep his stomach down, Blackburn peered ahead and jabbed his finger.

The valley ran straight for another five miles before another mountain spur formed a barrier across it. As Harvey climbed a couple of hundred feet for better visibility, a distant clearing among the firs on the left bank of the river could be seen. In its centre was a white target. As Harvey opened the bomb doors, his growl sounded in Blackburn's earphones. 'I'll drop the bloody things myself. Four at a time.'

Blackburn's nod expressed profound relief. To miss the target with the Yorkshireman in this mood did not bear contemplation. The Mosquito's nose dropped again and the tops of the firs shivered like green water in its slipstream. With both main and selector switches on, Harvey waited then began counting as the clearing flashed towards him. 'One, two, three – gone.'

The bombs fell away and were flung like stones into the clearing, but Blackburn made no attempt to see where they burst. His eyes were glued on the mountain spur that was hurling itself at terrifying speed towards them. For a moment it seemed Harvey's plan was to fly straight into its boulder-strewn slopes. Then sky and earth tilted dizzily and Blackburn felt as if his stomach was sagging to his knees. A moment later the Mosquito came shooting out of the valley like a sky rocket.

Glancing back Harvey saw columns of smoke rising only a few yards from the white target. His orders to the planes circling above were gritty with sarcasm.

'That's the way I want it doing this time. No poncing about at 2,000 feet – get right down on the deck. You don't have to worry about the Laird's gamekeepers – they've been told not to shoot to kill.'

In T-Tommy Gabby glanced at the tousle-headed Millburn. 'Our Tike's in a happy mood today. You think he might be constipated?'

The American grinned as he followed St Claire in the squadron's orbit above the valley. 'Could be. If he is, he's going the right way to shake it loose.'

In numerical order the Mosquitoes followed one another down. Mutters and curses filled the radio channel as planes came shooting out like corks from bottles, their nervous pilots fighting clear of the mountain spur. The old hands felt misgivings about the severity of the exercise which reminded them of the training they had received before the Swartfjord raid.

The strain of flying the fast-moving Mosquitoes in the narrow confines of the valley was considerable, but Harvey's orders had been to work the crews hard and he was in no mood to compromise. The older hands had little difficulty in planting their bombs within the clearing but the new members found the threatening mountain spur a distraction and Harvey kept them at it until the last of their bombs had been dropped. By that time jumpy nerves had become abrased ones, and when at last the crews formated to return home, the mood of some almost matched that of their deputy leader.

CHAPTER **27**

Millburn flipped a coin and slapped it down on the back of his hand. 'Heads you've got the back seat. Tails you're in the bushes. Call.'

Gabby, sitting behind him in the car, eyed his hands suspiciously. 'What's that coin you're using?'

'A Coin of the Realm, kid. One of your English pennies. What does it matter anyway? You're calling.'

'Heads,' Gabby said impulsively.

Millburn removed his upper hand. 'Tails! Into the bushes, my young love birds.'

The girl sitting beside Gabby let out a wail of protest. Small but buxom, she had a chubby face and a mass of curly fair hair. 'That's not fair. We should take it in turns. I got prickles all over me on Sunday.'

Millburn grinned at her. 'Try another position, honey. Teach our little Welsh friend to share and share alike.'

The girl next to the American turned with some impatience. A taller girl, she was modelled on Veronica Lake, the current sex symbol, from the long blonde hair that half hid her face to her pseudo-sophisticated voice. 'For heaven's sake, Dolly. . . . Don't be such a bad sport.'

'Who's a bad sport?' Dolly demanded. She jabbed her finger at the grinning Millburn. 'He fiddles that coin. I don't know how, but he does.'

Millburn tut-tutted. 'You'll never go to heaven if you have thoughts like that, Dolly.'

'It's you who should be worrying about heaven, Tommy Millburn. I know you're cheating.'

Veronica Lake, whose real name was Gwen Dawson, gave a cry of impatience. 'Please, Dolly. You're just wasting time.'

Millburn's twinkling eyes ran suggestively down the taller girl's shapely body. 'That's right, Dolly. You're wasting time. So what about it?'

Grumbling, Dolly swung her stubby legs out into the afternoon sunlight. 'This is the last time, Tommy Millburn. You're cheating – I know you are.'

Eyes glinting like a stoat after a rabbit, Gabby followed her into a clump of bushes, an army blanket over one arm. Watching them, Millburn leaned his good-looking tousled head from the car window. 'Watch out for the thistles, you guys. They look the kind that could do you a real mischief.'

Veronica Lake tinkled. Millburn grabbed her round the waist, and planted a kiss in the centre of her very low-cut dress. Then he jerked a thumb at the empty rear seat. 'Come on, honey. Let's be comfortable.'

The American's car was parked on a rough hillside covered with clumps of bramble and broom. Below it the grassy common sloped down to a small lake that had once been a gravel pit. The two airmen had brought the girls to the village the previous week and found it ideal for their needs. Seldom used by the villagers, the common offered privacy for their present activities while Fenleigh's two pubs were on hand for refreshment later.

Millburn helped the girl into the rear seat and slid in after her. As he put an arm round her waist she pushed him back. 'Don't be in such a hurry. It's all you Yanks think about. Can't we talk for a while?'

Millburn looked shocked. 'Talk? What about?'

'Well – there's you and me, isn't there?'

'You've got a point there, honey.'

'Well, go on then. Talk about yourself first.'

'O.K. I'm an American. I was born in El Paso. I'm 23 years old and I'm in the RAF. Oh yeah, and I'm a man. How's that?'

She suppressed a giggle with difficulty. 'Neither of you seem to do much in the Air Force. How do you manage to get so many afternoons off?'

'You get half-days. We get half-days. Union regulations, honey.'

'But we only get one a week, like today. Are you both on leave?'

Millburn put a finger to his lips and glanced furtively around. 'Can you keep a secret?'

'Yes. Why?'

'We're in training, honey – that's why we're getting time off just now. It's a special mission. When we're ready we're flying straight to Hitler's Chancellery in Berlin. We're going to land on the roof, capture him, and hand him over to Churchill. Not bad, uh?'

Her long hair, slanting across her face, was preventing her seeing his expression. She tossed her head. 'You're pulling my leg. Aren't you?'

He grinned. 'Don't be like that. In a couple of months you'll be able to go and see the guy in the London Zoo. Will you believe me then?'

She pouted. 'Aren't you ever serious?'

Behind her back Millburn was undoing the buttons of her dress. 'I'm serious now, honey. Deadly serious.'

'You haven't said a word about me yet,' she complained as he slid down one shoulder of her dress.

'That's right, I haven't.' Millburn slid down the other shoulder and took her bra off with it. As he eased her down and lowered his head, his voice took on a muffled sound. 'That's easy, honey. You're beautiful.'

Her hands clamped behind his back. 'Do you think so?'

'No doubt about it.' Half a minute more and Millburn came up for air. 'Mind you, I'll be able to tell you more when we get this dress off.'

She felt Veronica would forgive her one small giggle. 'You're very naughty, Tommy Millburn.'

Millburn was too busy with the dress to answer. Although blessed with considerable expertise, he had learned long ago that every new case presented its own problems. As the girl's wrigglings made matters worse, the American was tempted to throw open a door and undress her outside. Then, to his relief the dress slid to the floor.

Millburn was discovering he was breathing hard and doubted if it was all passion. 'Thank God for that.'

The girl had taken refuge behind her mask of hair. 'Don't sit there staring, Tommy Millburn. Do something.'

Millburn complied by climbing out of his own clothes. When he was down to his vest and underpants, she drew him down. 'Give me a kiss first, darling.'

Millburn had to part her hair twice to find her mouth. Her deep sigh was Veronica Lake at her best. 'That's wonderful, Tommy. Do it again.'

Millburn was obliging when there was the sound of a heavy vehicle braking on the road above. A moment later it began trundling down the hillside. Beneath him the girl stiffened. 'What's that?'

Millburn peered cautiously over the window sill. To his consternation a bus was following the track through the bushes. For a horrendous moment it seemed it would halt nose to bumper with the car. Instead it swung past and continued down the hillside. Before he ducked down the American caught a fleeting glimpse of a full load of passengers.

'What is it?' the startled girl asked again.

'It's a bloody bus,' Millburn hissed.

'A bus? It can't be.'

'It's a bus, I tell you. Christ knows where it's going.'

The two of them peered over the front seats. At the lake fifty yards away the bus halted and its doors opened. Millburn blinked. 'I don't believe it!'

The passengers who were disembarking were all women aged between forty and sixty. Chattering and laughing they formed into groups alongside the lake. Millburn stared at the girl. 'Who the hell are they?'

'It looks like a works' outing.'

'A what?'

'A works' outing. You know, a factory giving its staff a day in the country.'

Before Millburn could react the bushes near the car twitched violently. A moment later wearing nothing but her dress, Dolly appeared and flung herself into the driver's seat. 'You do what you like, Johnnie Gabriel, but I'm not risking being seen by a bunch of old women. If you want me, you can come back into the car.'

Hastily buttoning up his trousers, Gabby climbed in beside her. 'They couldn't see us from down there,' he complained.

'You don't know old women. They've got eyes in the back of their heads. Anyway, I was getting bitten. There are ants out there.'

Millburn tapped the back of the seat. 'What's the matter with you guys? You think talking's more fun?'

Gabby grinned, then turned towards the indignant Dolly. 'He's right. We're wasting time.'

Dolly sniffed. 'It's all right for him. He fiddles it so he always has the best spot.'

Her complaints died as Gabby nibbled at her ear. Soon whispers and giggles could be heard as the two of them began undressing again. For a few seconds there was silence. Then the car rocked violently and Dolly let out a yell of pain. 'Look out! Something's sticking into me.'

Gabby fumbled beneath her. 'It's only the handbrake.'

'Only! Can't you put something over it?'

Gabby could see nothing suitable, then remembered the army blanket. Seeing the party of women were still clustered round the lake he threw open the door and dived into the bushes, an apparition wearing only a pair of regulation underpants and blue socks. Running back to the car with the blanket over his arm he

314

stumbled, gave a howl of pain, and clutched his foot. Millburn, his cheeks reddened by Veronica Lake's lipstick, gave him a withering glance. 'You want to bring those old women on top of us?'

Groaning, Gabby hopped back into the car and slammed the door. 'Those bloody thistles!' He shoved the blanket beneath Dolly's ample buttocks. 'How's that?'

'A bit better,' she muttered. 'But it's still sticking into me.'

Gabby's retort was interrupted by a hiss of fury from Millburn. 'Sonofabitch, there's no wonder you two can't make it. You're worse than two old women.'

The insult stung Gabby into action. To the accompaniment of grunts, giggles, and sighs of ecstasy, the car began to rock in unsynchronized rhythm. A minute passed and then a stifled groan came from Dolly. 'I can't. . . . It's sticking into my back. Get off me!'

In concert with Millburn on the back seat Gabby was far enough gone to make such a request unthinkable. Fumbling under the squirming girl he found the handbrake and pushed it to the floor. Dolly gave a sigh of bliss. 'Oh, that's better, luv. That's better. . . .'

Millburn, who was half-way to the summit of his joy, did not even know the handbrake had been released. At first the car moved no more than a couple of inches. Then, as its rocking became more uninhibited, it began to roll forward, slowly at first, then faster as the declivity of the hillside steepened.

It took a heavy bump as the car ran over a ridge to alert Millburn that something was wrong. His startled voice came over the mounting rumble of the wheels. 'Gabby! We're moving. Goddamn it, we're moving.'

For the little Welshman the entire world was moving at that moment and he wanted it no other way. His ecstatic mumble was an attempt to reassure. 'That's all right, boyo. . . . That's how it feels sometimes.'

With self-preservation having an edge on sex, Millburn was now trying to extricate himself. 'The bloody brake's slipped, you Welsh moron! Do something, for Christ's sake.'

Alert at last to danger, Gabby fumbled beneath the pulsating Dolly, only to discover her plump buttocks were anchoring the handbrake firmly to the floor. He gave a desperate tug. 'Get up! Get off the brake.'

Wooed one moment and unwanted the next, Dolly's reaction was bitter. 'How can I get up? You're lying on top of me.'

Wriggling sideways Gabby tried again but the girl appeared to be jammed between the two seats. With the car now in full flight down the hill, Gabby had no time for niceties. Grabbing a piece of flesh between his finger and thumb he nipped hard. With a howl of indignation the girl shot into the air, only to drop back on the brake and trap Gabby's arm. Behind them Millburn had struggled to his knees. 'The foot brake,' he yelled. 'Get your bloody foot on it.'

He could have asked nothing more difficult of Gabby. With his left arm trapped beneath Dolly, the Welshman's skinny bare legs were kicking feebly at

315

the car roof. Down by the pond the party of women were gazing with astonishment at the runaway car. Bouncing and bucking over the uneven hillside, gathering speed with every second, it was plunging straight for them.

Millburn, baulked from climbing over the front seats by the couple lying across them, could see the startled women and the pond through the windscreen and his yell was hoarse. 'Do something! Get that footbrake down.'

With a desperate heave Gabby managed to free his arm from Dolly's buttocks and with a contortion that would have done credit to Houdini managed to reach the foot pedal. Closing his fingers round it he pressed down as hard as his restricted position would allow. To his surprise the car came to an abrupt halt. Screams and curses followed as Veronica Lake and Millburn collapsed in a heap on the floor. Dolly was likewise pitched forward, taking Gabby with her. Although her fleshy charms wrapped themselves round his face and almost suffocated him, Gabby miraculously kept his hold on the pedal until he was able to drag up the handbrake. With a groan of relief, he sagged back.

With the two couples fully occupied recovering themselves, it took a scream from Dolly to give the alarm. 'Oh, my God. Look!'

Women's faces were pressed against every window. As they saw the tangle of nude bodies, there was an outburst of laughter, screams and cackles. Gabby's nerve broke. Dragging Dolly to one side, he squeezed past her into the driver's seat. There, clad only in his socks, he turned towards the equally horrified Millburn. 'The keys! Where are the bloody keys?'

Agonized seconds passed while Millburn sought for his trousers which were buried beneath the sobbing Veronica Lake. Finding the keys in his tunic pocket instead he pushed them at Gabby. As the Welshman fumbled to insert them in the lock, there was a loud cackle from an old woman standing alongside the American's door. 'Let's get 'em out and take a better look at 'em.'

Millburn grabbed the door handle and hung on tightly. 'What the hell are you doing? Get the bloody thing off the ground!'

For an answer the car lurched forward, scattering the group of hysterical women. Swinging round it fled back up the hill, followed by a storm of boos and cheers. Dolly, whose crossed hands were struggling unsuccessfully to contain the bouncing of her charms, glared tearfully at the pale-faced Gabby. 'That's it, Johnnie Gabriel. That's absolutely the last time.'

Too shattered to think of a reply, Gabby swung the car on to the road and drove as if the entire German Air Force were on his tail.

CHAPTER **28**

Sitting in Henderson's swivel chair, Davies discovered his feet barely touched the floor. Reaching down for the height adjustment knob, he found it was jammed. His instant tetchiness betrayed the lack of sleep he had suffered during the last few days. Bloody raw-boned, hairy-kneed Scot! Why the hell couldn't he keep his equipment serviceable? As he leaned down and put both hands to the task, there was a tap on the door. Cursing, the small officer straightened. 'Come in!'

Harvey appeared in the doorway. The sight did nothing to improve Davies' temper. 'Afternoon, Harvey. Come in and close the door.'

The Yorkshireman obeyed and approached the desk. A less-prejudiced observer would have detected signs of diffidence in him. Davies was wondering suspiciously why he'd asked for a private interview. He debated whether to invite the Yorkshireman to sit down, then decided against it. Let the bloody-minded bolshie stand. 'All right, Harvey. What can I do for you?'

Harvey's nervousness showed itself in a defiant tightening of his features. 'It's a personal request, sir.'

'Personal?'

'Yes, sir. I'd like you to give me Miss Reinhardt's address.'

Davies jumped. 'Say that again.'

'I'd appreciate it if you'd give me Miss Reinhardt's address.'

A sudden wariness superimposed itself on Davies' irritability. 'Why didn't you get it from her yourself?'

'She left before I'd a chance to ask her.'

'You're saying she left without telling you?'

A muscle twitching on Harvey's swollen cheek was the only indication of his grief. 'Yes, sir.'

Davies sat back. Although secretly conceding it was rough on Harvey he could see no other course of action open to him. 'In that case I'd try to forget about her. If she'd wanted you to keep in touch she'd have made it possible.'

Harvey, who had suffered the same thought a hundred times already, managed to keep his pain hidden. 'If it's a brush off I shan't pester her. But I'd like to write to her to make it certain.'

'Why haven't you asked me before? She's been gone over a week now.'

'You haven't been here, sir. You left the same morning she did.'

Davies realized that was true. 'What else could it be but a brush off?'

'I don't know but I want to find out. That's why I need her address.'

'Well, I can't give it to you. Not without her consent.'

'All right, then ask her. Will you do that for me?'

Davies was beginning to breathe hard. 'You think I've nothing better to do than sort out your love life? It's clear as a duck's arse she wants to drop the whole thing. So why can't you accept it?'

Frustration and pain brought out all that was aggressive in Harvey. 'I'm asking you for her address, not the bloody moon. But you wouldn't help a lame dog over a style, would you?'

Feeling guilty already, Davies needed to hear no more. He came out of the chair like a sprinter from his blocks. 'One more word out of you and you're under close arrest. If Anna Reinhardt's had a bellyful of you that's all right with me because I've had a bellyful too. Now get out of here!'

For a full five seconds Harvey stared him right in the face. Then with a growl of hatred he strode from the office, leaving the door wide open. Davies stood glaring after him. 'By the bloody centre. . . .' His yell brought a sergeant running into the officer. 'Go and get the C.O.! At the double.'

Henderson hurried in fifteen seconds later. He found Davies glowering beside the swivel chair. 'What is it, sir?'

'That bastard Harvey – Christ – I've a bloody good mind to put him under close arrest.'

'What happened, sir?'

'The stupid sod's got a crush on Anna Reinhardt and wanted me to give him her address. When I wouldn't he was bloody rude.'

'I'm sorry about that, sir. Do you want me to discipline him?'

Davies cursed again, then appeared to relent. 'No, leave it,' he muttered. 'I gave him a fair old bollocking before I kicked him out. What time's Moore back today?'

Used to the Air Commodore's moods and aware of his dislike of Harvey, the Scot was astonished how quickly Davies' temper was cooling. 'He's back now. He phoned me twenty minutes ago.'

Davies gave a start. 'He is? Then get him here right away, will you?'

Henderson put a call through to the squadron office. 'He's just changing. He'll be here as quick as he can.'

Davies wandered restlessly round the desk and ended up at the window. 'You'll be glad to have him back.'

'Of course,' Henderson said, watching him.

Davies' eyes were following but not seeing the trim figure of a Waaf who was walking past the block. 'Sorry about those two ops. Group pushed on you this week but I couldn't persuade 'em to keep you in reserve any longer. But you got off lightly, didn't you?'

'Yes. Only one kite damaged.'

'No one injured?'

'No, sir.'

'That's what we can't afford while we're waiting – the loss of trained men. Who led 'em? Harvey?'

Feeling considerable sympathy for Harvey, the Scot took the chance to raise his credit. 'He did a good job both times. He's also kept the training up. Allowing for the way he must be feeling, I think that's pretty commendable.'

Davies' only response was a grunt. 'Keep all the kites serviceable you can, Jock. We can't say when we're going to need 'em.'

Five minutes later Moore entered the office. Although he was newly-bathed and changed, his appearance caused the Scot concern. 'You're not looking too good, Moore. Is anything wrong?'

Wheeling round, Davies saw the young pilot's face was paler than usual and bore considerable signs of strain. He broke in before Henderson could question Moore further. 'Hello, Moore. How were things at home? Is your mother bearing up all right?'

Although his questions seemed amiable enough – even considerate for one of Davies' temperament – Henderson imagined there was resentment in Moore's glance. 'She's taken it very well, thank you, sir.'

'That's good.' Courtesies over, Davies got down to business. 'Does Harvey know you're back yet?'

'I don't know. I haven't seen him.'

'He's just been in here. He wants Anna Reinhardt's address. I wouldn't tell him anything, so he might try you. If he does, you're not to discuss her with him. All right?'

This time Henderson was not surprised to see Moore's face tighten, although the pilot's reaction suggested bitterness rather than resentment. 'If that's what you want, sir.'

'It is what I want,' Davies snapped. 'In fact it's an order.' Seeing Henderson staring at him he stared back challengingly. 'She's obviously given him the brush off. So why should he go on pestering her?'

When Davies defended his actions to subordinates, the Scot knew it had to be an unreal afternoon. Wondering if he ought to comment, he was relieved when the red telephone on the desk began ringing. Answering it, he glanced at Davies. 'It's that call you've been waiting for.'

As Davies took the receiver from him, Henderson jerked his head at Moore and the two men left the office. Davies waited until the door closed before speaking. 'Davies here. Yes, sir. I got back an hour ago. What's that? They have? Already?' As he listened Davies gave a jump of excitement. 'That's the luckiest break we've had so far. Yes, of course I'll come round. Give me forty minutes. Goodbye, sir.'

Both Henderson and Moore noticed the change in him as they were called back into the office. An elderly puppy given a rubber bone could not have looked more bouncy or pleased with itself. 'I've got to run off,' he told Henderson. 'Can I borrow your car?'

More mystified than ever, the Scot nodded. 'Do you expect to be long, sir?'

'A couple of hours. Maybe less.' Slapping on his cap, Davies almost bounded to the door. 'See you both at dinner.'

As his footsteps hurried down the corridor, Henderson gave a groan. 'First he

319

tells us this operation is our pigeon. Now he's acting like a spy in a fifth-rate thriller. What the hell's going on? Do you know?'

When Moore did not answer the Scot walked moodily back to his desk. 'I'm not happy about the way he's treating Harvey either. The poor bastard was a different man after meeting that girl and I think he's entitled to some explanation why she dropped him flat like that.'

When Moore still did not answer Henderson gave him a hostile glance. 'Well. Don't you think so?'

To his surprise the good-looking pilot gave a shiver of disgust. 'Don't ask me what I think. All I know is that war's a filthy business.'

Henderson's brows came together. 'You're starting to act like Davies. I don't see what the war has to do with a man finding out why a girl's dropped him. He's been on the piss every night since she left.'

Moore turned sharply away and lit a cigarette. With the pilot's mood as enigmatical as Davies', Henderson could not decide whether the impulsive act was related to his question or not. Then, as the sunlight from the window emphasized the lines of strain on the younger man's face, the Scot drew his own conclusions and became sympathetic.

'The last few days can't have been easy for you. Are you sure your mother's all right?'

He saw Moore start, then draw in smoke. 'Oh, yes, thanks. She's taking it very well, considering.'

Having just made up his mind he understood Moore's behaviour, Henderson felt his question had come as a surprise. There were bloody undertones everywhere today, he decided. With a growl of frustration he made for the door. 'It's early but I'm going for a drink. You coming or not?'

Harvey ran Moore down on the airfield. The Squadron Commander was at the dispersal point of A-Apple, listening to his Flight Sergeant explaining why a new magazine was needed for its starboard cannon. Harvey gave the N.C.O. no more than a couple of seconds before breaking in. 'I'd like a word with you. In private. It's important.'

Giving him a curt nod, Moore turned back to the N.C.O. 'Strip the panel off, Chiefy, and I'll take a look. I'll be back in a couple of minutes.'

The indignant Flight Sergeant watched the two officers move away from the dispersal point. 'You see that?' he demanded of the three mechanics clustered around the nose of A-Apple. 'No apology – nothing. Just broke right in. I hope Moore tears a strip off the bad-mannered sod.'

Neither officer spoke as they tramped across the grass. It had been cut that day and had a sweet smell in the late afternoon sunlight. A flock of birds, grubbing for worms, rose and flew away. The dispersal point was a good forty yards away before Harvey halted. His hostility, fed by a week of brooding, prevented his noticing the strain Moore was showing.

'I'm putting in a recommendation that Peter Marsh is grounded.'

320

Braced for questions and a possible quarrel about Anna, Moore was taken by surprise. 'How is his wife?'

'She's conscious again. But that's about all. The doctors are afraid she doesn't want to go on living.'

Moore gave a wince of sympathy. 'I must get over to see her. How is Marsh taking it?'

Harvey's glance expressed contempt such a question was necessary. 'I haven't seen him for a couple of days. I asked the Adjutant to bring his leave forward. He's spending it visiting her in hospital.'

'When is he due back?'

'Next Monday. That's why I want him grounded this week.'

'Has he applied to be grounded?'

'No. The poor bastard can't face it. That's why we have to take it out of his hands.'

'But you know we can't do that. A man has to make the first move himself.'

Harvey needed nothing more to justify his personal animosity. 'What do you mean – we can't do it? This isn't some kid who's just started operational flying. He's done nearly as many ops. as we have. He's entitled to a rest.'

'If you mean a rest between tours, I agree with you. I'll see he gets one as soon as his present tour ends.'

'You know bloody well that isn't what I mean. The kid's been suffering hell for months. What's he going to feel like now, knowing the next time he goes on an op. she might finish herself off. For Christ's sake, we've got to help him.'

'We will, if he helps himself. Tell him to put in a request and I'll add my recommendation. There's no other way. You know the rules.'

Harvey cursed. 'I know effing rules can be broken if there's a will to break them. You're a personal friend of Davies – why won't you talk to him?'

Moore was trying to imagine Davies' reaction at this moment in time to the suggestion one of his most experienced pilots was grounded. 'He wouldn't wear it, Harvey. Not for a minute.'

'You mean you won't ask him? Right?'

'It's not that. You've just picked the worst possible time to ask. Give it a month, perhaps only three weeks, and I'll do what I can. But not now.'

Harvey's suspicious eyes were searching his face. 'What's so special about now?'

Aware how the Yorkshireman's questions were endangering security, Moore's voice turned unintentionally curt. 'I've promised I'll do all I can later on. Now let's drop it, shall we?'

In spite of his animosity, Harvey's urgent need to learn Anna's address had determined the Yorkshireman to keep his self-control until his questions were asked. But with his concern for Marsh high up on his list of priorities Moore's curt rejection was like petrol vapour coming into contact with white-hot metal. In a sheet of flame his resentment exploded.

'You're really something, aren't you? The big businessman, used to pushing his workmen around like effing pawns. Never mind about their personal problems! Work the sods until they drop, then sack 'em and get in a fresh lot. Success and profit first, last, and all the time. Jesus Christ, your kind make me bring up.'

A cloud shadow, drifting slowly across the field, reached the two men and isolated them in their hostility. Although Moore's good-looking face turned very pale, his reply was astonishingly quiet and controlled.

'I'm sorry I can't help you, Harvey. I really am very sorry.'

Conscious now that pride would never allow him to ask any favours of this man, Harvey let all his self-destructiveness burst to the surface. 'You know something, Moore? The Japs and the Nazis operate the way you do. Cannon fodder for the Fatherland. Chuck 'em in and let 'em die. That's where you ought to be – on the other side.' A shudder of desire ran through the Yorkshireman. 'Christ, don't I wish you were.'

It was an orgasm of bitterness that gave him no chance to read Moore's expression. When the retaliatory attack that he was thirsting for still did not come, Harvey gave a snarl of fury, swung away, and began trudging across the grass towards the billet.

Henderson was propping up the bar in the Mess when Davies found him. Although clearly excited and in a good mood, the small Air Commodore gave a glance of disapproval at the glass of whisky the Scot was holding.

'I've been hunting all over the station for you. Bit early for that stuff, isn't it?'

Henderson, who had already seen off two glasses, was in no mood for apologies. 'It's been that kind of day, sir. Can I get you one?'

'Not bloody likely. I never drink before dinner. Where are Adams and Moore?'

Henderson rebelliously drained his glass before replying. 'I don't know, sir. Probably in their offices.'

'Well, put out a call for them,' Davies snapped. 'I want the three of you in your office in thirty minutes. And lay on full security precautions in the meantime.'

Alcohol made the Scot's question overtly sarcastic. 'That couldn't mean you're going to give us an idea at last what's going on, could it?'

Davies gave him a sharp stare. 'What's the matter with you? You feeling the-little-boy-nobody-loves all of a sudden?'

Henderson's grin expressed both embarrassment and defiance. 'Would you blame me if I did?'

Davies' satisfaction at the news he had received proved adequate for the occasion. 'For Christ's sake, Jock, you know how these things are – these last few weeks I've even had to tell lies to myself. We haven't got all the problems solved yet – the last one might prove to be the biggest – but although it's still strictly hush-hush, things have gone far enough for you to be brought in. Give me thirty minutes and you'll get the full story.'

Henderson's voice was heavy with feeling as he pushed himself away from the bar. 'Thank God for that.'

CHAPTER 29

Adams was almost past the billet door when he heard the dog whimpering. Turning, he listened. It came again, an anxious, entreating sound. Hesitating for a long moment Adams tapped on the door.

There was a loud, relieved bark and the sound of the dog scampering across the floor. As Adams tapped again its paws scratched on the woodwork. Waiting no longer, Adams pushed the door open.

The dog leapt up in relief against his legs, then ran back. The shadowy billet reeked with the smell of whisky. Reaching the bed the dog turned its head and barked impatiently.

Crossing the floor Adams patted the dog absent-mindedly. His eyes were on Harvey sprawled out face downward on the bed. In his shirtsleeves the Yorkshireman had one arm doubled beneath him and the other dangling over the bedside. An empty whisky bottle and a glass stood on the nearby locker. The dog had awakened him and his face, unshaven since the previous day, lifted a few inches from his pillow as Adams approached. 'What do y' want?'

Adams found it was difficult to know what to say. 'Are you all right, Frank?'

'Course I'm all right.'

'Is there anything I can do?'

Harvey dropped back on his pillow. 'Yes. You can bugger off.'

Irresolute, Adams stood back. Tail wagging, the dog gazed up at him. Feeling unable to meet its eyes, Adams hesitated, then retreated to the door. As he closed it behind him the dog's disappointed whimpering commenced again. With his movements suddenly full of purpose Adams went looking for Moore.

Moore was in his office writing a letter when Adams found him. The chain of a block and tackle had broken that afternoon and a young fitter working beneath it had been badly injured. The Adjutant, on whom the unpleasant task of notifying relatives usually fell, had been surprised and gratified when Moore had said he would write the letter himself. He did not know it was a responsibility Moore had taken on himself since his early days of command at Warboys.

With a shaded desk lamp concentrating its light downwards, Adams' myopic eyes could not distinguish Moore's features clearly as he approached the desk. 'Sorry to bother you at this time of the night, Ian, but I've come about Harvey. I heard his dog whimpering a few minutes ago and took a look in his billet. He's in a hell of a state – plastered to the wide.'

There was a pause before Moore answered him. 'I noticed he wasn't at dinner tonight.'

323

'Tonight? I don't know when he ate last. It's been going on for weeks. Christ knows how he manages to do his job.'

There was the click of the lighter as Moore lit a cigarette. Still not able to see his expression, Adams drew nearer the desk. 'This thing's destroying him, Ian. He must have loved that girl to distraction.'

There was a sharp exclamation, then the sound of a chair pushed back. 'Just what the hell are you trying to say?'

Coming from one as controlled as Moore, the outburst both dismayed and startled Adams. At the same time the Intelligence Officer had his own brand of tenacity which became evident now. 'I'm wondering if it's necessary to let the poor devil suffer any longer. After all, unless the final stage is a failure, the big show must be on soon. I know it means breaking orders and security, but the hell with it. There's a limit to what a man can see another man suffer.'

Bitter and resentful, Moore's reply was not the one Adams expected. 'Do you think he'll suffer any less if he hears the truth?'

'Perhaps not,' Adams admitted. 'Perhaps it might make some things worse. But at least he won't go on believing the whole world has betrayed him.'

'Won't he? He's capable of going berserk and grabbing Davies by the throat.'

'No. He'll realize that any stupid move might harm Anna. He'd sooner shoot himself than let that happen.'

'There's still Davies. If he discovers security has been broken he'll be ruthless.'

It was Adams' turn to explode, an event totally out of character. 'Damn Davies! He's nothing but a military machine. No feeling, no pity – just eyes down and on with the job.'

'The type of man that wins wars.'

'God damn his war and God damn his type. I can't sit back any longer and let a man like Harvey destroy himself. You've said often enough he cares about others. Then isn't it time someone cared about him?'

There was a brief silence, then a clatter as a pen was thrown on the desk. 'Fair enough. Only let's hope you're right and it doesn't make things worse for him.'

Adams showed dismay as Moore came round the side of the desk. 'I don't want you to do it. I just wanted to talk to you first, that's all.'

Ignoring him Moore made for the door. Adams hurried after him. 'Ian, wait. You're needed for this operation. If Davies finds out I've broken security it won't matter.'

At the door Moore glanced back. 'You were right to come. I'll let you know how he takes it.'

Before Adams could protest again Moore had disappeared.

Followed by the relieved Sam, Moore approached the bed. 'Harvey, I'd like a word with you. It's important.'

The sound of the voice he hated brought Harvey's eyes open. As consciousness seeped back into them, he twisted round and recognized the man standing over him. With a curse he switched on his bedside lamp. 'Wha' the hell d'you want?'

'I want to talk with you. Mind if I sit down?'

Bruised, black-jowled, ravaged by alcohol, the Yorkshireman's face was a forbidding sight in the lamplight. 'I'm off duty, Moore. So piss off out of here.'

Moore was hardly aware of the deep breath he took. 'I'm not here on service business. I've come to talk about Anna.'

The girl's name was like an electric shock to the man, making him start violently, then lift up on his elbows. 'You heard from her?'

'No, it's not that.'

Harvey cursed again, then sank back. 'Then what the hell is it?'

Needing a moment to compose his thoughts Moore dragged up a chair to the bedside. A radio in the billet next door could be heard playing 'As Time Goes By'. Seeing the dog wagging its tail, Moore reached impulsively down to stroke it. Immediately Harvey's voice leapt at him.

'If you've got something to tell me about Anna, then bloody tell me. Or is this some dirty new game you're playing?'

The intensity of the man, the way the girl's name had sobered him, made Moore wonder if he had been wrong to take Adams' advice. Pushing back his forebodings he straightened in his chair.

'What I'm going to tell you is top secret. If Davies ever finds out I've broken security, we'll all be for the high jump. Worst of all it might put Anna in great danger. So for God's sake don't go haywire, and keep everything you hear to yourself.'

From Harvey's reaction there appeared to be only one sentence he understood. 'Put her in danger? What do you mean?'

Moore had already decided that the quicker the knife went in the less prolonged the pain. 'Frank, Anna isn't the girl we thought she was. She's a German working for British Intelligence.'

Harvey's cheeks drained of blood. Sensing his shock, the dog leapt up and tried to lick him. For a moment, the Yorkshireman was too stunned to resist. Then he pushed the dog away. 'It's a joke, isn't it? A bloody sick joke.'

As Moore shook his head, beads of sweat began forming on the man's unshaven face. 'Who told you?'

'Davies, the night before she left here. He ordered me to attend her briefing at Tempsford before they flew her back into Europe. That was the reason we left together the next morning.'

Harvey let out a muttered 'Christ' and dropped back on his pillow.

'She was under the tightest security orders while she was here – that's why she could say so little in the letter she left you. Also, as she knew she was going back to Germany, she felt it was fairer to you if she made a clean break. She knew it would hurt you at first – but what choice did she have?'

Moore saw the Yorkshireman's sunken eyes close. Moved and wanting to inflict no more pain, he knew one last thing had to be said or the pain already inflicted was without purpose. 'It hurt her like hell to leave you that way – she broke down twice in the car. As she wasn't a girl to show her feelings, it could mean only one thing. You couldn't be more wrong about the way she felt about you.'

A glance showed Harvey to be lying very still. Rising quietly Moore started for the door. He had almost reached it when a curse of protest echoed round the billet.

'For Christ's sake, you can't go now. If she's an agent there must be a connection between her and the training we've been doing.'

Turning, Moore saw the Yorkshireman had swung his feet to the floor and was sitting facing him. 'I've told you all you need to know, Frank. The rest doesn't concern you.'

'Doesn't concern me! You'd better believe this, Moore – if you don't tell me everything you know, I'll go straight to Davies and get it out of him. Tonight!'

Knowing he had lost, Moore walked heavily back to his chair. 'You must have felt the same as me – I couldn't believe she was only a schoolteacher. But I never guessed the truth until Davies told me the night before she left. Most of her background story was true enough – she had spent a number of years in England and she had worked in Bavaria. But her parents were German, not Swiss, and she was born in Munich.'

Jumping up, Harvey pulled another bottle of whisky from his locker. As he swilled the spirit into his glass, Moore noticed the violent trembling of his hands. 'I don't get it,' the Yorkshireman muttered. 'If she's a German, why is she working for us?'

The signs of distress that both Henderson and Davies had noted in Moore on his return to the station showed again as he sank back into his chair. 'I'd have thought that obvious. She's too intelligent and fair-minded to fall for that damned adage "My country, right or wrong." She's fully aware the majority of Germans would see her as a traitor but she feels that's a small price to pay if she and her friends can help to rid Germany of Nazism.'

There was the cartilaginous sound of Harvey swallowing. 'You still haven't told me how she's connected with the training we've been doing.'

Knowing that all escape routes were now closed, Moore told him about the experiments being conducted inside the valley. 'All that can be seen from the air is a railway track disappearing into a dense forest. That's bad enough but a few days ago Davies learned the establishment is built underground.'

'Underground? Then how the hell can it be bombed?'

'It seems there might be a way but Davies is keeping that up his sleeve for the moment. He says he hopes to have something definite any time now.'

Sidetracked for the moment by the news of the rocket establishment Harvey returned to his original question. 'I still don't see where Anna comes in all this.' Then he noticed Moore's expression and his breath sucked in. 'You're not telling me she's inside the bloody valley?'

Moore found he could not meet his eyes. 'None of the men agents could infiltrate the security screen. So she came up with an idea herself.'

'What idea?'

Moore felt he had had enough. 'Leave it there, Frank. Please.'

A hand like a vice gripped his wrist as he attempted to rise. 'If none of the men could get inside, then how the hell could she? I want to know.'

It was one of the few times in his life that Moore felt panic. 'I don't know that, Frank. She didn't tell me.'

The grip on his wrist tightened. 'You're lying! She went over there to offer herself to one of the bastards, didn't she? If none of the men could get in, it has to be that.'

It was Moore's own feelings for the girl that betrayed him. Staring at his expression, Harvey sank slowly back on the bed. 'Oh, Christ,' he muttered. 'Oh, Jesus Christ.'

The music next door had started again. A man was singing 'All The Things You Are'. Still on the bed, the dog tried to scramble on to Harvey's knee. Blind with grief, seeking relief in movement, the Yorkshireman jumped to his feet and walked round the bed. When he turned at last his appearance shocked Moore. His facial lines looked as if they had been slashed with a razor and his eyes were bloodshot with torment.

'Do you know who the bastard is?'

'No. Some executive officer, I suppose.'

'How soon can we make the raid?' Harvey's question was full of a terrible hunger.

'That depends on her coming up with the answers Davies wants.' The suddenness of Moore's decision surprised himself. 'You won't be going. Not now you know she's in there.'

'Not going?' Harvey looked horrified. 'But I've got to go.'

'No,' Moore said again. 'We can manage without you.'

The big man looked panic-stricken. 'If it's so important to her, I must go. Surely to Christ you can see that.'

Moore could see it as clearly as if he were in the man's mind but it still took him another thirty seconds to reach a decision. 'If I let you go, do you promise to play it straight from the book? No emotional gestures or any nonsense like that?'

'I'll play it straight,' the Yorkshireman muttered.

'Very well. We'll leave things as they are.' Held by the man's appearance Moore hesitated. 'Are you going to be all right?'

In Harvey's harsh world a man hid his wounds, knowing the indication of them was all that the predators were waiting for. Muttering something he sank down on the bed and began stroking the relieved dog. 'Of course I'm all right.'

As Moore nodded and went to the door, Harvey looked up. 'This raid's going to be a rough one, isn't it?'

'It depends. It might be.'

'Yet you did say you could spare me?'

'Yes. I can use one of our reserve crews?'

'Then, as I'm coming along, you could spare someone in my place?'

'What are you getting at?'

327

'I want you to leave young Marsh behind. Will you do that?'

Moore gazed at him in astonishment. Bloody, his head bowed, he still tried to protect others. It was suddenly very clear to Moore what Anna had seen in this man. 'All right. Marsh won't go. Satisfied?'

Harvey's nod was sullen, yet his every word reached the door. 'I appreciate what you've done, Moore. And the chance you've taken. Thanks.'

Strangely moved, Moore opened the door and stood on the step outside. 'I'd get some sleep if I were you. The green light could come at any time.'

This time Harvey nodded without speaking. Moore's last glance showed him bent over the dog as if ashamed of his gratitude.

Moore's last words to Harvey were more prophetic than he knew. Not fifty minutes later Henderson was called by the Duty Officer to the red telephone in his office. Davies was on the line and his excitement alone told Henderson the weeks of waiting were over.

'She's done it, Jock. I'll give you all the details later but the big show's on tomorrow. I want your lads briefed and your air-tests completed by 09.00 hours. All right?'

Henderson could feel his heart beating rapidly. 'Yes, sir. When will you be coming?'

'I've a few things to clear up with the Yanks and then I'll be on my way. Should arrive before midnight with luck.' Davies' enthusiasm came over the line as if he were in the office himself. 'Thank Christ we've got word at last. I was getting scared they'd got on to Anna and arrested her. You'll be getting your operational details through the usual channels. See you later.'

In fact the teletype in the Operations Room was already clacking. Fetched by the Duty Sergeant, Adams began taking down the details while S.P.s stood guard at the door and windows. The Duty Officer, making certain outside communications were cut, began to alert ground-crew N.C.O.s. At the same time all available S.P.s were driven at high speed to Highgate and adjacent villages where they rounded up indignant airmen and officers and shepherded them into waiting transports. The scene of intense activity at Sutton Craddock on their arrival convinced the most phlegmatic of them that something big was afoot. They were soon to learn how big that something was.

CHAPTER 30

The only men at Sutton Craddock who slept that night were the aircrews, and with the excited speculation at what the morrow might bring added to the activity around them, their sleep was only fitful. They were called at 05.00 hours, given breakfast half an hour later, and at 06.27 the station tannoy ordered them into the Operations Room. There, on the platform beneath the huge map of Europe, Davies, Henderson, Moore, and the rest of the briefing officers were waiting for them.

Only Moore, who was to fly with the squadron, had enjoyed more than two hours' sleep. The rest had been kept busy by Henderson and the dynamic Davies as they made certain the squadron was in one hundred per cent state of readiness. In fact, as far as the aircraft were concerned they had only to be air-tested and bombed up and they would be fully operational.

The state of the crews was less desirable. Caught by surprise at the speed of the emergency, allowed only a few hours' sleep to counter the effects of the previous night's beer, the rows of young men looked bleary and bewildered as they stared at the large cloth-covered mound that stood on a table in the centre of the platform. As Davies and the other officers conferred behind the table, the men's nervous eyes pulled away and wandered round the slogan-covered walls of the room. Whispers sounded, nervous laughs broke out, and matches scratched. Cigarette smoke, drifting into a misty layer beneath the ceiling, made the dangling models of German aircraft look as if they were flying through high-level cloud.

The group on the platform ended their conference and after a brief introductory comment from Henderson, Davies stepped forward. Murmurs died away and tension caught at the throat as his ferret-sharp eyes travelled along the rows of expectant faces. His high-pitched voice, trying to ease the tension, ironically only drew it tighter.

'You chaps are not exactly Strength-through-Joy boys in the morning, are you? I've never seen so many dogs' dinners at one sitting. Never mind. In a couple of minutes I'll guarantee to have you as wide awake as if I'd dumped you into a tub of cold water.'

On this highly expectant note Davies walked back to the table and laid his hand on the cloth that covered the large mound. 'Before this briefing's over you're all going to have the chance to take a closer look at this thing. But first I'm going to explain what it's all about.'

With that he jerked off the cloth. Leaning forward in anticipation, the crews

329

saw a large, papiermâché model of the Ruhpolding valley. Their blank stares were shared by Young and Harvey, sitting in their isolated chairs on the other side of the aisle. Leaning towards Harvey, the Australian muttered a question. Harvey, whose face showed the ravages of a sleepless night, shook his head curtly.

Davies moved behind the scale model and picked up a pointer. 'This is the valley you're going to. Your target is somewhere in a dense forest along its floor. I'm not allowed to tell you what Jerry's making there, but I can say that they are devices that could make our invasion hellishly costly or even impossible. So it's an establishment we must destroy and we shall destroy it. But there are snags.'

He paused so that his young audience could assimilate his words. Their faces were a study of their characters. Some looked pale and tensed. Some looked excited. In the second row of chairs, for all the world like a mischievous schoolboy being given details of a day's outing, Gabby was whispering something to Millburn, who grinned broadly. Further along the same row the Byronic features of St Claire were calmly attentive. Sue Spencer, sitting at the large table alongside Adams and the only member on the platform unbriefed about the raid, had her eyes on the young pianist. One of her slim hands, holding a pencil, was doodling on a piece of paper as if it had a life of its own.

'Snag Number One is the distance,' Davies went on. 'You've been nearly as far before – I've seen that – but not in daylight, and for reasons I'll explain in a moment, that's when the job must be done. The establishment is in a Bavarian valley south-east of Munich.'

There was a loud buzz of consternation. A voice called out: 'Christ, that's impossible!' Used to demonstrations of shock, Davies used the shout to advantage.

'Someone's surprised? You shouldn't be. You're an élite squadron with a record no other unit in the RAF can match. So what's surprising about a daylight raid into Bavaria? You should be glad I'm not sending you to Tokyo.'

A ripple of nervous laughter ran through the general alarm. 'Snag Number Two,' Davies said. 'The target's underground. Snag Number Three adds insult to injury. The target's somewhere in this bloody great forest. A railway track runs to it but Jerry's been clever as always – the firs grow tall in this part of the world and so he's only lopped off the lower branches. Add camouflage to that and it means you can't see the track from the air.'

In their bewilderment men began to forget discipline. Loud murmurs of protest and even a muted cat-call could be heard. A born actor, Davies allowed the hubbub to run on for a full ten seconds before walking to the front of the platform and holding up his hand. His grin was wicked.

'I said I'd wake you up, didn't I? Now you're awake, let's see how we can get round these snags. Number One first. We all know that if you fly that deep into Germany in daylight, Jerry will have half his Air Force waiting for you. But what if you fly on the backs of a hundred and fifty American B.17s going out to bomb Jerry's Me.109 factory at Regensburg? Jerry will throw everything at the B.17s, who'll be screening you from his detectors, and you'll have a cushy ride nearly all the way to your target.' At the stares of amazement he was receiving Davies grinned again. 'That's how it's going to be. The Yanks are going out at 29,000 feet and you're going to ride 'em piggy back at your maximum ceiling. They'll drop their bombs on Regensburg and keep going straight on to North Africa. When they reach Munich you'll peel off and with any luck at all, you'll have a free dive down to the target.'

The muttering among the crews died down as the feasibility of the scheme sank in. 'It'll work,' Davies assured them. 'The Yank daylight raids have been hurting Jerry and a hundred and fifty heavies penetrating into Bavaria will cause a hell of a reaction. All right, snag Number Two. This has been our biggest headache. We've known for some time that a tanker train containing thousands of gallons of highly-explosive fuel arrives every nine or so days and discharges into underground tanks. What we haven't known is when the next tanker is due. Last night we heard it should reach the establishment at 13.00 hours today and will start discharging fuel fifteen minutes later. The job takes about ninety minutes. Our boffins calculate that for maximum effect we want fifty per cent of the fuel left in the tanker and fifty per cent in the underground tanks when we clobber the train. After that it doesn't take much imagination to realize what will happen. The burning fuel will pour down, the underground tanks will explode, and up goes Jerry, establishment, and all. Nasty but necessary if we're to win this war and get back to our families again.'

The attention of his audience was now fully held. As a few faces, St Claire's prominent among them, winced at the method of destruction Davies allowed no time for reflection.

'That leads us to snag Number Three – how do we find the tanker in the first place? The answer there is that some very brave people in Germany have got an agent inside the valley and that agent will indicate to you the position of the train when you arrive. With everything happening in a hurry because of the train's arrival today they haven't been able to work out yet what the signal will be but we're assured we'll get one.'

From the platform Moore was watching Harvey. Until this moment the Yorkshireman's face had shown little expression as if the long night had burned his emotion to ash. But as Davies spoke of the lone agent in the valley the tell-tale muscle in his cheek began contracting.

'From all this you'll realize timing is vital,' Davies went on. 'You'll strike the tanker at 14.00 hours precisely and the entire operation, Yanks and all, is scheduled around that time. You'll top up your tanks at Manston and wait for the Yanks to formate over Dungeness. After they've had a good start you'll follow and climb up on their backs. Both of you must be at your maximum operational height before you reach Mons. You have an escort as far as our fighters' extreme range – after that you'll be on your own.'

'As for diversions, 12 Group will be on the offensive in the Netherlands and 11 Group will be on a similar sweep in Central France. One way and another' – Davies' grin moved along the row of faces – 'you're being mollycoddled all the way. That's the general picture. Any questions before I pass you over to your specialist officers?'

To Adams the Operations Room felt cold that morning. Davies had a knack of making the most hazardous operation sound routine, but Adams knew there was no guarantee the enemy controllers would not guess the Mosquitoes' target when they broke away from the B.17s. Even if they did not, the marauding German fighters would be on them like wolves if they wasted any time over the target. The sight of Teddy Young rising to his feet interrupted Adams' forebodings.

'What are your contingency plans if this agent doesn't get his message up to us, sir? I take it this could happen?'

Young did not notice the black look Harvey gave him. Forced into an admission he did not want to make, Davies displayed irritability. 'If you don't get a signal your leader will use his initiative. You'll get full details of the alternatives in a minute, but, briefly, one method is to try to estimate the line of the railway track and each kite to plant bombs along it until the tanker's reached. The other way is to pattern-bomb the area. Operational conditions would decide which method to use. But we're feeling confident neither will be necessary.'

Young opened his mouth again, then changed his mind and sat down. Adams read his thoughts as if they had been expressed. If they had to spend time looking for the target, the hostile fighters must reach them. Across the room MacDougall lifted a hand.

'Won't the Germans shunt the train away from the target the moment they get warning of us, sir?'

This time Davies was more at ease. 'They can't. We've established they're using steam locomotives. So any attempt to move the tanker would immediately give its position away.'

A question came from Ross, an ex-Edinburgh student. 'The underground tanks won't have access to oxygen, sir. So how can you be sure they'll explode?'

Davies conceded the shrewdness of the question. 'The answer is it's a fuel that contains its own oxygen content.' Aware it was a give-away reply to anyone who was technically-minded, Davies moved on swiftly. 'All right. I'm now going to pass you over to your specialist officers. Then you can take a look at this model and the photographs we've got.'

If any man among the crews remained unconvinced of the importance of the mission, the detailed briefing that followed put an end to his doubts. It was ninety minutes before the men returned to their seats and Moore spoke to them for the first time. Although sharing Harvey's concern for Anna, he gave the appearance of being relaxed and confident.

'We are using our full operational strength of sixteen Mosquitoes. Going out we shall fly in sections of three, line abreast. As we're hoping to go unnoticed above the B.17s we shall keep radio silence all the way. When I break it over the target, don't talk unless you've something worth saying. I don't want the channel cluttered up with comics, so all those with guilty consciences take note.' As Moore's eyes rested on the hurt Gabby, rows of tensed faces began grinning.

'Study your charts carefully. I want all navigators to keep individual logs so they can get home alone if necessary. In other words don't think this is a doddle and all you have to do is follow the Yanks to Munich.'

'You think there'll be any left by that time, skipper?' The mordant quip came from Stan Baldwin.

'Let's hope for our sakes there are,' Moore said dryly. 'Once we break from them at Munich we'll fly in line astern until we reach Ruhpolding. In case anyone should fall asleep and come adrift, your marker is a bloody great castle on an island in the Chiemsee. Ludwig II, the mad king of Bavaria, built it and it's a near replica of Versailles. So when you see it don't think you've gone mad or the Yank navigators have ballsed things up and taken you back to Paris. We enter the valley at the Ruhpolding end and follow the railway until it disappears into the forest. At this point, if all goes well we'll get our indication where the tanker is. The first kites will make their attack, the rest will orbit and give cover in the usual way. With any luck we'll have the job done and be away before Jerry can get his trousers up!'

'Supposing we don't get our signal, skipper.' It was Young again, still worried about the problem of location. 'It seems a hell of a big forest. How can we be sure which way the railway runs?'

Moore's honesty brought a scowl from Davies. 'I suppose the answer to that, Teddy, is that we can't. We'd have to play it as it came. If we'd used up all our bombs and still hadn't clobbered the train, we could still try cannon fire, so we'd have quite a few bites at the cherry. But this is looking on the black side. The chances are the first wave will blow the thing sky high and the rest of you will be stuck for a target.'

The thought of Mosquitoes strafing a tanker loaded with explosive fuel at tree-top height made Adams turn pale. Moore gave the crews no time for such speculation.

'My guess is that the hardest part of the operation will be in one sense the easiest. I don't need to tell any of you that Jerry's air defences have made a big come-back recently and their tails are right up. So it's a safe bet the Yanks are going to get a hell of a clobbering and it's not going to be much fun for us riding on their backs and watching over it. However' – and Moore was gazing straight at Millburn – 'it's imperative we conserve ourselves and our ammunition for the job in hand. So no gallant gestures. The Yanks won't hold it against you – they've been told what to expect.'

Heads nodded dubiously, Millburn's among them. 'The squadron call sign will be Longbow and the station call sign Harry. When you hear me transmit Crispin you'll know you'll be drinking champagne tonight. Any more questions?'

When none came Davies returned to the front of the platform. Solemn after his earlier enthusiasm, he brought a hush to the room.

'I've this last thing to emphasize. If these new weapons come into production they won't just affect the grand strategy of our combined Air Forces, they could delay the invasion itself. The cost of that in human lives and misery doesn't bear thinking about. Also some very brave people, among them the Americans who are setting themselves up as decoys, are taking some frightening risks for us. So I know you'll all do your best. Now off you go and get your kites air-tested. Take off time is 10.45 prompt.'

The tap on his billet door made Adams turn. With the briefing over he had slipped back to rummage for a letter he wanted to answer that day. As he straightened he saw the tall figure of Harvey standing in the doorway. The York-shireman was wearing flying overalls and had an oxygen mask and earphones slung over one shoulder.

'Sue Spencer said I'd find you here,' he muttered. 'You got a minute to spare?'

'Of course. Come in.'

Turning his head, Harvey whistled. A moment later Sam appeared and gazed up at him expectantly. Without preamble Harvey led the dog into the billet.

'I want someone to leave Sam with. Will you take him on? You seem to like dogs and he seems to get on well with you.'

Adams gave a start. 'Then you're not taking him with you today?'

The man's laugh was hard and humourless. 'All that way? What would the poor sod do for a lamp post?' Bending down he cuffed the dog's head. Reacting immediately, Sam leapt up against him. Ashamed of the demonstration of affection, Harvey pushed the animal back. 'Sit down! Stay!'

Wagging his tail, the dog sat back on its haunches. The Yorkshireman turned his grim face towards Adams. 'Well, will you have him? You'll find he does as he's told.'

Adams, who had drawn closer to read the man's expression, pulled himself together. 'Of course. I'll be glad to look after him until you get back.'

Harvey showed resentment. 'You wouldn't take him for longer?'

'If it were necessary, yes. But it won't be. You'll want him yourself again this evening.'

Harvey relaxed. 'Fair enough. Thanks. We're taking off soon so I'll leave him here. O.K.?'

'Yes. I'll shut him in when I go to the Control Tower.'

Nodding his appreciation, Harvey moved towards the door. The dog, eyes full of worship, gave a sudden anxious bark. As the Yorkshireman turned, his expression betrayed him. 'Shut up, you stupid old bugger. Behave yourself.'

The dog barked again. Moved by the scene, Adams forgot the rules and took a step forward. 'You feeling all right, Frank? You will be back for a drink in the Mess tonight?'

The man's expression changed. 'What the hell are you talking about? I'm just taking precautions, that's all. Of course I'll be back.'

Without another word he turned and closed the door behind him. Jumping to its feet the dog ran forward and began scratching the woodwork. Adams took a precious bar of chocolate from his locker, broke off a couple of pieces, and held them out in his hand. Although well known for his love of chocolate, Sam ignored the offer and continued to scratch at the door.

CHAPTER 31

At 36,000 feet the vast dome of the sky was a pitiless blue and the sun blinding even through the smoked goggles Moore was wearing. Behind him, in five ranks of three aircraft apiece, the Mosquitoes were like a troop of horsemen. Painted PR blue for the occasion, with the brilliant sunlight giving a halo to their spinning propellers, they yawed gently in the rarefied air. With the crews airborne long enough for the roar of engines to have faded into a neutral background, the sensation was one of almost disembodied detachment. In this bright beautiful world of the stratosphere, war was nothing more than an obscene thought in the mind.

Until a man gazed down and saw the massive armada of war 7,000 feet below that was heading relentlessly towards the heart of Germany. With each one of the 146 giant bombers emitting condensation trails from its wingtips, the effect was that of enormous rockets pouring out gas as they streaked through the sky. The great trails linked together and formed a wash that spread back into the windless stratosphere as far as the eye could reach.

An English voice on a low signal strength drew Moore's attention. 'Sorry but that's as far as we can go, Oklahoma Leader. We'll buy you tea and muffins when you get back. Good luck. Out.'

A humorous voice with an American drawl followed. 'We can't wait for those muffins, Turpin Leader. Thanks for your help.'

Moore and Hopkinson exchanged glances. The German monitoring service, picking up the heavy activity over the American airfields, would have guessed from the B.17s' assembly point at Dungeness that the operation was aimed at central or southern Europe. Fighter groups would have been moved to airfields west of Reims and those same fighters would certainly be airborne and in visual contact by this time. Their brief was to wait until the Allied fighter escort reached the limit of its range and then hurl their unimpaired strength against the unprotected bombers. The ground below was hidden by a thin film of mist but the news the escort was turning back gave a general indication of the armada's position. Within minutes it would be crossing the German frontier.

Pouring out their tell-tale wake, the Fortresses droned on while their crews peered out into the dazzling, deadly sky. Flak, which had followed them right across Belgium and France, grew fiercer as they turned south in a dog-leg. As predictors got their range and ugly black mushrooms burst into the heart of the

335

formation, a Fortress was hit in its inner port engine. Yawing clumsily, it began to sideslip, then to gyrate as the port wing broke up. The white puffs of two parachutes appeared but before more could follow there was a vivid flash and an eruption of oily smoke. Fragments flew in all directions and the fuselage, a metal coffin for the eight men still strapped inside, plummeted down and disappeared into the veil of cloud. Above, the armada closed its ranks and droned on.

Inside the huge planes gunners were either standing or crouched behind their heavy-calibre Brownings. With each Fortress carrying thirteen machine guns the concentration of fire directed on an enemy aircraft attacking from the rear or even below could be devastating. The weakness, as the Americans knew too well, was up front. Still not modified with a two-gun 'chin' turret, the Fortresses were vulnerable to a head-on attack. This weakness had been discovered by the Focke Wulfs of 11/JGI earlier that summer and they were the first to attack the armada just as it crossed the German frontier. A highly-experienced unit, they came straight at the Americans like a pack of wolves attacking a stampede of bison. Sweeping down from head-on and above, they opened fire with cannon at 800 yards. Guns firing until the last split-second before collision, they dived beneath the formation and swung violently away to avoid the fire from the bombers' ventral and side gun positions. Then, while the second wave made its attack, the first wave climbed back into position for a repeat performance.

The result of the first attack was instantaneous. One of the leading Fortresses took a burst of cannon fire full in the forward cockpit. The effect on flesh and bone was indescribable. With its controls locked by the explosions the bomber did not fall at once but like a blinded animal reeled from the main pack and began a bizarre course of its own. With the side and rear gunners unaware of the carnage up front, they continued to defend the doomed plane against the triumphant wolves that came snarling after it. One gun after the other ceased firing: then the entire massive structure lurched, turned over, and disappeared into the haze below.

The entire sky became threaded with cannon and machine-gun tracer as the ferocious battle continued. With their homeland threatened by the armada and the hideous carnage of Hamburg still fresh in their minds, the German fighter pilots displayed the same desperate courage as their British counterparts of three years earlier. Some Focke Wulfs, ignoring the massive fire-power of the Fortresses, plunged straight into the formation, spraying cannon fire in all directions as they dived. One, hit by at least fifty heavy machine guns, literally disintegrated in mid-air. Another crumpled like a shot pheasant and dropped as lifelessly. Yet another collided with a Fortress and the two planes, welded together, fell in a welter of flame and oily smoke. The radio channel, on which the Mosquitoes above were tuned, was filled with the sounds of battle.

'Bandit, Tex! Three o'clock high!'

'Close up, you guys. Keep formation.'

'I got the bastard! See that, Stan? I got the bastard!'

The minutes of fury seemed endless to the B.17s' gunners. When at last the

Focke Wulfs' ammunition ran out and they had to withdraw, some of the younger hands believed a victory had been won. The older hands dragged out new ammunition boxes, reloaded, shifted their gum from one cheek to the other, and waited.

They did not have to wait long. Two more fighter *gruppen* were already hurling themselves towards the armada. Others, Hans Klaus's night-fighter unit among them, were lined up on airfields waiting for their turn to attack. Aware the Americans would not be making such a deep penetration unless they had a target of high importance, the Germans had called up their night-fighter units to augment their defences, a build-up of strength that was massive and intimidating.

One of these two *gruppen* about to attack the armada was another of these night-fighter units. Equipped with 110s, its crews made up in courage what they lacked in daylight training. The other unit was an experienced squadron of 109s. Both units carried 21cm. rockets on their wings and as the first wave swept in they released the rockets at 900 yards. Two Fortresses were hit. One kept going with smoke pluming from an engine. The other had a wing shorn clean off and its asymmetrical remains went spinning earthwards.

Seven thousand feet above the running battle, the Mosquito crews were reacting according to their temperaments. While every man wanted to go to the help of the Americans, some had enough phlegm to accept the situation. Others, Harvey, Moore, St Claire, and Baldwin among them, found their passive role painful to a degree. In T-Tommy, Gabby was eyeing Millburn with concern. With his forehead above his oxygen mask furrowed and beaded with sweat, the American was clearly in torment as he watched the trial by fire of his fellow countrymen. Noticing Gabby's glance, he stiffened and reacted belligerently.

'What the hell are you afraid of? That I might give the poor bastards a hand?'

It was one moment in his life when Gabby knew that silence was golden. The American glared at him, then indicated the chart strapped to the Welshman's thigh. 'How much further, for Christ sake?'

Gabby decided it was unwise to tell him the truth. 'Not much further.' In an effort to take the American's mind off his equivocal answer, he pointed at an Me.109 that was plunging earthwards trailing smoke. 'Anyway, your lot are giving as good as they get.'

'You expect anything else?' Millburn muttered, gazing down again.

It was an unfortunate moment to choose. A B.17 had just received a direct hit from a 21cm. rocket and the mutilated body of a gunner could be seen dropping out of the ruptured fuselage. The curse that broke from Millburn was bitter and unprintable.

Beside its usual complement, the Operations Room contained two extra officers that afternoon. One was the Brigadier, a dignified if somewhat pale figure sitting beside Henderson and Adams at the large table. The other man was the Texan, General Staines. He had telephoned Davies the previous night to say he would

337

like to be at Sutton Craddock during the operation, and when Davies had expressed surprise as well as pleasure, the American had made the wry comment
that as he had accepted the pigeon he might as well see it home to roost. It was a
comment of such ambiguity that Davies had felt unable to pursue it further. The
Texan's one request was that a telephone should be connected directly to his
USAAF Headquarters, and Marsden had set this up during the night. The benefits
were now evident. 633 Squadron were still bound by radio silence but now the
Americans were under attack it was expected of them to report successes and
losses to their headquarters. Reports were coming in almost by the minute and
these were being passed on by Staines to the grateful Brigadier and Davies.

An unlit cigar in his mouth, the Texan had the receiver clamped to his ear.
Davies was pacing restlessly beneath the huge map of Europe. As he heard a
metallic crackling in Staines's earpiece he halted. Half a minute later the
American turned to the motionless Brigadier.

'They've reached Wiesbaden. Losses – eight so far and six damaged. The
Krauts are throwing everything at them.'

Catching the Brigadier's glance, Davies opened his mouth, then discovered he
had nothing to say. Adams, the most imaginative man in the room, was mentally
counting the losses in human terms. Eighty young men lost already and that did
not include the casualties on the damaged B.17s. His eyes moved to the large
clock above the map. At least another forty minutes to ETA. He could see the
massive Fortresses rising and falling in the afternoon sky, the attacking fighters
with their lethal cannon and rockets, the agonized cries of wounded men, the
flames that swept into choking lungs, and the silence of the room seemed to mock
him. Once again Adams hated the age and infirmity that had relegated him to a
role in which he felt so ashamedly safe.

The painful, loss-filled minutes dragged by. Behind the table Davies had resumed his restless pacing. The occasional glance Staines gave him indicated that
the Texan was not as free from strain as his extrovert appearance suggested.
Down the room the earphones of the Signals corporal who was waiting for the
first message from Moore remained silent. It was Staines, expressing a pride that
Davies understood well, who gave the news that the armada had reached its target.

'Regensburg – Prufening! You hear that? They've broken through!'

Davies gave a little skip of relief, then remembered himself. 'Well done. That
means our boys won't be idle much longer.'

The Texan waved him silent as he listened. 'The Krauts are pouring it in but
we're hitting the target O.K. Your guys are going on to Munich with the first
wave.'

Reports of the air battle raging over Regensburg were now coming in thick and
fast and Staines's tough face seemed to grow older by the minute as he listened to
his B.17 losses. 'Sonofabitch, this is costing something,' he muttered. At 13.37 he
glanced at Davies. 'Your guys have broken off contact. So they can't be far away
from the valley.'

With the photographs of the district etched in his mind, Adams was instantly there. Dry-mouthed navigators trying to identify the valley as the blue Chiemsee swept towards them. The lake shivering in the air-blast of thirty-two propellers. The island ahead with its columns of trees, statues, and bizarre halls of Versailles. Brief glimpses of terraces and flower-beds, then belly down on the lake again with spray hissing on red-hot engines. Over the autobahn and on towards the great semi-circles of mountains that lay between Bavaria and the Austrian Alps. . . . Adams' graphic vision was shattered as the sudden blip of Morse sounded down the room. Moving as fast as a man half his age, Davies jumped down from the platform and ran towards the corporal who was scribbling the message on a pad. Davies scanned the signal, then read it jubilantly aloud.

'Longbow leader to Harry. Valley identified. Stand by.'

Red spots glowing in his cheeks, Davies turned back to the corporal. 'Harry to Longbow leader. Have you a contact with Lorenz? Over.'

Over three minutes passed before the Morse blips came again. As Davies bent eagerly down, Adams saw his expression change. Henderson rose sharply to his feet. 'What is it, sir?'

Looking frail and anxious, the elderly Brigadier moved up alongside Davies. Turning as if his small body had become arthritic, Davies tore off the top sheet of the pad and offered it to him. As the soldier gave a start, Staines frowned and removed an unlit cigar from his mouth. 'What's the problem? You two lost your tongues?'

Forgetting both courtesy and rank in the stress of the moment, Davies conferred urgently with the Brigadier. As the soldier nodded, Davies scribbled on the pad and thrust it at the corporal. 'Send this! And make certain they receive it.'

As the tap of the Morse key began again, he walked towards Staines and laid Moore's message in front of him. When the American gave a curse of dismay, Davies walked back to the Signals bench. As he and the Brigadier stood waiting for news, their appearance made Adams think of two men who had gambled their all on a throw of the dice and the throw had failed.

CHAPTER 32

Hopkinson's sharp eyes were busy identifying the prominent features of the small Bavarian village as it swept towards him. The river, the Byzantine-style church steeple on the right, the railway station, the Steinberg Alps ahead. . . . 'Ruhpolding, skipper! Bang on the button.'

Moore nodded. Two valleys lay ahead and he was already banking A-Apple towards the narrower. Flying in tight line-astern formation the string of Mosquitoes curved and followed him. The village swept past and a few seconds later the sunlit plain gave way to high mountains that closed on either side. A road and single-track railway followed a stream that wound through isolated hill farms and grassy meadows. Ahead the bearded chin of a mountain split the valley into two branches. A wooded spur half-blocked the entrance to the eastern branch. The stream and road ran on into the western branch which was wider. The rail track parted company and looped round the foot of the spur to enter the eastern valley.

Nodding at Hopkinson, Moore followed the railway. Dense firs flowed beneath him, then he was over the spur and into the valley. His first glimpse of it confirmed all Davies' deductions. Seven or eight miles long, flanked by high mountains and with an even higher mountain sealing its far end, it could only be entered from its northern entrance by highly-manoeuvrable aircraft flying at low level. Once the target was located every Mosquito would have to circle back to Ruhpolding before launching its attack.

Moore switched on his R/T. 'Longbow leader. Orbit the valley and stand by. Keep watch for bandits. Red Section Leader, follower me into the valley.'

Conscious his time in the valley was governed by his speed, Moore throttled back. Harvey, summoned up by his call, was swinging into position alongside him. Both men had their eyes on the single track rail that had now straightened out and was running along the floor of the valley. Afternoon sunlight, filtered by the thin mist above, glinted dully on the massive steel gates that lay across it. Two tiny uniformed figures could be seen running into the massive blockhouse that stood close by. The shape of the security fence could be traced by the scars that ran along the lower slopes of the wooded mountains. The sheer size of the cordoned-off area and its impression of brutal efficiency added a nightmarish quality to Harvey's fears for the girl.

Moore's voice crackled in his earphones. 'You see anything?'

'Not yet,' Harvey muttered.

Scattered haphazardly among dense trees were a few small farms and handkerchief-sized meadows. Alpine-yellow in the sunlight, hay was already stooked for the winter feed. Here and there were foresters' huts and the thread of paths and fire breaks. Otherwise the valley was a dense forest of trees, sweeping down from the mountains and covering the ground in a vast, bottle-green carpet.

To gain a better view the two Mosquitoes climbed another four hundred feet. Below them the railway had already disappeared into the trees. Searching for unspecified instructions, Harvey was unsure whether he wanted those instructions or not. They would be evidence Anna was still free but their implementation might put her in mortal danger.

He glanced at Blackburn, who shook his head. 'Sorry, skipper, but I can't see anything either.'

The huge mountain at the end of the valley, with a boss of naked rock at its summit, was sweeping perilously close. The carpet of forest, reaching in all directions, was ominously still. Harvey's guess was the Germans were playing it canny to make certain first that the valley was the Mosquitoes' target. With an establishment of such importance hidden there, heavy defences must be present to guard it.

Like Harvey, Moore was growing increasingly anxious. Apart from concern for Anna, which he shared with the Yorkshireman, he realized that her role in the operation was more important than perhaps anyone had believed. Commonsense dictated that the Germans would not have continued the rail track in a straight line once it disappeared into the forest. The rocket establishment could be anywhere beneath the green quilt, perhaps even in the shadow of the bald-topped mountain itself.

A few more seconds and that same mountain was a threat the Mosquitoes could not ignore. With a word to Harvey, Moore banked steeply and began climbing up to the orbiting squadron. His decision was made. With only minutes left before enemy fighters reached them he could afford no more time waiting for Anna's instructions. However remote, there was the possibility the rocket establishment was within a mile or so of the forest fringe and the possibility had to be catered for. 'Longbow leader to Zero Two, Three, Four, and Five. Adopt Scheme A. In you go!'

The four Mosquitoes named peeled away and dived towards Ruhpolding. As he waited for them to return through the mountains Moore shared his attention between the valley and the sky above. The thin layer of mist worried him. Fighters could assemble behind it and attack with the minimum of warning.

Circling with him Harvey had settled his own private dilemma. If no message came from Anna the chances were high her role had been discovered, and the thought of her, a German, in the hands of the Gestapo made the Yorkshireman's hands sweat. A signal would at least mean she was free. But although Harvey was now scanning the valley with binoculars he could see nothing that remotely suggested a signal.

The first of the four Mosquitoes Moore had dispatched was now winging back through the mountains. Flown by Teddy Young it leapt the spur and made for the visible end of the rail track. The sight of its open bomb doors was what the hidden German gunners had been waiting for. Half a dozen prongs of tracer lunged at the plane as it rocketed past the steel gates. Young, who was holding the release button himself, pressed it a couple of seconds later. The automatic selector released his full complement of eight bombs at one second intervals. Delay-fused, they began exploding along a half mile stretch of forest as the Australian came corkscrewing out of the valley. Trees were flung upwards and fire blazed around the points of impact, but from the height Moore and Harvey were flying the forest looked as dense and invulnerable as ever.

Zero Three followed twenty seconds later. It had the bad luck to cross the mountain spur three hundred feet higher than Young where a 20mm. crew were crouching. As the Mosquito swept past a fork of tracer raked it from nose to tail. Turning over like a gaffed fish it somersaulted among the trees in a tangle of wreckage. Seeing the danger Moore dived down on the spur. The Mosquito could not drop bombs in a twenty-degree plus dive, but it could strafe with its cannon and Brownings. Crouched behind the nest of rocks, intent on spearing the next plane that swept past them, the gun crew were late in seeing the threat from above and before they could swing their gun-mounting round, Moore opened fire. The hose of shells severed branches from trees and hurled the men aside like broken puppets. Giving the sweating Hopkinson a word of reassurance he did not feel himself, Moore climbed back into orbit.

Zero Four crossed the spur safely and jinked towards the fires ahead. Now that the Mosquitoes had declared their intention, flak posts were springing up like dragons' teeth on every side of the valley. Jinking to evade the blizzard of fire, the Mosquito laid its stick of bombs ten degrees east of the line laid down by Young. All eight bombs burst as it climbed from the valley but the limited size of the explosions made it obvious the train had not been hit.

By the time Zero Five made its strike tracer was rising in sheets from the valley floor. Rolling in the dense explosions it laid its bombs ten degrees west and clawed for the safety of height. From above, the pattern of the bombing was a Y branded on the fringe of the forest. Catching Moore's eye, Hoppy gave a grimace. 'It's hopeless, skipper. We'd need a thousands kites to find it. And now they know what we're doing they'll shoot us down like bloody ducks.'

Moore knew he was right. Had the tanker been located, the losses incurred in its destruction could be justified. As things were the cost would be senseless. 'Get base on again,' he told Hopkinson. 'Tell them we've been in the valley nearly three minutes and there's still no signal from Lorenz. We've tried Scheme A but the flak is heavy. Ask permission to operate Scheme B.'

The answer that caused Davies so much heartbreak came thirty seconds later. Formating the squadron in sections of three, Moore led them back along the valley. With the need for pinpoint accuracy gone, they flew a couple of hundred feet above the surrounding mountains. Guessing their intent the gunners below fired as fast as their loaders could feed the guns. K-Kenny received a direct hit just as Moore gave the order to jettison bombs. As the sticks of bombs fell in an extensive pattern and disappeared among the trees, K-Kenny turned in an instant from a bird of grace and power into a miscellany of wings and broken spars falling out of a ball of smoke.

Moore was holding his breath and counting as he led the Mosquitoes to safety over the western mountains. As he dipped a wing, the bombs began exploding in rapid succession among the trees. The air-blast made the Mosquitoes rock like canoes in rough water. Waiting in case the train exploded, Moore swept along the valley rim. Although columns of black smoke were rising and drifting together, the fires, smothered by the dense trees, looked as innocuous as a hundred burning cigarettes scattered over a lawn. Hiding his feelings from Hopkinson, Moore lifted his face mask. 'Longbow leader. That's all we can do. Let's go home.'

He had barely finished speaking when a lone Mosquito dived past him. Certain that Anna had been killed or captured Harvey had no intention of leaving the valley until the cause of her sacrifice was found. Afraid for his safety Moore banked after him. 'Harvey! You're disobeying orders. Get back into formation!'

He expected no answer nor did he receive one for a full six seconds. Then Harvey's eager shout made him start. 'Moore! Something's happening down here. Come and take a look.'

Ordering Young to keep watch, Moore dived into the flak after the Yorkshireman. He saw D-Danny three thousand feet below, banking steeply towards one of the handkerchief-sized Alpine meadows. With two columns of smoke rising from the meadow Moore thought for a moment that two bombs had fallen on it. Then Hopkinson, who was gazing through binoculars at the field, turned his sharp face towards him.

'They're hay stacks, skipper. Someone's set them alight.'

The throttles of A-Apple nearly went through the gate as Moore rammed them forward. As the meadow grew larger in the windscreen he saw that two stooks of hay were pouring off black smoke. A shadow swept across the ground as at zero height Harvey flew over the meadow and waggled his wings violently. As the Yorkshireman swept away Moore saw a tiny figure crouched beside a stook of hay wave back. Hopkinson, staring through the binoculars, saw something else. 'Soldiers, skipper! Coming out of the woods on the other side!'

Moore switched on his fire-and-safe button. The party of soldiers, six in all, had now run out of the meadow. Urged by an N.C.O. they dropped down and took aim at the girl fifty yards from them. As she tried to find cover Moore opened fire. His first burst, fired at extreme range, served only to draw the soldiers' attention. His second burst, fired from less than two hundred yards, caught them as they were running back towards the trees. Like blades of grass beneath a reaper's scythe they were flung in all directions. Keeping his thumb on the button until the last moment Moore drew back the stick and went rocketing up the wooded mountainside.

Across the valley Harvey had banked steeply to return to the field and was in time to see Moore's devastating attack on the soldiers. As he came raging back he saw the girl wave her acknowledgment to Moore and run across to a fourth stook of hay. Three were now burning and as Harvey skimmed the field smoke began pouring from the fourth. For a moment, in spite of Blackburn's imploring glance, it seemed Harvey would attempt to land on the tiny field. Then, as the girl waved her arms frantically and pointed towards the woods, he abandoned the suicidal idea and headed across the valley.

In A-Apple Hopkinson was jabbing an excited finger downwards. 'It's the French Resistance trick, skipper. Giving us a bearing.'

Moore saw he was right. The four fires, set in converging lines, were aiming at an imaginary point deep in the forest. Debating whether to bring the squadron back into the valley, Moore decided there was time for that if his own attack failed. Giving Young instructions to keep the squadron out of flak range unless he was shot down, Moore turned to Hopkinson. 'Have you got a fix?' When the Cockney nodded Moore put A-Apple's nose down.

Below, the track of Harvey's Mosquito could be traced by the brightly-coloured pins of tracer that were trying to spear it. Aware their attackers were on the scent at last, the enemy gun crews were throwing everything at D-Danny. Black-faced and tormented, Harvey was driving the plane through the torrent of fire as if by will-power alone. Blackburn, helpless in his role of navigator, could do nothing but cling to his seat and pray. A deafening explosion almost turned the Mosquito over; a 37mm. shell tore a gaping hole in its starboard wing. Yet ironically it was a light machine gun which neither man saw that did the most damage. Opening up as D-Danny swept past, it stitched a line of holes the full length of the fuselage. Flung against his safety straps, Blackburn stared with disbelief at the charred holes in his overalls. Harvey, grunting with pain and doubling up like a boxer receiving a blow in the stomach, recovered and went raging on.

An isolated farmhouse appeared. It would be years before men would learn the secret of its hinged roof and the motor testing beds that lay beneath it. But as Harvey swept north of it he caught a glimpse of two green, cylindrical wagons standing beneath the firs. As the stricken Blackburn tried to draw his attention to them, Harvey put D-Danny into a climbing turn and came sweeping back.

Like some enormous green snake hiding from predators, the train was stretched out beneath the trees almost as far as the farmhouse. Switching on his firing button Harvey pushed the stick right forward. Still out of range Moore called an urgent warning.

'Harvey, you're too low. Attack at extreme range.'

Nothing but a bullet in the brain would have diverted Harvey at that moment. This was the prize Anna was risking her life for and Anna was going to have that prize. As the first wagon entered his sights he thumbed the firing button and held it down. The ashen-faced Blackburn closed his eyes as the Mosquito flew along the line of wagons. Twenty cannon shells a second, packed with high explosive, smashed through the skin of the tankers and ran on in a series of bright explosions. Overalled figures, working on couplings beneath the train, gave hoarse cries of warning and ran for their lives into the trees.

To Moore and Hopkinson time seemed to slow down in the breathless moment that followed. They could see Harvey's fire spearing into the trees but at first without result as if the rearmost wagons had already been drained of fuel. Then an odd cascade of liquid fire squirted into the sky. With black smoke pluming from its edges, it resembled a bizarre fountain. The pyrotechnical display seemed to last for seconds before a shimmering flash ran through the trees below. It was followed by a ball of fire that expanded at terrifying speed in all directions. The blast that followed it, a deafening peal of thunder, shot A-Apple upwards as if on the back of some gigantic lift. As Moore righted the aircraft a dense monolith of smoke, shot by fresh explosions and debris, began to cover the floor of the valley. Glancing at his watch Moore saw it was 14.14. Incredibly they had been over the valley only eleven minutes. About to order Hopkinson to send the message that would transform Davies from a shattered man to a euphoric one, Moore saw the navigator was already tapping the Morse key.

The R/T channel was swamped by shouts of triumph from the orbiting crews. Warning them not to relax their vigilance Moore turned again towards the dense column of smoke. Guessing his intent Hopkinson showed scepticism. 'He'd never survive that explosion, skipper. Not from that height.'

Parabolas of coloured shells soaring up among the black smoke proved Hopkinson wrong. Flak crews who had survived the tanker explosion had now recovered and were trying to take their revenge on D-Danny. Like a naked man who had lost half his skin in a fire the Mosquito was a hideous sight. Most of its paint was burnt away, great holes gaped in its wings, and its tail fin and one elevator were only naked spars. As Moore, ignoring the flak, drew in closer he could see Harvey's head lolling against the heat-blistered canopy.

'Harvey! Are you hurt?'

The Yorkshireman sounded dazed and far away. 'Aye. I've been hit.'

'What about Blackburn?'

'He got it too. But he's alive.'

'Can you make it home?'

There was no reply. A second wave of massive explosions was hurling up trees and debris from the tortured valley floor but Harvey had eyes only for the empty meadow in which the hay stooks were still smoking. Moore's voice turned sharp. 'She got away. In any case there's nothing more you can do. You've Blackburn to think about. Head for home and we'll give you cover.'

For a long moment D-Danny went circling the field. Then, with immense reluctance, it began to climb painfully from the valley where the rest of the squadron closed around it. Like a party of soldiers carrying away a wounded and valued comrade they rose and disappeared into the veil of clouds.

CHAPTER 33

Davies waited to hear no more than the word 'Crispin'. Like a man reprieved from execution he swung round on the onlookers who had risen to their feet. 'They've done it! They've bloody well done it!'

Adams was the first to find his voice. 'But how, sir? They'd already dropped their bombs.'

In his euphoria Davies forgot code words and everything else. 'The girl got a message through to them at the last minute. So someone went down and strafed the train.'

Adams' jubilation came to a dead halt. 'Who, sir?'

Davies turned back to the corporal. 'Does the message say?'

'Yes, sir. It was Flight Commander Harvey.'

Davies jerked violently. 'Who?'

'Flight Commander Harvey, sir.'

'My Christ,' Davies said blankly.

Henderson pushed forward towards the corporal. 'Is he dead?'

'The message doesn't mention losses, sir.'

'He must be dead,' Adams said.

'He'll get a decoration,' Davies told them. 'Posthumous or otherwise.'

As the two men stared at him, Staines's gravelly voice drew their attention. Alone alongside his telephone, the big American was frowning heavily. 'So the Rhine Maiden won't get airborne and my boys haven't given their lives for nothing. Congratulations.'

The bright-eyed Davies hurried over to him and shook his hand. 'Sorry, sir. We were carried away for a moment. It was your lads who made it possible for us to get there. We're deeply grateful.'

The mollified Texan shook hands with the Brigadier and Henderson in turn. 'In the long run we're the ones who'll profit. Those rockets would have knocked hell out of us if they'd gone into production. I'm putting your whole outfit up for Congressional Commendation, Henderson. In the meantime, if any of your boys get thirsty and drop into our airfields, I've a hunch they'll do all right.'

Even his Scots phlegm could not hide Henderson's delight as he nodded at the phone the American was picking up. 'Thank you, sir. What's the latest news from your end?'

'The serviceable ships are on their way to North Africa. It's the crippled ships we're concerned about. They've no choice but to turn back for home and it's a hell of a way before they get fighter cover.'

'How many are there, sir?'

'Twenty.' The Texan did not notice the look Davies gave Henderson as he put his ear to the receiver again. 'And some are in bad shape. The way the Krauts are hammering 'em we'll lucky if half of 'em get home.'

After a whispered word to Davies, the Brigadier walked over to a red telephone at the far end of the room. Adams was the nearest to him and although the soldier's clipped voice was low, its semi-reverential tone suggested a distinguished presence on the other end of the line. 'Hello, sir. Yes, the news is good – they've done it again. A complete success as far as we can gather. Losses? We don't know yet but I'll keep you informed. Thank you very much, sir.'

In the minutes that followed Adams' feelings were mixed – jubilation at the squadron's success was tempered by lack of details of its losses. Nor could Adams, a humanitarian, banish from his mind the gruesome deaths hundreds of workers must have suffered in the underground factory as the raging fuel swept in. Another harrowing factor was the stream of reports Staines was receiving about his crippled B.17s. Even Davies, once his euphoria had cooled, showed sympathy as he sat down alongside the Texan.

'Where are your boys now, sir?'

'Just short of the Rhine. Still a long way from fighter cover.'

'I shouldn't worry too much. Things mightn't turn out as badly as you think.'

Adams felt the resentful glance Staines gave him was justified. Jumping to his feet as if too excited to stay in one place for long, Davies went over to Henderson and began whispering to him, both men continually throwing glances at the American. Two minutes later a sharp exclamation from Staines sent both men hurrying over to him. 'Well, I'm a sonofabitch!'

Eager red spots were back in Davies' cheeks. 'What is it, sir?'

The Texan remained glued to the telephone for another fifteen seconds. Then his tough, incredulous face lifted up to the grinning Davies. 'My crippled B.17s report those boys of yours have caught up with them and are giving them fighter cover. You never told me this was part of the deal.'

Davies transferred his twinkling glance to Henderson. 'We weren't certain they'd have any ammo left after the Rhine Maiden affair. But assuming they had, we made the private point to Moore that as your lads had carried the can all the way there, it would be a nice gesture if we carried it part of the way back.' As Staines grinned appreciatively, Davies felt that in the circumstances an American-ism would not be out of place. 'In other words, sir, we're an outfit that likes to pay its debts.'

From above, the tightly-packed formation of B.17s looked like a school of wounded whales being attacked by killer sharks. Bleeding from a hundred wounds, they were defending themselves desperately but the attackers were hungry and ruthless. Boring in, snapping and tearing, they would strike at one aircraft until, dazed and blinded, it lost the security of its own kind. Immediately half a dozen shark-like fighters would close in for the kill.

Two units of German fighters were engaging the crippled B.17s. One was a Focke Wulf squadron recently withdrawn from the Italian front: the other was Hans Klaus's 110 squadron, thrown into action at last. On first sighting the formation of B.17s the young pilot's mouth had begun watering. Here, surely, was his tenth kill at last. Picking out a Fortress he went after it like a gun dog after a wounded boar.

It was a reckless attack that exposed Klaus's inexperience against the heavily-armed B.17s. Although some of their comrades were wounded or dead, the remaining American gunners were still full of fight and the hail of fire that greeted Klaus made him dive hurriedly for safety. Flushed with embarrassment and anger he remembered the instructions given him before take-off and turned west to catch the formation head-on as it made for home.

At the same moment Klaus turned west, Moore sighted the air battle ahead. His order made Millburn clamp his jaw in satisfaction. 'I think it's time we showed the Yanks our appreciation. Green Section Leader, prepare to attack. I'll stay and give Harvey cover.'

As Teddy Young led the squadron into the sun, Moore dropped behind Harvey. From the rear the Yorkshireman's aircraft was a hideous sight with its parboiled skin and skeleton holes.

'How are you feeling, Frank?'

The man's gruff voice gave nothing away. 'I'm all right. But the kid came round so I had to give him morphia.'

The two Mosquitoes were now four thousand feet above the air battle. At any moment Moore expected an attack but the fighters seemed drunk on the blood of the mammoths they were engaging. In his earphones Moore heard an Australian yell. 'Green section leader to Longbow. Pick yourself a target and let's go.'

Freed from their bombloads, the Mosquitoes came dropping out of the sun like a pack of gannets. Believing no hostile fighters within seventy miles, the Germans were caught by surprise. On the first strike three of them went reeling earthwards trailing smoke and fire. In T-Tommy Millburn was displaying relief that was near to ecstasy as he came climbing back and fastened his sights on a 110. Out-manoeuvred by the faster Mosquito, the Messerschmitt's propellers looked like waving arms in the sunlight as it tried to escape. Closing in, Millburn fired a burst full into its tanks. The acrid smell of the explosion entered the cockpit as T-Tommy flew right through the fireball. Yelling his triumph Millburn went in search of a fresh victim while the American gunners, resigned to death even as they were putting up a gallant fight for life, rubbed their eyes in astonishment at seeing the British squadron reappear in the role of fighter escort.

This new phase of the battle had been reached when Klaus returned on his head-on course. His shout of disbelief made Fritz start. 'Mosquitoes! Where the hell have they come from?'

Acutely aware that without the cover of darkness a 110 was no match for a Mosquito, Fritz felt his heart miss a beat. 'If you're right, be careful how you attack.'

With his personal enmity against the aircraft impairing his judgment, Hans was contemptuous. 'What the hell for? We still outnumber them two to one.'

Although duels between fighters were taking place far from the Fortresses, the epicentre of the main battle was now some miles away. As he aimed to dive on the approaching B.17s, Klaus saw two Mosquitoes a thousand feet below and heading in his direction. Snatching up a pair of binoculars he took in the tattered condition of the leading aircraft. Immediately he turned into the sun. He could dive on the two Mosquitoes, continue on and wheel into the path of the B.17s. It was a safe enough manoeuvre; even if he missed the rearmost Mosquito it would not dare to leave its charge and follow him.

Fritz made an immediate protest. 'Our job is to go for the heavies.'

'We are going for them,' Hans grinned. 'We're just going to swat a Mosquito or two on our way.'

The vectors of the 110 and the Mosquitoes were shortening fast. Banking tightly and allowing the crippled plane and its escort to pass westward beneath him, Klaus confirmed their speed was less than his own. Manoeuvring with great care so that the sun was directly behind them, Klaus launched his attack.

It was the greatest mistake of the young German's life. With years of combat experience behind them, both Moore and Hopkinson had been keeping special watch on the sun. Moreover Hopkinson's binocular-sharp eyes had picked up the 110 seconds before A-Apple had been spotted by Klaus. Bracing himself, Moore spoke quietly to Harvey.

'We've got company, Frank. Break when I tell you.'

Above them a blurred, black shape was growing rapidly larger in the dazzling orb of the sun. Moore waited another two seconds, then shouted his warning. 'Corkscrew starboard!'

Sluggish on its controls, Harvey's Mosquito fell into a side-slip as he swung it away but the manoeuvre was still effective. As Moore banked to port three lines of tracer appeared past his wingtip. It was followed a couple of seconds later by the 110, already banking steeply in a desperate attempt not to overshoot.

But in the deadly way of air combat, there was to be no second chance. No longer aided by darkness, the 110 was as doomed as a rabbit chased by a stoat as the graceful, more manoeuvrable Mosquito closed up behind. In vain Klaus hurled it about the sky. Inexorably its tailplane came creeping into Moore's sights. The fuselage followed and then the cockpit canopy. Steadying the Mosquito like the precision instrument it was, Moore fired a single burst. The 110 crumpled and began spinning earthwards, and one of the war's many millions of minute issues was resolved. Fritz Neumann would never learn if his mother was to survive her embolism – in fact she was to outlive him by only two days. And it was now very certain that Hans Klaus would not attend his wedding wearing the Iron Cross.

CHAPTER **34**

Pouring smoke from both its starboard engines the B.17 lurched drunkenly from the tight formation. As its pilot tried to bring it under control, two Focke Wulfs attacked from opposite sides. With five gunners already slumped over their weapons, the end was near. Cannon shells blasted huge holes in the massive wings and tore off the weakened tail assembly. With air screaming eerily inside its fuselage, the B.17 began its long fall to earth. Incredibly a gunner in the upper turret, his parachute pack blown to ribbons by gunfire, went on firing defiantly as the two Focke Wulfs followed the bomber down.

It was the first B.17 to be lost since 633 Squadron had come to the Americans' aid but all the Mosquito crew knew it would not be the last unless help came soon. In spite of the wing tanks they had carried to Bavaria, the extra demands of combat were a massive drain on fuel reserves. Two Mosquitoes had already been lost and there were wounded among the surviving crews. Gabby would no longer need to fake wounds to glamorize his image: blood from a wound in his thigh was splattered over the cockpit floor and on Millburn's overalls. Young Flemming of B Flight had been struck on the head by a cannon shell and his hideously mutilated body kept nudging his ashen-faced pilot. Blood was running down St Claire's left arm, but the calm young artist continued to attack every Focke Wulf that came within range. The battle had now moved into France but the enemy fighters had been reinforced by a crack *gruppe* from the Paris area and the odds were now heavily in their favour.

Six miles to the north Moore was keeping an anxious eye on the battle. Three hundred yards ahead of him Harvey's crippled plane was also causing him concern. During the last five minutes it had been flying an increasingly erratic course. As Hopkinson glanced at him, Moore addressed his microphone.

'You're off course again, Frank. Five degrees.'

A thick curse answered him. 'We're not going to make it, Moore. So get over and help the lads.'

'How badly wounded are you?'

'How the hell do I know?'

'Where is the wound?'

'Somewhere in my guts.'

'Are you losing much blood?'

'Enough.'

'Have you put a field dressing on it?'

'Yes, I've stuffed one down.' A pause and then another curse. 'Who the hell cares. Piss off, Moore. It doesn't matter.'

Above his face mask Moore's face was drenched in sweat. 'Stop talking like a bloody fool. If you don't care about your own life, think about Blackburn.'

There was a long pause and then D-Danny swung sullenly back on course. Alongside Moore, Hoppy gave a start and pointed ahead. A swarm of liverish black spots were swimming in the bright sky. Hopkinson snatched up a pair of binoculars, then sank back in relief. 'Spitfires. We've come into their range.'

A few seconds more and shark-like bodies, waggling their wings, streaked past and hurled themselves into the battle. Three flights of Thunderbolts were next. One detached itself and an American voice drawled in Moore's headphones. 'You don't mind my company, do you, Limey?'

'I love your company,' Moore told him. 'Stick around.'

The Thunderbolt began patrolling the sky a mile behind him. Seeing the Allied escort was now engaging the German fighters, Moore gave the order that brought relief to his hard-pressed crews. 'Longbow Leader to Green Section Leader. Disengage as soon as you can and take the boys home.'

Ahead D-Danny was flying like a bird with a damaged wing. 'Frank! You're losing height. Keep her nose up.' A pause, and then: 'Frank! Can you hear me?'

The voice that came sounded very distant and very drunk. 'What d'you want?'

'I said you're losing height.' Moore turned to Hopkinson. 'How much longer to the coast?'

The Cockney looked apologetic. 'At least fifteen minutes, skipper.'

Moore winced. 'Frank, listen. Use your oxygen. Turn it up until your head clears. All right?'

After a long pause Harvey's voice sounded louder. 'The Spitties have come, haven't they?'

'Yes. We should make it now.'

'That's good. The boys deserve it. Go and join 'em, Moore. You're sticking your necks out flying alone like this.'

'The same way you left Marsh?'

When there was only a growl for a reply, Moore went on: 'Frank, for all you know Anna could have got away. They'd have more than her to worry about when those tanks went up.'

To one as deep in despair as Harvey, an offer of hope had to be rejected swiftly unless it was to bring more pain. 'Why don't you piss off? And take that bloody Thunderbolt with you.'

Moore glanced back. The dogfight was now little more than a dancing cloud of gnats in the summer sky but the American fighter was still behind them. 'Anna wouldn't quit, Frank. If there's a way out of that valley she'll find it.'

There was a sudden snarl from D-Danny. 'What's that supposed to mean? That I'm quitting? All I'm saying, Moore, is that I can do without you.'

This was better, Moore thought. 'Why do you tykes love being independent? Does a piece of help stick in your gullet?'

'We get by without it, Moore. We always have.'

Hopkinson was peering into the sun. Glancing back Moore saw the Thunderbolt was coming down like a blunt-nosed meteor. As his earphones rattled to the American's warning, Moore yelled his own to Harvey. 'Break, Frank! Fast!'

Acting purely on reflex, Harvey sent D-Danny slithering round. Moore side-slipped to port, corrected A-Apple, and took a full deflection shot at the Focke Wulf that dived in front of him. The hastily-aimed burst missed but the German pilot, aware the Thunderbolt was also making towards him like an infuriated bulldog, continued to dive into the haze below. Harvey, who had lost nearly two thousand feet in the sharp action, was struggling to get D-Danny on an even keel again. Moore closed up behind him.

'You all right, Frank?'

He could hear Harvey's heavy breathing and knew loss of blood was taking its toll. 'Aye, I think so. Thanks.'

'Watch your compass. We're off course again.'

The slow minutes dragged past. With the Focke Wulf pilot deciding the air battle to the east offered easier pickings, the American pilot had climbed back into station again. In D-Danny Harvey's sunken eyes were half-closed. The rise and fall of the Mosquito, the limitless blue sky, the background drone of the engines, were all becoming a part of the light-headed world into which he was slipping. Beside him the unconscious, blood-stained figure of Blackburn was slumped against his straps. Frowning, Harvey turned to him. 'You're quiet, kid. What's wrong?'

Moore exchanged glances with Hopkinson. 'He's turning delirious. Frank, turn your oxygen full on!'

Once again the erratic course of D-Danny began to steady. 'That's better, Frank. Can you hear me all right?'

'Aye,' Harvey muttered. 'Just about.'

'What are your plans after the war?'

'After the war! What the hell are you talking about?'

'Like a job in my company?'

There was a silence, then a disbelieving laugh. '*Your* company! What as? A lavatory attendant?'

Moore relaxed again and smiled. 'No. I might do a bit better than that.'

'All right. A bloody sweeper. No thanks.'

The grim humour, coming from a tortured body, moved even the hard-bitten Hopkinson.

'Tell me what makes you tykes so bloody-minded?' Moore asked.

'That's easy.' Harvey had to pause for breath. 'It's living with toffee-nosed bastards like you. Turns anyone's milk sour.' Another pause for breath, and then: 'I thought you didn't fancy taking on your old man's job.'

'Who told you?'

'Anna.'

Moore's answer, although spontaneous, came as a surprise to himself. 'I seem to have different feelings about it now.'

'What's changed your mind?'

'I'm not sure. Maybe it's one or two people I've met recently.'

Hopkinson was jabbing a relieved finger at the coast that had appeared ahead. Although Moore knew its packed defences represented a last major threat, he had never seen a sweeter sight. 'We're nearly there, Frank. Hoppy will guide us through. Keep your oxygen full on and stick right on my tail.'

With A-Apple now in the lead the two Mosquitoes swept over the coastal defences. For half a minute the sky around them turned lethal with black explosions and lashing steel. Then they were through and the blue water of the Channel was below them. Dropping back Moore took guard behind Harvey again.

A few more minutes and the chalk cliffs of the Isle of Wight rose on their starboard side. They crossed the coast near Christchurch Harbour and swept over the green-quilted New Forest. By this time D-Danny was down to five hundred feet and slithering all over the sky. Sweating with fear for the Yorkshireman, Moore tried to revive him. 'Don't crack up now, Frank, for God's sake. Holmsley airfield's only a minute away.'

There was no reply. D-Danny's nose was dropping like the head of a weary animal. Taking a deep breath, Moore closed right in.

'Harvey, you cowardly Yorkshire bastard! Wake up or I'll splatter your guts all over the forest.'

Harvey jerked against his straps and his blood-streaked eyes opened. Behind him Moore switched on his firing button. Before the startled Hopkinson could protest he took careful aim and sent a long burst just below D-Danny's fuselage. A second burst ripped no more than fifteen feet above its canopy. Crash crews, standing by on the emergency landing field, heard the firing and gazed at one another in astonishment when they saw only two Mosquitoes sweeping towards them.

The reflexes of a man who had learned to fight almost before he could walk brought life back to Harvey. Ahead of him he saw the airfield with crash wagons and ambulances waiting alongside its east-west runway. With an enormous effort he steadied the Mosquito and made for it. As his eyes kept losing focus he heard Moore talking him down.

'Watch your flying speed as you lower your flaps. Left, left – steady. Your starboard wing's dropping. Up, up – that's better. Now back on the throttles. Back, back. . . .'

The runway was now streaming beneath Harvey like a black ribbon. Forty feet . . . thirty feet . . . he was sinking to a safe landing when his damaged control surfaces suddenly betrayed him and D-Danny dropped like a stone. A tyre burst immediately, pitching the plane off the runway and digging one wingtip into the soft ground. With a massive snapping of spars the Mosquito went spinning round and round, tearing off an engine in its gyrations.

Hoppy gave a horrified murmur: 'Oh, my God!' Ignoring traffic rules and personal safety, Moore put his wheels straight down on the runway. Behind him crash wagons, with sirens howling, were bearing down on the smoking wreckage. With brakes squealing and pouring off smoke, A-Apple bucketed down the field, turned off the runway, and came back at almost take-off speed.

As both men leapt out they saw a party of medical orderlies were carrying Harvey away from the crumpled cockpit while a crash crew struggled to free Blackburn. Leaving Hopkinson to see if the crew needed help, Moore ran on to the orderlies who were lowering Harvey on to a stretcher.

The Yorkshireman's appearance horrified him. His overalls were soaked in blood from the waist downwards and his face was hollow and ravaged with pain. He appeared unconscious but as Moore knelt beside him, his eyes opened.

'The kid! Young Blackburn! Is he all right?'

Glancing back Moore saw the crash party were bringing up metal-cutting equipment. Hopkinson, approaching from the wreckage, shook his head. Bending down again Moore tried to hide the scene from the supine Harvey. 'They're taking care of him, Frank. Lie back and relax.'

A medical orderly was trying to unbutton Harvey's blood-stained overalls. The Yorkshireman pushed him back impatiently. 'Wait a bloody minute!' Fumbling for Moore's hand he gripped it and drew the Squadron Commander closer. Seeing he wanted to keep his words private, Moore bent over him. 'What is it, Frank?'

The man's hoarse whisper seemed louder than a cry of pain. 'What do you really think? Could she have got away?'

Moore would gladly have lied his soul into Purgatory at that moment. 'Why not? After all that hell you raised, they'd be too busy to bother about her.'

The man's eyes, blood-streaked and oddly vulnerable, stared up at him. 'I'm grateful, Moore. Particularly for helping her.'

Over their heads airfoils were whining as battle-scarred Mosquitoes came in to unload their wounded and to re-fuel. Moore discovered the Yorkshireman was still gripping his hand. 'It's time they got you to hospital, Frank. I want you back on duty in three weeks' time.'

Harvey's lips quirked in grim humour. A Mosquito with a line of blackened shell holes running from a wing root to its cockade came bumping down the run-way less than thirty yards from them. The air disturbance swung one of the ambulance doors on its hinges. As the sound of the airfoils faded, Harvey's slurred voice arrested the orderlies who were about to pick up his stretcher.

'You know what I'd do, don't you, Moore? Probably the first day I was there.'

For a moment Moore thought he was turning delirious again. 'What, Frank?'

'I'd call a bloody strike, mate. You hadn't thought of that, had you?'

Moore gazed in awe at the ravaged, undefeated face. As the orderlies bent down again, there was a coughing roar from D-Danny followed by shouts of alarm as asbestos-clad figures scattered in all directions. Seeing the ball of fire that had suddenly engulfed the wreckage, Harvey cursed frantically and tried to push the orderlies aside. It took four men to hold him down as he fought to reach the fire that was incinerating Blackburn. Feeling deathly sick and telling himself it was caused by the stench of burning glycol and rubber, Moore knelt alongside Harvey again.

'I'm sorry, Frank. They did all they could. He didn't suffer. They think he was dead when you landed.'

Astonishingly, a muffled sob broke from the Yorkshireman. For a moment the column of black smoke seemed to darken the entire sky for Moore. Then, taking a deep breath, he rose and faced the senior medical orderly.

'Tell your doctors they've got to save this man's life. Make certain they under-stand that. Do you hear me?'

The N.C.O. glanced at his face, then looked away in embarrassment. 'We'll do our best, sir.'

Moore could not control his trembling. 'You'll do more than your best! You'll save his life!'

It was Hopkinson who hastily drew him away. 'It'll be all right, skipper. They'll take good care of him.'

The orderlies lifted the stretcher into the ambulance and closed the doors. Moore turned to watch the vehicle as it drove away. Ammunition was now ex-ploding in D-Danny, a lethal pyrotechnical display that brought shouts of warning from the crash crews. When Moore took no notice, Hopkinson touched his arm.

'Hadn't we better get moving, skipper? Most of the boys are down by this time.'

Moore's eyes remained on the departing ambulance. It took another anxious reminder from Hopkinson before he turned and took in the dense smoke and the bursting cannon shells. Giving the Cockney a curt nod, he started across the airfield towards the Control Tower.

Standing aside for the Brigadier to enter the staff car, Davies glanced at the two men standing on the kerb. No gnome or gremlin could have looked more maliciously wicked than the small Air Commodore at that moment.

'Pity I can't stay for the party. But think of me when I get back to Group tomorrow. The bastards wanted to shove you back into Main Force! I can't wait to see their faces now.'

With that Davies jumped gleefully into the car. Henderson gave Adams a rueful grin as the car disappeared through the station gates. 'See that look in his eyes. He's had a successful operation and this time the casualties aren't too heavy. That means in the future he'll volunteer us for every sticky job that comes along.'

The same thought had occurred to Adams. 'Eight dead and three wounded – I wouldn't call them light casualties.'

'No, but he expected far higher ones. He told me so this morning.'

'He nearly got them,' Adams said. 'If the girl had given her signal earlier and Moore had kept to the original plan, they'd have been shot down like partridges. Our estimates of the number of guns sited along the valley were miles out.'

'Could she have done it deliberately?'

'No. If she'd known there were so many guns she'd have told us. She probably ran foul of the soldiers on her way to the field and was late in escaping from them.'

Black against the evening afterglow the Mosquitoes looked like resting birds on the airfield. Although it was growing too dark for them to be seen, Adams knew that four of the dispersal points were empty. Down the road the sound of music and high revelry was coming from the Mess as the crews celebrated their victory. Davies had stood everyone down except essential personnel and there were similar celebrations in the N.C.O.s' and airmen's Messes. In the shadows between two huts opposite something moved and a moment later the figure of Sam slunk dejectedly across the road. As Adams called its name, the dog gave a whimper of recognition and made towards him.

'He keeps going back to Harvey's billet,' Adams said, bending down to stroke the dog. 'Did Moore phone the hospital again?'

'Yes. Harvey's had an operation and they gave the usual spiel that he's doing as well as can be expected. We're going to phone again in a couple of hours.'

An outburst of cheering floated towards them. Adams glanced in its direction. 'Moore has gone to the party, hasn't he?'

Henderson nodded. 'The boys didn't give him a choice this time. They practically carried him there. Not that he appeared that keen,' the Scot added as an afterthought. 'This business of Harvey and the girl seems to have got under his skin.'

355

Adams was rubbing the dog's ears. Before the senior officers had left, he and Henderson had shared a bottle of malt whisky with them. Never one who could take much alcohol without the effects showing, Adams was showing them now. 'It's a funny thing about those two. In a way they both had a love-hate for their countries. I suppose that was one of the things that first drew them together.'

Henderson's eyebrows knitted. 'Love-hate?'

'Yes. Harvey's hardly rapturous about our society, is he? And Anna hates the Nazis.' Needing someone to talk to tonight, Adams did not notice the big Scot's expression. 'She was a lovely girl. But I know I'm going to wish she'd never come here.'

Overhead the heavy drone of engines was moving across the late evening sky. Lost to Adams' meaning, the practical Henderson gave an impatient grunt. 'We'd have been bloody pushed to do the job without her, wouldn't we?'

Behind his thick spectacles Adams looked surprised. 'Oh, I didn't mean that. I meant that after a few years of war you manage to convince yourself that all the people on the other side are bad. After knowing Anna you can never think that again. So she's made everything that bit more difficult.'

Thinking what a load of bullshit Adams could talk after a few drinks, Henderson decided it was a night to be charitable. 'Don't go soft on me, Frank, for Christ's sake. There's a lot more war to go yet.'

Adams winced. 'Do you think so?'

'I'm sure of it. Jerry might be retreating here and there but he'll fight all the harder when we get near his frontiers.'

'I suppose you're right,' Adams muttered dejectedly. Another outburst of cheering down the road made the dog lift its head and bark. Taken to the confessional by three large glasses of whisky, Adams forgot whom he was talking to as he nodded at the source of the sound. 'That's where I'll be in a couple of minutes. And I won't be thinking of our dead boys or the dead Yanks or the dead Germans. I won't even be thinking about Harvey and Anna. I'll be downing the drinks they pass me, singing the old songs, and I'll feel so proud of this squadron and what the lads have done I'll feel fifteen feet tall.'

'Is that bad?' Henderson asked, staring at him.

To his dismay Adams realized he was going to be misunderstood again. 'I don't mean I shouldn't be proud of the squadron or the boys themselves. They're a fine crowd and they've done a wonderful job. It's just that I don't feel one should. . . .' Suddenly realizing that whatever he said tonight would sound wrong, Adams' voice trailed away. 'I think I've had too many glasses of whisky.'

It was a capitulation that brought Henderson relief. 'You know what's wrong with you, Frank? You're only half-sloshed. Have a few more drams and it'll all swing back into place again. Now let's get over there before those young buggers drink the place dry.'

Trying to match the big Scot's strides as they headed for the Mess, and with Sam pattering at his heels, Adams glanced up again at the evening sky. Another bomber was trundling across it, its passage only visible by the stars it extinguished. Soon it would join the main stream that would already be sweeping across the skies of occupied Europe. The armada would reach its target without undue difficulty because night one thousand, four hundred and thirty-nine of the war was calm and starlit. For the same reason enemy night fighters would have no difficulty in finding the Lancasters and Stirlings. As he pushed into the deafening, smoky carousal that was the Mess, Adams was reflecting what fine sport the War Gods would have tonight.

It took only two of the large glasses of whisky that were thrust at him from all sides to bring about the change in equilibrium that Henderson had predicted. Fine sport or not, Adams reminded himself, the bastards still wouldn't be having it off with those Rhine Maidens in the months ahead. Eyes glinting triumphantly behind his spectacles, he carefully located the piano and steered Sam and himself towards it. Half a minute later, his head back and his cheeks pink, Adams was singing the roof off with the best of them.

OPERATION CRUCIBLE

To

Mac, Boy, Pat, and Monica

with love and happy memories of Clifton

CHAPTER I

The 21cm rocket struck the B.17 full on its starboard inner engine. The explosion was followed by a ball of black smoke. A few seconds later the wing sheared away and the Fortress began spinning earthwards. Three parachutes blossomed out into the tracer-streaked sky. Within seven men still trapped inside, the B.17 disappeared into the clouds that hid the earth.

The clear sky above was filled with the frenzy of battle. Over 150 B.17s, flying in three tight boxes, were pouring out contrails that spread back as far as the eye could see. Darting in front and around them like swifts avid for food were countless German fighters. Black threads of tracer criss-crossed the sky like some surrealistic spider's web. Columns of smoke, ephemeral monuments to shot-down comrades, shredded in the winds of the stratosphere as the remaining B.17s fought for survival.

The enemy units attacking them, products of experience and German ingenuity, were formidable. The 21cm rockets, designed to create havoc among tightly-packed formations, were carried by Me.110D 'destroyers'. Mixed in with them were veteran units of Focke Wulf 190s heavily armed with 20mm cannon. Formidable enough on their own, these units were augmented by aircraft from the 3rd Air Force based in France. The Americans had made another penetration deep into the heart of the Fatherland. Every effort was being made to punish them for their temerity.

A new wave of destroyers was sweeping head on towards the B.17s. At 1,000 metres lances of smoke and flame darted from their wings. No attempt was made to aim at specific Fortresses: the enemy pilots knew, as with duck-shooting, that the laws of chance guaranteed some hits among such a dense target.

Struck just ahead of the pilot's cockpit, one B.17 swung off course like a blinded animal and crashed into the starboard wing of a companion. Locked in a tangle of broken spars and sheared metal, the two huge aircraft went spinning helplessly down. No parachutes emerged from the wreckage and a massive explosion before the aircraft had fallen two thousand feet made certain none would.

A second B.17 had ten feet of its port wing severed. Lurching perilously, it seemed about to slide to certain death when its desperate pilot brought up the wing by strength and prayer. Ignoring the danger of collision, his comrades on either side closed in to give him protection.

Since leaving their fighter escort on the Franco-German frontier the B.17s had been under constant enemy attack and during the long morning over half of them had sustained damage. Jagged holes let in icy blasts of air that froze bare hands to metal. Oil ran like black blood from severed pipe lines and formed slippery pools on the metal floor. Soot and blackened metal showed where frantic men had extinguished fires. As gunners strove to follow the lightning turns of the German fighters, their feet slipped on hundreds of spent shells. Above oxygen masks, paths of sweat ran whitely through the stains of cordite and oil. A few men found relief in cursing the leaders who had sent them against such massive odds. Most men, numbed by the discomfort and the fury of battle, fought on mechanically and doubted if safety would ever be reached. They had, they felt certain, already fought a thousand years.

Yet, in the way of air combat, the end came suddenly. At one moment the sky seemed full of deadly hornets, in the next it was empty as the German pilots, sighting the eager Spitfires and Thunderbolts at their rendezvous, withdrew out of range. Cowardice played no part in their withdrawal. Aware that the Allies were attempting to bleed them to death by attrition, the Luftwaffe was under the strictest orders to avoid contact with enemy fighters unless the occasion was justifiable.

Justification was clearly impossible here. A continuance of the attack that had carried the German fighters within range of the Spitfires and Thunderbolts would have resulted in as many losses to the Luftwaffe as to the Allies, and the mathematics of 1943 did not permit such extravagance. With the Allies still possessing no long-range fighter that could escort the USAAF on its raids into Germany, it was better sense to wait until the B.17s once again ventured into the Fatherland. The hundreds of B.17 wrecks that already littered Germany bore witness to the success of this policy.

Yet although the German withdrawal brought relief to the hard-pressed crews, for some the ordeal was not over, as wounded men fought to keep crippled aircraft flying. Back at an airfield in East Anglia two men were out on the field watching the grim assembly of crash wagons and ambulances. One of the men, bearded and wearing a greatcoat with the shoulder flashes of a war correspondent, was Ernest Lambert, American novelist.

A middle-aged man, short and stocky of build with a square aggressive face, Lambert's appearance did nothing to suggest he was one of America's lions of literature. His rise to world fame had been extraordinary. Until 1936 his name had been unknown to the public at large. Then MGM had filmed his fifth novel, *The Rains of Rajapur*. The film had been a massive success and from then onwards every book of Lambert's had received rapturous acclaim. With his work extolling the virtues of self-reliance and manliness, it was hardly surprising that the Hearst newspaper empire, for a fee that was said to be astronomical, had claimed his services for the duration of the war. The fact that most of Lambert's syndicated articles to date had either implied or stated that America's Allies were not pulling their weight appeared in no way to have affected his standing with the Hearst empire. Indeed suggestions had appeared in the American Press, brave suggestions because Lambert was a formidable adversary, that this very chauvinism was the real reason for his engagement.

His companion was the Station Intelligence Officer, George Hodgkinson. New to his appointment and awed by Lambert's reputation, Hodgkinson had felt it incumbent on him to offer Lambert a seat on the mission. His vague surprise at Lambert's curt retort that he had more to do than sit on his ass over Germany had not been assuaged by the constant sight of the correspondent propping up the Mess bar.

With the massing of the crash wagons and ambulances along the runways complete, an apprehensive silence had now fallen over the airfield. Taking his eyes off the eastern sky, Lambert turned to Hodgkinson.

'Why aren't they getting Mustang support?' His voice had the abrasive accent of a New Englander.

Hodgkinson, stringy in build and aware of it, showed some discomfort at the question. 'We find they're underpowered, sir. The Alison engines only develop 1,150 h.p.'

'I know that. But what about those fitted with Merlins?'

'They're O.K. In fact they'll outfly a 109. But we haven't enough to provide a worthwhile escort.'

He received an aggressive stare. 'Maybe you haven't. But what about the British?'

Hodgkinson misunderstood him. 'They've been providing escorts, sir. They're doing it now over France.'

'What the hell's the use over France? It's over Germany we need them.'

'Their Spitfires haven't the range, sir. They were built for Metropolitan defence, not escort duty.'

'That's why I'm asking about Merlin-powered Mustangs. The British have enough by this time. Why aren't they using them?'

Hodgkinson, who had no idea and in any case had a couple of drinking buddies in the RAF, was grateful for the siren that took away the need for an answer. Harsh and portentous, it caused an apprehensive stir among the onlookers who were standing beside the crash wagons. Engines began revving and a green Very light soared up from the Control tower.

Fifteen seconds later a far off drone could be heard. It grew heavier and men pointed at the eastern sky. Black specks, some trailing smoke, had appeared and became larger by the second. With at least half their number damaged, the intact B.17s began to orbit the airfield to give them landing priority.

The air was now shuddering under the impact of fifty engines. The first B.17 had gingerly manoeuvred to the western side of the airfield and was settling down to land. Airfoils whining, it swept past the two watching men and set its wheels on the runway. As its tyres screamed and screamed again, spray came up in clouds from the wet tarmac. As the pilot applied the brakes the B.17 slewed to the left and ran into the grass. It was the moment for two crash wagons and an ambulance to speed across the runway and halt alongside the smoking engines. Within seconds foam was spraying on to them and the danger of fire averted.

With a nod of approval Lambert turned his attention to the second B.17 which, wobbling perilously, was settling down on the same runway. As it drew to a halt, an ambulance and a crash wagon raced up. Asbestos-clad figures climbed into the rear gunner's shattered cupola and hacked their way inside. A minute later they lowered something in a sheet to the medical orderlies below.

The third B.17 was a grotesque sight. Half of its tail fin was shot away, huge holes gaped in its fuselage, and the entire port wingtip was missing. Moreover its undercarriage was hanging down like a bird's broken claw. Both men ducked as its shadow slanted obliquely over them. Frantic red Very lights from the Control Tower were calling for a second approach but the wounded crew, with a shattered radio, were in no condition to respond. Fighting pain, loss of blood, and an aircraft that seemed held together only by will power, they had reached home and could do no more. As the wheels missed the runway and touched the grass there was a scream of shearing rivets as the undercarriage collapsed. The aircraft was thrown into the air by impact, only to crash down as heavily again. For fifty yards it skidded forward, throwing off mud and pieces of metal. Then its nose dug in and the huge machine stood on end. For a moment it appeared about to somersault, then the fuselage crashed back with an impact that shook the ground. As Hodgkinson muttered 'Oh, my God', there was a coughing roar and a fireball that hid the entire wreck from view.

'Oh, my God!' Hodgkinson said again and began to run forward. Lambert caught his arm.

'Forget it. There's nothing you can do.'

The fireball was swelling like a giant balloon. Incredibly, thin screams could be heard through the thunder of engines and the howl of sirens. Hodgkinson looked as if he were going to be sick. 'Some of them must still be alive.'

Looking as shaken as the Intelligence officer, Lambert turned away. 'I want to use your Communications Room. Right now.'

Hodgkinson looked embarrassed. 'We never allow outside contact until the debriefing is over, sir. It's standard procedure throughout the Command.'

'I'm an official war correspondent, Major. That means I have a priority on communications.'

Hodgkinson's glance in the direction of the Control Tower was a plea for help. 'They'd never let you in without the C.O.'s permission, sir.'

'Then get his goddamned permission. I've got a story I want in tomorrow's papers.'

Hodgkinson's eyes were drawn back to the B.17 inferno. 'He'll be busy right now. But I'll do my best.'

'You do that, Major. Because there'll be some hard questions asked if this story isn't sent.'

Smoke from burning rubber and oil made Hodgkinson gag as he hurried away. Lambert watched him for a moment, then started towards the Signals Centre. His walk suggested an incensed and revengeful bantam cock.

CHAPTER 2

The camouflaged staff car pulled up outside the Administration Block of RAF Sutton Craddock with a squeal of brakes. The Air Commodore who jumped out was a small man with the alert movements of a squirrel. Wearing no overcoat although there was a chill in the late September wind, he nodded to his Waaf driver and marched briskly up the neat path that led to the door. A sergeant and a corporal, watching him from the safety of the Guardhouse, grimaced at one another. The appearance of Air Commodore Davies at Sutton Craddock rarely failed to denote trouble of one kind or another.

Trousers flapping round his legs, Davies hurried down a corridor. An Aircraftsman Second Class, on his knees scrubbing the linoleum floor, saw him coming and hastily drew his bucket aside. Ignoring his salute, Davies strode past and halted outside the C.O.'s office. Seeing the door was ajar, he gave it a single rap of his knuckles and pushed his way inside.

There were three men inside the office and it was clear they were all expecting Davies. The big, broad-shouldered man who stepped forward was Henderson, the Station C.O. Nicknamed 'Pop' by the squadron at large, he was a middle-aged, benign Scot who had taken command of the station after the death of Barrett in the Swartfjord. He was experiencing his usual ambivalence at the sight of the choleric Davies. The Air Commodore's terse phone call that morning had by implication warned him that Davies was coming up with some specialist mission for the squadron. He could find no complaint in that: his élite unit of Mosquitoes existed for that purpose and Davies brought with him a devotion to duty and a single-mindedness that the Scot, a professional airman himself, could only commend. His one reservation was that sometimes Davies could be over-zealous in achieving his objectives.

The other men were a contrast in types. The portly officer in his middle-forties was Frank Adams, the Station Intelligence officer. With his build and thick-lensed spectacles he could not be accused of looking a military figure, a fact the self-critical Adams had long accepted. Not a professional airman, and blessed or cursed with a vivid imagination, Adams' feelings towards Davies were more loaded. Although he shared Henderson's respect for the man's drive and enthusiasm, he occasionally deplored the ruthlessness that could weigh success against the lives of men who were his friends. At the same time Adams knew it was those very objective qualities that made Davies such an effective field commander.

The third man, considerably younger than his two fellow officers, was Ian

Moore, Squadron Commander. With a small combat scar on his right cheek, Moore was slimly-built with a fresh complexion and fair, wavy hair. As always his uniform was immaculately tailored. The recent inheritor of his father's chain of footwear shops, Moore was not short of money and more than a penny of it went into keeping him the best dressed officer on the station. Yet his was no case of the frills out-matching the package. Moore was an ex-Pathfinder and the ribbons of the DSO and Bar, and DFC, and the more unusual American Congressional Medal of Honour beneath his pilot's brevet testified to his outstanding combat record. Davies, by pulling strings as only the wily Air Commodore knew how, had worked his transfer from Pathfinders and given him command of 633 Squadron after its near annihilation in Swartfjord. Although at this time internal strife had been bringing the squadron to the point of disintegration, by the use of charm that could only be described as charismatic and leadership that had been inspired, Moore had welded the squadron into an élite unit again that had eventually destroyed the notorious Rhine Maiden establishment in far-off Bavaria. It was a feat that had gained for Moore a respect from the crews that had previously been given only to Roy Grenville, the leader of the Swartfjord raid who was now a German prisoner of war. The destruction of the Rhine Maiden plant had also earned Moore and the squadron the gratitude of American bomber crews who were only too aware of the losses they would have suffered had the proximity-fused rockets ever reached production.

Henderson's voice had a slight Highland burr. 'Good morning, sir. You're looking well.'

It was not Davies' way to indulge in formalities when the pressure was on. Pulling a newspaper from his briefcase he slapped it down on the desk in front of the Group Captain. 'I don't suppose you've seen this, have you, Jock?'

Henderson picked up the newspaper curiously. 'The *New York Daily Mirror*? No, I haven't. They don't stock it around these parts.'

Davies ignored the gentle sarcasm. 'Take a look at page 3.'

As Henderson opened the newspaper, Moore and Adams saw him give a slight start. As he began reading, Davies moved impatiently forward and tried to regain the paper. 'You can read the details later.'

The big Scot was not a man to be hurried when he chose otherwise. With his eyes still on the print, he moved away from Davies. A full six inches shorter than the Scot, Davies realized that in a confrontation of this kind he was outclassed and, like the good soldier he was, he turned his attack elsewhere.

'You two have heard of Ernest Lambert, haven't you?'

Both officers nodded.

'Did you know he's become a newspaper correspondent?'

Moore answered him. He had a laconic, cultured voice. 'Yes, sir. Doesn't he have a roving commission?'

'Too right he has. And he's roving around the U.K. at the moment.' From the corner of his eye Davies saw Henderson lift his head and was on him like a flash. 'Well! Have you finished?'

Henderson relinquished the paper at last. 'Not all of it. But I've got the drift.'

'Bloody disgraceful, isn't it?' Davies demanded.

The big Scot gave an indifferent shrug. 'Isn't it just the usual sensational rubbish the newspapers dish out?'

Davies stared at him. 'You know who Lambert is, don't you?'

'Yes. He's an American novelist.'

'Do you know what books he's written?'

Henderson was beginning to look resentful. 'Yes. They filmed one of them a few years back, didn't they?'

'They've filmed damn nearly all of his work, man. He's the biggest name in the business.' Davies transferred his stare to Adams. 'You must have read his books, Adams?'

Noticing Henderson's expression, the highly-sensitive Adams shifted uncomfortably. 'I've read one or two, sir.'

'Which ones?' Davies demanded.

Cornered, Adams tried to avoid Henderson's aggrieved eyes. 'I think one was called *The Rains of Rajapur*. Another was something to do with the Middle East.'

'*The Desert of God?*'

Adams brightened. 'That's the one.'

Davies gave an impatient grunt. 'Stop being so coy, Adams. You've read the lot and so has Moore. Even I've read three of 'em. And to be fair they weren't bad.' He turned back to the red-faced Henderson. 'He's known as the hairy-chested novelist. Hard, tough, but also literary. I suppose that's why he's been enrolled for the duration, so he'll keep the lads marching and the factories humming. The only snag is, if he keeps this up America won't have any Allies left.' Seeing the other two men's curiosity, he thrust the newspaper at Moore. 'The article's a direct attack on the RAF. He's sniped at us before but this time he's gone too far for us to ignore it.'

With Adams peering over his shoulder, Moore was trying to get the gist of the article and to listen to Davies at the same time. Thirty seconds later he handed the paper to the curious Adams. 'I assume it's the political implications you're worried about, sir?'

Davies nodded. 'You can say that again. There are always plenty of people on both sides of the Atlantic eager to find faults with the other, and this character's playing up to both. Only this time he's working on a particularly sensitive nerve. I don't suppose any of you have heard of Operation Pointblank that the Head of State drew up at Casablanca early this year?' When all three men shook their heads, Davies continued with a grunt: 'Nor should you have done. Basically it set out two principles. One was that Allied operations should start in North Africa to take pressure off the Russians. The second – and this is the one that concerns us – the strategic bombing of Germany was to be intensified. In June this year this order was broken down into specifics. Both Harris and Eaker were told to seek out and destroy factories devoted to enemy aircraft production. You know something about that – the B.17s who gave you cover on your way to Bavaria last month were after the Messerschmitt factories in Regensburg.'

Seeing he had fully captured the attention of his listeners, Davies walked over to a large map of Western Europe that hung on the office wall. 'This new directive didn't please Arthur Harris. As you must have gathered by this time, he believes area bombing can win us the war by itself. The Yanks have different views: they think they can hurt Jerry much more by bombing specialist targets in daylight. How much these different views are governed by necessity I'll leave you to guess. In the early years of the war we suffered so heavily in daylight raids that we turned to night bombers and now, with our factories tooled to produce them, we've no alternative but to continue their use. The Yanks are in exactly the opposite position. Lacking our experience of '39, '40 and '41, they came into the war as we did, believing the day bomber could always get through. Which is true as far as it goes but, as we learned the hard way, only at a hell of a price. So they're as committed to their B.17s as we're committed to our night heavies and neither side can turn back now.'

The faces of the three listening men were a study as Davies paused. As in any war in history, unit commanders in 1943 did not enjoy the confidences of their Commanders-in-Chief, and overall strategy could only be guessed at by intelligent observation. That Davies, a stickler for military security, seemed prepared to lift a veil or two made the moment one of high significance. Adams found himself giving a nervous cough as the Air Commodore continued.

'I'm not going into all the pros and cons because most of 'em don't concern you. But there's no denying that until recently the Yank daylight raids have pleased the boys at the top because one of the objectives of Pointblank was to destroy as many fighters as possible before the invasion, which we all know must come soon. Jerry's being clever in not committing his fighters to our own fighter sweeps over France but when the Yanks penetrate in daylight into Germany and attack big cities or vital factories he is forced to react. Of course he attacks our night forces just as energetically, but at night and with our .303 armament we can't hope to destroy as many of his fighters as the Yanks can with their ten .5 Brownings per aircraft. In theory, then, the Yanks can do heavy damage to his numerical strength but in practice they're the ones who are suffering the most. You know what their losses were the other day? Thirty-five B.17s with another fifteen damaged beyond repair. And sixty partially damaged. All that out of an initial force of one hundred and sixty aircraft.'

Henderson let out a shocked whistle which Davies answered with a grim nod. 'Terrifying, isn't it? Eaker's blaming the losses on insufficient front-line strength and he's probably right. Eight hundred or a thousand B.17s in one raid could probably out-gun Jerry fighters. But let's get back to Lambert. One of his bleats is that Harris should be co-operating more with Eaker in twenty-four-hour raids on specific targets. That way he argues the German defences in each area would be over-stretched. But now he's grinding another axe. Rumour has it that General Arnold over in the States is complaining our Fighter Command isn't doing enough to defend the B.17s and Lambert is making the complaint in public. In fact, as you see, he's saying our intransigence is costing American lives.'

'We know Fighter Command's problems – the Spitfire was designed for short-range interception and even with wing tanks and modifications it can't reach further than the German frontier. But Fighter Command do have a number of modified Mustangs and Lambert's also complaining we're not releasing enough of them to the 8th Air Force. I can't say how true or false this is, but I do know the RAF has been receiving bad publicity in the States recently and for all kinds of reasons this is causing both Portal and Eaker headaches. Something must be done quickly to bring back the old love affair and you're the unit chosen for the job.'

The atmosphere in the office was one of high expectancy as Davies' eyes moved from one man to the other. 'It's not difficult to understand why. Firstly, you're not part of Bomber Command whose policy of area bombing has lost favour with the Yanks. Secondly, you're not associated with Fighter Command either. Thirdly, and the best reason of all, your Swartfjord raid and your recent destruction of the Rhine Maiden Project made you the blue-eyed boys of the Yanks.' Davies, whose comments on the Americans had so far been a model of objectivity, back-slid for a moment into jingoism. 'And so it bloody well should. If you hadn't wiped out those anti-aircraft rockets, Christ knows the state they'd be in by this time.'

It was Henderson's turn to cough. 'Can I ask a question here?'

Davies frowned. 'If you want to.'

'Are these criticisms of the RAF coming from the American crews themselves or only from General Arnold and his staff officers? Because we've not found any resentment among the American boys we know.'

Disliking interruptions when he was in full flow, Davies tended to slide into sarcasm. 'I thought I'd just explained that. Next to Betty Grable, you're the Yanks' favourite pin-ups. It's the poor bloody artisans of Bomber and Fighter Commands who're taking all the stick.' Seeing Henderson's expression, Davies modified his tone. 'No, I don't think the average Yank crewman thinks any of this. He knows we're just doing the job we're told to do, the same way he does his. But who is he compared with the Pentagon, Ernest Lambert, and the public at large who don't know an aileron from a joystick? Our job is to discredit Lambert by showing the American public how wrong he is.'

Henderson was looking doubtful. 'And you've got an operation for us that can do this?'

'I'm expecting to have, Jock, if things turn out the way we're hoping. And I ought to know that by Friday at the latest. In the meantime don't be surprised if you get a visit from our newspaper friend. Rumours are going around he wants to see the set-up here.'

The Scot looked horrified. 'Lambert? Here?'

Davies grinned. 'Why not? He can hardly visit RAF units without taking a look at us, can he? Don't look so worried. Give him plenty of whisky and you might even win him over without a shot being fired.'

'I'll get some warning when he's coming, won't I?'

'Oh, Christ, yes. I'll contact you as soon as they request permission for his visit.

In the meantime you can stand your boys down. Not that I want 'em swigging beer in the Mess all day.' Davies switched his gaze to Moore. 'Get 'em on the ranges and give 'em plenty of low-level practice.'

Henderson's ears pricked. 'Low-level?'

Davies picked up his briefcase from the desk and took the newspaper from Adams. 'No luck, Jock. Security's as tight as a bull's arse in fly time on this one. It has to be; there are Allied lives as well as our own involved. You'll get all details as soon as permission is given.' The spry Air Commodore moved to the door where he grinned again. 'Cheer up, Jock. If we pull this off, you might get Veronica Lake sent over as a squadron mascot. And the rest of us might get a spare tin or two of Spam.'

With a wink Davies disappeared, leaving the three officers staring at one another.

CHAPTER 3

Millburn grinned at the girl behind the desk. 'Hiya, kid. How's life this morning?'

The girl, a pretty Waaf with freckles, eyed the dark, tousle-headed Millburn with some caution. Of Irish descent, the good-looking American had a reputation with women that was a legend on the Station. 'Life's fine, thank you – sir.'

'It is? That's great. Let's keep it that way.' Millburn lowered a leg over the corner of the desk. 'How about doing a movie with me tonight?'

The girl drew hastily back. 'No, thanks.'

The American slid another six inches across the desk. 'What is it, honey? You still holding a torch for that Limey boy friend of yours?'

'What if I am?' she asked defiantly.

'It's a waste, honey. He's two thousand miles away in Africa. You're losing precious flying time.'

'And it wouldn't be a waste if I went out with you?'

Millburn's grin broadened. 'That's for sure, honey. You'd be getting experience. And that's money in the bank for a girl.'

The girl opened her mouth, glanced at the closed inner door, and dropped her voice into an exasperated whisper. 'Tommy Millburn, you are the most conceited man I've ever known.'

'You've got the wrong word, haven't you, honey? You mean confident. There's a world of difference.'

'Not to me there isn't.'

The grinning Millburn lifted his six-foot, well-proportioned frame from the desk. 'You'll see the light sooner or later. And when you do, you know who'll help you.'

The girl gave a sniff. 'That'll be the day. Will you see the Wing Commander now? Or have you something more important to do?'

Millburn waved an indulgent hand. 'No. If he promises to hurry it up, I guess I can fit him in.'

Hiding her smile, the girl opened the door. 'Squadron Leader Millburn is here, sir.'

Moore, who was sitting at his desk signing papers, glanced up and smiled. 'Thank you, Tess. Show him in, will you?'

Millburn's entry typified the informal atmosphere of an RAF operational squadron. 'Hello, skipper. Teddy Young said you wanted to see me.'

Moore indicated for him to draw up a chair. 'Yes, there are a couple of things. Did Teddy tell you that we're standing down for a few days?'

'Yeah. What's the reason? Have we something big coming up?'

'We might have. But there's nothing definite at the moment. So if your boys start asking questions, let them think they're being given a rest.'

Millburn grinned. 'They're not fooled as easily as that.'

'All right, tell them they're getting sloppy and need some practice. Take them over the gunnery range and let them have a go at the low-level targets.'

Millburn looked disappointed. 'How many sessions?'

'Just the mornings. You can take the rest of the day off.'

'Great. They'll think it's Christmas.' The American pushed a packet of Lucky Strike across the desk. 'What's next on the list?'

'I've had news of Harvey. He phoned me this morning. He's made such a good recovery the hospital's discharging him in a couple of days.'

'You're kidding. He's had three operations, hasn't he?'

Moore nodded. Although busy lighting his cigarette, he was studying the American's expression. 'He has to convalesce for a while, of course, but he ought to be back with us around the middle of October.'

'That's great,' Millburn said. 'I wonder if the nurses down there have mellowed him.'

Moore smiled. 'I wouldn't think it's likely, would you?'

'Not much. He'll probably give me a bollocking as soon as he gets back for not keeping his office tidy.'

Moore exhaled smoke. 'You do realize I'll have to give him his flight back?'

To his gratification the American looked surprised rather than upset. 'What else? Hell, he practically destroyed that rocket plant single-handed. You know something? The boys'll be pleased. He's a better mother hen than I'll ever be.'

'We all agree he's a fine flight commander. But you've done a good job yourself. That's something else I want to talk about. You're a cert for the job if you do what the Yanks want and move over to them. In fact, with your experience you might get a squadron command. I know you've flattered us before by staying here

371

but this time the situation's different. We can't hang on to you at personal cost to yourself.'

Millburn's affability turned to wryness. 'Let's get it straight, skipper. Are you trying to get rid of me?'

'Don't be a damn fool. I'm trying to be fair to you.'

Looking embarrassed and defiant in equal parts, the American took a few seconds to respond. 'One thing I'd like to make clear, skipper. I think my guns are doing a great job.'

Guessing what was coming, Moore tried to hide his amusement. 'So do I. So do we all.'

With that important point made, Millburn's tone changed. 'So it's not that. It's just that a guy gets used to one unit.' Terrified of appearing sentimental, Millburn searched for a more harmless reason and found one. 'What about girls? A guy can lose out if he's always moving around.'

'That's true. Mind you, there are plenty of girls in East Anglia. And from the stories I hear, they don't exactly dislike the Yanks.'

'But the ones I've got here are house-trained. And that saves a man a lot of time.'

Moore lifted his shoulders expressively. 'Why didn't we think of that?'

Millburn grinned as their eyes met. 'So I stay. O.K.?'

The young squadron commander made no attempt to hide his satisfaction. 'Of course you stay. The last thing I want is to lose you.'

'Then do me a favour, skipper. Don't do me any favours. Just let me soldier along as before.'

Moore's laugh reached the Waaf in the anteroom. 'All right. But don't let me hear you moaning when Harvey gives you that bollocking. And don't get prickly when one of your war correspondents asks you what a clean, upright American boy is doing in the RAF.'

'War correspondent?'

'Yes. We've got one visiting us any day now. Ernest Lambert, the novelist.'

Millburn whistled. 'Lambert? Has it to do with the Rhine Maiden job?'

Realizing he could say little about Lambert's visit without endangering security, Moore prevaricated. 'If it is, he's a bit late. The dust from that settled a month ago.'

'Maybe he's just getting round to it.'

Moore nodded. 'I suppose it's possible.' Changing the subject, he picked up a form from his desk. 'I see you've put through McKenny's request for leave. You don't know he's still got two months to go?'

'Yeah. Only he's been pressing me hard and he's been hitting the bottle recently.'

'What is it? Girl trouble?'

'Search me. He won't talk about it.'

'Has the M.O. seen him?'

'I made him take a medical last week. The M.O. says there's nothing wrong with him physically. He says he's a bit highly strung but then who isn't?'

372

Moore glanced down at the form again. 'If I authorize this I'll have every man jack on the squadron slapping applications in. Try to find out what's troubling him, will you, and then we'll see what we can do.'

'Fair enough. Anything else?'

'No. That's the lot for the moment.'

The American nodded and stubbed out his cigarette. As he reached the door and the Waaf appeared, he turned. 'You know the real reason I'm staying here, don't you, skipper?'

'No. Tell me.'

Millburn winked and patted the cheek of the girl who was holding the door open for him. 'It's Tess here. She's driving me wild, skipper. A woman like her's worth anything. Even flying with a tribe of Limeys.'

The girl's expression told she had forgotten the presence of the laughing Moore. Before she could vent her feelings, the ebullient American had pulled the door closed and vanished.

The small officer standing beneath the naked light bulb that hung from the billet roof was trying to put a shine on his service cap badge. Halfway through the operation he turned and scowled at Millburn who was lying full-length on one of the beds. 'If you used Harvey's quarters instead of still kipping in here, maybe that lazy young sod Wilkinson would give me better attention.'

Millburn lifted his head. 'It's not rank that does it, mush. It's personality.'

'What do you mean – personality? You've got more cash to bribe him with, that's all.'

'Jealousy'll get you nowhere, my little Welsh binder. Why don't you accept that some guys have it and some don't? Anyway, what's all this moaning about? I thought you'd be happy to get a couple of days off duty.'

The small officer was in no mood to be placated. 'Don't worry; we'll pay for it. I saw Davies coming out of the Admin Block this morning. When he pays us a visit there's always trouble.'

Johnnie Gabriel, nicknamed Gabby or The Gremlin because of his wiry frame and sharp features that could look either comically old or young at will, was one of the Squadron's characters. Somewhat older than his aircrew colleagues, with a thirst for excitement that was insatiable, he had enlisted in the Thirties as a fighter pilot for the Government in the Spanish Civil War. Before crashing into enemy territory he had shot down three Fascist planes. Threatened with execution by the Falangists, Gabby had volunteered to fly for Franco and by some miracle of persuasion had been accepted. On his first solo mission he had flown straight out of Spain into France.

On the outbreak of World War Two he had not unreasonably expected the RAF to accept him as a trained pilot. Instead his offer to fly had been rejected and he had been kept waiting eighteen months before he was offered training as a navigator. His disgruntled acceptance had eventually led him to a Mitchell squadron where he had become Millburn's navigator. Set alongside the powerful

American with his devil-may-care features and shock of black hair, the Welshman looked more like a gnome than ever. Yet the two ill-assorted characters had become inseparable friends and notorious in every squadron in which they had served for their mad pranks and tireless pursuit of women. To date they had been in 633 Squadron just over four months. In spite of their wild reputation on the ground, they were highly capable crew and had been an almost automatic selection to lead A Flight after Harvey had been wounded and hospitalized.

Millburn yawned. 'What's wrong with a bit of trouble?'

'What are you looking for?' the Welshman gibed. 'Another DFC to show those Yank buddies of yours?'

'Coming from you, that's really something,' Millburn grinned. 'Who's the guy I once found polishing a scratch on his arm with a toothbrush so he could show it to his dames?'

Gabby, who had been wounded during the Rhine Maiden operation, gave a sniff of indignation. 'Some of us have had more than scratches, mate. You forgotten I was a stretcher case when we got back from Bavaria?'

'You've never let anyone forget. From the line you shot in the hospital, the nurses thought you'd captured Hitler and brought him back in the bomb bay.'

'So what? I got some dates for you, didn't I?'

'Yeah, you did. And I haven't got over 'em yet.'

Back on his favourite topic, Gabby tried blandishments. 'Change your mind and come tonight. Both of those kids have fallen for you.'

'Not a chance, mush. You're on your own.'

'But Betty's friend's not that bad. A bit skinny, perhaps, but she's got good legs.'

'A bit skinny? She's like Olive Oyl in one of those Popeye movies. I know why you want me along. So you can use my car.'

'It's not that at all. Four's more company than two.'

'You mean more company than three. I'm on to you, you little bum. That dame of yours won't go out with you unless Olive Oyl tags along and I don't blame her. So I'm supposed to provide the car and pick up the bills.'

Gabby looked hurt. 'You've got it all wrong. We've just more fun when we're out together, that's all.'

'More fun for who?'

'At least you could lend me the car,' the Welshman muttered.

'That's more like it. Well, I could but I won't. I'm going out myself on a recce after dinner. So the car's out.'

'Sod,' Gabby muttered, putting on his forage cap. Millburn guffawed as he watched him set it at a jaunty angle. 'You're wasting your time, mush. With Olive Oyl keeping a beady eye on you all night, you're never going to make it.'

'I'd do it for you, Millburn. You know I would.'

'Like hell you would. What about the time I picked up that dame in Scarborough? You ran out on me as soon as you saw her friend and I was stuck with the two of 'em for the rest of the day.'

'That was different. She had bad breath and bow legs.'

'At least she had legs. This dame walks on sticks.'

Gabby had a last try. 'So I've got to take the transport into town?'

'That's right. And back. You've got a tough night ahead of you.'

The small Welshman quivered with indignation. 'I've never picked up a girl yet without asking if she had a friend for you. And this is the thanks I get.'

'That's right. I've been stuck with so many plain Janes it's starting to affect my morale. From now on you take the rough with the smooth, boyo. Starting from tonight.'

Seeing it was hopeless, Gabby started for the door. He threw his last punch from the step outside. 'Now I know why you're still in our mob, Millburn. The Yanks are too smart to have you.'

Millburn's guffaw reached the Welshman before he slammed the door closed. 'You've got it wrong as usual, kid. The girls here won't let me go.'

CHAPTER 4

The Mess was unusually quiet that evening. With no operational flying that day, the crews were making the most of the occasion. Teddy Young, seasoned Commander of B Flight, had proved himself a dinkum Australian by going to the last of the season's flat races and taking a party of ten with him. Other airmen were visiting their girl friends in the local market town of Highgate or farther afield in Scarborough. Older and senior officers would arrive later but at this moment Timber Woods, the barman, was yawning and wishing he had something to read.

When Adams appeared in the doorway only two men were propping up the bar. One was Jack Richardson, the heavily built, ginger-headed Equipment Officer, the other was Paddy McKenny of A Flight. Neither was in conversation: in fact they were standing at opposite ends of the counter. The sight came as no surprise to Adams. Richardson, who drank heavily and told particularly dirty jokes, was not the most popular man on the station and his usual drinking partner, Marsden, the Signals Officer, had gone to the races with Teddy Young. McKenny was one of the many Irish volunteers who resented their country's neutrality. A strong-featured man with the abundant black hair and fair complexion that favoured so many of his race, he had been posted to 633 Squadron shortly after its near annihilation in Norway. Bernard Ross, a member of the original squadron whose pilot had been killed, had been teamed up with him. Both men having received training for the role, they were recognized as the squadron's photographic specialists.

With McKenny not one to wear his heart on his sleeve, Ross, a Scot from Ayrshire, was probably the only man on the station who knew of the sensitive streak that ran through the Irishman. To the squadron at large, McKenny was a rugged man who, having volunteered to fight the Nazi menace, was playing his part with skill and tenacity.

In the four months the Irishman and the Scotsman had been crewed together they had developed the kind of comradeship that men would look back on with nostalgia in the days of peace ahead. One common link was undoubtedly religion. Both men were Catholics and although neither paraded his faith before his less pious colleagues, they both observed their religion's more important conventions.

Nothing therefore could have emphasized more the change in McKenny's personality than his ceasing to attend Mass and Confession. In addition, he had started drinking heavily and, to Ross's secret hurt, begun showing a preference for his own company. The Scot's absence that evening was a result of this. An uncle of his, visiting Scarborough on business, had invited both men to have dinner with him. With McKenny having repeatedly rejected the invitation, Ross had been left with no option but to go alone.

To date this change in the Irishman had not affected his combat efficiency and so it had been noted by his fellow officers but no more. Adams, however, who had protective leanings towards the young aircrews, had made discreet enquiries of Ross, only to learn the Scot was as mystified as anyone at its cause. Inevitably rumours were beginning to circulate among the ground crews that McKenny was losing his nerve.

Two other officers shared the room. One was Sue Spencer, Adams' assistant Intelligence Officer, a willowy, graceful girl, gentle of disposition but highly efficient at her work. Her companion was Tony St Claire, another of the squadron's pilots. St Claire was sitting at the piano in the far corner of the room; the girl was standing at his elbow.

Adams was unashamedly envious of St Claire. An ex-student of the Royal College of Music, the young pilot had been making a name for himself on the concert platform before the war had called him into service. He was unquestionably the handsomest man Adams had ever seen: tall and slim, with a Byronic head and an artist's hands. Waafs went faint at the knees at the sight of Tony St Claire and yet he had eyes for no one but the girl at his side. In turn she showed a devotion to him that sometimes gave Adams nightmares. One of the girl's tasks was to help him de-brief the crews after an operation, which meant they shared together the excruciating wait before the surviving aircraft landed. In Adams' experience the girl's disciplined face had never betrayed her dread, nor had she ever expressed it to him, and yet to the sensitive Adams it seemed to fill every corner of the Nissen hut that served as his Intelligence office. The fact that Sue Spencer happened to be the kind of woman Adams' lonely nature admired did nothing to help him at such moments. Gentle, understanding, undemonstrative, she was the antithesis of the waspish and unsympathetic woman his wife had become.

As Adams paused in the doorway he saw Richardson was throwing hostile glances as McKenny. A man who needed company to fulfil himself, the Equipment Officer clearly resented the younger man's unsociability. Not wishing to disturb the couple at the piano and so forced to choose between lasciviousness and moodiness, Adams chose the latter and made towards McKenny. A black mongrel dog that had been sniffing at the Mess entrance padded after him across the stained carpet. Before the Rhine Maiden operation Adams had promised to look after Harvey's dog if anything should happen to the Yorkshireman and by this time the lonely Adams had come to need the dog perhaps more than it needed him.

Contenting himself with an amiable nod at Richardson, Adams leaned against the bar at McKenny's elbow. His tone of false heartiness jarred him. 'Hello, McKenny. So you haven't gone to the races with the others?'

Although clearly resenting the intrusion, the young pilot straightened himself. 'No, sir. I'm not keen on horse racing.'

The electric light glinted on Adams' spectacles as he nodded. 'That makes two of us. And anyway I always lose.' Seeing the barman waiting for his order, Adams glanced furtively at the Irishman's face. All the signs indicated he had drunk enough already and yet Adams did not see how he could deny him a round.

'I'll have a beer,' he told Woods. Then: 'What about you, McKenny? Do you want another?'

'I'd rather not if you don't mind, sir.'

Although aware why his offer was refused, Adams felt relief. 'I don't mind. It keeps my Mess bill down. Are you staying on for dinner?'

'I don't think so.'

Adams proceeded cautiously. 'You're going out, then?'

'No, sir.'

Adams pulled out his pipe and knocked it against the bar. 'From what I've heard it's not a bad meal tonight. Lamb, mint sauce, and all the trimmings.' At the pilot's indifferent shrug, he went on: 'What's wrong? You're not off colour, are you?'

The stare he received was decidedly hostile. 'No, sir, I'm not. Why?'

Hiding his embarrassment, Adams began packing his pipe. 'Isn't it the most obvious question when a man misses his meals?'

McKenny muttered something and turned towards the bar. 'There's nothing wrong with me, sir.'

Conscious he was making a hash of things and uncertain what to do next, Adams took refuge in a sip of beer. 'I'm glad to hear it. How's that kite of yours? You've been having an engine problem, haven't you?'

The pilot's expression suggested that he could not care if the engine fell out of its mountings. 'It keeps losing revs. Chiefy hasn't pin-pointed the trouble yet.'

'It must be a tough one if Chiefy can't find it,' Adams offered.

He received a morose nod. Adams had a last try. 'I suppose you've heard that Squadron Leader Harvey is now convalescing.'

'Yes, sir.'

'With luck we ought to have him back with us in three or four weeks. The boys are planning quite a party.'

There was no reply. Aware he had run out of conversation, Adams put a match to his pipe. The clouds of smoke he emitted brought a cough from Woods behind the counter and an injured glance. In the silence Adams heard the soft notes of the piano. Half-hidden in the shadowy corner of the room, St Claire was playing a melody of singular beauty that Adams could not place. As he ceased playing Sue Spencer bent impulsively down and kissed his cheek. Richardson, also watching the couple, gave a grunt of disgust. Why, Adams thought, did men with minds as prurient as Richardson's always gibe at demonstrations of affection? He was turning back to McKenny when Sue caught sight of him and waved him to join them. Adams hesitated, then tapped McKenny's arm.

'Excuse me, will you? Sue wants a word with me.'

The young Irishman had difficulty in hiding his relief. 'Of course, sir.'

Adams picked up his beer and crossed the room. The black mongrel, which had curled up at the foot of the bar, rose and padded after him. Sue, who was looking excited for one so disciplined, caught his arm and led him towards the piano. 'I didn't see you come in. Have you been in long?'

'Only a few seconds,' Adams lied.

'Why didn't you come over and join us?' Before Adams could reply, the girl went on: 'Tony's just finished playing part of a concerto he's written. It's beautiful.'

Adams waved the young pilot back into his seat. 'I heard the last few bars of it. I'm impressed.'

The girl, whose hand had been drawn to the pianist's shoulder as if by a magnet, laughed happily. 'You see! I told you.' She turned back to Adams. 'It's Teddy Young's birthday next Tuesday. I want Tony to play the concerto at the party the boys are giving him.'

The handsome young officer glanced up at Adams, one eyebrow quizzically raised. 'Can you imagine it, sir? A concerto at an aircrew party? She can't wait to get me drawn and quartered.'

Perhaps because of his own complex nature, Adams found the mixture of art and masculinity in St Claire one of the pianist's most attractive features. 'It is chancing your arm a bit,' he grinned. 'And anyway, it sounds too good for those young barbarians. Why don't you give a recital to us more mature, more civilized types? It shouldn't be difficult to reserve the Mess for an hour or two one evening.'

Sue showed her pleasure. 'Would you do that?'

'Why not? We're the ones who'll enjoy it.' Then Adams noticed St Claire's expression. 'That's if you're willing, of course.'

'If you don't mind, sir, I'd rather not.'

Sue gave a cry of disappointment. 'Why?'

St Claire lit a cigarette. 'I'd rather not, darling. Just leave it there, will you?'

It was a refusal Adams understood and respected. While the young officer could not avoid using the Mess piano – his only opportunity to keep in practice – for him to have given a recital might have suggested to some men that he was parading his talent. To lighten the moment Adams bent down to pat the dog that was nuzzling his foot. Seeing an escape in his action, the girl took it without thinking. 'I wonder how Sam will react when Harvey gets back.'

'He'll do cartwheels and somersaults,' Adams told her.

The sensitive girl was already regretting her words. 'He'll be glad to see him again, of course, but he's also grown very fond of you.'

Hiding a sigh, Adams gave the dog a final pat and straightened. 'No. We've got along all right but he's really a one-man dog. You'll see what I mean when Harvey appears.'

A shout made all three of them look round. Richardson, whose resentment at his isolation had been growing by the minute, was staring with hostility at McKenny. 'You! McKenny! What's the matter with you tonight?'

Adams noticed the young pilot had another drink in front of him. Sensing the danger, he gave the couple at the piano a warning look and crossed the floor. 'How about a drink, Jack?'

The belligerent Equipment Officer gave him a scowl. 'I've got a drink. I was talking to that toffee-nosed kid over there. Doesn't he know it's rude to stand in the Mess and ignore everybody?'

Adams kept his voice down. 'He doesn't mean to be rude, Jack. Forget about it and have a drink with me.'

Spoiling for trouble, the beefy Richardson pushed him aside. 'I'm not having a bloody pilot officer igore me. He needs a lesson in manners. McKenny, come over here!'

The pilot hesitated a moment. Then, face pale, he moved along the bar. 'What do you want, sir?'

'You've been standing there over half an hour without saying a word to anyone. Don't you know that's bad manners?'

'I'm sorry, sir. It wasn't intentional.'

'Wasn't intentional? I heard Squadron Leader Adams invite you to have a drink and you refused him. Yet the moment he walked away you ordered one yourself. What kind of behaviour do you call that?'

'It didn't worry me,' Adams said. 'In fact I never noticed it.'

'Well, I did. And I don't like young kids being rude to senior officers.' Richardson swung back on the pale McKenny. 'You've been acting this way for weeks now and drinking like a fish. For Christ's sake pull your socks up and start acting like a gentleman. Don't you realize that's what you're supposed to be?'

The Irishman stiffened. 'Is that all – sir?'

His delayed use of the title was all that Richardson needed to turn hostility into outright aggression. 'Don't try to be funny with me, McKenny, or you'll be in serious trouble!'

'I'm not being funny – sir.'

Adams threw a fervent glance at the door, hoping against hope to see new-comers whose presence might break up the scene, but the Mess remained disturbingly empty. The hoarseness of Richardson's voice told he had lost his self-control. 'Don't think I don't know what's wrong with you, McKenny. Just as everyone else on the station knows.'

For a moment the wrought-up pilot looked puzzled. 'I don't know what you're talking about.'

Adams heard a gasp from the watching Sue. It was a sound that brought perception to McKenny. As he gave a violent start and took an aggressive step forward, Adams seized his arm. 'That's enough! We're going outside.'

The young Irishman was deathly pale and breathing hard. Fearing he might be unable to restrain him, Adams felt relief as St Claire ran up and grabbed his other arm. 'Get a hold of yourself, Paddy,' the pianist muttered. 'Do as the Squadron Leader says.'

For a moment it seemed McKenny might resist them both. Then he pulled away and made for the door. Giving Richardson an expressive look, Adams followed him.

They reached the path that led to the junior officers' billets before Adams, who was conscious his role so far had been an inept one, felt it was safe to speak. 'He was half-drunk, you know. And he had no one to tell his filthy jokes to.'

In the evening gloom the Irishman looked grim and shocked. Although Adams felt fulminate of mercury would have been safer to handle, he tried again. 'All the same, he was right in saying you haven't been yourself these last few weeks. Wouldn't you like to talk about it? I promise it won't go any further.'

He received an aggressive glance. 'What is it, sir? Have you got the same idea he has?'

'Of course I haven't,' Adams protested. 'But any fool can see something's bothering you. Sometimes it helps to talk. That's all I meant.'

'It's not important enough to talk about, sir.'

'But if it affects you so much, it must be important.' Then, seeing the futility of argument, Adams compromised. 'At least promise me one thing. If you do feel like having a chat about it, come and see me.'

To his surprise McKenny halted. 'There is one thing you can do for me if you want to help.'

Adams felt gratification, 'What's that?'

'You could try to get me some leave. Even a couple of days would be better than nothing.'

Adams felt disappointed. 'Have you put in an application?'

'Yes. And it's been rejected.'

'Did you give a reason for requesting it?'

'No.'

'There you are,' Adams muttered. 'No one can get special leave without a reason. If you'll give me one I'll have a talk with the Squadron Commander.' The bitter glance he received made Adams frown. 'I'm sorry but I didn't draw up the rules, McKenny.'

'No, sir. May I go now?'

'I'm not stopping you. There is just one thing, though. I'd keep out of Richardson's way for a while if I were you.'

McKenny was already walking away. 'I tried to do that, sir, but it didn't help very much.'

Adams opened his mouth, then desisted and watched the Irishman disappear into one of the wooden huts ahead. The complex Intelligence officer had long felt that men were the victims of their stars and those who tried to help them achieved little but disappointment. At the same time it was a hypothesis that in no way repressed his better instincts.

With a sigh he started back for the Mess, with Sam pattering somewhat mournfully after him. A late September fog was drifting in from the airfield and was already diffusing the dim lights of the Control tower. Autumn was arriving early this year, Adams thought. In earlier wartime years he had tended to prefer autumn and winter, feeling that war in the gold of summer when the earth was burgeoning with its fruits was too monstrous a sacrilege. Tonight, however, with the damp fog setting down and the leaves dripping moisture, the combination of autumn and war seemed an unholy alliance.

He led Sam back to the Mess, only to pause again in the doorway when he saw how it had filled up during the last few minutes. With two general duty officers to share his jokes with, Richardson was now oozing bonhomie at the far side of the room. Another group of officers were clustered round the tall figure of Henderson. Driven from the piano by the invasion, St Claire and Sue Spencer were lost in a world of their own by the window. As he watched them, Adams suddenly experienced a feeling of isolation. With a sigh he called Sam to heel and made his way towards his office.

CHAPTER 5

The red telephone on Henderson's desk rang just before ten the following morning. Waving back his Waaf typist, the Scot picked up the receiver. The somewhat high-pitched voice that greeted him could have belonged to only one man. 'Henderson? Listen! I was right about that fellow Lambert. They phoned here a few minutes ago to ask permission for him to visit you. When will suit you best? Today or tomorrow?'

Henderson was showing dismay. 'If he has to come, today is better, I suppose.'

'Then it'll probably have to be this afternoon. That O.K.?'

'Yes, sir. But what's he coming for?'

'How the hell do I know? Because you're one of our most famous units, I suppose.'

Henderson glanced at the Waaf, who had resumed typing, and lowered his voice. 'It couldn't be about this operation you're planning, could it?'

Davies' hesitation suggested he had asked himself the same question. 'It's possible someone in Staines' outfit might have leaked it out. These Yankee Pressmen are powerful and this one's bound to have collaborators everywhere. But I wouldn't think it likely. So not a word unless he brings it up and even then play it canny.'

'I can't be anything else seeing I don't know what it is, can I?'

'Then you're lucky,' Davies said caustically. 'You don't have to watch your tongue.'

Henderson grimaced at the rebuke. 'What do you want me to say to him?'

'Keep off politics. Just give him plenty of spiel about the squadron's achievements, stressing the Swartfjord and Ruhpolding raids.' At times like this Davies could sound like a malicious elf. 'Rub it in that if we hadn't destroyed that Rhine Maiden plant, the Yanks mightn't have an 8th Air Force left by this time. Then, when you've softened him up, show him round. Only keep him away from the SCI dump. We don't want him giving Jerry the impression we're about to drop mustard gas on him.'

It was clear from Henderson's expression that he would rather face three Me.109s single-handed than the redoubtable Lambert. 'Will you be able to get here, sir?'

'Not this afternoon. I'm meeting Staines. But you can cope. Give him plenty of bullshit: it's important he goes away impressed. And whenever you can, steer him towards the Mess. They say he likes tanking up and the more drinks the fewer questions he'll ask. All right?'

'Yes, I suppose so.'

'For God's sake, cheer up, Jock. It's not the C.-in-C. visiting you.' When Henderson did not answer, Davies went on: 'There's one thing. If all goes well with Staines this afternoon, I shall want you all briefed and ready to go from the first light on Friday onwards. It's going to be one of those operations. So don't let your boys out on Thursday night. All right?'

'Yes, sir. Is that all?'

'All for the moment. I'll be in touch as soon as I get the all clear. In the meantime, good luck with Lambert.'

Henderson replaced the receiver and sank somewhat heavily back into his chair. His Waaf sergeant, a healthy-looking country-bred girl from Dorset whose vital statistics were enough to make any middle-aged officer reflective, pulled a letter from her typewriter and laid it on a pile of others on his desk. 'That's the lot, sir. Is there anything else you want?'

At any other time her question would have appealed to the Scot's sense of humour. Instead he nodded at a cabinet that stood near the girl's desk. 'What's the whisky situation like?'

She opened the cabinet. 'The bottle's almost empty, sir.'

'It is? Then be a good girl and slip along to the Mess for another, will you? I think I'm going to need it.'

The Waaf smiled as she moved towards the door. 'Are things as bad as that, sir?'

'They're a damn sight worse,' Henderson said gloomily.

The billet door swung open, letting in a shaft of weak sunlight. The man who entered, freckle-faced and ginger-headed, was Bernard Ross, McKenny's navigator. Coming straight in from the morning sunlight he did not immediately notice the man lying on the bed.

'You in here, Paddy?'

McKenny rose reluctantly on one elbow. 'Yes. What do you want?'

'Moore's buying the boys drinks to celebrate stand-down. Don't you think you ought to come over?'

McKenny dropped back on his pillow. 'He won't miss me.'

'He might. In any case it's a bit rude, isn't it?'

McKenny did not answer. Ross threw down a letter on the blanket that was covering the Irishman. 'This came in the morning post.'

McKenny sat up with a jerk. 'Why the hell didn't you give it to me straight away?'

'I've only been in the billet ten seconds,' Ross pointed out.

Tearing open the envelope, McKenny pulled out a single sheet of notepaper. As he began reading it, Ross tried again.

'Then what about going to Scarborough with us this afternoon? We might as well make the most of this stand-down: they'll probably change their minds tomorrow. We're doing a movie, then having a meal afterwards. Millburn says he'll find room for us in his jalopy.'

Devouring the letter, McKenny showed no signs of hearing him. Although good-tempered by nature, Ross began to show irritation.

'You could answer me, couldn't you?'

When the Irishman still ignored him, the young navigator shrugged and made for the door. 'All right; make yourself unpopular. Why should I care?'

A muffled curse as McKenny reached the end of the letter made him halt and turn. Seeing the Irishman crushing the letter in his hand, Ross approached his bed again. 'What is it, Paddy? Bad news?'

McKenny's bitter eyes lifted up to him for a moment, then he sank back on his pillow. Seeking a way of reaching him, Ross gave a start. 'It's nothing to do with that recent Baedeker raid, is it?'

It took a moment for his question to sink through the Irishman's misery. 'What raid?'

'The one on Lincoln. I thought you knew about it.'

'Was it a heavy one?'

383

'Nothing like we're handing out to Jerry. Only thirty or so kites. So I don't think you need worry too much about Joan or your sister.'

To his surprise the Irishman was now looking excited as he swung his feet to the floor. 'Are you sure about this?'

'Of course I'm sure. We're claiming five were shot down.'

Cramming the letter into his pocket, McKenny slipped into his tunic. Ross watched him in bewilderment. 'Are you coming to the Mess, then?'

The Irishman snatched his cap from a peg on the wall. 'No. I'm having another go at getting a 24-hour pass.'

'But I thought you'd just been turned down?'

'I have. But I'm going to try again.'

Ross showed concern as McKenny tried to pass him. 'You can't try twice in two days. You'll get all their backs up.'

'Who cares about their backs? I want a pass.'

Ross tried a last time before he was pushed roughly aside. 'You know you won't get it. So why make trouble for yourself?'

There was no reply. McKenny was already outside and hurrying down the path that led to the Administration offices.

The large American staff car was already parked in the courtyard of the country house when Davies' more modest Hillman emerged from the tree-lined drive. The challenge the Air Commodore received at the entrance was his third since entering the estate. As the Hillman moved forward again and parked near the American car, a young lieutenant, waiting at the foot of an imposing flight of steps, hurried forward and snapped a salute at the emerging Davies.

'Good afternoon, sir. The Brigadier's in the library. General Staines is with him.'

Nodding, Davies pulled his briefcase from the car and made for the steps. The young lieutenant, who had caught the eye of the Air Commodore's pretty Waaf driver, hesitated a moment before following him. The Waaf lit herself a cigarette. In the world in which Lynne Barker moved, second lieutenants were ten a penny.

Davies reached the top of the steps and turned right along a terrace. As the courtyard fell back, lawns and flowerbeds appeared below him. Among the elms that surrounded the gardens, rooks were cawing angrily at a pigeon that had settled in their midst. Smoke from a bonfire gave the afternoon air the scent of autumn. A jackdaw, perched on one of the large flower pots that lined the terrace, watched his approach with bright, curious eyes. Its hop on to the wall as he drew level was its only concession to his presence. Davies' thoughts were quizzical as he heard the second lieutenant hurrying after him. Security at High Elms was so tight that even the birds felt safe.

The lieutenant led him down a panelled corridor patrolled by an M.P., tapped on a side door and opened it. 'Air Commodore Davies is here, sir.'

The room Davies entered was all hide-bound books, panelled walls and dark oak furniture. At the far end french windows gave a view over the terrace and gardens. As the lieutenant withdrew, Davies saw two men occupied the room. One of them, sitting at a long table that ran down the centre of the room, was wearing the uniform of an American Air Force General. Ed Staines had once played quarterback for West Point and it showed even today in his fifteen-stone, granite hard body. Beneath spiky, iron-grey hair, he had a leathery face with bushy eyebrows and a solid chin. In one tobacco-stained hand he was holding an object that resembled a toy airship but in fact was a cigar.

The English Brigadier who was his companion could hardly have provided a sharper contrast. Elderly, slimly-built with a sensitive face and trimmed moustache, he had an appearance that was both military and distinguished. An Officer in Special Operations Executive, he had been working on and off with Davies ever since the Swartfjord raid in the spring of that same year. Although he was by nature a quiet, reserved man and Davies was nothing if not volatile and quick-tempered, the two men had discovered, secretly to their surprise, that their natures were complementary rather than conflicting and that they worked well together.

The Brigadier was approaching Davies with outstretched hand. 'Hello, Davies. General Staines got here earlier than he expected, so I've been able to give him the outline of our plan.'

Davies, whose last encounter with the American General had been during the Rhine Maiden affair, saluted, then took the huge hand that reached across the table to him. The American was grinning cordially. 'Remember me, Davies? I'm the guy you conned into sending one hundred and fifty B.17s all the way to Bavaria to cover sixteen of your Mosquitoes.'

Davies was heartened by the greeting. 'You have to admit it was worth it, sir.'

Staines dropped his bulk back into his chair. His gravelly voice had a strong Texan accent. 'I think you can say that. If we had those rockets to contend with on top of our other problems, I'd be in the bread line by this time. Davies, where the hell are those Heinies getting their ships from? Every time we go over, there are more of the bastards.'

The speed at which Staines moved on to this highly sensitive ground told Davies something of the big American's urgency and he chose his reply with care. 'I suppose it's due to their policy of avoiding our fighter sweeps and conserving their strength until we penetrate into Germany itself.'

'That's right. We haven't fighter escorts, so we get clobbered. And how we're getting clobbered. Do you know what our losses were on our last mission?' Although Davies nodded, the American told him regardless. 'That's nearly a thirty per cent loss rate, Davies. And that's about it. We can't go on much longer until we get more B.17s or adequate fighter cover.'

Davies gave a start. 'You're not thinking of suspending operations, sir?'

'What goddam choice do we have?' Staines demanded. 'No Air Force can take those kind of losses for long.' As the shaken Davies dropped into a chair, the American went on: 'You can see now why certain characters back home are asking why your Fighter Command, with its thousands of front-line ships, isn't giving us escort protection.'

Uncertain of Staines' stance in the controversy, Davies prevaricated. 'I take it you're referring to this campaign Lambert, the novelist, is leading, sir?'

The Texan scowled. 'Who else? The sonofabitch saw some of our ships coming back from Munich and the articles he sent back to the States were almost hysterical.'

Davies took heart from this attack on Lambert. 'What can Leigh Mallory do? The Spitfire was designed for short-range defence, not escort duty.'

The Brigadier was offering Staines another glass of whisky. The American nodded his acceptance before turning back to Davies. 'No one's arguing about that. But we can't ignore public opinion back home. Everything's at stake here, including our allocation of B.17s. We haven't half enough already: we're going to get fewer if Congress decides they're throwing good money after bad. Don't forget we've a powerful body in the States who want us to concentrate on the Japs first, and this propaganda of Lambert's is playing right into their hands.'

Although Davies seldom drank before dinner, he felt a need for the whisky the Brigadier was now offering him. 'It's even more serious than I thought.'

'You'd better believe it. It's turning into the kind of disillusionment that could spread throughout all the Services and even affect decisions in the White House itself. That's why I'm interested in this idea the Brigadier has put up to me. If you could pull it off, you'd be guaranteed the kind of publicity that would knock Lambert's campaign to hell.'

Davies threw a delighted glance at the elderly Brigadier. 'Then you're prepared to give us the green light?'

Staines's raised cigar checked him. 'Not until you've cleared up two points for me. How are your boys going to escape detection on their way out? To me it looks damn nearly impossible.'

'They're all specialists at low-level flying, sir. And don't forget they've already done it once.'

'What do you mean – already done it?'

'When they bombed the servomechanism factory at Hoffenscheim. They'd be flying at least two-thirds of the way along the same track.'

The Texan seemed about to say something, then shrugged instead. 'All right. They'll be the ones who'll get clobbered if they're picked up. But what about my boys? What guarantee can you give that half of 'em won't be killed?'

Davies had already decided to make no rash promises. 'Naturally we can't promise there'll be no casualties. For one thing we don't know what the German reaction will be. But my boys are experts at this kind of attack and we don't think the risks are very high.'

Staines studied his face for a moment, then turned to the Brigadier. 'Can we rely on your partisans?'

The Brigadier's quiet voice was an assurance in itself. 'We've used them before, sir, and they've always proved trustworthy.'

There was the sound of sandpaper on wood as Staines rubbed his chin. Then, giving a grunt of decision, he nodded at Davies. 'All right, show me the nuts and bolts.' As the delighted Davies dug into his briefcase and began pulling out photographs and statistics, the Texan checked him. 'As you're doing this as much for our sakes as your own, let's get one thing straight. This is a political mission as well as a military one. Which means that if it turns out a shambles, Lambert will skin you, your squadron, and the entire RAF alive. As I've sanctioned it they'll probably have me shovelling snow for Christmas too, but at least I know what I'm doing.'

Davies glanced at the silent Brigadier before answering. 'We're aware of the risks, sir. But if you're prepared to take them, so must we. Without allowing things to get worse, I don't see what alternative we have.'

Staines gave a grin of appreciation. 'I'll order a couple of shovels, Davies, just in case. Now fill me in with the details.'

CHAPTER 6

The large American car halted outside the wicker gate. The driver, a young and loquacious G.I., turned in his seat. 'The Black Swan. I guess this is the pub, sir.'

His passenger, the bearded Lambert, was gazing at the old country inn alongside the road. Solidly built with white-washed walls and a grey slate roof, it was reached by two gravel paths, one leading through a garden to a private porch, the other to the saloon and public bars. A large crab apple tree, bearing its September fruit, stood just behind a picket fence.

The G.I. was grinning. 'You know you won't get a drink? The Limeys have this crazy thing about licensing laws.'

'I know.' Climbing out, Lambert surveyed the airfield opposite. Hangars and the Control Tower could be seen over the long wooden fence that served as its perimeter. Fifty yards down the road a 25-cwt transport emerged from the main entrance, paused outside a sentry box, then accelerated towards Highgate. The autumn sun was already low in the sky and a sullen bank of cloud on the horizon hinted there would be fog again that night. Hiding a shiver, Lambert walked down the private path to the front porch. Finding the oaken door locked, he swung down a heavy iron knocker. About to knock a second time, he heard the sound of a bolt being withdrawn and a couple of seconds later a girl appeared in the doorway. 'Good afternoon, sir. What do you want?'

Lambert's eyes flickered over her appreciatively. She was a big handsome girl with bold features and dark hair. The sweater she was wearing and the short apron beneath it, drawn tightly round her waist, accentuated her large breasts.

Seeing Lambert's interest, she lifted a hand and touched her hair. Maisie, the barmaid of the Black Swan, as generously natured as she was well-proportioned, was a girl whose feminine instincts were triggered automatically when a man entered her orbit. When one appeared with the flashes of an American war correspondent on his greatcoat, Maisie's reflexes were as acute as a seismograph.

'My name's Lambert,' the correspondent told her. 'Ernest Lambert. Are you Maisie?'

The girl looked surprised. 'How do you know my name?'

'You were engaged once to a Canadian, weren't you? A pilot who won the VC.'

Maisie's expression changed. It was only six months since Gillibrand had been killed defending the airfield and the reminder was still painful to her. Before she could reply Lambert nodded towards a field that lay alongside the inn. 'You can still see scars in the stubble over there. Is that where he crashed?'

As the girl nodded there was a shout from inside the pub. 'Who is it, Maisie?'

'An American,' Maisie shouted back. 'A war correspondent.'

'A what?'

'An American war correspondent.'

A man wearing braces and an open-necked shirt appeared in the hall and came to the girl's side. Joe Kearns, the genial owner of the inn and a friend of Adams, was in his middle fifties with a countryman's ruddy face and thinning white hair. He gazed curiously at the bearded Lambert. 'What can we do for you, sir?'

In spite of being a New Englander, Lambert had never been able to take cold weather and was secretly cursing the chilly afternoon that no one appeared to be feeling but himself. 'I'm visiting a few RAF stations. Can you spare me a few minutes?'

Pushing forward, Kearns saw the man's shoulder flashes. Although looking puzzled, he nodded. 'I reckon so, sir. Come inside.' He turned to Maisie. 'Take him into the private lounge, lass, while I find my jacket.'

The room Lambert entered had a mullioned window set in an alcove. The walls were oak-panelled and blackened beams crossed a low, whitewashed ceiling. With shadows gathering in the corners and the thick stone walls defying noises from the airfield, the atmosphere was that of a bygone age. Lambert's nod expressed his approval.

'This is all I expected. How old is the inn?'

Maisie had all the indifference of her kind to her heritage. 'I dunno. Hundreds of years, I suppose. Won't you sit down?'

Lambert settled into a high-backed chair and pulled out a packet of Camel cigarettes. 'Will you have one?'

Maisie examined the packet as he offered it to her. 'Gillie used to smoke these.'

'Sit down and tell me about him.'

Maisie accepted a light, then dropped somewhat reluctantly into a chair at the opposite side of the window recess. 'What do you want to know?'

'Tell me how he won his VC.'

'It was the morning the Jerries raided the camp. Gillie was waitin' to go on a met. flight and managed to get his plane off the ground. He shot down two, maybe three of 'em and then he must have run out of ammunition because he crashed into a Jerry who was goin' to bomb the Control Tower.' The girl lowered her head and pretended to adjust a high-heeled shoe. 'They both crashed into that field over there.'

'He was alone in his ship, wasn't he?'

'His ship?'

'I mean his aircraft.'

'Yes,' Maisie muttered. 'His regular navigator, Jimmie, had been killed a few days before, and he left his new one on the ground. I suppose he didn't want him killed as well. Not that it made any difference. He was killed later when they did the raid in Norway.'

'That's how it's been for years, sir.' The voice came from Kearns in the door-way, now wearing a tweed jacket with leather elbows. 'We just get to know 'em and then they're killed. Sometimes you forget who's dead and who's alive.'

'You must have known Grenville,' Lambert said.

'Of course, sir. He's the squadron leader who led the raid to Norway. He got the VC too, you know. Would you like a drink?'

The American saw Kearns had a glass in his hand. 'I thought you English weren't supposed to serve drinks in the afternoon.'

Kearns put the glass beside him. 'We can't sell 'em, sir. But there's nothing to stop us giving one to a visitor.'

Lambert discovered the drink was whisky. 'Aren't you two joining me?'

'If it'll make you more comfortable, sir, we'll have a small one.' Kearns glanced at Maisie. 'I opened a new bottle, luv. You'll find it under the counter in the saloon.'

With an inviting swirl of her skirt and a backward glance at Lambert, Maisie withdrew from the lounge. Lambert watched her go, then offered Kearns a Camel. The innkeeper shook his head. 'No thanks, sir. I'm a pipe smoker myself.'

Lambert's tone was casual as he put his cigarettes away. 'I guess the boys use this pub as much as they use their Mess?'

'Yes, sir, I think they do. And we try to make 'em feel as much at home as we can.'

'In other words you're almost one of the family?'

'That's one way of putting it, sir.'

'So you must know as much about them as anybody?'

'I'm not quite sure I follow you.'

'They come and drink here. So you'll hear both their private and professional problems.'

Kearns, who for all his amiable exterior was nobody's fool, was instantly on his guard. 'What we hear we forget, sir. It's wartime, you know.'

A quick learner himself, Lambert realized he was not talking to some country pushover. 'We have that problem in my job every day – what it's safe to publish and what we should hold back. So don't get me wrong. I don't want any state secrets but I'd appreciate one or two harmless stories for my newspaper.'

'Is that why you're here, sir? To write about the squadron?'

Lambert lifted an eyebrow. 'What else? 633 Squadron's a big name in the States. People can't read too much about it.'

With his affection for the squadron on a par with Davies', Kearns was mollified by the flattery. At the same time he was too much of a Northcountryman to lower his guard that swiftly. 'They deserve a bit of credit. I've never met a finer bunch of lads.'

'Tell me about their new squadron commander. How do you reckon he stands up alongside Grenville?'

'Mr Moore?' Kearns hesitated to find the right words. 'He's a different man in one way and yet he's alike in another. If you know what I mean.'

'I'm not sure I do.'

'Well, Mr Grenville was more forceful in his ways whereas Mr Moore is quieter like. But from all I hear he's every bit as good a leader. The lads have come to think the world of him.'

'He's got a bit of money behind him, hasn't he?'

Kearns was instantly on guard again. 'I wouldn't know much about that, sir. All I know is he hasn't any side and treats everyone the same.'

'What about Frank Harvey, the guy who was wounded bombing that ammo factory? Did you know him?'

The phrasing of Lambert's question was deliberate. With the need to hide from the public the Germans' lead in rocketry, the Allied Governments had instructed the Press and radio to describe the Rhine Maiden exploit as a raid on a huge enemy ammunition factory. Kearns, who because of his friendship with Adams knew more than he was supposed to know, was equally cautious in his reply. 'Aye, we knew the lad well. He was one of us.'

'One of you?'

'Aye. A Yorkshireman. His home isn't that far from here.'

'What sort of a guy is he?'

'A big feller. Dour but as straight as a die. And a hard man to stop if he gets the bit into his teeth.'

'Didn't he have a girl friend staying here?'

Kearns was wondering how much the war correspondent knew. Anna Reinhardt, the German girl working for the Allies, had stayed a week in the Black Swan before returning to Europe to organize the Mosquito raid. The innkeeper decided the Yorkshire dictum of 'when in doubt say nowt' was the wisest course.

'He might have had, sir. But plenty of lads bring their girl friends here.'

An expert on interrogation, Lambert could see he was getting nowhere with the canny innkeeper. Downing his whisky, he rose. 'I'd like to stay longer but the C.O. might show me round the arifield today and there isn't that much light left. Can I have a room if I need one tonight?'

Maisie had just appeared in the doorway and answered for Kearns. 'Yes; we're empty at the moment. Aren't we, Joe?'

Kearns could do nothing more than nod his head. At the front door the American turned to him. 'I'll phone you from the airfield as soon as I know the score. In about an hour's time.'

He gave a shiver as Maisie opened the door for him. 'Is it always as cold around here in September?'

'We can get early winters,' the innkeeper confessed. 'This looks like being one of 'em.'

Maisie watched the American climb into his car before withdrawing from the porch. Kearns frowned at her as she closed the door. 'Why did you tell him we'd plenty of room? If he stays the night he's going to be asking more questions.'

Maisie shrugged. 'So what? He's a war correspondent, isn't he? What can we tell him he can't find out somewhere else?'

Kearns was wondering at his unease. 'I don't know. But be careful what you say to him until I've had a word with Frank Adams.'

Back on the road the G.I. had reversed the car and driven through the station gates to the guardroom. As a young S.P. conferred with him, an enormous shout made a nearby puppy drop its tail and run for its life. A massive middle-aged sergeant had emerged from the guardoom and was making towards the car. 'You, lad! What do you think you're doing?'

The young S.P. stiffened and turned an embarrassed face. 'It's the American war correspondent, sergeant.'

'And you're telling him how you're winning the war, are you? Get back to your duties, lad, and leave this to your betters.'

As the red-faced youngster backed away, the sergeant bent down to the driver's window and pointed at a gravel strip opposite. 'That's where you park, lad. You can wait there while I take your gaffer to the C.O.' Turning, he threw open Lambert's door. 'Mr Lambert, sir?'

Lambert's bearded face gazed out. 'Yes, sergeant.'

'The C.O.'s expecting you, sir. Follow me, please.'

Curious eyes followed the two men as Lambert obeyed. Six feet three inches tall, without one speck of mud on his white gaiters and polished boots, the sergeant was a figure straight from the War Manual. Behind him the forty-six-year-old Lambert, at least nine inches shorter, was finding his hairy-chested image suffering from the contrast. In an instinctive effort to compensate, he was walking with longer strides than usual, with his iron-grey beard thrust forward like a cow-catcher of a Western locomotive.

The sergeant marched off the road, opened a door, and stood like a granite statue while Lambert passed through. The N.C.O. then led the way down the corridor, the impact of his boots bringing Lambert visions of typewriters leaping into the hands of startled Waafs. His rat-tat-tat on the C.O.'s door sounded like a burst of machine-gun fire. A second later he threw the door open, whipped up a salute like a karate chop, and made his announcement.

'Mr Lambert-sir!'

Henderson, who seemed singularly unruffled by this display of military efficiency, rose from his desk and came forward. 'Thank you, sergeant. Please come in, sir.'

The impassive S.P. whipped up another salute and vanished. Shaking hands with Lambert, Henderson closed the door. 'Welcome to Sutton Craddock. Shall I take your coat?

Lambert's eyes were on the small coke stove that served to heat Henderson's office. With fuel in short supply at this stage of the war, general orders forbade fires until October 1st and the Scot was not one to steal a march on his men. 'No, thanks, Group Captain. I'll stay put for a while.'

Henderson drew up a chair for him. 'Would you like a cup of tea?' Then, remembering. 'Or a cup of coffee?'

Lambert hid another shiver. 'Make mine coffee.'

Henderson opened the ante-room door. 'Get us a couple of coffees, will you, Laura?' He glanced over his shoulder. 'Black or white?'

'Black and strong,' Lambert told him. His gaze followed the big Scot as Henderson returned to his seat behind the desk. With Americans generally the taller of the two races and yet with the first men he had encountered at Sutton Craddock both dwarfing him, Lambert felt it was not one of his better days. Shaking his head at the cigarettes the Scot was offering him, he pulled out his pack of Camels. 'I like 'em toasted. You care for one?'

Henderson reached out amiably. 'It'll make a change. We used to get these in our Mess at one time but they seem to have dried up recently.'

As the men lit their cigarettes they took the opportunity to size one another up. Too goddam easy-going like so many of the other Limey's he had met, was Lambert's assessment. And this was supposed to be one of their crack units. When the hell were they going into top gear? Or hadn't they got a top gear?

Henderson's impression was even less favourable. A professional airman, he had found it distasteful that a civilian should have the power to investigate and criticize the force he served in. That the investigator should also be a foreigner and a scribbler of fiction to boot seemed the final insult to the Scot. Although conscious of his prejudice, he liked neither the man's aggressive manner nor his somewhat protuberant eyes. As for his untrimmed hair and beard, the clean-shaven Scot decided they epitomized the undisciplined Press world from whence he came.

The smoke both men exhaled suggested a certain satisfaction with the assessments. Lambert moved his gaze round the austere office with its large wall map of Europe, its charts, graphs, and photographs of aircraft and airmen. 'So this is the unit that received a special commendation from Congress! That doesn't happen every day of the week.'

Henderson was wondering if there was any irony in the abrasive New England voice. 'We're aware of that. Naturally it's something we're very proud of.'

'They gave you a lot of coverage in the States. More in fact than they gave our own boys. Did you know that?'

'No, I didn't. If it's true your Press were at fault. It was a joint operation and we certainly appreciate the help your boys gave us that day.'

The correspondent gave his characteristically impatient nod. 'What are your views on those rockets, Henderson? Were they the menace they were made out to be?'

Henderson shrugged. 'I can only go on what the boffins say. According to them no daylight formation would have stood a chance once they were in full production.'

'You think they'd have done more damage than their fighters are doing now?'

It was a question that reminded Henderson he was dealing with a professional interrogator, and he proceeded cautiously. 'I'd say a great deal more. They would also have left Jerry's fighter force intact for the invasion when it comes.'

The correspondent leaned forward. 'Do you know what I find particularly interesting about the Rhine Maiden mission, Henderson?'

'No. What?'

'I'm fascinated by the escort job you did on our B.17s on their way back. All the crews I've spoken to said if you hadn't given them fighter cover until they reached our Thunderbolts, their casualties would have been twice as high.'

Henderson almost relaxed his vigilance. 'It's generous of them to say so. But then we've always had good relations with your aircrews.'

With his victim lured over the trap, Lambert pulled the trip lever. 'I'm sure you have. But it does raise a question a lot of folks back home are asking. If your unit was able to give such effective fighter cover on the Rhine Maiden job, why can't it be done more often? The Mosquito is in full production now and you're getting more and more squadrons equipped with them.'

Annoyed at the way he had been trapped, the Scot almost over-reacted. 'That's just what amateurs would think. Made of wood as she is, the Mosquito is something of a miracle plane but her main strengths are her speed and her high-altitude performance. If she had to take on German fighters in daylight at the altitude your B.17s fly at, she'd be at a disadvantage, particularly if she had to carry auxiliary tanks.'

For one so aggressive, Lambert was looking almost bland. 'And yet I've got dozens of witnesses who say she was a match for the Heinies over Bavaria.'

It was not like Henderson to brag about his squadron but the moment seemed to call for it. 'You're forgetting this is one of the RAF's specialist units. Many of my boys are on their second tour of operations and some are on their third. That's the reason they did so well.'

'Couldn't other squadrons receive the same training?'

'It's not just training – it's experience. And experienced men are in short supply. Most die before they can get it.'

'So you don't think Mosquitoes are the answer to the losses our boys are suffering?'

'I'm sure they're not,' Henderson said bluntly. 'What you want is a long-range, single-seater fighter that can go all the way there and all the way back. Failing that you need more Forts in your formation to increase your fire power.'

Lambert's smile was innocuity itself. 'I see you're quite a strategist.'

Henderson knew he ought not to retaliate but the temptation was too great. 'Aren't we all? At least I've got the excuse that flying is my business.'

It was the moment when the Waaf sergeant brought in the coffee and for that Henderson blessed her. 'Thanks, Laura.' Guiltily remembering Davies' orders not to get involved in argument, Henderson hastened to his cupboard and brought out the new bottle of Scotch. 'What about a shot to keep out the cold?'

Lambert shrugged. 'Why not?'

Somewhat surprised the correspondent was showing no rancour, the Scot poured a generous shot into both cups. 'If you want to take a look round the station, we'd better start in a few minutes or it'll be too dark.'

Lambert picked up his cup. 'Is it all right with you if we go round tomorrow?'

Henderson stared, dismayed. 'Are you staying overnight?'

'I can't very well get back to London tonight, can I?'

The Scot recovered with an effort. 'No, I suppose not. All right, let's do that. Do you want us to find you a billet now or later?'

With an eye on the empty stove, Lambert reacted quickly. 'There's no need. I'm staying in that pub across the road, the Black Swan.' Before the Scot could show his surprise, the American went on: 'If it's O.K. with you, I'd like to attend your briefings tomorrow. What missions have you lined up?'

The embarrassed Henderson felt aggrieved that Davies was not there to handle his own chickens. 'I'm afraid that won't be possible. We're on stand-down at the moment.'

The correspondent stared at him. 'Stand-down? I thought things were at crisis point right now?'

'We only got the order yesterday.' Unable to give the true reason, the pink-cheeked Henderson could only curse inwardly at the flaccid excuse he had to make. 'They must have decided the boys needed a rest. They've been on maximum effort for nearly a month.'

Lambert's silence seemed to say it all. Fumbling inside his greatcoat he pulled out a notebook. 'I'm told you've got an American pilot on your establishment. A guy called Millburn.'

'That's right. He's acting as flight commander at the moment. He's one of our best men.'

'I'd like a talk with him. Can you arrange it?'

'Yes. In any case you'll probably see him in the Mess tonight.' A malicious vision that embraced violent aerobatics and air-sickness brightened Henderson's expression. 'If you'd like to take a closer look at the Mosquito, why don't you ask Millburn to take you up? I can't think of anyone who could demonstate its performance better.'

CHAPTER 7

Condensation gave the carriage window the texture of frosted glass. McKenny felt its chill as he rubbed it with the palm of his hand. The autumn evening was almost over and night was settling over the flat Lincolnshire fields. The train rattled over a bridge and the young pilot caught sight of a car with blinkered headlights passing along a road below. A solitary house with darkened windows swept past. Then the fields returned with their trees and fog-shrouded hedges.

McKenny blamed the shiver that ran through him on the unheated train. With rolling stock neglected by the demands of war, its progress suggested that the driver was afraid that any higher speed than 20 m.p.h. would result in its disintegration. To the young Irishman, whose failure to keep the appointment he had made for that evening would mean the waste of his hard-won leave, the dragging minutes were torture. As the train halted for the umpteenth time at a country station, he forgot the elderly couple sharing the compartment and muttered a curse. Glancing round, he saw neither the man nor the woman had taken any notice of him. Grey-haired, tired-faced, both looked too occupied with their own problems.

The clatter of boots made him turn back to the window. A sizeable party of American airmen, hellbent for a night out in Lincoln, had burst into the dimly-lit station and were boarding the train. Half a dozen of them clustered outside his door, then saw the elderly couple and moved into the next compartment. As the hiss of steam quickened he could hear their voices and laughter. Their gaiety seemed to mock him and he huddled deeper into his greatcoat.

It was another half hour before the train pulled into Lincoln. Grip in hand, McKenny was waiting at a door and leapt down to the platform before the train stopped moving. Even so a party of Americans were first at the barrier and before he reached the taxi rank every cab had gone. A big American top sergeant left behind gave him a friendly grin. 'Hard luck, bud! But it's always this way on pay days.'

McKenny realized now that he was going to be late no matter what happened. Fighting back panic, he lowered his grip to the pavement. The light had long gone and wisps of fog were drifting into the forecourt. The American gave a shiver. 'Jesus, it's raw. Why the hell had they to post me to a dump like this?'

McKenny was watching the fog and wondering if it would add to his problems. The American, who by this time had recognized his gaffe as well as McKenny's rank, tried to make amends by offering him a cigarette. 'This your home town, sir?'

Behind McKenny a dozen other Americans were assembling.

'No,' he muttered. 'I'm Irish. My sister lives here.'

The sergeant relaxed. 'They told me it didn't start getting cold in these parts before October or November. So what's wrong this year?'

McKenny sucked in smoke. 'It happens this way sometimes. It could warm up again in October or it could be an early winter.'

'Jesus, I hope it warms up. I come from New Mexico and . . .'

To McKenny's relief a taxi entered the forecourt. 'Maybe we can share,' the American offered. 'Which way are you going?'

'The Western Hospital.'

'Is that near the American Services Club?'

The Irishman thanked God. 'It's on the way.'

'Then jump in and let's go.'

The taxi drew away. With the recent raid having enforced a blackout, traffic was at a crawl. The American noticed the glances McKenny kept giving his watch. 'Does your sister work in the hospital, sir?'

The pilot's voice was curt. 'No. I'm seeing her later.'

About to ask a further question, the American noticed his expression and gazed out of the window instead. Five minutes later the taxi halted and the driver glanced back. 'Is this all right, sir, or do you want to go inside?'

McKenny saw the taxi standing outside the hospital entrance. Dragging out his grip, he began fishing into his pockets for money. The distant sound of traffic was muffled by the settling fog. His urgency made the good-natured American tap the driver's shoulder. 'I'll see to it, bud.'

Thanking him, McKenny ran across the road to a pub that stood on a street corner. Pushing aside a blackout curtain he entered a large saloon bar with a long counter and glass-partitioned alcoves. Girls and servicemen, many of them Americans from East Anglian bomber bases, packed the floor and clamoured for drinks at the bar. The alcoves with their leather window seats were occupied by civilians, most of them elderly.

The impact of glare, smoke and noise halted the Irishman for a second before he started forward. To his relief he caught sight of the girl when he was halfway across the bar. Wearing the uniform and cape of a staff nurse, she was sitting in one of the alcoves with her back to a window. As McKenny struggled towards her a young American corporal, with a crew cut and a face like a newly-picked apple, left his grinning friends and edged by an elderly couple into her alcove. The girl's reply to his invitation was a smile and a shake of her head. When the American's second attempt failed he grinned bashfully and returned to the bar.

The youngster's friends were chaffing him as McKenny pushed past. By this time the girl had seen him and her look of relief matched his own. 'Thank God,' he muttered, bending down to kiss her. 'I was afraid you might have given up by this time and gone back.'

'What happened?' she asked.

With a groan he dropped alongside her. 'Nothing really. Just the damn train took twice as long to get here as it should.'

'You're looking thinner,' she said. 'And very tired.'

His gaze was devouring her, moving from her short, dark hair to her large expressive eyes, and down to her shapely mouth. McKenny, who was as deeply in love as a man can be, had long ago decided he would never anywhere see another girl as beautiful as Joan Williamson.

'I was afraid I was going to miss you,' he muttered. 'How long can you stay?'

'Only until nine. It was difficult enough to get an hour off at such short notice.'

'I couldn't phone you earlier – I only got the 24-hour pass this morning. And then I had to use the excuse I was worried about my sister.'

'How is she?'

It was a measure of McKenny's infatuation for the girl that he had hardly given a second thought to his sister during the journey. 'Haven't you phoned her to find out?' she asked when he did not answer.

'She's not on the phone,' he muttered.

'Couldn't you have phoned one of her neighbours?'

He shifted guiltily on the window seat. With the minutes as precious as jewels, his love begrudged every moment spent on anything but their problem. 'Can't you stay until ten?' he urged. 'Surely the girls would cover up for you.'

'I can't, Paddy. We're hopelessly under-staffed and we've got air raid casualties and casualties from the bomber bases as well as our normal intake. We're working fourteen and sometimes sixteen hours a day. So how can I take another hour off?'

'You can't or you won't?' he asked bitterly.

'That isn't fair, Paddy.'

'Why isn't it fair? I'm as sorry as the next man for those poor devils over there but I don't think a bit of feeling for me would come amiss. I'm in the Forces and I bleed too, you know.'

Her dark head lowered. 'I know how hard all this is for you. And I'm desperately sorry.'

'I don't think you do know. I happen to be so much in love with you that the stinking world isn't going to be worth living in if I lose you.'

In a world at peace she would have chided him for self-pity. In a world at war, with him in one of its most dangerous occupations, she could feel nothing but apprehension. 'You mustn't talk like that.'

'Why not? Don't tell me you care.'

'Of course I care. I care very much.'

'You've a strange way of caring, haven't you? Is it true what you said in the letter I received this morning? That you're going overseas soon?'

She gave a hesitant nod. 'Yes. We hope to leave sometime in the middle of November.'

His exclamation drew the attention of the elderly couple at the far side of the table. 'You *hope* to leave. And yet you've just been telling me about all the casualties you're getting in. What are you trying to do? Escape?'

Her eyes lifted. 'You can't believe that of me.'

397

'How the hell do I know what to believe? When we got engaged six months ago you told me you'd never been so happy in your life. Now you can't get away from me fast enough. What have I done? I've hardly seen you in that time.'

'How often must I tell you that you haven't done anything? I can't help what has happened to me. I've even tried to fight it but it's no use.'

There was a torment in his bitterness that made her wince. 'So I have to be dumped like a load of ballast. My Christ, it turns you people callous. You don't give a damn what you do to people who love you.'

Before she could protest a middle-aged couple pushed past, forcing both of them to their feet. When they dropped back she fumbled for his hand beneath the table. 'It has nothing to do with you, Paddy. You must believe that.'

When he did not answer she saw he was staring down at her hand that no longer wore his ring. At his look her voice broke. 'What else could I do? I can't let you go on hoping. It's too cruel.'

He snatched his hand away. 'Cruel? What do you think this is?' Pain made him want to hurt her as he was hurt. 'Do you know what I think? You're not satisfied to be like the rest of us, doing our small bit to win the war. You have to be the Lady with the Lamp, shining it through Darkest Africa. Have you ever thought of that?'

The girl turned pale. Alongside her the middle-aged woman nudged her husband to listen. 'I know how it must seem to you. But that's the problem. Until one's had the experience it is difficult to understand.'

There was no reaching him in his bitterness. 'You couldn't put it better. You're something special now. I'm just one of the cattle who isn't worth a damn to anyone.'

For a moment she showed anger. 'That's a wicked thing to say. You're just as important as I am. Perhaps much more important.'

'Who to?' he sneered. 'God?'

She flinched. 'Don't talk like that, Paddy.'

'Why not? It's a fair question, isn't it?'

She tried to catch hold of his hand again. 'Talk to your priest about it. Why didn't we think of that before? Tell him everything and I'm sure he'll make you understand.'

His laugh sounded like a file on metal. 'That old hypocrite? All he'll give me is a mouthful of cant. Anyway, what makes you think I still go to Church?'

'You haven't stopped going?'

'Of course I've stopped. I haven't been since you gave me my cards.'

She was showing more distress than she had shown all evening. 'You mustn't do that, Paddy. You were brought up in the Church. You need it more than people over here.'

His eyes burned at her out of his dark, embittered face. 'If you do this to me I shall never go near the Church again. Never!'

Her voice dropped into a whisper. 'That's blackmail, Paddy.'

'If it's blackmail, it's what you're doing to me.'

'Speak to your priest,' she begged. 'At least try it.'

He saw he had found a way of hurting her. 'Since when do you go to enemies for help?'

A shudder ran through her. 'Don't talk that way, Paddy. Please don't talk that way.'

'Why not?' he jeered. 'Are you afraid a thunderbolt might strike me down?'

She rose to her feet. 'I'm going to get you a drink. Wait here for me.'

He pulled her down. 'I don't want a drink. I want you to postpone that trip until you can see things more clearly. It's only a few months' delay. You can always go next year.'

Biting her lip, she allowed her eyes to touch the clock over the bar. Instantly he leapt to his feet. 'You can't get away from me fast enough, can you? Come on then – let's get it over!'

Turning, he pushed his way through the crowd of servicemen. The middle-aged woman, her face alight with vicarious excitement, leaned towards her husband as the girl ran after him. 'Paddy, please! Don't run off like this!'

He halted only when they were outside in the dark street. Two slow-moving cars went past with a hiss of tyres, then there was only the muffled murmur of traffic in the city centre. She hesitated a moment, then pulled him round to face her. 'Keep quiet and listen to me for a moment. You're wrong in thinking I don't want to marry you. I know you'd make me happy and I've always wanted children. That's why this is the hardest thing. . . .'

It was a mistake. Before she could finish his arms were around her, crushing her as if to fuse flesh against flesh. 'Then let's get married right away. I'll make the arrangements as soon as I get back.'

Relief made his words brittle. 'God, you've had me frightened these last few weeks. Don't frighten me like that again.'

Voices sounded behind them as the pub door opened. A soldier and a girl, their arms wrapped round one another, walked past. Watching them go over his shoulder, she knew that if she lived a hundred years nothing would be harder to say.

'You didn't let me finish, Paddy. I have to go through with this. I have to because it's so much stronger than I am. Won't you try to understand and not think badly of me?'

She felt she had driven a knife into his unguarded body. The white blur of his face stared at her, then he pushed her roughly away and started down the road. In the distance the cathedral clock was chiming the hour. Frantic for his safety, she ran after him. 'You can't just walk away like this. First you have to promise to take care of yourself. And you mustn't give up the Church. Please promise me you won't.'

He snatched his arm away. She knew the look he gave her would haunt her for the rest of her life. Sobbing, she followed him. 'Now you're being cruel. How can I help what has happened? Paddy, please! Say something.'

Hands driven into his greatcoat pockets, he was walking faster and faster. She ran another dozen yards after him, then halted. Behind her there was laughter as a party of servicemen filed out of the pub. As they moved in the opposite direction she realized the clock had stopped chiming. Ahead of her McKenny had not looked back and was beginning to merge into the dark shadows that lay across the pavement. She watched him a moment longer and then turned away. Her young face looked blinded with grief as she crossed the road and walked towards the hospital entrance.

CHAPTER 8

Henderson was chatting to Adams and Lambert in the Mess when he saw Millburn enter. Leaving Adams to hold the fort for a moment, he walked over to the American pilot and lowered his voice. 'Remember what I told you. Watch what you say.'

The tousle-haired Millburn grinned. 'Take it easy, sir. In a couple of days they'll be featuring us on the cover of *Time* magazine.'

Henderson was in no mood for jokes about Pressmen and publicity. 'The only pictures he's likely to publish are you lot clustered round the bar downing double Scotches. So don't go getting dreams of glory.'

He led the American to the bar. 'Lambert, this is Millburn, my American flight commander that you asked to meet.'

Lambert held out a hand. 'Glad to meet you, Millburn.' He indicated the ribbons of the DSO and DFC on Millburn's chest. 'It looks as if the British are taking good care of you.'

Millburn squinted down at the ribbons and grinned. 'We play poker for these. And I'm the best poker player on the squadron.'

Henderson scowled and intervened. 'I hate to say it but he did win them the hard way. Mind you, if he had ribbons for the women he's laid he'd look like an American general.'

Adams winced at the gaffe. Wondering what masochistic kink in his subconscious had let the words loose, Henderson did his best to make amends.

'It gets a bit expensive in pregnant Waafs. At the same time, if you were to offer me a half a dozen more Americans like him I'd think it fair exchange.' When Lambert made no comment, Henderson gave it up and made for his whisky that was standing on the bar. After conferring a moment with Millburn, Lambert turned to the Scot. 'You don't mind my having a private word with him, do you?'

Henderson motioned Adams towards him. 'No, go ahead. You can use my office if you like.'

Declining the offer, Lambert led Millburn away from the bar and pulled a couple of cigars from his battledress pocket. 'Havanas! I picked up a box yesterday.'

Millburn shrugged and took one. 'You been over here long?'

'Three weeks. Ten days in London and the rest of the time at our bomber bases in East Anglia. It's murder down there, Millburn. We're getting shot to hell.'

'Yeah,' Millburn muttered. 'We've heard about it.'

'They've got to have the same fighter protection you gave Staines' bombardment group down in Bavaria. If you could do it, why can't other Mosquito squadrons?'

Millburn's spontaneity owed nothing to the few words Henderson had slipped to him earlier. 'It's a long-range fighter's job. There's no other answer.'

'And yet you held them off. Why?'

Millburn had no effete English inhibitions about singing his unit's praise. 'Because the boys here are the best in the business. Haven't you done your homework?'

'Is that why you haven't moved over to the Yanks?'

The directness of the question made Millburn frown. 'I don't know. I haven't thought about it.'

'What else could it be?'

'Maybe I like the girls here!'

'Don't make a joke of it, for Christ's sake.'

'What do you want me to say? That I make more money here?'

'O.K. I'll spell it out to you. You've got years of combat experience. You ought to be giving the fruit of that experience to your own country. Period.'

The hot-tempered Millburn was showing resentment. 'What difference does it make? We're fighting the same enemy, aren't we?'

'That's not an answer and you know it.'

'Why do I have to give you an answer? I've nothing against my own guys: they're doing a great job. But I've been over here nearly three years and a man makes friends in that time. Anyway, what would I do on a heavy bomber unit? I'd be a fish out of water in a B.17.'

'You might get more respect in one,' the correspondent said dryly.

Millburn's black eyebrows came together. 'What does that mean?'

'There's a strong feeling back home that the RAF isn't doing all it could to protect our boys. As a member of the RAF you have to share that blame.'

'Blame? This is the outfit that destroyed the Rhine Maiden plant and got a Congressional commendation. You forgotten that?'

'That was an isolated incident. In general the British don't appear concerned about our losses. In fact some of us believe they're not sorry.'

'Not sorry?'

'That's right. It helps them to argue their night bombing policy is the correct one.'

Millburn was beginning to breathe hard. 'That's the biggest load of bullshit I've heard in years. Everyone here is as concerned as hell for our boys.'

'All the same, that's what's being said in the States. From the top downwards.'

Obeying Henderson in his own way until this moment, Millburn broke free of the leash. 'If it is, you're one of the guys who's handing out the poison. I've heard all about you, Lambert. You're the sonofabitch who's trying to split the Allies down the centre and give the Heinies the war on a plate.'

All conversation in the Mess ceased as men turned to stare at the incensed Millburn. Henderson, who had been keeping an anxious eye on him during the dialogue, gave Adams a horrified glance and hurried forward. 'What's all the shouting about, Millburn?'

The American was too irate to mince his words. 'Nothing, sir. I just hadn't met a Fifth Columnist before, that's all.'

Henderson's shocked face was a study of emotions. Half of him wanted to kiss the American on both cheeks and pin another medal on his chest; the other half was trying to imagine Davies' reaction if news of the incident reached him.

'You gone out of your mind, Millburn? Mr Lambert is a guest of the squadron. I want an apology immediately. And it had better be good.'

To the Scot's surprise, the bearded correspondent shook his head. 'Forget the apology, Henderson. I represent the free Press. That means any man's entitled to his views.'

Henderson damned his need for gratitude. 'That's very generous of you, sir.' He glared back at Millburn. 'In that case you'd better go to your billet and get your good manners back. Bloody disgraceful behaviour!'

Still angry, Millburn made for the door. Hesitating a moment, the Scot followed and caught him outside. 'What the hell are you trying to do, Millburn? Get us drawn and quartered over there?'

'Didn't you hear him?' the American demanded. 'He thinks we're glad when the Yanks have heavy losses.'

'He's not going to change his mind if we accuse him of being a Fifth Columnist, is he?' Henderson grunted. 'Pull yourself together. Things are bad enough as they are.'

Millburn relaxed as his temper cooled. 'I'm sorry, sir. But no guy should say things like that.'

Henderson felt a grin coming, battled hard, but it broke through. 'There's one good thing. Being a Yank yourself, he can't say it's Limey prejudice. But no more arguments with him, Millburn, or I'll bounce you all the way to East Anglia!'

Davies came on the telephone next morning while Henderson was showing Lambert round the airfield. Leaving the correspondent in Adams' care, the relieved Scot jumped into the jeep sent for him and was in his office four minutes later.

'Hello, sir. Sorry to have kept you waiting but I was out on the airfield with Lambert.'

Davies' voice was full of suppressed excitement. 'He arrived, did he? How are you getting on with him?'

'Not too badly, I suppose. Although in one way it's a pity we're on standdown. I've the feeling he thinks we're a pack of scroungers.'

Davies could contain his news no longer. 'He won't be thinking that for long, Jock. The job's on tomorrow morning. I got clearance from Intelligence ten minutes ago.'

The Scot felt his pulse quickening. 'Do I cancel all passes, sir?'

'Yes. And make sure any lads who're already out are back by 18.00 hours. I'll want your senior officers this afternoon. We'll also need the advice of your armament officer on what stores to carry.'

'What about Lambert? He's sure to want to attend.'

Davies' grunt betrayed how his decision hurt. 'Seeing one purpose of the exercise is to move public opinion in the States I suppose he has to be. All right, Jock, let him come. But don't let him leave the station afterwards. He's subject to the same security regulations as the rest of you.'

'What time can we expect you, sir?'

'I'm waiting for the last of the photographs and then I'm on my way. Say around 15.00 hours.'

In fact Davies arrived half an hour earlier. Henderson escorted him to the Operation Room where his senior officers were assembled. Among them were Moore, Teddy Young and Millburn. Lambert, more curious than anyone, was talking to Adams when the two men appeared. Waving everyone closer, Davies climbed on to the platform that stood beneath the huge map of Europe. The two red spots high up on his cheeks told those who knew him he was more than usually excited.

'Good afternoon, gentlemen. I've called you to this preliminary briefing because I've got a rather special operation for you tomorrow.' For a moment Davies' eyes rested on Lambert before sweeping round the arc of curious faces. 'It won't be news to you that our American colleagues have been suffering heavy casualties in recent months on their deep penetration raids into Germany. They've stuck at the job with all the guts in the world but without fighter escorts their losses have been frightening. Last week alone they lost over four hundred men.' As somebody whistled Davies nodded grimly. 'It doesn't take long to run up that score when every B.17 carries a crew of ten. We wish to Christ we could help them but the only fighter capable of escorting them is the Mustang and until enough of them get the Merlin engine, the Yanks are having to go it alone.'

With that punch delivered at Lambert, Davies changed his tone. 'However, there are more ways of killing the cat than shooting it. Our agents in France tell us that it's Jerry's practice these days to take all aircrew prisoners shot down in northern Europe to a special compound north of Paris where they've assembled a team of interrogation experts. Because this interrogation is very thorough, men are sometimes kept there for weeks. When they are finally released they're shipped away by special train to prison camps deep in Germany or Poland. Some of these trains carry two to three hundred prisoners.' Seeing Lambert give a start, Davies gave his imp-like grin. 'That's right, gentlemen. We're going to give one of these trains our special attention.'

Taking a pointer from the desk, he moved to the large map of Europe. 'Our agents in France informed us about this compound and the trains six week ago. When we expressed interest they began a detailed surveillance. All the trains so far have taken this route, Noyon to Guise, then through the Ardennes to Liège, Aachen, and so into Germany. We believe they're using this secondary route because of the attention our fighter-bombers are giving to the main-line tracks. We've now been informed the largest shipment of prisoners to date is moving out tomorrow. So this is your mission. To halt and disable this train so that a large band of partisans assembled close by will be able to free the prisoners and through their escape network help them to return to this country.'

A buzz of excitement filled the room as Davies walked back to the desk and picked up a pile of photographs. 'I want you to pass these round. They were taken by our agents of the stretch of line where your attack will take place, a valley deep in the Ardennes. We've chosen it because the Ardennes is both mountainous and heavily-wooded: ideal country for an ambush and an escape because communications are relatively poor.' He passed the first photograph to Henderson. 'You'll see the stretch of line ends in a tunnel. Two flak posts guard it. Your first job is to knock out these posts so that the partisans can block the tunnel with explosives without incurring too heavy casualties. Then, when the train is forced to halt, you'll disable the engine and knock out the flak wagons that protect it. Once you've done this the partisans will break open the wagons and with any luck get the prisoners well away before Jerry can react. As the partisans are bringing transport with them, we're hoping this shouldn't be too difficult. Any questions so far?'

There was a short silence as the photographs changed hands. Millburn was studying a blurred, long-range photograph of a train. 'What's the armament on these trains, sir? Do you know?'

'LMGs and 37mms,' Davies told him. 'One wagon in the front and one in the rear.'

'No 88s?'

'No.'

Moore and Young were conferring. A few seconds later the squadron commander's quiet voice stilled the buzz of conversation. 'It's difficult to judge from these photographs how wide the valley is. I take it the agents know we need plenty of width to make a broadside attack?'

With Moore having put his finger on the item that was worrying him most, Davies frowned. 'Of course they know.'

Young, knowing nothing of the politics behind the operation, put his foot in it with typical Australian aplomb. 'Let's hope they've chosen right, sir. Because I wouldn't like to be those prisoners if we have to attack fore and aft.'

It was all Lambert needed. 'I have a few questions, Air Commodore. Are all these prisoners Americans?'

Davies' dislike of the man betrayed itself in his reply. 'Not all, Mr Lambert. The RAF suffer losses too. But as it seems most of our survivors are sent to a compound near Rheims, we can expect the majority to be your countrymen.'

'Isn't this a rather unusual operation?'

Davies gave himself time to think. Although both he and Staines had known all along the correspondent was too shrewd not to guess the raid had political aspects, both had gone to considerable lengths to ensure he could not prove it. Davies' reply when it came was appropriately innocuous.

'Not for this squadron, Mr Lambert. They are specialists in precision operations.'

'All the same, it seems odd you're going to all this trouble to free our boys and doing nothing for your own in Rheims?'

'It's not odd at all, Mr Lambert. There isn't a railhead near our boys' compound: they have to be shipped away by motor transport.'

Lambert shrugged. 'O.K., so you want to free our boys. But then why don't you attack the compound instead of the train? Wouldn't that be safer for them?'

At this juncture Davies realized he was enjoying himself. 'It would certainly be safer for the prisoners, Mr Lambert. Unfortunately it would also be pointless because with German troops everywhere, the partisans couldn't assemble to get them away.'

The correspondent seemed unshaken by the grins of the airmen around him. 'As it's a job that concerns American lives, I can take it our own people have given you permission to go ahead?'

'Right from the top, Mr Lambert. General Staines himself has authorized it.'

Lambert threw a glance at Teddy Young. 'Then, although one of your flight commanders appears to have doubts, you yourself are quite confident no prisoners will be harmed?'

'Only a damn fool would make a promise like that,' Davies grunted. 'This is a war operation and like all war operations, it is a calculated risk. A few men might be injured or killed but many others might escape. General Staines is aware of this and prepared to take the gamble. So would the men on the train if you were able to ask them. That's what being a soldier instead of a civilian is all about, Mr Lambert.'

Someone let out a low whistle that was instantly suppressed as Davies glared round. Seeing Lambert still appeared unmoved, Davies decided to open up with all his guns.

'For an important representative of the American Press you seem remarkably unenthusiastic about our plan to help your boys escape, Mr Lambert.'

With the question pushing Lambert right out on a limb, the watching Henderson silently applauded as for the first time the correspondent hesitated. 'Not at all, Air Commodore. With the reservations I've made, I'm all for it.'

Like the good soldier he was, Davies pushed his advantage home. 'I'm glad. Because we do care about your boys, you know. If we pull this off I'd like the American public to know that.'

Lambert's expression told Henderson beyond doubt that the correspondent knew the name of the game. 'If you pull it off, Air Commodore, the public will certainly hear about it. Why shouldn't they? It's my job.'

With the majority of the officers present knowing nothing of the politics behind the operation, there was more than one puzzled face. Feeling he had won one small victory, Davies turned to Moore.

'As Jerry's unlikely to neglect you the way he neglects our fighters, I've got plenty of diversions laid on for you. The Banff Wing will be out over the coast of Jutland and II Group have promised to play hell over Northern France. So one way and another Jerry's defences should be well stretched. As far as the route goes, I thought you could use the Hoffenscheim one you used last month, although that's for your navigational officer to decide.'

'I take it you're not thinking of giving us a fighter escort, sir?' Young asked.

Davies had not yet forgiven the Australian for his gaffe. 'How the hell can I? The essence of this operation is to keep below Jerry's radar detectors. A gaggle of Spitties above you would be a dead giveaway. When you get over the target you'll have to provide your own cover.' When no one spoke, Davies turned to Lindsay, the Armament officer. 'I suppose you'll have to use rockets?'

'I'm afraid so, sir. Those flak wagons are cannon-proof.'

Davies' question betrayed his fear of a faultily-aimed rocket. 'You couldn't use armour-piercing shells?'

Both Lindsay and Moore shook their heads. Seeing Lambert's expression, Davies let the point drop. 'All right, let's move on to the flak posts. To be on the safe side one of your sections had better carry a couple of 250-pounders apiece. You can always jettison 'em later if you don't need them.'

Moore was studying a photograph of the valley again. 'Does anyone know if the gunposts have radios, sir?'

Davies was quick to guess how the squadron commander's thoughts were running. 'No. We don't know about the train either. But it shouldn't matter if our timing's right. By the time the crew can stop the train they'll be in reach of the partisans anyway.'

'I take it they won't be able to see the explosions?'

'The partisans say not. The track winds through the hills like a snake before it enters the valley. With any luck they won't see or hear anything.'

As Davies had feared, Lambert was not through with him yet. 'You've told me this unit specializes in this kind of mission, and of course I take your word for it. But I'm still not clear how they can take out those flak wagons without doing un-acceptable damage to the rest of the train.'

Davies' patience was beginning to run out. 'I haven't the time to give you a lec-ture in aerial tactics, Mr Lambert. Perhaps later on one of my specialist officers will go into details for you.'

'All the same, this is what the mission is all about. Suppose for example the Heinies change the make-up of the train and put a flak wagon in the middle. Will your boys still go ahead?'

'In all operations of this kind the squadron commander makes the final de-cision. If on seeing the train he decides the risks are unacceptable he is allowed to abort and return home. Does that make you any happier?'

'I'd be a lot happier if I knew what you consider an unacceptable risk, Air Commodore.'

Davies kept calm with a superhuman effort. 'I must be wrong but I keep on getting the feeling you don't want us to try to rescue your boys. If I'm right, as you've attended this briefing you might want to put your objection in writing. I'm afraid we shall still go ahead because High Command still controls these decisions but at least it will ensure your objection is made public.'

The intimidation his words contained angered even the case-hardened correspondent. 'No one's objecting to an attempt to rescue our boys, Air Commodore, and you know it. All I'm doing is objecting to any risks being taken with their lives.'

'And I've told you no unnecessary risks will be taken. Now do I have your permission to continue with this briefing?'

The two men's eyes held for a full five seconds before Lambert turned and made for a row of chairs along one side of the room. As he sat down, Davies glared round the arc of whispering men. 'Perhaps we can get down to business now. Lindsay, how many AP rockets have you got in that store of yours?'

CHAPTER 9

The only light shining in his Intelligence Room when Adams returned that evening was one near the door. With the far end in deep shadow and his myopic eyes taking time to adjust from the dusk outside, he was a moment before he noticed Sue Spencer sitting at her desk.

'Hello. What are you doing sitting in the dark like this?'

Her uncharacteristic embarrassment told him immediately something was wrong. 'I've got most of the material over to the Operations Room. I've been waiting for the Photographic Section to finish the extra prints.'

'Are they done?'

'Yes. They came a few minutes ago.' The girl rose. 'I'll take them over now.'

He waved her back into her seat. 'There's no hurry. Davies has just put the briefing back half an hour. There are still a few technical details he and Moore can't agree on. I left them to it.' As she sank reluctantly back he pulled out his pipe. 'It wasn't a bad meal tonight, was it?'

She shook her head, appeared about to say something, then changed her mind. Without quite knowing why, Adams said it for her. 'But then they always do put on a better meal before an operation, don't they?'

Her eyes met his own in the shadows. 'Yes. I suppose it's the Eat, Drink and Be Merry philosophy.'

Sinking down behind his desk, Adams began packing his pipe. 'What do you think of Lambert?'

He had the feeling only a part of her was talking to him. 'I couldn't make him out. At one moment I felt he was genuinely concerned about the American prisoners and in the next that his real objection to the operation was the harm it might do his case.'

'You were probably right both ways. He'll be like the rest of us: good in parts and bad in others. I think he is concerned about the American losses and he does believe we're dragging our feet in providing escorts.'

'He's not right about that, is he?'

'Not from all the information I've been given or found out. But it's easy to imagine how it must appear from the American viewpoint.' Adams' shrug told why he had always found it difficult to find a niche in life where he could operate without doubting his integrity. 'Anyway, how can any of us, Lambert included, ever know what goes on at the top? They probably don't know themselves.'

She managed a smile. 'You can sound quite cynical sometimes, Frank.'

As Adams gave a somewhat shamefaced grin, the scream of an electric drill could be heard. With the strike imminent, fitters were working throughout the night. The girl turned away with a shiver. 'Why do men fight, Frank?'

Tempted to give a bitter answer, Adams took another glance at her and thought again. 'Because the human race is stupid, I suppose.'

'Is that what you call it – stupid?'

Adams put a match to his pipe. 'It's as good a word as any on a dismal autumn evening.'

He sensed her resentment as she turned to him. 'Am I embarrassing you, Frank?'

'No.'

'I think I am. I'm sorry.'

Adams chose his words carefully. 'You don't have to be sorry. You've every right to be worried about Tony. You wouldn't be human if you weren't.'

'But I shouldn't show it when I'm on duty, should I?'

'You don't. You're astonishingly brave.'

'But I'm showing it tonight, aren't I?' When he did not answer her voice rose. 'Aren't I?'

'If you say so.'

'Why, Frank? Why tonight?'

'Because you can't hide fear all the time. Because you're human like the rest of us.'

She appeared not to be listening to him. 'They've done operations like this before. Often. So why am I so afraid tonight?'

'You're probably tired. Off you go and rest. I can manage without you at the briefing.'

She refused almost angrily. Then her tone changed. 'How much longer is it going on, Frank?'

'You mean the war? Oh, it can't last much longer. Not once we invade and we all know that's coming soon.'

'You mean it can't last more than another year? Or two years?'

'Stop being such a pessimist. Once we've got troops into Europe they could crack quickly.'

'The Germans? Never. They'll fight all the harder once we get near their old frontier.'

Adams, who had said much the same to fellow officers in the past, felt the odds were stacked against him that evening. 'We can't see into the future, Sue. So it's better not to try.'

Once again she appeared not to hear him. 'It's my own fault. I shouldn't have fallen in love. Only fools fall in love in wartime.'

Adams cleared his throat. 'Sue, be honest with both of us. Would you like to be posted?'

Her eyes widened. 'Posted?'

'Yes. You can't go on being tortured like this. Nobody can.'

She was staring at him as if he had suddenly become an enemy. 'Do you think it would be better not to know? To spend every minute fearing the worst?'

'It wouldn't be like that, Sue. Millions of people have loved ones in the war but they don't suffer the way you're suffering here.'

'How do you know that?'

'It's obvious they don't. And it's equally obvious why.'

'It's not obvious to me. I'd go out of my mind if I didn't know what was happening.' She was looking almost panic stricken as she gazed at him. 'You won't do it, will you, Frank? Please say you won't.'

Adams sighed. 'I ought to. In the long run it would be the best thing for you.'

The way she pulled herself together was a measure of her fear. 'Don't be silly. You said yourself everyone gets a bit depressed now and then. Now we've had a talk I feel better already.' Jumping to her feet she picked up a pile of photographs from her desk. About to carry them away, she paused. 'You won't do anything, will you, Frank?'

Adams sighed. 'No. Not if you don't want me to.'

Glancing down the hut to make certain it was empty, she bent down and kissed his cheek. 'Thank you, Frank. You're a wonderful person. Now I'll take these photographs over.'

Smiling at him, she tripped down the hut and deposited the prints in a cardboard box. Carrying the box to the door she turned and gave him another smile before disappearing. Adams, who could still feel the imprint of her kiss on his cheek, sat a minute before switching on the light. The irony of the kiss had not escaped him. She was afraid of him now.

The morning of the 27th was in keeping with the rest of that autumn week. A light drizzle of rain during the night gave way to a dark and grey dawn. The Met. Forecast promised some improvement in visibility later but with a depression anchored over the Low Countries there was no likelihood of clear skies that day.

With the operation scheduled for low-level, most of the air-crews were delighted: a low cloud base greatly diminished the chances of fighter interception. Senior officers, Davies in particular, were less pleased. Poor visibility meant difficult target identification, and that could affect the exact timing on which the mission rested.

Visibility notwithstanding, the squadron made its preparations with its usual high efficiency. With Davies expecting his 'scramble' call at any time after 09.00 hours, the Mosquitoes were already tuned and airworthy when the aircrews arrived at 07.30 to test them. After the pilots and navigators went off for breakfast, final checks were made and the aircraft were handed over to the armourers. Bombs were hoisted into bomb bays; rockets slung beneath wings. Magazines were snapped on to the 20mm cannon; shiny belts of .303 shells fed into the ammunition tanks. In a final act as significant as the closing of a visor, the safety pins of both bombs and rockets were withdrawn and the bomb doors closed. When the aircrews returned equipped with parachutes, revolvers, survival kit, foreign money and all the other paraphernalia they carried, their Mosquitoes had been turned into sophisticated and deadly war machines.

By 08.30, to Davies' great relief, the cloud base had lifted enough for the poplars at the far end of the airfield to be clearly visible. At 09.05 a terse call on the red telephone in Henderson's office sent a green Very light soaring up from the Control Tower. Within seconds the first Merlin gave its characteristic cough and fired. Other engines began firing as A-Apple, Moore's Mosquito, rolled from its dispersal point and began taxi-ing down the north-south runway. As other Mosquitoes followed it, the concentrated roar of thirty-two Merlins made every loose window on the airfield rattle.

At 09.09 a second green Very light soared up from the balcony on the Control Tower where Davies, Henderson and Lambert were standing. Immediately A-Apple's engines went into a higher octave and water began spraying from its tyres as it gathered speed. Heavy with its load of rockets and bombs, it dipped its wheels twice on the runway before breaking free and lifting with a crackling roar. As it banked away from the Control Tower the rest of the sixteen Mosquitoes followed at six-second intervals. All circled the airfield once. Then, slotting behind one another's starboard wings, the squadron headed south over the poplar trees. As the deep drone began to fade, Lambert glanced at Davies.

'They look good. I'll give you that.'

'They are good,' Davies declared. 'Complete professionals.' He turned to Henderson. 'Isn't that right?'

The undemonstrative Scot wished Davies would keep his pride to himself. 'We like to think so.'

'You are,' Davies assured him. 'No question about it.'

Lambert was pointing at the aircraft that were now little more than dots against the grey sky. 'Why are they flying in echelon like that?'

Davies was only too happy to emphasize his unit's expertise. 'We've found out that Jerry's long-range radar can pick us up almost as soon as we leave our airfields. By flying in echelon our images superimpose themselves on his radar screens and give him the impression we're heavies. When the boys dive down at Manston on the south coast and fly ultra low level, he'll think we've just been airtesting and we've landed again.'

The bearded Lambert gave a grimace of respect. 'Who thought that one up?'

'It's one of the tricks Moore brought with him from Pathfinders.'

'You think highly of Moore, don't you?'

Davies glanced at Henderson, who nodded his agreement. 'If anyone can do this job, he's the man.'

Lambert opened his mouth to say something, then closed it again. A morning breeze, fresh from the North Sea, was gusting into the balcony. 'You think we can go somewhere a bit warmer now?'

For an embarrassed moment Henderson believed the correspondent's discomfort was going to bring a grin from Davies. To his relief the Air Commodore stifled the impulse. 'Why not? There's nothing we can do for the next two hours. Let's go and have coffee in the Ops. room.'

CHAPTER 10

Hopkinson jabbed a finger at A-Apple's windshield. 'Hallé, skipper! Eleven o'clock.'

Moore took a quick glance at the crenellated skyline and eased A-Apple a couple of degrees to starboard. Adams had warned him there were heavy flak defences guarding the town's industries. Behind him the line of fifteen Mosquitoes curved like a piece of string and then straightened again. As the haze of smoke fell behind, a road appeared flanked by trees. At Hopkinson's nod Moore latched on to it, his wingtips no more than fifty feet above the tree tops. A man on a bicycle seeing the aircraft were Allied, wobbled alarmingly as he tried to wave to them. A convoy of enemy transports coming in the opposite direction braked and white faces stared upwards. Moore caught a split-second glimpse of a soldier throwing a rifle to his shoulder but A-Apple's speed swept the image away.

The road went past a farmhouse and ran straight as a die for a couple of miles. With a slip in concentration at that height meaning certain death, pilots had to keep their eyes focused at an imaginary point half a mile ahead. Images leapt into vision and swept as rapidly away: a stretch of cobblestones, two schoolgirls skipping excitedly, a narrow canal. A thump on Moore's arm was followed by Hopkinson's yell. 'Power cables ahead!'

A-Apple waggled its wings and switchbacked over the cables like a car in a fun-fair. Ahead, Moore saw a large bridge approaching. Hopkinson jabbed out a satisfied forefinger. 'There's the river, skipper.'

Moore was already swinging towards it. Striking the railway line that ran close to the river a few seconds later, he squatted A-Apple down on the track. 'How are we for time Hoppy?'

The navigator glanced at his watch. 'Just about bang on. We should reach Namur in three minutes.'

The thin-faced but sprightly Hopkinson was a Cockney who had been Gren-ville's navigator. Having missed the Swartfjord raid because of a wound received earlier, he had been one of the survivors of the old squadron when Moore had been sent to take Grenville's place. Shocked by the loss of his friends and in parti-cular his skipper, Hopkinson had at first resented Moore and made it clear he did not want to fly with him. Moore, who was never one to give orders when he could use persuasion, had not forced the Cockney to become his navigator but in-stead had pointed out how his exceptional navigational skills could save the squadron lives as well as wasted missions. His patience had been amply re-warded. Today Hoppy, as he was universally known, was as much an asset to him as he had once been to Grenville.

The railway track and its telegraph poles were blurred by speed as the sixteen Mosquitoes headed down it. Freed for the moment from the tyranny of dead reckoning, Hoppy was able to examine the grey sky above. Since they had left Sutton Craddock the cloud base had been steadily lifting and on the navigator's estimate was now at least 3,000 feet high.

The track sank into a cutting. Moore was now flying only a few feet above the trees that grew on the high banks. A startled crow, trying to escape, struck his port wing and was flung away, a tangle of bone and feathers. A road bridge ahead brought a signal from Hopkinson and he eased back on the wheel. The superbly trained pilots behind him reacted as one man and the line of Mosquitoes rose and dipped again. With 633 Squadron existing for precision operations of this kind, Moore had put his men through many hours of exacting practice and it was doubtful if there was another squadron in the Allied Services that could have flown at such a height for so long. Without doubt they were too low for radar detection and yet Moore was only too aware of the efficiency of the German Ob-server Corps. If they flew much longer down the railway track, fighters would be vectored on to an interception course.

Hoppy's ETA for Namur was only seconds adrift. As chimneys and then build-ings appeared ahead, Moore banked away from the track and flew south of the town. For a few seconds puffs of black smoke burst among the Mosquitoes as an alerted battery of 37s alongside a marshalling yard opened fire, and T-Tommy flown by Millburn shuddered as a piece of steel tore through its fuselage. Then green and brown fields were flowing below again as Moore's flight path took him out into the country. Hoppy nodded at his quick glance. 'Any second now, skip-per.'

Although their height prevented them seeing it, the crews knew the great plain of Liège lay on their left, with the forest-clad foothills of the Ardennes ahead. As the town's skyline disappeared behind them, Moore again took the Mosquitoes down to ultra low level. Startled cattle reared and fled as the sixteen thunderbolts roared past. Grass shivered and flattened under the air-blast of propellers. A clump of high trees appeared ahead. Like a line of horsemen taking a fence, the Mosquitoes soared over it and down. Hundreds of starlings, feeding in a freshly-ploughed field, rose in a startled cloud and swept away. In T-Tommy Gabby leaned towards Millburn. 'What's he trying to do, boyo? Turn us into moles?'

Millburn grinned. 'You know something? I always thought you were a mole.'

Gabby glared at him. 'You think that's funny.'

Millburn grinned again. 'I'll lay odds a mole wouldn't think so.'

Ahead in A-Apple Hoppy was jabbing a finger upwards. Nodding, Moore rose a hundred feet to extend the navigator's field of vision. Peering out, Hoppy checked his watch again. Five seconds later he gave a nod. 'O.K. skipper.'

Moore waggled his wings four times. Behind him, with Young in the lead, the fifteen Mosquitoes swung away north-east. The plan was simple; the timing complex. To avoid making the train crew suspicious, Moore would fly alone along the track, survey it, then turn north-east towards the tunnel, so completing two sides of a rectangle. Teddy Young would lead the squadron to the Meuse east of Namur and follow the river almost to Liège, when he would turn south-east, thus completing the other two sides of the rectangle. With distances and speeds precisely calculated, the squadron would be able to rendezvous with Moore the moment he broke radio silence. In later years sceptics would sneer at the suggestion that men could achieve such accuracy after flying hundreds of miles from their base. In fact it was quite common for aircrews to be within seconds of their ETAs.

Fields gave way to forests of pine as the lone A-Apple swept into the Ardennes. Compelled to fly higher than he would have liked because of the need to find the rail link between Namur and Marche, Moore could only hope the hill tops were screening him from the vigilant radar detectors. With both men keeping a wary eye open for fighters, an anxious minute passed before Hoppy gave an exclamation. Following his pointing finger Moore saw a double thread of steel running along the foot of a steep valley. The note of the engines rose half an octave as he put A-Apple's nose down.

Levelling off two hundred feet above the track he followed it round a wooden hillspur. Beyond the spur the valley widened and a small hamlet appeared. A man digging in a garden recognized the aircraft and waved his spade. Beyond the hamlet a column of white smoke was rising from a sawmill. Hoppy, among whose jobs was the monitoring of the aircraft's speed, tapped Moore's arm. 'You haven't allowed for the dive, skipper. Throttle back a bit.'

Realizing he was right, Moore obeyed. Ahead, the track ran around another wooded spur. As A-Apple swept over it Hoppy gave a grunt of satisfaction. 'Marche ahead, skipper.'

413

Skirting the town, Moore made contact with the railway again as it swung north-east. The floor of the valley they entered was dotted with small farms fed by a meandering stream. As they rounded a shallow hill Hoppy gave a yell. 'There she is, skipper. Just as the Old Man said.'

A mile or so ahead a train was steaming eastwards. Moore had already banked to port and was flying along the pine-covered hills that flanked the valley to the north. A lone Allied aircraft close to a prisoner-of-war train might arouse suspicion. One flying a couple of miles away could be dismissed as a chance encounter.

Hopkinson had his binoculars to his eyes. 'She's the one all right, skipper. Only she's got two flak wagons at the back instead of one.'

'Two? Are you sure?'

'Yes. The rear one seems to be carrying an 88. The other two look as if they've got 37mms and LMGs.'

By this time Moore could pick out some details of the train with the naked eye. Although diminished by distance, it still had an air of brute power with its huge locomotive belching out smoke, its thrusting metal wheels, and the massive flak wagons at the front and rear. A sign its appearance did not belie its potential came five seconds later when a heavy explosion made A-Apple reel. Hoppy lowered his binoculars and gave Moore a wry grin. 'It's an 88 all right.'

Before Moore could reply flak began bursting all around the aircraft as the 37mm guns got their range. With all the information he needed, Moore swung into a tributary valley. Hoppy, watching the train until it vanished from sight, turned back to him.

'Everything seems O.K., skipper – it hasn't slowed down. But it's going to be a tougher nut than we thought.'

'I'm afraid you're right, Hoppy.' Moore replied dryly.

A minute later they rejoined the track. There was no risk of being sighted by the train crew: two hill spurs now separated them. Conscious they were now flying along the far side of the plotted rectangle, both men knew the tunnel must appear soon. Below, the railway track was leading them into wilder country. Rocky outcrops and fast-flowing streams mingled with forests of pines. A hawk was hovering over a scabrous hilltop. As the thunder of A-Apple's engines reached it, it dipped a wing and fell away.

The track curved round a bend and entered a wide valley. Three miles or so ahead the hills swept in and turned the valley into a cul-de-sac. Moore met Hoppy's eyes. 'This must be it.'

A-Apple went into a shallow climb. As the boulder-strewn floor of the valley swept past, the two men could see no sign of life. Hoppy gave a grimace. 'Let's hope the partisans have arrived, skipper.'

The words had barely left his mouth before something white fluttered among the thick belt of trees that clothed the northern side of the track. Nodding at Hoppy, Moore gave his attention again to the hill ridge ahead. Covered in trees, it appeared about five hundred feet in height at the point where the rail tunnel ran through it.

The branches of the pines shivered as A-Apple leapt over the ridge. Three seconds later the ground fell back to the floor of the valley and the railway track. Sweeping up the northern hillside, Moore banked steeply and flew back towards the tunnel. As the ridge passed below him an explosion made the Mosquito shudder. 'See it?' Moore shouted.

Before Hoppy could answer a fork of tracer stabbing out from the southern hillside confirmed the gun post's position. It was sited high enough to defend the tunnel from both air and ground attack. Since the Mosquito had appeared, the crews of the flak posts on either side of the tunnel had been frantically stripping the covers off their guns and warming up their radar predictors. The western gun crew had won by a short head.

Both Moore and Hopkinson saw that Davies was right: the post had to be destroyed or the partisans could never reach the tunnel. As black puffs of smoke burst around A-Apple, Hoppy's voice sounded over the intercom. 'O.K., skipper. Bomb fused. Left, left, steady . . .'

The gun battery was on a small rocky ledge half-hidden by trees. As A-Apple, with bomb doors open, swept towards it, the battery's LMGs opened up. Appearing to start slowly at first, the tracer suddenly accelerated like an unfurling whip. Forced to fly straight and level as Hoppy lined up his bomb-sight, Moore felt his toes clench up inside his flying boots as the steel lashed past.

The Mosquito's head-on approach was not lost on the German gunners. It was a simple situation of kill or be killed, and the barrels of the pom-poms were jerking like the heads of striking cobras. To Hoppy, squinting down, it appeared that the gunners were giving a pyrotechnic display. Both he and Moore winced as a burst of LMG fire pierced the open bomb doors and ricocheted in a series of banshee screams from the bombs cradled there.

'Right a bit, skipper. Right . . . Steady, steady . . . bomb gone!'

The 250-lb bomb, tail-fused with a five second detonator, fell away. With the vengeful flak still following him, Moore swung away immediately and dived down into the valley. Trying to look back, Hoppy was counting . . . 'three, four, five!'

The explosion came half a second later, hurling trees and debris high into the air. It was followed by a minor avalanche down the hill. The black explosions and parabolas of tracer that had been following A-Apple were snuffed out as if by a magician's wand. On the intercom Hoppy's voice had a note of relief. 'First time lucky, skipper!'

Moore drew an arm across his sweating face. 'Let's hope so.'

He put the Mosquito into a high climbing turn and gazed back. Gambling that the gun battery was completely out of action, six partisans had already run out of the surrounding trees and were urgently attaching explosives to the tunnel entrance. As A-Apple circled just below the hilltops a series of jolting explosions made its crew turn their eyes sharply on the stricken battery. A second later Hoppy gave a shout of relief. 'It's O.K., skipper. It's the other battery waking up.'

A parabola of LMG tracer, arching over the tunnel but falling well short of the orbiting A-Apple proved the Cockney right. Hidden from the battery by the ridge, the tough partisans continued their work. With the explosives in position, they ran out an electric cable to the side of the track. One man paused to wave at A-Apple, then all six disappeared into the trees.

Glancing back to ensure the train had not yet entered the valley, Moore and Hopkinson waited for the explosion that threw dust and rocks high into the air. When the smoke cleared, the tunnel entrance appeared to be partially blocked and earth and rocks covered a ten-yard section of track. Satisfied, Moore swung A-Apple towards the ridge.

'Let's put that other gun post out of action before the boys arrive.'

It was a decision so typical of Moore that Hoppy made no attempt to argue although his expression was wry. The order of battle, as agreed between Davies and Moore, was that Moore would attack the western battery and then keep watch for the partisans on the train's progress. In the meantime Millburn, leaving the rest of the squadron orbiting in a valley two miles away, would fly in from the opposite direction and attack the eastern battery. Only if one of them were to lose his personal duel would the other Mosquito attack both gun posts. By using only two aircraft initially, it was hoped that neither the oncoming train nor the enemy radar detectors would be alerted.

As it happened, Millburn was the first to reach the surviving battery. With the American's natural aggressiveness stimulated by the prospect of aiding his compatriots to escape, he was nearly thirty seconds ahead of schedule. Seeing the battery squirting tracer at A-Apple, Millburn went at it bald-headed.

The post was a secondary one and unlike the crews of the western battery the gunners had no concrete bunker to protect them. With Millburn's attack coming from the lower reaches of the valley and with the crew concentrating on A-Apple, the American was able to fire two rockets before a shot was fired back at him. One rocket narrowly missed but the second smashed through the armoured shield of the pom-pom as if it were cardboard, killing the crew instantly. The LMG mounting was also damaged and its crew critically wounded.

With the valley now safe for the next phase of the operation, Moore and Millburn began orbiting the valley at the eastern side of the tunnel. From there they could see the train enter the valley without the likelihood of being seen themselves. As the long seconds ticked past, Moore felt tension winding like a spring inside him. The possibility had always existed that the train might carry radio and so have been alerted by the gun posts. A second, more lethal possibility was that the hill tops had not screened the two Mosquitoes from the enemy radar detectors. Intelligence believed the nearest fighter airfield was at Maastricht, fifty miles away. If the airfield's scramble system was efficient – and German defence systems usually were – this meant enemy fighters could reach the train approximately ten minutes after their initial warning. If all had gone according to plan, the Mosquitoes had that number of minutes to disable the train and free the prisoners. If the plans went awry, the valley would turn into a death trap for them.

Twenty more agonizing seconds passed before Hoppy's sharp eyes spotted puffs of smoke rising above the distant hill spur. Fifteen more seconds and the train appeared, a black caterpillar crawling into the wide valley. Letting out his breath in relief, Moore signalled Millburn to close up behind him and spent the next minute making the two Mosquitoes as inconspicuous as possible against the vast backdrop of the hills. Alongside him Hoppy kept surveillance on the train through his binoculars. Puffing black smoke through its stack, it was hauling its bulk along the valley without suspicion of the obstacle ahead. When he estimated it was halfway down the valley, Hoppy tapped Moore's arm. Clicking on his R/T, Moore broke radio silence at last.

'Swordsman Leader to Zero Two. All obstacles cleared. Bring your boys over now.'

As Moore heard Young's twangy voice acknowledge, he was conscious it was the crossing of the Rubicon. Whatever might have happened earlier, it was now certain sirens would be screaming and enemy pilots racing for their Messerschmidts and Focke Wulfs. Satisfied that the train's weight and speed must now carry it within range of the partisans, Moore swung A-Apple's nose westwards.

'Swordsman Leader to Zero Eight. While we're waiting for the boys, let's have a crack at that first flak wagon. The usual drill. Let's go!'

It was a snap decision that neither Hoppy, Millburn nor Gabby thought reckless. The quicker the train was attacked at this juncture, the less prepared its gunners would be. And the swifter its disablement, the quicker the squadron's escape.

As the two Mosquitoes swept over the tunnel, the train driver spotted the debris ahead of him and slammed on his air brakes. Long sparks flashed as, with a hiss of air, wheels locked and screeched along the rails. Prisoners in the central wagons were flung into heaps by the sudden deceleration and gunners in the flak wagons, hurled from their seats, hid their faces as loose shells slid murderously across the steel floors.

It was a moment of confusion that could not have been more fortuitous for the two Mosquitoes. As sparks flew from the train half a mile ahead, they separated, Moore climbing steeply to port, Millburn to starboard. It was a tactic Moore had made his crews practise many times and it was to prove invaluable today. Banking in unison they came plunging down from opposite sides of the valley, their targets being the engine and foremost flak wagon in which bruised and cursing gunners were only just climbing back to their feet. With the need for accuracy imperative, both aircrews came in at a slight angle to the train so that any overshots would fly past the engine and not hit the central wagons.

With the flak guns not yet manned and the explosive content of their rockets small, both pilots were able to close well inside the prescribed safety distance before firing. As the rockets darted out like luminous lances, the two aircraft banked yet again to port and swept safely past one another. Moore's rocket, striking the now stationary engine, sent a huge column of steam and boiling water high into the air. Aft of the coal tender, Millburn's rocket pierced the flak wagon just behind and below its main turret. To Gabby, gazing back as T-Tommy rocketed upwards, the damage appeared to be slight. In fact the steel projectile, ricocheting around the inner steel walls until its high velocity was exhausted, had smashed machinery and men indiscriminately and turned the wagon into a charnal house.

To Teddy Young and the rest of the squadron, now pouring into the valley, the sight was like two gannets attacking a huge snake. Catching sight of the aircraft as he levelled off from his climb, Moore wasted no time in giving orders. 'Give us cover, Red Section Leader. Zero Nine- take the 37mm wagon. Ten – take the 88. In you go.'

Young led his flight upwards and began his patrol at the base of the clouds. The two named Mosquitoes took station on either side of the valley and prepared to attack. Ideally Moore would have preferred to send in two aircraft against each flak unit but with the two wagons coupled together the danger of collision was too great. His compromise would at least ensure neither wagon could be certain from which side its real threat came. As the two Mosquitoes began to dive, Gabby, seeing no flak radiating from the wagons, gave Millburn a grin. 'A piece of cake, boyo.'

It proved a rash prophecy. The tough German gunners had now scrambled back into their seats and their menacing gun barrels were swinging round on their attackers. The 88, with its heavier shells but slower rate of fire, turned on the remainder of the aircraft orbiting above. The 37mm of the foremost wagon and the LMGs that both wagons carried shared themselves out between the two diving Mosquitoes.

Zero Nine was Andy Larkin, the rangy, satirical New Zealander, and Richards; Ten was Frank Day and Clifford, both survivors of the squadron. With the 37mm pointing in his direction, Larkin took the brunt of the flak; to the crews orbiting above, his Mosquito seemed to disappear into a rectangle of bursting shells. Miraculously it survived and went rocketing up the opposite hillside with no worse than blackened wounds in wings and fuselage. Not surprisingly, however, its rockets missed the 37mm wagon and lanced harmlessly into the trees.

Frank Day, having to face only LMG fire, was able to aim his rocket more accurately and it struck the revolving air-vent of the 88 wagon. It smashed the vent away but the tough armour prevented more damage and the projectile ricocheted away.

Shouts and curses on the R/T channel betrayed the crews' reaction to the defence the train was making. Moore's calm voice silenced them. 'Your turn, Eleven and Twelve.'

Eleven was McKenny and Ross; Twelve was Lester, an ex-London University student, and Thomson, a building society clerk. As the two Mosquitoes began their dive Moore tried to draw some of the fire by flying lengthways along the train. Only one LMG gunner allowed himself to be diverted; the others concentrated grimly on the real threat above them.

Fire was now radiating from the two wagons like the quills of a porcupine.

Although both Mosquitoes had to fly through sheets of LMG tracer, Lester had also to face the dreaded 37mm pom-poms. Before he could fire his rocket, a shell hit his starboard engine and another exploded an auxiliary fuel tank. Blazing fiercely, the entire wing folded back and broke away. The asymmetrical remains spun down and exploded among the trees. Emotion brought a curse from Hopkinson. 'This is murder, skipper. Two kites at a time haven't a snowball's chance against that kind of flak.'

His sharp reply betrayed Moore's own anger. 'Keep your eyes open for bandits!'

For McKenny and Ross, now facing the combined fire from both wagons, it was like flying into an erupting volcano. Tracer clawed at the cupola and drummed viciously on the Mosquito's stressed skin. An explosion shattered the compass and ignited its alcohol. Kicking his rudder bar to make the Mosquito as difficult a target as possible, McKenny fought to get within range. As he levelled off to take sight on the 88 wagon, there was a jolt and a terrifying scream as the starboard propeller was shattered. As the Irishman cursed and switched off the engine, Ross saw his intention and gave a shout of protest. 'That's enough, Paddy! Break away, for God's sake!'

Ignoring the Scot, McKenny flew on into the sheets of tracer and released his rocket at almost point-blank range. It flew straight and true, piercing the armoured side of the wagon just below its gun turret. The immediate cessation of fire from all its guns told its own story. Keeping control by will power as much as skill, the Irishman leapt over the train and struggled to gain height.

The shouts of triumph from the orbiting crews were stilled by Moore's urgent voice. 'How are you, Paddy?'

'We're all right, skipper. But I've only got one engine.'

'You got the 88 wagon, Paddy. Well done. Get off home and we'll try to catch you up later and give you cover.'

'O.K., skipper. Thanks.'

Up on the hilltops Thirteen and Fourteen were preparing to launch their attack. Thirteen was a blond young South African, Van Breedenkamp, and his English navigator, Arthur Heron. Fourteen was Tony St Claire and Simpson. Witnesses to what lay before them, all four men were pale and grim. Orbiting above, Moore was acutely conscious that the stubborn defence of the last flak wagon was endangering the entire operation.

'Millburn! Let's share this one. You go in low after Van Breedenkamp and I'll follow St Claire.'

Aware how close enemy fighters must be and that the release of his compatriots below hung on a knife edge, Millburn could not have heard an order more to his liking. Breaking from his orbit almost before Moore had finished speaking, he made for the hillside from which the South African was preparing to launch his attack. At the opposite side of the valley Moore swept round to follow St Claire. 'In you go, Thirteen and Fourteen. We're right behind you.'

The two leading Mosquitoes dropped their noses and began their dive. As the

419

scream of engines and airfoils grew louder, the quadruple 37mms of the flak wagon opened fire on St Claire. To the tormented partisans hidden in the woods its rhythmical pounding sounded like the drumbeats before an execution. Three seconds later the wagon's LMGs began firing at Van Breedenkamp. Both Moore and Millburn, flying half a mile back and only a hundred feet above the valley floor, were left unmarked as the enemy gunners concentrated on their nearest threat.

Van Breedenkamp was the first to release his rocket. It struck the wagon's armoured skirt, ricocheted on to the stricken 88 wagon, and made a fiery trail along the track. As the South African swung away, the LMGs immediately lowered their barrels on to the advancing T-Tommy. Coming in like a charging bull and totally ignoring the danger of collision with St Claire, Millburn fired his rocket. It struck one end of the LMG turret and swung the heavy structure round on its axis. At the same moment the machine guns ceased firing. Millburn's yell of triumph made R/T earphones rattle. 'See that, you guys! We've got the LMGs.'

Yet although the impact of the rocket inside the steel hull must have sounded like the end of the world to the surviving pom-pom gunners, they ceased firing for only a couple of seconds. As they recommenced, the sky around St Claire and his navigator turned into a hell of explosions and screaming steel. A red-hot fragment ripped a two-foot hole in the aircraft's port wingtip. Another lethal fragment ripped off an engine fairing and hurled it away. A third shell made a large hole in the nose cone housing the cannon and Brownings. Screaming like a banshee, air entered and flung an icy blast into the cockpit. One of the calmest men in the squadron, St Claire still managed to steady the Mosquito and when a clear view of the wagon appeared through the bursting shells he fired a port rocket. Aimed at close range, it would almost certainly have hit its target had not a shell struck the starboard engine at precisely the same moment. Although half-stunned by the explosion, St Claire managed to pull the nose up and the aircraft passed a few feet over the wagon. Trailing smoke and glycol, it staggered a few hundred feet up the hill. Then its crippled wing dropped and it fell among the trees.

The tragedy was visible to all the orbiting crews. With the 37mm shell swinging the Mosquito off course at the exact moment the rocket was fired, the rocket had struck one of the nearby wagons containing American prisoners. Although its explosive charge was small, it was sufficient to blow out almost all the opposite wall. As men spilled out on the track, some clearly dead and others badly mutilated, Millburn let out a horrified 'Oh, my God!'

At the opposite side of the track heavy explosions rocking A-Apple told Moore he was now the gunner's target. Before Machin, the last member of the flight, could grasp his opportunity, the revengeful Millburn stole it from him. Banking on a wingtip he headed straight for the wagon again. Seeing him coming, Moore held the gunners' fire until it became suicidal and then banked sharply away. As the pom-pom followed A-Apple, Millburn released two rockets. One ricocheted from the wagon's armoured skirt but the second one struck it squarely and disappeared inside. The guns stopped firing immediately and a few seconds later smoke escaping from the turret told the battle was over.

There was no jubilation among the circling crews. The enemy gunners had died valiantly and down on the track the sight was harrowing as wounded men helped one another from the burning wagon. As one man paused to shake a fist upwards, the tough Millburn winced and turned his head.

Partisans, who had been anxiously scanning the sky for enemy fighters, now began pouring out on to the track. A dozen of them ran to help the wounded Americans, the rest, armed with tools and crowbars, began working frantically on the bolts of the intact wagons.

Their urgency was shared by Moore. Every professional instinct in him was screaming to pull the squadron out of the death trap while there was still time. Yet if he gave the order and the fighters came before the prisoners were released, the dead would have died for nothing.

To his relief the partisans appeared to have cracksmen with them because the locked doors were opened with almost magical speed. As the last one slid back and uniformed men leapt out and ran into the trees, a green Very light soared upwards.

It was a signal that came just in time. The light had barely reached its full trajectory before Young's voice rattled in Moore'e earphones. 'Bandits, skipper! 190s.'

Glancing upwards Moore saw a blunt-nosed shape diving at incredible speed towards his orbiting aircraft. It was followed by a Mosquito firing all four guns. Deciding it was wiser to wait for his comrades than lose height to aircraft as formidable as Mosquitoes, the 190 pilot swung past and disappeared into the clouds. Moore's welcome order came a second later. 'Swordsman Leader to squadron. Line astern. We're going home.'

Diving A-Apple to tree-top height he headed back up the valley. Peeling away, the survivors of his flight followed him. Up aloft Teddy Young's flight gave a last snarl at the 190s that were harassing them, hid in the clouds for a few seconds, then dived into the valley themselves. Full speed and at zero height, their camouflaged bodies merged into the green hillsides and the wolves who tried to follow them discovered only shadows on which to vent their fury.

CHAPTER 11

The Mosquito leapt over a line of poplars and sank down on its belly again. Below an uneven grassy field flowed past. Half a dozen grazing cows reared up and then broke into a terrified gallop. A narrow stream and a cobbled road swept past in quick succession. A minute later a church steeple and a number of chimneys appeared on the skyline at two o'clock. Ross pointed a finger. 'Calais!'

Instead of answering him, McKenny changed course a few degrees. Glancing ahead, Ross saw a major road had appeared on the flat landscape. Enemy transports preceded by a motor-cyclist were making their way along it and McKenny was heading straight for them. Hiding his alarm Ross indicated a map strapped on his knee. 'Forget the transports,' he shouted. 'Let's get back home.'

Even within the terms of the RAF's code of practice, which since the days of Trenchard in the First World War had been attack, always attack, Ross's caution was justified. Although the Mosquito was an extraordinary aircraft capable of a high performance even on one engine, it was the pilot's duty in a damaged machine to do everything possible to return to base so that both valuable aircraft and its highly-trained crew could live to fight another day. To risk that achievement for a few easily replaceable transports was poor military judgment and made Ross grip McKenny's arm when the pilot took no notice.

'You're taking us among the flak posts, Paddy. Get back on course.'

McKenny muttered something and flung his hand away. Staring at him, Ross's apprehension grew. Whatever the events that were changing the Irishman's character, one result appeared to be an alarming increase in his aggressiveness. Another, if one could analyse his expression, was a perverse desire to intimidate his navigator. Before Ross could protest again, McKenny lined up his reflector sight on the rearmost transport and opened fire.

The massive recoil of four automatic guns blurred both men's vision and seemed to halt the Mosquito momentarily in mid-air. As grey-clad figures leapt down from the transports and tried to reach the shallow ditches, they were cut down like grass before a scythe. A petrol tank exploded in a fireball of oily smoke that blackened the sky around the Mosquito as it went snarling down the row of transports. Cursing men flung themselves flat on the road; others rolled into the icy water of the ditch. A few, one of them a tough grizzled sergeant, knelt in the centre of the road and began firing back. Earth and sky swung dizzily as McKenny banked steeply and thumbed his gun button again. A second truck exploded, throwing flaming debris in all directions. As earth and sky tilted again, Ross let out a yell of anger. 'What's the matter with you? You'll have fighters on us in a minute.'

The horizon steadied and to his relief Ross saw they were heading for the coast. He jabbed an urgent finger to the south. 'We can't cross here. Get back on our track.'

If McKenny's revenge against the world was momentarily satiated, his self-destructive impulses were as strong as ever for he continued straight ahead. After trying twice more to dissuade him, Ross gave up and concentrated on pin-pointing flak posts they were approaching. Dunes of sand were appearing now in the grassy fields. Here and there were wooden bungalows, once occupied by summer holiday makers, now empty and abandoned. Other less innocent structures nestled into the sides of hillocks and sand dunes. Difficult to spot from the air because of their camouflage and low profile, they were as dangerous to aircraft as massed shotguns to low-flying pheasants. As the Mosquito flew past one of them, four lines of tracer leapt out and impaled it.

The swiftness of the attack took both men by surprise. One hose of bullets took half of the starboard aileron away. A second struck sledgehammer blows along the fuselage. Although the burst of fire swept from end to end of the Mosquito at lightning speed, Ross, whose navigator's seat was unprotected by armour, felt the blows lasted for minutes as his cringeing body waited for bullets to tear up through his buttocks and spine. As the Mosquito staggered away, a second bunker fifty yards away opened fire. Bullets smashed into the silent engine, tearing off a piece of cowling before ricocheting eerily away. Another burst of fire cut the stabilizing controls. Reeling like a drunken man, the Mosquito crossed the deserted beach with its coils of barbed wire and tank obstacles and flattened over the grey sea. Frustrated that their victim had escaped, gunners followed it with parabolas of tracer that splashed sullenly among the waves.

Ross, finding it hard to believe he was still alive, took a full fifteen seconds to find his voice. 'What the hell's the matter with you? Are you trying to get us killed?'

Although the nearness of their escape had turned McKenny pale, his face was as sullen as before. 'What was I supposed to do? Go past those transports without firing a shot?'

Tension, spring-tight within Ross, had to find release. 'Don't tell me that was for the war effort. You've been doing some odd things lately but that was the craziest thing yet.'

McKenny's head turned. 'What's all the fuss about? Did I scare you?'

The taunt added fuel to the Scot's anger. 'If I was scared, I wasn't the only one. You know what Moore would do if he heard about this, don't you? He'd ground you faster than that.'

It was a blow that struck home: McKenny's glance was a mixture of defiance and alarm. 'What are you turning into? A bloody informer?'

'I'm your navigator, remember? And you're supposed to follow the track I give you when we cross the coast.'

'Oh, for Christ's sake stop bellyaching! We got out all right, didn't we?'

Ross, whose training had kept him scanning the gauges and sky above even as he quarrelled with McKenny, gave a sudden start. 'We're not out of the woods yet. Have you noticed our oil pressure?'

McKenny stared at the pressure gauge of the remaining port engine, then glanced sharply over his left shoulder. As he sank back, Ross tried to see past him. 'What is it? A cut feed line?'

'I don't know. I can't see any spray.'

Not for the first time that morning Ross blessed the grey sky that still stretched from horizon to horizon. Had it been cloudless there was little doubt fighters would have already pounced on them. As it was they were not halfway across the Channel. Only a few minutes from safety but the needle of the pressure gauge already on the fringe of the danger quadrant.

The white cliffs of Dover were distinct on the horizon when the men's sensitive ears picked up the sudden labouring note of the engine. With oil pressure down towards zero, the temperature gauge was in the red as friction began to heat up the oil-starved engine. Jettisoning his remaining rockets, which traced a fiery path over the wavetops before plunging into them, McKenny nodded at Ross's enquiry. 'Yes, give them a fix. We're not going to clear the cliffs.'

Praying the radio was not damaged, Ross called in Air/Sea Rescue and to his relief got a reply almost immediately. Giving them as accurate a fix as possible, he tightened McKenny's seat harness and then his own. The overheated engine was now thumping alarmingly and giving off smoke. With the wavetops snapping less than a hundred feet below them, the pale-faced McKenny gave Ross another nod. 'I'm putting her down now. Jettison the hood.'

With a series of bangs that threatened to tear the wing away, the engine seized and died. As Ross released the cupola, a rush of cold air and a scream of airfoils entered the cockpit. Handling the unstable Mosquito like a crate of eggs, McKenny put her nose down a few degrees. Gripping his seat tightly, Ross saw the choppy waves rushing towards him. As spray splattered against the windshield, McKenny hauled right back on the wheel. The Mosquito lifted her nose briefly, then dropped belly flat into the sea. The massive jerk threw both men forward against their straps. Alongside them there was a fierce hissing and a great cloud of steam as the white-hot port engine sank under the waves. Recovering his breath Ross snapped open his harness and pushed himself upwards. 'Come on! Let's get out of here.'

There was no answer from McKenny. His body was limp and blood was oozing down one side of his face. Dropping back, Ross unfastened his harness and with a superhuman effort heaved him out of his seat. By this time McKenny had opened his eyes but he seemed incapable of helping himself. Bending down, Ross somehow managed to get his head and shoulders under the pilot's legs. Bracing his arms against the seat he straightened his back and heaved McKenny to the cockpit rim. Steadying him there, he climbed on to the seat and pushed again. Tumbling like a limp sack over the rim, McKenny fell on the flooded wing and into the sea. Gasping from his efforts, Ross dropped on the wing himself and tried to grab McKenny's overalls as the swell washed him away. With the wing offering no handhold, the Scot was dragged into the sea himself. With their Mae Wests keeping them afloat, Ross was content for a moment to keep McKenny's head above the waves while he regained his breath. Recovering, he saw the wooden-framed Mosquito still afloat. Unsure how long it would remain that way but deciding it would be a better target for Air/Sea Rescue to locate, he struck out and dragged McKenny round to the tail section.

By the time he reached the tail the Irishman had recovered sufficiently to be able to help himself. Kicking and scrambling, the two men dragged themselves over the half-submerged elevators and clung to the fin. With their weight depressing the tail even lower, they had some difficulty in keeping their heads above the choppy waves. Blood was making pink rivulets down McKenny's face and both men were shivering from the cold. The Irishman coughed water from his lungs. 'You think they'll be long?'

'They shouldn't be,' Ross shouted back. 'They've a base only a few miles away.'

In fact rescue was already on its way. On permanent standby, an Air/Sea Rescue launch and a Lysander aircraft had been despatched within a minute of receiving the Mayday call. Spotting the Mosquito almost as soon as it crossed the coast, the Lysander had given the launch a radio fix. Already sniffing about like a wolf for scent, the power boat had changed direction and now, with a bow wave as high as her bridge, was bearing down on the sinking aircraft. Five minutes later, wrapped in blankets, McKenny and Ross were on their way to hospital.

'They should never have got us involved in politics, sir,' Henderson muttered. 'Something was bound to go wrong.'

The Scot's criticism was aimed at Davies, who was standing at the other side of the large desk in Adams' Intelligence Room. Moore and Adams were also present at the private inquest. Davies, who had just spent some of the most uncomfortable minutes of his life closeted with Lambert, answered, with a scowl. 'Someone had to do it, Jock. And we were the obvious choice.'

'I know that, sir. But it carried too many risks for the prisoners.'

'Everyone knew that,' Davies snapped. 'And no one more than the Yanks. But they still gave us their permission. And they probably would again. You're talking as if the raid was a failure. Don't you realize two to three hundred valuable aircrew have escaped?'

Having made a point, the big Scot was not one to withdraw it without good reason, 'I know that, sir, but how many will get back to the U.K.? Probably not more than a dozen or so.'

'You're a bloody pessimist today, aren't you, Jock? If the Resistance play their cards right, they could get a hundred over to us. Maybe more.'

Henderson looked sceptical. 'I don't see Lambert stressing that, do you? It isn't as if he didn't warn us there was a risk of American lives.'

'He's not the only one who issues bulletins! Staines is arranging for a Press release that will emphasize the hundreds of American boys we've freed. That can't look bad in the American headlines, can it?'

The Scot stuck to his guns. 'Not if it goes in the headlines, sir. It's Lambert that's worrying me. After all, you said yourself he's the most influential correspondent in the States.'

Knowing from all Lambert had told him that the Scot's fears were justified, Davies lost his temper. 'What is all this, Jock? Are you blaming me for carrying out my orders? Or are you blaming me because a bloody flak shell hit St Claire and spun him off target?'

Suddenly realizing that beneath his testy façade the Air Commodore was as upset as he was, Henderson turned contrite. 'Of course I'm not, sir. It just seems so damned unfair that after all Moore and his boys did, they should get such a lousy break.'

One of Davies' best qualities was his quickness to forgive. 'That goes without saying. It was a brilliantly-executed operation and everyone is to be congratulated for their part in it. The first man to say that was Staines when we spoke over the phone.'

'I suppose he'll be one of Lambert's major targets?'

'He will be. But Staines can take care of himself. I gather he's already working on something that could put the ball right back into Lambert's court.'

The Scot showed instant alarm. 'We wouldn't be involved in this, would we?'

Davies' defiance was a giveaway in itself. 'Why not? We're as keen to clear our name as anyone else, aren't we?'

'You suggested a minute ago we'd nothing to be ashamed about!'

'You know damn well what I mean. There's no question that Lambert's going to blow up this accident to further his own ends. So our job is to do something that'll K.O. him once and for all.'

Henderson's alarm was manifest now. 'I don't like it, sir. We're getting deeper and deeper into politics.'

As apprehensive himself but seeing no way out, Davies became testy again. 'Where the hell do you get this political stuff from? All we did this morning was try to free a few hundred American prisoners and we succeeded. All we'll be doing if Staines wins this additional job for us will be to work with the Americans instead of with our own forces. What's political about that? We're both on the same side, aren't we? To me these are war operations pure and simple and any political capital that comes out of them is just a fling-off.'

Henderson half-opened his mouth to protest, then decided enough was enough. Self-guilt brought him a glare from Davies before the Air Commodore turned challengingly to Moore. 'You've been very quiet so far, Moore! Don't you think the operation was worth while?'

Although Moore had bathed and changed, his good-looking face was still showing the strain of the fierce engagement. His answer was typically candid. 'It's difficult for me to answer that, sir. I lost four of my men with another three in hospital. But if war is just a matter of mathematics, then I'd have to say it depends on how many Americans get back to the U.K.'

'War *is* a matter of mathematics,' Davies snapped. 'And I've good reasons for believing a high percentage of 'em will get back.' Noticing Moore's fatigue, his tone changed. 'You did a great job, Ian. And I'm sorry about your men. Particularly St Claire. It's a hell of a thing to happen to a man.'

Standing just behind Moore, Adams thought of Sue Spencer and winced. When it had been confirmed St Claire was missing, he had stood the girl off duty and taken the debriefing himself. Clearly in a state of shock, she had protested bitterly at his decision. It was the kind of courage that had gone straight through the defences of the sentimental Adams but when he had learned about the Americans St Claire had killed he had been adamant. Hearing the grim details of how her fiancé had been shot down would be agony enough for her. Learning of the cruel trick fate had played on him might be too much.

Her absence had meant a long de-briefing session for Adams. An additional factor had been the condition of the crews. Flying long distances at low-level was always a heavy strain, and G.D. Waafs had been kept busy bringing in cups of sweet tea and sandwiches as the men had filed singly into Adams' 'Confessional'. All had carried in with them the smell of battle: the odour of cordite, burnt oil, sweat, petrol, and other less definable smells that Adams had grown accustomed to over the war years. As always, they had stirred conflicting emotions in him. Condemned by his age and poor eyesight to ground duties, Adams had never lost his envy of these young men whose missions brought hope to the oppressed people of Europe. At the same time his envy often disturbed and puzzled him because another side of Adams hated war with its waste of young and promising lives.

'When are you expecting to hear from General Staines again, sir?' It was Henderson, still worried about being drawn deeper into the world of politics and journalism.

'I'm seeing him tomorrow morning,' Davies told him. 'He's hoping to have some news for us then.'

A tap on the door made all four men turn. As Sue Spencer appeared in the doorway, the room went quiet. Seeing the three senior officers with Adams, the girl drew back.

'I'm sorry. I thought Squadron Leader Adams was alone.'

Henderson damned the heartiness in his voice. 'That's all right, Sue. Come in.'

For a moment it seemed the girl would withdraw in spite of his invitation. Then she closed the door and walked uncertainly towards Adams. Henderson pulled out a chair for her but she appeared not to see it. Adams, who had stepped forward, cleared his throat nervously. 'What is it, Sue?'

The girl was clearly still in shock. Her face looked frozen as she gazed at him. 'I want to know if it's true that Tony killed some Americans before he was shot down.'

Davies cursed beneath his breath. 'Who told you that?'

Her gaze turned on him. 'I overheard two of the crews talking. Is it true, sir?'

For once Davies seemed to be short on words. Moore came to his aid and to the embarrassed men his cultured voice struck exactly the right note of sympathy. 'It is true but it wasn't his fault, Sue. A shell swung him round just as his rocket was fired. It could have happened to any of us.'

'But it didn't happen to any of you, did it, sir? It happened to Tony and everyone's going to blame him for killing those Americans.'

'No, Sue. Nobody will blame him. Certainly not American aircrews. They understand how these accidents can happen in combat. That's something you don't have to worry about.'

Her voice sounded as if it were struggling upwards through layer after layer of anguish. 'A man loses his life trying to rescue others and he kills them instead. It's very ironical, isn't it?'

Henderson cleared his throat. 'Aren't you looking too much on the black side, lassie? All we know so far is that they crashed into the woods. As the partisans would be near enough to give help, they could be as right as rain.'

His words of comfort seemed to antagonize the girl. 'As right as rain, sir? After going down with a wing shot away?' She turned to Moore. 'They say you were just behind him when he was hit. Won't you tell me exactly what happened?'

Adams, who knew the girl better than any of them, was wondering if it might not be wise to tell her everything while she was in a state of shock. Moore's reply showed he was of the same mind.

'I think you're right not to hold out too much hope, Sue. Both of them were too low to bail out. On the other hand they didn't seem completely out of control. And they hadn't that far to fall.'

If his words gave the girl any hope, she killed it immediately. 'He's dead. They both are. You're all certain of it. But do you know what I believe? Tony's not going to rest. Not when he knows about the men he's killed.'

As Adams felt himself stiffen, Henderson gripped his arm and put his mouth to his ear. 'Get her out of here and take her to the M.O.! Tell him to put her to sleep. Go on — move it!'

The girl tried to resist Adams. Deciding it was one of those occasions when it was kinder to be cruel, Henderson turned authoritarian. 'Flight Officer Spencer, you'll leave this office with Mr Adams. At once. That's an order.'

None of the three remaining officers looked at one another as Adams steered the white-faced girl outside. Grunting with relief, Henderson fished into his tunic for cigarettes. 'Poor wee devil,' he muttered. 'What a hell of a thing to happen.'

Davies was frowning heavily. 'That's the trouble with having love birds on the same unit. Everyone gets hurt twice as much.'

Taking the remark as a criticism and with his nerves still raw, Henderson responded with some heat. 'They got involved after they were both posted here, and the regulations only apply to married couples. And it's never affected their work.'

Seeing how feelings were running, Davies let the matter drop and glanced at his watch instead. 'I've got to be moving. Try not to worry about what happened. You've all done a great job and I mean it. I'll be in touch again tomorrow. Probably in the afternoon.'

Stiffening, the two officers watched his brisk figure march down the hut and disappear. With a groan Henderson sank into a chair. 'Try not to worry! With Lambert sharpening his knives and he and Staines cooking up another operation for us.' The Scot's aggrieved eyes settled on Moore. 'Don't you think it's crazy involving us in politics like this?'

Moore hesitated. 'If he's right in what he told us earlier, I suppose things couldn't have been allowed to drift.'

'Yes, but why us? Hell, there are hundreds of squadrons in the RAF.'

'We are his brain child, so we were a natural choice,' Moore reminded him. 'And I suppose the Rhine Maiden job did make us the most likely candidate for a public relations exercise.'

Henderson sighed. 'I suppose so. But if this is fame, give me anonymity. No one's quicker than the public to yank down their heroes and Lambert's sure to do a hatchet job now.'

'It does look that way,' Moore admitted.

'Then wouldn't it be wiser to cut our losses?'

'If that accident this morning made things worse, Davies can hardly do that, can he?'

'But has it made things worse? What about all those Yankee prisoners you helped to escape?'

Moore smiled. 'That wasn't the way you were arguing a few minutes ago.'

The Scot groaned. 'You're right. I'm so mixed up I can't tell my arse from my elbow.' His tone changed. 'Forget what you said to Sue just now. How do you think the Yankee crews are going to react when they hear about the men we've killed?'

'What would our reaction be if an American operation killed around twenty or thirty of our men?'

The Scot nodded gloomily. 'Right. We'd say it was another Yankee cock-up. Let's hope they're more generous.'

'They might be. But that's not likely to make any difference to what Lambert says to the American public, is it?'

Henderson made a gesture of distaste. 'No, it isn't. So whether we like it or not we've got to take on another dicey job. Like kidnapping Eva Braun from the Eagle's Nest. Or towing the *Tirpitz* into Scapa Flow.' An alarming thought brought an end to the Scot's sarcasm. 'What if this one goes sour too? Christ, we could go down in history as the unit that split the Allies right down the middle and won Jerry the war. Have you thought of that?'

Tired though he was, Moore had to smile at the Scot's dour humour. 'No. And I don't intend to until I've had some sleep.'

A glance at the young squadron commander's face brought Henderson out of the realms of speculation. Heaving his bulk from the chair he took Moore's arm. 'The hell with it. Let's go and have a quick whisky. Then you'd better get off to bed.'

CHAPTER 12

Halting the battered saloon by the kerb, Millburn whistled and turned to Gabby alongside him. 'You're sure this is the place?'

Jumping out, Gabby walked towards a pair of large, wrought-iron gates. 'Kashmir House. That's the address Wendy gave me.'

Millburn joined him and peered through the gates. A circular drive, well-kept flowerbeds and a large house showed through the dusk. Millburn whistled again. 'What did they say their Pappy is? A colonel?'

'A general,' Gabby corrected. 'Twenty-five years in India.'

Millburn grinned. 'A pukka sahib. I wonder what Mammy's like?'

'According to Wendy all Memsahib and Roedean.'

'Roedean?'

'A posh girls' public school,' Gabby explained, then showed impatience. 'You going to talk here all night? The girls will be wondering what's happened to us.'

Millburn took another glance through the tall gates. 'You're sure there are no butlers or maids there?'

'No. They've all been given a half day. The girls have everything fixed.'

'And Mom and Pop aren't due back until tomorrow afternoon?'

'That's right. What's the matter with you? You're not usually as cautious as this.'

'I don't go to bed with debutantes every night in their Mammy and Pappy's stately home,' the American pointed out. 'If Pappy's an ex-Indian General he might have planted tiger traps in the drive.'

Gabby swung open a gate. 'All right. If you're worried, leave the car outside.'

The small Welshman had met the girls two days ago. With Millburn on duty, Gabby had drifted in to a charity dance organized by the local Women's Voluntary Service. Trained in observation, he had noticed two attractive girls helping out in the kitchen, and, ever the opportunist, had zeroed in. In no time at all he had discovered they were the high-spirited daughters of General Richards, ex-Indian Army, local J.P., and very much a part of the county society. On extended leave while repairs were being carried out to their private girls' college and with their parents away for a few days in Manchester, the two girls were clearly out to enjoy themselves and Gabby had taken full advantage of the situation. With self-assurance making up for his lack of inches and membership of the famous 633 Squadron to give him glamour, the navigator had quickly made a date for himself and Millburn. When Wendy had innocently suggested the men could come round to the house if they wished, Gabby's satisfaction had been immense. 'We're in, boyo. For the whole night if we like.'

Millburn, who found it hard to believe in fairies, had been more cautious. 'Don't build on it. Kids like that are protected. Their idea of living it up is lemonade and snakes and ladders.'

'Society kids? They're doing it before they go to school! I tell you, boyo, we're in. It's going to be bath salts, Bells Whisky, and bed, bed, bed.'

The two airmen's shoes were crunching on the gravel. Halfway to the house, they heard the faint yapping of a dog. A few seconds later a light showed as the large front door was flung open. As giggles and upper-class voices could be heard, Millburn lifted a comical eyebrow. 'Debretts? Or Burke's Peerage?'

Gabby grinned expectantly. 'Probably both.'

The girls had now appeared on the porch. A yapping Pekinese shot out after them, ran towards the two men, then scuttled back as Millburn tried to stroke it. Before either airman could speak, the taller of the two girls approached the American with an extended hand. 'You must be Tommy Millburn. I'm Hilary and this is my sister, Wendy.'

Millburn discovered Hilary's hand had a certain upper-class assurance. Wendy's hand had a more schoolgirlish wriggle. Millburn, caught more times than he cared to remember by Gabby's blind dates, was surprised to see how attractive both girls were. Hilary was tall and slender with long, blonde hair. Wendy, two inches shorter, had a slightly fuller figure and wore her hair in pageboy style. The family's wealth showed in their fashionable dresses.

Wendy had already taken possession of Gabby and was leading him into the house. Deciding the Welshman was starting to pay his debts at last, Millburn followed the delectable Hilary into the hall.

His feet sank into a deep pile carpet. On his right the crystal contents of a glass cabinet twinkled with the light from a huge ceiling chandelier. Ahead, a wide staircase ran up to a balcony. The panelled walls and balcony were lined with portraits of stern-faced soldiers with topees on their knees. A stuffed tiger's head and a huge Bengalese hallstand gave evidence of the family's background. A cocktail cabinet, a large sofa and two armchairs completed the furniture.

Giggling, Wendy pushed Gabby forward and dropped on the sofa with him. Giving her sister a sharp look, Hilary led Millburn to one of the armchairs. 'I hope you find this comfortable.'

Millburn hesitated. 'What about you?'

She drew up a leather stool and folded gracefully down on it. 'I'll sit on this. I often do.'

The Pekinese dog was sniffing at Millburn's leg. Reaching down to stroke it, the American drew back his hand just in time as the dog took a snap at him. He managed a smile. 'What's his name?'

'Pouchi,' the girl told him.

To Millburn's relief Pouchi took a last sniff at him and then moved petulantly away. His gaze returned to the girl. Her posture on the low stool showed him she had long and shapely legs. Unlike her sister, who had a fuller face, she had a slender chin and high cheekbons. With her blonde hair falling across her face in

431

the fashion of the time, she had an enigmatic expression as she gazed up at the American. 'May I have a cigarette?'

Millburn began fishing in his tunic. 'Sorry. I thought perhaps you didn't smoke.'

She lifted a plucked eyebrow. 'What on earth made you think that?'

When Millburn only shrugged, she accepted a cigarette and put it somewhat speculatively between her lips. Across on the sofa where Gabby was looking as smug as a cat with cream, Wendy turned. 'Can I have one too, please, Tommy?'

Millburn lit both their cigarettes before dropping back into the armchair. As he lit his own, Wendy began to cough. 'These have a funny taste, haven't they?'

'They're toasted. Don't you like them?'

Wendy pulled a face but persevered. On the leather stool, with her cigarette held elegantly in one slim hand, Hilary was eyeing Millburn again. 'Are you really an American?'

'That's what my birth certificate says.'

'But then what are you doing in the RAF?'

Millburn grinned. 'Round about 1939 I got a hankering for a trip in a boat and it brought me over here. Then I met a guy in a pub one night and he told me the RAF would teach me to fly for nothing. He didn't say a thing about having to stop on and fight the war. Just shows you can't trust guys in pubs.'

'I think it's wonderful you came over at that time to fight for us. Daddy would think so too.'

Millburn blinked. 'Would he?'

'Or course he would. Poor Daddy. He's been trying to get back into the Army ever since the war started but they won't have him because of his heart.'

'That's tough,' Millburn agreed.

'It upsets him because we're not doing more as a family. I know he'd give anything if we were boys. If we were, he'd have us in the Army tomorrow.'

Millburn took another look at her shapely legs. 'Sing hallelujah you're not.'

'Not what?'

'Boys. There are too many boys around, don't you think?'

'We don't think so. Where we are in Harrogate they all seem to have been called up.'

'There are still a few around,' Millburn suggested. 'Ready and rarin' to go.'

She slanted a cool glance at him and then, with a flash of silken knees, rose. 'Would you like a drink?'

'I wouldn't mind. What have you got?'

He received a stare. 'Anything you want. Just say.'

'Then I'll have a Bourbon.'

'That's a whisky, isn't it?'

'Kind of. Yes. Whisky'll be fine.'

The girl turned to Gabby who was deep in puissant conversation with the giggling Wendy. 'What about you, Gabby?' When the Welshman did not hear her, Millburn spoke for him. 'Women always do this to him. Give him a whisky too.'

Jerking her head at Wendy, Hilary crossed the large room to the cocktail cabinet. Wendy, who, unlike Gabby, was missing nothing, hesitated a moment and then followed her. Watching the two of them whispering as they searched among the bottles for whisky, Millburn caught Gabby's eye and motioned him over.

'You're sure you've got the right age of these girls?' he muttered.

Gabby looked surprised. 'Of course I have.'

'Well, I'm not so sure. That upper-class stuff and sophistication can fool you but I don't put Hilary any more than eighteen or nineteen. And if there's two and a half years between 'em, that could put you into the red zone, mush.'

Looking uneasy, Gabby glanced round at the whispering couple. 'You're crazy. Wendy's got more on the top than Hilary.'

'So what? They can have 'em as big as that when they're fourteen. You'd better watch it, boyo. I don't want you doing a stretch in Wormwood Scrubs.'

Gabby glared at him resentfully. 'Trust you to spoil it. Here we are, right among the fleshpots, and you have to give me a worry like that.'

'You? Worry? That'll be the day. You check on her, buster, or the old man might do a tiger chase on us.'

Across the room Wendy had found the whisky and was busy pouring it out. Seeing Hilary had noticed them talking, Millburn nudged Gabby who went back to the sofa. A minute later Wendy crossed the room carrying a tray. Giving a glass to Gabby, she approached Millburn. The way she eyed him made it clear she found the American's rugged good looks attractive. 'We don't seem to have any Bourbon, so I've given us all Scotch whisky. Is that all right?'

The glasses on that tray, all half-filled, strengthened Millburn's suspicions. 'Are those raw?'

'Raw?'

'Is that neat whisky?'

The nubile Wendy stared down. 'Yes. Why?'

Looking uncertain for the briefest moment, Wendy glanced at Hilary who was at her elbow. With a light laugh the elder girl picked up a glass and sank elegantly on the stool. 'Don't worry about us. There's always lots of drinking at the parties we go to. One gets used to it.'

Waiting until Wendy had returned to Gabby, Millburn leaned foward. 'How old is your sister?' he muttered.

'Eighteen. Why?'

'Are you sure?'

There was a sudden upper-class chill in the stare he received. 'Of course I'm sure. What a silly question.'

Lifting a hand, Millburn sank back. 'O.K. O.K. I just want to be certain.'

'Certain of what?'

'Certain she can handle whiskies of that size,' the American countered.

'You seem very interested in Wendy.'

Millburn decided he had done enough in the line of duty. 'Wendy's Gabby's problem, not mine. Tell me about yourself. Have you got a boy friend?'

The girl's tone told him he was still not forgiven. 'One or two.'

'Here?'

'No.'

Millburn grinned. 'I always think it's here that counts, don't you? When do you expect your folks back?'

He found the look she gave him difficult to interpret. 'Somewhere around noon tomorrow.'

'Is that a fact?'

'Yes. They're staying with my mother's sister in Manchester.'

'They're taking risks, aren't they?'

'Why?'

'Leaving two beautiful daughters on their own.'

He received that look again and this time wondered if it could be a challenge. 'Why should that be taking a risk?'

Millburn shrugged. 'Life being what it is.'

'How is life with you?'

Millburn finished the last of his whisky. 'It's getting better all the time.'

She took the glass from him. 'Then you'd better have another drink.'

Millburn watched her graceful figure cross over to the cocktail cabinet where Wendy was already giving herself and Gabby a refill. Returning to the sofa the younger girl handed a glass to Gabby and then dropped giggling on his knee. Seeing the triumphant look Gabby gave him, the frowning Millburn, who liked to be second to no man, decided that different temperaments though the girls might have, this was the time to act. As Hilary returned and handed him another large whisky, he patted his knee. 'How about sitting here for a change? You'll find it more comfortable than the stool.'

Her smile froze. 'On your knee? We hardly know one another.'

'That's why, honey. Give my knee a try and we'll put that right.'

She sank down on the stool with some hauteur. 'I'm perfectly comfortable here, thank you. May I have another cigarette?'

Conscious he was getting the hot-and-cold treatment, the American consoled himself by remembering a full night lay ahead. Avoiding Gabby's grin, he prepared himself for a long siege. 'O.K. Let's get to know one another. Were you born here or in India?'

'India,' she muttered.

'Was Wendy born there too?'

'No. She was born in England.'

Millburn made the comment without thinking. 'You'd have thought it the other way round.'

She stiffened. 'What does that mean?'

'Nothing,' Millburn said hastily.

'Yes, it does. You were hinting something.'

'Was I?'

'Yes, you were. And I don't like people who hint things.'

Never a man to be made a fool of, Millburn began to lose his temper. 'There doesn't seem to be much you do like, does there?'

She was staring at the sofa where her sister and Gabby, with half a bottle of whisky inside them, were well past the need of conversation. The sight appeared to annoy her, for with an exclamation she jumped to her feet. 'Would you like to look round the house?'

'You mean you're going to show me round?'

'If you'd like to see it, yes.'

The American rose philosophically. 'O.K. Let's go.'

As they passed the sofa Gabby gave the American a licentious grin before sinking his face into the giggling Wendy's neck again. With heightened colour Hilary led Millburn into the library, the dining room and the kitchen quarters. As they came out in the hall again, she paused sullenly at the foot of the staircase.

'Would you like to see the rooms upstairs?'

Millburn shrugged. 'Why not.'

Giving him another stare, the girl led him on to the balcony where he was introduced to her parents' rooms, Wendy's room, a couple of guest rooms and the bathroom. She passed by one door that stood in the centre of the balcony but on their way back she paused outside it. 'I don't suppose you want to see my room?'

Puzzled by her behaviour but an eternal optimist, Millburn kept a low profile. 'Why not? We've seen everything else.'

With the balcony giving a clear view of the hall, Gabby and Wendy could be seen sprawled out full length on the sofa. As a loud giggle followed by a squeal floated upwards, Hilary gave an impatient exclamation and threw open the bedroom door. 'I don't see any point in it but you can go in if you want to.'

She did not switch on the light, giving Millburn only a glimpse of expensive furniture and a silken bed. As he walked forward across the thick carpet to gain a better look, the door closed behind him. As he turned, a sullen voice sounded in his ear. 'Well. Isn't this what you wanted?'

As Millburn stood there, too surprised to speak, the girl's voice came again. 'What's the matter? You're not just all talk, are you?'

Coming to life, Millburn found the girl in the darkness and kissed her. The effect astonished him. With her sullenness falling away like an unwanted cloak, she pushed him towards the bed. As he dropped on it, she fumbled to unbutton his clothing while her mouth osculated against his neck and face. 'Don't just sit there,' she muttered impatiently. 'Take your clothes off.'

As he obeyed, Millburn could hear her heavy breathing and the urgent hiss of silk as she tore off her dress and underwear. Seconds later he was flat on his back on the bed again with the girl poised over him. In the darkness he could see the white blur of her face. When he tried to roll on top of her, she pushed him back, slid down, and lowered her head. The earth exploded for Millburn and bursting stars took its place in the heavens. A minute later her moist mouth returned and osculated against his own. He hardly recognized her throaty voice. 'Now it's your turn, darling. Do anything you like. Hurt me if you want to. Only do it, do it!'

Grabbing her long, slender body, Millburn obliged. Her sobs quickened, then rose into a crescendo. 'Yes, yes, yes ... Don't stop ... Don't stop. ...'

When nature forced him to stop, the astonished Millburn found himself upturned once more. Lowering her head, Hilary caught the lobe of his ear in her teeth and tugged. As the American jumped, her hand slid down his body. Almost to his surprise Millburn discovered her squeezing, probing fingers awakened his passion yet again. The springs of the bed protested as the two of them rolled over and over. When he sank back at last, Millburn was panting as if he had run a marathon. As the girl put her arms around his neck, he pulled away. 'Hold it, honey. You think I'm superman or something?'

Smiling, she drew his arms across her breasts and snuggled herself into his thighs. Deciding the world was more full of surprises than Christmas cake with currants, Millburn was about to fall into an exhausted sleep when he heard a car engine outside. He sat up sharply. Hilary's eyes opened. 'What is it, darling?'

Leaping out of bed Millburn ran to the window but, with the bedroom at the side of the house, he could see nothing but trees. He turned back to the startled girl. 'Did your folks go to Manchester by train?'

'Of course. One can't get enough petrol for long journeys.'

Millburn almost relaxed, then went tense again. 'That means they'd have to take a taxi from the station.'

Before the girl could answer he heard a door slam, followed by the sound of a departing car. Millburn began climbing frantically into his trousers. 'They're back. They must be.'

The naked girl leapt out of bed. 'That's impossible. They definitely said they were staying until tomorrow.'

Tucking in his shirt, the American slipped into his shoes. 'Someone's arrived. And who else would it be at this time of night?' As the alarmed Hilary stared at him, Millburn remembered. 'My God! Gabby and Wendy! They'll run right into them.'

Motioning Hilary to keep quiet, he drew back the bedroom door. The chandelier had been switched off and only the faint glow of an electric fire stained the darkness below. Listening, Millburn heard voies outside, followed by the sound of a key in a lock. The yell of warning he was about to deliver Gabby died in his throat as the hall lights suddenly blazed on.

The scene that leapt out of the darkness was like a tableau for some blue comedy. Down on the sofa, where Wendy had proved that fast beginners are not always the quickest finishers, Gabby was starting to have his way at last. Naked except for his socks, he was poised over the pulsating Wendy, whose bare legs were wrapped passionately around him. To the horrified Millburn, the Welshman's white buttocks resembled some exotic mushroom against the green cloth of the sofa. Frozen in nature's most ridiculous posture, Gabby in turn was staring back aghast at the intruders framed in the doorway.

One was a woman in her middle forties, amply-built and wearing a fashionable hat and coat. The sight of Gabby's buttocks leaping out of the darkness had brought a high-pitched scream from her. Now, hypnotized by the vision, she was clutching her throat. The florid General was alongside her, twelve to fifteen years her senior and sporting a white moustache, looked hike a hirsute Victoria plum as he gazed uncomprehendingly at the sofa.

Time, which had stopped for all concerned, suddenly caught up with itself in a hasty whirring of cogs and dials. Confronted by Gabby's nether regions, the Memsahib had only one course open to her. With a muted sigh, she slid down to the carpet with elephantine grace and lay motionless. The General, looking more than ever like a Victoria plum about to burst, glared down at her. 'Which one is it? Damn it, I can't tell from this end. Which one, woman?'

Memsahib kept her eyes tightly closed. Straightening, the General let out a bellow that made the crystals on the chandelier jingle. 'You young scoundrel! I'll have you flogged. No, damn it, I'll have you shot! I'll shoot you myself.'

Dancing with rage, he glared round for a weapon. Seeing nothing that would inflict the mutilations he had in mind, he charged for the library. Torn rudely from heaven to earth, Gabby rolled off the sofa and hopped frantically up and down as he tried to climb into his trousers. Wendy, panic stricken, dragged down her skirt and fled weeping towards the kitchen. With the hall momentarily empty of all but the hopping Gabby, Millburn leaned over the balustrade. 'Never mind your clothes, you moron,' he hissed. 'Get the hell out of there before he shoots you.'

Taking the American at his word, the Welshman grabbed his clothes and bolted for the front door, leaping over the prostrate Memsahib in the process. Unsure whether the General had overheard him or not, Millburn withdrew into the bedroom. The panic-stricken Hilary followed him. 'He'll shoot you both! He's got a shotgun in the library!'

Aware there was no escape downstairs, Millburn threw open the window. To his relief a drainpipe ran down the wall a couple of feet away. Stuffing his socks and tie into his tunic pocket, the American climbed out on the window ledge. As more threatening bellows were heard downstairs, followed by the yapping of Pouchi, Hilary's white face stared out. 'Hurry! In case he comes upstairs.'

Suspecting the girl was more concerned for her own safety than for his, the sweating Millburn gripped the window sash with one hand and reached out gingerly with the other. To his relief the fall pipe seemed firm. Squirming round on the narrow ledge, he released the sash and grabbed the pipe with both hands. Shoes scrabbling against the wall, he began lowering himself down. He was passing a lower window when there was the crash of a shotgun followed by a startled yell. Aghast, he glanced up at Hilary who was leaning out the window. 'My God!' he muttered. 'He's shot Gabby.'

She motioned him frantically to keep quiet. 'Don't let him know you're here or he'll shoot you as well.'

It was advice Millburn hardly needed. Yells and blood-curdling threats were followed by another thunderous blast from the shotgun. Feeling soft earth beneath his feet Millburn edged to the front of the house and peered round.

In total defiance of the blackout the lights of the porch were ablaze. They enabled Millburn to see the formidable figure of the General, shotgun at the ready, stalking along the left-hand drive. Half-expecting to see a mangled body nearby, the relieved Millburn could see no sign of Gabby. Another roar from the General provided the explanation.

'Come and face your medicine, you scoundrel! I know you haven't got away.'

Millburn realized Gabby could be hiding on either side of the circular drive. For his part, the trees and shrubs that flanked the right-hand drive were his nearest cover. As he wondered how he was going to cross the lighted frontage of the house without detection, Pouchi, who until now had been cowed by the roar of the shotgun, suddenly burst out from the porch and flew yapping towards the left-hand gate. Recognizing help when he saw it, the General gave a roar of welcome. 'Good boy, Pouchi. Find him! Find the scoundrel.'

Genuinely alarmed for Gabby's safety, Millburn acted promptly. Grabbing up a large stone he hurled it at a clump of trees near the right-hand gate. As it struck a tree and fell, the yapping dog changed its course and scampered across the intervening flowerbeds. The triumphant General ran after it. 'Good boy, Pouchi! Flush him out!'

The moment dog and master vanished among the shadowy trees, Millburn put his head down and flew down the opposite drive. 'Gabby!' he hissed. 'Where the hell are you?'

He was halfway to the gate when a shaken figure emerged from the shrubbery. Grabbing the Welshman's arm, Millburn kept running. He had just reached the gate when there was a roar of fury, followed by a stab of light and an explosion from the clump of trees. As both men ducked, pellets rattled among the dry leaves behind them. Gabby let out a yelp. 'He's mad! Stark raving mad!'

Millburn dragged him through the gate and down the pavement towards the car. Bundling him into it, he threw the car into gear and ignoring the danger of collision, backed at full speed away from the house. As he braked and turned the car across the road, the General reached the gate. Giving another Imperial bellow, he threw the shotgun to his shoulder and fired. Pellets rattled against the side of the car and glass showered over the startled Millburn. Spinning the wheel, he put his foot down hard. 'Jesus,' he muttered, 'This is worse than Happy Valley!'

They were a mile away before Millburn eased off the accelerator and turned to the shaken Gabby. 'You hurt?'

Gabby who had miraculously held on to his tunic but lost his shirt, slid a finger beneath his buttocks and felt gingerly. 'I think I've got a few pellets in me. ' His voice rose indignantly. 'The old bugger would have killed me. You realize that?'

As relief welled up in Millburn, so did anger. 'You've done it to me again, haven't you? What was it going to be – bath salts, whisky, and bed? You never told me their old man was a homicidal maniac.'

The resilient Welshman was recovering fast. 'What are you moaning about? You got what you came for, didn't you? I saw you go into Hilary's bedroom.'

Millburn had never felt more vindictive. 'But you weren't so lucky, were you, boyo?' He grinned at the glare he received. 'I warned you all that giggling was probably just wet knickers and wishful thinking. Maybe the next time you won't be so quick to keep the hot numbers to yourself.'

CHAPTER 13

Staines and the Brigadier were talking beside the french windows when Davies was shown into the library at High Elms. As the young lieutenant announced him, the American General turned, then gave a wry grin.

'Davies! What the hell are you still doing in uniform? I thought you'd have been sent your dungarees by this time.'

Uncertain what undercurrents might be lying beneath the humour, Davies decided to accept it at face value and ran his eyes over the General's uniform. 'They issue smart dungarees in your outfit, sir.'

Staines grinned again. 'We don't do badly, do we?' He thrust out a big hand. 'If you don't like yours when they arrive, I'll send you a pair. At least they help morale.'

With the man's handshake firm, Davies began to feel the interview wasn't going to be the ordeal he feared. 'I'm sorry things went the way they did, sir. But the boys did their best. If it hadn't been for that one damn shell the operation would have been a complete success.'

Staines dropped his bulk into a chair. 'I know that, Davies, and so do my staff. In fact I'll let you into a secret. I don't think there's another unit around that could have done such a precision job. Even getting there undetected was a small miracle.'

Generosity on this scale exceeded Davies' wildest hopes. At the same time it increased his embarrassment. 'Thank you, sir. But I hope it hasn't made any difficulties for you.'

Staines gave a shrug. 'That depends on which side of the fish pond you're standing. If the Brigadier's partisans get fifty or so of our boys back, I won't miss my share of drinks over here when Christmas comes. But if you've got Congress in mind, I might not be so popular when Lambert's finished with me. I had a telex cable this morning saying he's already done his first hatchet job. And there's plenty more to come.'

Davies could not hide his dismay. 'But won't your Congressmen take into account the prisoners we've freed?'

'The one's who're backing us will. But the hawks who want the Japs finished first are going to have a field day. Can't you see Lambert's headlines? RAF KILL

AMERICAN PILOTS. RECKLESS MISSION TO HUSH CRITICS. Whether we like it or not we've given him the chopper to kill the chicken.'

As Davies sank heavily into a chair, the Brigadier's quiet voice made both men glance at him. 'I feel the same responsibility as Davies, General. We can't undo the accident but you have my word that every effort will be made to get as many men as possible back to the U.K.'

The Texan lifted his big shoulders. 'I'm not blaming you. It was a great idea. But now it's backfired on us, I'm thrown into the ball game myself. If we don't counter Lambert's campaign smartly, our entire air strategy over here could be affected.'

Eager to re-burnish his unit's international reputation, Davies was looking at a large map that was lying folded across the desk. 'The brigadier says you already have something in mind, sir?'

'That's right. By luck we've an operation due in a week that will hit the head-lines of every paper in the States. I thought if I could get you involved, we could knock Lambert out cold before he can do too much damage. So I spent all last night arguing with the U.S. Army and the Navy. Lucky for us they share my view of your mission yesterday; in fact they're full of praise for it. Add to that your Rhine Maiden reputation and I managed to get you into the team. But don't think it was easy because originally this was meant to be an all-American occasion.'

As attentive as an excited terrier, Davies watched the big Texan unroll the map. It proved to be a large-scale representation of the French Cotentin peninsular. Anchoring the map with two glass ashtrays, Staines motioned Davies to his elbow. 'If you agree to play in this game and you pull it off, we're right back on base again. So don't say no until you've got all the facts. O.K.?'

Seeing he had the small Air Commodore's undivided attention, Staines turned back to the map and dropped a tobacco-stained forefinger on a point near the north-western tip of the peninsula. 'X marks the spot! Up above the cliffs here near Omonville the Heinies have almost completed a large radio-location station. Apart from giving early warning of air raids, its job will be to scan and plot all Allied shipping movements along the Channel in the Plymouth-Southampton area. A Yank task force is going to blow it up. It's going to be a big operation. At least 3,500 troops are taking part. Your job, if you take it on, is to provide air support. In turn you'll receive high cover from our 8th Air Force Thunderbolts. If the job's a success, the news value will be sensational. FIRST AMERICAN TROOPS INTO EUROPE ... INVASION IMMINENT ... you can see the headlines in every newspaper from New York to Los Angeles. Best of all from our point of view is the publicity the RAF will receive as the British unit who gave our boys protection. Every Mom in the States will send the British an extra food par-cel and Lambert's campaign will get a lethal kick up the ass.' Staines turned and gazed up at Davies. 'Well. What do you think?'

Davies coughed and drew away from the cigar smoke as if blaming it for his hesitation. 'What exactly would our role be again?'

'Ground support. That way all the Army and Navy as well as any war cor-respondents present will see you doing your stuff. You'll ground strafe any Heinie reinforcements who might be rushed up while our boys are blowing up the station. That shouldn't be too difficult. The station stands on an isolated site on the cliffs and there's only a narrow support road leading up to it.'

Davies asked the obvious question first. 'But why can't you attack it from the air?'

'That's easy. We don't want to.' Seeing Davies' expression, Staines threw a grin at the Brigadier. 'Remember the Dieppe raid of '42? Its purpose was to blood the British and Canadian troops and to probe the enemy's coastal defences. Now it's our turn. Someone up top has decided our divisions stationed in the U.K. must get some battle experience before the invasion. Also it's important we know what new defences the Heinies have up their sleeve. This radio station gives us the perfect excuse to launch a raid on this coast without anyone guessing we have other motives. With all the intelligence the station is intended to feed back, a raid of this size will seem completely justified.'

Davies' face cleared again. 'But won't the fact we haven't tried to bomb it look suspicious in itself?'

'No. Fortunately for us, our B.17s did have a crack at the early installations before this scheme was mooted and found the bunkers took everything they could hand out. Since then our agents have discovered they're nine feet thick and can only be destroyed by charges planted inside. So one way and another we don't think the Heinies will get on to us.'

Knowing Davies better than the American and reading more from his expression, the Brigadier thought it prudent to add a few words of his own. 'Apart from your unit's reputation, Davies, which has persuaded the American Army and Navy to fit you in, we do feel you're well equipped for the role. You can carry 250-lb bombs, rockets, even anti-personnel bombs if you think them necessary. You've also got machine guns and 20mm cannon for strafing troops and tanks if the Germans can get them to the station in time!' A sensitive man, the Brigadier made it clear he appreciated what was being asked of the Air Commodore. 'We're fully aware of the risks involved in ground support. However you will be patrolling the road, which is some distance from the station itelf. And it is going to be impressed on the assault troops that the elimination of flak posts is a top priority.'

Although Davies' face cleared somewhat, it still betrayed a conflict of emotions. Pride that 633 Squadron, the élite unit of his own creation, should be invited into an all-American operation was there in full measure. At the same time the small Air Commodore was too much of a professional to let pride take precedence over commonsense, and his doubts showed as he glanced back at the Texan.

'I appreciate your confidence in us, sir. But as the real purpose is to restore the RAF's image over in the States, wouldn't a couple of Typhoon squadrons do as good a job and also present smaller targets for ground fire?'

Staines frowned. 'I'm going to have to recap, Davies. Someone in our Joint Air Staff decided for political reasons that Lambert's propaganda had to be countered and so your squadron was thrown in at the deep end. Because the operation needed my permission, I was thrown in too. Now the scheme has backfired

and given Lambert a new stick to beat the RAF with. So now you, me and everyone else concerned with weakening the Heinies' Air Force before the invasion,
has to clear up the mess and quick. Otherwise God knows what damage will be
done.'

Davies countered frown with frown. 'I know all that, sir. But Typhoons are
specially designed for ground support. If they do as good a job, won't that reflect
just as well on the RAF?'

'Goddamn it, Davies, you keep on missing the point, never mind the facts of
life. Armies, Navies and Air Forces hate one another's guts. Yours do and ours
do. Half the time they're expecting us to bomb and strafe them instead of the Heinies. So imagine their faces when I come along and ask them to use RAF ground
support. Now they know I'm a Fifth Columnist! I had to argue all night, Davies,
and pull every con-man's trick in the book before they agreed. But what chance
would I have had if I'd suggested using a couple of unknown Typhoon squadrons? I got you in because of your reputation but even then it was touch and go.'

A realist, Davies saw he had no choice. 'All right, sir. We'll take it on. What's
the date of the raid?'

Staines' rugged face betrayed his relief. 'Good man. Granted the weather's
favourable, a week today. The assault craft are due on the beaches at first light. I
know it's short notice but that can't be helped. The raid was originally scheduled
for the middle of September, so we're lucky to get into the act at all. You can be
ready, can't you?'

'We can be if we get all the operational details in time.'

'That'll all be taken care of this week. It'll probably mean your going down\to
Portsmouth to meet the Army and Navy but that can't be helped. I'll fix up a
briefing session as soon as I can and we'll meet there. Keep everything between
the three of us until I give you the green light. In the meantime I understand you'll
be getting a few interim details from your own Intelligence.'

The Brigadier nodded as Davies glanced at him. 'We've asked our French
agents to take a few photographs. They're working on it now.'

Davies turned back to the Texan. 'I take it there's an alternative date in case the
weather plays up?'

'That's right. The following night. If that also proves rough it's off until the
spring. The weather men reckon it'll be too hazardous later in October.'

Davies was thinking of the recent inclement weather. 'Let's hope the weather
settles down before then.'

The big Texan's grunt betrayed the importance he attached to the operation.
'Amen to that.' He turned his chair towards Davies. 'Smoke?'

Davies saw he was holding up his cigar case. Remembering that the last time he
had smoked one of the American's massive cigars he had survived without injury,
and feeling it was a gesture that sealed the entente, the small Air Commodore
took one. Applying a match with confidence, he let out a strangled cough. 'My
God!'

Staines looked innocent. 'Something wrong?'

It was a full six seconds before Davies could vent his accusation. 'This isn't the brand you were smoking before.'

'That's right.' The Texan was grinning. 'The war's getting rougher all the time. Leave it if it's too strong for you.'

Davies would have died rather than make such an admission. Drawing on the miniature airship again, he emitted a cloud of acrid smoke and unsteadily rounded the table to collect his briefcase. His effort to suppress a fit of coughing showed in his reddened eyes and halting voice. 'They just take a bit of getting used to, that's all.'

Staines winked at the Brigadier who, relieved at the outcome of the meeting, was hiding a smile. 'O.K. Davies. We'll get you briefed as soon as we can – certainly before the weekend.' As Davies saluted and reached the door, the big American's quizzing voice made him glance back indignantly. 'Maybe by that time you'll have got that smoke finished.'

The pretty Waaf opened Moore's ante-room door. 'Pilot officers McKenny and Ross are here, sir.'

'Good. Send them in, Tess, will you?'

Ross, entering the room first, looked uncertain as he approached the desk. McKenny, pale-faced and with a large plaster showing beneath his cap, had the expression of a man who had just had crippling news and was still stunned by it. The handshake they both received from the smiling Moore put Ross at ease but made no impression on McKenny, whose thoughts seemed to be in another world. Moore studied him for a moment before he invited the two men to draw up chairs.

'It's good to have you both back. The truth is I didn't expect you until tomorrow. I thought the West End might have tempted you to break your journey.'

Although a man who found small talk difficult, Ross made the effort if only to counter McKenny's black mood. 'Wouldn't you have minded, skipper?'

Moore's eyes twinkled as he sank back into his chair. 'Officially, yes. Unofficially, I might have blamed it on the transport system.' His tone changed as he turned to the silent McKenny. 'How's your head, Paddy?'

The question had to sink through McKenny's preoccupation before he responded. 'It wasn't much, skipper,' he muttered. 'There's no fracture or anything like that.'

'So the M.O. says. All the same he'd like you to have a couple of days off.' As McKenny gave a start, Moore turned to Ross. 'As you're part of the same team and you got the same ducking, I don't see why you shouldn't have a couple of days as well. Only hang around the station. I might be needing every man I have quite soon.'

McKenny's face clouded again. Curious to know the verdict on the operation, Ross failed to notice it. 'Was the job a success, skipper? Or did St Claire's accident foul it up?'

Moore's shrug gave nothing away. 'We released a train load of prisoners. So I don't think we did too badly, do you?'

'I know, skipper, but what about the ones we killed? How are the Yanks taking it?'

'As far as I know, the Yanks are taking it very well. I had half a dozen phone calls yesterday afternoon asking me to congratulate you all on what you did. You'll find details on your flight notice board.'

The freckle-faced Ross grimaced. 'They're being generous, aren't they?'

'Very generous so far,' Moore said truthfully.

'I don't suppose you've heard anything more about St Claire and Simpson?'

'Nothing that didn't come out at the de-briefing. It looks as if they have a chance but only a slim one. Arthur Heron was wounded but he should be all right in a few weeks.'

'So if St Claire and Simpson bought it, we lost four men?'

A man who felt his squadron losses without showing it, Moore gave a terse nod. 'That's right. And one way and another I think we were lucky. Particularly over you two.' To Ross's dismay he picked from his desk a de-briefing report that the two men had filled in half an hour earlier. 'This report from Adams says you think your port engine must have had an oil pipe nicked when you attacked that flak wagon. Are you sure of that? Because it took a hell of a long time to run dry, didn't it?'

Ross was careful not to glance at McKenny as he answered. 'We can't think where else it can have happened, skipper.'

Moore, who had been secretly watching McKenny, now turned to the Irishman. 'Then you didn't run into any other flak on your way home?'

Once again it took McKenny a moment to realize he was being spoken to. 'We'd have put it on the report if we had, skipper,' he muttered. 'Everything's down there.'

'You're quite sure of that?'

'Yes. Of course I am.'

Moore gazed at him, then shrugged. 'I suppose stranger things have happened. But it does make you the luckiest couple on this side of the Channel. All right, I'll tell Adams he can send in your report with the rest of them. Congratulations on getting back safely and have a rest for the next couple of days. That's all.'

Both men rose but only Ross turned for the door. 'Can I have a word with you, skipper?' McKenny muttered.

Moore sank back into his chair. 'Of course. Sit down.'

At the door Ross paused and threw an uneasy glance over his shoulder before disappearing. Moore pushed a packet of cigarettes across the desk. 'What's the problem, Paddy? You're looking right under the weather. Is it that bang on the head or is something else troubling you?'

McKenny made certain the office was empty before answering. Resentment that service life should force him to take Moore into his confidence made his voice sullen. 'There was a letter waiting for me when I got back today. From my fiancée.'

Wondering if he was going to get at the root of the Irishman's troubles at last, Moore played his cards carefully. 'She's the pretty girl who's a nurse, isn't she? In Lincoln?'

'Yes. She's a staff nurse there. But she'll be leaving soon. She's joined a nursing unit that's going to the Middle East. They were expecting to go in November but this letter says they'll now be leaving in the middle of October.'

'Is she the reason you wanted leave so badly last week?' Moore interrupted.

Although McKenny nodded, he avoided Moore's eyes. 'I wanted to try to talk her out of it.'

'I take it you didn't?'

'No.'

Moore picked up a pencil from his desk and studied it a moment before speaking. 'This is happening all over the world, you know, Paddy. Single men sent abroad have to wait four years before they see their girls again. So yours isn't a special case.'

The Irishman's sudden passion made Moore's eyes lift. 'It's special to me, skipper. If I can see her again, there's still the chance I might change her mind.'

'You know they need nurses in the Middle East, Paddy? Pretty badly from what I hear. She probably knows that too.'

McKenny's expression made it clear he could not care less what the Middle East needed. 'I must have one more chance, skipper. You said I can have two days off. Then why can't I spend them in Lincoln?'

Moore was studying him closely. 'Is this your only reason for wanting to see her? Or is there something else?'

The Irishman's outburst made Moore wonder for a moment if he were right. 'Only reason? Christ, she's my fiancèe and she's going abroad for God knows how long. And I'm in aircrew with only one chance in three of surviving the war. What other reason do you need?'

Deciding he must be reading more into the affair than he should, Moore sighed and sat back. 'All right, Paddy. You win. When's your next train?'

The change in the man was almost miraculous. 'I can catch a connection in Highgate at 20.30.'

'Then you've got plenty of time to get ready. But I want you back at 24.00 hours tomorrow. Not a minute later. Is that understood?'

The Irishman was already halfway across the room. 'I'll be back, skipper. I appreciate it. Thanks.'

As he ran out into the corridor, Moore entered the anteroom. The Waaf, gazing with surprise at the slammed door, turned to him with raised eyebrows. 'What did you do, sir? Give him a thousand pounds?'

Moore's smile was wry. 'Tess, I'm going to ask you a question and I demand a straight answer. Am I getting too old and crotchety to appreciate the agony of young love?'

The girl ran her eyes down his youthful figure and giggled. 'Hardly, sir. I'd say you understood it very well.'

Moore grinned at her and then withdrew thoughtfully into his office. 'Thanks, Tess. I was beginning to wonder.'

Ross was waiting anxiously in the corridor. 'What was all that about?' he asked as McKenny hurried towards him.

He received a cheerful slap on the shoulder. 'Come outside and I'll tell you.'

Puzzled at this change of mood, Ross obeyed. 'He didn't bring up that business about the engine again, did he?'

McKenny laughed. 'No. He believed the fibs we told him. All we spoke about was leave.'

'Leave?'

'Yes. I've got until midnight tomorrow.'

'You mean to go to Lincoln again?'

'That's right.'

The Scot whistled. 'How did you pull it off?'

In a rare good humour McKenny winked at him. 'I think he's pleased with the job we did.'

He was leading the navigator down a path that led to the junior officers' billets. 'What time's your train?' Ross asked.

'8.30 from Highgate.'

'Then we've time for a drink before you start getting ready, haven't we?'

Shaking his head, McKenny continued walking. 'I want to get ready first. If there's still time we can have a drink before the transport leaves.'

Heartened by the Irishman's change of mood, Ross followed him into their billet. As McKenny stripped off his tunic and began removing his shoes, the Scot dropped on the bed opposite him. 'I suppose you'll be seeing Joan,' he ventured.

McKenny grinned. 'What do you think I'm going for?'

With moments of good humour a rarity these days, Ross decided to exploit this one to the full. 'Has this something to do with that letter you got today?'

Unlacing a shoe, McKenny paused, then appeared to make a decision. 'Yes. She's written to say she could be leaving Lincoln in a couple of weeks.'

Hardly able to believe he was enjoying the Irishman's confidence, Ross proceeded with great care. 'Where is she going, Paddy?'

McKenny dropped his second shoe before replying. 'She's going with a nursing unit to the Middle East. The latest date of sailing is the middle of October.'

Without being certain why, Ross was feeling relief. 'Is that what's been worrying you lately?'

Turning to drape his tunic over a hanger at the head of his bed, McKenny took a moment to reply. 'What do you think?'

'But why haven't you told me before?'

'What was the point? You couldn't do anything.'

Ross found that hard to deny. 'Are you going to try to talk her out of it?'

'If I can, yes.'

'Do you think you can?'

446

There was no answer from the Irishman who still had his back to Ross. Unable to see the effect of his question, the Scot asked it again. 'Do you think you can, Paddy?'

McKenny let out a sudden curse and slumped down on the bed. 'No,' he muttered. 'I haven't a chance in hell.'

Ross was showing dismay at this relapse. 'Why not? Can't she get out of it?'

'She can get out of it if she wants to. But she doesn't.'

'Why? Does she feel it's her duty?'

McKenny's laugh was harsh. 'That's one way of putting it.'

In his eagerness to help, Ross made his fatal blunder. 'Have you talked to Father McBride about it?'

McKenny glanced up sharply. 'What can he do?'

'He might offer to talk to her.'

'You think that would make any difference?'

'It might. Isn't it worth trying?'

McKenny's eyes were suddenly full of dislike. 'You still believe in fairies, don't you? That a priest has only to open his mouth and the walls of Jericho come tumbling down. I suppose you'd like me to go down on my knees and pray as well?'

The Irishman's hostility was bewildering Ross. 'What's wrong with prayer? You've turned to it often enough in the past.'

'That's right. And where the hell has it got me?'

Ross thought he understood. 'If people make decisions that hurt others, Paddy, you can't put the blame elsewhere.'

'You mean you can't put the blame on God. Right?'

The young Scot's voice did not falter. 'If you want to put it that way.'

'I do want to put it that way. He claims to have made the world and everything in it. He claims to be omnipotent. So he has to take the blame for all the suffering in it. He can't have his cake and eat it.'

'That's ridiculous. People were given free will. If they use it to start wars and cause misery, they're the ones who must shoulder the blame.'

'So God isn't to blame for this shambles? It's you and me and all the other guys?'

'In a way, yes, I suppose it is.'

'Then why don't you set a good exmaple? I know how you hate dropping bombs on women and kids. If this is all about free will, why don't you use yours and quit?'

'That's a stupid question.'

'No, it isn't. If you're right about free will, everyone of us ought to stop killing one another.'

'You know as well as I do that the people who started this war won't quit. They have to be stopped.'

'You mean they act as if they're possessed?'

Ross fell into the trap. 'Perhaps they are. By the power of evil.'

McKenny's grin mocked him. 'Then they're not free agents, are they? They're just pawns in a power game. Which brings us back to the question – why doesn't God put an end to it? You're prepared to fight evil – why isn't he? I thought he was supposed to love his children.'

Unused to theological arguments, Ross was losing his way. 'I've just told you – God can't interfere without taking away our free will. We have to clean up our own mess.'

'But you've just agreed the power of evil is involved. Where's the free will in that?' When Ross remained silent, McKenny's voice rose contemptuously. 'You and your kind make me sick. You know why? Because you haven't the guts to put the blame where it belongs. And in my book that's cowardice.'

It is doubtful if anything but an attack on his religion would have provoked Ross into retaliation against McKenny. 'At least we know now why you attacked those transports, don't we? Joan has decided to nurse in the Middle East and so you hate the world, the Germans, your friends, even God himself. Have you ever thought that's the way children act when they can't have what they want?'

McKenny stiffened. For a moment it looked as if he might strike Ross. Then, muttering something beneath his breath, he snatched a towel from his locker and made for the washroom. The slam of the door made the unhappy Ross wince.

CHAPTER 14

The wind, keening down the narrow country lane, made the two cyclists strain on their pedals. Dressed in the ubiquitous blue of the French farm labourer, both men were in their middle thirties. One, Pierre Lefray, was powerfully-built with a square, dogged face and a thatch of brown hair. His companion was thin to the point of emaciation, with hollow cheeks and lank black hair. A Breton like his friend, Jean Arnaud was a product of the slums of St Nazaire, cynical, tubercular, and fanatical in his hatred of the German invader. The narrow lane ran up a steep hill and the exertion of climbing it against the wind was clearly taxing him, yet his cycle was a full length ahead of Lefray's. As they passed a large proclamation carrying a legend in both French and German, he glanced back and gave a shout. 'We're in the prohibited area now. So keep your eyes open.'

Pierre Lefray contented himself with a nod. Vigilant before, the two men now glanced back over their shoulders every few seconds. Reaching a gate almost at the hill crest, they hurriedly swung it open and carried their cycles over the muddy entrance into a field. Hiding them in the thick hedge, both men crouched down to recover their breath and study the view before them.

Fields, divided by stone hedges, swept down the hillside to a distant beach. The sea was a grey line at the edge of an equally grey sky. The view was desolate except for a curious complex of buildings that towered into the sky a mile or more to the men's right. Reaching back into the hedge, Arnaud pulled out a small, telescopic camera and a pair of binoculars from his saddlebag. Stuffing the camera into a pocket he focused the binoculars on the installation.

A massive squat blockhouse leapt into vision. It supported a tall steel mast that terminated in a large, rectangular aerial. Two smaller dish aerials stood a hundred yards or so at either side of the parent building. Other blockhouses, all massively constructed, formed an irregular pattern inside a perimeter wall. Outside the wall pillboxes were cunningly sited to give maximum covering fire. The entire complex was surrounded by tank traps and dragon's teeth.

Arnaud passed the binoculars to Lefray. At the bigger man's grunt of shock, Arnaud gave his street-Arab grin. 'There's a minefield too. Two hundred metres in depth right up to the strong points.'

Lefray was watching grey uniformed figures moving inside the perimeter wall. 'It must be important to them. Why the hell can't London bomb it? Surely it would be cheaper in lives.'

'They already have. But those blockhouses are three metres thick.'

'All the same, it's going to be an expensive job. Louis says the beach defences are the worst he's seen along this coast.'

Arnaud's shrug betrayed his cynical indifference to death. 'At least the Yanks'll learn what to expect when the invasion comes.' Straightening, he pointed at a tall oak whose branches reached out over the field. 'That must be the tree Etienne told us about. Let's get the job over.'

His thin chest was still rising and falling rapidly from his earlier exertions. As a sudden fit of coughing doubled him up the good-natured Lefray tried to take the camera. 'Let me handle it. I know how to use that thing.'

His deep-set eyes feverish, Arnaud pushed him roughly aside. 'The hell you will! You'll obey orders or you'll be in trouble when we get back.'

The chastened Lefray followed Arnaud to the base of the oak and helped him on to its lower branches. He then ran back to the gate to keep watch on the road.

Gasping with his exertions, Arnaud was halfway up the tree when a shout from Lefray made him freeze. Listening, he heard the hum of an engine through the sound of the wind and the rustle of dry leaves. Glancing around him, he edged into a large fork in the branches and made himself as inconspicuous as possible.

At the gate Lefray was watching an Sdk/2 armoured car making its way slowly up the hill. Its purpose was clearly surveillance: an officer with binoculars was standing up in the turret scanning the surrounding fields. Behind him were the menacing barrels of a 20mm cannon and a machine gun. Slipping back through the gate Lefray took cover behind the hedge.

The armoured car's engine took on a sterner note as the hill steepened. Thirty yards away a flock of starlings broke cover from a tree with a clatter of wings. Able to hear voices now, Lefray threw an anxious glance at the oak. To his horror one of Arnaud's blue-trousered legs was visible through a gap in the branches.

Cursing the impulse that had made him take cover at the wrong side of the gate, Lefray was considering a dash past it when the armoured car reached the gate and halted.

Gazing frantically along the hedge, Lefray saw a clump of bramble and edged towards it. In the lane a door slid metallically back. As boots clattered down on the lane Lefray pulled an automatic pistol from the waistband of his dungarees and sank down behind the bramble.

The gate rattled as a corporal climbed over it and jumped down into the mud. His expression told his views of an officer who delegated such jobs to his subordinates. Picking his way gingerly to one side of the gate, he rubbed one muddied boot against the other as he surveyed the field before him. Peering through the bramble, Lefray saw that Arnaud's leg was still visible.

He ducked back as the soldier began moving towards him. As the footsteps came within a few paces of him, he braced himself. Then they halted and he heard the sound of a man relieving himself.

An impatient shout came from the lane. Grunting something, the corporal adjusted his clothes and started back towards the gate. Aware it was the most dangerous moment of all, Lefray was frantically trying to decide whether a suicidal attempt to rescue Arnaud would have any point or purpose if discovery came when a jackdaw broke out from the hedge and flew squawking past the corporal's head. With a start the German turned his head and watched it fly towards the cliffs. By the time he looked back his eyes were fully occupied by the glutinous mud that surrounded the gate. Stepping gingerly through it, he swung a leg over the gate and dropped out of Lefray's sight. His relaxed voice as he addressed the officer told the Frenchman all was well. A moment later the armoured car drove away. Waiting until it had cleared the hill crest, Lefry ran forward. 'Are you all right?'

Arnaud's reply was caustic. 'All right? You think I'm a bloody chimpanzee? The wind's nearly killing me.'

'We were lucky. You had a leg showing.' The anxious Lefray watched Arnaud edge out along an upper branch. 'Don't fall, for God's sake.'

A curse followed almost immediately as Arnaud, in lifting the camera to his eye, almost lost his balance. Wrapping an arm around a branch, he braced himself and tried again. In all he took six photographs before pocketing the camera and climbing down. Leaving his observation point at the gate, Lefray joined him.

'You think the light was good enough?'

Short of breath after his exertions, Arnaud's reply was curt. 'We'll have to find out, won't we?'

Lighting foul-smelling cigarettes, the two men moved behind the clump of bramble and waited. Once they heard the sound of a passing horse and cart and the murmur of voices. It was followed ten minutes later by the armoured car. This time it did not stop at the gate but continued down the hill.

Although by this time Arnaud was shivering with cold, still the two men waited. Dusk was now closing in and shadowing the distant radiolocation station. Once more the patrolling armoured car returned and disappeared over the hill crest. This time Arnaud gave Lefray a nod and the two men dragged their bicycles from the hedge. Before wheeling them out on the lane, they stood a moment listening. Then, running forward, they began free-wheeling down the hill. Dusk closed around them and in a few seconds they disappeared.

'Was this Staines' idea, sir?' Henderson asked.

Davies gave him a sharp look. 'Yes. Why?'

No one could be more blunt than Henderson when he felt the occasion demanded it. 'Then I think he's picked the wrong squadron for it. This is a Tiffie job.'

'What makes you so sure of that?'

'The job itself. Ground support. Isn't that what Tiffies are for?'

Davies had the expression of a man defending a shaky position and knowing it. 'The job might call for a long patrol over the target area. Typhoons couldn't stay out that long.'

'They could go over in relays, couldn't they?'

With a snort of exasperation, Davies turned to Moore. 'I suppose this is your opinion too?'

The three officers were the only men present in the Operations room that day. Acutely aware of his responsibility, Davies had asked for full security measures to be taken and two S.P.s were on guard outside.

Challenged into giving an opinion, Moore chose the most tactful one possible. 'If we were talking in purely military terms, sir, the answer would have to be yes.'

Davies scowled at the admission he was forced to make. 'Well, we're not talking in purely military terms. Staines wouldn't have stood a snowball's chance in hell of getting the Yanks to agree to any other squadron but us. So for Christ's sake let's cut out the quibbles and make the best of it. If we can do a good job here, the publicity will be tremendous and a crisis will be averted. In the long run that could be more important than sinking a couple of Nazi battleships.'

Henderson gave a long-suffering sigh. 'All right, sir. We'll do our best, of course.'

'Good man. That's the spirit.' Looking relieved, Davies turned back to Moore. 'I shall want you and Adams to come down with me to Portsmouth when they convene the briefing. You'll get plenty of warning.'

Moore nodded. 'You say our job will be to patrol the coastal road?'

'That's right. If Jerry doesn't get his reserves up in time, it'll be a doddle. Even if he does, you ought to be able to handle 'em easily enough if our Intelligence hasn't misled us.'

'I'd like a preliminary look at the road and the station, sir.'

'I'd rather you didn't. Jerry might get suspicious if he sees too many kites flying over the station.'

'I can get round that easily enough. I'll take a flight path that will make it seem I'm photographing the Cherbourg docks.'

Davies frowned. 'I've already had Benson on the blower. They'll be sending a photo-reconnaissance Spitfire over the station as soon as the weather improves.'

'I'd still like to take a look at it myself, sir,' Moore said quietly. 'It could make quite a difference on the day.'

Davies gave in testily. 'Oh, all right. Only you're not going alone. You'll take a minimum of four kites. And you'll stay at maximum height. That's an order.'

'If I take men with me I'll have to give them some reason for the trip,' Moore reminded him.

He received a scowl. 'You see how you're complicating things.'

'Can't I just tell them we're checking on all the radiolocation stations? There's nothing unusual in that to stir their curiosity. In any case my men won't talk. I'll take three of my most experienced crews.'

'Mind you do that,' Davies grunted. 'If anything was to leak out we'd all be crucified.'

CHAPTER 15

The young S.P. standing in the doorway looked embarrassed. 'Sorry to bother you, sir. But Maisie says it's urgent.'

Eyes still dazzled by the light, Ross stared at him. 'What time is it?'

'11.20, sir.'

'And you say she's waiting in the guardhouse?'

'Yes, sir. Shall I tell her you're coming?'

Ross swung his pyjama-clad legs to the floor. 'All right. Tell her I'll only be a couple of minutes.'

The S.P. nodded and disappeared. Ross, who was still feeling the effects of the crash, began dressing. With McKenny not due back until midnight, he had left the Mess early and been in bed by 10.30. As he slipped into his tunic he wondered what possible reason the girl could have for wanting to see him at this hour.

Most of the blacked-out billets were silent as he hurried past them, although muffled sounds of gaiety from the Mess ahead told him Millburn, Gabby and company were still in action. A chill in the night air made him wish he had put on his greatcoat. The shortcut took him past the Intelligence hut and the enquiring bark of a dog and a chink of light in a window told him Adams was working late.

He found Maisie inside the guardroom talking to the duty corporal. The corporal, a mechanic from the airframe section with the furrowed brow and doleful expression of a retriever, was clearly disappointed by his swift arrival. Guard duty, hated by all and sundry, was seldom relieved by the presence of an attractive woman. He moved reluctantly away as Ross crossed the room. 'What is it, Maisie?'

The girl, who was wearing a fawn mackintosh thrown over a skirt and blouse, gave the corporal a bright smile. 'Thanks for getting him for me, love. Ta ta.' Before Ross could question her further she took his arm and drew him outside. As she closed the door, her expression changed.

'We've got your friend over in the pub, love. Paddy McKenny.'

Ross gave a start. 'Paddy! What's he doing there?'

She gave him an impatient push towards the station gates. 'I'll tell you everything later. Let's get there first.'

Ross had a quick word with the sentry at the gates, then hurried down the dark road after the girl. 'What's going on?' he muttered. 'When did he get to your place?'

She was already halfway to the inn. 'Just over an hour ago. A taxi brought him.'

The darkness made it difficult to read her expression. 'What do you mean – brought him?'

She pushed open the wicker gate. 'You'll see in a minute.'

The heavy front door was unlocked. Closing it, she switched on the light and gave a shout. 'Joe! Bernard Ross is here.'

The white-haired Kearns came hurrying into the hall. Shirt-sleeved and wearing an apron, he was clearly relieved to see Ross.

'Hello, lad. Maisie will have told you. We've got your pal upstairs.'

Ross's forebodings were growing. 'Upstairs? What's the trouble?'

Kearns gave a grimace. 'He's in a bad way, lad. We've been worried about him.'

Ross started immediately up the stairs. Hesitating, Maisie turned to the innkeeper. 'I'll finish washing those glasses if you want to go up with him.'

'No, lass. You were with the lad when he was talking. I'll see to things down here.'

The girl followed Ross up the crooked staircase. Although the Scot was not tall, the ceiling beams made him duck his head. As he reached the landing, Maisie pushed past him and opened the door of a front bedroom. Leaving the room in darkness, she motioned Ross inside.

His first impression was the acid smell of spirits. Although the light from the landing was shining into the room, the bed was in a shadow and it took him a moment to recognize McKenny lying there. The Irishman was asleep and his heavy breathing told the rest. The puzzled Ross turned to the girl.

'How did he get here in this state?'

She drew up a couple of chairs and accepted the cigarette he gave her. 'He must have been drinkin' on his way back because they found an empty bottle of whisky on him. So maybe he wasn't incapable all the way. But he was bad when he got to Highgate. They looked at his identity card and put him in a taxi for the camp.

Lucky for him, the driver was old Bert Leeson. We sometimes use him on Sundays when the buses aren't running. He's got a son in the Army, and thinking Paddy might get into trouble at the camp, he dropped him off here to see if we could pull him round first.'

Ross glanced at the bed. 'I take it you didn't have much luck?'

As the girl drew hard on her cigarette, he noticed her expression for the first time. Normally a bold and breezy girl who had a riposte for every pass made at her, she had a look of disquiet that puzzled him. 'That's the funny thing,' she muttered. 'After I got some black coffee down him, he started talkin' all right. Almost too much. But then he suddenly went off again. That's when we thought we'd better get in touch with you.'

Her face held his attention. 'What do you mean – almost too much?'

She glanced away. 'Joe didn't hear him. He was too busy lookin' after the bars. But it scared me, I can tell you.'

'Scared you?'

For a moment she looked defiant. 'It would've scared anybody, the things he was saying.'

'Was it about this girl?'

'At first it was.' Maisie paused. 'Did you know she'd broken off their engagement and is going abroad?'

Ross nodded. 'That's why he'd got this two-day pass. He was hoping to talk her out of it.'

'Well, he didn't,' Maisie muttered. 'He didn't even see her. Apparently she'd been on night duty this week and was sleepin' when he got to the hospital. When he asked the matron to wake her up, she told him she insisted her nurses got their full sleep or they'd be in no condition to work.' In the half-light Maisie's eyes were huge with disbelief. 'Can you believe it? He's fightin' for his country, with a last chance to see his girl, and the old cow wouldn't wake her up. I don't blame him for what he did. I'd have felt like shooting the old bugger.'

Ross was erect in his chair. 'What did he do?'

'The way he told it, it was all jumbled up, but I gather he went berserk and tried to find her by throwin' open doors in the nurses' quarters. So the old bitch put three orderlies on him and had him thrown out.'

Ross was actually experiencing relief. 'So that's what happened.'

'It's enough to make any man turn to the bottle,' Maisie said. 'All the same, I can't understand some of the things he said to me afterwards.'

Her tone brought back the Scot's apprehension. 'What things?'

'Horrible things. I'm not religious myself, 'least not more than most people, but I can tell you he scared the life out of me.'

'What did he say?'

'Oh, horrible things about God and how he hated him. He got himself into a terrible state. I though once he was going to hit me.'

Ross cleared his dry throat. 'You know the reason, don't you? He's blaming God for it.'

454

'For losing his girl? But why should he do that?'

'I can't think. But he is.'

Womanlike, Maisie was immediately captivated. 'Just think how he must love her. Nobody's ever gone off God for me. When did all this start?'

'He's been moody for weeks, but I only found out two days ago.'

Maisie was gazing with respect at the sleeping McKenny. 'There can't be many men who feel that way about women. It reminds me of that film they made about the moors up here. The one with the chap called Heathcliff. What was its name?'

In his concern for McKenny, Ross had to concentrate on her question. 'You mean *Wuthering Heights*?'

'That's the one. He must have hated God too for keepin' the two of them apart. I remember wondering afterwards if a man would ever feel that way about me.' Maisie's lowered eyes were almost sullen as she drew hard on her cigarette. 'Sometimes I had the idea Gillie was that kind of man. You know – the kind nothing can stop. But it looks as if when you're dead, you're dead.'

Coming from a girl he had always seen as a cheerful extrovert, the sentiment came as a surprise to the religious Ross. About to protest, he rose to his feet instead. 'I suppose I'd better try to wake him up. Can I have some black coffee?'

Maisie nodded and crossed over to the door. 'I won't be long, love.'

Sitting on the bedside, Ross shook the Irishman's shoulder. The only response was a groan. He shook again, harder. 'Paddy! Wake up!'

This time, to his surprise, McKenny's eyes opened. At first they were blank. Then recognition seeped into them. 'Bernie?'

'Yes. I've come to take you back. Can you walk?'

The Irishman lifted his head from the pillow, then dropped back with a groan. 'I feel sick,' he muttered.

Pulling and heaving, Ross managed to get him into the bathroom and over the water closet. For a full five minutes the Irishman retched and vomited. When at last he staggered back, Ross swung him over the wash basin. Although the cursing McKenny tried to strike him, Ross doused his head and neck with cold water. Finally he rubbed him with a towel and steered him back across the landing. When Maisie entered a minute later the drenched and trembling Irishman was sitting on the bed. She pushed a cup of black coffee into his hands.

'Drink this, love. You'll soon feel better.'

The bitter coffee made the pilot grimace. His bloodshot eyes roamed round the bedroom. 'Where are we?'

'You're all right, love. You're in the pub.'

'How did I get here?'

'Bernie'll tell you later. If I were you I'd go back with him now and get a good night's sleep. You'll feel better tomorrow.'

With the girl's aid, Ross got the Irishman down the stairs and out on to the path. At the wicker gate she read his glance. 'Don't worry. Neither of us will tell anybody.'

Reaching back, he gave her an impulsive kiss. 'Thanks, Maisie. You're really something.'

Her dark eyes were on the unsteady McKenny. 'It's little enough for what you do for us, love.'

The night air appeared to fuddle the Irishman's senses again and on reaching the guardhouse Ross was forced to call on the young S.P. for assistance. Supporting McKenny between them, they half-carried him to the billet. To Ross's relief they passed no one of authority and five minutes later he thankfully lowered the Irishman down on his bed. He threw the S.P. a dark look as he straightened. 'Not a word of this, young Conroy, or we'll take you out and bomb Berlin with you.'

The young S.P., who unlike most of his breed had a hero-worship for the squadron's aircrews, gave him a conspiratorial smile. 'Anyone can fall and twist their ankle, sir, can't they?'

Ross grinned back. 'For an S.P. you've got a lot of imagination, Conroy. Remind me to recommend you for a DSO.'

As the delighted youngster went out and closed the door, Ross began to undress McKenny. At first he believed the Irishman had fallen asleep again but as he began unlacing his shoes, McKenny cursed and tried to kick him away. 'I want a drink.'

'We haven't got a drink. So shut up and keep still.'

Pushing him away with surprising strength, the Irishman lurched towards his cabinet. 'Who says we haven't?' Yanking the door open, he turned triumphantly with a bottle of gin in his hand. 'What's this? Scotch mist?'

Ross tried to take it from him but was pushed violently away. Dropping on his bed, McKenny unscrewed the cap and tilted back the bottle. About to use brute force on him this time, Ross saw the bottle was almost empty. A few seconds later there was a curse and the crash of glass as the Irishman flung the bottle across the billet. Muttering something Ross could not catch, he fell back with his wet hair on the pillow. Deciding this time he would leave well alone, the Scot was beginning to undress himself when he heard an ugly laugh.

'The bastard's won. Did you know that?'

For a moment Ross was puzzled. 'Who's won?'

'That God of yours.' As he glanced back, Ross saw the Irishman's head had lifted from his pillow. With the bruise dark on his face, his expression was almost evil. 'I'll tell you something else. He plays dirty too. He didn't even give me a chance to see her.'

Turning, Ross hung up his tunic. 'Go to sleep, Paddy. Things'll look better in the morning.'

'Those bloody priests have got you taped, haven't they?' McKenny sneered. 'Upside down and sideways. There isn't a God, you superstitious fool, and there's never been one.'

Ross began unlacing his shoes. 'Then he didn't prevent you seeing Joan, did he?'

'Oh, yes he did. An' do you know why? Because he's bloody vicious and ruthless.'

Ross walked across and laid a blanket over him. 'I'm putting out the light now.'

There was a curse and then, with the swift change of mood that characterizes drunkenness, McKenny reached up and fumbled for his hand. 'Good ol' Bernie! Nobody like you, Bernie. You're all right. It's just you've got so many weird ideas and . . .'

As the Irishman's voice dropped into a mumble, Ross released his hand gently and threw another blanket over him. He then sat on the bedside and waited until the man's breathing steadied before climbing wearily into bed. Expecting to fall asleep almost immediately, he kept on hearing McKenny's taunts and accusations and when sleep did finally come to him, it was fitful and disturbed.

CHAPTER 16

From 35,000 feet the coast of France was like a low cloud clinging to the edge of the sea. The dome of sky was a cold blue and the brilliant sun made McKenny's eyes throb in spite of his smoked glasses. He was flying J-Jimmie, the squadron's photo-reconnaissance Mosquito fitted with an F.53 camera. Behind J-Jimmie the exhaust gases were streaming out like the wake of a ship.

Three other Mosquitoes were arrayed beyond the Irishman's port wingtip. Flying in fingers four, they belonged to Moore, Young and Millburn. The morning after McKenny's return to the station, the day had dawned clear and bright. With the Met. people anticipating excellent visibility until the early afternoon, Moore had not wasted a moment. The four Mosquitoes had been air-tested before breakfast and on their way towards Cherbourg by 08.30.

It was an early call that could hardly have been more unfortunate for McKenny. With only six hours' sleep behind him, the Irishman still had alcohol in his blood. Fearing at one time he might have to report him unfit, Ross had feverishly plied him with black coffee and douched him twice beneath a cold shower. The result was success only as far as the pilot's ability to fly was concerned. His mood remained as black as a towering thunderhead.

In spite of the urgent preparations Moore had to make, McKenny's condition had not gone unnoticed by him, and he had questioned both the Irishman and Ross before allowing them to make their air-test. Careful to say nothing about McKenny's experience in Lincoln, the young Scot had vouched the pilot was fit enough to carry out the operation. In other circumstances Moore would have taken no chances and grounded the crew. As it was, with the operation needing his two photographic specialists, it was a difficult decision to make. In the end, after giving McKenny a reprimand which he had taken in sullen silence, Moore had given him permission to fly.

With time for questioning at a premium and Ross covering his friend with half-truths, Moore had no way of knowing it was a mistake. Perhaps because of the bitterness that compounded it, McKenny's hangover was not clearing. His head still throbbed with hammer blows and his mood was as unstable as fulminate of mercury. In addition the residual alcohol was affecting his blood vessels. His hands and feet ached intolerably from the bitter cold and as it affected his nerve centres, the rows of dials before him kept blurring. Sitting beside him, the uneasy Ross noticed how the Irishman kept turning his oxygen fully on to clear his vision.

Flying at point in the fingers four formation, Moore was gazing down on the congealed sea where the wake of two ships, probably mine layers, looked like the excrement from two caterpillars on an enormous leaf. He was wondering what the German response would be. There was no doubt the four Mosquitoes were being monitored: at this height half a dozen radio-location stations would have picked them up fifteen minutes ago. And fifteen minutes was a long warning if any of Jerry's latest FW.190 A-6s were in the neighbourhood. Intelligence had discovered he was using a new fuel additive that greatly increased his fighters' rate of climb. It meant, if the 190s had been despatched immediately, they could already have reached 20,000 or thereabouts. After that their power curve would rapidly fall away but they could still be a deadly threat if the Mosquitoes dallied too long over the coast.

The question was whether the enemy would risk his 190s encountering Allied figher patrols to intercept four Mosquitoes whose great height made it obvious they were not going to launch an attack. He might turn a blind eye to them or, uncertain why they were tracking along the coast at that height, he might decide to play safe and intercept. Equally, with the morning so clear after weeks of poor weather, he might even think them an excellent excuse to test his air defences. With no need to keep radio silence, Moore had a word with his crews. 'Starfish Leader. Keep your eyes open for bandits. We might be tempting them into a little practice.'

The experienced crews had already been searching every corner of the brilliant sky until their eyes watered but could see no tell-tale contrails. Below, the Pointe de Barfleur slid beneath their starboard wingtips. By leading the flight in a westerly direction that would take it across the tip of the Contentin peninsula, Moore was hoping the Germans would believe they were doing reconnaissance of the important port of Cherbourg.

Ahead the peninsula reached out into the Channel like the leg of a huge animal. Smoke puffs began opening out like evil blossoms as the coastal batteries, stretched to their extreme range, began to put up a probing barrage. Moore changed course and altitude, flew straight for thirty seconds, then swung 20 degrees to port again. Feeling their aircraft yaw in the rarefied air, the pilots opened formation to lessen the danger of collision.

The smoke puffs multiplied as they neared Cherbourg. Hoppy's needle-sharp eyes could see ships, tinier than matchsticks, lying alongside wharves and jetties.

At the end of the port's long mole the submarine boom stretched across like a knotted hair. As A-Apple rocked to an explosion, Moore changed course again and dropped five hundred feet.

To further the deceit, the mosquitoes circled Cherbourg twice before heading west again. As they swept along the northern coast, Moore's hope was that the Germans would assume the reconnaissance was over and they were making for home.

Ahead, the Cap de la Hague looked like the rounded back of a sea monster. Beyond it could be seen the Isle of Alderney. Below, the countryside was well-wooded but as the Cap drew nearer the hills and cliffs took on a more barren aspect. After winding through wooded hills, the communication road the Mosquitoes were detailed to patrol had now emerged a couple of miles behind the cliffs and was running parallel to them. As Moore's eyes followed it, Hoppy leaned forward against his straps. 'There's a cloud ahead, skipper. It could foul things up.'

The cloud the Cockney was pointing at was a haze of strato-cirrus. As it drifted below the crews saw it was thin enough for the coastline to be traced through it. At the same time all of them knew it would fog up details of the radiolocation station on the camera film.

The station was now dead ahead of them, standing on a barren hillside a mile from the sea. 'What are you going to do, skipper?' Hoppy asked.

Moore was trying to estimate the height of the cloud. 24,000 feet . . . possibly a couple of thousand less. If 190s had been scrambled as soon as the monitors had picked up the mosquitoes, they could already be at that height or even above it. A cool strategist, Moore decided that with photo-reconnaissance Spitfires already briefed to take photographs he had no right to risk his crews' lives. He would content himself with a survey of the area he was detailed to patrol.

He gazed down again. Hazy though the view was, he could pick out the salient features. A support track ran from the coastal road to a cluster of mounds at the cliff edge that he took to be the gun battery. Below the battery was a rocky bay with a semi-circle of sand. Although the beach ran westwards, the cliffs straightened and grew steeper as a hill range ran out into the sea. Eventually a rocky promontory, reaching almost to the water's edge, separated the beach from a large, sandy bay that indented the coast for another two kilometres. The radiolocation station stood on the hillside above this beach. Still further west, where a shallow valley ran between low cliffs, was a third and smaller bay.

As Moore lowered his binoculars, Hoppy, who had been scanning the coast road, turned to him. 'Is that all we're supposed to do, skipper? Just patrol that road? It looks like a piece of cake.'

Moore's comment was dry. 'It could be a tough old biscuit on the day, Hoppy.'

Back in J-Jimmie McKenny was showing increased impatience when no order came from Moore. 'We haven't come all this way for nothing, have we?'

Ross nodded at the haze below. 'Moore knows I can't get photographs through that.'

'Then let's go beneath it. We're doing no good up here.'

Ross stared at him. 'We can't go down there. Jerry could be waiting for us.'

In his present self-destructive mood, any challenge was fuel to McKenny. 'So what? They keep saying they want his fighters destroyed, don't they?'

Knowing how acute the Irishman's hangover was, Ross made the mistake of not taking him too seriously. 'Don't tell me you feel like being a hero. Not after the state you were in last night.'

The pilot's masked face turned towards him. 'I can't do anything right these days, can I?'

'Not when you keep on disobeying orders. If you go on this way you'll either get us shot down or court-martialled.'

'I thought you were the Christian soldier who wanted to win this war and give evil a kick up the backside?'

Suddenly aware how dangerous the Irishman's mood was, Ross ignored the gibe. 'Have a word with Moore and ask what he wants. That's the simplest answer.'

'Why bother about Moore? God'll always take care of you, won't he? Or aren't you so sure about the Old Guy anymore?'

Ross was apprehensive now. 'Stop clowning about, Paddy. If we disobey orders, Moore will jump on us with both feet.'

McKenny needed nothing more to curse and peel away from the formation. Moore's voice rapped out sharp and urgent in the men's earphones. 'Get back into formation, Zero Three! At the double!'

In J-Jimmie, now in a thirty-degree dive, Ross was staring at McKenny in disbelief. 'Have you gone crazy? You can be court-martialled for this.'

Once more they heard Moore's authoritative voice. 'McKenny! This is an order. Get back into formation!'

McKenny's response was to switch off the R/T. 'We've come all this way: we're taking those photographs,' he told Ross. 'So get your camera ready!'

The altimeter needle was swinging rapidly back round the dial. 27,000 feet . . . 25,000 . . . 23,000. As he watched the film of cloud leaping towards them, Ross felt his hand sweating. If there were any Focke Wulfs climbing up to intercept, they would be licking their lips at the dish being offered them.

For three seconds the sunlight dimmed, then J-Jimmie was through the haze and the cliffs were sharp in detail. Levelling off at 22,000 feet, McKenny nodded tersely at the camera. Deciding that now the risk had been taken it might as well serve a useful purpose, Ross began filming. By this time the flak was heavy from both the coastal defences and the radio-location station, and twice McKenny had to steady the Mosquito as explosions threw it off course.

As the buildings fell behind, Ross decided one pass was enough and climbed back into his seat. 'We've been lucky so far. Now let's get out of here.'

For a moment it seemed the aggressive Irishman would make another run over the station. Instead he muttered something and turned towards the sea. With the sun shining through the tenuous cloud, it had a glare that hurt the eyes. As Ross squinted up at it through his tinted goggles, he saw a black speck suddenly darken beneath it. Another speck appeared a second later. As he gave a yell of warning, tracer flashed past their starboard wing.

In spite of his hangover McKenny's combat reflexes were good. Before the Focke Wulf pilot could make his correction, he swung J-Jimmie violently to port. The 190 banked after it and for a few seconds, with their relative speeds reduced to a low vector, the Focke Wulf seemed to be swinging almost lazily in the sky. In his mirror the fascinated Ross could see its stubby wings, long cupola, and a halo of yellow light around its radial engine.

With combat joined, McKenny's training cleared his mind of everything but the task in hand. Survival depended on keeping the curve of pursuit so severe that the enemy pilot, who had to turn inside the curve to line up his guns, would either black out from the g-forces or break off his attack.

J-Jimmie's wings tilted more and more as McKenny increased the angle of turn. As elevators took the place of rudder, the Irishman drew the column back into his chest, forcing the aircraft into a circle as tight as a death ride in a fun fair. Ross felt the unnatural weight of his head pressing down on his spine, the drag on his eye sockets, and the leaden weight that was sinking into his bowels. Behind them, the German pilot fired one abortive burst before settling down grimly in pursuit.

It was a classic air combat situation in which the manoeuvrability of the aircraft decided who should live or die. It so happened McKenny and Ross had the good fortune to be in a twin-engined aircraft that had the manoeuvrability of a fighter. As the Irishman increased his turn until the Mosquito's wings were almost bowing with the strain, the 190, forced into an even steeper bank to line up its guns, suddenly faltered as its pilot blacked out from the crushing g-forces. Before McKenny could voice his triumph there was the sound of a pneumatic drill pounding metal as the second 190 took over from the first, whose pilot was recovering a thousand feet below.

For Ross, helpless to do anything but cling to his straps and pray, the next few minutes were a mad confusion of spinning sea and sky. From the glimpses he caught of diving aircraft and black crosses, it appeared an entire flight of 190s had dropped on them and some calm cell in his mind told him to prepare to die. The sudden sight of Mosquitoes and Spitfires diving past made him wonder if he were having hallucinations. A moment later sea and sky levelled off and in the way of aerial combat the sky was abruptly empty of aircraft. As the sweating McKenny sank back in his seat, the bewildered Ross turned to him. 'What happened?'

The Irishman jerked a sullen thumb upwards. 'Moore came down to help. And then a crowd of Spitfires arrived. They're chasing Jerry back to Berlin.'

Glancing up Ross saw Moore's trio of Mosquitoes a thousand feet above. As McKenny began climbing towards them, the Scot's anger exploded.

'What made you do a crazy thing like that? If those Spitties hadn't been around we might have all been killed.'

He expected another gibe but the shock of combat had temporarily exorcised the Irishman's inner demon and he made no comment as Ross raged on.

'That's the third time you've nearly killed us. If you want to commit suicide, jump off a cliff or shoot yourself. But stop trying to do it when I'm flying with you.'

The glance McKenny gave him was full of sullen contrition. Reaction made Ross neither notice nor care.

'I've had you. Right to the top. If Moore doesn't ground you I'm going to ask for another pilot. And when they ask me why, I'm telling them everything.'

With his expression hidden by his mask, McKenny swung into position along-side Millburn. Gabby was gazing across at the jagged holes that the second 190 had punched into J-Jimmie. 'What do you think came over him, boyo? You think he was drinking poteen last night?'

Millburn, who for all his carefree behaviour on the ground was a highly professional pilot, growled his disgust. 'I hope the skipper takes the hide off the sonofabitch.'

Henderson, who was standing thoughtfully at the window of his office, turned as Moore entered. 'Hello, Ian. Sorry to disturb you but I had Davies on the phone a few minutes ago. Among other things he read out an extract form the *New York Daily Mirror* that Staines has passed over to him.'

'How was it?' Moore asked. 'As bad as we expected?'

Henderson scowled. 'Worse if anything. Lambert says we knew from the beginning there was a risk to the prisoners. And that the entire operation was politically motivated. What the bastard doesn't say is that if he hadn't been carry-ing out a poison-pen campaign against the RAF, the operation wouldn't have been necessary in the first place.'

When Moore only nodded, Henderson showed a bitterness rare in one so phlegmatic. 'We pull off one of the most skilful low-level operations of the war. We free maybe two hundred American aircrews and give a massive boost to the morale of the partisans. And all we get for it is a bollocking. And Davies still wonders why I don't like playing politics.'

'Did he have any news of the other operation?' Moore asked.

The Scot nodded moodily. 'He's full of it. He's certain this time Lambert is going to be dumped right on his arse. I wish I was as confident.'

'Is he going to be on the HQ ship?'

'Yes. Plus dozens of American top brass, war correspondents, and Lambert.' Henderson could not help the malicious thought. 'I hope they use the same Operations Room or whatever they call it in the Navy.'

'Did he say when he wants Adams and me to go to Portsmouth?'

'That trip's off.' When Moore gave a start, Henderson continued: 'Apparently one of the major naval units taking part in the operation has been under refit in Scotland and there's been a hold up. Nothing serious but to avoid a last-minute rush when it reaches Portsmouth, two Yank officers have flown up to Scotland to hold the briefing there. As we're on their flight path back, Davies has arranged for them to drop in here as well.'

'Good. When do you expect them?'

'Sometime tomorrow afternoon. So make sure Adams and your two flight commanders are within call, will you?'

As Moore nodded, Henderson's tone changed. 'What's all this I hear about McKenny? There's a rumour going round he disobeyed your orders this morning and nearly dropped you all in the brown stuff. Is it true?'

Moore, who had ordered his flight commanders to say nothing about the incident until he had interviewed McKenny, guessed the source of the rumour. On landing he had gone straight over to the Irishman and the words they had exchanged must have enabled the mechanics to put two and two together.

'I'm afraid it is. I've just had him in my office.'

'What happened exactly?'

Moore told him. When he finished Henderson looked shocked. 'That's blatant insubordination! What are you going to do? Court-martial him?'

'I'm not sure yet,' Moore said quietly.

'Not sure?'

'No.'

Knowing that in spite of Moore's affability, he could be ruthless with conduct that endangered his crews' safety, Henderson was looking as much puzzled as indignant. 'Why not?'

'I had a word with Ross beforehand. He wouldn't deny or confirm what happened this morning but he did tell me what happened to McKenny in Lincoln yesterday. And I suppose in fairness one must take it into account.'

'Lincoln?'

Moore gave details of the hospital incident. The frowning Henderson rubbed his chin. 'It's rough, I'll give you that. Bloody rough in fact. But it still doesn't excuse his going haywire and risking all your lives. Men are getting Dear John letters all the time. You forgotten the Yanks are over here?'

'I agree. But I can't help feeling there's something else behind it.'

'What else?'

'I don't know.'

'Doesn't Ross have any ideas?'

'He says he hasn't.'

The big Scot made an impatient gesture. 'Insubordination's too serious a crime for excuses, Ian. I know his country isn't at war, that he didn't have to fight, and the rest of it, but I feel you still have to make an example of him.'

Moore's good-looking face turned expressionless. 'I've got it in hand. I'll decide if a court martial is called for after he's seen the M.O. again. I also want to make a few more enquiries. In the meantime he's been grounded.'

Aware how adamant the young squadron commander could be when his mind was made up, Henderson gave no more than a grunt of disapproval. 'All right, he's your responsibility. But as I'm still the C.O. around these parts, I don't want you making any decision until I've seen the M.O.'s report myself and heard the result of your enquiries.'

*

463

McKenny slammed the billet door and made for his locker. Ross, who had been anxiously waiting his return, sat up on his bed. 'Well! What happened?'

The Irishman cursed and jerked open his locker door. 'He's grounded me.'

Ross showed no surprise. 'What about a court martial?'

'He's going to make up his mind about that after I've seen the M.O. again.'

The young Scot sank back in relief. 'Then you're all right.'

A half-bottle of gin in his hand, McKenny stared at him in dislike. 'How do you work that out? You think the M.O. is going to find something wrong with me?'

'It's not that. Moore's a decent officer and if he was going to court-martial you, he'd have done it right away. I think he's sympathetic about what happened in Lincoln yesterday.'

'Why did you tell him about that? I don't want his sympathy.'

'I had to tell him something. You nearly got the flight wiped out this morning.'

'You're talking as if he's let me off. He's still grounded me.'

'He couldn't do much else, could he? Not after you disobeyed his orders in front of both his flight commanders.'

McKenny's look of dislike grew. 'You're glad about it, aren't you?'

A man who hated lying, Ross could not help his brief hesitation. 'Of course I'm not.'

'Yes, you are. You were getting scared to fly with me. It stood out a mile.'

Ross saw no point in more lies. 'Is it surprising after the way you've been acting lately?'

McKenny tilted the bottle and took a long drink. Ross watched him uneasily. 'When are you seeing the M.O.?'

'In twenty minutes.'

The Scot gave a start. 'Then you're crazy. If he finds out you've been drinking this time of the day, you'll be in even worse trouble.'

'How can I be in worse trouble?'

'Don't be a fool, Paddy. If you play your cards right, you could be flying again in a few weeks.'

McKenny lowered the bottle. 'You'd love that, wouldn't you? If you're smart, you'll keep a bottle of gin in that locker.'

Ross ignored the comment. The Irishman's taunting gaze remained on him. 'Although, come to think of it, it doesn't make any sense, does it? Not when you're the one who's supposed to believe in God and all his Angels.'

Ross's young face set. 'Don't start all that again.'

'Why not? It fascinates me. If God is so wonderful and good to his children, what are you so scared about? All he'll do if we're hit is put a magic carpet underneath you and lower you to the ground.'

'Stop talking bloody nonsense,' Ross gritted.

'Why is it nonsense? Don't you believe he can do it?'

Ross rose to his feet. 'I'm going to the Mess.'

'What's the matter,' McKenny jeered. 'Can't you face the truth?'

Ross took a deep breath. 'It's time you faced the truth, Paddy. Because of this girl you've gone to pieces and turned against everything and everybody. But it's not that easy to lose God, is it? It's twisting your guts out so much you want to destroy my faith too. Isn't that what all this is about?'

For a moment the Irishman went very pale. Then his harsh voice echoed round the billet. 'You need a home truth or two yourself, Bernie. The Church has conditioned you to genuflect, eat biscuits, and act out the rest of the bullshit but none of it helps when the shit's flying about. I know it doesn't – I saw your face this morning. You won't admit it because of the implications but it's a fact just the same. You've no more faith than I have.'

The young Scot had also turned very pale. 'I believe in God, Paddy. I believe in his mercy and his love.'

'But not in his protection, right? And what about his mercy? He didn't show much to St Claire and Simpson the other day, did he? Or to Lester and Thomson. And according to you they were also fighting against evil.' There was a look on McKenny's face that made Ross shudder as the Irishman leaned forward. 'I'll tell you something, Bernie. If this is the way God behaves to people who're fighting his war, I'd rather ask the Devil for help.'

Ross crossed himself involuntarily. The gesture brought a jeer from McKenny. 'Look at yourself, you stupid bastard. You're as superstitious as an African pygmy.'

It was an effort for Ross to keep his voice steady. 'You won't destroy my faith, Paddy. No matter what you say or do.'

The Irishman tossed the bottle of gin on to his bed and went to the door. Hand on the latch, he turned and gave another laugh. 'You want a bet? Wait and see.'

CHAPTER 17

Moore was in No. 1 hangar standing alongside a stripped-down engine of A-Apple when a flushed young ACII stiffened in front of him. 'Your sergeant's been looking for you, sir. She says you're wanted in the Intelligence Room.'

Tight security was in deployment around Adams' 'Confessional' as Moore approached. S.P.s were standing outside the windows and a third was on guard at the door. The reason was obvious the moment Moore entered. Apart from Davies, Henderson, Adams and the two flight commanders, two American officers were present. One was a naval commander; the other an Army colonel. All were gathered around Adams' desk, which had been cleared for the occasion.

Davies' slight testiness told Moore he was excited. 'What happened? Your sergeant didn't know where you'd got to.'

465

As composed as always, Moore glanced at the two Americans. 'Sorry, sir, but I didn't hear the aircraft fly in. I've been over in No. 1 hangar. I've had a bit of trouble with my starboard engine recently and Chiefy asked me to take a look at it.'

Grunting something, Davies turned back to the two American officers who had straightened from the desk. 'Gentlemen, this is our Squadron commander, Wing Commander Moore. Moore, this is Commander Runcorn of the United States Navy and Colonel Tilsey of the United States Rangers.'

Moore shook hand with each man in turn. Runcorn, slim and dark, was a man in his early forties with observant eyes. Tilsey was a fair, good-looking man of athletic appearance who looked a few years younger than his compatriot. As Davies gave Moore's name, Runcorn stubbed out a cigarette. Adams, watching the introductions, noticed the Americans' eyes flicker over the ribbons Moore was wearing. The behaviour told him both were acquainted with Moore's record and had respect for it.

With introductions completed, Davies wasted no more time. 'Before we start talking about the job we've got for you, I want to impress on you all the need for security. You won't mention a word of this outside this room, not even to one another. Is that absolutely clear?'

As all the squadron personnel nodded, Davies glanced at the Americans before turning to the two flight commanders. 'If you were wondering why representatives of our major ally are present, it's not just because they're involved but because it is their operation. We are going to be the only British unit taking part, so you will realize we're being given quite an honour. I know you'll play your part by being worthy of it.'

The puzzled glance Young exchanged with Millburn added to the tension of the moment. Motioning them both nearer the desk, Davies picked up a pointer and prodded a huge photograph lying there. 'Here is the Americans' objective. One of Jerry's largest radiolocation stations, powerful enough to scan every ship that passes down the Channel and to pick you up almost before you leave your airfield. It isn't new to you: I let you fly over it yesterday so you could take in its main features. What you didn't know is that it's not going to be bombed but raided from the sea by the Americans. I won't say any more because that's why our American colleagues are visiting us. But you'll see in a moment that you are taking part in an extremely important operation. Now I'll hand you over to Commander Runcorn and Colonel Tilsey.'

As the two Americans glanced at one another Runcorn picked up the pointer and handed it to Tilsey. Grinning at him wryly, the good-looking colonel walked over to a large map of the western seaboard of France pinned to a blackboard behind the desk. His accent told Adams, who prided himself on voice identification, that he came from the South West, probably California.

'Firstly, gentlemen, I would like to say how glad we are that your squadron is taking part in this mission. By this time it's something of a household name in the States, so we feel it's an honour we're in this job together.'

Winking an eye at the absent Staines, Davies accepted a cigarette from Henderson. With the courtesies over, Tilsey got down to business.

'From the nature of the target you might be visualizing the kind of raid the British carried out on Bruneval in 1942. A drop of paratroopers, a surprise attack, and withdrawal in assault boats before enemy reserves could arrive. Although this station is more ruggedly built and has better defences we might have thought on the same lines if we hadn't other reasons for the raid. With the invasion of Europe on the horizon, we need battle experience that we can disseminate among our invasion troops and up-to-date knowledge of the beach defences we're likely to face. This raid should satisfy all these objectives while also getting rid of a station that because of its range could warn the enemy of our pre-invasion shipping movements. In other words we're really doing a Dieppe job like the Canadians and British did in 1942. At the same time we can justify to the enemy the forces we're deploying because of the exceptional defences of the station. Has anyone any questions so far?'

'How long does the tide give you ashore, Colonel?' Henderson asked.

'Three hours. Three and a half at the most. So we have to move fast.'

'Exactly how strong are the station defences?'

The American waited while Adams pinned up an artist's impression of the station on a second blackboard. 'In effect it's a cluster of strongpoints supporting the aerial masts for good measure. Round them is this perimeter wall and armed pill-boxes. Outside the perimeter is a minefield. In addition,' and Tilsey's pointer returned to the map and ran along the cliffs, 'there is a gun battery here. We're assuming it's part of the coastal defences but its positioning shows they've also had the station's defence in mind. Add to that heavy beach defences and you'll see we have a pretty hard nut to crack.'

'What about enemy reserves?'

'Intelligence tells us they have an infantry unit of unknown size on manoeuvres somewhere around Bricquebec. They also have a squadron of tanks in Les Pieux. Add to that the strength of the station itself and it means we're having to put tanks ashore as well as light artillery.'

Young was making thumb measurements on the map. 'What about Cherbourg? We're pretty close to it, aren't we?'

'Yes, but most of the defences there are static ones, heavy artillery and the like, although of course they might rush some infantry towards us. The main Panzer defences of the peninsula are down in St Jores where they can be moved quickly to any coast under attack. However, as they couldn't possibly reach us under three hours, the local reserves in Les Pieux seem to be our main threat.'

'How are you figuring to cross those minefields, Colonel?' Millburn asked.

'We've got thirty B.17s flying in ahead of us. We're not expecting them to damage any strongpoints but they should hand out a few headaches and blow gaps in the minefields for our tanks to exploit.'

Millburn, who had shared a few beers with Young at lunchtime, went beyond his brief, to Davies' displeasure. 'If it's anything like Dieppe, you're going to lose a lot of men, Colonel.'

Tilsey nodded. 'You could well be right. But our troops have been in England a long time now and they need battle experience. What other way is there of getting it?'

The American's frankness and modesty was clearly impressing his British audience. They encouraged a twangy quip from Teddy Young. 'You could always teach 'em to fly and lend 'em my Mosquito. You wouldn't hear me fretting if I could put my feet up for a year or two.'

The Australian's levity brought a glare from Davies but before he could intervene the young Colonel laughed. Expecting more formality from the British, both Americans appeared delighted at the relaxed atmosphere. 'I'll tell them that. You never know – some might take up the offer.'

'Any time, sir,' Young grinned.

As Davies coughed, Tilsey got back to business. 'Our total strength will be around 3,500 men of which 800 will be Rangers – our equivalent of your Commandos. We're also shipping thirty-odd tanks along. We've been training down in Cornwall for the last couple of months, so we're in reasonable shape. Our first job, which will be done by the Rangers, will be to destroy that coastal gun battery and any other gun emplacements that block the way. Then we shall put tanks ashore in a gap in the cliffs two miles west of the station. In the meantime troops will be coming ashore and clearing the cliff defences. If all goes according to schedule we'll then be able to launch an attack on the station from the three sides. When we take the station the strongpoints will be destroyed from the inside by plastic explosives. While all this is going on our engineers will be studying the gun battery and the coastal defences we've knocked out. When they've got all the information they need, we pull out our tanks and troops and come home. That's our side of it. Now I'll pass you over to Commander Runcorn who'll tell you what our junior service will be doing to sabotage our plans.'

Grinning at the crack, the slim, dark naval officer exchanged places with Tilsey. 'Good afternoon, gentlemen. Our junior service would first like to add its own appreciation and pleasure that your squadron is sharing this operation with us.' As laughter broke out Runcorn laid his pointer on the map of France. 'For operational purposes the landing sites have been given the following code names. Blue Beach, here, is a bay beneath the gunbattery where the Rangers will land. White Beach, to the west, is a larger, sandy bay where the main bulk of the infantry will come in. Further west still is Red Beach. It stretches across a gap in the seafront through which we're hoping our tanks can deploy. Reference maps of these sectors giving their exact positions have been given to your Intelligence Officer, who will distribute them later. O.K. so far?'

As men nodded, the naval officer went on: 'Our task force will consist of destroyers, infantry landing ships, assault craft, gun-ships, and minesweepers. Our HQ ship will be the destroyer *Brazos*. Our first job will belong to the minesweepers who will clear a passage through the fields and mark it. In the meantime we'll be embarking troops. The minesweepers will then return and lead us to a point seven miles off the enemy coast. As the radiolocation station isn't operational yet, hopefully we'll arrive there undetected.'

At this juncture Adams hesitated, then raised a hand. 'What about the other monitoring stations along that coast? Won't they pick you up?'

Runcorn nodded apologetically. 'Sorry, I forgot to mention that. Fortunately the normal radar site is far less stoutly constructed, and a couple of days beforehand your air boys and ours are going to carry out a blitz on them. As you know, it happens periodically, so shouldn't cause too many German eyebrows to raise, but to be on the safe side we're also going to blitz sites in the Pas de Calais and Fécamp areas. In addition, in the same area, we've got aircraft flying up and down the coast carrying some kind of jamming device. They'll start operating only at the last minute to avoid alerting the coastal defences prematurely. That side of it is a bit too complicated for me but our scientists assure us it should work.'

As Adams nodded, Runcorn turned back to his main audience. 'Once there our destroyers will fan out to protect the convoy and the landing parties. These parties will embark at 05.00 hours and try to hit the beaches at first light. In the meantime the destroyers will be laying smoke and bombarding the coastal defences. They can't hope to do much more with four-inch guns than harass the batteries and strongpoints but they can also turn their guns on any reserve coming up to aid the station. Naturally all ships will remain in position throughout the operation and re-embark the troops when it is completed. We don't know whether the Heinies will commit the Luftwaffe during this time but if they do we've got twelve squadrons of Thunderbolts to take care of us. Any other questions so far?'

For a couple of minutes Young and Millburn had been exchanging puzzled glances. Young beat the American to the question by a short head.

'It's all clear but for one thing, sir. What are we supposed to do?'

Before Runcorn could answer, Davies moved forward. 'Perhaps you'll let me answer that, Commander?' When the naval officer nodded, Davies took his place before the map. Aware of the insecurity of his position, his voice was sharp as he ran a finger along the coastline.

'As you see, there's only one main road in these parts and it runs a mile or so back from the station. So if Jerry rushes up any troop transports or tanks, this is the way he must come. Your job will be to stop him. And if any of his tanks try to take the short cut across the cliff top, you stop him there as well. All right?'

Unaware of the deeper issues at stake, Young was looking flabbergasted. 'You mean it's a ground support job, sir? But why us? It's a cut and dried job for Typhoons.'

By this time Davies had a craw full of Typhoons. 'What the hell gives you that idea, Young? You can carry more stores than Tiffies and just as important you can stay longer over the battle area. That could be crucial.' Seeing Young opening his mouth, Davies moved in quickly. 'You won't have any worries about enemy aircraft. The 8th Air Force will be giving you top cover.'

The Australian muttered a chauvinistic quip at the grinning Millburn. Remembering how little the two flight commanders knew, Davies got his temper back under control.

'You've been chosen because you're the most flexible and highly-trained unit we have. Moreover' – and Davies felt it was safe to go that far – 'the Americans know your reputation and wouldn't be using you unless they felt you were the right men for the job. As I said earlier, you're being paid a high compliment.'

Prompted by his mid-day beer, Young could not resist blowing a raspberry at Millburn. With the sound coming out louder than the Australian intended, those who knew Davies expected a sharp response. Instead Davies craftily used the gesture as a distraction. 'You want to watch that drinking at lunch time, Teddy. All that wind could do you a mischief at 20,000 feet.'

The two visiting Americans joined in the laughter. Moore, aware of Davies' dilemma, made a tactful intervention as it ceased. 'Might I make a suggestion, sir? As we don't know how heavy the enemy response will be, wouldn't a couple of Typhoon squadrons on stand-by be a good insurance? Then we'd be in no danger of letting the Americans down if Jerry springs any surprises.'

Standing alongside Adams, Henderson muttered his approval. 'That's not a bad idea. It's something the Yanks might accept.'

Watching Davies' expression as he glanced at the two Americans, Adams felt certain the Air Commodore felt the same way. When Runcorn gave a nod, Davies turned back to Moore with some gusto.

'We'll work on that idea, Moore. It has promise. All right, let's leave the rest until next week. For security reasons we're not briefing the crews before Monday. By that time they'll all be down south at Holmsley, which will be your base during the operation. I've already arranged for a Bombay to pick up your maintenance crews and their stores on Monday morning. In the afternoon Commander Runcorn and Colonel Tilsey have kindly agreed to pay us another visit when they'll give us and the crews a final, detailed briefing. Any more questions until then?'

When no one spoke Davies turned to the two Americans. 'Then that only leaves me to thank you two gentlemen for coming today.' He glanced at Henderson. 'I think before they leave we ought to crack a bottle of Scotch, don't you?'

The Scot grinned as he produced a full bottle from a drawer in Adams' desk. 'I thought you never drank before dinner, sir.'

Davies' sense of humour was nothing if not astringent. 'I wish I could say the same about you, Jock.'

As the laughing men separated into small groups, Moore found himself alongside Tilsey. The young Colonel's bearing and handling of the briefing had impressed him. 'Might I ask what part you're playing in the operation, Colonel?'

'I'm in charge of the Rangers. We're the ones landing at Blue Beach below the battery.'

'That means you're spearheading the raid, doesn't it?'

'Not really. You could say the B.17s are doing that.'

Never one to seek the limelight himself, Moore found the good-looking American's self-effacement likeable. 'I know it's none of my business but it does seem you're making this hard for yourself. Wouldn't it be cheaper in lives to probe a more normal stretch of coast and clobber the station again with Lancasters or Forts? At least we should be able to keep knocking the aerials down.'

'Hardly. If we went in without a definite objective the Heinies would smell a rat and our own Press would crucify us for throwing away lives. Besides' – the American's shrug was fatalistic – 'I'm only a colonel and ours isn't to reason why.'

Moore pursed his lips, then nodded. 'No, I suppose not. Anyway, good luck.'

Tilsey toyed with his glass a moment, then gave a wry smile. 'I'll come clean with you, Moore. Originally I was one of those who resisted the idea of using anyone but our own men. Now, having seen your outfit, I'm glad I was talked round. I think you'll take good care of us.'

With the telephone to his ear, Adams gave a start and sank into his chair. Sue Spencer, packing maps and photographs into a large crate, paused to listen.

'How many, sir? That's very good, isn't it? You're right – they're doing a fine job. I take it you've no further news from the Red Cross?' Adams listened for a few seconds, then nodded. 'I see. Thanks for keeping us posted, sir. I'll inform the C.O. right away.'

Replacing the receiver, he was about to pick it up again when he felt the girl's eyes on him. 'That was the Brigadier. The first of the American escapers has got back. Five of them – smuggled over from a Belgian fishing port. It's quicker than anyone dared hope, so there's an excellent chance there'll be more within the next few weeks.'

'That's good news, Frank,' she said quietly. 'The crews will be pleased too.'

Knowing the news she hungered for, Adams did not keep her waiting. 'There's also word from the Red Cross. They've confirmed the deaths of Lester and Thomson.'

As her face paled, Adams went on quickly: 'But they've no news of Tony and his navigator. They've been asked to carry on the search, of course.'

Without a word she turned and continued to pack the crate. Feeling clumsy and inadequate, Adams cleared his throat. 'It could be good news, Sue. If they'd been killed in the crash their identification tags would have been found. As it is, the partisans could have pulled them out of the aircraft and taken them away with the Americans.'

For a moment she sat very still. Then she crossed the Nissen hut and picked up a pile of de-briefing forms from a table. 'Don't humour me, Frank. You know as well as I do that if their aircraft caught fire and exploded, their discs could have gone anywhere.'

Adams opened his mouth, then closed it again. Since St Claire had gone missing, the element that sustained life seemed to have drained from her. He had lost weight and the dark shadows under her eyes betrayed her grief. Yet when Adams had suggested she took leave or even a few days off duty, her reaction had been almost hostile. He had the feeling that, consciously or subconsciously, she was determined to go on working for St Claire as well as herself.

She returned to the crate, hesitated a moment, then turned. 'Shall I tell you something, Frank?'

'What?'

'At times like this it's almost a relief.'

Adams pretended not to understand. 'A relief?'

'Yes. Aren't you shocked?'

Adams shook his head. 'No.'

'I am. I hate myself for it. Yet that's how I feel.' When Adams said nothing she went on. 'If Tony had been here I'd have gone half-crazy for the next two nights. Now that's all over.'

Adams cleared his throat again. 'Do you think it's going to be that dangerous?'

'Don't you?'

'Not necessarily. If the flak posts get knocked out early – and the Americans are giving them top priority – it shouldn't be too bad if they keep to the road.'

'You know them better than that. They'll help the Americans in every way they can.'

Adams was afraid she was right. 'Moore's not going to throw their lives away. He's too responsible a squadron commander.'

'I know that. But he's also not the kind of man who'll let the Americans have losses if his intervention can help them.'

'It might never happen,' Adams muttered. 'Let's hope it doesn't.'

She was gazing through the window as if she had not heard him. 'Every man in this squadron is as important as Tony. And yet I'm feeling relief because this time I know he's safe. I'm selfish, aren't I, Frank?'

Adams sighed and removed his spectacles to clean them. 'No. As I said once before, you're human like the rest of us.'

'That's just another way of saying I'm selfish.'

'No. We can't bleed for everyone or we'd bleed to death.'

To Adams' horror her shoulders began shaking. 'We should bleed for everyone. Otherwise we're nothing. Oh, God, Frank, I wish this war was over. I'm terrified of what it's doing to me.'

CHAPTER 18

The aged MG sports car contained two drunken pilot officers and their girl friends. With its hood down, the wind was buffeting their faces and ruffling their hair. Both girls squealed as the car skidded round a corner and rocked violently before straightening again. The driver, not yet twenty-one, glanced back over his shoulder and gave a yell of pride.

'Isn't she a beauty?'

The second pilot, equally youthful, gave his girl friend a wink. 'She's not bad. But I still think that old jalopy I had last year could go faster.'

'Don't talk bull, man. This'll do eighty if I push her.'

'Then start pushing her. Otherwise it's going to be closing time before we make the Saxon Arms.'

The driver put his foot down and the note of the engine rose a full octave. The country road ahead was flanked by trees and high hedges. The sun had long set and dust was stealing over the fields. A couple of crows, settling down for the night, cawed indignantly and rose with a clatter of wings as the car roared past.

The driver reached out and put his arm around the waist of the girl beside him. As she snuggled against his shoulder, he began singing lustily. A second later the other pilot joined in. The girl at the back was showing alarm at the speed they were travelling but quietened when she was also pulled into her boy friend's arms.

Fifty yards ahead the road swung into a sharp left-hand bend. With his attention diverted by the girl alongside him, the driver failed to see it until the girl let out a warning scream.

It was the last sound any of them were to hear in their young lives. A second later the car leapt across the road and slammed into a tree with an impact that could be heard a mile away. Two bodies catapulted out, crashed into the hawthorn hedge, and hung motionless. Two others lay mangled among the jagged wreckage. In the silence that settled over the countryside, the only sounds heard through it were the hiss of hot metal and the dripping of petrol.

Moore was in No. 2 hangar when Henderson found him. With the move south scheduled for the morrow, he and his two flight commanders had been busy all day checking their specialist officers were sending everything needed for the operation. All heavy equipment, including bombs and rockets, had already been despatched by road transport. The Bombay, due at Sutton Craddock the following morning, would airlift the more fragile equipment and it was these items the ground crews were now packing into crates. The men had been working hard all day, and with only a privileged few knowing the reason for the move, rumours were rife and complaints many.

Teddy Young was the first to notice Henderson as the big Scot steered his bulk through the orderly chaos. 'The Old Man looks in a paddy. I wonder what's up.'

Henderson came to a halt in front of them. 'Did any of you give your lads permission to go out this evening?'

Moore glanced at the two flight commanders, who shook their heads. 'No, sir. The station's on stand-by.'

'That's what I thought,' Henderson said grimly. He turned to Young. 'No one asked you for a quick trip into Scarborough or Whitby?'

The ginger-headed Australian looked puzzled. 'They know better than that, sir. What's the problem?'

'The problem is two corpses on a mortuary slab in Highgate. Jennings and Stuart. Killed instantly in a car crash.'

Young's jaw dropped on to a packing case. 'I heard Jennings was going to buy a jalopy. They must have gone over the fence and picked it up. The stupid young bastards.'

Henderson turned to Moore. 'You realize what this means? With Heron wounded, Illingworth sick and McKenny grounded, even if we use our reserve crews we're going to be two kites shy. We might get away with one but two – hell, Lambert will crucify us.'

Moore guessed the way the Scot's thoughts were running. 'Are you asking me to lift McKenny's suspension?'

Henderson scowled. 'You don't think I like it, do you? But has anyone got any other ideas?'

Teddy Young gave a resigned shrug as Moore glanced at him. The young squadron commander stood deep in thought for a moment, then moved away. 'I'll go and have a talk with McKenny.'

With all passes cancelled, the Mess· was crowded when Moore entered. Although the bar was as busy as usual, he could see that news of the car accident had preceded him. The aircrews were gathered into small groups and there was a total absence of their usual gaiety. The irony did not escape Moore as he caught sight of Ross talking to Hopkinson and Stan Baldwin at the bar. Men could die in combat almost daily and their comrades would mourn them in wine and laughter. Yet when they were killed in commonplace ways the shock was felt by all.

Ignoring the questions put to him, he pushed his way towards the young Scot. 'I want a word with you, Ross. It won't take a minute.'

He led Ross into the corner where the piano stood. With St Claire missing, Lindsay absent, and the only other pianist on the station, Illingworth, down with 'flu, it was the quietest corner of the room.

'I've got a problem, Ross. As you must have heard, Jennings and Stuart have just killed themselves in a car crash. Yet we've an operation scheduled for the day after tomorrow that calls for full squadron strength. If I were to rescind McKenny's suspension, would you be willing to fly with him?'

Ross's surprise disguised his apprehension. 'Are you giving me a choice, skipper?'

'In fairness I must. How do you feel about it?'

'How important is the operation?'

'It's very important. If it wasn't, I wouldn't be letting McKenny off the hook.'

'Then it's O.K. I'll fly with him.'

The young Scot's willingness to do his duty made Moore join Henderson in damning the political side of the operation. 'You don't have to, Ross. No one will think the less of you if you refuse. In fact no one will know.'

'It's all right, skipper. Have you had a word with Paddy yet?'

'Yes. I've just left his billet. I told him if he put one foot wrong I'd skin him alive. He swore on the Bible he'd behave. Can I trust him, Ross? Don't cover him because he's your friend. His life as well as yours could be at risk if he acts like a damn fool again.'

Ross cleared his throat before replying. 'I think he'll be all right, skipper. I know it hurt him like hell to be grounded.'

'That's what I'm banking on. He knows this is his last chance. All right, Ross. You'll both join the rest of the boys in the morning. If we can't get your kite cleared in time, you can take either Jennings' or Stuart's aircraft. We've no problem there, worse luck.'

Ross checked him as he moved away. 'Are you going to tell Paddy, skipper, or shall I?'

'You leave that to me,' Moore told him. 'It'll give me another chance to warn him of the consequence if he wanders off the straight and narrow.'

CHAPTER 19

His chubby face pink from the effort, the young aircraftsman Ellis heaved a box of camera gun films from the 25-cwt Bedford, lowered it to the ground, and sat heavily down on it. Towering over him was a huge Bombay transport that had flown in just after dawn. A second Bedford in the process of being unloaded was standing at the opposite side of the aircraft.

As the young ACII mopped his face, a lanky Leading Aircraftsman ducked under the tail of the Bombay and approached him. The newcomer, wearing a filthy pair of overalls and a shoestring of a tie, was clearly an old sweat. 'What the 'ell are you doing, Ellis? Takin' a holiday?'

'I'm bushed,' the youngster muttered. He gazed up resentfully at the huge aircraft. 'What's all this about anyway? Where are we going?'

The old sweat gazed furtively around, dropped on the box beside him and pulled a fag end from the pocket of his overalls. Lighting it, he sucked in smoke greedily. 'The Middle East, mate. A pound to a penny.'

The ACII looked shocked. 'You mean the desert? But what about all the things we're leaving behind?'

'That's the way the mob does things. Some stupid bastard wakes up and then it's all rush an' panic. We'll probably get our kit in a couple of months' time, full of flies and sand.'

'I don't want to leave England,' the youngster wailed. 'I've got a girl here.'

McTyre gave a lascivious grin. 'They've got girls over there too, mate. Real women – all tits and bottom. I had an oppo' once who did a tour round Alexandria. They used to go to a café where they put on shows for the lads. You know what the women did?'

Ellis shook his head. Leaning towards him, McTyre gave the gory details. When he finished, the cherubic-faced Elllis looked both fascinated and horrified. 'He must have been pulling your leg!'

McTyre shook his head triumphantly. 'Naw. I've heard the same thing from other bods who's been there. In a couple of weeks you're goin' to see things that'll make your hair curl.'

'I still don't want to leave England,' the youngster muttered.

McTyre gazed up with distaste at the grey October sky. 'You must be off your marbles, mate. Who's your girl friend? Mae West?'

A yell from the second transport made him glance round. A corporal had ducked beneath the Bombay. 'What the hell are you doing, McTyre? Havin' a game of cards?'

Ellis jumped to his feet as the corporal strode towards them. Nipping out his fag end, McTyre rose more slowly. 'Listen to the bastard,' he muttered. 'He's been sittin' on his arse for the last half hour while I've done all the work, and now he's yelling for action. Roll on the revolution, mate!'

While 633 Squadron was preparing to move down to Holmsley, a week of intense activity was being culminated on the south coast of England. For days massive air patrols had kept the skies clear of enemy reconnaissance aircraft while 3,500 American troops arrived and settled into specially prepared camps in the Portsmouth/Southampton area. At the same time hundreds of tons of equipment, guns and ordnance were loaded on to supply ships assembled in local docks and on to tank landing craft.

Other sections of the services were equally busy during this time. Minesweepers, whose task would be to clear a channel to the enemy coast, began assembling off Southampton. Four American destroyers positioned themselves in the Portsmouth roads. The HQ ship *Brazos*, straining every steam pipe and rivet to make up lost time, arrived only forty hours behind schedule. Thunderbolts of the 8th Air Force touched down at selected airfields and prepared themselves for a showdown with the Luftwaffe. High-ranking officers of all services and a large coterie of war correspondents began to arrive at an hotel on the outskirts of Portsmouth where a reception hall had been converted into a Communications Centre.

The 6th October dawned cloudy but bright. In the early evening the first of the American troops began to file on to their assault craft. As each vessel filled up, it moved out into the Solent. The minesweepers lifted anchor and began their perilous outward journey. Although for the majority of the assault force the 6th was only a day of discomfort, for some men the operation had already begun.

633 Squadron, the only British unit involved, flew their Mosquitoes into Holmsley airfield in the New Forest during the morning. The Bombay transport, carrying ground crews and specialist officers as well as essential spares, arrived half an hour later. To unaccustomed eyes the scene would have appeared chaotic as the Station Warrant Officer, known to one and all as 'Bert the Bastard', bawled orders and men ran around as if chasing their tails. Yet the chaos had an order of its own and by the late afternoon, to the indignation of its permanent residents, 633 Squadron was in full possession of the airfield. Evidence of this was provided by McTyre. The old sweat had brought with him a kitbag of tea, sugar and tinned milk, and before darkness fell was doing a roaring trade dispensing tea at 2d a cup from one of the dispersal huts.

To their surprise and gratification, the aircrews and non-flying officers were billeted in a small hotel that stood just off the Lyndhurst-Bournemouth road. All the crews had been given a briefing by Moore and Adams just before leaving Sutton Craddock and in the late afternoon received their promised visit from Runcorn and Tilsey, who were doing a tour of the operational squadrons. After being given all the latest intelligence, the crews were allowed to stand down on the condition they did not stray outside the hotel grounds.

In the meantime, to the anxiety of those responsible for the operation, the weather began to deteriorate. The wind started to freshen and rain squalls began sweeping in. To the troops who, for logistic reasons, had already been embarked on their assault vessels, discomfort turned to distress as more and more of them became seasick. In the large Portsmouth hotel, tension grew apace during the night as the half-hourly weather reports came in. Among the high-ranking American officers and the war correspondents who crammed the Communications Room, the huge figure of Staines and the bearded face of Lambert were conspicuous. A few British liaison officers were also present, among them Davies. Made even more aware of the importance of 633's role by a VIP phone call he had received just before midnight, the small Air Commodore was suffering an anti-climax as the night wore on. 10.00 hours was the absolute deadline for a decision if the convoy was to sail on the 7th and yet by dawn the meteorological reports were still unfavourable. With the first two weeks in October the absolute limit for amphibious operations in the Channel, Davies was in a dispirited and testy mood when the Met. Officer returned yet again to the Communications Room. Although everyone was too tired to notice it, this time he was showing some excitement.

'I've some good news for you at last, gentlemen.' As weary heads jerked up, he went on: 'Our latest reports indicate the winds will start decreasing during the forecast period and will veer west-south-west in the late afternoon. The rain and the poor visibility should gradually clear during the day and the swell will moderate.'

The Chairman of the Executive Committee, a distinguished-looking American with a tanned face and white sideburns, rose from his chair. 'What does all that mean? That we can go?'

The Met. Officer's reply had all the caution of his breed. 'We have reason to hope that by the time the convoy reaches its station across the Channel, conditions should be reasonable to fair, sir.'

The Chairman grinned at his expectant officers. 'When translated, I guess that means yes. So get the machinery moving gentlemen.'

A cheer sounded, followed by a rush of feet as officers scrambled for telephones. Back in the small hotel near Lyndhurst, Henderson grabbed up his bedside telephone the moment it began ringing. 'Yes. Henderson here.'

'I've good news, Jock. It's on.'

Henderson, who, between cat-naps, had been listening to the rain squalls lashing against his window, was surprised. 'They're taking a hell of a chance, aren't they?'

'Not according to their Met. boys. They predict reasonable weather by this evening.'

'Let's hope they're right,' the Scot said dryly.

'They usually are. Jock, listen! Lambert will definitely be covering the operation in the *Brazos*. Staines is also going out, which means you'll be right under the microscope. So tell your boys to do their best, will you?'

'They usually do, sir.'

'I know that. But this support job is becoming more important by the minute. The C.-in-C. himself phoned me just before midnight, so you'll see how big the political snowball has grown.'

The Scot almost asked if it was expected that his men flew their aircraft straight into the enemy strongpoints, then checked himself in time. 'They'll be told to do their best, sir.'

'Good man. You don't need to rush them off their feet today. You've plenty of time.'

Henderson was the last man to flap when there was no need. 'You can leave all that to me, sir. Do you still intend going aboard the *Brazos*?'

'What a damn silly question, Jock. Of course I do.'

The Scot had his reasons for feeling a trifle malicious that morning. 'You do realize the Luftwaffe might come out in strength?'

Davies' yelp made the phone rattle. 'If Staines can go and Lambert can go, I think I can go too, don't you?'

'Yes, sir. But then why can't I come along as well?'

'Oh, Christ, don't let's have that again. You know why. You should be glad: we'll all probably be seasick. Now I'm going to get a couple of hours shuteye before things get under way.'

In fact the operation was already under way. With the all-clear given, minesweepers returned to their dangerous task of clearing and marking channels across to the Normandy coast. As the news filtered down to the rank and file, men shook off their malaise and looked again to their responsibilities. Sailors hurried about ships checking everything from Oerlikons to ship hoists. Tank crews examined their armour again; artillerymen checked their pieces. Unit commanders repeated briefings while infantrymen cleaned their firearms for the fourth, fifth, or sixth time. In short, with the prospect of action only a few hours away, the task force became a fighting unit again.

The aircrews of 633 Squadron began the day less arduously. Aware they would get little sleep the following night, Henderson allowed them to stay in bed until 09.00 hours. After a leisurely breakfast, they were transported to the airfield to airtest their Mosquitoes. As each aircraft landed, mechanics swarmed around it to carry out final checks. Lastly, trolley trains arrived carrying 250 MC bombs and wing rockets. When armourers had finished hoisting these into position, each of the fifteen Mosquitoes was ready for its dangerous and exacting role.

With great care being taken in every step of the preparation, the autumn afternoon was fading before the final Form 700 was signed. When at last the crews were driven back to their hotel they discovered Henderson had organized a first-class meal for them. The irony was not lost on the crews and grins ran round the tables as the deep voice of Stan Baldwin, the only coloured man in the squadron, could be heard remarking to his pilot, Paddy Machin, that it was the best Last Supper he had ever tasted. Coffee was taken in an adjacent room where Henderson, Moore and Adams gave the men a final talk, an interview that provided an opportunity for last-minute questions. The bar was then opened until 21.00 hours with drinks strictly rationed. When it closed Henderson had a quick word with Moore and his two flight commanders and then addressed the men. 'All right, lads, that's it. An early night will get shot of those bags under your eyes. You'll be called at 04.00 hours sharp.

With good-natured grumbles the crews filed off to their rooms. When the last man had gone, Henderson closed the door and turned to the two flight commanders who, along with Moore, had remained behind.

'This'll only take a few minutes. As Moore has already told you, this isn't just a highly responsible operation for us, it has strong political overtones as well. So it's important we do our best to stop reinforcements reaching that station. But that doesn't mean any of you play Tom Mix and attack the strongpoints or gun-posts. The Yanks don't expect it and neither do we.'

The Scot's eyes shifted to the impeccably-dressed Moore. 'If you have any problems or need support, don't hesitate to call for it. You'll get a quick response because both Davies and the Typhoon squadrons will be tuned in on your wavelength.'

'Are you joining Davies on the *Brazos*, sir?' Millburn asked.

The disgruntled Scot shook his head. 'He won't let me go in case I'm wanted here when you come back. But I'll be standing by in the Ops. room. All right, I'll see you in the morning.'

The party of men took the lift up to their rooms on the second floor. Reaching his room first, Moore drew Millburn to one side. 'Take it easy tomorrow. Don't think that because they're Americans down there you have to go in and spike Jerry's guns single-handed.'

Millburn grinned. 'I'll be a good boy, skipper.'

'Mind you are. I don't want half my squadron littered over the cliffs.'

479

Shouting goodnight to one another, the men dispersed. For ten to fifteen minutes the corridor was silent. Then a door creaked open and the furtive figures of Millburn and Gabby appeared. Motioning to one another to keep quiet, they tiptoed to the end of the corridor and disappeared.

Five minutes later, looking disappointed, they tip-toed back and entered a smoke-filled bedroom. The shirt-sleeved figures of Teddy Young and Hopkinson were sitting on the bed with a cabinet laid on its side in front of them. Opposite were the New Zealander Larkin and Frank Day. A bottle of gin and a dozen bottles of beer littered the floor nearby. As Millburn and Gabby entered, Hopkinson was shuffling a pack of cards in preparation to deal. Young, a glass of gin in his hand, turned to the newcomers with a grin. 'I thought you two were hoping to bed down with those waitresses?'

Millburn helped himself to a beer. 'This bum navigator of mine lost his way again. He got us into the laundry room.'

The perky Hopkinson jerked a thumb at the ceiling. 'They're on the top floor. In the last two rooms.'

The American stared at him. 'How do you know that?'

'I asked the night porter.' As Millburn made for the door, the Cockney grinned. 'I wouldn't bother. He said one sleeps with the secretary and the other with the receptionist.'

'Those two poofs?'

'That's the way it goes, Yank. The ones near the camps get too much and those out in the sticks have to take what they can get.'

'But they've got camps round here. Camps of red-blooded Yanks.'

Gabby joined in the chorus of cat-calls. 'You know why your lot get more than your share, don't you? It's those fat wallets of yours. Take 'em away and you'd be more frustrated than a pisspot on a Welsh Sunday.'

'*I'd* be frustrated? I'm on the same pay as you, remember? RAF starvation pay. And have you noticed me short of dames?'

'That's the line you shoot 'em,' Gabby declared. 'A couple of oil wells and a half a dozen ranches. You're the biggest conman in the business.'

The American gave a wicked grin. 'And who kept rubbing that scratch he got over the Frisians, so he could show off his war wound to his girl friend? Go on, boyo – who?'

As Gabby glared at the American for this revelation, Young gave Hopkinson a wink. 'I don't know why you guys don't stick to horses. At least you don't have to bullshit 'em.' He slapped a pocketful of change on the cabinet. 'All right, get your starvation pay on the table. You might not be needing it tomorrow night.'

In other rooms men were reacting differently to the ordeal on the morrow. A few lucky ones, Stan Baldwin and Machin among them, were already asleep. Roberts and Preston had finished a half-bottle of gin that Preston had sneaked into the room and with the sharp edges of life pleasantly blurred were now dozing off. Butterfield and Foster, both soccer fanatics, had found an argument about the relative merits of Dixie Dean and Stan Mortensen a useful prelude to sleep.

Others were finding sleep more difficult. By mutual consent Smith and Paget had given up the effort and were playing a game of pocket chess. Monahan and Evans, both ex-students, were reminiscing about their days at college and the girls they had known. Matthews was wondering if he would ever achieve his ambition of becoming a jazz drummer, while his navigator Allison, ex-£2-a-week clerk from Gateshead, was wondering how his widowed mother was managing on the money he sent her weekly. In their pre-battle behaviour, most of the crews were running close to form.

Among the exceptions was Moore. A complex man, sensitive and intelligent on the one hand, painstaking and disciplined on the other, the squadron commander left nothing to chance before an operation and so was usually able to rest with a satisfied mind. Finding sleep difficult tonight, his first thought was that there must be some technical or tactical point he had overlooked but although he racked his brains for a full hour he could think of nothing significant.

He wondered if McKenny could be the reason. After the Irishman's behaviour, all Moore's military instincts had demanded the pilot remained grounded, not least to safeguard Ross. Yet Moore could be a pragmatist when the occasion demanded it, and he could not feel guilty for a decision that had been forced on him by demands outside his control.

His thoughts moved on to Harvey and then, by chain reaction, to the girl Harvey loved, Anna Reinhardt. Since the Yorkshireman had been wounded, Davies had received only one item of news about her – that she had escaped from the Ruhpolding valley after the Rhine Maiden establishment had been destroyed. As soon as the news had reached Moore he had visited Harvey in hospital. He had arrived just before Harvey's most serious stomach operation and Moore was not the only one who believed the news had saved the Yorkshireman's life.

Lying there in bed Moore could see the girl as she had appeared at their first meeting in the Black Swan: oval-faced, dark hair swept up in a French roll, dressed like a queen in a black dress with no jewellery except an emerald brooch. A beautiful woman who was to prove as capable and courageous as any man. Moore had no illusions about his feelings for Anna Reinhardt. She was all he admired in a woman and hardly a day had passed since she was dropped into Occupied Europe that he had not remembered her.

He wondered where she was now. With enemies searching everywhere for her, she might already be in a prison cell. A German girl, a traitor in Nazi eyes, in the hands of the Gestapo. As he winced, Moore knew it was a nightmare that must have haunted Harvey throughout the long weeks he had spent in hospital. Although he had shared the thought with no one, Moore was glad Harvey had not returned to the squadron in time to take part in the present operation. Secretly he often wished the Yorkshireman's injuries would ground him permanently. With Anna operating as an SOE agent behind the Nazi lines, the odds against the couple meeting again were heavy enough. With Harvey flying in a squadron reserved for highly-specialized and dangerous missions, at times they appeared hopeless.

Another man finding it difficult to sleep was Ross, who was sharing a room with McKenny. Until an hour ago the Irishman's relief at the lifting of his suspension had seemed a guarantee in itself that he would behave responsibly the following day. Yet when the two men had come up to their room, all Ross's misgivings had returned. During their absence someone must have noticed their room did not contain its obligatory Bible because one copy had been laid on each bed. The sight of them had brought about an immediate change in McKenny. Cursing, he had snatched up his copy and flung it down the room where it had struck the corner of a desk and fallen to the floor with its binding split open.

It was a sight that had made Ross cross himself. From McKenny's glance he had expected a new onslaught of taunts and ridicule. Instead the Irishman had turned away and climbed into bed without comment.

Although greatly distressed by the incident, Ross had been equally relieved it had not led to a quarrel that could have disastrous consequences on the morrow. The sense of duty that had made him volunteer to fly again with McKenny in no way meant the home-loving young Scot had aspirations to glory. For him the golden sands of the Galloway coast, the mist-shrouded peaks of Ailsa Craig and Arran, and the green Heads of Ayr around which he had often walked with a bonnie lass called Maggie Andrews were all he wanted out of life. These last few weeks they had never seemed more precious and he desperately wanted to see them again.

It was this yearning that had committed Ross to the act that was now denying him all chance of sleep. Terrified of another quarrel with McKenny, for the first time in his young life Ross had not knelt down at his bedside and prayed. Instead, like a man ashamed of his faith, he had crept between the sheets and silently said his prayers there.

After the taunts and threats McKenny had made, Ross found this act full of frightening implications. Turning his head towards the Irishman's bed, he listened. Believing McKenny was asleep, he tip-toed to the window and drew the blackout curtains aside.

Although the night sky was still overcast, here and there stars were shining through breaks in the clouds. The wind had dropped and had a plaintive sound as it sobbed in the eaves. Gazing out into the darkness, wondering what the dawn would bring, Ross had a sense of loneliness as sharp as a wound.

A voice at his elbow made him start violently. 'What's the matter, Bernie? You looking for fairies?'

Ross tried to smile. 'I couldn't sleep so I was checking on the weather.'

McKenny glanced out. 'It won't be perfect but it's improving. What's the time?'

'Half-eleven.'

'Then the convoy will be on its way.'

'Yes, I suppose it will.'

'I'll bet a lot of them will be seasick. There's bound to be a heavy swell after all this wind.'

Ross was finding comfort in the Irishman's amicability. 'I'm glad I'm not crossing with them. I get sick on a boating lake.'

McKenny's eyes had lifted to a large break in the clouds through which stars could be seen. As he gazed up, his mood changed. 'A hell of a lot of them are going to die on that beach tomorrow. And I'll bet a week ago half of them had never heard of it. It doesn't make any sense, does it?'

Caught unawares, Ross could only shake his head. In the dim light McKenny's face had turned bitter. 'Look at those stars. They don't give a damn, do they?'

Ross was feeling a familiar dryness in his throat. 'They're only stars, Paddy.'

The Irishman's hard stare turned on him. 'How can you of all people say that? They're God's stars. And they'll look down on all those bodies rocking in the surf tomorrow and they won't give a damn. You don't learn very fast, do you? That's what life's all about. Total cosmic indifference.'

Ross wanted to protest but his courage failed him. As if ashamed of his outburst, McKenny pulled the blackout curtains back into place. 'We'd better get some sleep or we'll be bushed tomorrow.'

Back in bed, Ross lay listening. When he was certain McKenny was asleep, he slipped out and went down on his knees. His prayers were feverish and full of shame and yet when at last he crept back between the sheets it was as if a load had fallen from him and he fell asleep almost at once.

Far away across the Channel the American convoy was standing in readiness off the enemy coast. Troops embarked on their landing craft were watching the eastern horizon for the first sight of dawn. Some were still retching from seasickness. Others were whispering to their comrades to hide their nervousness. All were totally isolated in their thoughts.

Banks of mist drifted over the restless sea. Through them the ghostly hulks of tank landing ships could be seen. Occasionally men felt drizzle touch their faces. The muted throb of engines came through the splash of waves. On the Rangers' landcraft, craft that carried Colonel Tilsey, a sergeant pointed eastward at a fog bank that was turning grey. Following his eyes, men swallowed to lubricate their nervous throats.

Less than a minute later the sound of aircraft engines could be heard. As the roar grew into deafening thunder that swept overhead, the spell that had gripped the convoy was broken. Men straightened their chilled bodies, cheered, and waved their arms at the invisible B.17s.

The thunder moved southward and became a heavy grumble. Feeling their heartbeats in their wrists and temples, the assault troops waited. A brilliant light lit up their white faces. As the parachute flare sank downwards, the horizon that until now had been a solid wall of darkness was bisected into cliffs and sky. A flash ran across the night clouds, followed by a dozen others in rapid succession. The explosions, sounding like heavy doors being slammed, held a brutal threat that made more than one man cross himself. Bows awash with speed, a destroyer came sweeping through the ranks of bobbing ships. As an officer yelled orders through a megaphone, a hundred engines roared into life and the landing craft started for the beaches. Operation Crucible had begun.

CHAPTER **20**

Flying line astern with A-Apple in the lead, the fifteen Mosquitoes crossed the English coast near Highcliffe and dropped immediately down to the wavetops. Men on an inshore fishing boat were buffeted by air displacement as the line of screaming engines and fishlike bodies hurtled past. A startled gull, rising from the swell, struck the windshield of T-Tommy and slid off in a tangle of blood and feathers. To the west the visibility was poor as the night made its reluctant retreat. To the east the sky was rapidly brightening over the Isle of Wight.

With fuel reserves an urgent consideration, all Mosquitoes were carrying auxiliary tanks. As a further conservation measure they were flying at economical cruising speed without boost. To confuse the enemy's radar scanners, Moore had led them in a short dog-leg after leaving Holmsley. Now he was taking them so low over the Channel their slipstreams were scuffling the grey wavetops.

The lighthouse and Needles of the Isle of Wight had barely fallen behind before they ran into a rain squall that reduced visibility to half a second's reaction time. With radio silence in force, the crews' response was based on the high level of training Moore had given them. Instead of increasing the interval between aircraft, they closed up almost nose to tail. It was a manoeuvre only superbly-experienced and confident crews could have attempted. While each pilot shared his attention between the Mosquito ahead and the tossing sea below, navigators strained their eyes to pierce the grey curtain that swept horizontally past.

The squall died two minutes later. In A-Apple, Hopkinson touched Moore's arm and pointed. Far ahead, sheets of light that resembled a summer electric storm were illuminating the horizon. The cessation of the flashes a minute later told the crews the destroyers were lifting their fire to allow the beach parties to land. With the Mosquitoes now halfway across the Channel, which was a hundred miles wide at this point, navigators were keeping an eye open for flak ships. Although fewer ships guarded this wider section of the Channel than the Dover Straits, there had always been the danger one might have spotted the convoy during the night and alerted the coastal defences. In fact this had not happened but now it was daylight, and with bitter experience of the massive firepower these floating gun platforms contained, crews kept a wary eye open in case one should be on the move and cross their flight path.

The reappearance of flashes ahead told the crews a duel was now being fought between the naval escort and the coastal defences. Daylight was advancing fast and eight minutes later a dark line began to separate sea and sky. Ships, hull down on the horizon, grew into toy vessels and then into towering hulks of camouflaged steel. Columns of water were erupting around them and over to the right a heavy explosion followed by an enormous mushroom of smoke marked the death of a destroyer.

Shivering the waves with their slipstreams, the Mosquitoes weaved their way through the assault craft while each man gathered his own split-second impressions. Landing craft, full of huddled men, heading for the beaches. . . . A body floating face down in the surf. . . . Canisters of smoke, intended to conceal, blowing away in the dawn breeze like tattered rags. . . . Men running clumsily across glistening shingle. . . . Two rag dolls sailing into the air as a shell exploded. Ominous lines of tracer sweeping like whip lashes towards the aircraft as the cliffs flashed past.

Staring back through the perspex blister, Hopkinson was trying to take a count of the aircraft. 'I think they've all got through, skipper.'

When Moore judged his aircraft were out of range of the coastal light flak, he led them in a tight orbit and gazed down. On Blue Beach to the east, Tilsey's Rangers appeared in charge of the situation. Uneven ground around the gun battery had enabled them to close in, and as Moore watched, a tongue of fire from a portable flame-thrower licked out and enveloped one huge bunker.

Straightening from his orbit, Moore flew west along the coast road. From his height of 2,500 feet he could see over both sides of the hill behind the radio-location station and although he knew reinforcements must already be on the move, at present both ends of the road were empty of traffic.

With the station now only a mile or so to his right he could see the damage the B.17s had done. Outhouses and billets had been reduced to rubble, the perimeter wall was broken in a dozen places, and the cliff top outside was pock-marked with craters where mines had been detonated by exploding bombs. The main buildings and strongpoints, however, appeared intact, as did the three aerials of the scanners. The burnt-out wreckage of four B.17s testified to the ferocity of the defences.

That most of the heavy flak towers were still operational was soon evident from the murderous fire now pouring upwards. The brightening sky was peppered by white and black puffs of smoke as the radar-controlled guns followed the Mosquitoes along the cliffs. Young swore an Australian oath as his Mosquito almost turned over to the concussion of a 37-mm shell. To lessen fire Moore swung sharply to port and led his file of aircraft as far inland as visibility of the coast road would permit.

White Beach, where the main body of the infantry was pouring ashore, fell behind. Ahead was Red Beach with its shelving valley where landing craft were putting armour ashore. Seeing the road ahead was clear, Moore was about to lead his patrol back along the battle area when his earphones crackled. 'Guard Dog Leader. Do you hear me?'

Moore would have known Davies' voice anywhere, 'Guard Dog Leader to Ramillies. You are loud and clear.'

Davies sounded as excited as a schoolboy on sports day. 'What's the position on the road?'

'So far it's clear in both directions.'

'Good. Now listen. There's a foul-up on Red Beach. Do a recce, will you, and report back as quickly as possible.'

Relieved that Davies had broken radio silence, Moore called in Teddy Young. 'Take over and keep patrolling the road, Teddy. I'll join you in a few minutes.'

As Young led the squadron into a tight 180-degree turn, Moore put A-Apple into a shallow dive. Picking up speed he crossed the cliffs two miles to the west, and headed back over the sea towards Red Beach, where two tank landing craft had their ramps down on the beach. One had been hit and had dense smoke pouring from its quarterdeck. The other had a crippled amphibian lying at the foot of its ramp which men were struggling to drag aside. On the beach itself tanks and gun carriers ran in a drunken line towards the gap in the seafront that was their only escape route. Three of the vehicles were ablaze and trapped soldiers were trying to find cover behind others from murderous fire that was sweeping the bay.

Higher up the beach a dozen or so Americans were crouched behind a shingle ridge that lay at one side of the gap. As A-Apple swept towards it, a soldier jumped up dragging a Bangalore torpedo behind him. He had not run five yards before a hail of bullets cut him down. A comrade jumping up to give aid was killed before he cleared the top of the shingle.

Before A-Apple swept past Moore spotted the obstacle and the origin of the murderous fire. Conscious the gap in the seafront repesented a weakness in their defences, the Germans had bridged it with a thick concrete wall. A camouflage net, ripped almost in half by shell fire and fluttering in the morning breeze, explained why aerial reconnaissance had failed to detect it. The gunfire came from two large bunkers built into the low cliffs at either side of the wall.

As A-Apple flashed over the gap, one of the flak posts gave it a vicious burst of tracer before concentrating again on the pinned-down soldiers. Hopkinson's Cockney voice echoed Moore's thoughts. 'If their tanks can't break out, skipper, they'll never be able to take that station.'

Back on the HQ ship *Brazos* the usual muddle of communications that seems to plague all large-scale military operations had kept Davies ignorant of the reason for the debacle on Red Beach. Now, as the details reached him, he forgot his earlier orders for the Mosquitoes to concentrate only on the support road.

'Ramillies to Guard Dog Leader. The problem's a reinforced wall blocking the gap. Can you distract the gun posts for a minute or two?'

Moore, who had already decided on his line of action, acknowledged tersely. 'Message received, Ramillies. Guard Dog Leader to Zero Seven, Zero Eight, and Zero Eleven. Join me on Red Beach at the double.'

Zero Eleven belonged to McKenny and Ross, Zero Seven to Machin and Baldwin, and Zero Eight to Millburn and Gabby. All three Mosquitoes arrived in less than a minute and formated behind Moore who was orbiting over the road. A few words were all the experienced crews needed. McKenny had Machin banked away, swept out to sea, and came back on a reciprocal course towards Red Beach. Thirty seconds after their departure Moore and Millburn, flying almost wingtip to wingtip, aimed their Mosquitoes at the distant gap in the coast. The tactic was to be the diversionary one used against the flak wagons in the Ardennes. In the few seconds left for reflection before the action began, the usually chirpy Hoppy sounded apprehensive. 'If I mess this up, skipper, I'm going to kill a couple of dozen Yanks.'

Moore's reply hid his own apprehension as the slopes of the shallow valley flashed past. 'They'd die anyway if we leave them there, Hoppy. But you won't mess it up.'

'Let's hope you're right,' the Cockney muttered.

Opening the bomb doors, Moore could feel them quivering beneath him. Alongside him the doors of T-Tommy opened at almost the same moment. 'Main switch on, skipper,' Hoppy said. 'No. 1 bomb tail-fused.'

The second pair of Mosquitoes were less than two miles away and approaching from the sea at a combined speed of nearly six hundred miles an hour. As their bomb doors opened, the enemy gunners accepted them as a threat and both heavy and light automatic guns swung upwards to cover them. At 1,000 yards the two Mosquitoes began firing with their 20-mm cannon and although for the sake of the American soldiers as well as the second pair of Mosquitoes the shells were aimed wide, the ground gunners took the fire as further proof the two aircraft were a major threat and gave them their full attention.

It was an opportunity the pinned-down American soldiers did not miss. Dragging Bangalore torpedoes behind them, two men jumped over the ridge and hurled themselves to the foot of the wall. Two more followed a few seconds later. It was a display of zeal that none of the Mosquito crews wanted but there was nothing they could do to recall the men.

The ground fire was both fierce and accurate. With his diversionary task completed, Machin broke away, a thin trail of white smoke coming from his port engine. To Ross's alarm, McKenny held on course for three more endless seconds which gave time for both bunkers to fire on them. For a moment the Mosquito seemed to stagger in mid-air. Then J-Jimmie recovered and joined Machin in circling round as if to make a second attack.

As a decoy ruse, the manoeuvre worked perfectly. With the enemy gunners fully occupied, the second pair of Mosquitoes sweeping towards the opposite side of the wall were allowed an almost uninterrupted run-in. Neither Hoppy nor Gabby was using their bombsights; at zero height they were a handicap rather than an asset. Instead, with the bomb releases in their hands, they were watching their pilots intently.

The Mosquitoes were flying so low their slipstream was shivering the dry gorse and ferns that lined the valley. As gorse gave way to sand, Hoppy held his breath. Moore, whose eyes were fixed on the left-hand bunker, saw it flash into his windshield and gave a shout, 'Now!' Hoppy pressed the bomb release and the

250-pounder plunged down, bounced once, then buried itself in a mound of sand little more than ten yards from the bunker.

Forty yards to the right Millburn and Gabby had a similar success with their own attack. Yet because both crews entered the bunkers' field of fire the moment they swept over the wall their need to take violent evasive action prevented them being certain their bombs had not bounced over the wall and landed near the pinned-down Americans. Necks twisted to watch as they swept out of range, all four men were mentally counting: 'Eight . . . nine . . . ten . . . eleven. . . .'

The two explosions came within a second of one another, hurling fountains of sand upwards. When the smoke blew away it looked from above as if little damage had been done to the massive bunkers. What no outside observer could see, however, was the effect of the concussion inside them. With blood oozing from their mouths and eardrums, men were sprawled in grotesque postures beside their guns. Of the four American soldiers who had reached the wall, two were dead and the other two half-stunned. The rest of the advance party, however, did not waste their opportunity. Running forward with demolition equipment, they quickly had charges planted beneath the wall. Orbiting above, ignoring the vengeful flak from other gun posts, Moore saw explosions throw rubble high into the air. As tanks and mobile guns began moving eagerly forward, there was a yell in the R/T from Millburn.

'We've done it, you guys! They're on the move again.'

Relaxing, Moore gazed back and saw only two Mosquitoes were orbiting with him. His terse question quietened the American's jubilation. 'Where's Machin?'

Hopkinson pointed seaward where an aircraft trailing white smoke could be seen making towards the convoy. Moore lifted his mask. 'Zero Seven! Are you all right?'

Machin's voice sounded far away. 'Our port engine's running hot, skipper, and we're losing revs with the other. I'm trying to ditch near the ships.'

In the meantime there had been another breakdown in communications on the *Brazos* that had prevented Davies hearing the outcome of the action from Moore. When he received it from Army sources his delight at his squadron's important contribution showed in his semi-abandonment of Signals procedure. 'Ramillies calling Guard Dog Leader. Good work, Moore! Everyone here is as relieved as hell. Now get back to that road and away from the flak!'

Before Moore obeyed, he noticed that the American assault troops had broken through the lighter cliff defences and were now massing behind bushes and in hollows. His guess was that now the tanks had broken out of Red Beach, the assault on the station itself would wait until the armour arrived to spearpoint it, a move that would reduce casualties both among the remaining minefields and within the perimeter wall itself.

As the three Mosquitoes swept eastwards to join the rest of the squadron, Gabby pointed at a huge pall of smoke that hung over the cliffs ahead. His quip was aimed at Millburn.

'It looks as if they've finished off that gun battery. You know something, boyo? They must have some of our Commandos with them.'

The jubilant Millburn laughed. 'You're seeing something today, you little punk. Hard-nosed Yankees on the prod. Maybe they won't bother to get back into those boats. Maybe they'll go straight on to Berlin.'

Gabby grinned maliciously. 'Maybe they still will. Straight into prisoner-of-war camps.'

About to answer, Millburn caught sight of American Rangers hurrying westward along the cliffs. Having neutralized the powerful gun battery, which both reduced the enfilading fire sweeping White Beach and took pressure off the fleet at sea, Tilsey was now leading his men forward to tighten the noose that was closing around the radiolocation station. Millburn jerked a thumb at the Rangers. 'See that? It's going to be over in half an hour. This invasion when it comes will be like taking candy from a kid.'

Gabby sniffed. 'It doesn't take much to make you cocky, does it?'

'Jealousy will get you nowhere, boyo,' Millburn grinned. 'Nowhere at all.'

Millburn's jubilation was shared by almost every officer on board the *Brazos*. Apart from the hold-up on Red Beach, now satisfactorily resolved, every step in the operation was on schedule. The only question men were asking themselves – and it seemed like looking a gift horse in the mouth – was what had happened to the German infantry and tank reserves? Allowing for almost any contingency they ought to be within sight by this time.

To older soldiers who had experienced German military efficiency it was the one mystery that threw a shadow over the operation. As a consequence some men actually showed relief when Davies, after clapping his hands over his earphones to shut out extraneous noise, glanced round at them. 'My men report tanks and infantry ahead.' He leaned over his microphone. 'Ramillies here. I want map references of those tanks and their number. Over.'

Men crowded closer as Davies listened. When he finally glanced at them there was not a cough in the Operations Room. His gnome-like face seemed to have sharpened and there were two red spots high up on his cheekbones.

'It seems as if our Intelligence has been wrong, gentlemen, unless the enemy has brought up reinforcements during the last two days. My men report dozens of tanks moving up the road from the south-east and equally heavy infantry re-inforcement behind them.'

'What are you saying?' The question came from a greying, two-star general. 'That we're in a trap?'

Davies hesitated. 'It's too early to say that, sir. But this report does suggest your tanks will be heavily outnumbered.'

CHAPTER 21

The tanks were coming up the lane like a column of bulldogs with their teeth bared. A pennant was fluttering from the leading vehicle's turret. As the Mosquitoes came screaming over the hill, tank commanders ducked their heads and watched the aircraft stream past and soar into a climbing turn. The troop transports that were following halted and grey-clad soldiers swarmed into the thick hedges that flanked the road.

Although his instinct was to attack immediately, Young knew it was vital first to alert HQ of the threat and he dipped a wingtip to gain a better view. The tanks appeared to be a mixture of Panther Ds and Tiger Is, both extremely formidable fighting machines and in another class to the light armour the Americans had been forced to bring. It was their number, however, that startled the Australian. They stretched down the hill and beyond it, giving the impression an entire armoured regiment was on the move.

The explanation, had Young known it, was simple. For many months the Germans had been disturbed by the French Maquis' activities and the almost daily reports they were known to be giving the Allies about German defence dispositions. With the forthcoming invasion making it vital this information was stopped or, even better, rendered incorrect, new and elaborate security measures had been introduced. Only one-third of the armour available on the Western seaboard was now left visible to prying eyes: the rest was hidden in innocuous shelters or specially-constructed underground parks. Unfortunately for the Americans, the local hide-out for the Panzer Group defending that area was a large turf-covered bomb dump only seventeen miles away. With the huge coastal guns needing large reserves of ammunition, even Arnaud's efficient partisans had assumed the well-guarded dump was what it seemed and so had gravely underestimated the enemy armour available.

It was the Tank Commander's reluctance to throw his forces in piecemeal that had delayed his response. Instead of advancing immediately with his visible reserve, he had made a rendezvous point and waited there until his main force of armour had joined him. In the meantime, knowing an infantry division was on manoeuvres near Rocheville, he had put in a request that a contingent should be rushed up at once. After appraising the American raid, German HQ had granted his request and the troop transports had caught up with his column five minutes ago. A second contingent of troops was standing by on red alert.

This brief delay had in no way worried the Tank Commander. Indeed, to give the Americans time to extend themselves and so become sitting ducks for his heavy counter-attack had seemed good military strategy. What he had not expected was the wall at Red Beach to be breached so quickly. Even this news had not shaken his confidence because he knew his armour not only outnumbered but could also outgun the lighter amphibious armour of the Americans. His concern at this stage, then, was not the outcome of the battle but whether he could reach the radiolocation station in time to give it support.

Expecting an immediate attack by the aircraft, the tanks had halted like the transports behind them. With the Mosquitoes peeling away and then orbiting above, an observer with romantic tendencies might have imagined the two units were paying tribute to one another before engaging in mortal combat.

If it was a tribute, it was a short-lived one. Finishing his report, Young wasted no more time. 'Leader to Red Section. Line abreast and pick your target.'

Like a line of cavalry changing direction, the Mosquitoes banked round and came swooping down on the road. At the same moment tank turrets spun round and automatic guns began pumping out shells. Weaving to make themselves a difficult target, the Mosquitoes launched their first rockets at 900 yards range. Seconds later they opened fire with their 20-mm Hispanos. One rocket struck a Panther on its most vulnerable spot, just beneath its armoured skirt. The puff of smoke that erupted from the turret gave no real hint of the shambles inside as the warhead exploded. The fireball that burst out five seconds later and rose to a hundred feet above the column gave a better indication of the kill. A second rocket struck a Tiger's starboard track and immobilized it. Bright flashes along the column denoted hits by the 20-mm shells.

The more manoeuvrable LMGs of the tanks raked the Mosquitoes as they swept across the road. Before they could attack again the tanks slewed round on their tracks and made for the hedge that stood between them and the cliffs. Built without a Bocage earthwork, it proved no obstacle to the heavy armour. Crushing it aside, the tanks broke out on the open cliff top and the danger caused by their high concentration was over.

To the west Moore had heard of the crisis on his R/T. As he led his small flight past the embattled station to join his main force, he saw that some American tanks had crossed the minefields and were already nosing through the station perimeter. On the northern flank exploding mortar shells suggested the American infantry were also closing in. The battle for the station, then, appeared to be going well. At the same time Moore was under no illusion how quickly the situation could change if the heavy tanks Young reported were to reach the scene.

The flashes of rockets and tracer, the pock-marked morning sky, and the drifting smoke ahead told him he was less than a minute from them. In T-Tommy behind him, Millburn was showing uncharacteristic concern. 'Where the hell have all these Jerry tanks come from? We were told they'd have less than twenty.'

'Jerry's always smarter than you think, boyo. If those tanks break through, it'll be that prisoner-of-war camp for sure.'

Millburn gave a muted curse. In the Mosquito opposite him, McKenny had turned to glance at his starboard wing. Jagged holes disfigured it and part of the aileron was shot away. Alongside the Irishman, Ross was showing reaction. During the shell-shocked seconds it had taken him to launch his decoy attack on the gunpost, all McKenny's self-destructive impulses had surfaced again. Teeth clenched and lips drawn back, he had made the young Scot believe he intended to crash the Mosquito against the bunker. When he had levelled off only a few feet above the spitting guns, Ross's eyes had been tightly closed and his body rigid with fear. His voice betrayed that fear now.

'Why didn't you break off sooner?'

McKenny shrugged. 'That wall was important. Any fool could see that.'

'That didn't mean we had to fly down the barrels of the guns. You should have broken off when Machin did.'

'For Christ's sake, I can't do anything right these days. We got away with it, didn't we?'

'How many more times do you think we can get away with it? We've over-played our luck already.'

The Irishman threw him a mocking glance. 'I didn't think you called it luck. I thought it was divine protection.'

Ross found he was shaking with anger. 'Stop sneering at me, Paddy! Stop it!'

McKenny's laugh chilled the young Scot. 'What will you do if I don't? Get out and walk home?'

In A-Apple ahead Moore was in contact with Davies. 'Have you called up the Tiffies yet, sir?'

Davies sounded anxious. 'They're on their way, Moore. Is it bad?'

Blue Beach was directly ahead of Moore and he could see American soldiers running westward along the cliffs. Alerted that heavy tanks and infantry were on their heels, Tilsey's men were making for two stone hedges that ran across the fields to the cliff edge. Moore could only hope the Rangers carried adequate anti-tank weapons. Troops caught out in the open by tanks were like meat caught in a meat grinder. 'It's very bad, sir,' he told Davies. 'We're going to need all the support we can get.'

Half a mile or so from the gun battery the Rangers had destroyed, the German tanks had halted to allow their infantry to catch up with them, a respite that gave the Rangers another minute to reach cover. Jumping behind the low stone hedges, the Americans lined up their anti-tank weapons and waited.

Ahead of them the German infantry, veterans from North Africa, were all experienced in working with armour. Packing behind the tanks, they thumped their rifle butts on the steel plating to indicate their readiness. Through the explosions and general din of the battle, Tilsey's Rangers heard the cough of engines and the chilling, never-to-be-forgotten grinding of tracks as the giant tanks rolled forward once more. Only here and there could their grey hulks be seen. Panthers flanking their advance were laying smoke that the prevailing wind was sweeping across the battle zone.

Young's Mosquitoes had taken full advantage of the short delay. Their rockets were darting like fiery lances into the dark smoke. Aware that the armour of both the Panthers' and the Tigers' petrol tanks were carried there, they were attacking from that quarter whenever possible. Moreover the arrival of the German infantry made the tactic reap even grimmer rewards.

Leading his small flight down the cliffs, Moore joined in the attack. Flying at almost zero height he launched his first rocket well within safety range at a Tiger that loomed out of the smoke. An orange flash followed by a balloon of fire brought a cry of success from Hopkinson. A couple of seconds later a blast of heat flung the Mosquito upwards.

A hundred yards away Millburn was attacking with the urgency of a man who knew his compatriots would be overwhelmed unless the armoured advance could be checked. The rocket he released flew off the armoured skirt of a Panther in a ricochet of sparks. Cursing, Millburn held his dive until smoke was swirling past the cockpit blister. Grey-clad figures appeared, their faces lifted apprehensively. Thumbing his firing button Millburn opened up with both cannon and machine guns. Men stumbled and fell and the Panther slewed round as a 20-mm shell blew a section off its track. Holding his dive until the last second, Millburn pulled out less than a dozen feet above the tank. Gabby's indignant voice attacked him over the intercom. 'What're you trying to do? Frighten the bastards to death?'

With the tanks drawing within range of the first stone hedge, American bazooka teams were now in action. Columns of black smoke signalled a couple of hits but the tough German armour kept on rolling forward. As Moore circled back for a second attack, the sight of a burning Focke Wulf 190 falling past him told him another battle was being fought overhead. Although by this time the German High Command had satisfied itself the raid was only a local one, they had decided the Americans must have their noses bloodied or they would return for the invasion with a dangerous confidence. Accordingly suqadrons of 190s and 109s that for the last few months had been used only in defence of the Fatherland were now descending in swarms on the covering Thunderbolts.

The battle both on land and in the air had now reached the stage where all seemed confusion to those taking part in it. In the air men were assailed by sights and sounds the human senses are ill-equipped to withstand: parabolas of lethal tracer, shell bursts of jagged steel, the scream of engines and airfoils, the judder and crash of cannon fire. Behind the hedges Americans, firing desperately at the juggernauts advancing to crush them, had eardrums and lung tissues ruptured by the blast of shells. In the tanks Germans were loading guns, firing and loading again in a hell of sweat, din, and cordite fumes. For all of them time lost its meaning. Even fear withdrew into the background, although its hideous presence was never far away. The dominating emotion was urgency: the urgency to kill before one could be killed.

In J-Jimmie McKenny was fighting like a man to whom life had lost all value. As he traded cannon fire with Tigers and Panthers at point-blank range, Ross, conscious of the need for desperate counter-attack, was denied even the relief of condemnation as the ferocious attacks continued.

In A-Apple Moore was growing concerned about the ammunition problem.

Already three of Young's flight had reported they were low on rockets and 20-mm shells. The thought of having to withdraw and leave the troops below to their fate distressed Moore and he took A-apple up to 1,500 feet to reappraise the situation. From that height he could see American tanks moving about in apparent freedom within the station perimeter. A quick check with Davies confirmed that the station was now in American hands and that explosive charges were being laid within the blockhouses. Within minutes, if all went well, the withdrawal to the landing craft could begin.

Heartened by the news and the possibility his squadron might still be in at the death, Moore gave his attention again to the threat from the east. As the smoke-covered cliffs swept back, Hopkinson gave a start. 'Take a look over there, skipper! Aren't those Jerry tanks down on the beach?'

CHAPTER 22

Moore saw that the Cockney was right. Somewhere back along the eastern cliffs the Germans had found a way down to the sand and their light tanks were racing along it towards White Beach.

Tilsey was already reacting to this threatened outflanking of his frail defence line. Rangers were sliding down the cliffs and taking cover on the blunt promontory Moore had noticed earlier. With the tide high, it reached out to within ten yards of the seas. If the tanks were allowed to pass this neck of beach, they would be in a position to pour infilading fire on the infantry landing craft and menace the withdrawal of the entire task force. Shells bursting among the tanks and on the promontory told Moore the Rangers and the armour were already engaged.

Away on Moore's left the Typhoons had arrived. He could see their heavily-muscled shapes diving in and out of the smoke. Welcome though their arrival was, it only compensated for the troops Tilsey was being forced to draw out of his defence line. Trying to estimate how many Mosquitoes he dared pull out, Moore lifted his mask. 'Guard Dog Leader to Zeros Six, Eight and Ten. Join me over Blue Beach.'

Young, sounding weary, answered him. 'Day and Clifford have bought it, skipper.'

'Then send me No. Eleven.'

Without waiting for the aircraft to arrive, Moore banked round and attacked. He received the full attention of the tanks that were heading along the beach in ever-greater numbers. Scoring a hit on one that crippled its tracks, Moore opened fire with cannon and machine guns on the infantry following the armour. As he swept towards the cliffs a sudden fork of tracer made him bank steeply away. Grimacing at the startled Hoppy, he tried to pin-point the source of the gunfire.

It proved to be a flak post half-buried in a high sand dune. Deciding it was too well-protected to make an attack worth while, Moore gave a warning to the three Mosquitoes now formating behind him. 'Keep clear of that flak post half a mile east of the promontory. Follow me.'

Circling out to sea, the four Mosquitoes separated and came at the tanks line abreast over the surf. Shells laid a curtain of steel before them. All four aircraft released a rocket apiece and then banked steeply away. Two scored direct hits: two missed their targets. The rocket that lanced out from McKenny was heading straight and true for a Panther when a fault in the projectile made it veer away at the last moment. As it harmlessly showered a tank with wet shingle, the flak post on the cliffs picked on J-Jimmie and raked it with tracer.

It was a provocation the cursing Irishman could not resist. Soaring into a tight turn, he headed back for the cliff. Realizing his intention, Ross gripped his arm. 'Moore told us to ignore it!'

It is doubtful if McKenny heard him. Hands gripping the control wheel as if it were the throat of an enemy, he aimed the Mosquito's nose at the concrete bunker. As a sheet of tracer swirled towards them, Ross made his last appeal. 'Paddy, for God's sake! It's suicide.'

A second later J-Jimmie seemed to halt in mid-air as the tracer struck her. At the same moment McKenny fired two rockets. One struck the bunker but failed to penetrate the reinforced concrete. As McKenny banked steeply away there was a massive rat-tat-tat on the underside of his armoured seat. Forgetting the navigator enjoyed no such protection, McKenny failed to notice the agonized jerk Ross made against his straps. The gun post was swinging back into the Irishman's sights and his sole obsession was to destroy or be destroyed.

This time he opened fire with his cannon and closed to point-blank range. Ironically, the smaller projectiles were more effective, penetrating the visor through which the bunker's LMGs were firing. As the gunfire abruptly ceased, McKenny went into a climbing turn and glanced at Ross triumphantly.

'What do you mean – suicide? We've knocked it out, haven't we?'

Ross did not reply. As his eyes cleared from the fight, McKenny saw the Scot was sagging limply against his seat harness.

'What's wrong, Bernie?'

When Ross again made no response, McKenny reached out and tried to tug him round. For a moment the Scot's limp body resisted, then it lolled towards him. There was fear now in McKenny's voice.

'Bernie, can you hear me? How bad is it?'

The young Scot was trying to speak. Instead blood spurted from his mouth and ran down his overalls. His left leg began kicking spasmodically. A moment later his head fell back and his dead eyes stared up through the perspex blister. McKenny's cry was one of pure terror. 'For Christ's sake, Bernie. Say something!'

In A-Apple Moore had noticed McKenny's reckless attack on the gun bunker but an American voice in his R/T had checked his reprimand.

'Brooklyn to Guard Dog Leader. Do you read me?'

Moore had already recognized Tilsey's voice. 'I read you, Brooklyn.'

'You got any bombs left?'

'Yes. Why?'

'Drop them on this headland. Try to block the beach.'

It was a tactic fraught with danger. 'We can't be that accurate with bombs. It could put your men at risk.'

Tilsey was still cool enough for irony. 'You could say they're at risk now. Drop your bombs.'

Beside Moore the usually cheery Hopkinson was looking apprehensive. 'Does he know what he's askin', skipper? If we kill any more Yanks we'll be at war with 'em.'

The perils latent in the request were obvious enough to Moore but with the entire withdrawal threatened he could see no alternative. 'Guard Dog Leader to Zeros Six, Eight, and Eleven. Bomb tip of promontory at ten-second intervals.'

Warned of the forthcoming bombing, half of Tilsey's men were falling back to fresh positions along the low cliff face. Moore's guess was that Tilsey was staying with the rearguard. On the opposite side of the promontory, shells were falling among the tanks as the American destroyers reacted to this new threat to the withdrawal.

WIth J-Jimmie back in formation again, Moore led the Mosquitoes across the cliffs. His plan was to attack the promontory from its landward side in the hope that the forward plunge of the bombs would hurl debris over the neck of beach.

As he made for it he glanced down to see how the wider battle was progressing. The confrontation between the Rangers and the German tanks and infantry was reaching its climax as the weakened line of Americans fought gallantly to hold their positions. Hideous tongues of flame licking through the smoke told Moore the tanks were within flammenwerfer range of the Rangers. Mosquitoes and Typhoons were still plunging in and out of the smoke like dolphins in a sea. A near collision rocked A-Apple as one Typhoon, its pilot intent on a marauding tank, missed it by less than thirty feet.

Glancing further west Moore could see great columns of smoke rising from the radiolocation station and landing craft lining up on the beaches. If the enemy's eastern thrust could be held for another twenty minutes or so, the mission could still be a conspicuous success.

Down on the beach Tilsey and his rearguard kept their positions until A-Apple with its bomb doors open could be seen approaching at 1,500 feet over the cliffs. Then, bending double, their boots slipping in the shingle, they ran back and took cover with the rest of their party behind a ridge seventy yards from the promontory. Moore's urgent voice reached down to Tilsey. 'You're too close, Brooklyn. Drop back another hundred yards.'

Ducking as a shell showered him with sand, the panting Tilsey crouched over the microphone his Signals corporal was holding out to him. 'We're O.K., Guard Dog Leader. Just get those bombs dropped.'

With the promontory sweeping towards him Moore had no further time to argue. Conscious he was flying well below safety height with a nose-fused bomb, he banked steeply away as his 250-pounder dropped. It burst on the western side of the promontory and threw up a shower of rocks. As A-Apple recovered and went into a climbing turn, Hopkinson gave a grunt of approval. 'It might work, skipper, if we can get enough bombs down there.'

But the tough German armour had recognized the threat, and reckless of their safety, tanks were making at speed for the neck before it could be closed. Pushing aside a clay boulder, a leading tank rounded the promontory and came in sight of Tilsey's men. In the exchange of fire that followed a bazooka shell tore off one of the tank's tracks and left it grinding impotently in the sand. Yet two others were already rounding the promontory and more were in eager pursuit.

Anxious for his colleagues below, Millburn chose to go in next. Although flak was heavy around him, the experienced American laid his bomb not thirty yards from Moore's. This time half a dozen large rocks rolled down on the debris-covered beach. Tilsey's encouraging voice crackled in Moore's earphones. 'You're doing great, Guard Dog Leader. Keep it going.'

Zero Six followed Millburn. It was flown by the two soccer fanatics, Butterfield and Foster. Realising the outcome of the battle might depend on their making the breakthrough along the beach, the tanks put up their fiercest barrage yet. The youthful Foster, trying to concentrate on the low-level bar of his bombsight, saw chains of shells swirling towards him. He was just about to press the bomb release when a 75-mm shell burst full in the main fuel tank. Two seconds later all that remained of Zero Six was a rotating ball of fire that fell into the sea in a cloud of steam.

Moore's voice had a flat sound as he spoke to McKenny. 'Let's try this another way, Zero Eleven. Tail-fuse your bombs, go in low, and drop them both together.'

Moore saw Hopkinson wince. It was an order the squadron commander hated giving but if the beach was to be blocked, it was now clear that only pin-point accuracy would achieve it. If McKenny survived the gauntlet of fire at zero height, Moore's hope was that the tail-fusing of the bombs, with their eleven second delays, would enable J-Jimmie to escape the heavy explosions.

Had Moore seen McKenny's expression he would have realized that his concern for the Irishman's safety was academic. Brought back to the hell of sanity by Ross's death, the Irishman was waiting only for a chance of redemption. Before Moore had finished speaking his hand reached out and fused the two bombs. As he took J-Jimmie over the cliff top at 1,000 feet, Hopkinson gave Moore a puzzled look. 'Didn't he hear you tell him to go in at low level?'

The explanation came two seconds later. As every tank in the vicinity opened fire on him, McKenny pushed both throttles through the gate and went down like a meteor. A 75-mm shell blew off half J-Jimmie's tail fin and another set fire to its port engine but it is doubtful that anything could have stopped the Irishman in that moment of expiation. Trailing flame like a torch, the Mosquito struck the far end of the promontory and exploded, fuel tanks, bombs, and all. As scraps of aircraft, sand and boulders were flung upwards on the periphery of a huge ball of fire, A-Apple, a thousand feet above, shuddered to the massive explosion.

Hoppy's murmur was hoarse. 'God in Heaven!' His pale face turned to Moore. 'He meant that, skipper. Those bombs were nose-fused! Why?'

Below, the huge smoke cloud was beginning to drift away and the circling men could see that the neck of the promontory had been severed and tons of earth and rock were blocking the beach. After their initial shock, enemy tanks were on the move again and one was rearing up like a dog as it tried to pull itself over the rubble. When it slid back and crashed heavily on its side, it was clear that in spite of the German infantry who were already attempting to move the rocks, no tanks would round the promontory in time to affect the American withdrawal. However, the reaction of the American Rangers was not triumph as they rose from behind their bank of shingle. Like the airmen above, they seemed stunned by McKenny's sacrifice.

Moore led Millburn back over the cliffs. The sight that met them was heart-rending, for with their line weakened the Rangers were suffering greatly for their valour. With the German armour having broken through at last, anti-tank teams were still firing as tanks reared over them and crushed them with their pitiless tracks. Other Rangers, risking incineration from flame-throwers, could be seen running through the smoke and endeavouring to drop grenades down tank visors and turrets. Two things were being learned at heavy cost that morning on the bloody cliffs of Omonville. One was that the Germans were going to fight with their usual tough determination when the invasion came. The other was that the New American Army waiting in England for its day of destiny need fear comparison with no army in the world for its courage and fighting qualities.

Over on White Beach, with the Americans conscious it was a race against time, shuttles of landing craft were frantically ferrying infantrymen out to the waiting ships. Disregarding the dangers to their rearguard, destroyers were now pounding the advancing German armour and in a final effort to gain time, the American tanks were thrown into the battle. Out-gunned and lighter-skinned than their German counterparts, they were doomed from the onset but went into combat like terriers harassing a stampede of bulls. Soon the cliffs above Blue Beach were dotted with their blazing hulks but there is no doubt their courageous sacrifice earned the Americans the extra few minutes necessary to ferry the last of their infantry out.

Above the bloody battle the surviving Mosquitoes and Typhoons had run out of ammunition one by one. No units had played their part with more distinction, as their heavy losses showed. The final and ironic tragedy for 633 Squadron came when Millburn and Moore, having sent their surviving aircraft home, were taking a last look at the shrinking perimeter to see if there was anything more they could do. As they swept over the wrecked radiolocation station, Millburn, who was flying fifty yards behind Moore, saw a single line of tracer soar up from a shattered bunker. Before he could yell a warning, the tracer ran the full length of A-Apple. A second later the Mosquito reeled and began to side-slip towards the cliffs. As it cleared them it seemed to recover for a moment, only to crash in a huge shower of spray in the surf a couple of hundred yards from the last of the American landing craft. Diving down, Millburn swept less than a hundred feet above the wreck. 'See anything?' he yelled at Gabby.

The distressed Welshman shook his head. Millburn did another pass but neither man saw any movement in A-Apple. With the beach littered with wrecked vehicles and mounds that had once been men, there was nothing Millburn could do except send an emergency call to Davies in the *Brazos*. With heavy hearts and a last glance at the wreck, the two men started back for England.

CHAPTER 23

By the noon of that same day Holmsley looked like a battlefield. At the far end of one runway a tractor was feverishly dragging a crippled Mosquito out of the way of incoming aircraft. Seven other battle-scarred Mosquitoes were dispersed around the airfield. Having spoken to their ground crews, the weary pilots and navigators were now tramping towards Henderson, who was standing at the edge of the tarmac apron. Adams was at his elbow. The rest of 633 Squadron, plus the airfield's regular personnel, were waiting in anxious groups and watching the southern horizon.

Someone gave a shout and pointed an arm. Seconds later the uneven throb of engines could be heard. As a Mosquito appeared over the pine trees, crash wagons began throttling up and a siren gave a scream. With smoke pouring from one engine and huge holes in both wings, the Mosquito was keeping in the air with the greatest difficulty. Once clear of the pines it ignored the wind direction and sank down on the runway like a man at the end of a marathon. For fifty yards its landing appeared successful. Then its undercarriage collapsed and it crashed down on its belly. Two crash wagons and an ambulance accelerated as the aircraft skidded on to the grass and ground-looped with a snapping of spars and a shearing of metal.

Henderson took a couple of steps forward, then halted. 'Half of my squadron scattered over a bloody cliff in France and the other half pranging itself on a satellite airfield. And all to nail a pack of lies from a paranoiac war correspondent.'

Adams was sharing his bitterness. 'This will be the end of it, surely.'

The Scot was watching the first crash wagon scream to a halt with its nose only inches from the Mosquito's smoking engine. As white foam squirted out and killed the fire risk, he relaxed and turned to Adams. 'It had better be or they'll be wanting a new C.O. as well as a squadron commander.'

Adams winced at the reminder. By this time the first of the surviving aircrews were arriving. Visibly moved by their hollow faces and battle-stained appearance, Henderson moved among them. 'You've done a great job, lads. And although I don't expect it means a damn to you right now, the operation was a big success.'

The weary men showed no reaction. Stunned by the brutality of battle, they could feel only in personal terms. Larkin was the first to express the anxiety all were feeling. 'What's the latest news of Moore and Hoppy, sir?'

'Better than we first feared,' Henderson told him. 'Air Commodore Davies says the Yanks picked them up and got them to the hospital ship. The last he heard they were both undergoing surgery.'

It took a moment for his news to sink into the exhausted crews. Henderson's eyes were on a Mosquito that had just landed safely. Instead of taxi-ing to its dispersal point, it was jolting across the grass towards them. As its propellers jerked to a stop, Millburn and Gabby dropped to the ground. Releasing his parachute harness, the American, whose oil-stained right cheek was bady contused, began running forward. Henderson met him halfway.

'You two all right?' When Millburn nodded, the Scot went on: 'You saw Moore go down, didn't you? What happened?'

No one was more anxious for news of the popular Moore than Millburn. 'He wasn't a hundred yards ahead of us when an LMG got him. He didn't seem right out of control when he hit the surf. What's the latest news? Did the Yanks pick them up?'

'Yes. They're on the hospital ship having surgery. That's all Davies could tell me.'

By this time Gabby had joined them. 'Does that mean they're bad, sir?'

Anxiety made Henderson irritable. 'I've just said – I don't know. We'll have to wait until the convoy gets back.'

The survivors, who had clustered round Millburn to hear his news, were now looking as if the effort had drained them of their remaining strength. As Henderson's eyes ran round them, his tone changed. 'I've never seen a crowed of men look so knackered. Forget the de-briefing – we'll handle it later. Go off and get yourselves some grub and coffee.'

Millburn remained behind as the crews trudged off. 'Did Davies tell you about McKenny, sir?'

Overhearing his comment, Young moved back. Henderson shook his head. 'He's one of those who got the chop, isn't he?'

'Yeah. But it wasn't an accident.'

The Scot frowned. 'What does that mean?'

Millburn told him. Henderson exchanged a shocked glance with Adams. 'Are you telling me it was suicide?'

'What else could it be? Nobody goes in at zero height with nose-fused bombs.'

'But why would he do that?'

The American shrugged. 'Search me. If the tanks had gotten past that headland they'd have cut off our withdrawal for sure. But no one was asked to commit suicide.'

'And you're sure that's what it was?'

'It had to be. Even if he'd dropped his bombs from that height, he'd still have blown himself to hell.'

Henderson's bitter eyes moved to the surviving aircraft. Deciding it was all too much to take at one sitting, he gave a sigh. 'It's been that kind of day, so I suppose it all fits. Do you expect any more kites in or are you the last?'

'We're the last,' Millburn told him.

Henderson winced. 'God Almighty.' With an effort he pulled himself together and led the three men towards a distant Nissen hut. 'Let's go and have a bloody drink.'

Adams halted the staff car outside Sutton Craddock's Administration Block and made his way down the corridor to Henderson's office. He found the Scot just replacing the telephone receiver. At any other time he would have noticed the satisfaction Henderson was showing. 'Can you spare me a few minutes?'

Henderson sat back. 'As a matter of fact, you're just the man I wanted to see. What's happened? Have our spares and replacements arrived?'

Adams grimaced. 'Nothing seems to have arrived.' He nodded at the pile of requisition forms on the desk. 'I see you're still signing them.'

'I've been doing nothing else since we got back,' Henderson grunted. 'At this rate it'll be Christmas before we're back at full strength. The only consolation, I suppose, is that this time the job wasn't for nothing. Staines says that over in the States Lambert's campaign has collapsed like a house of cards. In fact we made such a good impression that he's been forced to join in the chorus and praise us.'

Although seldom malicious, Adams could not contain his grin of pleasure. 'So that's the end of it.'

'It has to be, hasn't it? He can hardly switch round in a week or two and start slanging the RAF again.'

'It must have lost him some credibility over there.'

'I hope it's lost him his bloody job,' Henderson muttered.

'Davies must be pleased.'

'Davies? He's like a dog with two tails. Particularly after the C.-in-C.'s congratulations.' Then the Scot's tone changed. 'Harvey phoned me this morning. He's been down to Southampton to see Moore.'

'What's the latest news?'

'Much better than we hoped. They think Moore could be back on his feet in about two months. Hoppy's going to take longer but should be operational soon after Christmas. Guess what? Harvey's staying down in Southampton until the end of his leave.'

'Why? So he can visit Moore?'

Henderson grinned. 'Being Harvey, he made some other excuse but that's his

501

reason all right. Funny, isn't it, when you think how he used to dislike Moore.' It was then the Scot noticed Adams' expression. 'What was it you wanted to see me about?'

'I've got news about McKenny,' Adams told him. 'I think it explains everything that happened.'

Henderson showed immediate interest. 'You mean why he committed suicide?'

'Yes, I think so.'

The Scot motioned to a chair. 'Then let's have it.'

Adams sank down somewhat heavily. 'I've just come back from Highgate. A Catholic priest there, a Father McBride, phoned me early this morning to ask if he could see me. He'd just heard about McKenny's death and thought we should hear the background story.'

'A priest?'

'McKenny's priest,' Adams explained.

Henderson's face cleared. 'Go on.'

'I think he got in touch with me because not long before the train operation I had a word with McKenny about his heavy drinking, and he must have mentioned my name to McBride. It seems McKenny had stopped attending Mass and Confession but wouldn't give McBride a reason. So eventually McBride had a word with Ross. Ross didn't want to talk at first but when McBride convinced him it was for McKenny's good, Ross told him about an ugly incident they'd had back in the summer. Do you remember the low-level raid we made on the Rutenbreck?'

Henderson had to think. 'Was that when we clobbered a machine tool factory?'

'That's the one. McKenny had a hung-up bomb and it fell on a row of houses. Both he and Ross saw women and children running out. One child was blazing like a torch.'

'Did they mention this at de-briefing?' Henderson interrupted.

'They only said they'd hit the row of houses. They probably didn't want to think about the child.'

'Go on,' Henderson said again.

'Also back in the summer they were both witnesses when Taylor and Gibson were trapped in their crashed aircraft and burned alive.' Inclined to digress when the psychological aspects of war were involved, Adams digressed now. 'To an irreligious old sod like me, a few incidents like that seem more than enough to destroy anyone's faith in a just and kindly God. It makes me wonder how many men are going to come out of this war with any faith at all. To some that's surely going to be a far gerater loss than an arm or leg. Yet because it's not a loss people can see, they're not going to get much sympathy or understanding.'

Henderson shifted restlessly. 'I've got the point. The priest believes these experiences caused his breakdown.'

To his surprise Adams shook his head. 'No. Perhaps because McKenny was a Catholic, McBride wasn't satisfied his faith could be undermined that way. I think he's wrong and that was the beginning of it, but that's neither here nor there. McBride went on making enquiries and eventually found out that McKenny's girl friend had broken off her engagement and was going overseas. Even that didn't satisfy McBride and he went to Lincoln to see the girl. You'll never guess what he found out.'

Henderson's attempt at humour was only half-hearted. 'Don't tell me she'd shot the Pope.'

'Just the opposite. She'd turned religious herself.'

The Scot's square face frowned at Adams. 'What is this? Some kind of sick joke?'

'No. When you think about it, it makes sense. McKenny's girl friend was a Protestant and according to what she told McBride, she'd hardly given religion a second thought since she went to Sunday school as a child. But sometime during the summer she got "the Call".'

Henderson's eyebrows rose. 'The Call?'

'You know – the sudden impulse to give up all earthly things and spend the rest of one's life serving God. In her case it meant joining a group of nursing missionaries who in a week or two are going out to a leper colony in West Africa.'

'But McKenny told Moore she was going to the Middle East.'

'That was to conceal what had happened to her. He didn't want us all to know she was giving him up for God.'

The Scot was frowning again. 'All right, I can see it would be a blow. But if he was such a religious kid at the time, how could her turning religious too cause him to break down?'

'Turning religious is one thing, having a conversion so complete that it ended their relationship is another. Although, unlike McBride, I believe other factors were already turning him against religion, it must have been a hell of a shock, and when he finally realized she was leaving him for God, he began to see God as his rival. His enemy, in fact. And it's not difficult to imagine what this would do to anyone as fundamentally religious as McKenny. In his pain he'd begin turning against everything and everybody, including his best friend, Ross. Ross more than anyone because deep down he'd be jealous that Ross had managed to keep his faith intact.' When Henderson slowly shook his head, Adams allowed his imagination a moment's indulgence. 'It's a bit like the story of Lucifer, isn't it? One of God's brightest angels becoming his deadliest enemy.'

Henderson gave a grunt. 'That's a bit fanciful, isn't it?'

Remembering whom he was talking to, Adams felt his cheeks turn warm. 'I suppose it is. But even in wartime it's not every day you run into something as profound and harrowing as this.'

Henderson conceded a nod. 'Then you think that was why McKenny committed suicide? To destroy Ross as well as himself?'

'Oh, no. Not to kill Ross. In one way they were closer than brothers. When I did the de-briefing, young Evans said he heard McKenny over the R/T a few minutes before he killed himself. The reception was poor but Evans said he was asking Ross how badly hurt he was and sounded half-crazy on finding he was dead. Why he then crashed into the promontory is anyone's guess. It might have been revenge on God, an impulse of self-destruction, expiation for getting Ross killed, or simply a self-sacrificial act to save hundreds of American lives. I like to think it was the last two but who can ever say?'

Henderson pushed a telex form across the desk. 'I know what the Yanks are saying. Both he and Ross have gone up for a posthumous Congressional Medal of Honour.'

Adams removed his spectacles and began wiping them. 'I'm glad. If medals mean anything, both boys deserve them more than most. Ross knew the danger when he volunteered to fly with McKenny again, and the damned war had already destroyed McKenny before it killed him.'

For once Henderson did not find Adams' sensitivity an embarrassment. 'It might be a good idea to keep this quiet, Frank. At least until the dust settles. But it's not all doom and gloom, thank God. Do you know who was on the telephone when you came in?' As Adams shook his head: 'It was the Brigadier. He's got news of St Claire and Simpson. They're both alive and well.'

Adams was sitting bolt upright in his chair. 'Is he sure?'

'That's what his agents have told him. The Resistance can't get either of 'em across yet but they'll be giving it a crack in due course. Do you want to tell Sue yourself?'

Adams jumped up. 'Do you mind?'

'No. You're her Father Confessor. Off you go.'

The interval between his leaving Henderson's office and reaching his 'Confessional' was a blank to Adams although his thudding heart told him he must have run most of the way. When he threw back the door, the girl was filing photographs into one of the steel cabinets. Seeing his exhausted condition, she showed concern. 'What on earth's the matter, Frank?'

Before Adams could get his breath back she suddenly halted and put a hand to her throat. The panting Adams nodded and entered the hut. 'Yes. I've got news for you . . . Good news. Put those photographs down and come over here.'